THE QUEEN OF LIGHT AND SHADOWS

THE FALLEN QUEEN

J. D. Marcella

Bluebonnet Books

Edited by: Chelsea Schermerhorn

Art Credits:
Cover Art: Martyna Szpil-Augusiewicz and J.D. Marcella
Lizen Barrymore
Isabela Guinart

First edition 2025

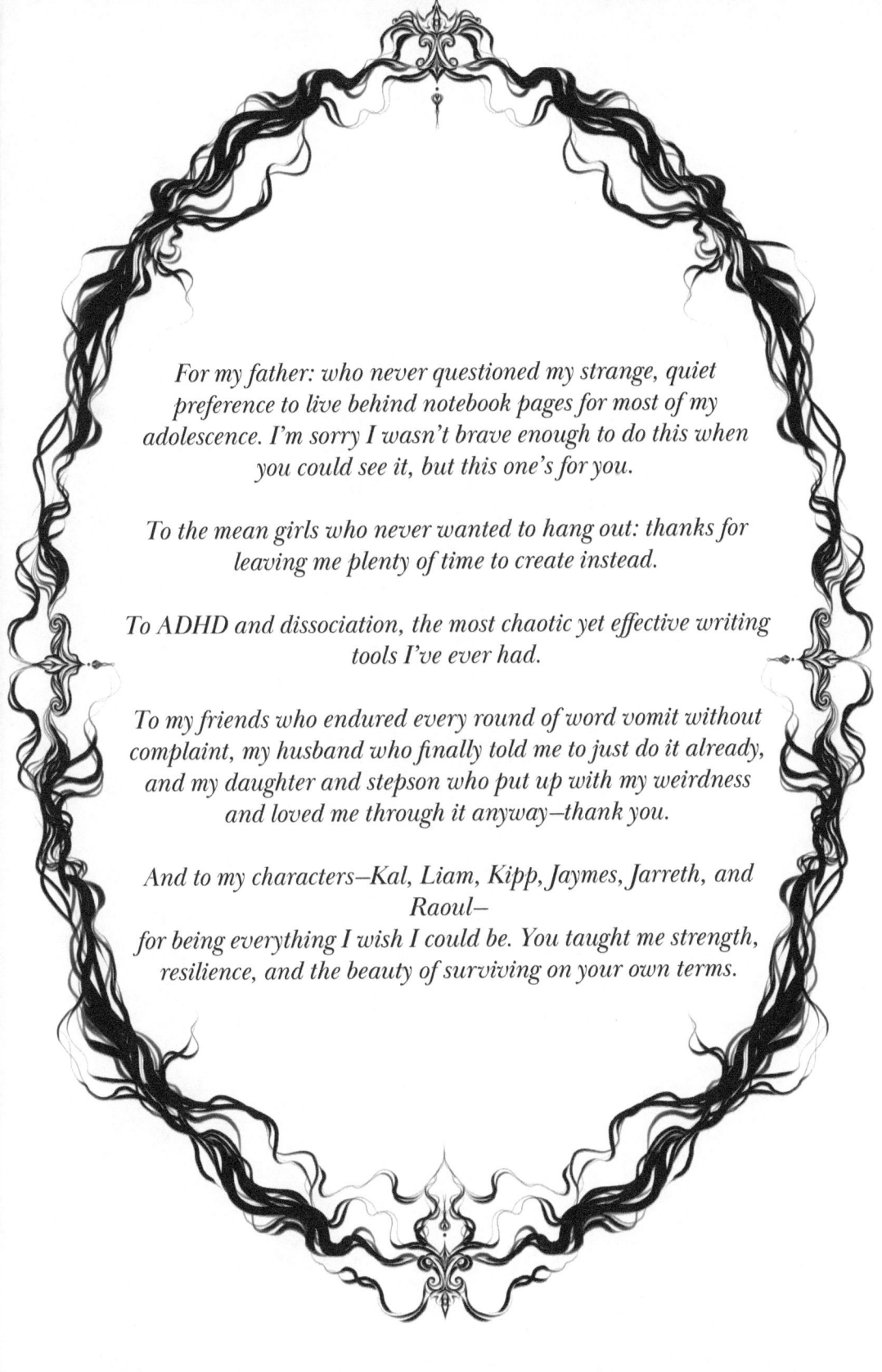

For my father: who never questioned my strange, quiet preference to live behind notebook pages for most of my adolescence. I'm sorry I wasn't brave enough to do this when you could see it, but this one's for you.

To the mean girls who never wanted to hang out: thanks for leaving me plenty of time to create instead.

To ADHD and dissociation, the most chaotic yet effective writing tools I've ever had.

To my friends who endured every round of word vomit without complaint, my husband who finally told me to just do it already, and my daughter and stepson who put up with my weirdness and loved me through it anyway—thank you.

And to my characters—Kal, Liam, Kipp, Jaymes, Jarreth, and Raoul—
for being everything I wish I could be. You taught me strength, resilience, and the beauty of surviving on your own terms.

Contents

PROLOGUE: THE FALL

The gods are gone.

Some fell in silence, their temples left hollow and their names forgotten. Others vanished in storms of blood and fire, their passing leaving scars upon the land that never healed. In the wake of their ruin, the world did not find peace–only hunger.

Men clawed for meaning where none remained. Priests sought explanations, scholars argued over fragments of scripture. Kings promised purpose to restless subjects. Yet in the shadows of uncertainty, others found opportunity. Power untethered from heaven was power waiting to be claimed.

From the northern wastes, where winter never loosens its grip, Rhaen rose. He broke the clans and bound their savagery beneath his banner until all of the north lay crushed at his feet. But he was not satisfied with the meager lands of the north, nor of the power a mere mortal man could hold.

Rhaen believed the gods' might had not vanished, only shifted, waiting to be seized. He sought it in the ruins of their temples, among altars blackened by frost and blood. There he scoured broken idols and fractured scripture, hunting for the remnants of divinity–something he might twist into his own ascension. He dreamed of becoming beautifully and ruinously divine, a god born of ash and iron, before whom all the world would either worship or bleed.

What he uncovered was no blessing, but a truth buried in silence.

Iron.

The eternal fae, untouched by age and unbroken by time, bore a secret frailty. Iron unmade them. Seared their flesh, stripped their magic, and bled their immortality into dust. Rhaen had found no godhood, but he had found a weapon to erase all of those who would stand above him, and it was enough.

His alchemists soured their craft into cruelty, blackening chains and shaping blades meant to tear eternity apart. Armed with this knowledge, Rhaen turned his horde south, to the place where the last god had fallen.

Elandra.

A kingdom sanctified by divine touch, a citadel of wonders where magic still lingered after the heavens grew silent. It should have been unassailable. Instead, it became his prize.

The north came with iron and fire. They burned the groves, salted the rivers, and hunted the fae, hell-bent on their extinction. One by one, they fell, until only echoes remained.

Elandra fell.

Its towers became pyres, its streets ran red, and its royal family was slaughtered on the throne. What remained of its people were ground beneath northern boots, while Rhaen gorged on ruin.

But conquest does not rest. The kingdom still smolders, its rot seeping outward, blackening the borders of every land it touches. Fire spreads. Ash follows.

And beyond the smoke, whispers stir that this is only the beginning...

The Blade and the Broken

The screaming had ceased. Not from mercy, nor because the pain had passed. Her voice was simply...gone. Burned out, broken and swallowed by the dark.

Liam crouched beneath the shadow of a stone archway, just beyond the iron-bound doors of the chamber. His breath came shallow, each inhalation a grind of pain through broken ribs–remnants of the beating he'd earned for defying his father again. His fists clenched so tightly his nails cut into his palms, but he felt none of it. The pain had become background noise.

He had stood in the path of her suffering, as he always did. Silent, unflinching, already knowing it would make no difference. The blows still landed. The pain found her anyway. And she endured it; because there was no other choice. Mercy did not exist in this place.

The two guards stationed at the door made no sign they had heard the screams. One idly picked at his fingernail, while the other leaned on his pike, half-asleep. Neither spared a glance at the room they were meant to guard. To them the girl within was nothing more than livestock. Just something to be used, discarded, and forgotten.

Cold rage coiled within Liam, slow and suffocating. A steel-forged hatred sharpened over years of helplessness. He wanted to tear them all down, every last one of them. From the bored guards to the men in the council chamber. From the grinning courtiers to the man who sat on the throne.

Especially him.

The iron doors creaked open, the sound loud and final, like the toll of the bell to announce a hanging. Liam's breath caught in his chest. Two of the king's personal guards stepped through the door, dragging a broken shape between them.

Her hair, once carefully combed, hung in knotted strands across her blood-smeared face. Her garments were torn, stained, and clung to her like gauze, offering no modesty nor protection. Her limp body hung between the men holding her up, her feet dragging on the floor behind.

Liam's stomach turned.

She wasn't moving.

He lurched forward, reflex outweighing caution. Despite the pain, his body moved as if to throw itself between her and the men who held her. He would fight, even if it meant dying.

A hand seized his shoulder.

"Not yet."

Liam spun, ready to lash out–and stopped.

Arjun stood behind him, his expression hard as flint.

"Tonight." He whispered. There was no hesitation in the fae's voice. "We will take her tonight."

For a moment, Liam could only stare. They had whispered of a successful escape before–in that quiet dark, the space between hopeless days–but those were only dreams. A fool's hope really. The castle was layered with traps. Magic wound through every stone, every corridor was lined with iron and watched by guards...or worse.

But the tone in Arjun's voice wasn't hopeful. It spoke of a plan.

Liam's gaze shifted back to her as the guards hauled her down the hall towards the gilded cage they cruelly called her quarters. He could see her breathing was faint, her arms hanging useless at her sides. He knew what that meant and he knew what would happen if they waited.

"She won't survive another night," he said, the words brittle.

Arjun's reply was faint, but final. "He's never going to stop."

Liam nodded. He had always known it. Though tonight, for the first time, he believed they might finally do something about it.

They waited until silence filled the castle.

When the drunken laughter behind velvet curtains dwindled to nothing and the last footsteps faded into stone, Liam moved. Somewhere deep within the keep, the usurper had retired...sated, smug, and blind to the blood spilled below his feet.

There would be no second chance. One misplaced breath, one echo too sharp, and the night would end with slaughter.

Liam advanced through the corridors like a shadow unmoored, each step measured, each movement bound by tension. Pain burned under his skin, his ribs flaring with each breath, but he pressed forward.

This wasn't heroism; this wasn't even hope. It was duty, and it had a cost he'd long ago accepted. Better to die beside her than to stand idly by while she was broken apart, piece-by-piece.

He reached her chamber and opened the door, stepping inside with the care of a man defusing a trap.

She lay on the cold floor, curled in on herself, more shadow than flesh, the iron chains pooling around her frame. The fragments of her dress hung in shreds, torn and bloodied. She faced away from him, but the damage was clear. Bruises marked her limbs, some fresh, others long settled. Across her body, welts rose in deliberate lines, each burn and cut placed with the precision of someone practiced in the art of pain.

She was breathing, but barely.

Liam took another step and the smell reached him. Blood. Sweat. Iron. And underneath it, a darker scent—one he refused to name.

His knees threatened to fail, but he forced himself to continue forward until he stood in front of her.

Her hair stuck in clumps to the stone. Her fingers twitched against the floor, curled as though bracing for a blow. The bruises on her wrists and ankles were deep, framing the burns the iron manacles left.

But it was her eyes that struck deepest. They were open and empty. She wasn't there.

He knelt at her side, his voice raw. "Kal?"

No answer.

"Kalithea."

A flicker. Barely that. But it was something.

He reached forward, brushing the hair from her face. Her skin was cold to the touch.

"We're leaving," he whispered.

For a moment she stayed silent, hardly breathing. Then, her lips parted and a rasp slipped out, "He's coming back tonight."

It wasn't the guards she spoke of; it was their father she feared, the man who ruled their bloodline like a curse.

Liam's chest tightened. Rage returned hot, and deep. A storm ready to split open his bones. He gathered her into his arms, gently, reverently, as though she were made of glass.

"Not tonight," he said, voice breaking with the force he used to contain his rage. "Not ever again."

She made no sound, didn't cling to him. She simply...existed. Her breath soft against his chest, almost too light to feel.

Arjun entered without warning, soundless as a wraith. He knelt beside them, placing one hand at Kal's brow. She closed her eyes at his touch. Whatever magic he could summon against the oppressive iron walls whispered through the air...ancient, steady. With the last bit of his magic, he snapped the manacles off her, doing his best to muffle the noise.

Liam spoke low. "She can't run, not like this."

"She won't have to," Arjun replied. "You carry her."

Liam stood, lifting her with care. She weighed almost nothing. Her head fell to his shoulder, her body loose and unresisting, and he held her as if she were the last thing left worth holding.

They left the chamber and passed through empty corridors, slipping between the guard rotations. Down stone steps slick with cold. Out into the wind of the first interior courtyard, to the place they had made it to so many attempts before, but never further.

The dark opened before them like a waiting mouth, dangerous, vast, but it was theirs. As Liam stepped into the night, he made no prayer. No vow to gods. Only to the blood in his veins.

She is my sister. She is my queen. And I will be her sword until my last breath.

Let the world come. He would tear it down to raise her back to her throne.

The night was wrong. Not silent in the way of peace, but hollow. Brittle. Liam could feel it, the wrongness, the kind that made skin crawl and breath catch in the throat. A stillness stretched too thin, like the world itself had paused to see if they would reach the end or die in the attempt.

He ran through the castle, his lungs burning. His arms began to ache beneath Kalithea's weight, her body limp against him, as she drifted in and out of consciousness. Still warm. Still breathing. That was all that mattered.

Arjun ran beside him, noiseless and relentless. His steps never slowed. Every turn, every narrow corridor they slipped through, he took without hesitation. He moved like a man who had long studied the palace not as a home, but as a prison, and learned every keyhole, every crack in its walls.

But something pressed in around them. The darkness no longer felt empty. It felt watchful.

Then Arjun spoke, his voice calm in a way that made Liam's blood run cold, "We're out of time."

Even before Liam heard the sound, he knew. Then it came, steel on steel. Shouts. Pounding of boots on stone.

They'd been found.

Liam's grip tightened around Kalithea instinctively, "We can still make it– "

"No," Arjun said, "*you* can."

Liam stopped, "What the hell does that mean?"

But Arjun had already turned, facing the direction of the noise, hand resting on the hilt at his side. "It means I stay."

The words hit like a punch. "The hell you do," Liam hissed.

Arjun didn't flinch. He stepped close, shoving a pack into Liam's hands then pressing his hand to Kalithea's forehead. A small whisper of magic stirred in the air—old, careful, protective.

"You don't have a choice, Liam."

"I'm not leaving you behind."

"Yes, you are."

Their eyes met. In Arjun's gaze, there was no fear, only certainty.

And Liam understood. This had always been the plan. Arjun had made his decision long ago and now it was too late to change it.

"They'll take you," Liam said, voice strained, "You know what they'll do."

"I've survived worse."

It was a lie. One not meant to be believed, only to soften the edges of goodbye. The sounds of pursuit grew louder, orders were shouted and the rhythm of boots crashed nearer.

Arjun turned and drew his blade in a clean, practiced motion. The steel caught what little light the corridor offered. He placed himself between them and the storm.

"Run,"

Liam didn't move.

"*Run.*" Arjun said again, no longer a plea, but a command. Then he was gone.

The fae met the oncoming guards like a hammer striking steel, sword flashing, what little magic he could muster rising with a pulse of power. The noise exploded behind them—shouts, metal, bodies slamming against stone.

Liam didn't look back.

He couldn't. If he did, he would falter. And Arjun's choice would mean nothing. So he ran. Into the cold. Into the dark. Into whatever freedom remained beyond the reach of the throne.

Liam didn't stop running until the castle was behind them—far enough to be swallowed by the dark, a nightmare blurred by distance. He didn't stop when his lungs wanted to give out, or when his legs buckled under the strain. He didn't stop until the horizon began to shift and the first pale threads of dawn crept across the sky in streaks of gold and muted rose.

Only when Kalithea stirred in his arms, barely more than a flicker, did he let himself collapse.

He dropped to his knees, the earth hitting hard, but it barely registered. His breath came in ragged gasps, chest heaving as though his heart meant to tear free. Kal lay against him, her body too still, her skin cold to his touch.

But she was breathing. And that was enough.

He folded his arms around her, holding tight to that small, steady rhythm—the proof that she was still alive. The wind stirred the trees, brushing the leaves with soft sound, and for a moment, the world felt real again.

Liam lowered his head, his voice barely above a whisper. "I swear it..."

Rough. Broken. But firm.

"I swear on my life, Arjun. I'll avenge you."

He didn't say it for comfort. It wasn't a hope, he knew what awaited Arjun when he chose his fate. But it was a vow etched into his bones, sharp enough to cut through whatever came next.

Deep in the woods, he sat with his back to the cracked stone of a half-collapsed outpost, what had once been a watchtower. The ruins had offered just enough cover to hide them, just enough shelter to dress her wounds. It wasn't safe, but nothing was. And it would do.

He hadn't slept. Not really. Even as the adrenaline faded, even as his body trembled from exhaustion and pain, he stayed awake. Watching. Guarding. Listening to the rise and fall of her breath and the hush between.

Crickets chirped in the quiet. but the sound felt distant.

Kal lay on a pile of leaves, wrapped in torn cloth and whatever clean fabric he could spare. Fever flushed her cheeks, her expression slack, her eyes closed but restless beneath the lids.

Liam rubbed a hand across his face, dirt and dried sweat gritting against stubble. He winced as his fingers passed over bruises. Souvenirs from the night before. Cuts, burns, and battered muscle all throbbed under his shirt. But he ignored it, pain could wait.

Then movement. A small breath.

"Liam?"

His head snapped toward her. Her eyes were open, unfocused,

bloodshot–but open.

A breath tore free from his chest, raw with relief.

"You're awake," he said, voice rough from disuse.

She blinked slowly, trying to remember how to see. As her gaze found him, it narrowed with confusion when she took in the sight of him.

"You look like hell," she murmured.

A weak laugh escaped him. "Yeah, well," he said, shifting closer, "hell tends to follow you around. So that makes sense."

She tried to move, too fast, and pain struck. Her breath hissed out between her teeth.

"Don't," Liam said, hands out, hovering just above her shoulders. "You're still healing."

Her hand drifted to the bandages at her collarbone. Fingers traced the edges slowly, then stilled. Her breath caught. He saw it then, the moment the fog broke. The moment that memory returned.

"Liam..."

He didn't answer. He already knew what was coming.

"Where's Arjun?"

It was barely a question. Still, it landed like a blade in his gut. He said nothing. Couldn't. He just looked at her and she saw the truth in his silence.

Her lips parted, trembling, breath turning uneven as the weight of it struck her fully. Her shoulders curved inward, hands twisting into the leaves below her. She tried to swallow the sound, to hold it down like she always had, but a muffled sob broke from her chest.

Liam didn't move at first. He had never seen her cry. Not when she was beaten, starved, or dragged in chains before the court. Not when she was locked in darkness or forced to kneel at their father's heel. Through it all, she had never let the world see her break.

But now, for Arjun, she wept–and it shattered something inside him.

He crossed the space between them, drawing her carefully into his arms. She didn't resist. Her body folded into his, trembling as she buried her face in the torn fabric of his tunic, her hands fisting at his chest. The sobs came harder now, low and unrelenting, years of grief suddenly unbound by the loss of the only other person who had never failed her.

He held her as tightly as he dared, not to hush her, but to offer the only shield he had left to give. And when her breath hitched, when her sobs slowed just enough for her to lift her tear-streaked face, he pressed his forehead gently to hers.

"Kal," he said, voice hoarse but steady. "Listen to me."

She didn't speak, but her eyes met his, raw, red-rimmed and un-flinching.

"You are my queen. You are my sister. And from this moment forward, I am yours. I will not leave your side. I will not let them take you again," Liam said.

Tears slid freely down her cheeks, but she didn't look away.

"If I must die for you, I will," he said, not as a dramatic oath, but as the simplest truth, "But I will not fail you."

He leaned in once more, the press of his brow against hers grounding them both, and with a voice carved from the marrow of loyalty itself, he finished the vow that had lived in his blood since the day she was born.

"I am your sword. I am your shield. And until my last breath, I will protect you."

ᚦHE ᛈAᚦH ᚠORWARD

Dawn draped itself around them, cold, but no longer cruel. For
the first time in their lives, the dark carried no threat. There
were no footsteps behind the door, no iron locks clamped to her
ankles, no cruel whisper of threat waiting at the edge of dawn.
Only stillness.

Liam sat beside Kalithea, closer than they had ever dared before
when their lives were separated by her iron chains, their shoulders
brushing with an ease that felt unfamiliar. They leaned against the broken wall of the ruined outpost, the stone at their backs rough and chill,
their limbs sore from flight, their bones heavy with exhaustion. Yet the
silence between them did not press down like it once had. Instead, it lay
gently like an unspoken truce between everything they had endured and
everything still ahead.

Neither spoke, they simply sat, leaning into the feeling of something almost too fragile to name.

Comfort. Safety.

It felt strange. Unnatural, even. The world outside stretched vast
and uncertain, wide with paths and possibilities they had never dared to
imagine. It should have felt like freedom. Instead, it felt like something
borrowed. Like a dream they might still wake from, at any moment.

"What do we do now?" Kal asked her brother.

Liam didn't answer right away. He shifted beside her, reaching for
the battered pack they'd carried with them through forest and ruins,
his fingers slow and stiff with cold and weariness. He pulled it close and
began to dig through it, taking quick stock of the supplies with the grim
practicality of someone who knew better than to hope.

"We head east, towards the mountains of Dulthair," he said
eventually, his voice rough but certain. "We have to find food. Shelter.
Something better than this. And then–"

He stopped. His fingers brushed against something unexpected. A smooth, stiff shape tucked underneath the worn contents of the pack. He paused, brow furrowed, and drew it free.

A letter. Still sealed.

For a moment, he didn't breathe.

Kalithea shifted beside him, the alertness in her posture sharpening as she leaned closer. Her gaze settled on the folded parchment now trembling slightly in his hands.

"What is it?" she asked.

But Liam didn't reply. His eyes had fixed on the handwriting inked across the parchment. Every stroke was familiar, every curve unmistakable. He knew that script as surely as he knew the rhythm of his own heartbeat.

"Arjun," he said, the name escaping in a breath, scarcely more than a whisper.

He broke the seal with shaking fingers. The parchment was creased and weather-worn, the edges soft and crumpled from being buried beneath rough fabric and fast movement. It resisted unfolding, as though reluctant to give up its message. But eventually it yielded, and the words revealed themselves with brutal clarity.

> *Kalithea. Liam.*
>
> *If you're reading this, it means I was right. It means I didn't make it out with you.*
>
> *Don't waste time mourning me. Your path lies ahead, not behind. I know what you're thinking–you'll want to turn back. You'll want to fight. But not yet.*
>
> *Kal, remember what I taught you. Remember who you are. That shadow inside you, it isn't a curse. It's power. Yours to wield. But you must learn to hold it without letting it hollow you. Use it, or it will use you.*
>
> *Liam, keep her grounded. Keep her from doing something reckless in the name of saving the world too early. And Kal, for all our sakes, don't let him throw himself at danger just to prove he's unafraid.*
>
> *I had a plan. I made arrangements with the King of Varis before any of this began. He agreed to offer sanctuary but only if you reach him. Make your way to the base of Veylorin Lake. There, you'll find enough supplies to carry you through the mountains.*
>
> *You must get to Varis. This pack isn't meant for comfort. It's packed for speed. Don't stop. You know they'll be on your trail. Hopefully I bought you enough time. Hopefully this time, it's different.*
>
> *Reach the capital. Find the king. Don't rest! Don't trust*

anyone! Not until you're standing before him.
This is your only chance.
Make it count.
—A

Liam stared at the page, the words blurring as his eyes burned. Beside him, Kal waited silent. She hadn't spoken but he could feel the stillness in her.

For a moment, he said nothing. But the letter, like everything Arjun left behind, had already carved its mark. Liam folded the letter carefully, as though it were something that would crumble if handled too roughly. Then, without a word, he held it out to Kalithea.

She took it from him without hesitation. Though her movements were measured, there was tension in her fingers. Her eyes moved slowly over the page, taking in each word as if memorizing them. Liam watched as her grip tightened, the paper creasing from the force of her hold, her knuckles whitening under the strain.

Her shoulders squared. Her jaw set.

He recognized the expression that began to take shape—the same guarded look she always wore when the world demanded more than it had any right to. It wasn't weakness. It was armor, forged through years of endurance, tempered by silence and scars.

He leaned toward her slightly, letting his shoulder brush against hers.

"Hey," he said softly.

She gave no reply.

His voice lowered, a thread of quiet defiance under the weariness. "We'll make it."

Still, she said nothing.

"I don't care what it takes, Kal. We'll make it."

That, at last, drew her eyes. She turned her head just enough to meet his gaze, and in that glance—brief though it was—he saw everything the words had not named. The grief she hadn't spoken. The fear she refused to voice. The weight of a loss that felt like it might never ease. And beneath it all, the stubborn battle she fought against the despair that was clawing at the edges of her resolve.

At that moment, he wasn't just her brother. He was the only tether left that kept her anchored to what remained of hope. So he gave her a half-smile—crooked, familiar, nothing too grand. Just enough to crack the stillness.

"Besides," he said, leaning back and stretching his arms behind his head with exaggerated nonchalance, "the sooner we get there, the sooner we can start pissing off an entirely new kingdom."

She blinked once, her expression blank. Then, slowly, a sound escaped her, not quite a laugh, but close enough. A breath caught between disbelief and amusement, light enough to be real, fragile but genuine.

Liam rose to his feet, shaking the stiffness from his legs as he stood. The ache in his muscles flared briefly, but he ignored it. They didn't have the luxury of rest, not for much longer.

He extended a hand toward her, "Come on, sister."

For a moment, she didn't move. Her eyes lingered on his outstretched hand. Then, without a word, she placed her fingers in his. He closed his hand around hers and pulled her up.

And side by side, with the last of the letter's words still in their hearts and the first edge of dawn glinting faintly on the horizon, they turned toward the light–and began walking toward whatever waited beyond it.

The Hunt Never Ends

The forest stretched outward in every direction, an ancient sprawl of trees whose twisted limbs reached like skeletal arms toward the sky. Their shadows stretched long across the fading light, folding the underbrush into silence. No roads cut through the thickets. No game trails softened the earth under their boots. There were no ruins, no broken stones, no markers at all to suggest that men had ever passed this way—and that, more than anything, was why Liam had chosen it.

They had been running for days.

No rest. No warmth. No fire to chase away the biting cold. They avoided roads and trails, navigating only through ravines and overgrown gullies, doing whatever was necessary to stay beyond the reach of the men sent to drag them back.

Liam knew his father. He knew the speed and severity with which the king would act now he knew Kalithea was gone. There would be no delay. The orders would already be issued, the hunt already begun. Every scout in the territories, every tracker with a hound, every soldier born to move silently through the woods—they would all be in motion. Closing the distance. Tightening the net. This was no escape. It was a pursuit. And they were the prey.

If they stopped, even for a heartbeat too long, they were finished.

"Keep moving," Liam murmured, his voice just loud enough to reach her ears, no further. The words rasped against the cold, rough with strain and long hours without sleep.

Kalithea didn't speak. She nodded once and pressed on, her expression drawn, her lips pale with cold, her steps heavy with exhaustion that had sunk deep into her marrow. Her wounds had not fully healed. Every motion came with effort, but she moved forward nonetheless. She had always been stronger than anyone gave her credit for. Stronger, even, than she had any right to be. But strength, he knew, had limits—and they were both nearing theirs.

Liam could feel it in the hollow weight of his limbs, in the dull throb behind his eyes. In the sluggish ache that dragged behind every breath. The hunger gnawed deeper than the bruises. It coiled in his stomach like something feral, refusing to be ignored. He pushed it down. He didn't have a choice. Kal hadn't eaten in two days. What little he'd managed to find—roots pulled from the frozen earth, bitter berries, a raw half-rotten hare more bone than meat—had all gone to her. And even that had not been enough.

The cold worsened with each passing night. The wind cut through their thin clothes like blades. It slipped beneath collars and sleeves, settled against skin like frostbite waiting to claim its due. Their boots were soaked through, their fingers numb, and without fire, they had no way to dry what the rain took from them.

But fire meant light. And light meant death. So they kept walking.

Dusk fell like a shroud—the fading sky bleeding into twilight until the trees seemed to shift and lean, becoming a maze of shadows and whispering limbs. Liam's eyes scanned the forest ahead, but his mind was already elsewhere, listening more than looking.

That was when he heard it. A howl. Distant and thin but unnatural. It echoed with too much precision, held too long in the throat. Not a wolf. Not even a beast.

A signal.

He stopped. His hand shot out, closing around Kal's wrist with sudden urgency. She halted instantly, her breath rising in faint white puffs between them. Her eyes searched his face.

"That's not a wolf," she whispered.

"No," Liam replied, his tone gone cold. "It's a call."

A hunter's cry. A warning. A message passed between predators. And it meant only one thing. They were close.

Too close.

Kalithea swore beneath her breath, the words sharp with anger and fear. "They're tracking us."

Liam's mind was already moving, turning over routes and mistakes. They had been careful—so careful. They had crossed rivers, backtracked their trail, masked their scent with crushed leaves and mud, and still it had not been enough.

"Move," he said, his voice steady but firmer now, his hand tightening on her wrist before releasing it. She didn't question him.

They ran, branches clawing at their skin. Thorns tore at their cloaks. The underbrush rose around them but they kept moving—faster, harder, lungs burning, feet slipping, hearts pounding.

And then came the sound they had feared. Voices, faint but

growing. Shouts echoing through the trees, boots slamming against the frozen ground, the rhythm of the hunt crashing through the forest like a wave. Light followed next. Torches. Dozens of them, weaving through the woods in sweeping arcs, flickering flames like serpents sliding through the dark.

"They're cutting us off," Kalithea said, her breath labored.

"I know." Liam didn't hesitate. "We split."

Her head snapped toward him, disbelief flashing in her eyes. "*What?*"

"Circle back toward the ridge," he said, voice clipped but clear, already shifting direction in his mind. "We will meet there."

She caught his arm, pulling him half around to face her. *"Liam—"*

"Go."

There was a pause, brief but weighted, as her eyes locked with his, something hard and furious rising in her throat. But she didn't argue again. She turned, and without another word, vanished into the trees, her body low, her steps swift and silent. She moved like someone born in shadow, like someone who had survived too much to be caught now.

And Liam, alone now in the deepening dark, turned the other way. He turned away from the path Kalithea had taken, his boots grinding deliberately over frostbitten leaves, making no effort to conceal his steps. There was no attempt to mask his trail, no care taken to move silently. Every snapped branch, every rustling limb, every heavy footfall served a single purpose.

He wanted them to hear him. If they chased him, they would not be chasing her, and for now that was enough.

The first arrow cut past his ear with a sharp whistle, the kind of sound that promised death by inches. He dove instinctively, crashing into the underbrush, heart slamming against his ribs in a frantic rhythm. Behind him, a voice rang out, too near for comfort.

"There! I see him!"

Another arrow followed, the string's snap echoing like a drumbeat across the trees. Liam twisted sharply, the shaft thudding into a tree trunk just inches from his side. Bark exploded outward, splinters slicing through the air. Too close.

He hit the ground and rolled hard, his body already bruised from days of flight. His mind raced through his options. He needed cover. He needed height. His gaze lifted to the branches above him. They were thick, their gnarled arms strung with moss, heavy with leaves and shadow. Strong enough to hold weight. Close enough to reach.

He didn't hesitate. With a surge of effort, Liam leapt upward, fingers locking around the lowest limb. A second arrow struck the ground beneath him as he swung his legs up and climbed, fast and silent. The cold bit at his hands, the wind clawed at his cloak, but he pressed higher, until the trees became a fortress. The canopy enveloped him completely and he was able to start jumping from limb to limb, leaving the place he entered the trees far behind him.

Then he stilled.

The forest floor below shivered with movement. Torches glowed faintly through the leaves. Hunters spilled into the clearing, blades drawn, boots heavy against the earth. Their breath misted in the air, harsh with exertion.

"He's here somewhere," one growled. "The dogs scented him. Spread out!"

"Search the trees," another barked. "Don't let him vanish again!"

They moved like predators, quick, efficient and disciplined. Liam didn't blink. He counted footsteps. Counted heartbeats. Waited. And when the last man held back for one last pass and stepped directly under his perch, Liam struck.

He dropped silently in a controlled fall, blade drawn before he hit the ground. The slash was clean, across the neck, just above the collarbone. The soldier let out a strangled gasp, staggered once, and dropped into the leaves without a sound.

Liam was already moving.

He stripped the corpse swiftly, pulling the man's bow from his back, slinging the quiver over his shoulder, grabbing a belt dagger and any tool he could carry. His fingers moved with the speed of necessity, his body already retreating before the others even noticed their numbers had thinned.

By the time the call of alarm rose behind him, Liam was gone.

He didn't stop until the ground began to slope upward, the trees thinning slightly as the ridge revealed itself in the growing dark. Wind rushed between the rocks, the cold keener now. But not nearly as sharp as the fear that had gripped him since they'd separated.

Then he saw her.

Standing against the wind, one arm drawn tightly around her torso, her cloak torn and her hair tangled from running–Kalithea waited. Her face was pale beneath a sheen of sweat, her eyes hard and clear. *Alive.* He exhaled, relief hitting so hard it almost dropped him.

She was upright. Breathing. Her injuries had worsened but not broken her. Bruised, bleeding, battered but still standing. He stepped forward, lifting the bow he'd stolen in silent offering.

"You good?" he asked, his voice rough.

Kal's eyes scanned him once, checking for injuries, before she gave a small nod. "You?"

Liam let the corner of his mouth turn upward just enough to be a smile. "Better than them."

She huffed a breath. Not quite a laugh, but close enough. There was a flicker of pride in her eyes, of shared understanding. But already, she was turning to the forest behind them, to the shadows.

There was no time. No victory here. Only survival, moment by moment.

Liam gave her a final glance, nodding once.

"We will survive tonight."

She didn't blink. "We will survive every night."

It wasn't bravado. It was a fact. A truth forged in fire, carried in blood. And without another word, they turned and ran, together–vanishing once more into the wild, because the hunt had not ended.

It never would.

Liam's lungs burned with every breath, each inhale a struggle edged with ice, but he forced his body forward, refusing to yield. The ache in his legs had long since passed into something deeper–beyond pain, beyond fatigue. His steps had grown uneven, each one pulled forward by nothing but willpower and the grim knowledge that if he faltered now, if he stumbled even once, it would not be his life that ended.

It would be hers.

The forest gave way suddenly, the trees thinning into open air as the ground dropped into a sheer cliff face. Stone fell away into a chasm so deep the mist at the bottom swallowed everything. There was no path forward, no narrow trail to skirt the edge, no ledge to climb. Only rock, wind, and the empty gorge yawning beneath their feet.

Liam skidded to a halt at the cliff's edge, gravel scattering. His breath ragged in the cold air as he turned sharply to face the tree line behind them. He could already hear the pursuit–the crash of boots through underbrush, the urgent bark of orders, the telltale ring of drawn steel. And then came the flicker of light. Torches wove through the darkened woods, dozens of them, flickering between the trees.

"They're trapped–surround them!" A voice cut cleanly through the woods, sharp with satisfaction.

Liam stepped forward, placing himself between Kalithea and the encroaching line of flames. His chest still heaved with exertion, but his hands were steady as he drew his blade. Behind him, Kalithea remained still, her breathing slow and steady. He could see the tension in her frame. Her fists had curled tight at her sides, her jaw locked hard enough to crack bone.

He could feel it too. Something shifted in the air around her, barely perceptible at first, but unmistakable to him.

Her magic was stirring.

It coiled deep within her like a waiting storm, the pressure of it building with every passing second. It was not wild, not yet, but it was close. He could see it in the faint dark shimmer along her skin, feel it in the way the wind had begun to shift its path, subtle currents circling her like the pull of a tide turning inward. It was power, ancient and volatile, held just beneath the surface.

And she was holding it back.

Barely.

"Hold on Kal, don't let it go, just stay behind me!" Liam called back, his voice firm and unyielding.

Kalithea turned toward him pulling twin daggers, her eyes blazing beneath the tangle of her hair. "Like hell."

There was no time to argue. A hunter burst from the trees, blade already raised, and Liam met him mid-stride. Steel rang out, the clash of metal sharp and punishing in the still air. The force of the blow echoed up Liam's arms, but he didn't falter. He turned with the momentum, ducked underneath a second strike, and drove his own blade forward in a clean, brutal arc.

Another man came through the trees. Then another. Liam moved without thought, his body responding to instinct and necessity. Each parry and counter came faster than the last, his blade carving a path through the chaos with the desperation of a man who knew the end was already coming. He didn't fight like a soldier, but as something more dangerous...a brother with nothing left to lose.

Still, he could feel the tide turning. For every man he dropped, two more followed. These weren't common guards. They fought with precision, with coordination, and above all, with purpose.

"Orders are to bring the girl alive!" someone shouted over the clamor. "Kill the boy!"

The words struck harder than any blow. It had never been about both of them, he had never mattered at all.

And Kalithea heard it.

He saw the shift in her face, the realization settling in behind her eyes. She tightened every line of her posture, her fear dissolving, leaving only cold, calculated conviction.

The wind sharpened. The ground beneath their feet vibrated faintly, a tremor not caused by footfalls or impact, but by something darker– something elemental. The torches, once steady, flickered violently, their flames bending away from her as though even fire understood what was coming and refused to meet it head-on.

Her magic rose.

It moved like smoke and shadow, curling around her until the air itself seemed to recoil. The hunters faltered for a breath, their steps slowed as instinct surpassed training and fear whispered to the edges of their resolve.

"Kal, no!" Liam yelled, panicking.

And then–without warning–the world began to unravel.

THE DARKNESS UNLEASHED

The world convulsed the moment her magic broke free.

It did not rise slowly, nor did it shimmer like starlight or drift like mist. It tore from her–violent and unchecked–as something ancient awakened within her chest and refused to be bound a moment longer. The scream that followed was not one of pain, but of release. A raw, tearing sound that ripped from Kalithea's throat as the world recoiled from her power.

The earth buckled. The wind dropped as though strangled. The torches winked out in a single, soundless instant. And the air itself turned heavy, so thick with magic it suffocated the body like smoke. For a heartbeat, everything stopped. Even the air itself seemed to sag beneath the weight of what she had become.

Liam had no time to think. The force struck him like a hammer to the chest. An invisible shockwave that lifted him from his feet and flung him backward. The breath was stolen clean from his lungs, as his body hit the frozen ground hard enough to jar every bone, pain flaring bright and fast through his injured ribs.

The darkness poured from her, thick as oil and twice as fast. It curled through the air in long, writhing tendrils that moved with heavy intent. It pulsed with power, devoured light and warmth and breath itself. And in its wake came a wrongness so profound that even the trees seemed to lean away.

Liam struggled to rise, but his limbs felt heavy. He was pinned by something heavier than fear. He could only watch.

The hunters, those closest, froze in place with dread. One man, eyes wide and mouth slack, tried to step back, his arm outstretched as if reaching for something that might save him. His fingers never met anything. His body shuddered, spine arched with a sickening crack, and then folded inward with a sound like wet parchment torn in half. His limbs twisted unnaturally, flesh pulled taut and then snapped by an unseen force. A second later, he was gone, nothing left but blood and shards of bone.

Another cried out, a scream that didn't rise from pain, but from horror, high and feral. The shadow reached him before he could turn. It slipped beneath his skin, and in the next breath, he began to unravel. His tendons snapped, muscles tore from his bones as if flayed from within. His skin split along invisible lines, clean as if carved, revealing raw sinew and pulsing tissue before the darkness shredded it into dust.

The next man fell to his knees, blade forgotten, arms raised in surrender. His mouth opened to plead, but his jaw opened wide, stretched open by a force that didn't stop. The shadow poured in, silencing any sound before it was born, filling him with darkness until his chest collapsed inward and his body toppled like a doll emptied of its soul.

More followed.

They ran. They screamed. Some tried to fight.

None succeeded.

The darkness moved with purpose, faster than breath, faster than thought. Bodies dropped in every direction, collapsed into twisted heaps of snapped bones and organs crushed under the weight of this darkness. The very ground blackened where the shadows touched it. Stones cracked. Roots recoiled. The forest shuddered as trees split down their trunks, the bark curling away from rotting wood, their leaves shriveling in an instant. Veins of corrupted energy spidered through the soil, staining the clearing with the mark of something elemental—something broken.

Liam pushed himself upright on shaking arms, coughing violently as he tried to reclaim his breath. His throat was raw from ash and power and fear. Even though his eyes burned, he forced them open, forced himself to look. He shouted her name. Once, then again, then a third time. Each word was more desperate than the last.

She didn't answer.

Kalithea stood at the heart of the destruction, her body encircled by a vortex of shadow that spiraled outward in trembling pulses. Her hair floated weightlessly as it was lifted by the power she could no longer contain. Her skin glowed faintly, not with light, but with dark veins that shimmered like obsidian beneath the surface. Each one pulsing in time with a force that did not belong to this world.

Her eyes, when he saw them, were no longer her own. They were black. Not just dark, but void. Hollow and endless, as if every trace of who she had been had fallen inward, devoured by the very thing she had tried so hard to control.

She was no longer screaming. She was silent now, and in that silence, the world itself held its breath.

But the storm did not subside.

It raged around her. The magic given form, a wild and consuming force that tore through the world as if it had never belonged. It moved without direction, without mercy, unraveling stone, earth, and life in equal measure. Liam could feel it now, the magic turning on her, feeding not from her strength but from her grief, her fear, her pain. With each pulse, it deepened, darkened, until the power no longer felt like it belonged to her at all.

And he understood, with perfect clarity, that if he didn't reach her now—if he didn't stop her—it would consume her completely.

With no space for fear, no time for reason, he moved without thought. Liam threw himself into the center of the storm—past the grasping coils of shadow, past the warning cries of instinct—wrapping his arms around her as the magic lashed at his skin, as pain surged through every nerve like fire. He pulled her close and held her, though it felt as if the very air sought to tear them apart.

It was madness. It was suicide, but it was the only thing that mattered.

He pressed his forehead to hers, anchoring her with touch, with his presence, his voice cracking as it forced its way out.

"Kal, stay with me!"

Her body writhed against him, muscles locking in violent convulsions. Her breath came in short, ragged bursts. Her head thrashing from side to side as though fighting something only she could sense. The magic surged again, this time not in a single pulse but in a burst of fury, ribbons of shadow tearing through the air like claws slashing at prey. It was not just power. It was rage given form, grief made tangible.

"*Kalithea!*," he gasped, tightening his hold even as the magic flayed across his spine and seared through his muscles. "Look at me! You're safe. You're here. Come back!"

But she didn't hear him. She didn't feel his hands bruising her arms, didn't register the desperation in his voice or the blood now soaking into his sleeves. Her eyes were wide, but they saw nothing. She was lost, deep inside the place where her power had taken her, a void from which there was no return unless someone pulled her free. The magic burned through him like molten steel, flooding every part of him with blinding heat. But he did not let go.

"*You have to stay with me!*"

Another pulse rippled outward. The clearing shattered beneath it. Trees cracked at the base, scorched bark exploding outward. The ground split along jagged lines as blackened stone gave way under their feet. Shadow tore through what little remained. And for one terrible moment, Liam felt the world tilt, as if the ground itself might fall away.

"*Kalithea!*"

He shouted her name again, louder this time, hoarse with pain and defiance. But still she didn't answer. Her eyes remained unfocused, locked on something far beyond this world, far beyond him. She was slipping, falling further into the magic with every breath.

Teeth clenched against the pain. He pulled her tighter into his arms, shielding her body with his own. He leaned forward until his brow met hers again.

"I'm here." He whispered, almost to himself, wishing with all his soul that she would just hear him.

A tremor passed through her.

"I'm here. We're here. *I'm safe Kal.*"

Something shifted in the air around her. The magic flickered, just for a moment, a brief disruption in the storm. He felt it, a note of recognition, a fracture in the madness.

Her hands twitched.

"Come back to me, sis."

She gasped. The sound was jagged, involuntary, a desperate breath ripped from her chest. Her back arched once, her limbs seized under the force of it, and then–just as suddenly–it ended.

The magic collapsed inward like a star imploding. One instant it filled the world, and the next, it was gone. The shadows vanished. The storm quieted. The wind died. Kalithea went limp in his arms. Liam's knees gave out, and they fell together onto the blackened earth. As shadowed ash billowed around them, he cradled her carefully, holding her close. Her body was cold and slack against him. For a heartbeat, he couldn't breathe. The world had gone so quiet it felt hollow.

There were no enemies left. No cries, no footsteps. The hunters hadn't fallen.

They had been erased.

His arms tightened. He pressed his fingers to her throat. *Nothing...* but then–there. A flutter, a pulse. Faint but alive.

Relief hit him so hard he nearly doubled over with it. He pressed his forehead to her temple, barely able to hold back the sound caught in his chest.

"You're okay," he whispered. "You're okay."

She jerked against him, a breath breaking from her lungs. This one fuller, deeper, the sound of a life dragged back from the edge. Her hands gripped the front of his tunic. Her breath came in uneven sobs. Her body pressed close as if she needed to feel his heartbeat to believe she was still here.

He held her without speaking, his arms firm, grounding her with every part of himself. His jaw pressed against her temple, his eyes closed against the tears threatening to rise.

He didn't let go.

Around them, the clearing lay silent. Broken, scorched, scattered with the remnants of what her power had done. The scent of ash and blood lingered in the air, thick and metallic.

When he finally spoke again, his voice was faint, low and hoarse.

"We'll figure this out." He didn't loosen his arms. "Together."

The Night Before Sanctuary

By the time they reached the final town before the capital of Varis, the sun had already begun to sink beyond the rooftops, casting long shadows that stretched across the cobbled streets. The last embers of daylight painted the worn stone in molten gold that softened the edges of cracked shutters and crooked walls. It was a peaceful place, folded between the arms of wooded hills and a slow-moving riverbend. And for the first time in weeks, the silence did not carry threat with it.

They had taken the long road, doubling back more than once. Avoiding the main thoroughfares, skirting the edges of merchant caravans and patrol roads, always keeping to the trees. The detour had cost them time and it had drained the last of their strength. But now they were too close to sanctuary to risk speed over caution. And even weariness had its place when survival was on the line.

With the last of the silver recovered from Arjun's hidden cache at Veylorin Lake, they had purchased three things: horses, time, and warmth. A modest meal from a forgettable tavern and access to a quiet bathhouse tucked into a narrow street just beyond the main square. The coin had barely covered the cost, but the man who opened the door had taken one look at their faces and asked no questions.

Kalithea slipped into the steaming water without a word, her movements slow and careful—each one drawn from the tension of a body pushed well past its limits. The heat wrapped around her like cloth, sinking into her bones. But it did not reach the fatigue etched deeper than flesh. Blood and dirt spiraled away from her skin, clouding the water, but the marks beneath remained untouched.

Scars did not wash away.

She sat still, eyes closed, shoulders bowed as the water lapped gently at her collarbone. The bruises ached. The shallow cuts whispered along her ribs and arms. Her entire body was a ledger of violence—a record of survival. And still, the ledger grew longer.

Across from her, on the smooth stone ledge that flanked the bath, Liam sat with his back to her. His sword rested flat across his knees. He had not spoken since they arrived. Had not moved except to take his place at her side, silent as always but unyielding. She had grown used to the quiet he carried with him like armor.

When she finished and dressed, she turned toward him and watched the way his eyes shifted. His gaze fell to the exposed skin of her arms, to the marks—some old, some fresh—where silver lines crossed over raw red. And in that moment, she saw it: the way his jaw locked, the slight twitch in his fingers as his hand curled into a fist against his knee. Rage, carefully caged, barely kept there.

"Liam."

He exhaled sharply and turned away again. His fingers tightened around the hilt of his sword before he forced himself to release it. His jaw worked for a moment before the words came.

"You should put a glamor spell on your scars to hide them."

The tone was too controlled. Too even. The kind of control that came at a cost.

She stilled. He had never said that before. Never suggested she should be anything other than what she was.

"Why?" she asked quietly.

He turned his head. His gaze met hers without hesitation.

"You know why."

The clothes they had made her wear in the palace had never been meant to protect—only to display. Silk so thin it vanished in light, chains that draped like jewelry but locked like shackles. The metal filigree was designed to frame her like an artifact, not guard her like a queen. The court had not seen her as a woman, only as a spectacle. And now, even dressed by her own will, even armored in her own dignity, the scars would show. They would speak before she did.

"They'll see what they did to me," she said, her voice steady, the truth laid bare in the simplicity of the words.

"And they'll see *weakness*," Liam answered. "You need them to see you as untouchable."

She swallowed, her throat tight. "You hate that I have to hide them."

His hand returned to the hilt of his sword, and this time, he didn't release it.

"I hate that they're there at all."

After a long moment, Kal lifted her hand and traced her fingers through the air, slow and purposeful. Her voice followed with a whispered invocation and the glamor settled over her like smoke. Her skin shimmered, flickered, and then cleared.

The scars were gone. As though they had never existed.

Liam said nothing, but when she looked at him again, the rage remained. Not loud, not shaking—but buried deep, wedged into his chest, cold and constant.

Something he could not exhale.

Later, when the bathhouse had emptied and the steam had faded from the air, the hush returned. The heat had long since retreated from the pools, leaving only the faint warmth that clung to stone and skin.

Liam settled onto the narrow bench behind her, the cushion thin and worn beneath him. He said nothing. Just reached forward and began to work through Kalithea's damp hair with steady hands. His fingers moved slowly, untangling each knot with patient ease, as if smoothing the chaos might somehow ease the weight of the past she carried with it.

Kalithea sat cross-legged before him, back straight despite the exhaustion within her. Her eyes remained closed, her breath faint. She said nothing at first, content to let the moment stretch into silence.

"You'll need to act like a queen," Liam said eventually, his voice steady, his hands still moving gently through her hair. "Even if they don't call you one yet."

Kal didn't open her eyes. "And you'll need to act like a prince. Like the son of Elandra. Not just my shadow."

He paused, fingers resting lightly at the ends of her hair. "This isn't about me. It's *your* crown they stole."

Kal's voice was quiet, but it cut cleanly. "They didn't just steal it from me."

Another breath passed between them—thick with memory, heavy with truth.

"So stand like it's yours, too."

He exhaled in resignation. His fingers continued their quiet work. And then she felt the soft clink of metal as the first strand of silver brushed her shoulder.

Without ceremony, he began to weave the fine chains—relics from Arjun's hidden pack—into her braids. He threaded them with the same care he had given before. The strands caught the lantern light as they moved, glinting like tempered starlight against black silk.

"They'll expect me to be grateful," she murmured, voice calm, but edged with steel.

"They'll expect a girl in exile," Liam said, the chain slipping through his fingers. "One desperate for mercy."

"And what should they see instead?"

He clasped the final link.

"A queen who does not kneel," he said quietly. "A fire they cannot stop"

Kal opened her eyes.

Before her, the polished silver basin reflected their images in the low, flickering light. She studied the mirrored version of herself—the dark braid threaded with silver, the shadows beneath her eyes that no amount of rest could erase, the stillness in her shoulders.

Liam's reflection sat just behind her, eyes steady, jaw set, the sword still resting across his knees. She looked at him through the mirror, her gaze holding his.

And in her eyes, the fire had returned.

"Then that is what they'll see. You burn, I burn. Let the rest of the world pray they don't," she said.

Even though the palace had not yet revealed itself on the horizon, it pressed against her as a heavy, unrelenting presence, growing heavier with each step that brought her closer to its gates.

It was not the sight that warned her. It was instinct, the same instinct that had carried her through the corridors of gilded cages and silk-draped cruelty. The same quiet knowledge that danger did not always arrive with raised voices or drawn steel. Sometimes it came with smiles, with soft voices and polished manners. With banquets and bowed heads and an open hand moving to close around your throat.

They were riding into such a place now.

A foreign court, ruled by a foreign king, governed by foreign laws dressed in civility and custom. But Kalithea knew better. She had walked through halls like these before, beneath ceilings painted with myth and stained-glass saints. Past the noblemen whose greetings wrapped silken threats. She had learned to read the shape of power where no blood was spilled, but battles still raged all the same—on the floor of council chambers, behind drawn curtains, in whispered alliances and calculated betrayals.

Varis would be no different.

She knew what would be waiting beyond its carved doors. Eyes that watched too closely. Hands that offered aid with conditions unspoken. Courtiers who smiled too easily, who looked at her not with respect, but assessment. They would not see the woman who had clawed her way from ruin. They would see an opportunity. An orphan. A dethroned heir in need of sanctuary, whose loyalty might be bought or bent or broken.

She had been trapped in a cage once. This time, she walked toward the trap with her eyes wide open.

The man who had built the first cage was behind her. But others like him would be waiting. They always were. Power drew them like blood in water. And they wore masks of courtly grace—men who would drape their hunger in kindness and wield politeness like a weapon. Monarchs, generals, ministers, they all played the same game. Only the board changed.

So she would give them nothing. No emotion. No vulnerability. No glimpse of the girl who had once been broken and made to kneel. She would bury every fracture deep until even she could not reach it. The court would not see her grief, or her magic, or the rage she still carried like embers burning with every breath.

They would see control. Measured steps. A mind too sharp to dull. A presence that neither flinched nor begged. There could be no mistakes. No missteps. No misplaced trust.

She would build her alliances, yes—but not attachments. She had no use for soft edges, no need for sentiment. What she required were weapons—individuals who could be shaped, directed, and placed. Informants, tacticians, power-brokers. She would measure every name, every face, every offer, and decide which could be bent to serve her cause. When the time came and the court turned to look at her, it would not see a girl returned from exile, but a queen who had never stopped planning.

Trust, she knew, was a luxury—and she afforded it to only one.

Liam.

He remained the one constant in the shifting landscape of her life. He had stood with her when she had nothing. He was her brother, bonded by the pain they shared, by the history they both bore in silence. A boy who had thrown himself between her and harm so many times that Kalithea had lost count. Who had taken the punishments meant for her, who had bled in her place, and never once asked for thanks.

She hadn't pulled him into this war. The court had done that. The crown. The man who wore the title of royalty like armor while destroying everything it once stood for. They had turned Liam into what he now was—a blade honed on injustice, sharpened by loss, wrapped in the grim patience of someone who had endured far too much far too early.

She had lost Arjun. She would *not* lose Liam.

Even now, Arjun's name drifted through the corners of her thoughts. She had forced herself not to linger on him, not to carry the weight of that loss where others might see it. But in the hushed moments, when silence settled and the road stretched ahead without sound, she remembered. The way he had walked into death without hesitation.

She had failed to save him, but she would not fail again.

The sky above Varis had faded into a deep, bruised violet by the time they reached the lower edges of the palace district. The last warmth of the sun long surrendered to the authority of night. Sconces danced with life along the cobbled roads, in cheerful succession. Pools of golden light spilled across the stones, catching in the slick edges left behind by the evening mist. The scent of flowers mixed with the sharper tang of damp soil rising from the gardens that skirted the lane.

They rode side-by-side, their cloaks drawn close against the cooling air. They moved with purpose down the lesser-traveled alleyways that curved like veins through the capital, to avoid the broader roads where merchants and nobles were still finishing their rounds. The hour worked in their favor; the shift-change among the guards would leave gaps, however brief, and fewer eyes meant fewer questions. And fewer questions meant fewer risks.

"The north gate should be quickest, from what I remember on the maps," Liam said eventually shifting in his saddle, his voice just above a breath, reluctant to break the hush that held around them. "Should take us through the garrison courtyard—less traffic, fewer nobles."

Kalithea nodded without looking at him, as her eyes swept the darkness ahead trying to determine if the shadows might just yield a threat. "But more soldiers," she murmured.

He didn't answer. Arjun's word had brought them here, and Arjun's word had never failed them—but the world had, again and again. Trust was a fragile thing, precious and brittle. They had both learned that it often broke in the hands of kings just as easily as in those of killers. Even now, with the promise of sanctuary ahead, her instinct recoiled like a hand brushing too close to fire. There was always a price. Even kindness exacted one.

She exhaled and forced her shoulders to relax under the weight of the damp cloak. Her back however remained taut. "We don't bow," she said, an order that reaffirmed something buried deep within. "We don't kneel. We represent no court but our own."

Liam's mouth pulled into a line that wasn't quite a smile. "You mean yours."

"No," she said simply. "I mean *ours*."

She let it settle there. He didn't challenge it—not truly. His voice hadn't held resentment, only weariness. His eyes hadn't left the gate since it came into view. It was tall and broad, flanked by four guards in deep blue and silver, their spears upright and burnished to gleam in the torchlight. They shifted at the sight of strangers approaching in foreign-cut cloaks, their posture sharpening even before a word was spoken.

Kal felt their gaze touch her. Assessing, calculating. They noted the damp braid falling over her shoulder, the slight weight in her motions masked by exactness. The way she held herself straight, regal in bearing yet unadorned by any crest or sigil. Liam drifted closer as they passed between the guards, not shielding, only in such a way that if blades came, they would strike him first. The guards did not halt them, though their eyes lingered.

The second gate admitted them with a slight groan, revealing a courtyard cleaner than the streets behind them, the broad stone tiles polished smooth by time. Iron sconces held steady flames, casting quiet halos across the colonnades. A pair of horses crossed in the distance, their hooves striking in rhythm, their riders unconcerned with the two hooded figures now moving through the palace grounds.

They found the stables without interruption, though Kalithea kept one hand within easy reach of her blade. She dismounted first, her boots touching the ground in near silence. Liam followed with the same ease and took both reins before raising his voice.

"You there," he called out to the boy who had dozed into a slouch near the stable wall, his head tucked into his collar.

The boy startled upright, blinking rapidly, no more than fifteen, though trying hard to seem older. He rose quickly at Liam's approach, eyeing the horses, then their riders—his gaze lingering on the worn leather gloves, the absence of any identifying crest. What they wore was not common, yet neither did it speak of ceremonial arrival. But they moved like people accustomed to command.

"Feed, water, and brush them down," Liam said, handing off the reins. "Make sure it's done before dawn."

The boy gave a short nod, then hesitated. His eyes flicked between them once more. This time he caught the subtle stiffness in Kal's stance, the edge in her silence. A ripple of caution, more than fear, passed through him and he took the reins without protest.

"Far stall," Liam added, quieter now. "They don't like company."

The boy's hesitation stretched half a second longer before he nodded again and turned away. He walked with the clipped efficiency of someone trying to convince himself he was being useful, not dismissed.

Kalithea watched him disappear beneath the arch, then tilted her chin toward the carved passage that led into the palace proper. "We'll be watched now," she said, her voice steady, almost detached.

Liam's reply came with the ghost of a grim smile, "We'll see them first."

The courtyard unfurled before them in a broad sweep of stone and shadow, its expanse framed by high walls laced with ivy and torch brackets, flames flickering low in the evening wind. The scent here was different than in the gardens above—less perfumed, more grounded—a mingling of dirt and clean sweat, of oiled leather and sharpened steel. It was a soldier's space, functional, disciplined, and free of pretense.

Kalithea's boots made no sound across the stone, but she felt the shift in Liam. His hand brushed the edge of his cloak— in a quiet movement that's been bred into men who had learned to live prepared. She slowed, only a breath's width, her gaze cutting sideways just as he stilled entirely.

Then she saw the man.

He stood half in shadow near the arch that led into what must have been the barracks. He had no weapon drawn, there were no words offered, but his presence held weight. He didn't watch them with challenge or with hunger, but with a narrowed gaze that assessed, categorized, and waited.

He was tall, his build broad in that unpolished way only years of real battle could carve. The set of his shoulders spoke of readiness, not ceremony—his stance relaxed, but deceptively so, as if coiled for motion at a moment's notice. His short hair was dark, curling longer at the top than the sides in an unruly rebellion against whatever discipline held him in check. His short-trimmed beard gave his broad but angular face the edge of something handsome touched by hardness.

But it was his eyes that held her—longer than she meant to allow. They didn't flash or leer; they didn't attempt charm or project threat. They simply held—depthless, still, like the surface of deep water that gave away nothing of what waited below. She had seen eyes like that before. Eyes that had looked into violence and didn't blink.

A weathered cloak hung over one shoulder, fastened with a simple clasp made for utility. Under it, his shirt collar was open just enough to reveal sun-worn skin peppered with scars. Around his neck, a leather cord bore a golden medallion—worn with time, but not without meaning.

She did not stop walking, but she let her eyes linger on him the way one might pause before a dagger left unsheathed on an unfamiliar table. Not fearful. Not curious. Just watchful. Measuring. And then, as quickly as she had noticed him, she dismissed him with cool disinterest. Her chin lifted in a small, decisive motion, and her hand shifted slightly—barely a gesture, but Liam understood. He fell in step once more, silent, and they continued across the courtyard.

A young page rounded the far colonnade, distracted, likely en route to nowhere of consequence. Liam moved before the boy could pass them, stepping into his path with an unshakeable, unyielding finality.

"Boy," Liam said, his voice low, without menace but a firmness that halted questions.

The boy froze, wide-eyed.

"Go to the King. No one else. Tell him only this: the one he was expecting has arrived. You will not speak those words to another soul—not in the hall, not in passing, not even to yourself. You will find him. Alone. And you will say exactly what I told you."

The boy's mouth parted slightly, some response forming, but Liam didn't raise his voice. He simply let the next words fall.

"If you value your life," he said, his tone still and cold, "then you will forget our faces the moment you turn away. Not a whisper. Not a glance. Not a shadow."

The page swallowed hard, nodded with a jerk, and cast one glance between the woman who stood regal and mysterious and the man who radiated danger—then fled toward the inner corridors with steps that quickened once he was out of earshot.

Adjusting the fall of her cloak effortlessly, she stepped through the stone archway that marked the threshold of the palace proper. The torches cast warm gold against cold stone as her shadow slipped across the floor and into the halls of Varis.

Inside, the palace breathed elegance with every line and surface. The floors were laid in veined marble—silver threading through stone like rivers frozen in time—while the vaulted ceilings rose in arching spires overhead. The chandeliers hung with glass teardrops that caught the torchlight and scattered it like fractured stars. The walls gleamed in polished stone, cool and dusky in color, like storm skies trapped in the mineral. Silver filigree danced across each surface in curling patterns. Every arch bore the symbol of Varis, the white stag, crowned in golden antlers that cradled a flame suspended just above its brow—never touching, never consuming, as though it bore some sacred burden too holy to extinguish.

It was beautiful. Too beautiful.

Kalithea's eyes moved through the space—not drawn to its splendor but cataloguing its risks. Beauty was no measure of mercy. She had walked through halls gilded in gold before and still heard the echo of chains.

They paused in a recessed alcove along the northern wall, partly screened by tall metalwork sculpted into a tangle of antlers. The screen provided concealment without cutting off their view, the perfect blend of art and advantage. It was a place designed for courtiers to linger unseen—but for Kal and Liam, it was a place to observe, calculate, and plan for the worst.

"That corridor," Liam murmured, his voice nearly lost in the hush, "loops back toward the courtyard. If they block the main entry, we can cut through and reach the stables."

Kal didn't answer immediately. She was listening. Feeling the air shift.

"That window," she said at last, nodding toward an arched pane of tinted glass inset between two columns, "has a hinged base. Opens inward."

Liam didn't look. "Would you jump from that height?"

"I'd throw you first," she replied, dryly.

His breath caught on something that might have been a laugh, had it been allowed to grow.

They stood together in the hush. Shadows clothed them as they watched the court unfold from its outer edges. Creatures of grit and grief standing poised at the border of a world made of gold.

"You think he'll be soft?" Liam asked, quieter now. "A king who wears silver and rules through the bottom of his goblet?"

Kal's gaze landed on the stained-glass panel at the end of the chamber, the white stag half-turned as though watching her.

"Arjun said he was kind," she murmured.

"That doesn't mean he's harmless."

"No," she agreed slowly, her voice cooling. "It doesn't. We don't trust him. Not yet. But we show strength. Discipline. He's already made the first move. He opened his gates."

"And if he wants more than words?"

Kal's answer was steady. "Then he'll learn that the tales about us are true."

She turned her head, eyes catching the flicker of firelight in the glass, "We burn."

THE KIND KING

The soft scuff of boots stirred the still air as Kalithea turned her head. She glimpsed the page returning, this time with another figure following in his wake. The second man was taller, clad in tailored robes of navy trimmed with silver, the fabric pressed so sharply it seemed as if it had never been worn. A medallion marked him for what he was: a senior herald, his insignia polished to a gleam.

He didn't speak at once. His gaze moved over Kal and Liam with open scrutiny, passing from the scuffed edges of their boots to the heavy weight of Liam's travel-worn cloak. His brow furrowed, mouth tightening with an uncertainty that flirted with hesitation, as though deciding whether to speak... or summon steel.

Then his eyes met Kalithea's. She didn't blink. Her chin remained high, tilted with a quiet defiance that did not need to announce itself. There was power in her presence—unvarnished, unapologetic. Liam mirrored her without effort, quieter in his stance but no less imposing. His hand rested casually at the hilt of his sword—not as a warning, but as a statement of fact.

The herald faltered. There was nobility here, yes, but of a type unfamiliar to him. He cleared his throat and bowed with just enough of an incline to acknowledge a rank he could not name and dared not dismiss.

"His Majesty requests your presence in his private study," he said, his voice crisp with rehearsed decorum. "If you would follow me."

Kal gave no verbal reply, only a nod, cool and guarded. Liam did not move until she did, falling into step just behind her left shoulder. The three of them turned and passed through the high arch of the corridor's inner threshold.

The palace enveloped them at once, a structure of soaring grace and meticulous design, every inch built to proclaim not only wealth but heritage. Gilded cornices crowned the hallways, their filigree catching the soft gleam of pearl-lacquered walls. Sconces lined each stretch of marble with calculated symmetry, casting long shadows that layered over one another. No corner existed without intention; every alcove had been carved with reverence and pride.

Kal's stride was smooth, her bearing unshaken by grandeur. Where others might pause to marvel, she studied instead–her gaze skimming each wall and ceiling arch, counting the spacing between doors, the height of windows, the intervals between light and shadow. She had long since learned that beauty often masked danger, and palaces were the most elegant traps of all, designed to distract and disorient.

Liam walked beside her. His fingers curled loosely over the pommel of his sword, his steps silent but solid, a rhythm attuned to danger. He watched everything—the servants who passed with their heads bowed, the change in echo as the corridor curved, the shift in airflow near vented alcoves. With every step, he revised the map he was building in his mind: five turns, two stairwells, a side passage that bent northward behind an unguarded door.

The herald glanced back once, and in the moment his gaze touched Liam's intense expression, something in his posture stiffened. He said nothing, but walked a shade quicker than before. They continued deeper into the palace's inner sanctum. Past a series of mosaic columns inlaid with stag motifs, under domes painted in metallic hues, where torchlight scattered in reflections too intricate to be accidental.

When the herald turned again, they entered a wing of different character. The guards here were fewer, but more dangerous. Older, quieter, more precise in posture and uniform. Their tabards bore sigils Kal did not recognize, but the implication was clear. These were not men assigned to decorate a hallway. These were trusted protectors of something sacred...or royal. Her eyes flicked once toward Liam. He returned a nearly imperceptible nod. He'd marked them too.

The corridor narrowed into its final stretch. It ended at a set of towering double doors carved from metal-veined wood, silver threads gleaming through the grain like lightning caught in ancient bark. They rose high, their surface carved with leaping stags and curling flames. The antlers gilded with gold leaves that shimmered even in low light. This was no mere entry. It was a legacy. Authority carved into architecture.

Two guards flanked the threshold. They stood like statues, halberds polished to mirror-sheen, tabards without a single crease, expressions devoid of distraction. These were not ceremonial watchmen. These were men who had killed before and would do so again without hesitation.

Without a word or gesture, one moved to the handle, and the other mirrored him. Together they pulled the doors outward with a smooth, deliberate sweep. The herald stepped forward while casting a final look over his shoulder before he cleared his throat and raised his voice, the words echoed with perfect formality.

"Your Majesty, the guests have arrived, as requested."

He turned, bowed halfway, and extended an arm to usher them inside.

Kalithea did not pause, though every instinct within her wanted to. This was the place where games began. The air was wrong–the silence too rehearsed, the lighting too careful–but she knew how fear presented itself. And how others watched for it. So she moved forward as though the floor beneath her had been laid for her feet alone. Liam followed a breath behind. He didn't look toward the center of the room, or the rich furnishings that likely lined the chamber, instead his eyes moved to the shadowed corners, to any possibility of hidden threats or danger. His hand never strayed from his sword, his posture never softened. He would not pretend ease where none was earned.

The study smelled of parchment and firelight, a space steeped not in pageantry but in quiet authority. Warmth radiated from the hearth, where flames curled steadily against carved stone, casting an amber glow across the chamber's worn splendor. Shelves lined the walls in dark-stained oak, their contents neither staged nor pristine, but lived-in. Books softened at the corners from long use, scrolls bound with leather thongs that bore the marks of repeated untying, maps folded so many times the vellum creased like skin. A brass astrolabe rested beside an open atlas, both left mid-consultation, and nearby lay a harp with one cracked tuning peg, its presence more personal than decorative. A sword leaned against the far wall, unpolished but lovingly kept. It was a room not arranged to impress but to be thought in, commanded from. At the center of it all stood the desk, half-buried underneath documents, scattered wax stamps, and curling edges of correspondence–at once chaotic and controlled. Behind it sat the man they had come to meet.

King Alden Llewelyn did not rise at their entrance, but lifted his eyes from the page before him, the flicker of the hearth light catching on the gold embroidery along his collar. Though seated, he gave the immediate impression of breadth–his frame wide at the shoulders, posture alert but at ease. Silver streaked the edges of his short-trimmed beard, and though time had begun its slow march through his temples, it had yet to diminish the presence he carried. He was the kind of man who had not yielded to age but had learned how to wear it. He looked not like a king out of stories, but like a man who had endured long enough to rule with something deeper than strength. His mouth might have seemed stern if not for the ghost of amusement tucked into the corners, as though he were someone more inclined to laughter than judgment. The lines below his eyes bore the evidence of a life well-lived and fully seen. But it was the eyes themselves that stilled Kal's breath, if only for a moment.

Clear blue. Steady, warm, watchful. The eyes of a ruler who had not allowed the years to harden into cruelty. They did not flicker with pity, nor narrow in suspicion. They simply saw her.

Kal stopped before the desk, Liam a half-step behind. Neither bowed. Neither offered their names, nor proffered titles, nor explained their presence. They stood as they were, unapologetic and unmasked.

The king considered them for only a moment more before speaking.

"Leave us."

The herald bowed and retreated at once, disappearing behind the silent sweep of the closing doors. The guards followed suit without a murmur. Only the click of the latch broke the room's breathless hush.

Alden raised a hand before either of them could speak. "Please," he said, gesturing to the chairs before his desk, his tone gentle. "Sit. You've done enough standing for one day."

Kal did not move immediately. Her eyes traced the gesture, then returned to the king, weighing him for threats. Finding none, she lowered herself into the seat, not nervous. Prepared. Liam followed suit, slowly positioning himself at an angle that kept Kal within arm's reach. His shoulders squared, his body tight with readiness. Even seated, he looked less like a guest and more like a watchtower.

The king studied them both in silence for a beat longer, then said, with no grandeur or artifice, "I'm sorry."

Kal's eyes narrowed, though her voice stayed even. "For?"

The question slipped out more sharply than she intended. The syllables shaped by suspicion born of those who had spoken softly only to twist softness into chains.

Alden's expression didn't falter.

"For whatever path the world forced you to walk to reach my door in this condition," he said. "Whatever it took from you along the way. I cannot restore what was lost. But I can say that I am sorry for it."

She held his gaze without blinking, her face vacant.

"We didn't come for sympathy," she said.

"I know," Alden replied, his voice carrying the edge of a chuckle. "I doubt you'd know what to do with it, even if I offered it."

He leaned back, the gesture not one of arrogance but of a man creating space, inviting truth to breathe between them.

"I don't offer sympathy. I offer rest. And the hope that, behind these walls, you might find what you have not been given in far too long–*safety*. Stillness. The freedom to be."

Kal's jaw tightened, though the words came without venom. "Those who believe in safety are often the first to fall."

Alden's smile was unshaken, tempered by understanding. "Then don't believe in it," he said simply. "Feel it. In time."

The fire crackled behind him, a gentle punctuation to the quiet.

"You'll be quartered in the east wing," Alden continued. "It borders the royal family's wing. Few pass through there. Only those I permit."

Kal said nothing, but she listened, the shift of her eyes giving her away.

"That wing belonged to my wife's kin," he went on. "When she passed, I closed it. The rooms are yours, if you'll take them. No one enters that wing without my word. No courtiers. No spies. Only my most trusted—myself, my son Jarreth, and his champion, Raoul Sahir. No others."

The silence stretched, taut but not hostile.

"You may remain anonymous," Alden added. "For as long as you wish. No declarations. No announcements. No one beyond this room needs to know you've set foot in Varis."

Liam's breath escaped in a sound too dry to be called a laugh, too sharp to be entirely mocking.

"True anonymity?" he said. "Rare commodity in a palace."

Alden gave a small, rueful smile. "Rare, yes. But not unachievable. Not when the one who holds the throne is willing to guard your name himself."

Then his voice dipped lower—not for secrecy, but for sincerity.

"Whatever trust you choose to give me, let this be known: I will never use your presence here as leverage. I will not speak your names. You've lived too long with the weight of war on your shoulders. I won't add my own."

Liam spoke first, his voice careful. "What do you want from us in return?"

Alden did not flinch. He did not bristle, preen or hedge the truth in diplomacy. He simply leaned back, fingers steepling beneath his chin and said, "Nothing."

Kal's reaction was slight but unmistakable. Her eyes snapped into sharper focus, the wariness in them intensifying. When she spoke, her voice held the caution of a woman who had been offered too many honey-eyed traps.

"Kings do not give without cost. Even the ones who smile. They want favors. *Leverage.* Future obedience."

Alden met her words not with denial, but with quiet sorrow. His expression softened into grief.

"I am sorry," he said again, and this time the words carried weight. "Sorry, that you've come to believe that. And I am even more sorry that the world has justified it."

His eyes met hers, steady and open. There was no guile in them. No cunning. No ask.

"But not all power is a leash. Not all refuge is a cage."

Kal watched him apprehensively. She had heard too many promises, seen too many hands held out with something hidden behind the fingers. Even now she searched–scanned the way his mouth curled, the angle of his shoulders, the subtle cadence of his breath–for the edge of the blade he hadn't shown. She found nothing, and that unsettled her more than any trap might have.

"I offer this," Alden said softly, "because someone should have, long before now. If it begins with me, then so be it."

She did not respond. The silence wrapped around her, brittle and gleaming, dangerous in its restraint. Beside her, Liam remained equally still, offering no answer of his own. Though the suspicion that burned within him had not lessened, merely folded in on itself, soundless and coiled under the same unease that gripped her.

Alden allowed the pause to stretch between them, neither hurried nor hesitant, and when he spoke again, his tone had softened, his cadence almost conversational. "Arjun sent word ahead. More than words actually. Supplies. Clothing. Coin enough to ensure neither of you would need to rely on the charity of strangers. He said–" a flicker of a smile played across his face "–that neither of you would accept kindness unless it had been disguised as something earned."

At the mention of that name, Kal's throat tightened with something sharp and sudden. She hadn't expected to hear it, not so soon, not spoken so casually. It felt like a thread being drawn loose from a wound still stitching itself shut. Her hands clenched together in her lap, fingers folding tightly until her knuckles whitened from the strain.

The King gestured toward the nearby table where a satchel lay neatly sealed, his voice grew quieter, edged with the care of a man delivering something sacred. "There's enough for all three of you. He thought of everything. Said you would never want to owe anyone. That if you came here, it had to be on your own terms."

Then, as if the question were nothing more than practical curiosity he asked, "When will he be joining you?"

Beside her, Liam shifted. The first movement he'd made in minutes. His mouth parted slightly, the beginning of an answer struggling to form but nothing emerged. His throat worked, brow furrowing, but the words refused him. They were caught somewhere deep, unspoken and unwelcome, anchored in pain too raw to speak aloud.

Kal answered in his place. Her voice emerged flat and distant, devoid of emotion. Her fingers moved slowly, lacing together with forced calm atop her thigh.

"He fell." The words were sharp and absolute.

Alden stilled.

Kal's gaze remained steady, her expression fixed with careful discipline. "He stayed behind at the palace. Rhaen's men were already coming through. He knew they would never stop hunting us. He... chose to give us a head start. Held them off long enough for us to reach the Eastern Road."

She paused, but not to breathe, to fight off something deeper. Grief pressed against her chest with quiet, ruthless persistence.

"He knew he would not survive."

Liam's hand curled tighter around the hilt of his sword until the leather creaked beneath his grip. His jaw clenched, muscles ticking with restraint. And though he did not speak, the angle of his face–turned slightly toward the fire–betrayed the storm gathering behind his eyes.

Kal could feel her own grief moving through her, not a wound but a second pulse, rhythmic and relentless. And still, her face held. No break. No weakness. Not here. Not in front of a king.

Alden inclined his head with a solemn grace, the lines at the corners of his eyes deepening. "You have my most sincere condolences," he said, each word thoughtful, not performative. "From every letter he sent, every scribbled note or update passed to me, it was clear what kind of man he was. Clever. Brave. Tireless in his care for you both."

He looked between them now, his voice low with something that came close to solemn respect.

"You meant the world to him." The quiet that followed held a shared understanding of loss that no kingdom or crown could alleviate.

Then Liam spoke, voice rough and worn at the edges. "We... were the only family he had left. After the purge..." His throat bobbed as he swallowed hard. "And he was all we had too."

He left it at that, because to say more would be to break entirely.

Alden's shoulders lifted with a long breath, the weight of their story settling into the space around them. "You've both seen too much," he said softly. "Far more than anyone of any kingdom should have to bear. It is my hope that you'll find some measure of peace here. And in time... perhaps even happiness."

Kal's chin lifted, her poise untouched by the heaviness pressing into the room. "We appreciate the sentiment, Your Majesty," she replied, the words cool and clear. "But so long as my people bleed... so long as the purges continue and Rhaen's shadow darkens even one inch of my homeland, there will be no peace for us."

Her eyes locked with his.

"We will learn what must be learned. Forge whatever alliances are necessary. And one day, we will march."

Alden did not flinch from the declaration. In truth, he smiled–just a fraction, showing a glimmer of respect. "Then may the gods be wise enough to stand out of your way."

He rose then, slowly, gesturing with a subtle sweep of his hand. "Come. I imagine your journey was longer and far more perilous than you'll ever confess to. Let me show you to your quarters, Queen Kalithea."

The title landed without ceremony. It rang as a simple truth spoken aloud as though it had never been in doubt.

Kal did not move. Not immediately. Though her expression remained composed, something shifted behind her eyes. The word echoed in her chest with the distant gravity of a tolling bell. *Queen.* It was a title ripped from her with blood and ash, a crown shattered and scattered in pieces across a dying land. And yet Alden had spoken it without pause as if no other name fit.

She said nothing of it. Instead, she arched her brow, her voice dry with incredulity. "A curious thing, that a king would show us to our chambers himself. Not a servant. Not a slave."

Alden chuckled, already making his way toward the doors. "There are no slaves in Varis, Queen Kalithea. And as for servants..." He paused at the brass handle, fingers hovering with idle grace. "I'd prefer to keep the number of people who know your true identities as small as possible. Even my son will only be told that you are honored guests. Guests to be treated with the utmost veneration...but nothing more."

Liam's tone was edged with disbelief. "You're not even going to tell your heir who we are?"

Alden said nothing, still smiling faintly as he opened the doors without fanfare and stepped through. He didn't look back. He simply moved forward, his back unguarded, his pace slow. A wordless display of trust so rare, it struck more deeply than any oath spoken aloud.

Kal watched him go, expression clouded. Liam hesitated for a beat longer, his hand still resting near the hilt of his sword. But at length, he allowed it to fall away, and followed.

The corridor unfolded before them in subtle majesty, its polished stone floors gleamed faintly beneath their boots as warm light spilled from the sconces affixed along the walls. Each flame swayed gently in its cradle of gold.

King Alden walked ahead without haste, his gait steady. When they reached a branching corridor, he gestured with an easy motion down the right-hand passage.

"My quarters lie just beyond there," he said, his tone casual, though not without weight. "As do my son's, and his champion's. Should ever the need arise."

Kalithea offered no reply, but the detail lodged itself quietly in her mind, another thread to pull when the time came. Information was its own currency, and she had long ago learned to value even the smallest coin.

They continued on. The main corridor remained empty and unmarred by foot traffic. No servants swept around corners bearing linens or wine, no guards loitered in half-shadowed alcoves pretending not to watch. It was, as Alden had promised, kept utterly bare. Only at the end, where the corridor intersected with the royal wing, stood a silent formation of armored sentinels. Present, yes, but stationed far enough away to neither intrude nor overhear.

Eventually, Alden drew to a halt before a pair of carved wooden doors, tall and elegant, with an arching threshold between them that led into a shared sitting chamber beyond. The wood was dark and rich with age, the panels inlaid with a subtle silver filigree that caught the lanternlight without calling attention to itself. The entire space breathed refinement, but never ostentation.

He turned to face them then, and something in his posture shifted. Formality gave way to something more human, less king than caretaker.

"These are yours," he said quietly. "Everything Arjun sent ahead has been placed inside–clothing, coin, supplies. He thought of everything. You'll find no detail overlooked. He made certain you'd have what you needed to begin again."

He paused, understanding the enormity of what 'beginning again' could mean. Especially to those who had bled to reach the threshold of safety.

"Take your time. There's no schedule to meet here. No demands to answer until you're ready to be seen."

He gestured faintly toward a silver-cast bell affixed beside the door frame, its rope coiled with blue thread. "If you need anything, ring this. My head of staff is the only one who'll come, and only when summoned. His name is Dodder. He's been with me since I was a boy–loyal, discreet, and as safe a soul as you'll ever meet."

A brief smile touched his mouth then, wry and knowing. "Though I suspect the pair of you will test his patience soon enough."

He said nothing more. No further reassurances. No lingering platitudes. With a final, respectful incline of his head, King Alden turned and walked away down the corridor. His pace was unchanged–unhurried, unguarded, never once glancing back. He left them as he had received them: not as fugitives to be managed, but as sovereigns who had not yet reclaimed their crowns.

ALONE AT LAST

O nly when the soft echo of Alden's retreating steps had faded into silence did Liam step forward and press his hand against the door. It opened without resistance, swinging inward on well-oiled hinges to reveal the chambers beyond–rooms meant for comfort, though neither of them quite knew what to do with comfort.

He entered first, gaze sweeping across the interior warily, instincts trained by hardship. The suite was elegant. The floors gleamed with a mirrored polish, their surface broken by thick-woven rugs in hues of slate and garnet. Heavy curtains framed high windows, their embroidered edges stirring faintly in the draft. Carved furniture in dark wood flanked a low-burning hearth, the fire casting its glow across marble and brass. There was an unfamiliar peace to the space, a kind of reverent quiet that spoke of isolation rather than opulence.

Liam moved through it like a shadow; checking each archway, each corner, each entryway with the diligence of someone who expected danger even in sanctuary. When he returned, his nod was short and tight–enough to signal all was well, though the tension in his shoulders didn't ease.

Kal lifted a brow, her tone dry. "You do realize I'm perfectly capable of protecting us."

"Yes, yes, I know," he said, brushing past her with the tired cadence of an oft-repeated exchange. "You're the nightmare everyone checks for."

A faint smirk tugged at her mouth. "Exactly."

But whatever humor might have followed faded the moment his gaze caught on the table at the center of the sitting room. Neatly arranged bundles lay stacked in rows; clothing folded with care, straps of armor polished and oiled, satchels drawn and knotted, pouches of coin glinting faintly in the firelight. Weapons wrapped in oilcloth sat beside scrolls and tomes, their presence obscured but unmistakable.

He froze, his expression tightening.

Kal followed his line of sight and stopped beside him, her breath caught in her throat. It wasn't the wealth or the resources that silenced her. It was the intention behind them—the foresight, the meticulousness. These were not gifts hastily thrown together. They were pieces of a life reassembled by hands no longer here. Preparations made by Arjun before they had even dreamed they would need them.

Her eyes moved slowly across the items, noting the careful attention to detail—everything accounted for, nothing forgotten. Armor. Robes tailored in the cuts of Elandra's ancient court, before the fall, their deep hues unmistakable. Jewelry once used to dress her like a weapon now reclaimed as tools of diplomacy, leverage, strategy. Even the coins had been bundled, separated from jewels from the fae halls. But it was not any of that which undid her. It was the realization that he had seen it this clearly. That he had known, long before they had admitted it, what would come next.

The ache that rose behind her eyes was sudden, fierce, but brief. There would be no collapse, no unraveling. She had long since learned how to bind grief below the surface, how to keep it from drowning the task ahead. And still... she stepped forward, closing the distance between them until she stood beside Liam. Then, quietly, she leaned her brow against his shoulder.

Liam stiffened, unprepared for the gesture. But after a breath, his arm shifted, settling gently at her back. They stood like that for a while, not moving, letting the fire burn low in its grate, and the silence stretched on between them.

Eventually, it was Liam who pulled away first. He crossed to the table with the steady efficiency of a soldier returning to duty and crouched beside two oil-wrapped bundles. The unfolded cloth revealed steel, well-balanced, honed to a gleam. Identical to their blades left behind in Elandra. Kal joined him, her eyes moving from the swords to the smaller weapons beside them. Curved daggers, gifts from the fae court, lay nestled in black velvet, their edges glinting. The weight of them was perfectly balanced in her hands.

Beyond the weapons lay the rest of Arjun's legacy: books, scrolls, and painstakingly gathered research that was wrapped in leather and bound with twine. Kal recognized several titles at a glance: arcane studies, leyline charts, treatises on containment and rune theory. Some bore the sigils of fae archives long thought closed to outsiders. Others had been annotated in Arjun's hand. Underlined phrases, marginal notes, glyph corrections written in a tight, slanted script. A few had corners blackened from testing wax seals and binding runes.

She did not touch them. Not yet. It felt too much like trespassing. Instead, she let her gaze linger on the bindings, on the corners he had marked, on the faint signs of wear. They revealed just how many nights he must have spent reading, studying, preparing her for the power she had refused to name.

Liam, ever pragmatic, tested the weight of the coin pouches and laid the weapons in their proper order. Kal remained still, her fingers trailed just above the topmost scroll.

They didn't speak, there was no need. Everything that mattered had already been said by a man who wasn't there to say it.

Liam carried the blades into his chamber first, and placed them carefully at the bedside. He found a floorboard near the hearth that lifted slightly under pressure, and, without hesitation, concealed the coin pouches beneath it. In his mind, he already catalogued the room as if preparing for siege. It was the instinct of someone who had never trusted safety to last.

Kal moved with equal purpose, her hands ghosted over the books before she carried them into her own chamber. A cabinet near the wall served well enough. She aligned the spines with meticulous care, though she knew she wouldn't read a word of them tonight. Not with Arjun's notations still echoing like phantom voices beneath the bindings.

By the time the last of the packages had been sorted and put away, the fire had guttered low in the hearth. Its once-bright flames reduced to an amber glow and shadowed embers.

Their weapons lay within reach, polished and waiting. Liam stood near the door that linked their chambers, one hand rested lightly against the frame, the other drifted unconsciously toward his belt where no blade remained. Kal stood across from him, her back against the arch of her doorway, arms folded tight across her chest, eyes unfocused. It was a familiar silence, one forged in the long nights of shared hunger, sleepless marches, and narrow escapes. It carried the memory of nights when the dark had not been empty. When it crawled with shadows that did not stay outside. When sleep had been a danger, not a reprieve. When the dark had meant chains, and waking meant remembering that no help was coming.

Eventually, Kal pushed off from the doorframe. "We'll stay in your room."

Liam turned toward her, expression serious.

"If anyone tries the corridor," she continued, her voice sharpening slightly, "they'll expect me to be laid out behind silk and linen. Not curled at the foot of your bed with a barricade in place and steel within reach. If we're to sleep at all tonight, it'll be with a door locked and a chair under the handle."

He let out a breath, long enough to be considered a sigh. "I was hoping you'd say that," he admitted. "Didn't want to be the one to suggest it."

Kal's mouth tilted, a faint echo of humor glinting at the edge. "Afraid I'd accuse you of coddling me again?"

He gave her a long-suffering look. "More afraid you'd accuse me of needing company to scare off the shadows."

Her gaze turned dry. "If you drool on me again, I swear I'll cut out your tongue."

Liam snorted, but the sound was soft, "Still so dramatic, even when you're barely upright."

She didn't dignify that with a reply, only moved past him, as one hand reached for the nearest chair. It scraped softly across the floor as she dragged it toward the door, angling it to brace beneath the handle. "This won't stop anyone determined," she said, "but it'll give us the seconds we need to draw steel. Maybe more."

"Gods," Liam muttered, watching as she shoved the table into place behind it, "you make it sound so welcoming."

Kal pushed her hair out of her face, fatigue weighing her down more than she let on. "Come now, brother. These Varisian beds are the size of siege towers. I doubt your snoring will echo quite as badly as it did when we were sleeping on stone and straw."

He rolled his eyes and scratched at the back of his neck. "That was only when I was concussed."

"Which was... often," she said, mockingly thoughtful, lips curved slightly.

He laughed then, hushed and unguarded, the sound scraped at something in his chest that hadn't fully settled since they arrived. It wasn't enough to shake the weight in the room, but it shifted it slightly, and made it somewhat bearable.

He eyed the upholstered armchair near the hearth as if it might bite. "I'll take the first watch. That thing looks like a cloud stuffed with lies."

Kal shook her head, her own laugh softer. "Try not to die of comfort."

He didn't answer, only dragged the chair into position near the fire's dying glow. Kal shed her boots, stripped out of her outer tunic, and retrieved her dagger from where it leaned against the wall. She slid beneath the blankets, the layers of soft fabric unfamiliar against her skin, and lay still with her fingers curled tight around the hilt. The warmth was strange, almost disorienting. She didn't trust it, but she didn't reject it, either.

Liam wedged the chair tighter against the door, gave the barricade a nod, then lowered himself into the chair with his sword across his lap. His head tilted back, and he exhaled once, eyes trained on the ceiling.

The fire cracked softly, and the old stones of the palace creaked as night settled deeper around them. Kal lay on her side, blade nestled against her stomach, eyes open. Watching nothing.

Neither of them slept.

But they rested, and for tonight, that was enough.

A New Routine

The days passed without urgency, marked by the repetition of quiet rituals that soon became indistinguishable from one another. Time softened around them, until it was no longer measured in hours or days, but by the dull rhythm of habits worn deep into the bone.

They did not leave the royal corridor King Alden had given them. There had been no need. Everything they required arrived at their threshold. Water, food, firewood, bandages, candles, and once, even a small box of sharpened whetstones wrapped in cloth. The outside world was held at bay not by locks or guards, but by understanding.

Only Doddard came and went. He was always punctual–three visits a day without fail, always carrying a tray, a bundle, a bucket of steaming water depending on the hour. He made no conversation, asked no questions. His movements were careful, methodical, touched by the grace of long service. And with the slow caution of a man whose sight had dulled but whose purpose had not. Kal watched him closely in the first few days, her suspicion sharp. But there was nothing in his gait or tone that suggested deceit, only age, and a loyalty so ingrained it had become reflex.

So they were left alone, and in time, the corridor reshaped itself around their isolation. The lush furnishings of the shared sitting chamber were rearranged with purpose. Rugs were rolled and stacked against the wall. Tables, chairs, and ornamental benches were pushed aside until the center of the room became nothing but cold, open stone. Each morning, before the light reached the windowpanes, Kal and Liam rose to spar, a ritual forged through years of shared pain and unrelenting threat. Steel struck steel in practiced cadence, boots scuffing worn arcs into the polished floor.

And each night, without fail, they rebuilt the barricades. Their constructions changed by the day, refined with each passing dusk until the barricades became muscle memory, a defense woven into the fabric of their lives.

They watched the palace through the tall windows. They studied the shift changes of guards far below, the patterns of servants crossing the courtyards and galleries. Kal mapped the estate in her mind, filling in blanks with glimpses and instinct, matching her knowledge of structure with what little they could observe.

At night, when the fire dimmed and Liam sat sharpening his blades in the corner, Kal read. She consumed Arjun's books the way one might reach for a lifeline in the dark, clinging to each line of ink as if it might spell out a truth capable of pulling her out of the shadows. Fae magic. Ancient hymns to long dead gods. She studied them with a hunger born of desperation. The ache of needing to understand what had been buried within her since birth. Arjun's handwriting laced the margins, his thoughts folded neatly between the lines.

Once a week, a message arrived. Doddard delivered them without flourish, short scrolls bearing Alden's hand. No wax, no royal seal. Just words, brief and unadorned.

Do you require anything else? You are welcome to join us when you are ready. There are those in the court who would meet you with open hands, not blades.

Each time, Kal read the words, folded the parchment, and said nothing. She never sent a reply.

Still, silence began to wear on her.

It no longer felt like safety. It felt like weight. Like being buried beneath stillness. The air had grown thick with it, this quiet that was neither comforting nor dangerous, simply endless. She was sharp again, her body honed, her reflexes clean. Her grief had been stitched shut. Her magic had remained dormant, still and waiting. And yet something inside her paced like a caged beast, not from fear, but from anticipation.

Morning came with the low spill of pale light across the stone floor, the courtyard tiles beyond the window catching the first gold of dawn. Kal stood in the center of the room, blade freshly sheathed, breath steadying in her lungs. Across from her, Liam sat where he had fallen, one knee drawn up, his collar damp where the morning's sparring had left its mark.

She dragged her wrist across her brow and exhaled, then spoke without looking at him. "I need to move."

Liam tilted his head up, gaze sharp beneath the tousled fringe of hair plastered to his brow. "You just tried to carve a rib from my side. That didn't count?"

She bent, picked up a fallen strip of linen, and wrapped it around her fingers slowly. "I mean beyond this corridor."

The words hung there for a breath, weight pressed in from the silence that followed. It wasn't fear in her voice anymore. What hummed beneath her skin now was purpose.

"We've learned what we can from shadows and windows," she said, voice low.

He didn't speak right away. His hand reached for the waterskin, fingers tight around the leather as he drank. Then, at last, he said, "And if someone recognizes you? Or think they should strike before we're ready?"

Kal met his eyes, calm and unblinking. "Then we'll know who stands where." When she spoke again, it was softer, meant more for herself than for him. "I'm done hiding behind silk walls. I need to see what game we've walked into and who is expecting to play."

Liam gave a grunt as he moved to the tall windows, pushing the curtain aside with two fingers, peering down at the manicured garden below. The palace bustled in the quiet way of trained order; servants passed like whispers through the hedges, their movements organized, every step rehearsed. The world turned below them as though untouched by ruin or fire.

"If we're going to walk the palace," he said, still looking outward, "we do it carefully. Slowly. No names. No open truths. This court doesn't deserve our story."

Kal leaned her shoulder into the wall near the hearth with her arms crossed, gaze distant. "Agreed."

"And we do it together," he added, voice firmer now. "At least until we know how the guards rotate, who watches what, where the soft places are. If something goes wrong–"

"*No.*"

The word cut through the air. Liam turned toward her, a frown pulling at the edge of his mouth. She didn't soften her gaze.

"If we always move together," she said, "we're easier to recognize. A fae-marked girl and a scarred, brooding wraith with a death stare? We might as well carry a banner announcing our presence. They'll recognize us in two heartbeats."

He bristled but didn't argue the point.

"If someone's listening for rumors," she went on, "if even a whisper has reached the wrong ears, I'm the one they'll look for. Let them. Better I draw the eyes while you study their reach."

His jaw tightened. "And if they move first?"

"Then I'll move faster."

Liam's silence was louder now, thick with everything he wanted to say but knew she would not hear. Kal stepped forward, her voice dropping as she closed the distance.

"You know I'll draw attention whether I want it or not," she said, softer now, "I need to be a question people ask, not an answer. You're better in the shadows. Better at pattern, timing, structure. I walk the floor. You watch the walls."

"That's not the point," he muttered, more to the air than to her.

She arched her brow. "Then what is?"

"You're my sister." The words hung heavy, personal in a way neither of them enjoyed naming aloud.

Kal didn't flinch. But her smirk, when it came, was gentler than usual. "And you're not rid of me. But we play it smart, not sentimental. I walk alone. You map the guards. We meet back here after each circuit. If anything seems off, we pull back."

Liam didn't answer right away, but she could see the reluctant agreement settle into the shape of his body–the subtle tilt of his head, the shift of his weight. It wasn't consent so much as resignation, and perhaps, in that, a trace of trust.

He sighed and let his head tip back toward the ceiling, eyes closed. "You're still a pain in the ass."

Kal grinned, something almost mischievous flickering behind her eyes. "And yet I'm always right."

He muttered something under his breath that sounded vaguely like blasphemy, but she was already moving. She stretched her arms overhead as she crossed toward her chambers with the confidence of a woman who had just outmaneuvered her most stubborn ally.

"Don't worry," she said without turning. "Even here, among velvet and marble, I'm still the most dangerous thing in the room."

Liam gave her a look. "You hid four knives in your bathing robe yesterday."

She paused at the threshold and glanced back over her shoulder with a wicked smile. "Five. But who's counting?"

She vanished into her chamber, the door swinging shut behind her with a soft hush. Liam shook his head and crossed to the hearth, muttering beneath his breath as he reached for the nearest weapon and set it beside the fire.

The royal wing still slumbered beneath the hush of pre-dawn, its halls steeped in that fragile hush that lingers just before the world

wakes. The air held a clean chill, faintly scented with ash, stone and the last traces of night's hold.

She changed into her training leathers, matte black, supple and worn smooth by use, fitted close to the body with seams designed for movement rather than show. Over them, she pulled a pale cream tunic–loose and simple, the lacing at her collar left undone, the sleeves rolled just below the elbow for ease. Her bracers, leather reinforced with fine stitching, were laced with a pull on each wrist. The boots she slid into were silent by design. The soles stitched for stealth, the heels worn but reliable.

Her hair she bound with speed and ease, braiding it tightly from crown to nape. And though a few dark strands slipped free to frame the sharp line of her cheekbones, she left them untouched.

In the common room, the hearth had long since gone cold. She crossed it without hesitation, pausing only to lift the blade that always waited beside the doorframe.

Behind her, Liam's door creaked open. He appeared half-dressed, hair a mess, rubbing at sleep-heavy eyes. "You're dressed like you've got something to kill. Should I be worried?"

Kal didn't look up as she adjusted the strap on her bracer. "Going to find the sparring yard."

He leaned a shoulder into the doorway, posture loose but eyes alert beneath the haze of sleep. "So I've been replaced."

"As much as I enjoy planting you in the floor," she said, her tone dry but not unkind, "I need space. Open air. And someone who doesn't mutter every time I flatten them."

He made a noise of offense. "I let you flatten me. It's called morale building."

She cast a glance back at him with the faintest smirk. "Is that what it's called?"

Then she opened the door.

"Train without me," she added, already stepping into the corridor. "Try not to sprain something."

"Don't get arrested," he called after her.

She raised one hand in a lazy, dismissive wave and disappeared into the dim passageway.

She turned left and retraced the path she and Liam had taken on that first night. When they had stumbled through these same corridors hunted and half-starved, the taste of blood still fresh in their mouths and silence thick as armor at their backs. Eventually, she reached a corridor that narrowed. The ornamentation faded from gold filigree to carved stone, the carpets gave way to plain tile. She remembered this threshold; an outer passage near the servant's entry.

Then she saw it.

The training yard unfolded, wide and open to the morning sky, bordered on all sides by low walls and iron-grated balconies. The stone floor bore the scuffs of old combat, the pits worn smooth by a thousand hours of footwork. Dummies stood in orderly rows at the far end–some shaped like men in armor, others like lean targets for precision strikes. Racks along the walls bore swords, spears, maces, and practice staves. Sand pits yawned near the far edge for grappling, while a pulley track stretched across one wall, rigged with moving targets that could be reset with a crank.

Everything a soldier might need. Everything a commander might require.

The yard was hers alone. Kal stood at the center of it, unmoving, and let her breath release slowly. She circled the yard, her eyes sweeping over every line, every corner of the space. Torchlight flickered against exposed steel, catching on the curve of blades and spear tips, painting narrow shadows against the pale stone. The flagstones beneath her boots were uneven in places, smoothed by time and wear, sloping slightly toward a central drain where rainwater or blood might pool.

Only when the world was certain and accounted for did she begin. The first strike came without fanfare. A smooth draw of the sword into a diagonal arc that sang softly before it struck. The blade bit into the shoulder joint of the nearest dummy, splitting the wooden arm clean at the socket. The sound echoed briefly across the stone, then vanished, as if the yard itself had swallowed it.

She flowed through the space, each step purposeful, each breath in rhythm with motion. She pivoted, turned low on one heel, slashing upward into the air before she reversed into a downward cleave meant for a phantom neck. Her shoulders rolled smoothly, her weight shifted with control, her hips twisted through the follow-through of each cut. A pattern, ingrained over years of need and repetition. The kind of fighting that was learned in alleys, in cages, in places where mercy was a weakness. Where men taught her pain before they taught form and sometimes never taught form at all.

She advanced on a cluster of three dummies, each carved in rough resemblance to an armored foe. The rhythm of it was unrelenting, a dance of devastation–tight, efficient, lethal. Every movement designed to incapacitate or kill. The blade flicked through the air in rapid arcs, drawn from the memory of men who had tried to take her life and failed. She visualized them now–faces from Rhaen's court, armed and grinning, lunging for her throat. She felt the phantom weight of their blades crash into hers. Heard the breathless grunts of combat. Answered each imagined attack with lethality.

In her mind, she snapped necks, shattered ribs, crushed windpipes. Not from anger. From control.

The shadows that sometimes gathered behind her eyes—whispers of the past, faces she could not forget—lurched forward, only to break against the calm ferocity of her command. Here, in motion, she was not haunted. *She was whole.* For however long the yard remained hers and hers alone, she could be more than fear. She could be the weapon they had tried to make of her...and the mind that had reclaimed it.

An Unwelcome Intrusion

Kal moved through the training yard with efficiency, the weight of the sword in her hand was familiar, reassuring. It served as a reminder of who she was and of what she had survived. Her limbs obeyed without thought, the rhythm of her footwork matched to breath rather than emotion. She lunged forward, grounded and precise, then drew back into guard, only to pause mid-step. As one trained to recognize danger before it announced itself, she sensed the weight of another's attention. It clung to the air, unwelcome, however not unfamiliar.

She continued the motion through to completion, giving no sign she had noticed. But her awareness shifted and sharpened. Her next pass around the yard brought her within sight of the archway.

A man stood there. Not just any man, but the man who had watched her the first night they entered the palace, bruised and bloody.

He hadn't moved to interrupt, remaining still, framed by the light rising behind him, his arms loose at his sides. The cut of his coat marked him as a soldier. His posture was relaxed, there was no mistaking the readiness in the way he held himself. This was a man accustomed to battle. His expression revealed little, neither surprise nor arrogance. If anything, there was curiosity in his gaze. But it was the detached, analytical sort. He watched her, evaluating her footing, the angle of her blade, and the discipline in her stance.

Kal did not return his look. She resumed her drills without a word, offering neither acknowledgement nor invitation. If he wished to observe, so be it. He would find nothing soft in her display.

There was a faint creak of leather as he moved. A coat shrugged off and laid across the bench, gloves drawn on with ease. No challenge. No disturbance. Only calculated preparation.

Kal didn't turn to greet him, or feign ignorance of his presence.

She simply observed quietly. He walked with balance. A swordsman, clearly. But not a common one. On the left breast of his shirt was the gold stag of Varis. Beneath it, stitched in bronze thread, a second mark: crossed blades beneath a hawk in flight. A champion's crest perhaps.

He stopped beside one of the training dummies she'd torn apart earlier, resting a hand on its splintered shoulder with ease. He leaned into the wood, watching her with quiet interest, a slow grin forming on his face.

"This wasn't quite the dawn drill I expected," he said.

His tone was light, not mocking. Confident, but not overbearing. The kind of voice that filled a room without trying, because it had never needed to ask for space.

"I thought I'd be alone," he went on, casually gesturing toward the ring. "Stretch. Breathe. Maybe ruin a dummy or two. But it seems I've arrived to find the yard already broken."

Kal finished her last form with a clean arc of steel, then shifted into stillness. Not at ease, never that, but poised. She turned, her sword held low. Her gaze swept over him, once. Cool. Calculating.

"I'm surprised to see any knights training at this hour," she said at last, her tone dry. "I thought Varisian steel only stirred once the wine had dried up."

The jab landed. A grin tugged at the corner of his mouth, genuine and unbothered.

"That's the rumor," he said, his smile widening with easy candor. "But some of us still believe in discipline."

She let her gaze drift, taking in the empty yard with painstaking slowness. One brow arched.

The man gave a mock sigh, his voice dropped to something closer to theatrical offense. "In my defense," he said, gesturing loosely around them, "I'm not Varisian."

The answer slid the last piece into place. Raoul Sahir. The Crown Prince's Champion, the man from the Dunes.

It tracked. The posture. The poise. The lack of pretense in his gaze. He wasn't watching her like a man measuring beauty or threat. He was watching like a soldier who had walked too many battlefields to be surprised by either.

Raoul moved to the edge of the ring with a kind of quiet entitlement, as though claiming the space simply by standing in it.

"I always thought noblewomen preferred gentler mornings," he said. "Letters. Silk. A steward to glare on their behalf."

Kal's brow rose. "And I thought champions had better timing than interrupting a fighter mid-strike."

That earned another laugh, this one softer. "So that's what you are, then? Not a lady. A fighter?"

"I didn't ask you to name me."

"No," he said, tilting his head slightly, "but you didn't correct me either."

She held his gaze a moment longer, then turned away, returning to the center of the ring. She had no interest in indulging him but no intention of retreating either.

He stepped forward, unhurried. "If I didn't know better, I'd say you were ignoring me."

She pivoted just enough to glance at him sidelong. "If I didn't know better," she said, "I'd say you were used to being entertained."

That drew another laugh from him. "Most are, when they wear crests like mine."

She didn't even blink.

He let out a quiet chuckle. "Nothing? Not even a flicker? Gods. I may have to try harder."

That earned him a sidelong glance, weighing and brief.

"Is that what this is?" she asked. "Trying?"

He grinned. "Only a little."

Kal raised her blade again, the tip angling toward another practice form.

"Then stop. You are embarrassing yourself."

She pivoted back to the ring's center. Her movement was meant to end the conversation, to continue her focus. It dismissed him, without scorn, as though he'd proven uninteresting.

Raoul stepped closer, his gaze tracing the deep split she'd left in the wooden dummy's shoulder. The grin had faded. His tone dropped with it.

"You train hard."

Kal said nothing.

He moved again, as though this were casual, just two strangers sharing morning light. "So tell me," he said, eyes lingering on the damage she'd left behind, "is this just about moving beautifully before sunrise? Or do you actually plan to sweat? Bleed, if it comes to it?"

Kal turned and lifted the blade in one smooth motion, leveling it at his chest.

Her voice was soft. "Are you sure you can keep up?"

He blinked, then laughed, and something dangerous stirred behind it. Something that welcomed the challenge. He stepped back a pace and drew his blade in a clean arc, shoulders rolling loose as the steel caught morning light.

"Oh, I like you," he murmured, almost to himself.

"You know," he continued lightly. "Most people ask if I'll go easy on them."

Kal didn't flinch. "I wouldn't insult myself."

That earned a grin. "Then I hope you're as good as you look."

"Then stop hoping," she said, "And find out."

He raised his sword. The space between them vanished, not with motion, but with tension. Strategy took shape between them, alive in the quiet. Raoul's posture was relaxed but calculated. His sword hung low, inviting an opening.

She waited. Time stretched. And then, just beneath his jaw, a flicker. A shift in breath. Pressure met its mark.

He moved. The first strike came clean, a diagonal sweep, careful and precise. A textbook opener meant to provoke rather than land. Kal didn't step back. Her wrist turned, blade snapping upward. The parry met his strike with a jolt, metal ringing as she forced him off his pivot, momentum broken mid-flow.

She tilted her head, eyes flat. "If this is the best Varis has to offer," she said, "I'll need to look elsewhere for a challenge."

He straightened, laughing under his breath. "You wound me, my lady."

She leveled him with a bored look.

Raoul lifted his sword again, this time without theatrics. The circle he walked was smaller now, tighter. His voice lost some of its polish.

"Forgive me for wanting proof before I took you seriously."

Her eyes held his. "You're late to the realization."

That grin came again, but the ease was gone. This one belonged to a man who'd misjudged the battlefield. He came at her faster this time. No wasted motion. No lazy shifts. His stance adjusted, grip steadied, breath tightened. Kal saw it all, the shift from interest to intent. Like a commander reads a map. She read it in his feet, his shoulders, the tilt of his blade.

He struck again. This time, a feint high, then a drop to her hip—quick, precise. She caught it mid-arc, blades locking with a twist that sent his follow-through wide. He staggered half a step, correcting with a grunt. She didn't press the advantage. Just watched, expression unchanged.

Raoul stepped in again, faster now. His rhythm picked up, pushing her. Each blow was harder than the last. His breath dragged. Sweat lined his jaw. But she didn't yield. Kal's movements flowed, in a way that made violence look like art. Every strike answered. Every counter was clean. Her footing never faltered. Her breath stayed level. Not a single gesture wasted.

He pressed harder. The force of it began to show—his balance slipping by degrees, lungs burning, his form fraying.

"You're terrifying," he muttered between swings, laughing even as the edge of fatigue caught his voice. "Has anyone told you that?"

He pivoted, aiming a wide arc meant to draw her out.

"You really are–" steel rang "–the most thrilling woman–" clash, recoil "–I've nearly died fighting."

She turned his next blow with a sharp downward strike that rattled his arms.

He staggered back a pace. "Sweetheart," he said, catching his breath, "you make it damn hard to keep a man's dignity."

Sweetheart.

She moved to end it. Blade low. Then high. Then diagonal in a flash that carved the distance between them. There was no time to respond. His block came from instinct, not intent, and the force of it jolted through his grip. She didn't slow. He backpedaled, forced into defense. Her strikes came in a rhythm too precise to interrupt. No breath wasted. No misstep given. She was relentless–ice, not fire. Cold and exact.

"Wait–" he managed, teeth clenched, blade barely catching the next blow.

She didn't. Another strike forced his guard wide. Then her leg hooked low behind his knee. One shift of her weight and the ground took him. He landed hard, dust blooming around him. Kal stood over him, sword lowered. Unsmiling. Unmoved. She didn't offer a hand.

He lay still for a moment, breathing hard. Then, he laughed. It tore out of him without restraint, deep and startled, like a man who'd just seen his reflection in the teeth of a wolf and decided he admired it.

Kal stepped back, her sword steady at her side.

He wiped sweat and sand from his face with a grimy hand. "Well," he said, voice rough, "I stand corrected."

Kal's head tilted. "You never stood to begin with."

Raoul stayed where he'd fallen, one arm braced in the dust, his chest rising with the last of his breathless laughter. He stared up at the pale sky overhead with the kind of look a man wore after being reminded he was still very much alive.

With a low groan, he rolled onto his side and pushed himself upright. His grin shifted, less swagger now, less show. What lingered was something quieter. Earnest. He watched her walk away, his eyes following the steady, confident line of her back. He watched the way she moved without a trace of urgency, as if the fight had taken nothing from her.

He shook his head, dust curling at his shoulders. "I'll admit it," he called after her, voice still raw with the echo of laughter. "I underestimated you."

She didn't stop. Didn't look back. Only a pause–brief, nearly imperceptible–in her stride gave any hint she'd heard.

"But you won't get that from me again," he added, as he sat up straighter, one hand dragging through his hair to clear the sweat from his brow. "Sweetheart."

She paused a moment. "Surprisingly slow to learn a lesson, then."

She remarked, almost as if to herself.

He let out a short, rueful laugh. "Or just stubborn. Depends on the storyteller."

Raoul stood at last, brushing grit from his legs with one hand. He rolled his shoulders, flexed his fingers, and reminded himself that while the ground hadn't cracked his bones, it had done a fine job cracking his pride.

"Care to make it best out of three?" he asked, lifting his brow in her direction.

At the far edge of the ring, she paused, then turned slightly. Her expression remained unfazed, the faint trace of dust clinging to the edge of her jaw, her eyes sharp and level as they met his gaze.

"Don't be late tomorrow," she said.

He blinked. "For what?"

"To learn another lesson," she said as she turned again, her boots near-silent as they crossed into shadow. The stone arch swallowed her figure without fanfare.

And then she was gone.

Raoul stood alone in the ring, the quiet settling in around him. He stared after her, lips parted. The light breeze tugged at the open collar of his shirt. Then, slowly, a whistle escaped him, as if he'd just watched something sacred walk past and vanish.

"Gods," he murmured, dragging a hand along the back of his neck, as his grin returned—slower now, not amused but stunned. "What just happened..."

He stayed there a while longer, his heartbeat still finding its rhythm, the heat of the match still burning. It had been a long time since anyone had left him like this. Not defeated. *Awakened.* The arena was empty now, but the space still felt occupied—like she hadn't left so much as withdrawn her presence, leaving only the impression of motion and control behind her.

He exhaled slowly, dragging a hand down his jaw. The grit of dust clung to his skin, but it wasn't discomfort that lingered in him. It was disbelief. There had been no hesitation in her movements. No flare, no waste. She didn't fight to impress. She fought to end it. She moved like survival had been her only teacher and it had taught her well.

And still...that wasn't the whole of it.

He'd known women who were skilled, who held their own in battle and beyond. Some he'd fought beside, some he'd bedded. But this was different. She didn't draw attention because she wanted it. She didn't command the air around her through force of voice or gesture.

She simply *was.*

Beautiful? Yes...but not in any familiar sense. Not in the way men spoke of beauty. She held the kind of stillness storms did, that breathless silence before lightning breaks the sky. Her face didn't charm. It warned. And her eyes–otherworldly, enchanting–met him with the calm disinterest of someone already judging the worth of the conversation. She wasn't just a woman. Not to him. She felt like something dangerous. And she'd dropped him in the dust like it meant nothing at all.

He laughed under his breath, the sound quiet and shaken. He hadn't been ready. Not for that kind of fight. And certainly not for her. But even now, with the ring silent and the heat bleeding out of his skin, his pulse still thrummed with energy. With clarity. She had struck more than his sword. She had cut through something in him.

She had seen him. She had read him in a glance...and found him lacking.

And Gods help him, *he wanted more.*

GARNET AND STEEL

The royal wing stood hushed when she returned, the corridor dimly lit by torches that guttered low in their sconces. Morning light had begun to touch the high windows, casting a pale wash across stone and shadow. For most, it would have felt peaceful. But for Kal, there was no comfort in it. Not now. Not with her pulse still echoing the rhythm of motion.

Liam stood by the hearth as she entered. Arms crossed. Shoulders square. His shirt was damp from drills, his expression blank, save for the angle of his jaw and the flicker in his gaze.

He'd been watching.

She passed him without pause, pulling the leather bracers from her wrists as she moved, and dropping them on the bench near the corner. Her breath remained even. Her movements were exact.

"Why did you spar with him?" Liam's voice was low, roughened by restraint.

"I needed the practice," she said, not slowing down or stopping.

"That's not what I asked."

The last strap came free, and she laid her dagger beside the rest of her gear, the motion quiet and methodical.

Liam stepped forward. "You engaged him. You spoke with him. Then you fought like it mattered. Why?"

She let the silence stretch. Let him fill it with the weight he wanted it to carry.

Then, without turning or raising her voice, she said, "Because that man was Raoul Sahir."

That stopped him.

"The *champion*," she added, as she turned to face him at last. Her expression gave nothing away. "The one we discussed, that we'd need to assess."

Liam's mouth tightened. "He wasn't assessing you. He was undressing you with his eyes."

Kal didn't blink. But something colder slid beneath her expression. "And what would you have me do?" she asked. Calm. Controlled. "Run? Flinch? Pretend I hadn't noticed?"

"You didn't have to entertain him."

"I didn't." Her voice was flat as steel. "I measured him."

Liam scoffed. "Measured what? How fast he would finish if he found his way to your bed?"

Her eyes cut to him with the sort of look that stripped a man bare with its quiet fury. Liam had seen it before, and he knew what followed it.

"If we start breaking at every man who acts like a man," she said evenly, "we'll never get to the war."

He stared at her, jaw clenched. Then his voice dropped to something darker. "If he lays a hand on you, I'll gut him where he stands. I'll string what's left from the Varisian gate and let the crows decide what part they want first."

Kal held his gaze for a moment longer. Then her mouth curved, barely.

"If he manages to lay a hand on me," she said, "you'll need to move quickly."

"Why?"

"Because I'll have already broken both his wrists."

The silence that followed wasn't peace, but it was an understanding. She turned away again, removing the rest of her gear. Liam didn't argue further. He knew her truths too well. She didn't lie, not about threats, and never about survival. Still, he didn't move from the hearth. His arms remained crossed, his stance rigid. She could feel it. He wasn't finished.

"So what now?" he asked. The question was clipped, with tension in it. "You planning to duel the palace one noble at a time? Let every man with a sword test your patience?"

Kal didn't hurry her answer. She tied off the last strap, then turned. "No," she said. "Next, I'm going to let Alden show me his court."

Liam frowned. "What?"

"It's time," she said. "I need to see what I'll be dealing with. What are the politics and who are the players? Where does the real power sit?"

He stepped forward, already shaking his head. "Kal—"

She raised her hand. He stopped moving. The gesture cut the space between them with finality.

"I'll go as no one," she said. "No name. No title. No claim. That's the line I won't cross yet. But I will not spend another week in the dark while the world rearranges itself."

Kal crossed the chamber in silence, the stone cool beneath her feet as she stepped into the smaller room, where Arjun's parcels had been carefully stored. The light filtering through the high-arched window was faint, diffused with morning haze, casting a soft gleam over the open chest where metal glinted and fabric lay folded in ordered layers. She knelt without sound, her fingers trailing across the garments one by one, taking the measure of each as if assessing armament rather than attire. Arjun had chosen well. Of course he had. There were no Varisian flourishes here—no lace, no feathers, nothing made to flatter soft conversation.

She pulled one of the dresses free, holding it up to the morning light. Where the women of Varis favored full skirts, pastel colors, and embroidery thick as armor, Kal's wardrobe was something else completely. Dark jewel tones like sapphire, garnet, emerald. Each cut to wrap her form, whisper-slick and tailored to the hard-earned lines of her body. Silks that clung without restricting. Bodices cut just low enough to command attention, but never beg for it. Slits along the leg. Strategic cutouts at the curve of her ribs and spine, never enough to be called vulgar, only enough to leave a man wondering what he hadn't seen.

She chose garnet. The color of blood under torchlight. She drew it up over her hips and shoulders before fastening the back, the open-cut sides clinging perfectly against the arch of her waist. She moved like she'd done this a hundred times, because she had. But this time felt different.

This time, *she* had chosen the armor.

Next came the corset. Filigree metal, shaped like curling scrollwork, slid into place over her torso like a second ribcage. She tightened the clasps, unflinching as it cinched around her. It didn't hinder her breath, it *shaped* it. It drew the eye to the lines of muscle that curved like sculpture beneath. She knelt once more to retrieve the matched arm guards and fitted them into place with care. The lattice of steel hugged her forearms, gleaming faintly when she moved, and mirrored pieces clasped along her thighs and calves, visible only through the slit that ran high along her leg.

Adornment without fragility.

Jewels trained to catch the light and deflect stares. She wove them into her hair. Twisting fine strands of polished metal between her curls, so that they shimmered like chainmail as they fell in careful waves over her shoulders.

When she finished she stood before the mirror, she studied her reflection. What stared back was a contradiction: too refined for armor, too lethal for silk. Her beauty was not soft or inviting. It warned. Her expression was calm, composed. This was the shape she had chosen. For a moment she didn't move. Her gaze lingered on the figure in the glass, tracing the lines of exposed skin, the cool shimmer of steel, the deliberate construction of who she had allowed herself to become. She knew what the court would see, and what they would fail to name.

She would not be easily placed. Not Varisian, not foreign. Not modest, not scandalous. Not one of them. Just...some other.

Was this what she wanted? To be seen? To be noticed after trying to disappear for so long?

Kal turned from the mirror without another glance, the metal along her limbs gleaming with every step. She stepped back into the common room, the hem of her gown whispering across the stone as she adjusted the last hidden clasp at her thigh. The daggers slid into place beneath the folds of her dress, weightless but ready. One at the small of her back. Another tucked along her ribcage. One more inside her boot.

Every step was smooth. Controlled. Lethal beneath the illusion.

Liam turned–and froze. Whatever distraction had held him vanished. His expression shifting instantly from indifference to something akin to open-mouthed horror. His mouth opened, then closed again, as if he meant to speak but found himself briefly incapable of forming words. When he did recover, his hands came up in something that hovered between surrender and outrage.

"What part," he asked, already louder than the hour called for, "of...*that*–" he gestured wildly in an arc that encompassed her entire form, "–is meant to maintain *anonymity?*"

Kal lifted a brow, unmoved.

He didn't wait for her answer. He had already begun pacing, his words gaining momentum.

"I swear to every God I've ever cursed," he continued, pacing now. "I will be dueling *every* male in this court before sundown. All of them! One by one. *It'll be a bloodbath!* And when I'm finished, they'll need to rename the ballroom the Hall of Widows. They'll need to open an annex wing just for funerals."

Kal moved past him to retrieve the final clasp for her shoulder guard, her expression composed, though the faint twitch at the corner of her mouth betrayed her amusement.

"Dramatic," she tossed at him.

"I'm being *practical.*" Liam stopped pacing just long enough to point at her. "By the end of the week, there'll be so many corpses we won't *need* to worry about the height of the balcony anymore. We'll just step off gently onto the pile of dead suitors and descend the mound of flesh, pride, and egos like a staircase from hell."

Kal didn't bother suppressing the soft breath of laughter that escaped. She smoothed her palms down the fitted sides of her gown, then straightened, the movement smooth and unhurried.

"You've seen me before in far less."

His mouth shut, the protest dying as the words struck harder than any taunt. She hadn't said it bitterly. But the memory hung between them all the same–chains, collars, skin bared not by choice, but by force. He remembered every detail.

He turned to stare hard at the wall, muttering under his breath. "Doesn't change the fact that half the men in this court won't have the faintest idea what to do with you."

Kal tilted her head, sun catching in the jeweled strands she'd woven, the metal glinting faintly in the morning light. "You say that as if it's *my* burden to ease their confusion."

Liam didn't turn. His jaw flexed. "They'll stare. They'll stumble. They'll spill wine trying to look casual, and the moment one of them opens his mouth–"

"–we'll know who lacks composure," she interrupted smoothly. "Which, as you so often remind me, is useful information."

He muttered something that may have included *suicidal peacocks*, but she didn't press. Instead, she fixed him with an expectant, steady look.

"Well?" she asked. "Are you coming or not?"

He let out a long sigh and disappeared into his room.

When he returned a few minutes later, the transformation was clean and precise–dark linen coat, fitted trousers, polished leather. Arjun's tailoring had done its work. There was no crest, no house sigil, no mark of rank, only a soldier's silhouette wrapped in court-approved shadow.

He stood beside her without comment.

Kal looked him over, lips twitching into a smirk. "Well brother, you clean up well. Almost court-worthy. They won't know which direction to swoon in."

He rolled his eyes. "Don't talk to me."

She turned without waiting, silk trailing at her heels as she crossed the chamber and opened the door to the outer hall. The guards at the far end straightened instinctively, their attention flicking toward her and then quickly away, uncertain whether they were meant to acknowledge her presence at all.

Kal gave them no glance. Liam fell into step beside her, still silent, still tense. They moved through the corridors, the halls bathed in gold from the rising sun through arched windows. Kal's hair shimmered as she walked, the delicate strands of metal catching the light like starlight scattered across a dark sea. She looked like no one else in this place. Like something crafted from myth and steel.

As they turned the final corner, Kal spotted the tall carved doors of Alden's study just ahead.

Doddard had mentioned it weeks ago—

"If ever you wish to speak to the king before court begins, he's always there, just before the hour turns. He likes the quiet."

Kal paused once at the threshold, her fingers brushing down the length of her bodice, ensuring the blade at her side hadn't shifted.

Then she lifted her chin.

And knocked.

PIECES ON THE BOARD

T he knock echoed once sharply. From inside, a smooth voice answered without hesitation. "Let them in, please."

The guards exchanged a glance, and though neither spoke, the pause was telling. One reached for the latch, but not before his eyes slid to Kal—the sweep of dark silk, the gleam of filigree across her chest, the metallic elegance threaded through her hair. He looked away. Then, foolishly, he looked back. The second guard wasn't any better. His grip on the door wavered for half a breath as his gaze tracked the lines of her figure, a form built for conquest, equal parts seduction and threat.

Kal ignored them both. The dress whispered over the marble as she crossed into the king's private study, Liam following close behind.

The study was sunlit and warm, the hearth still glowed from an earlier fire. King Alden looked up and for a moment, he stilled. Surprise crossed his face, a brief flicker of unguarded reaction. His eyes swept over Kal first, cataloguing what he saw with barely suppressed amusement. Then his gaze shifted to Liam, and he laughed.

The laugh came easily. It was real, and it rang with the pleasure of something wholly unexpected.

"Well," he said, sitting back, eyes still bright with amusement, "the two of you certainly do know how to make an entrance."

His gaze returned to Kal, openly assessing and entirely unthreatened. "I'll have to double my efforts now, I think. If you walk the palace dressed like that, half the court will be clawing for your name by midday, the other half composing sonnets and scandals."

Kal tilted her head, watching him in silence.

He gestured lightly with one hand. "Don't worry. I've no complaints. Gods know this place could use some shaking up. I rather look forward to watching them scramble. A breath near the high table and they'll fall apart. *It'll be magnificent.*"

Her eyes stayed on him, sharp and level, reading him searching for cracks beneath the laughter. But there were none. No edge beneath the warmth. No pressure behind the charm. Only a man who saw what she was and found it entertaining rather than dangerous.

It was almost disarming.

Liam, ever the one to ground a moment before it wandered too far, cleared his throat beside her.

"We wished," he said formally, "to observe your court today. Your politics. If you would be inclined to allow it, without announcing us or drawing attention to our presence."

Alden nodded, the lines of amusement still present around his mouth.

"Of course. I'd be glad for it." He leaned forward, elbows resting on the carved arms of his chair. "You're welcome to sit where you like, though I'd caution against mingling too freely. Dressed as you are," he nodded toward Kal, still half-laughing, "you'll find little peace. There'll be offers of wine, flattery, possible duels by sundown."

Kal didn't flinch.

Alden's grin faded only slightly, the amusement still lingered behind his eyes. "If you want my advice, play into the mystery. Don't meet them in the crowd. Sit beside me. Let them guess. Let them wonder."

He nodded toward the corridor that led into the court chamber. "They won't dare approach if they think you sit above them. They'll chase ghosts before they approach a mystery on the dais."

Kal watched the king for a long moment.

Alden met the look without flinching. His tone softened just enough to feel personal. "And I won't name you. Not until you say it's time."

That earned him a single nod. Kal stepped forward, the firelight catching along the curve of her corset as she passed. Her footsteps made no sound against the polished floor.

Alden rose to follow, straightening his tunic with casual care.

"Well then," he said, a smile returning. "Let's give them something to talk about.

King Alden led them through the palace in silence. The halls grew grander with every turn—tall ceilings gilded in gold-leaf, banners hung along the way, mosaic floors polished to a gleam. Servants stepped aside at their passing. Some bowed their heads with grace; others stared outright. The shift in attention followed them like a ripple through still water.

Not all of it was for Kal.

She saw how the women looked at Liam–brazen, curious, some openly intrigued. He didn't return a single glance. Dressed in black from shoulder to boot, the coat cut close to his lean frame, he walked radiating restraint. His dark hair fell to his shoulders in loose waves, catching faint highlights beneath the high windows, framing his strong jawline. The shaved side of his head, a style favored by fae warriors, showed a large scar earned in battle. His features–hard, clean and unsmiling–gave away nothing, his pale grey eyes looked forward without once turning.

They stopped before a set of towering double doors, framed in carved oak and gold, behind which the low thrum of the morning court murmured like a hive.

Alden turned to them with a grin already tugging at his mouth. There was something almost boyish in it, like a mischievous child.

"Are we certain?" he asked, voice light, even as his eyes glittered with the anticipation of a man who knew exactly what sort of chaos he was about to unleash.

Kal met his gaze and gave a single nod. Liam mirrored it without pause, though his was sharper, more a warning than assent.

Alden chuckled under his breath. "Gods. This is going to be fun."

He turned to the herald standing stiff at the threshold. "Announce only King Alden and his guests."

The man blinked. "Only...Your Majesty?"

"Yes," the King replied, voice light but final. "Just like that."

The herald straightened, adjusted his robes and with a quick intake of breath he disappeared through the doors.

A moment later, his voice rang clear across the court chamber. "His Majesty King Alden Llewellyn of Varis...and...*guests*."

The great doors swung open. King Alden strode forward first, his crown caught the morning light, robes trailed in his wake as though he carried no weight at all. He offered no explanation to the gathered nobles. Just a pleasant nod and the easy confidence of a king who knew his court wouldn't dare question him.

Kal followed, her steps were unhurried, her posture unchanged. Each footfall fell like water against stone, soft, but leaving no question of its presence. She didn't scan the room for reaction. She *was* the reaction. The silence broke within three strides of her stepping into the hall. The sound of cloth shifting and chairs creaking rose in a scattered chorus as the court collectively tried to understand what they were seeing and failed.

She did not beg attention. *She commanded it.*

Liam walked a step behind, silent as ever, his gaze fixed forward. If any part of the chamber registered for him, it didn't show. He looked as if he'd already judged every noble in the room and found none worth the trouble. By the time they reached the dais, the room had grown louder. Whispers rose behind fans and gloved hands. Men leaned forward, women narrowed their eyes.

King Alden took his seat as if settling into an opera box before the opening act. One hand rested lightly on the arm of his throne, the other gestured toward the chair to his left. Kal ascended the step with smooth efficiency and sat beside him–straight-backed, composed, untouched by the rising noise behind her. The firelight glinted off the metal along her waist and shoulders. Her hands rested lightly in her lap, her posture perfect, her expression neutral. But her eyes, her eyes *moved*. She swept her gaze across the room, cataloging every face, every glance. Intrigue was everywhere. Lust, too. Whispers passed like a current between noble mouths, some sly, others enraptured. No one knew who she was, but they *felt* what she was.

She didn't smile, but her eyes paused on the man to King Alden's right. He had frozen mid-sip, a goblet hovered half a breath from his lips, forgotten. His mouth was slightly open. His eyes were wide. And he was *staring*. Not subtle. Not careful. Just...utterly undone.

He was perhaps her age, or not far past it, and beautiful in the way that statues sometimes were. Fine-boned. Golden-skinned. Hair a tousled, golden brown that curled in loose waves, as if the wind had its way with it and no one dared tame it. His white and gold court attire gleamed in the morning light, ornate and pristine.

But none of that made an impression. It was the look. The pure, awkward, *undeniable fascination* painted across his face, like a man who had just seen a star fall from the sky and hadn't decided which way to run.

Kal regarded him evenly. She held his gaze, and let him feel the full weight of being *seen*. He flushed instantly. Deep red bloomed up his neck, the tips of his ears coloring, and he quickly set his goblet down poorly. It clinked against the table with a hollow echo, as he immediately busied himself with pretending to listen to something that was no longer being said.

She dismissed him with a glance, her gaze moving forward again, uninterested. Another piece on the board. She would figure out what to do with him later. For now, she sat still, regal and enigmatic. She watched the court react, an entire chamber unraveling beneath a single entrance.

The first petitioner stepped forward reluctantly, shaken from whatever whispered theories or fantasies Kal's arrival had stirred. He bowed low, fumbled his words, then composed himself under Alden's steady gaze. The business of the day resumed, hesitantly at first, then with growing momentum as the court attempted to adjust to this mystery.

Kal watched in silence. She said nothing, made no movement to draw attention, but she observed everything. The King listened to each speaker with patience. His face was open but ambiguous, his posture relaxed without ever seeming informal. When he responded, it was with calculated words and precise direction. He was kind, remarkably so, but not pliant. His verdicts were firm. He did not bend to sentiment. And yet, she noted, he never lost their respect. They bowed when dismissed. They thanked him sincerely.

Strange, she thought. *Power without cruelty.* She had never seen the like. In Elandra, mercy had been a weakness. Kindness was a trap. Rhaen's court had been built on fear—on manipulation, punishment, and spectacle. Kal had lived under it, endured it, worn it like a second skin until she'd learned how to use it herself.

But this...this was something else. Not softness, but conviction. It unsettled her more than cruelty would have.

She kept her gaze forward, posture impeccable, but her mind never stopped moving.

Beside the king, the golden-haired man had not moved once since she'd sat down. Or rather—he had, but only in short, miserable bursts of self-conscious tension. His goblet, that had been returned to the table, was now ignored. Both hands were pressed to the table as if he needed an anchor.

Every time Kal shifted, every time her gaze swept even marginally in his direction, he flushed. A sharp pink across his cheeks, creeping red along his throat. He tried not to look at her, and failed again and again, each failure more graceless than the last.

She could only assume he was Prince Jarreth.

The crown prince of Varis, she thought, barely restraining the flicker of amusement that almost curled at the edge of her mouth. *Gods help them.*

But it was the man to Prince Jarreth's right who drew more of her attention. Raoul Sahir. Unlike the prince, Raoul didn't flinch. He didn't flush or fidget. But he watched her nonetheless, often and intensely. He was better at disguising it. His eyes only shifted to her when he thought she wouldn't notice. When he wasn't turning to whisper something to Jarreth or listening to a petition with a calculated stillness that suggested he was measuring every word.

But Kal saw him. Saw the way his shoulder tensed when she shifted. Saw the way his gaze returned to her when the court quieted. Not in awe or lust, or at least not *just* that, but in curiosity. *He's still trying to figure out what I am.*

She didn't offer him any clues.

A soft chuckle rumbled beside her, too quiet for anyone else to hear.

Alden leaned slightly toward her without turning his head, his voice pitched just for her ear. "It is," he murmured, "*utterly delightful* to see my son and his champion so thoroughly unraveled."

Kal's gaze didn't shift.

He continued, the amusement in his voice rich and unbothered. "Normally, they preen like peacocks. Controlled. Composed. Arrogant to the bone. And women? Gods, the women throw themselves at their feet. *It's exhausting.* But this?" He stifled another chuckle. "This is *art.*"

Kal made a faint sound in her throat, noncommittal, but she filed the observation away.

Prince Jarreth: anxious and undone. His knight: calculated but intrigued. Two game pieces on a board. One brittle, one watchful. And both of them were shaken. It was always useful to know who could be shaken, and by what.

COMPOSURE UNMADE

Gods," Raoul muttered under his breath, shifting in his seat. "You're staring again."

Prince Jarreth didn't respond at first. His jaw tensed, and he pulled his eyes forward, blinking hard like someone shaking off a blow. He sat straighter in his chair, adjusting the cuffs of his already perfect sleeves as if the act might reset something in him. Then he shot Raoul a look. Cold and controlled.

"I'm well aware," he said tightly.

Raoul's lips quivered in amusement, though he kept his posture stately, eyes still forward. "How many times have you composed yourself now?" he murmured. "Eight? Ten?"

"Enough."

"She hasn't even spoken," Raoul added, tone dry.

Prince Jarreth exhaled deeply through his nose. "Do you ever stop talking?"

"Only when I'm asleep," Raoul quipped "And even then, I've been told it's inconsistent."

Jarreth glanced sidelong at him, the edge of irritation in his gaze met the easy calm eyes of a man who knew exactly how far he could push. Raoul's expression shifted slightly.

"That's her," he said under his breath. "The woman from the ring this morning."

Jarreth stilled.

He turned his head an inch toward Raoul. "Are you sure?"

Raoul gave him a slow, withering look, as if the very question were an insult.

"Yes," he said flatly. "Unless by some tragic impossibility, *two* women like that have suddenly appeared in the Capital."

Jarreth rolled his eyes and faced forward again, his fingers tightening on the edge of the table. "Must you always be so theatrical?"

"You say that like it isn't deserved," Raoul muttered, glancing toward the woman seated beside the king. "Just look at her."

Jarreth didn't need to. He already had. Her dress was unlike anything the court had ever seen, jewel-toned and sleek, glinting with metalwork and shaped to a figure built from equal parts grace and strength. She didn't smile, didn't speak, didn't shift. She simply *was*–meant to be admired from a distance and touched only by fools.

"She looks..." The Prince started, then stopped.

Like a queen. Like a threat. Like someone born of myth.

Raoul arched his brow. "Dangerous?"

Jarreth pressed his lips into a line. "Intentional."

Raoul hummed, pleased. "Yes, that too."

They were silent for a breath as another petitioner finished his case and was dismissed. The court shifted, and the murmurs began again, but neither man looked away from the king's left side.

"She's sitting next to Father," Jarreth mused, brows drawing together. "That doesn't happen."

Raoul nodded once. "He knows her."

"Then why haven't we heard anything?"

Raoul tilted his head slightly, keeping his tone hushed. "That's the better question."

Jarreth let the silence stretch before whispering, "We need to find out who she is."

Raoul smiled faintly, the edge of calculation in his expression clear now. "We will. Corner the king. Corner *her*. Preferably after court ends and we're not under threat of making a scene."

Jarreth sighed, irritated by the sudden turn his morning had taken. "You just want an excuse to talk to her again."

Raoul's grin sharpened. "Well, I won't lie to you."

Their eyes flicked back to her once more. She was unmoving, radiant...and dangerous.

Court wound down slowly, the final petitions trailing off. But the low hum of speculation hadn't ceased since Kal entered. Even now, with the sun slanting higher through the windows and the day's business at an end, nobles lingered. Heads turned under the pretense of conversation. Eyes flicked upward under lowered lashes. They were still watching her.

King Alden stood with a brief statement, his voice calm and clear as he dismissed the court for the day. "We thank all who brought their voices today. You are heard. You are seen. The Court is now adjourned. You may now exit the hall."

He remained in place as the crowd began to disperse. They stepped down from the dais with slow reluctance, many of them still craning to sneak one final look. It wasn't until the last courtier trailed through the double doors–pausing for one lingering glance–that Alden exhaled a short, amused breath and turned to Kal. He didn't look at his son. Didn't even acknowledge Raoul.

"Now," he said lightly, the corners of his mouth curving, "what did you think of our little display?"

Kal didn't answer immediately. She sat still, back straight, her hands resting loosely in her lap. Her gaze drifted forward as if weighing something unspoken in the air.

"It's very different from what we've known." She responded calmly.

Neither she nor the king spoke of Rhaen. Neither spoke of Elandra. But the weight of her words hung between them, understood.

Alden hummed thoughtfully. "I would imagine it is." His voice softened, though it lost none of its clarity. "Still, I hope you saw something useful. Some strength in it."

She tilted her head slightly, watching him.

"It doesn't always take a blade or a clenched fist to earn obedience," he added. "Sometimes steadiness is louder. Sometimes kindness roots deeper than fear."

Kal didn't respond, she only nodded once, silent and thoughtful. She glanced at her side, but Liam wasn't watching her. His gaze was locked on the two men across the dais, eyes cold and narrowed. His expression was thunder made flesh, a storm drawn taut across his jaw. He hadn't missed the way the Prince and his knight had spent the entirety of the court session watching his sister like men facing the divine.

They were edging forward now, subtly repositioning themselves in anticipation of conversation.

Liam's glare darkened.

Alden chuckled under his breath, not bothering to hide his amusement.

"Oh, this is *delicious*," he murmured.

Before either of the men could speak, the king lifted a hand with theatrical patience. "Save whatever star-struck poetry is about to fall out of your mouths," he said dryly. "Truly. Jarreth, perhaps start by collecting your jaw from the floor before you lose it entirely."

Both men flushed, sharply and in unison. Jarreth stumbled forward half a step, his mouth opening–then closing–then opening again. He tried, bless him.

"Forgive me," he finally managed. His tone uneven, voice cracking on the tail end of the word. "It's just that–I–apologies, my lady, I didn't mean to–"

Raoul cut in before further damage could be done.

"Prince Jarreth Llewellyn," Raoul interjected, recovering the introduction with a well versed grace that almost–*almost*–covered the awkwardness, "and I am Sir Raoul Sahir, Llewellyn house champion." He gave a slight bow, which was just enough to acknowledge formality without groveling. "We're honored to have witnessed your arrival. Might we know your name, my lady?"

Kal rose slowly, her eyes flicking to King Alden.

"Your Majesty," she said, voice cool and smooth. "Thank you for your willingness to allow our observation."

He nodded, the corner of his mouth twitching in silent enjoyment.

Kal turned partially toward the two men, offering the barest tilt of her head, formal and distant.

"Your Highness," she said to the prince, voice neutral. "Sir Sahir."

And then she turned and walked away, silk trailing like smoke in her wake, Liam following immediately, his expression fixed in a scowl that needed no translation. He didn't so much as glance at either man as he passed, only let his presence speak in silence, solid and cold.

The door closed behind them with a final click.

A moment passed before the King laughed–loud, warm and unrestrained. He leaned back in his chair, hands folded over his stomach, and watched his son with his knight still staring dumbfounded at the place Kal had once stood.

"Oh," he sighed through his laughter, "I've waited *years* for something this entertaining."

The echo of the doors hadn't even faded before Alden turned to them, his smile stretching wider by the second.

"Well," he said with mock solemnity, clasping his hands. "That was... an absolute *travesty*."

Raoul groaned softly.

Jarreth narrowed his eyes.

Alden didn't stop.

"I've never seen anything quite like it," he mused aloud, as he stood to pace just slightly. Thoughtfully, like a general surveying the battlefield after an especially embarrassing rout, he said, "My son–*the* Crown Prince of Varis–reduced to a stammering schoolboy. And my most stalwart knight... actually attempting to use *charm*. Gods above, it was pitiful."

Jarreth exhaled hard through his nose. *"Father."*

"Yes?" Alden turned, eyes bright with amusement.

"Who is she?"

There was no teasing in the question, only tightly coiled irritation beneath the surface. A demand born of frustration and bruised ego.

Raoul folded his arms beside him. "I've *bled* for less, your Majesty," he added dryly. "She bested me this morning in the ring. I still can't lift my shoulder. That earns me *something*."

King Alden's grin turned wolfish.

"What it earns you," he said, "is the pleasure of knowing you were not simply bested, but *ignored*. And with that kind of display?" He looked between the two men, shaking his head. "You'll be lucky if either of you *ever* get a second glance."

Raoul arched his brow. "Then we'll just have to earn it."

"Indeed," Jarreth added, tone clipped. "We'll find out who she is. We'll find her. Ask her ourselves."

Alden barked a laugh.

"With *what* plan?" he asked, circling toward them like a lion mildly entertained by its cubs. "With the brilliant charm you displayed today? With the stammering and the blushing and the wine nearly sloshing out of your goblet?"

Neither man answered.

"And while you're chasing her down," the king went on, eyes dancing, "what will you do about the man beside her?"

At that, both men shifted uncomfortably.

"Ah yes," Alden nodded sagely. "The one dressed in black with eyes like winter and the expression of someone deciding where to place your bodies after snapping you in half."

"I noticed," Raoul muttered.

"Did you?" Alden smiled. "He noticed you, too. Especially *you*, Jarreth."

The prince grimaced. "I wasn't going to *touch* her–"

"Oh, I'm sure that would've made a lovely epitaph."

The room fell into a beat of silence. The amusement fading as Alden finally drew still. And then his voice shifted. Not cold but tempered. The tone of a man reminding them that, behind the wit and the smirking observations, he was still king.

"You are not to press them," he said plainly. "I will not be telling you who they are. They are my guests. My *personal* guests. They are here under my invitation and protection, and they are not to be questioned. Not followed. Not harassed. If they speak to you, you may answer. If not, you keep your distance."

Raoul's jaw tensed. Jarreth stiffened further.

Alden looked between them, his smile now faint. Almost pitying.

"I know you," he said. "I know how you chase what doesn't yield. But you'd do well to remember that not everything is yours to conquer."

He turned, his robes shifting with the movement, and strode toward the tall doors at the edge of the chamber. Just before he reached them, he glanced back over his shoulder, his tone suddenly bright again.

"And for the love of the Gods, both of you need to learn how to *keep your composure* around *real* women."

The doors closed behind him with a soft, definitive thud.

Jarreth stared after him, face strained. Raoul scratched the back of his neck, then exhaled a long breath through his teeth.

"Hell," he said.

Jarreth didn't answer. Raoul gave him a sidelong glance.

"She really *was* something though, wasn't she?"

Jarreth sighed. "Shut up, Raoul."

They stood in the echoing silence of the chamber long after Alden left them behind. Just two men, flanked by emptied thrones and the fading murmur of vanished nobility.

Jarreth finally broke the silence, as he dragged a hand through his hair.

"He didn't deny knowing who she was."

"No," Raoul agreed, following him down. "He very much did not."

"But he didn't confirm anything either."

Raoul let out a slow exhale. "Which means she's not just some noble cousin tucked away in the country."

"She's not *from* here," Jarreth murmured.

Raoul chuckled, "You sound sure."

"I am. You saw the dress."

Raoul gave a small, appreciative whistle at the memory. "Hard to miss. Not exactly Varisian fashion. Unless we've suddenly decided corsets made of armor are the height of seasonal couture."

"And she carried herself..." Jarreth's voice trailed off. "Not like a guest. Not like a woman visiting court for the first time."

"No," Raoul said thoughtfully, "she walked in like she already owned it."

Jarreth frowned. "That kind of presence doesn't come from nowhere."

"Which is exactly the problem," Raoul said, voice softer now. "There's nowhere I can *think* of that trains women to carry themselves like that. That kind of control? That calm?" He shook his head. "Even the generals' daughters we met at the war councils in the Dunes didn't walk like that. They postured. She didn't."

"She didn't have to."

Raoul gave a short laugh. "Exactly."

They were quiet again, the weight of it pressing between them.

Jarreth turned and looked toward the doors she'd exited through, his jaw tight. "Did you feel it? When she looked at you, it was like being measured. Not noticed. *Measured.*"

Raoul's smirk faded a little. "Yeah," he said. "I felt it."

They both stood in silence a moment longer. Then Raoul clapped a hand on Jarreth's shoulder with a grin that didn't quite reach his eyes.

"Well, I suppose we've found the new ruling mystery of the court," he said. "Who she is. Where she came from. And whether we're ever going to get the chance to say something *that* doesn't make us look like lovesick fools."

The prince shook his head. "Not likely."

Raoul's grin returned, a touch sharper. "Then I'll take the odds."

And with that, the two men turned from the empty chamber, still no closer to answers—only the certainty that *whoever* she was, she had shifted something in both of them.

And they hadn't even learned her name.

THE LESSON

K al shed the pageantry of court like a snake discarding its skin. The jeweled strands had been unpinned from her hair, the corset's ornate filigree set aside without ceremony. The gown lay across the back of a low chair. Now she sat curled in one of the room's cushioned seats, dark breeches tucked at the knee, a cream tunic loose across her shoulders. Her sleeves were rolled, her braid damp from a hasty rinse. Stripped of gold and ceremony, she looked more dangerous than she had in full regalia.

She was watching Liam. He paced the way a storm builds—silent, electric, barely restrained, the fury in his movements palpable. His jaw clenched, hands twitching once, twice, before curling into fists.

"*I knew it,*" he muttered. "The moment we stepped into that chamber. The way they looked at you...every man in that room! Like they were starving and you were the last thing left to eat."

Kal said nothing, waiting.

Liam spun mid-step, gesturing toward the air with a bitter edge. "All of them. Nobles, envoys, guards. But those two...Gods, Kal. They didn't even *pretend.* The prince looked like he'd forgotten how to breathe, and the other one—the knight—watched you like he'd found one of the old Gods."

Kal arched one brow, eyes tracking him with faint amusement. But, she didn't interrupt.

Liam's voice pitched sharper. "You saw it. Don't act like you didn't. Like dogs in heat. I should've taken a blade to both and let the rest learn from the example."

Kal exhaled faintly and raised a hand, in quiet dismissal. Liam halted as if struck still by the gesture.

"Are you quite finished?"

His glare was all the answer needed.

"Pity." She leaned forward, resting her arms on her knees, her gaze steady. "You were too busy plotting bloodshed to notice what mattered."

Liam narrowed his eyes.

"Alden," she said. The name hung for a moment. "The way he holds his court."

Liam frowned. "What about it?"

"It's different." Her voice dropped, softer but more certain. "He doesn't rule through fear. Doesn't need to shout to be heard. But they listened. They all did. Even the ones who resented it."

Liam's mouth tightened. "Sounds like weakness to me."

Kal's gaze cut to him. "No. It's something else, and whatever it is, it's *working*."

A heavy silence pulsed between them. Then Kal leaned back again, something flickering behind her eyes.

"Although," she added lightly, "you were a bit of a spectacle yourself."

Liam blinked incredulously. "What?"

Kal gestured toward him with casual amusement. "Did you miss the trail of sighing noblewomen? You've become a walking tragedy poem. The jaw, the scowl—*absolute bait*."

He made a sound of disgust, muttering under his breath as he turned away.

Kal's smile sharpened. "Shall I call for Doddard? We could request a registry of eligible daughters. Titles, dowries, dental records. I'll oversee interviews personally. Round two can involve fencing or embroidery."

A pillow hit the wall with a soft thud where her head had been seconds before.

"You're impossible," Liam grumbled.

"And you," she said, stretching out one leg, "are predictable." Her voice dipped, losing the humor. "Which is why you need to learn to rein it in. That rage of yours."

He didn't reply, but his shoulders tensed.

"Men will look," she said. "That's what they do. And it's not weakness in me that draws their gaze—it's weakness in *them*." Her voice was crisp now. "And if their hunger hands us even a sliver of leverage, I will use it. Without shame. Without pause. Until I take back what was stolen."

Kal rose well before the sun.

The air still clung to the chill of night, the horizon only just beginning to pale in the east. She wore a blouse of deep forest green, high-collared with laces left open, sleeves cinched above the forearms. Over it, a leather corset–not the molded sort favored by noblewomen, but a reinforced piece, fitted tight with buckles and cross-straps. Her trousers matched in shade and shape, tailored for motion, tucked into worn black boots.

She bound her hair back without fuss, tight and unbraided, the dark coils falling free behind her like a banner of shadow. Her hands moved to the weapons next, sword first, then daggers.

When she opened her chamber door, she nearly collided with Liam.

He didn't so much as blink. "Let me guess," he said, voice low, dry as the desert wind. "The training yard."

Kal gave him a look that said she had neither time nor patience for the obvious.

Undeterred, Liam went on. "And I'll wager–high, too, if I cared for coin–that your eager little shadow will be there as well. Right on time. Sword polished. Grin sharpened."

She stepped past him without ceremony, like he was simply part of the architecture.

"Yes, Liam," she said flatly. "I'm going to train."

He followed, boots silent beside hers. "And the knight?"

Kal adjusted the strap across her shoulder, eyes flicking his way.

"He'll be there. He's not exactly subtle."

Liam muttered something beneath his breath. She didn't ask him to repeat it.

Instead, her voice turned cool, thoughtful. "My interest in him is limited, I want to see what he is when stripped of charm. What's beneath the posture? If there's anything worth keeping, if he can be useful."

"If he's just another man with too much confidence and too little substance..." Her tone hardened. "I'll carve out the difference and move on."

Liam caught her arm, not rough, but firm. She turned, meeting his gaze squarely.

"You say that," he murmured. "But–"

Kal didn't flinch. "I mean it. You know I do."

A long pause stretched between them. His hand fell away.

"I'll be watching," he said.

Kal didn't look back. "I would expect nothing less."

The ring was empty.

Torchlight still clung to the edges of the yard, though the flames had dulled to embers. The first thread of morning painted the sky in pale steel. Kal stepped into the sand, setting her gear beside the bench. She rolled her shoulders once, then dipped into a long stretch.

She was halfway through a forward bend when the scrape of boots broke the hush.

"Fascinating," came Raoul's voice, smooth and just a shade too pleased with himself. "Your obsession with dawn is either admirably disciplined, or deeply concerning. Perhaps you have a tragic aversion to sleep." He paused a moment before continuing wryly, "You rise before the sun, take the ring without an audience, and yet you stretch as if every eye in court were watching."

Kal arched into the pose, arms reaching overhead as if greeting the sky itself. "And you speak as if you've just stumbled from a poem."

He stepped into the ring's edge, arms folded. "No poem," he said. "Though I'm told my presence inspires a fair number."

"Most of them end in creative curses, I imagine."

"Only the best ones." He winked.

She bent again, slower this time. "You're late."

"I'm never late," Raoul replied easily. "Time simply has the good sense to wait for me."

Kal reached for her boots, gaze fixed on the ground. "Does that line ever work?"

"It gets me invited back, which is more than I can say for most men."

Kal finally straightened, rolling her neck once. She moved into a deeper lunge, her back leg extended, her muscles shifting beneath the fitted leather. Her blouse clung to the shape of her waist, the corset defining every inch of her position.

Raoul unslung his sword from his back with an adept flick, followed immediately by the *clack* of it glancing off the edge of the bench.

A long pause. Then a cough. "A minor setback."

Kal looked over her shoulder, one brow lifting with imperial disinterest. "Need assistance?"

"Only if you're offering medical aid to my pride." He chuckled.

"Afraid I don't treat injuries, I merely inflict them."

Raoul gave a wounded look as he retrieved the blade. "Cruel and beautiful. That's just irresponsible."

Kal finally straightened, turning fully toward him, "And yet you showed up."

He tilted his head, shrugging. "Curiosity. Possibly self-destruction. One of those."

Kal's gaze moved over him once, expression incredulous. "I've inspired curiosity?"

He gave a small, theatrical sigh. "Learning your name is becoming something of a personal quest."

"I suggest choosing a better one."

"Absolutely not, my lady," he flourished, "I would perish from the unbearable torment of not knowing your name."

Kal's lips almost curved.

Raoul caught it, eyes glinting. "Ah, a crack in the armor."

Kal turned back to him, her gaze cool and amused as it swept over him. "Not knowing must be difficult for you.

That earned a laugh, richer now. "You have no idea."

She clicked her tongue lightly. "Truly taxing for the ego, I imagine. Poor thing."

"You do realize," he said, stepping into his own stretch with a grunt, "that this isn't how most women greet me at dawn?"

"Most women flatter," Kal replied. "I've never pretended to."

She turned back to the ring, drawing a practice sword free from the rack with ease.

Raoul followed, his eyes lingered a moment on her, watching the way she moved. Controlled. Dangerous. Beautiful in the way a blade is, before you realize too late that it's already cut. He moved into position across from her, his sword lifted, grin back in place. And somewhere beneath it all, a simple, dawning truth settled into his mind.

Gods, what have I gotten myself into?

Raoul stepped forward with easy grace, his blade spinning once in a lazy arc, catching the pale light of morning as he grinned–confident and just short of arrogant.

"I'm ready for my next lesson, my lady."

Kal didn't move. She simply lifted one brow, as if considering a rather unremarkable insect.

"*Next?*" she said.

That single word had weight to it. Raoul's grin faltered, if only by a breath.

Kal stepped toward him, voice level, "You haven't learned the first one. Today, I decide whether you're simply slow to absorb instruction... or a lost cause entirely."

Raoul's grin returned, sharpened at the edges, something more wolfish than charming.

"Well then, *sweetheart*" he said, tossing her a wink with galling ease, "only one way to find out how well I listen under pressure."

Kal stared at him with indifference, with that still, assessing silence that made most men flinch.

"Tough crowd," he muttered. "It must be hard pretending to be immune to my charm."

"If that's what passes for charm in Varis," she said, tone dry. "I have no faith left in its women."

Raoul raised his brows, mock-wounded.

"And to think," she added, circling him now, "someone let you live this long believing you were charming."

He opened his mouth–perhaps to offer something roguish in reply–but she moved. One moment she was speaking, the next she was striking. Steel whistled through the space between them, and Raoul's reflexes snapped into action on pure instinct. He blocked, barely. Her blade scraped against his, the vibration running down his arm like a jolt. She pressed forward immediately, her next strike angled for advantage. There was nothing polite in it. She drove him backward with cold, precise efficiency.

Raoul's smirk vanished. There were no flourishes now. No verbal parries.

She was *measuring*.

And Raoul, for all his well trained form, found himself reacting too late, too often. He pivoted, caught her next strike at the edge, but already she was past his guard again. Her movements were deliberately uneven, just enough to upset the rhythm, just enough to unseat his footing.

He tried to counter, Kal sidestepped the blow and turned it back on him in one smooth twist, pressing him another pace toward the edge of the ring. The sound of their blades rose and fell with the wind, each clash underscored by the soft thud of shifting sand. Raoul's chest heaved now with exertion, which meant it was time to adjust. He dropped the posturing–the crisp lines of Varisian court technique designed to win applause, not battles–taking up a lower stance, shoulders loosening, the tightness in his stance unraveling into something more instinctual. Smoother. *Real*. Something that must have been learned under the hot sun of the Dunes.

Kal noticed, saw it in the way his blade began to arc at unfamiliar angles, in the way he stepped inside her range to disrupt. There was grit in it now. Muscle behind precision. A shift in tempo. Something closer to a hardened warrior than a precise knight, which was *far* more interesting to her.

She let him come. For a time, she allowed the rhythm to shift. Their blades blurred, moving faster now, driven by breath and instinct. He struck at a sharper angle. She turned the blade aside. He feinted, spun, came back low but Kal never broke pace. She let him believe the tide was turning. Then she ended it. One wrong step. That's all it took. One overreach, subtle, but there. Raoul lunged too far, just a fraction, reaching for advantage. Kal pivoted, her blade catching his sword. Her weight shifted.

And Raoul's world turned.

She swept his leg out from beneath him, and the next thing he knew, the sky greeted him with indifferent clarity. He hit the sand flat, the air punched from his lungs, and lay there in silence for a beat–just long enough to question several decisions in his life. A hoarse laugh escaped him as he stared up at the sky, his chest rising, sword still clutched in one hand.

"Well," he said between breaths, "that was humbling."

Kal stood above him, her sword lowered but still in hand.

"You changed tactics," she said at last, her voice cool.

Raoul blinked up at her through the haze of exertion. "Thought I'd try something new."

Kal tilted her head slightly, a few loose curls sliding over her shoulder. "It almost worked."

He gave a crooked smile, wincing as he pushed himself up from the ground. "*Almost*," he said, "is doing a lot of work in that sentence."

"It usually does."

He chuckled as he straightened, brushing sand from his tunic and dignity alike. The ache in his ribs reminded him that this lesson would not fade quickly.

"Still not going to tell me your name?" he asked, his tone still laced with that infuriating charm, but edged with something quieter. Not pleading, he didn't beg. But hoping.

Kal paused. Just a breath. Just long enough to suggest she'd considered it. "*No.*"

He grinned despite himself. "You really do enjoy watching me suffer."

That earned him a flicker of her gaze, and it was enough to knock the breath from his lungs more effectively than any strike.

"If that's what you've taken from this," she said, "you've mistaken the lesson."

Raoul tilted his head, sword resting against his shoulder. "So?"

Kal arched one brow imperceptibly.

He motioned between them with a half-shrug. "Have you decided? Am I a lost cause? Or do I still earn the right to be taught?"

For a heartbeat, she regarded him. Then she turned fully, facing him.

"You're not a lost cause," she said. "You just...learn slowly."

Raoul groaned, "Gods, woman. At least let me die with a sliver of dignity."

Kal turned and walked from the ring, the rhythm of her boots steady in the sand. Her curls bounced with each step like a banner of disdain trailing behind her. Raoul watched her go, breath catching despite himself.

"Will you be back tomorrow?" he called. "Or should I assume this heartbreak is my final reward?"

She didn't turn but her voice drifted back, clean and clear.

"Your first lesson," she said, "is not to be late."

Then, just as she passed beneath the arching stone of the gate, she glanced back.

"You tell me if there'll be another."

And then she was gone, swallowed by the walls and morning haze alike.

Raoul stood still a moment, blade slack in his grip, his grin returning—slower now. A quiet, rueful thing.

"Not late," he murmured. "Gods help me, I'll be early."

He let out a breath, then turned back to the ring. He trained for another hour. Longer, if truth be told. But the rhythm was off. The balance was misaligned. No matter how he moved—no matter how he struck or stepped or corrected his form—his thoughts kept circling back to her. The lines of her face. The way she cut through posture and pretense both. The stillness that she carried was like a second weapon. *And those eyes.*

Gods above.

Those eyes were going to ruin him.

The halls were near silent, as Kal turned toward her wing. But as she rounded the next corridor, she found she was not alone.

King Alden stepped from a side hall, his presence almost casual. He wore no crown, no sash of state—only a dark tunic, a vest of muted embroidery, and the simplicity of a man unbothered by pomp before breakfast.

He paused when he saw her, offering a smile that crinkled at the corners of his eyes. "Training so early?" he asked, voice light with amusement. "Or should I assume you never stop?"

"The arena is well-equipped." she said evenly. "Even the flooring is maintained. I was...surprised."

Alden gave a short laugh. "That arena's older than my reign. Most of my predecessors used it for ceremonial duels, feast displays, and diplomatic entertainment. I keep it sharpened for more practical reasons, I do enjoy a good morning training every now and then." He shrugged lightly. "And a place of discipline deserves respect."

Her gaze narrowed, more intrigued than skeptical. "And here I thought kings preferred soft chairs and later mornings."

He chuckled. "I did. Once. But my wife used to rise before the sun. She claimed it was the only hour that truly belonged to her."

Kal said nothing, but something in her stance shifted subtly. Listening.

"I started rising with her eventually," Alden went on, his voice a touch wistful. "It became...our hour. Before the robes and the rings and the ministers. Just us. It taught me a great deal about how to rule, strangely enough. Quiet teaches more than noise ever could."

He glanced past her then, a flick of memory passing through his features. "I suppose the habit never left me. Even after she did. Some habits outlast the reason for them."

Kal watched him carefully. Still searching for the hidden edges, but she found none. Just Alden, smiling with the peaceful gravity of a man who had carried love and loss and still somehow stood without bitterness.

Alden looked at her again, his smile gentle. "It must be strange for you," he said. "Coming from what you endured, to this. I see it, you know. That look in your eye every time we speak. Like you're trying to solve a riddle written in water."

She didn't reply.

He offered a small shrug. "I'll take it as a compliment."

A ghost of a huff left her, barely a breath, but it was there.

He grinned faintly. "Will I see you at court today?"

"No." She replied. "No. I've no desire to be predictable."

"Wise," he said, nodding. "Though I hope one day you'll stop needing to live like that. Always alert. Always measuring."

Kal's gaze sharpened "That kind of life," she said quietly, "isn't one I was given the luxury to imagine, let alone want."

Alden nodded in understanding.

"Well," he said, adjusting the line of his vest, "if court doesn't tempt you, my private study might. There's a collection there that might suit you—treatises on law, diplomacy, military history. Even some agricultural theory if you're desperate."

Her expression flickered to almost a smile.

"A wise ruler," he said, "never stops learning. Especially about those they intend to protect."

Kal inclined her head. "Thank you."

He caught the edge of caution in her voice but pressed nothing.

"You're welcome to join me anytime," he said instead. "And I'll show you whatever you wish to know."

With that, he turned and continued on, his footsteps faded into the corridor's quiet. No farewell. No flourish. Just the sound of a king who knew when to leave a conversation standing.

MEASURED IN SILENCE

I t had been four days.

Not that Raoul was counting. Not in any obvious way. But he *knew*. Four dawns since she'd slipped from the training ring without a backward glance. Four mornings since she'd left his pride laid bare in the dirt and somehow made him feel as if he *liked* it.

He hadn't stopped showing up. Each morning, earlier than the last, blade in hand, his hope fraying by degrees. No one saw her. It was as if she'd stepped from myth into his life and then back out again with the same maddening grace. The yard sat empty, the torches burning low, the air still and unwelcoming in her absence. He trained anyway, letting his frustration fuel each strike, each step. But his rhythm never settled, not the way it had when she was across from him, pushing him back with that infuriating elegance.

Jarreth fared no better, though the prince would rather chew glass than admit it. He followed his father through court with grim efficiency, attending minor petitions, foreign complaints, even temple offerings to long dead Gods, *anything* that might yield a glimpse of dark curls or a glint of that fathomless gaze. Nothing. She'd vanished like smoke and left both men trailing after the echo of her absence.

By the fourth day, Raoul's knuckles were bloodied from training and Jarreth's patience hung by a thread. They sat at the king's table, one on either side of Alden—two men, both wounded, pretending not to limp.

King Alden, of course, noticed. He poured his own wine, perfectly unhurried. His eyes flickered between them like a man observing a private joke he wasn't quite ready to share.

"Saints above," he said, setting his goblet down. "You've seen her all of once—*twice*, maybe—and I've never seen two grown men so completely undone. Tell me something," he continued, his tone light. "Did either of you sleep last night, or are you determined to haunt the halls like widowed ghosts?"

"She's making a point," Jarreth muttered.

Alden lifted a brow. "And what point is that?"

Raoul smirked faintly, but the edge was gone from it. "That we aren't half as interesting to her as she is to us."

The king leaned back, clearly enjoying himself now. "Saints preserve us. Look at you two. My son, brooding like a jilted bard. And my warhound, pacing like someone broke his favorite sword."

"Almost did," Raoul murmured.

Alden laughed, utterly delighted. "Gods, my most composed men, reduced to brooding shadows and court-day sighs." He glanced at Jarreth with mock sympathy. "Did you write a sonnet yet? I assume that's next."

Jarreth leveled him with a flat stare. "You're *not* helping."

"I'm not *trying* to help," Alden replied, grinning as he leaned back. "I'm actually enjoying this immensely."

Raoul muttered something that sounded like "heartless old bastard," and Alden raised his brows.

Jarreth's jaw twitched. "That's not comforting."

"It's not meant to be." Alden swirled his goblet once. "You're both used to being seen. Noticed. *Admired.* She doesn't care for any of that. She looks at a man like she's checking his weight on a scale she built herself...and Gods help you if she decides you're lacking."

Raoul leaned forward, "And if she doesn't?"

Alden's gaze sharpened. "Then you'd best be sure you're ready."

Alden stood, stretching lazily. "Hopeless," he said, casting one last look between them. "Utterly hopeless."

Kal hadn't left the eastern wing in days, but whether for reflection or silence, even she was not certain. Now, the quiet had grown stale, and something in the air felt shifted.

She turned a corner near the southern gallery and halted. Alden stood mid-stride, not ten paces away. His hands were clasped behind his back, his bearing at ease, though the slight lift of his brow suggested he also hadn't expected the encounter.

"Well," he said, his voice warm, "the court will have to adjust its wagers."

Kal didn't return the smile, "I wasn't aware I'd become a subject of betting."

"Not formally," Alden replied. "Though your absence has been...

noted."

She studied him skeptically.

He offered his arm. "Walk with me?"

The question hung, not heavy, but after a moment she stepped forward and set her hand lightly on his sleeve. They moved in silence at first, their footsteps echoed faintly between the high archways. King Alden set a steady pace, not rushed, not ceremonial. If he meant to speak with purpose, he gave no indication of pressing for it.

"The solarium on the eastern side catches the morning sun before the rest of the court rises," he said at last. "Servants don't linger there until the first bell sounds. It's a good place for quiet, if you're inclined."

Kal gave no answer, but her attention stayed with him.

"The library is open to you," he continued. "All of it. I've given orders to the keepers. You'll find the lower archives unlocked."

They passed into a longer corridor lined with aged windows, their glass panes casting latticed shadows across the floor. Beyond them, garden walls rose, half-lost in ivy.

Alden gestured to a curved stair tucked beneath an archway thick with vine. "That leads to the outer gardens. Patrols are discreet, but thorough. It's quiet there as well. Peaceful."

Their path wound past colonnades and hidden balconies, corners of the palace that most nobles passed without thought. Alden spoke of each in turn, not with pride, but with invitation. He wasn't displaying a kingdom, he was pointing out choices. Spaces.

She turned toward him, expression guarded. "You're showing me how far I'm allowed to go," she said, voice flat. "Without actually saying it."

Alden blinked, surprised, then gave a short laugh. "Guilty as charged."

Her eyes narrowed, though not with anger.

"I'm not trying to coax you," he added. His tone shifted, lower now, more careful. "Not really. I just...want you to feel like you can go where you like. Inside these walls, I mean. If going outside is still too much."

She looked away again. Her hand slipped from his arm, folding loosely behind her back as she turned toward the gardens.

"Want," she murmured, "is a luxury."

His smile faded but his voice held steady. "The offer still stands."

He gestured ahead. They moved on, the sound of their steps soft against sun-warmed stone. Alden didn't press her. When he spoke, it was of small things—the day's weather, a dispute in court yesterday involving two noble houses and an unfortunate goat, and the running feud between the royal chefs and the steward over spice shipments from the coast.

Kal said nothing, but her posture changed gradually. Her shoulders lowered by a measure, and her eyes moved from the tree line to the cobbled path without expectation of pursuit. For the first time in days, she wasn't checking over her shoulder. The silence lingered between them, staying long enough to build an unknown pressure in her chest. And then, almost without thinking, she recognized it.

He was waiting. He was giving her the space to speak if she wished and accepting it if she did not. That unsettled her more than any question he could have asked.

She drew a slow breath, steadying it. Then, as if testing the sound of her own voice, she asked, "There's a hall near the west wing. Gilded doors. I saw it once, passing through. What is it?"

Alden looked at her, quietly pleased.

"The Treaty Hall," he said. "It's where foreign dignitaries are received. Where most of our formal alliances were signed."

She nodded once, thinking. "And the wing with the stone latticework near the royal chapel?"

"The historians' cloisters. The scribes keep the ancestral records there. And the deeper archives, some go back nearly to the founding of Varis."

Another silence. Shorter this time.

Then she said, slowly, "I'd like to join you again. At court. To observe."

Alden turned fully, surprise flickering for a moment before it gave way to something more honest. His smile creased the corners of his eyes.

"I'd be honored."

She held his gaze, wary still, but not withdrawn.

"There's a session today," he said. "Mostly light petitions, but a few worth hearing."

She didn't answer immediately. He saw the pause, the calculation behind her eyes, the search for strings.

At last, she inclined her head, barely a nod.

"I'll be there."

Kal's pace through the palace halls was steady, each step steady. The gown moved with her, cold blue silk trailing behind like meltwater over stone. The guards stationed at each threshold stood aside without question.

Liam said nothing. He walked a half-step behind her, alert in every line of his body. His eyes never stilled. Every servant who turned too quickly, every guard whose gaze lingered half a moment too long–he marked them all. Kal didn't need to glance at him to feel the silent tension that radiated off him.

They found Alden in one of the side vestibules off the eastern stair, his voice low as he conferred with a steward over court seating arrangements. The king looked up at their approach, and the expression that crossed his face was something between amusement and honest delight.

But it wasn't her he looked at first. It was Liam.

Alden dismissed the steward with a flick of two fingers and turned to greet them, hands loose at his sides, his posture open and without formality.

"Well now," he said. "The elusive shadow himself." His tone held warmth, and something quieter beneath it–curiosity, perhaps. "I was beginning to think your brother had retreated to only rumor and threat."

Kal offered a faint tilt of her head. "He joined me to observe."

Liam said nothing, silent as a shadow.

Alden didn't falter. If anything, he seemed faintly entertained.

He inclined his head instead of offering a hand, as if correctly guessing it wouldn't be taken. "Liam. I imagine there are few things less appealing than courtrooms and courtiers, but I hope you'll humor me again. These halls pretend to be dangerous, but the only threat tends to be to pride."

Still no reply. Just a flicker in Liam's eyes, not acceptance, not rejection. Just...awareness.

Unbothered, Alden turned and gestured for them to follow as he led the way into the corridor beyond. "Keep an eye on Lady Marwen today. She has a tendency to wear whatever color the most powerful person favors. She'll be in gold this morning, she heard a whisper Raoul had a good showing in sparring yesterday and thinks he's climbing further in noble rank"

"Baron Estel," Alden went on, as they continued down the corridor, "will be watching Jarreth's hands like a hawk. He believes gestures carry hidden signals. I once spent an entire week speaking only while gesturing with my left just to watch him panic. Nearly drove him into a fit."

She caught it then, a subtle shift at her side. A breath that wasn't quite a scoff. A tightening at the corner of Liam's mouth, the faintest pull of muscle that meant reluctant amusement.

They climbed the final flight toward the royal entrance above the court floor. Marble gave way to polished stone inlaid with silver. The vaulted ceiling stretched high overhead, lit by the filtered glow of the rising sun. King Alden stepped into position at the head of the landing just as the great doors before them creaked open. The hinges gave a low groan, followed by the hush of breath from the chamber beyond as light spilled into the corridor, bright and clear.

Beyond the threshold, framed in the arch beneath the carved seal of House Llewellyn, stood Prince Jarreth and Sir Raoul. Both men turned at the sound of approaching steps. Jarreth straightened, a tentative smile pulling at the corners of his mouth. Raoul's was more immediate, an arched brow, a flash of mischief lighting behind his eyes. Until they saw him. Liam stepped out from behind Kal, the light from the open court catching the sharp lines of his frame. The black of his coat casting him in contrast to the marble and gold around them. Whatever warmth had lingered on Jarreth's face vanished. Raoul's grin faltered, his gaze drawn–fixed not on Kal, but the figure at her side.

Liam didn't look at them, he didn't need to. His presence alone did the work. He moved like something coiled and patient, dressed in silence and shadow. A weapon disguised in formal wear.

The murmurs of nobles quieted as Alden crossed the threshold. Heads bowed in dutiful reverence. Kal trailed one step behind him, the folds of her gown catching in the morning light, silver filigree flashing with each turn like frost catching sun. Without waiting for a gesture or word, she took the seat to Alden's left. Her expression remained composed, cool, untouchable. She had the presence of someone who knew her place and saw no reason to explain it.

Liam took the chair beside her, posture loose but eyes sharp–tracking movement, measuring distance, noting exits. Across from them, Prince Jarreth and Sir Raoul moved to claim their usual places at King Alden's right. They began to incline their heads towards Kal in polite acknowledgement, only to stop mid-motion, struck by the full weight of the scowl aimed in their direction.

Raoul blinked and leaned back slightly. "Was that–? Gods, he *glared* at me."

Jarreth, slower to react, narrowed his eyes. "Are you sure it wasn't just his face?"

"I've had daggers look at me with more affection."

Jarreth looked again, sharply now. "He was with her at court before, but I haven't seen him since. Do you know who *he* is at least?"

"No," Raoul muttered, watching the pair across the dais, "but he is her hand. That's no guard's seat. Could be a lover."

Jarreth's posture stiffened.

"Or a husband," Raoul added, voice quieter, eyes narrowing. "Married, hidden, and now paraded into our path just so the Gods can laugh."

"If that's the case," Jarreth said under his breath, "she married a man who looks ready to kill us both."

Raoul gave a resigned nod. "Which would be fair."

Their hushed voices didn't go unnoticed. A low sound cut across the tension, amused. Alden turned slightly from the scribe at his side, fixing both men with a pointed look, his eyes glinting with humor.

"Careful," he murmured, voice pitched just above the hush, "you're not wrong about the look. But if you keep whispering like that, he might decide to see which of you flinches first."

Jarreth straightened immediately. Raoul, ever the braver fool, offered a weak grin.

Alden leaned back in his chair, entirely at ease. "Don't worry. He only hates you because you're staring at her like starving men at a feast."

Raoul's gaze drifted again to Liam, wariness tightening his shoulders. "So...a husband, then?"

Alden gave a quiet chuckle but offered no answer.

Kal had not turned once. The tension coiled in the air was tangible. She felt it in the way silence hung between glances, in the pulse of watchful breath across the chamber. The men across from her–crown prince and champion–radiated unease, wrapped in their own calculations, their interest poorly masked.

Let them wonder.

The court came to order without trumpet or fanfare, no ceremonial overtures or thundered announcements. Alden's voice alone was enough, calm, steady and familiar. The room fell silent.

Kal remained composed at his left, her back straight, her hands resting lightly on the carved arms of the chair. At her left, Liam sat silent in black, motionless as stone.

But he saw everything. Not just the words offered before the court, but the rhythm behind them. He marked tone as much as content. He saw how each noble stood with open posture, how they addressed Alden not out of fear, but with a deference earned by long steadiness. There was no false flattery, no veiled barbs. The debates were real–matters of trade routes, tax policies, skirmishes along minor borders. The language of government.

Alden listened with the patience of a man who did not need to speak loudly to be heard. His replies were soft-spoken, but his words carried weight, rippling through the chamber like stones dropped into a calm river. Only gentle power, by a man who did not need to prove his authority because it had already been accepted.

Even Liam, tense as ever, felt the difference. This was not the usurper King Rhaen's court. There were no games played with smiles and blades. No veiled threats behind wine cups, no nobles waiting for Kal to falter so they might strike. This was something else, something steadier. Something dangerous in a quieter way.

Yet all this power was not enough to pull Liam's attention away from the two men staring at his sister. Prince Jarreth and Sir Raoul were seated directly across from the dais–one heir, one soldier, both with rank enough to warrant attention. Their roles required focus, but their eyes betrayed them. They looked at Kal too often. Not long enough to be obvious, but with the persistence of men who couldn't help themselves. But even that confidence slipped now and then, when Liam caught them in the act. Each stolen glance was met with a look–subtle, sharp and unblinking. A warning. No words. No threat made aloud. Just the cold, constant pressure of being *seen*.

King Alden, for his part, observed all of it from the center, every bit the image of a serene king. Outwardly, he offered thoughtful nods, murmured assent, and tapped his approval for reforms throughout the kingdom. But inside...he was *thrilled*. The return of Kal's brooding guardian unnerved them both. And Alden–who had once thought Jarreth's composure beyond shaking, and Raoul's charm ironclad–was quietly delighted. These once clever men now both were losing their footing over a woman who hadn't said a word to them...and a man who looked capable of dismantling the court with a single glance.

Alden laced his fingers and leaned back, serene.

Yes, he thought. *This court season would be one to remember.*

As the court session drew to a close, the chamber's stillness broke into a rising current. Kal stood when Alden did, her expression unchanged–unbothered by the session's contents, yet not disengaged. Liam rose beside her, still silent, his presence more of a warning than a companion, a sharpened edge beneath tailored black.

They had just begun to follow Alden toward the side corridor when two figures stepped forward with unmistakable intent. Raoul reached them first. He moved easily, the picture of court-trained grace, his expression too open.

He bowed his head with casual polish. "You've been scarce."

Kal did not reply, she simply watched him.

Raoul pressed on, undeterred by silence. "We'd heard all manner of rumors. Some said you were off charting new realms. Others insisted you were hunting something monstrous in the wilds." He smiled. "As it turns out, they weren't entirely wrong."

His gaze slid to Liam. The grin didn't falter, but the edge in his voice sharpened. "And with a familiar shadow, no less."

Liam didn't blink. The look he gave Raoul was not hostile, it was worse. Dismissive.

A step behind, Jarreth lingered, visibly less prepared for the encounter. He opened his mouth as if to speak, then thought better of it. When Kal's gaze found him, calm and impassive, whatever confidence he'd gathered dissolved. He adjusted his cuffs with unnecessary focus and studied the floor as if the veining in the marble might offer counsel.

Raoul ignored the prince's retreat.

"We did miss your presence here," he said smoothly. "These halls are colder without you. I trust your time away was...rewarding?"

There was charm in the words, but Liam knew provocation when he heard it. Before Kal could speak, he stepped forward, just enough to draw a line between them. His voice was low, level, and cut clean through the air.

"We're done here."

He didn't address the two men. He spoke past them, to the King, who stood just behind.

"Thank you for your hospitality."

Kal inclined her head to Alden in polite farewell, then turned as Liam guided her from the room. His hand at her back was light, but there was no mistaking the message in his posture: no more words, no more games. They slipped into the corridor without another glance.

Jarreth remained still, watching them go, his expression a mix of frustration and unease.

Raoul let out a slow breath, his tone drier now. "That glare could peel stone."

Behind them, Alden folded his arms and grinned. "You two really thought that was going to go differently, didn't you?"

Jarreth's brow furrowed. "Who *is* he?"

Alden didn't answer immediately. He just chuckled, clearly entertained.

"Stars help you both," he said, stepping past them with the easy stride of a man enjoying the outcome more than he'd admit. "That man would kill for her."

Raoul tilted his head slightly. "I think he'd rather just kill *us*."

"Oh, without question," Alden replied, already halfway to the door. "And judging by the look on his face?" He cast them one last amused glance. "He'd get away with it."

The doors closed behind them with a soft, final thud. The murmurs of the court faded, swallowed by the corridor's high stone archways and glimmering marble. The hall stretched before them, lined with gilded sconces that flickered in the still air, casting long shadows along the polished floor.

"The audacity," Liam muttered, just above a whisper. "A prince and his champion, circling you like a well-dressed carrion. Smiling like they'd earned the right to breathe your air."

His jaw flexed. "I should've–" He cut off, the words unfinished, the thought too sharp to voice.

Kal didn't look at him. Her eyes remained ahead, calm. "Should've what?" she asked mildly. "Broken the prince's nose in front of the entire court?"

"Would've been worth it," he snapped. "The way they looked at you."

She exhaled, not quite a sigh, not quite amusement. "They didn't touch me."

"They *thought* about it."

Her lips twitched. "You plan to fight every man who has an unworthy thought?"

"If I have to."

A silence stretched between them. Her steps slowed just enough for her to glance at him, though her voice remained even.

"You're not entirely wrong," she said. "They were arrogant. But not cruel. Not like the ones we left behind."

Liam gave a stifled, derisive breath. But he didn't disagree.

Kal walked on a few paces before speaking again, her tone light, but pointed. "Tell me what you saw in Alden."

He said nothing at first. One hand flexed at his side, as though resisting the familiar weight of a hilt. Finally, he said, quieter now, "He's... different. Not weak. But not like the others either. Doesn't posture because he doesn't need to."

Kal gave a short nod, her eyes never leaving the end of the hall. "And?"

Liam let out a long breath, slower this time. Some of the heat behind his words had cooled. "I don't know what to make of it."

They continued in step, the tension of the court bleeding from their shoulders by slow degrees. Though Liam's gait still held an edge, watchful, bristling.

After a few more turns, Kal slowed, casting a glance sideways. "I'm going to the king's study."

Liam gave an indistinct grunt. "More books?"

"More insight," she corrected. "He's given me access to his private collection. It would be foolish not to see what he guards behind locked doors."

He scoffed. "And what am I meant to do? Wait outside like a leashed hound?"

She turned to him fully now, her voice steady. "Go to the training yard."

He frowned. "To watch half-trained nobles swing blades like sticks?"

"To *mingle*," she said pointedly. "To listen. To see who's worth watching and who's worth using. There are guards there who were raised in this court, men and women who've been watching nobles' posture since birth. That knowledge is more valuable than you think."

He sighed, long and weary. "Their form is an insult. If one of them tried to kill me, I'd die laughing before I bled."

Kal smiled, just barely. "Then try not to laugh too loud. You'll ruin the court's illusion of strength."

He didn't smile back but he didn't argue.

She stepped closer, lowering her voice. "You need to learn this court, Liam. We both do. If we mean to take back what's ours, it starts with understanding how the roots twist beneath the stone. Who serves what. Who watches whom."

He studied her, eyes sharp beneath the burn of restraint. But for once, he offered no deflection. Just a brief, clipped nod.

"I'll go. But I'm not wasting time sparring with children."

"Of course not," she said, turning away. "Just glare at them. That usually works."

The air in Alden's study was still—thick with the scent of old parchment, polished oak, and the faint trace of burned-out wax. The hush carried a kind of weight, not oppressive, but absorbing. Kal had long since lost track of time. Scrolls lay open across the broad desk in layered disarray—records of trade, disputes between border lords, long-forgotten treaty revisions penned in an impersonal, meticulous hand. A leather-bound volume on succession law sat propped open beside her, one edge anchored beneath her palm. Her fingers moved absently along the grain of the parchment as she read. Military texts had taught her terrain, movement, the rhythm of battle at a glance. But this, this was another kind of war entirely. Lines of ink charted not bloodshed, but strategy: grain shipments as leverage, land rights as inheritance traps, generational grudges hidden in polite civic records.

She read the way she fought, focused and methodical. Each passage filed away, another blade to wield when the time came.

She hadn't noticed the sun's retreat across the high windows. Hadn't heard the door latch shift. But the breath...that, she heard. A sharp inhale, caught mid-startle. Not loud. Just enough to break the silence.

Her gaze lifted.

Jarreth stood in the doorway, half-stepped into the room, with one hand still resting on the latch. His eyes met hers and widened, as if he'd stumbled into a lion's den and only now realized the danger.

Kal didn't rise. She leaned back in the chair, hands resting lightly on the carved arms. Her expression didn't shift. She let the silence settle around him like dust.

And waited.

"Are you coming in," she asked, voice smooth, "or are you content decorating the doorway like some newly commissioned bust?"

The jab startled him into motion. He blinked, stepped forward with too much haste, caught between retreat and recovery.

"My apologies," he said, the words tripping over themselves. "I didn't realize–I wasn't told anyone was here, I–"

She gestured to the chair across from her with a flick of her fingers. "Sit."

He obeyed, too quickly. The chair scraped softly against the stone as he adjusted, posture too straight, hands clasped tightly in his lap like a student awaiting judgment. He nodded once. A formality. Perhaps an anchor.

"It's...good to see you again," he managed. "I hope today's court wasn't–well. I hope it was informative."

He tried again, leaning forward slightly, voice lowered now.

"I realize we haven't had a proper chance to speak," he began, careful but sincere, "and I wanted to–"

Her gaze didn't shift. It didn't harden but it didn't soften either.

"Why do you try so hard to hide behind titles and decorum?" She asked, her voice smooth and sharp all at once.

Prince Jarreth blinked. Once. Then again.

"What?" he asked, not defensive, just caught off guard. There was confusion in his tone, light and genuine.

Kal remained seated, fingers still steepled in front of her, her voice even. "You dress the part. You speak in perfect register. Your posture is polished. But it's all surface."

She didn't raise her voice.

"Your spine holds too tightly," she continued. "Your tongue is measured down to the word. And your eyes..." She paused, letting the moment stretch. "Your eyes ask more than your mouth ever dares."

Jarreth stared at her as the silence stretched between them, long enough to force a decision. Most men would've shifted. Most would've filled the space with apology, or charm, or defense. But Jarreth didn't. Slowly, he adjusted his shoulders, his posture reassembling itself with the control of a man slipping back behind a wall of protocol.

"I'm afraid I don't understand," he said at last, voice calm, flat. "I am who I am. The Crown Prince of Varis."

"So," she said quietly, "you're a title." Kal tilted her head. The motion was slight, not dismissive or mocking. Just...considering.

His control held but she saw it fray at the edges.

"You speak like a man shaped by duty," she said. "Calculated, presentable. *Safe.* And yet everything about you reads as unfinished."

He parted his lips, as if to reply but she didn't give him the chance.

"Are you hiding him?" she asked, eyes narrowing slightly. "The man beneath the polish? Or is there nothing left? Did you bury him so deep beneath the crown that you've forgotten where the mask ends and he begins?"

The silence that followed was heavy, dense with the weight of something unspoken. Jarreth didn't flinch, but the breath he took stalled in his chest. And she saw it, recognition. The dawning realization that someone had seen too clearly, and found the thing he hadn't named.

He didn't speak. Couldn't.

Kal simply watched him, as if she were waiting to see whether the man would rise to answer her or whether the mask would. But he said nothing. So she didn't press, she let the silence hold. Then, she rose with the same grace she always carried, the faint rustle of silk and parchment the only sound as she closed the tome before her. She slid it aside with care.

"Good evening, Your Highness."

Her voice was smooth as ever, polite even, but it landed with finality. And then she turned and walked out, the study door clicking softly behind her.

Jarreth remained seated, unmoving. Not a shift of shoulder or flicker of breath. The study was quiet again, the hush folding in around him like dust settling. But her voice echoed still, relentless.

You're a title. Is there a man beneath it? Or is there no man at all?

He exhaled slowly, long and controlled. Then let his gaze settle on the empty chair across from him. He hadn't even asked her name. He wasn't sure that would have mattered. The door creaked open again a few minutes later but this time, the silence broke differently. Looser. Lighter. And entirely unwelcome.

Raoul entered with his usual ease, the kind that bordered on insolence. His coat hung open, hands shoved into the folds like he owned the place. His smile was already forming.

"Thought I'd find you buried in some dusty scroll," he said, eyeing the papers strewn across the desk. "Didn't expect to find you looking like a man who's just seen the heavens fall."

Jarreth didn't answer. His eyes remained unfocused, as if trying to replay a moment he couldn't quite hold onto.

Raoul's brow lifted, intrigued. He glanced from the empty seat to Jarreth's expression, and back again.

"Wait," he said, lips twitching. "Don't tell me. This is about the Haldren girl, isn't it? Hair like spun gold, voice smooth enough to fell a man at ten paces...ringing any bells?"

Jarreth blinked, as if the sound had finally pulled him free. His scowl was slow in forming. "No, it's not her."

Raoul grinned, pleased. "Ah. But someone *did* get to you..."

Jarreth hesitated, then ran a hand across his face. "*She* was here. I didn't know—walked in, and there she was, reading through my father's study like she'd built the place herself."

He exhaled again, the sound quieter this time. "She didn't say a word at first. Just watched me. And when she finally spoke..." His voice drifted off. "She said only a few things. But she..." He shook his head. "She took me apart. Like she already knew where to press."

Raoul gave a long, low whistle and dropped into the opposite chair with theatrical flair. "Gods. I've never seen you rattled like this."

"I'm not—" Jarreth began, then stopped, too quickly. "I'm not *rattled*."

Raoul propped his chin in one hand, unconvinced. "No, no. Of course not. You look positively radiant."

Jarreth shot him a dark look.

"But it's curious," Raoul continued, voice too light to be harmless. "Your legendary composure seems to have abandoned you. Along with your charm. And your words. And whatever royal dignity you usually drag into rooms like a trailing cloak."

"Gods, shut up," Jarreth muttered. "You haven't had any better luck."

"You know," Raoul added, gesturing lazily toward the desk, "*I* spoke to her. Full sentences, even. Might not have impressed her, but I didn't turn to stone."

"That's because you have no shame."

Raoul grinned. "It's my defining trait."

He leaned back in his chair, studying his friend with interest. "Where's the prince who could make half the court swoon with a glance? The one who dances like a dream, the polished heir who never stammers and always finds the perfect line? Did he flee?"

Raoul went on, eyes glinting with mischief. "Has he been replaced by this poor soul—undone by a single woman who never raised her voice?"

Jarreth groaned and dropped his head into his hands. "I hate you."

Raoul laughed, soft but not unkind. "No, you don't. You just hate being seen."

Jarreth didn't answer. He was too busy remembering the weight of her eyes, wondering, more than he cared to admit, if she'd been right.

The Only Game Worth Playing

Morning broke pale and cool across the stone corridors of Varis, the early light slanting through high windows in long bars of gold. Kal stood before the wardrobe in silence, pulling her sparring leathers into place. Each buckle fastened cleanly, each strap drawn taut. The dark fabric hugged her form without excess, built for movement rather than display. Her hair, pulled back and bound with brisk efficiency, fell into line without need for adjustment.

Her boots carried her through the halls, where the night still clung to the stone. The light grew with every step she took, brighter where the corridor opened to the southern arch. Beyond it, the palace gave way to the training grounds; open earth, old stone, and the familiar cadence of wood on steel. The scent of sand and sweat rose to meet her, and something in her eased as her feet met the packed soil. This was the only kind of peace she trusted—loud, honest, earned.

Beneath the high arch, Raoul was already moving across the sparring yard, his form easy and efficient. He trained alone, shirt damp at the collar, his movements stripped of theatricality. And yet, for all his focus, he turned the instant she arrived. His grin unfurled at once—sharp, pleased, too knowing by half.

"My lady," he called out, pausing just long enough to offer a half-bow, one arm extended in exaggerated courtly flourish. "Back from your kingdom of tomes and torchlight. I was beginning to suspect you'd vanished into the archives forever and forgotten about me."

Kal didn't dignify him with more than a glance. She stepped lightly onto the sand and began her own warmup, her limbs unfurling in long, languid stretches, her movements slow and sinuous.

She could feel his gaze. He didn't even try to hide it.

Raoul leaned his weight onto one foot, his arms folded lazily across his chest as he watched her. "You know, sweetheart, it's cruel to make a man wait so long just to be humbled again."

She rose fluidly from a deep stretch, brushing dust from her palms. "Waiting," she said without looking at him, "is a lesson."

Raoul raised a brow, intrigued.

She met his eyes then, expression cryptic. "Absence is a weapon. If you don't know how to wield it, you don't know how to fight it."

He stared at her for a long, quiet beat. Then, unexpectedly, he laughed. It was a low, rough sound–amused, pleased, a little disbelieving.

"So that's what this was," he said, shaking his head. "Gods, I thought you'd abandoned the ring. And here you've been dragging me through a game I didn't even know I was playing."

Kal stepped into position, the air between them already shifting.

"I don't play," she said.

He grinned wider. "That's the most dangerous thing you've said yet."

Raoul hadn't stopped watching her since the moment she stepped onto the sand. His grin had settled into something lazier now, his body loose and coiled with barely-contained energy. It was clear he'd come early not just to train–but in the hope that she would arrive. And now that she had, he didn't intend to waste the moment.

"You know," he said as she adjusted the strap across her chest, "there are rumors already. That you're Alden's secret weapon. Or an exiled noble. Or someone even the Dunes wouldn't cross."

Kal said nothing.

"I've also heard," he went on, circling idly to her right, "that you killed a man in another court just for touching your shoulder without permission."

Her hand slid down to check the balance of a shortblade. Still no answer.

"I've also heard," he added, "that you arrived by way of the north cliffs, barefoot and blood-soaked, carrying your man over your back and a war in your eyes."

Kal paused, gaze cool as winter glass. "You've heard a great deal."

Raoul grinned. "I listen well. Though I'd much rather hear it from the source."

She looked at him fully now, the weight of her stare flattening the air between them.

Then she stepped away towards the rack of swords. She didn't reach for her usual blade. Instead, her hand fell to something tucked at the back of the rack–an unfamiliar shape, long coiled and half-forgotten among more traditional weapons. She drew it with care, and as the light caught its form, Raoul's attention sharpened. A chained crescent blade. The steel curved in a half-moon, its edge gleaming despite the age of the weapon, bound to a length of braided chain and finished with a narrow grip wrapped in black leather. Foreign make. Rare. A weapon that demanded not only strength, but fluidity–requiring its wielder to balance movement against momentum, to control the weapon as if it were part of the body rather than something held in the hand.

Kal stepped into the open circle of the yard. She let the chain unwrap with a flick of her wrist, the arc of the blade singing once through the air. She shifted her stance, testing the weight, then moved. The weapon came to life in her hands. She controlled the chain through subtle, minute shifts of her wrist and forearm, adjusting tension like a second breath. The crescent blade spun in tight, whipping rotations around her before reversing direction mid-motion, slicing low, then high, then coiling into a spiral as she ducked beneath its arc and sent it flaring outward again. She advanced, turned, pivoted, changing direction with such controlled ease that it seemed choreographed.

Raoul said nothing, watching. He had seen arrogance in the training yard before. He had watched nobles overextend, hoping to impress. He had witnessed flourishes meant to display skill only to fail. But this... this was something else.

Kal wasn't performing. She was demonstrating.

He folded his arms across his chest, his earlier grin fading into something quieter. Respect, perhaps. And something bordering on wariness.

"Saints," he muttered under his breath. "She could kill a man with a ribbon if she felt like it."

Kal didn't look at him. The chain snapped tight around her forearm, the blade held still with a single twist of her hand. She lowered it slowly, breath steady, gaze calm.

Raoul shifted his stance at the edge of the yard, one brow arched, arms still folded across his chest. Whatever flicker of awe he might have shown seconds earlier had already begun to mask itself beneath familiar bravado.

"Good gods" he said, tone light, "If I'd known that's your idea of warming up, I might've sent for a priest instead of sparring gear. Remind me to only cross you when you're unarmed."

Kal unwound the chain slowly, the crescent blade still in her grip, though her gaze had already left it. She didn't rise to the bait.

"You mistake this for something I need," she said evenly, voice calm. "To best you, I could just use a stick."

Raoul blinked, then he laughed. It was a short, honest sound–half amusement, half wounded pride.

"Is that so?"

She met his gaze with a look as cool and composed as her breath. "You're welcome to test the theory."

His grin widened. "I always did have a fondness for losing with style."

He crossed to the weapon racks with easy steps and swapped out his twin practice blades for a simple short sword. He tested its balance once before returning to the center of the yard. Kal placed the crescent blade back onto its hook and reached instead for a slender, unadorned staff–oak, smooth-grained, the length of her own height. She spun it once, testing the weight, then stepped into position opposite him.

Raoul raised his blade in a light guard, a smile still playing at the corner of his mouth. "Do try to go easy on me. My pride's already limping."

The moment the signal came–a slight nod between them–she moved.

Her first advance was quick, but not rushed, the staff held low in one hand. She struck high, reversed it, brought the opposite end up toward his ribs before retreating just out of reach. Her grip was fluid, two-handed only when needed, her movements shaped by control rather than brute strength. Raoul adjusted fast. He had quick feet, faster reflexes. He blocked the next sweep and answered with a short jab meant to drive her back. But Kal ducked beneath it, turning the staff in a smooth arc that caught the inside of his wrist and sent the blade wide.

He came again, more focused this time. A feint high, a cut low, and a step meant to corner her against the sandbank–but she turned inside it, pivoting on one foot, bringing the staff down across his shoulders with enough force to stagger but not injure. Raoul recovered quickly, circling now, his earlier grin tempered by growing awareness.

Kal didn't circle. She stalked. Two steps. A faint shift of her weight. Then the staff lashed out–low, fast, aimed at his ankle. He jumped back a beat too late and caught the next strike across the hip. She spun once, dropped her center, and swept his legs out from beneath him in a clean, decisive arc.

Raoul hit the ground with a breathless thud. Dust lifted around him. He lay there a moment, staring up at the sky, chest rising with exertion–and something perilously close to admiration.

Kal stepped back, her staff lowered at her side, saying nothing.

Raoul exhaled, one arm flung across his chest. "Saints preserve us," he muttered. "You weren't bluffing about the stick."

Kal tilted her head, the barest echo of a smile flickering–too subtle to be called satisfaction. "I rarely bluff."

He looked up at her, squinting against the morning sun, still winded but grinning. "Remind me never to try and impress you again."

She didn't look back. But there was the faintest trace of a smile at the corner of her mouth.

"I'm beginning to think you enjoy this," he called after her, brushing sand from his shoulder as he sat up rising with a muffled grunt. He rolled his shoulder once, testing the bruise already blooming along the muscle, and turned to watch her.

She was across the ring now, cooling down with the same ruthless grace that had knocked him off his feet. Each motion was deliberate without the faintest flicker of triumph. No gloating. No sly glance in his direction. Just the discipline of a woman who hadn't needed to prove herself and had done it anyway.

That, somehow, made it worse. Or perhaps better...he hadn't yet decided.

"Well," he offered, brushing his palms together as he approached the edge of the ring, "I'm not too proud to admit it–that was impressive. Thoroughly humiliating, of course for me. But impressive nonetheless."

She didn't reply, her focus was still internal, measured in breath and muscle, not chatter.

Raoul stepped closer, careful not to intrude, but not pretending disinterest either. "Tell me something."

At that, her gaze shifted. Over her shoulder, one brow arched–not invitation, simply acknowledgement.

He tilted his head, offering a smile that was half charm, half genuine inquiry. "The man you're always with–the one who looks like he's five seconds from committing murder if someone breathes too loud."

Raoul hesitated a beat, then continued. "He's not a guard. Not just a guard, anyway. He watches you like..." He frowned slightly, trying to shape the right words. "Like something he lost once, and doesn't intend to lose again."

A faint curve touched her lips, not quite a smile, but the shape of something sharpened on the edge of knowing. It made his skin tighten, prickling under the weight of something unseen.

"Curious?" she asked, her voice light, but with an edge beneath it. Always, there was the edge.

Raoul offered a shrug, casual. "It's hard not to be."

She stepped toward him.

"Why?" she asked.

He blinked. "Why, what?"

"Why are you curious?" she repeated, voice still smooth, though now laced with something colder. "Is it the mystery that draws you? Or are you trying to assess the danger?"

He tried for a grin, cocky and warm. It came out thinner than intended. "Can't it be both?"

Kal studied him for a long moment. Raoul felt it, that weight behind her gaze. The way it sifted through his words, posture and breath as though they were puzzle pieces she'd already learned how to rearrange. She began to circle him. Slow steps over packed dirt, the sound barely a whisper. Her gaze never left his eye.

"You ask questions," she said softly. "But you don't want answers. You want categories. Titles. Boxes. Champion. Lover. Guard. It's easier that way, isn't it?"

His smile faded. Not entirely, but enough.

She stopped in front of him, head tilted, gaze fixed. "And what would you do," she murmured, "if none of those names fit?"

He opened his mouth, then paused. Thought better. "I'd...adapt."

Her head tilted the other direction. "No. You'd misstep."

And just like that, she was turning away.

"You want to know who he is?" she said without looking back. "Figure out who I am first."

Raoul took a step after her, his brow creased. "Is that a challenge?"

But she didn't answer. Her steps were soft over stone, each footfall erasing the conversation behind her. The sun caught the edge of her braid as she passed beneath the arch and disappeared into shadow, leaving nothing but dust in her wake.

Raoul stood in the center of the yard, one hand still loosely curled around the hilt of his sword, the other brushing absently against his ribs where she'd landed her final blow. The sky above was already brightening, sharp lines of gold slicing across the southern wall. Somewhere behind him, a knight barked orders at a page who'd dropped his blade.

He didn't hear it.

He was still smiling like a fool. Like a man thoroughly bested and already plotting the next round.

The door creaked softly on its hinges as Kalithea stepped into her chambers, the scent of dust, sweat, and oiled leather clung to her skin. Her bracers came off first, buckled straps sliding loose as she crossed the room toward the washbasin. Her mind was still half in the sparring ring—half in the feel of impact, breath, calculation.

But she wasn't alone. Liam stood near the window, arms folded across his chest, shadowed in the amber light slanting in from the courtyard. He didn't speak at first. But she felt his presence like pressure in the room, thick and coiled.

"You let him chase you."

Kal didn't flinch. She dipped her hands into the cool basin, watching the water cloud with dust and sweat. "I let him spar."

"You didn't shut him down," Liam said, voice tight with heat just beneath the surface. "Didn't stop the way he looked at you. Didn't end the game. You fed it. Let it stretch its legs. Let him think he had room to run."

Kal lifted her gaze, slow and level, catching his gaze in the warped brass mirror above the basin. Her expression didn't shift. "We need allies."

"He's not an ally," Liam snapped. "He's a dog–tail high, nose to the wind, sniffing after your warmth like it belongs to him. He doesn't see you. He sees the shape of a woman and the idea of conquest."

She dried her hands, taking her time as though the conversation were no more urgent than a misplaced button or a scuffed boot. "He can want whatever his heart or his loins desire," she said, calm and even. "It doesn't concern me."

Liam took a step forward, teeth clenched. "You think that makes it harmless?"

"I think it makes it predictable."

The shift in her tone was slight–but enough. She turned from the mirror, the cloth still held loosely in one hand, and faced him fully now. Her voice cooled, the edge returning with unmistakable clarity.

"If he turns out to be another empty man wrapped in compliments and performance, I'll discard him. Like I've done before. But until then..." She folded the cloth and set it neatly on the basin's rim. "He is the Champion of Varis. And, if what I've been reading in Alden's study is true, the blood-heir to the Warlord of the Dunes. That means he's leverage, a potential link to two kingdoms with divided loyalties. A blade pointed in the right direction. And I will not throw that away because his glances linger too long or his words come dressed in flirtation."

"You're letting him believe he's getting closer," Liam said after a long moment. This time, quieter. Accusation had dulled into something colder. Something closer to fear.

Kal tilted her head, the corners of her mouth unmoving, but her eyes gleamed, sharp and unreadable.

"I want him to believe that."

The silence that followed was dense, drawn tight between them.

Liam looked away first. Not in defeat–but in the way of someone who understood the terrain and still hated what it demanded. "You play a dangerous game," he said, his voice low.

Kal turned back to the basin, already reaching for the tunic she'd draped across the chair.

"It's the only one worth playing."

A Crack in the Wall

D ays passed in quiet procession, each indistinguishable from the last to the casual eye. Every morning brought the same rhythm—blade, breath, discipline. And in that rhythm, she kept the world at bay.

At dawn, the ring belonged to her, but Raoul was always there now. Sometimes he arrived before her, leaning on the railing like a man lounging at the edge of a battlefield. Other times he trailed after her in silence, boots crunching on dust covered stone, offering the illusion that he had arrived by chance. But Kal knew better. Men like Raoul didn't linger without purpose, and charm was never freely given.

Each morning he greeted her with a grin too bright for the hour and a title more absurd than the last. "My lady," he'd intone with exaggerated reverence. Or, "Sweetheart of Steel," or "Stormborn," or once, when particularly bold, "Her Royal Danger Wrapped in Silk and Spite." It never earned more than a glance, if that. Kal offered no name. No past. No invitation.

She spoke only in bladework. They moved in tandem, clash and pivot, sweat and silence. Her strikes were relentless, precise in a way that revealed not just training but survival. Raoul began to sharpen beneath that pressure, his footwork cleaner, his reactions faster. But he remained several steps behind, always just a beat too slow. And every time she bested him, he rose from the dust with that same infuriating smile, as though defeat were just another kind of conversation.

Jarreth fared no better. He tried, halting greetings at court gatherings, questions framed in careful neutrality when they passed in the palace halls. But his tongue stumbled the moment her gaze found him. Every word he managed to speak unraveled beneath the weight of her silence. She didn't need to raise her voice; a single look from Kal was often enough to leave the Crown Prince of Varis standing stiff and uncertain, like a boy still growing into his armor.

Her days unfolded according to her own design. She could often be found seated in Alden's study, his library, or one of the smaller private reading rooms where few dared intrude. She moved through volumes with the hunger of someone denied knowledge for most of her life—absorbing land disputes, family lines, trade tariffs, siege records, inheritance laws, everything that Rhaen had never shown because he had never cared to *rule*. His court had been a blade pointed at the world. Alden's court whispered of longevity, of alliances spun like silk and bloodlines woven into power, like a thousand unseen threads spun across generations.

Kal meant to master every thread.

To his credit, Alden didn't hover. He offered her space, and when she crossed paths with him, he rarely interrupted her reading beyond a dry observation or an unassuming suggestion. He would leave books on the corner of her table, never announced, never explained. Treatises on diplomacy, memoirs of failed kings, personal letters from border wars long forgotten.

At first, she asked no questions. But, then came the shift. She began to speak, precisely, pointedly. Not of herself, but of matters of state. Of unrest in the outer provinces. Of how to force concessions from stubborn nobles without igniting civil fractures. Alden answered with stories, not instruction—wry recollections of court missteps, victories won not by sword, but silence. His guidance was sharp, often laced with unexpected humor, and always handed over like a coin flipped into her palm. He did not demand gratitude.

She hadn't expected to enjoy his company, and yet...she did.

Their walks grew longer. Through the terraced gardens, down quiet halls hung with tattered banners, she questioned, he answered. Sometimes he questioned back, and she learned the art of withholding without lying. In him, she saw no hunger. No ulterior pull. Only satisfaction in watching her carve space in a world that had never invited her. Of course, she searched for the trap. She prodded his words, examined his silences. Weighed his kindness like a blade in her palm. But there were no hooks beneath the surface. Only depth. Sharp, steady, immovable.

It made her uneasy. She knew how to parry cruelty. She could predict desire. But this—authority without brutality, mentorship without possession—it unsettled her more than anything Rhaen had ever done. And though she would never name it, not even in the guarded silence of her own mind, she had begun to look forward to those walks. Those moments of wit traded for insight. Of watching a man rule not through force, but through patience.

And, slowly, she realized she started enjoying their walks.

The garden lay still beneath the waning afternoon light, its hedgerows casting long shadows across gravel paths and moss-laced stones. The air held that particular hush reserved for late hours when even the birds had grown tired of their own voices. The palace loomed beyond the high walls, its endless murmur softened by distance, reduced to nothing more than the whisper of power too far away to matter.

Kal sat beneath the sweeping limbs of a flowering tree, where pale blossoms stirred in the breeze. The marble bench beneath her bore the cool weight of silence, and though a book lay open in her lap, its words had long since ceased to hold her attention. Her gaze lingered somewhere beyond the page, fixed not vacant.

She heard him long before he spoke.

Footsteps, soft and uncertain, pressed into the gravel like second thoughts. The kind of tread that wanted to be heard but feared being noticed. She did not lift her head. Some part of her already knew who it would be.

"Afternoon," came Prince Jarreth's voice. Polite. Formal. As if court etiquette might spare him from judgment. "I didn't expect anyone to be out here."

Kal turned a page without hurry, her fingers brushing parchment with the same casual dismissal she might give a fly. "And yet," she said, not looking up, "here you are."

He paused. A breath, a wince, the sound of shifting feet. "I—well, I was just walking. Thinking."

Still, she did not respond. Her eyes flicked up once, sharp and fleeting, just enough to meet his gaze before dropping again. It wasn't curiosity, it was assessment.

He stood frozen on the path, caught between approach and retreat, like a man who had stumbled into sacred ground and suddenly remembered his shoes were muddy. For a long moment, he simply watched her—watched the way the wind pulled a strand of hair across her cheek, the way the tree cast shifting shadows across her expression. She offered no invitation to sit.

"I thought maybe..." he began again, then faltered. "Well, I was wondering... perhaps if you hadn't—maybe you'd like to—"

He trailed off, exhaling in frustration, then laughed softly to himself. "You know what? I tried."

That gave her pause. Not the words, but the way he said them. No court mask, no careful choreography of tone and posture. Just resignation, worn plainly, without shame. For the first time, he sounded like a man, not a prince.

Kal's gaze rose slowly, more pointed now. She studied him as one might study a flawed blade, evaluating not just the weakness, but what had caused it. A moment passed, then another. Finally, she closed the book with a soft, decisive sound and rose to her feet.

Jarreth stilled as she crossed the garden. No words, just presence. Her proximity was purposefully controlled. There was no heat in it, only weight.

"You should never try to be something you're not," she said softly, "least of all just a role."

He opened his mouth, but no words came. Her eyes held him where he stood.

"The man behind the title..." she continued, her tone colder now. Not cruel, but clear. "He's suffocating. Dying by inches. And if you don't figure out who he is—soon—there'll be nothing left but an empty name."

Jarreth's throat worked in a silent swallow. He didn't argue, didn't move.

Kal waited a moment longer, gaze unwavering. Then, without further word, she stepped past him. The faintest brush of her sleeve grazed his arm, a touch so light it barely existed, but it left the air changed in its wake.

Jarreth turned, and watched as she walked away. Her silhouette was framed by the low sun and the pale drift of blossoms falling from the trees above. He stood in the silence she left behind, breath tight in his chest, and felt—though he could not name it—that something within him had shifted.

Jarreth didn't hear the footsteps until the moment was lost. Until the hedge behind him rustled softly and his father stepped into view, clearly having been enjoying the spectacle far longer than decency allowed. King Alden had his hands clasped behind his back. His stride unhurried, his expression drawn in the familiar lines of mock sympathy, tempered by the unmistakable glint of amusement behind his eyes.

"Well," the king said, sounding far too pleased with himself, "you look like a man who's just been shoved off a cliff and landed squarely on his pride."

Jarreth groaned, scrubbing a hand down his face as though he could erase the moment from existence. "How long were you standing there?"

Alden tilted his head, feigning contemplation. "Long enough to hear the whole sad affair. Long enough to admire your courage, if not your execution."

"I didn't fail," Jarreth muttered, though the words rang hollow even to his own ears.

The king arched a brow. "Son, I've watched men take arrows to the lung that had more bravado than that conversation."

Jarreth flushed. He opened his mouth, thought better of it, then settled for a grimace instead. "You heard what she said?"

The smirk faded, just enough to show it had never been cruelty, only a father's fond indulgence. Alden stepped closer, letting the silence settle before answering. "Every word."

Jarreth's gaze dropped to the gravel. He kicked at a stray pebble, jaw working. "And?"

"And," Alden said, voice gentler now, "I think she was right."

Jarreth's head snapped up.

Alden held up a hand, forestalling protest. "I might have phrased it with a bit more *tact*. A touch less surgical precision. But the heart of it? She wasn't wrong."

Jarreth folded his arms across his chest, bracing for impact. "You've told me I represent the crown. That I have to be more. That I don't get to fail."

"And you don't," Alden said calmly. "But being crown prince is your duty. Not your identity."

He let that settle between them, his gaze steady. "You've spent your whole life perfecting the role. And gods, you've done it well, when you're not tripping over your own words, apparently. The court sees a title. They see discipline. They see a Prince in polished boots and tailored silence. But she..."

Alden's smile returned, quieter this time. "She sees through the mask. Past the polish. She sees *you*...and she's waiting to see if you've got the spine to meet her with something real."

Jarreth said nothing. The words landed like stones dropped in a still pond; no splash, just ripples that sank deep.

Alden stepped forward, lifting two fingers and tapping them lightly against his son's chest. "If you're set on chasing a storm like her–and I suspect you are, though I warned you not to–you might consider leading with the man, not the mask."

Jarreth let out a slow breath, rubbing the back of his neck. "And if that's not enough?"

Alden chuckled, already turning away. "Then try managing a full sentence before collapsing into apologetic stammering. *Gods*, you used to be charming. What happened to that man?"

Jarreth muttered a curse under his breath, though it lacked conviction. His father's laughter trailed behind him, fading into the breeze as Alden disappeared down the path once more.

Jarreth remained where he stood, framed by late sunlight and the soft drift of petals from the trees above. Around him, the garden resumed its hush. But the words lingered, both his father's and hers, circling like slow birds overhead.

ᛏO ᛖARN A ᛜAME

I don't even know your name."

Raoul stood in the middle of the ring, turning towards her at the sound of her footsteps. There was no jest in his voice, no lilt of mischief. The words landed heavily, and Kal raised a brow—not at the question, but at the fact that he'd bothered to drop the bravado.

He stepped closer, sword lowering to his side as though it had grown heavy. "It's been days now. And I keep coming back, like a fool with something to prove. I've been bruised, bloodied, humiliated...and not once have you offered a name. Not even a hint."

She watched him with the same unfathomable poise she always wore. Like the silence between them belonged to her.

Raoul let out a sharp breath, though it wasn't quite a laugh. "Do you know how impossible it is to flatter someone who knocks you flat every morning and refuses to be called anything but *my lady*? At least give me something. A syllable. A letter. *Anything.*"

That earned him something. Barely a flicker, but it was there. A subtle shift at the corner of her mouth, a glint in her eye. And to him, it was a victory worth the bruises.

Kal stepped into the ring quietly, her movement fluid, drawn tight by muscle and resolve. In one graceful motion, she unsheathed her blade. The steel sang as it left its home, a note as sharp as her gaze.

"If you want my name," she said, voice low, "then win it."

She nodded once toward the center of the ring.

"Knight."

Raoul blinked, then broke into a crooked smile that held more delight than frustration. "You know," he said, adjusting his grip on the hilt, "that's rather cruel."

Kal didn't answer, she didn't need to. Her stance said enough—

guarded, grounded, dangerous. She was ready.

And so was he.

They came together like storm winds colliding, his strength against her precision, her speed against his fire. The ring rang with the clash of blades, each impact a declaration, each retreat a gamble. She was faster, of course. Cleaner. But he forced her to move—forced her to adjust, to pivot, to narrow her eyes in the face of something that wouldn't fold.

He pressed harder than he had in days. And still, she broke through.

Once. Then twice. A third, a fourth. Each fall came quicker than the last, but each time he rose again, breathing heavier, eyes burning brighter.

The fifth bout left him flat on his back in the sand, sweat streaking his jaw, breath coming in sharp pulls through gritted teeth. Above him, Kal stood—unbothered, blade steady, gaze level. She sheathed her weapon and turned.

"Wait!" he called after her, propping himself up on one elbow. His voice carried more laughter now than desperation. "Will I see you tomorrow?"

She didn't look back.

But her voice floated over one shoulder, cool and sure. "Show up early," she said. "And find out."

Then she was gone again, a shadow melting into the mist. She left nothing but footprints in the sand and a man who, despite the ache in his spine and the sting in his pride, was already planning what time to arrive.

She hadn't reached the end of the northern wing before Liam emerged from the shadows. He fell into step beside her easily, though there was nothing relaxed about his presence.

"You've been giving him ground," Liam said, quietly, but with more heat. "Every day. You let him talk. Let him circle. And now you dangle your name like it's a gift to be earned."

Kal stopped cleanly, and turned to face him, meeting his gaze with cool, unshaken resolve. "How long do you think we can keep hiding?"

Liam's jaw tensed, a flicker of something bitter flashing behind his eyes.

"Truly," she pressed, voice calm but relentless. "How are we meant to gather allies, raise armies, ignite the kingdoms behind us—if we never even claim ourselves aloud?"

He said nothing but his silence was weighted.

Kal didn't falter. "We always knew it wouldn't last. That sooner or later, someone would have to see us. Know us. Not just the names, but the weight behind them."

She gave him a moment. One heartbeat. Then drove it home.

"I'm not talking about court," she added. "Not yet. But those two–the prince and his champion–aren't just palace ornaments. They're the bloodline and the blade of Varis. When the day comes and we march to reclaim Elandra, they could be more than allies. They could be the keystone of everything we build."

Liam's shoulders drew tight, arms rigid at his sides. But when he spoke, his voice was cold iron. "And if either of them thinks this is a game dear sister–if they touch you, or try to take something that's not theirs–if they so much as make you falter, Kal, I'll end them. No matter their title. No matter the cost." He didn't raise his voice.

Kal held his gaze. Her expression shifted, barely, but enough. A stillness crept into her features that wasn't distance, but gravity. Truth. The kind too heavy to run from.

"I'm not going to lose myself," she said, quietly.

She drew a breath and let it out slowly. "With Arjun gone...we can't afford that."

Her eyes dropped for a moment, just one, then lifted again, steady and clear.

"I'll keep that part of me buried, Liam," she said, voice soft now, but colder for it. "Even if it kills me." She paused for a moment, "We don't get to lose ourselves. Not now. Maybe not ever."

Kal turned from him without another word. Her steps were soundless, as her silhouette retreated down the stone corridor like smoke drawn by wind. And then she was gone. Leaving Liam alone in the corridor, his fists clenched and face carved in stone, with nothing but the silence of her absence and the ghosts of what she'd once been.

The fire in Alden's study had burned low, casting a muted glow across the stacked leather-bound volumes and the scattered papers that littered his desk. The room smelled of ink, old parchment, and the remnants of last night's rain drifting faintly through the open window. He was hunched over a map when the knock came. He looked up, brow furrowed in thought, just as the door opened.

Kal stepped through without waiting for the invitation, crossing to the chair opposite his desk.

Alden leaned back slightly, one brow lifting. "So early in the morning," he said, not unkindly. "Should I be alarmed?"

"No." Her voice was even. "Just thoughtful."

He set the quill aside, fingers lacing together as he regarded her. "You wear your thoughts like most people would wear armor. And they appear heavier than usual this morning."

A flicker of something–amusement, maybe–touched her mouth, but vanished before it could settle. She exhaled softly, then raised her gaze to meet his.

"I'm considering telling them."

Alden's eyes narrowed slightly, not in suspicion, but in interest. "You'll need to be more specific."

"Prince Jarreth. Sir Raoul." She paused. "Who I am. Who Liam is."

Understanding came without surprise. He nodded slowly, posture shifting subtly–less the sovereign, more the father, always the strategist. "I see."

"They follow me like shadows," Kal said. "If I'm not behind a locked door, they're circling. Asking. Guessing. It's becoming...tiresome."

Alden allowed himself the smallest twitch of a smile. "That's persistence, I'm afraid. They've always been relentless once they've set their minds on something."

"I've noticed."

He leaned forward slightly, his tone thoughtful now. "And you're weighing whether they can be trusted. With your name. With the truth."

She inclined her head.

"I'm not announcing it in court," she clarified. "Not yet. But if they're going to keep circling, I need to know they'll protect it. Keep it. Not turn it into leverage."

Alden considered that in silence. At length, he gave a small nod. "They can."

One of her brows rose. Slightly.

"In their own ways," he amended. "Jarreth will keep any confidence you place in him. Not out of calculation, but because he honors what he's been given. Raoul...is not as careless as he pretends to be. He tests. He pries. But once his loyalty is given, it's iron."

Kal sat back, arms folding loosely, expression uneasy.

Alden tilted his head. "Still, I have to wonder."

She met his eyes.

"You've endured their questions this long. Why now?"

There was no challenge in the words, only curiosity. But Kal's eyes narrowed in assessment, not defiance.

He pressed gently. "It's not just to stifle the noise. Giving them your name won't lessen their questions, it may only deepen them."

Her gaze drifted to thoughts beyond the room. The fire threw soft shadows across her face, and for a moment, Alden didn't speak. He knew how to wait for answers that came slow, weighted, and true.

"You haven't been leaving them quite so stunned," he said at last, his voice low. "Your silences used to be walls. Now they feel more like... pauses. And I suspect you've even started to enjoy their company."

He let the words hang before adding, almost offhandedly, "Even if my son continues to flounder like a fish tossed into a fountain."

That pulled a breath out of her. a kind of amused scoff buried beneath years of restraint.

Alden blinked, then grinned faintly. "Was...was that *amusement?*"

She didn't answer. But her mouth twitched again, unmistakable now.

"Well, then." He leaned back with a contented sigh. "Perhaps there's hope for all of us yet."

He studied her for another long moment, expression softening beneath the weight of something more personal.

"You know," he said, "if you keep coming in here speaking in full sentences and nearly-smiling, I may start to expect it."

Kal gave him a flat look, but the edge in it was dulled.

"I'll prepare the court poets," he continued breezily. "They've never had to rhyme 'miracle' with 'Queen of Silence' before, but I imagine they'll rise to the challenge."

This time, the curve of her mouth was clearer. Small but real.

Alden let the jest fall away as gently as it had come. "I'm glad you came to me," he said, quieter now. "Truly. I hope the day comes when you can walk these halls without so much weight on your shoulders."

Her eyes stayed on his for a long moment. Something sharper lived behind them still–defense, memory, the shape of pain not yet named–but it wasn't rejection. Not this time.

"One day," she said quietly. Not a promise...but not a dismissal either.

Alden nodded, saying nothing more. She rose, smooth and soundless, and crossed to the door. He watched her go, and when it closed softly behind her, the study fell still again.

He leaned back in his chair and exhaled, long and slow. *One day.* She would never have said that before. In the beginning, even a hypothetical future was something she carved from stone, brittle and unyielding. But now...now it was something softer. Not certain. But no longer made of ash and warning.

He looked toward the hearth, where the last of the embers stirred.

The court was shifting. His son was unraveling in the best of ways. His champion was bruised but smiling. And the woman who had arrived as a blade cloaked in shadow was now speaking softly of someday.

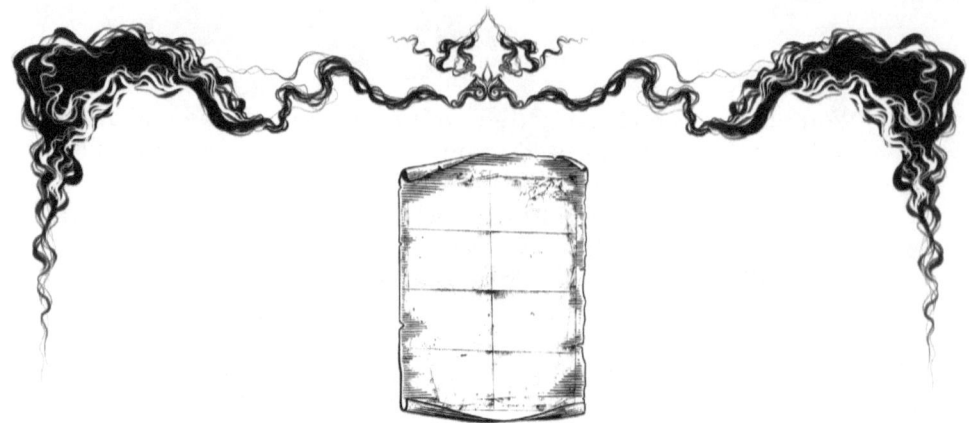

NAMES AND THEIR PRICE

aoul reached the sparring ring just as the faintest trace of sunlight brushed the tops of the eastern battlements. The courtyard still lay under the hush of morning. The scent of sand, old sweat, and forged steel clung to the air like memory. For once, he was early. Earlier than usual. Earlier, even, than her.

He stretched in silence, working the tightness from his shoulders, rotating each arm in slow arcs before dropping into the first of a dozen forms drilled into him since boyhood. Movements came easily, but his focus wandered. Each pass of his blade was interrupted by a glance toward the archway where she always appeared, silent and inevitable. But today, it remained empty.

He moved through another sequence, sharper this time, trying to shake the weight building in his chest. Still nothing. No footsteps. No shadow at the edge of the stone.

The sun began to rise in earnest, gilding the highest windows of the palace in a pale gold. A pair of guards passed beyond the colonnade, nodding to him in passing. He offered a return gesture without thinking, distracted. Then, after another few long minutes, he stopped entirely. Lowering his sword, he exhaled hard, dragging a hand back through his hair with the kind of frustration he rarely let show.

"She's not coming," he muttered, half to himself, half to the wind.

Turning, he crossed the ring toward his coat, which lay folded near a length of coiled rope on the stone bench. But something caught his eye, a slip of parchment tucked carefully beneath the cord. It wasn't the kind of thing left by accident. No torn corner or carelessness. This had been placed with intention.

He frowned and crouched, brushing the rope aside. The note was folded in thirds, edges precise, the paper smooth and heavy beneath his fingertips. When he opened it, the writing struck him first–clean, simple script, elegant but firm. There was no greeting, no flourish. Just six words.

In confidence–Queen Kalithea of Elandra

For a breath, nothing moved. Not the breeze. Not the ring. Not the man who held her name in his hands. Raoul stared at the words, as if they might shift beneath his gaze and reveal some alternative meaning–something other than the truth so plainly written. But the ink did not blur. The script did not lie. It said what it said, and every letter struck like a hammer.

Kalithea.

He saw her now in fragments, each moment reformed by revelation. The way she moved–too precise, too effortless, the economy of someone trained not to impress, but to survive. The way she measured every glance, every word, like each might cost her something she couldn't afford to lose. And her eyes–gods, those eyes–quiet but unsparing, like she saw through cloth and armor and masks alike. She hadn't needed to speak her name. She had worn her legacy like a second skin.

Queen of Elandra.

He thought of the stories. The royal house hunted to extinction. The usurper's banners flying over a broken kingdom. The last true heir taken in chains–or so the bards had said, their songs trailing into silence, because silence was safer than truth. And yet she was here.

Raoul looked down at the paper again. She could have kept it hidden. Instead, she had trusted him with something that could topple kingdoms.

In confidence.

It struck him harder than any blow she had ever landed. This wasn't a test. It was an offering, given in silence, left without demand. She had trusted him.

He sat there for a long while, unmoving, the world shifting faintly around him–the warmth of the sun creeping across the sand, the slow stir of palace life beginning behind stone walls. But Sir Raoul Sahir didn't move. Not yet.

Not until the name had settled fully into the hollow behind his ribs, until the weight of her trust had rooted itself into his spine. When he understood that nothing would ever be simple again.

Jarreth stood with all the stiffness of a man trying too hard not to pace. Arms folded across his chest, jaw clenched, he looked every inch the crown prince—except for the frustration leaking through the edges of his composure. It coiled in the set of his shoulders, in the twitch at the corner of his eye. He was used to answers. To access. To truth being a matter of inquiry and rank. And this, this dance around a woman he could neither outmaneuver nor fully understand, had begun to fray something fundamental in him.

"I'm not asking for her secrets," he said, his tone clipped. "I just want to know who she is. Where she's from. *Why is she here?*"

Alden Llewellyn, King of Varis and veteran of far more dangerous confrontations than flustered sons with too many questions, did not look up right away. When he did, it was with the arch of a brow and the faintest twitch of a smile at the corner of his mouth. "You've asked me seven questions in ten minutes, all asking the same thing, Jarreth. That one is just dressed up with different words."

Jarreth's frown deepened. "You know something."

"Oh, I know quite a lot of things," Alden murmured, setting down his quill. "Not least among them is how red your ears are getting."

The prince flushed a deeper shade almost on command. "You've given her access to your private library. She walks the corridors with you. You don't grant that kind of privilege lightly. If she's under this roof with your favor, I have a right to understand why."

Alden leaned back, hands folding lightly across his middle, expression mild. "*Ah.* So it's not about the woman. It's about being left out."

"That's not what I—"

"You were never this persistent when I brought the Haldren envoy," Alden mused aloud, tone sly.

Jarreth's mouth snapped shut.

The king chuckled. "And if memory serves, you were rather *curious* about her too."

The flush spread from his son's neck to the tips of his ears now, "That's not—this isn't—"

He coughed once, looked determinedly at the marble flooring, and said nothing.

"She's just..." he muttered after a long pause. "Intriguing. That's all."

The door opened with a soft click. Both men looked up. Kal stepped into the study with the poise of someone accustomed to entering rooms where she was not expected. The Lady of Silence, as some had begun to whisper. And her silence, as always, arrived first.

Her eyes found Jarreth immediately. There was no mistaking the gleam in them. Not cruel, but sharp. Amused.

"*Intriguing,*" she said, as if testing the taste of the word. "That's quite the compliment."

Jarreth looked like he'd just remembered how to breathe and

wasn't sure he liked it.

"I–I didn't–"

"What is it," Kal asked, stepping further inside, "that you find so intriguing about me, Your Highness?"

Alden settled deeper into his chair, already grinning behind steepled fingers.

Kal moved in a slow, soundless arc. She didn't stalk, no, stalking implied a predator with something to hide. She circled like a general inspecting a battlefield she already knew would be hers. Jarreth turned slightly as she passed behind him, but she was always one step beyond his reach.

"Is it your pride?" she asked, tone smooth. "Does it chafe, not knowing something in your own court? A thing in your court you can't read, can't bed, *can't charm?*"

Prince Jarreth stiffened.

"Or maybe it's simpler." Her voice dropped an octave. "Maybe it's that I don't look like the pale little court flowers who bat their lashes and wilt when you smile, that I don't fall into the roles your noble ladies have rehearsed since childhood. Maybe...it's that I didn't smile when you stumbled. That I didn't offer softness when you showed discomfort. *Maybe...*" she said, as she returned to stand before him again, "I didn't let you be ordinary. I wouldn't accept the 'I'm just a prince' answer? The mask you feed the world like it should be enough. Did that *rattle you,* Your Highness?"

Her words weren't cruel. They were too carefully aimed for that. They weren't meant to wound, but to dissect. To measure what lay beneath the crest and crown.

Jarreth held her gaze, and to his credit, didn't look away. But his fists had curled tighter, and the furrow in his brow deepened–not with offense, but with something else. Something like realization.

Across the desk, Alden was silent, with a slight glint of satisfaction in his eyes. He had no intention of stopping them, not when things were just starting to get interesting.

Kal finally stopped in front of Jarreth again, eyes locked to his, her gaze so intense it felt like standing in a flame that chose not to burn...yet.

"*Well?*" she asked softly. "Which is it?"

Jarreth didn't answer at once. He looked as though she had struck him, with an accusation wrapped in its own truth. His mouth parted slightly, some defense half-formed, but it withered before it left his tongue. Whatever reflex he had for cleverness, for court-trained charm or polished justification, it deserted him now under her gaze.

She sat gracefully, her eyes holding his, unwavering in their intensity.

"I didn't think you'd answer," he said at last, voice quieter now. "If

I asked directly."

She inclined her head, a slow, elegant tilt. "Then you don't know me at all."

That stung, though she hadn't raised her voice. Jarreth's fingers twitched at his sides. "I'm not trying to trap you. Or expose you."

"Then what are you trying to do?" Kal asked.

He didn't know. *That was the problem.* Or perhaps the answer. Jarreth Llewellyn, son of kings, had never been particularly unsure of anything in his life, until now. And in that moment, the full measure of her unsettled him more than he cared to admit. She was not like the women who filled the halls of his court, who learned early how to make their presence pleasing, their silences submissive. She didn't yield. Not in stance. Not in thought. Not in speech. And still he found himself returning to the question, circling it like a hawk unable to dive.

"I'm trying," he said, lifting his chin, "to understand you."

Kal leaned back further in her chair. *"Why?"*

He frowned. "Because you matter."

That stopped her. He saw the flicker of it, even if she masked it quickly. A narrowing of her eyes, subtle, assessing. Recalculating.

Alden made a quiet sound, a breath caught somewhere between satisfaction and caution. "Careful," he said, not unkindly. "That answer puts you in dangerous territory, son."

Jarreth shot him a glare, then turned his gaze back to Kal.

"I didn't mean it as a threat," he said. "I meant...there's something about you. You move through this court like you've already seen the end of every game we play. You don't chase favor or recognition, and yet people follow. My father listens. Raoul watches you like he *expects* to be outmatched."

"You command things without asking for them," he continued, steady now. "And I think... I think whatever it is you're not saying, it matters. Not just to you. T*o all of us.*"

She unfolded her legs, spine straightening, though the motion was still deceptively casual. "And you believe that gives you the right to know who I am?"

"No," Jarreth said. "But I believe I should be able to *earn* it."

There, that landed. Her expression didn't betray much, but the beat of silence that followed said enough. Kal turned slightly in her chair, repositioning, rebalancing. As if something had shifted in her estimation of him and she was still deciding whether to keep it or cast it aside.

"I've given you every reason to walk away," she said. "You didn't."

"Because I don't want to."

"And that," she murmured, "is usually where the danger begins."

Alden hummed softly from behind his desk. "She's not wrong."

Jarreth held her gaze. "I'm not afraid of danger."

Kal's brows lifted, and the faintest glint of a smile passed across her face like a shadow through light.

"No," she said, thoughtful. "I don't think you are."

Her words weren't an approval, but they weren't a dismissal either.

She turned her gaze back toward Alden then, and the moment between them broke. Jarreth exhaled, unsure whether he'd passed a test or simply survived it by breath alone.

Kal leaned back slightly, her gaze returning to him like she was peeling away layers of armor he didn't remember putting on. She said nothing for several seconds. She searched for motives, ones she knew well. Hunger, ambition, leverage. But what she saw, instead, was a man out of his element. A man who didn't know what to make of her, but hadn't run from it. Not yet. Curiosity wasn't dangerous on its own. Left unchecked, it could become a need. And *that* Kal never let anyone get close enough to feel.

Still...

She sat back a little farther, folding one leg neatly over the other, relaxed now, but only just.

Jarreth held her gaze, though it felt like staring into the heart of a storm. His fingers curled at his sides, but he didn't look away. Not now. Not after everything. She had seen through him with exactness, and still, she had offered the challenge.

"If you're so desperate to know..." she said, "then perhaps you should ask me." Her voice softened, but the edge remained. *"Not your father."*

Jarreth swallowed. He hadn't expected it to be so easy, nor to feel so impossibly difficult.

"Who ARE you?" He blurted.

Kal's brow arched slowly, expression cryptic.

He cleared his throat and corrected, this time more carefully. "What's your name?"

She didn't blink, didn't move. And for a moment, he thought she might dismiss him with silence. But then she spoke, and the simplicity of it nearly stole his breath.

"Kalithea."

Just that. No title. No pretense. A name heavy with something old and unspoken. He stared, not at her, but at the space between them. He had expected resistance. Evasion. A puzzle to unravel. Not this smooth surety.

"And where are you from?" he asked, voice faltering in the wake of her calm.

The quiet that followed was different now. No longer caution but weight. A pause heavy with memory.

"Elandra."

The name hit him like a blow. It was a name carved into the bones of history. A kingdom burned into legend and grave dust. A word that tasted of ash and iron and the silence of forgotten thrones.

"You're..." The realization shattered him like a stone striking glass. "Why did you come here? To Varis? To my father's court?"

Kal considered the questions. "To learn."

He frowned. "To learn what?"

"What could you possibly be learning that requires *this* much secrecy?" he asked again, more boldly than he meant.

Kal's lips twitched, barely, but enough. The barest breath of amusement.

"Bold today," she mused. *"How strange."*

Jarreth flushed immediately.

"Whatever is necessary," she continued, each word calculated, "to take my kingdom back."

The words rang out, quiet and absolute.

Jarreth staggered inwardly, his world shifting. Her name was no longer just a name, it was a flag raised above ruins, a fire rekindled in a place he hadn't known was still burning.

Alden laughed, a low sound thick with amusement and warning. "You're not giving her much faith in Varis as a future ally, boy."

Jarreth flinched, not from the scolding, but from the sudden understanding. Kalithea wasn't here to play court, she was here with purpose. And he, fumbling and curious, had stumbled blindly toward the heart of it.

Alden leaned forward now, the smile lingering, but his voice sharpening beneath it. "She is Queen Kalithea of Elandra. She stays in this court under my protection, in any role she chooses. Until the day comes when what was stolen is reclaimed."

The room felt colder. Branded with something ancient. Jarreth nodded, slowly, stiffly, the words sinking in.

Alden's gaze sharpened further. "And this conversation ends here. What Kalithea chooses to reveal, she will reveal. *On her terms.* Not yours. Not mine."

Jarreth opened his mouth, a thousand apologies and explanations tangled behind his teeth, but none of them made it out.

Then, without thinking, the next question spilled free.

"The man beside you," he said, quieter now. "At court. *Who is he?*"

Alden reached for his tea, eyes gleaming with the kind of mischief only kings and fathers were allowed to enjoy.

Kal turned her eyes on Jarreth again, and gods help him, he felt the weight of her gaze all over again. She tilted her head again measuring him–and after a long, silent beat, she spoke.

"He is my brother and my champion. Prince Liam of Elandra."

Jarreth blinked. He hadn't considered that, and hearing it confirmed so many things. The protectiveness. The fury. He stood rooted, the shape of her name still echoing in his mind like a bell.

She rose with that same uncanny grace, no rush in her step, no indulgence in farewell. At the threshold, she paused just long enough to let her final words fall into the silence.

"Next time you seek answers," she said, "seek them from the source."

Jarreth stared after her, the door clicking softly shut behind her. His mouth remained slightly parted, breath shallow, thoughts flying in every direction. The name she had given, the truths unveiled, the weight of her gaze–it all churned together in his chest with maddening force, a storm without form.

Behind the desk, Alden let out a long exhale and leaned back in his chair, the picture of amused exasperation. One hand swept idly across the desk, brushing aside a half-read letter.

"Gods," the king murmured, shaking his head. "How did you even exist before she arrived?"

Jarreth's eyes tore from the door, dragging themselves back to his father with effort. He didn't speak right away, just leveled him with a look of pure, soul-deep weariness. "*Please don't.*"

But Alden grinned wider, unabashed. "No, truly. I've watched you stand toe-to-toe with generals twice your age. I've seen you dismantle silver-tongued emissaries from Haldren, charm the high priestesses of Caerlyn, out-debate every noble who thought lineage made them clever. You've held this court together for weeks when I could barely stomach it myself. And now–" He gestured loosely toward the door. "One woman walks in, and you're blushing like a novice asked to dance."

Jarreth muttered something that sounded like a curse and collapsed into the chair Kal had just vacated. He sat heavily, elbows on knees, hands running through his hair as if trying to shake something loose from his skull.

"I don't know *what* it is," he said, quieter now, voice stripped of ceremony. "*It's maddening.* I go to speak and the words rot in my mouth. She looks at me, and I can feel every line I've ever told curling to ash under her stare. I try to sound composed, and all I hear is how foolish I've become."

Alden didn't mock him for the admission. His smile faded, replaced by something quieter, more thoughtful.

"That's because she's not interested in lines," the king said at last.

Jarreth looked up, brows knit.

"A woman like Kalithea doesn't care for practiced speeches or diplomatic charm," Alden went on, voice lower, slower. "She's lived through fire and shadow, boy. And came out shaped by it. You don't impress someone like that with polish. You impress her with the truth. If she chooses to let you."

Jarreth leaned back slightly, expression impassive, but the tightness in his jaw betrayed the churn beneath.

Alden waited, then continued, voice softer still.

"She sees people," he said. "Not the masks. Not the roles. But the marrow beneath. Whether they want her to or not. And a woman who sees like that... doesn't have time for artifice. She won't waste breath deciphering what you pretend to be. She'll measure the soul behind your eyes and weigh it. Quietly. *Brutally.*"

Jarreth's throat worked once. He sat straighter, but not taller. Not stronger. He looked like a man who had walked into a room certain of the destination but only now realized he had no idea where he stood.

"*I know who I am,*" he said defensively. "I've led councils. Negotiated treaties. Commanded—"

"Duties," Alden interrupted, his tone light but unyielding. "Those are duties, Jarreth. Not identity."

That struck deeper than expected. Jarreth's mouth pressed into a flat line.

Alden leaned forward, the weight behind his words settling between them.

"I'm not asking who you are as Prince of Varis," he said. "I'm asking who you are when the crown isn't in the room. When no one's looking. When it's just you. Because she will ask that without ever speaking a word. And if you don't know the answer..."

He let the sentence drift, unfinished, its shadow heavier than its end.

"She will decide for you."

Jarreth's gaze dropped, his posture rigid now with a different kind of tension, the pressure of self-recognition.

He didn't speak. The name still burned in him like an old truth freshly spoken:

Kalithea. Queen of the Fallen Kingdom.

Kal closed the door with a click, the sound almost dainty against the stone walls of their wing. The silence that followed was heavy. She crossed the chamber, already tugging loose the fine gloves that clung to her hands. Near the window, Liam sat sharpening a dagger with slow, methodical strokes, the whetstone rasping in time with his breathing. He didn't look at her as she entered. He didn't need to. He could always feel when something had shifted.

"I told them," Kal said, not looking his way.

The blade stopped mid-draw. The whetstone fell silent.

She turned slightly, casting him a sidelong glance as she unhooked the final clasp at her wrist. "Both of them. Jarreth and Raoul. They know who we are. Not the full history, only our names."

The silence that followed was a detonation held in suspension. Then the blade hit the table with a sharp clatter. Liam stood with sudden violence, the chair scraping back behind him. His entire body was drawn too tight, all muscle and fury wound into human form. His voice came low, quiet, and dangerous–the kind of low that preceded disaster.

"You *what?*"

She continued calmly, setting her gloves beside the basin, as if his voice hadn't just laced the air with steel. "I told you I would, and I didn't tell them everything."

"You didn't have to." he snarled. "That's not the point."

He stepped forward, each movement coiled with restraint, as if every breath cost him. "Those two? Of all people, those two? The ones who look at you like they've found salvation in your damn shadow? You think they'll stop at a name?"

Kal leaned against the cold lip of the stone table, hands braced. Still. Waiting.

"They'll want more," Liam continued, pacing now. "They'll want to know what lies beneath that name. Who you were. What they can reach. *What they can claim.* You gave them the thread, and they'll pull until they have the whole bloody tapestry–and by then, it's too late to take it back."

His voice cracked sharp across the room, echoing against the high stone. "They already watch you like you're something holy. You think giving them truth will humble them? It will *consume* them. Curiosity isn't benign, Kal. It turns. It twists. They'll want to touch the parts of you that don't belong to them. The parts no one should get to see."

Still she said nothing because she knew he had not yet finished bleeding.

Liam's hands were clenched at his sides, the pacing grown tighter now, more desperate than furious. "They'll press, Kal. They'll press too far. And when that happens...when your walls drop for even a moment, the shadows won't ask permission. *They'll come.* And then it isn't just your soul on the pyre."

He stopped short of her, eyes burning, the edge of grief cutting beneath every syllable.

"I can't watch you break again," he whispered.

The silence that followed was longer this time. It yawned between them like a wound neither of them wanted to name.

Then Kal exhaled, long and even. "Are you quite finished?"

Liam's glare was blistering. He didn't answer.

She arched a single brow in response, regal, unflinching. "I didn't give them our past," she said, voice smooth. "I didn't unearth what was done in the dark. I didn't show them the scars we never speak of. I gave them a name. That's all."

She stepped away from the table, slow and purposeful, her boots nearly silent against the stone. The air around her shifted again, more presence than movement. More command than threat.

"I need to know," she said, voice quieter now, though no less sure. "I need to weigh them. Raoul. Jarreth. I need to know what they are when stripped of politeness and pretense. Whether Raoul's charm is just hiding emptiness. Whether Jarreth is only a polished title wearing a man's skin."

Liam didn't move. His jaw clenched so tightly it looked carved from granite.

Kal stopped a pace from him. Her gaze settled on him fully now, steady and sharp. When she spoke again, her voice didn't rise.

"I am tired of waiting. Of silence dressed up as safety. If they are to stand beside me when the storm comes, I need to know if they will break."

She stepped even closer, her next words softer, but laced with steel. "I am not losing control. Not for them. Not for anyone."

For a moment, nothing passed between them but the quiet crackle of breath and the weight of memory. Then Liam turned away, because he could not bear to look at her and remember how many times he had seen her rise from ruin.

His hand dragged through his hair, slow and tense.

"Just don't let them in," he muttered. "Don't forget what happens when people get close."

Her answer came low and certain.

"I haven't and I won't."

It was late, torches cast soft amber light down long corridors, their flames flickering in rhythmic breath. Kalithea stood alone in the eastern gallery, a high curved stone balcony that overlooked the practice yard below. The sand was silvered by moonlight, each training dummy stretched into something long and distorted by shadow. Her arms were crossed loosely, her expression carved from deep thought, and the wind teased at the braids that crowned her head, stirring them just enough to give the illusion of movement to an otherwise motionless figure.

She had come for solitude. But solitude was rarely allowed to last.

"You always watch from above," said Jarreth behind her, his voice soft and thoughtful, more observation than intrusion. "Not just here. You do it in court too."

Kal didn't turn. Her gaze remained fixed on the sand below. "It's easier to read the game when you can see the whole board."

There was a pause, a hesitation, and then she felt the curve of a smile behind her, even before she heard it.

"So you admit it's a game," Jarreth murmured, almost sounding relieved.

"Everything is a game," she said, not unkindly, but without softness.

A second pair of footsteps echoed off the stone, this set was less cautious, more confident.

"Shame," Raoul drawled as he came into view, lounging against one of the stone arches with rehearsed indifference. "And here I thought you were up here seeking inspiration."

Kal turned just slightly enough to let her gaze cut toward him, cool and sharp. "Inspiration implies a desire for something beautiful."

He grinned, hand resting against his chest. "And I'm not?"

Jarreth gave a weary sigh. "Please stop."

Her gaze lingered, sweeping from one man to the other, assessing with that unnerving stillness she wore like armor. Then, slowly, she turned back to the arena, letting their banter fade beneath the weight of her silence.

"If you've come to offer amusement," she said without inflection, "I'm already familiar with your repertoire."

Raoul gave a short laugh, not offended. "You say that, but here we are. Undismissed."

"For now."

It was Jarreth who stepped closer then, shifting the tone, his posture straighter, his intent clearer. "We were hoping you might talk with us."

She glanced sideways again, one brow lifting. "About?"

"You," he said simply. "The woman behind the name."

That earned a longer look. She turned to face them fully, arms still folded, spine as straight as any blade she carried. There was no retreat in her stance, but no invitation either.

Raoul tilted his head slightly, his tone softer now. "Now that we know who you are...it feels strange, speaking only to a shadow."

"*Strange...*" Kal echoed, voice thoughtful. "Is that what it feels like?"

He stepped closer, slow and restrained, not encroaching but not backing away either. "You gave us your name. But names are only doors and you haven't opened yours."

Her gaze sharpened, but the voice remained level. "You're circling," she said. "Both of you. One wrapped in coyness, the other in laughter."

Jarreth flushed, his discomfort visible though he didn't look away. Raoul only smiled again, this time more slowly, as though acknowledging the hint.

"We're not trying to trap you," Jarreth said carefully, his voice more grounded.

"No," Kal said. "You're trying to see something that isn't yours to see."

Raoul leaned casually against the stone railing, his eyes on hers. "Then tell us what is something that *is* ours."

For a moment, she didn't answer. She studied them–the earnest prince who asked without knowing what he truly wanted, and the charming knight who smiled as he tested every wall she'd built. Their interest didn't displease her, but neither did it tempt her. It amused her, that was all.

"If I gave you something real," she asked, voice cool, "what would you do with it?"

Raoul said, after a pause, with shaken confidence. "We'd...understand you better."

"That," she said quietly, "is the problem. You keep thinking there's a version of me you'll like better than the one standing in front of you."

Jarreth's brow furrowed. "That's not what we think."

Kal tilted her head, voice nearly curious. "No?"

Raoul remained silent.

She took a couple steps, just enough to stand within reach. Not so close as to touch, but close enough for them to feel it. The shift. The pressure. The quiet demand of her presence.

"When you speak to a ruler," she said, voice low, each word carefully placed, "you see crowns and consequences. When you speak to a woman, you see softness waiting to be earned. But when you speak to me..."

Her eyes met Raoul's.

"You don't know what you're looking for. So you press."

She let that settle, watching them both. Neither interrupted. Neither dared.

Finally, her gaze held Raoul's. "You want to make me laugh."

She turned to look at Jarreth. "And you want to make me *trust* you."

She turned her head and cast one final look down at the sand of the practice ring–far below, pale and untouched in the moonlight, like a battlefield waiting for names. Then she spoke, quietly, without softness.

"Tell me," she murmured, as if only asking after the weather, "do you believe I look at people the way you do?"

Raoul shifted, the line of his jaw hardening slightly as his body took a half-step back before catching himself. Jarreth, still standing straighter than his friend, frowned deeply.

"What do you mean?" he asked, though the edge of his voice betrayed what he already suspected.

Kalithea didn't indulge them with explanation. Her gaze stayed level, mysterious, and strangely still. It was as if a deeper mechanism beneath her skin was turning, weighing, cataloging what could be said against what must never be.

"I think," she said at last, her tone deceptively light, "you expect to understand me through a lens shaped by want. What you desire. What the world owes you in return for your effort. But that's not how I measure people."

Kal took a single, calculated step toward them, and it was remarkable how such a small motion stole the air from the space around them.

"You ask," she continued, "as if answers are owed. But if you knew the cost of truth, you'd be more careful in how you sought it."

She paused, letting the silence stretch then, long enough to become uncomfortable. She was not cruel, but she understood the utility of discomfort, it made people honest.

"You want me to open up," she went on, her voice shifting, low and sharp as drawn steel, "but I've lived a life where opening doors gets you killed. And still, here you stand, pressing at thresholds like you've earned the right."

Neither man moved to respond. Raoul's mouth opened once, then shut again. Jarreth's fingers twitched at his side.

"I don't need attention," she added. "And I'm not interested in being understood by men who still think the most dangerous thing about a woman is what she refuses to share."

Then she turned smoothly. Without anger or haste, only finality. Her steps were soundless against the stone as she moved away. The wind tugged at the hem of her cloak, drawing it behind her like a whisper. And the silence she left in her wake stunned them.

Raoul recovered first following her, his stride longer, boots too loud in the hushed hallway. "You know," he said, almost casually, "most people don't walk away from a prince and a war hero mid-conversation."

Jarreth, slower to follow, winced. "Raoul—"

Kal didn't slow. "Most people..." she replied, her tone lazy, "tend to waste too much time trying to be liked."

Raoul laughed. "That sounds suspiciously like an accusation."

"It sounds like an observation," she countered, not breaking her pace.

Jarreth quickened beside her now, his voice lower, more reserved. "We weren't trying to interrogate you. We just wanted...something genuine. Something without layers."

That made her smile. Not fully, just a flicker of something dry. Wry. Dangerous.

"And you thought chasing me down a marble corridor like over-eager squires would earn it?" she asked, amused. "Gods, your kingdom's women must be more forgiving than I gave them credit for."

Raoul grinned, persistent as ever. "I was hoping our dedication to pursuing perfection might tip the odds."

This time, she did glance back, one cutting sweep of her eyes that froze him in place.

"Flattery," she said, almost sighing. "The last tool of men who have nothing sharper."

"But," Raoul said, matching her step again, "you still haven't dismissed us."

She stopped. Both men stumbled slightly before catching themselves. She turned on her heel slowly. She folded her hands before her with the poise of someone who'd once stood in front of executioners without flinching.

"So this is the tactic," she said. "Charm. Curiosity. A few self-deprecating remarks. You crowd close and hope something cracks."

Raoul smiled thinly. "That obvious?"

Jarreth looked like he might die from the shame. "It wasn't meant to be that–"

"Tell me something," Kalithea interrupted, stepping forward. "How often does this routine work for you?"

Raoul hesitated. Just for a moment, but it was enough.

"You want to impress me," she said, her voice softer now, but heavier for it. "You want me to laugh, or speak plainly, or slip and reveal something you can carry away as proof you were close. But you forget–" Her gaze pinned them both. "I am not trying to be liked. And I have learned that those who seek pieces of me rarely stop at the first cut."

She stepped around them without waiting for an answer. But her voice drifted back like smoke as she disappeared into the darkness of the corridor ahead.

"If you intend to play games, gentlemen, make certain you've studied the rules. For I do not lose."

This time, they did not follow. Raoul stared after her as though seeing something he didn't have the language to describe. Jarreth ran a hand through his hair and released a slow, uneven breath.

Raoul, voice a shade too reverent, finally spoke. "...I think I'm in love."

Jarreth groaned. "You're an idiot."

Follow at Your Peril

The great hall of Varis laid awash in golden light. The sort of light that filtered down through stained glass in narrow, fractured shafts–glorious in appearance, but uncomfortably warm, lengthening the court hours. The marble underfoot was worn to a quiet shine, each step echoing through the corridor as if the walls themselves were listening. The hum of voices, sharp and political, rose and fell like the tide, each petitioner a drop in the sea of obligation.

Kalithea sat at Alden's left in a high-backed chair of burnished wood. Her poise had become routine now, her presence expected but never explained. She was a study in contrasts: foreign, yet accepted; silent, yet impossible to ignore. She rarely spoke unless summoned. Yet when she did, the court stilled as though reminded that some blades, when drawn, did not sing–they whispered.

The current petitioner was one such fool who had mistaken titles for power and words for leverage. He stood with palms outward, voice pitched in the theatrical cadence of aged entitlement, presenting a tangle of grievances over the border tariffs between the southern estates and the marshland territories. It was inheritance dressed as policy. It was a veiled power grab.

When he finished, his bow was deep, precise, rehearsed. His gaze went first to King Alden, then to the prince beside him.

Then Prince Jarreth, in a move so deliberate it left even Raoul blinking upright from his post behind them, turned his head to Kal.

"What's your opinion on the matter?"

The silence that followed was deafening. Alden's brows lifted in faint, unsurprised amusement. One or two nobles in the upper galleries exchanged glances, uncertain whether this was error or brilliance. Kal, ever still, ever poised, did not so much as blink.

"Tariffs," she said, her tone light but edged, "are not about balance. They are about thresholds. How long one side can suffer before breaking, and how long the other can afford to wait."

A pause. Planned. Tactical.

"The marshes do not need southern trade. Their autonomy is survival, not indulgence. But the southern houses—" her eyes flicked, barely, to the seated nobility "—require grain to placate their lower provinces. If neutrality is your goal, remove the tariff. But if you seek to remind the southern lords where true authority resides—"

She didn't raise her voice. She didn't need to.

"Raise it. Offer a crown tithe to the marshes directly. Favor the hand that does not beg."

The silence this time was heavier. Sharper. King Alden laughed. Not loudly, but richly, like a man who enjoys when someone else sets the fire under his son's feet.

"Well done, Prince Jarreth," he said with a grin. "A perfect demonstration in handing a woman a sword and asking if she knows how to use it."

A ripple of laughter moved through the gallery, but it carried a new undertone, curiosity. Calculation. Those who hadn't taken Kal seriously now leaned forward. Those who had, listened harder.

Jarreth, to his credit, wore his embarrassment well. "I was...curious how she might respond."

"And now you know," Alden murmured. "Next time, choose your questions like you'd choose your allies...based on how dangerous their answers might be."

Kal said nothing. But the slightest tilt at the corner of her mouth suggested she was neither offended nor flattered, merely satisfied.

The rest of the day's court passed without spark. Petitions blurred together. Nobles whispered in corners, attempting to reshape their strategies around the new piece seated beside the king. Kal remained still throughout, as if no attention had touched her at all. But when the last decree was issued and the hall began to thin, she rose with the same grace she'd held all morning.

"You're following me again," she said without looking back.

"Stretching our legs," came Raoul's voice, all lightness and unrepentant grin.

"Coincidentally in your direction," added Jarreth, sounding vaguely pained by the admission.

Kal glanced over her shoulder. "Should I be impressed by this consistency?"

"Only if you're flattered," Raoul returned, undeterred.

She sighed, though it sounded more like weariness than disapproval. "You are both relentless."

"Persistence is underrated," Raoul said, shrugging easily.

"I'm beginning to think you'd trail me into battle."

"I've heard worse ideas," Jarreth said, a touch too quickly.

Kal stopped walking. Both men faltered, halting just short of her, one looking sheepish, the other expectant.

"If you're going to follow me like dogs," she said, her voice quiet but pointed, "at least learn to bite with purpose."

She turned and walked on. And, because they couldn't help themselves, they followed. They trailed her like shadows given thought and motive, never crowding, but never far. Kalithea walked with a steady gait, hands lightly clasped at her back, the hem of her gown sweeping silent over the marble. She never glanced at them, but she knew the distance between them down to the inch.

"Do you ever take compliments?" Raoul asked after a beat, his voice sliding easily into the space between them. "Or do you cut those down before they land, too?"

Kal didn't pause. "I find them tedious. Usually a precursor to disappointment."

Raoul gave a low whistle. "She's poetic when she's scathing. I admire that in a woman."

"Perhaps," Jarreth offered, tone more introspective, "she'd prefer if we dropped the charm. Just spoke plainly."

Kal's voice came back colder this time. "You assume I want to hear either."

"I think," Raoul said, undeterred, "you're used to men falling apart in your presence and mistaking that for control."

The sound she made was almost a laugh. Almost.

"No," she said at last, "I'm used to men trying to find the one version of me they think they can survive."

She kept walking. And still, they followed. Kalithea turned the corner of the upper gallery, the hall curved ahead like a blade readying its arc—and she paused.

Liam was already there. He came toward her with a storm in his stride, long coat splitting at the flanks like a banner cut loose in the wind. His boots struck the floor with uncompromising steps, and his eyes—dark, unyielding, already narrowed—cut straight through the air between them.

He saw her. Then he saw what trailed behind her, and the anger welled in his chest.

Raoul and Jarreth slowed as if struck by some invisible line. They weren't fools. The shift in the air was not to be ignored. Liam didn't speak. One hand came to Kal's arm—not rough, but firm, controlled—and turned her with that same deftness he'd used to steer her through enemy corridors and burning cities.

"We're going," he said, voice low, clipped, and dangerous.

Kal lifted a brow, neither surprised nor impressed. Her chin tilted slightly, her expression serene save for the cool amusement playing beneath it.

"Liam."

Behind her, both men had stopped mid-step. Neither moved. They read the angle of his shoulders, the calculated slowness of his breath. They saw the way he didn't even glance at them. Not until Raoul, too bold and always a step too close, leaned forward ever so slightly.

Liam turned. Not quickly. *Slowly.* The way a predator might shift its weight before the pounce. His eyes met Raoul's with the kind of silence that said more than threat. There was no rage in them, just absolute conviction. It wasn't that he could kill them.

It was that he would.

Neither man followed.

Kal allowed herself to be led, making it clear with the set of her shoulders and stride, that it was her choice to move, not his command. Liam didn't look back. He walked beside her as though every corridor they passed were a battlefield, and she, once again, the prize everyone thought they could win. They turned down a narrower hall, the muffled footsteps behind them fading away. Kal pulled her arm free, not forcefully, but with intent.

"That was dramatic," she said, voice light, though the steel beneath it rang clear.

Liam didn't break stride. "They were too close."

She exhaled softly through her nose, gaze drifting toward the wall as they passed. "They've been near me for days. It's becoming harder to avoid."

He stopped sharply, the motion sudden enough that his coat flared and fell. When he turned to face her, his anger wasn't loud, it was focused and honed.

"You speak of it like it's nothing," he said, low and tight. "Like it's an inconvenience. Proximity isn't the danger. *Intention is.*"

Kal turned toward him, expression neutral but eyes dark with warning. "You think *they're* dangerous?"

"I think men like that always are. Especially the ones who *think* they aren't. The ones who smile while they get close. The ones who believe they deserve to be close."

Her lips curved. Not with humor, more like familiarity. "And how many blades do you think I've danced around in my life, Liam? You really believe those two are the ones who'll break me?"

He didn't answer.

She stepped past him, slow, graceful, every movement dismissive without effort. Her hand trailed along the stone briefly as if anchoring her to the hall itself.

"These men wouldn't last a week in the courts we crawled out of," she said, her voice almost tired. "They wouldn't last a night in the rooms where power comes without pretense."

Liam caught up to her, his silence flint-edged now. The kind that ground against the inside of his teeth because words wouldn't help. Because he knew she was right.

"That's not the point," he said quietly.

"No, dear brother," she agreed, casting a glance over her shoulder. "But it's still the truth."

They walked the rest of the way without words. His pace matched hers exactly, his presence just off her shoulder like the shield he never laid down. But the tension had shifted. The storm had passed, no lightning, only the charged calm that followed.

She knew what he had done. Not dragged her away for her sake. He had done it to keep them from seeing too much. From seeing what he feared they might one day be allowed to touch.

They hadn't moved.

Raoul and Jarreth stood exactly where Kalithea had left them. Liam's parting glare still pressed against the back of their necks, a wordless reminder that he didn't miss much and forgave even less.

Raoul broke first, letting out a slow breath as he rested a hand against his chest. "I've faced warlords with more delicate threats."

Jarreth didn't glance over. His eyes remained fixed on the corridor ahead, where Kal had vanished without a backward look. "That *was* delicate."

Raoul gave a dry snort. "Which is precisely why it feels like a warning."

They might have lingered longer in their mutual discomfort, thoughts circling the same unsolvable problem, if not for the voice behind them–clipped and unmistakably unimpressed.

"Tell me...are you both naturally this dense, or is it something you've been practicing?"

They turned.

King Alden stood a few paces down the hall, arms folded across his chest. His expression carried the kind of disappointment usually reserved for treaty breaches and diplomatic dinners turned to chaos. One brow rose, the same way it had during Jarreth's younger days, when he'd tried to sneak a falcon into the royal chapel for instance.

Raoul straightened slightly. "Your Majesty," he said with mock formality. "Always a pleasure."

Alden didn't blink. "If that were true, you'd stop giving me reasons to question your judgment."

He turned his gaze on his son. "You're the crown prince of this kingdom. I assume you remember that?"

Jarreth nodded once. "I do."

"Then act like it." Alden's voice sharpened. "Because if you keep chasing that woman with that expression on your face, it won't be you inheriting this throne. It'll be your brother–after your unfortunate and entirely preventable disappearance into a shallow grave dug by a very loyal and very capable sibling who already has blood on his hands and no interest in diplomacy."

Jarreth stiffened. "You're exaggerating."

Alden took a step forward. "Am I?"

Raoul raised a hand. "He's not."

"Of course I'm not," Alden sighed. "You've both spent the last week trying to press a woman who's made it abundantly clear she has no interest in being *pursued*. She is not a puzzle to unravel or a storm to weather. And she is most certainly not waiting for one of you to break through her armor with the right combination of cleverness and charm."

He paused, expression darkening. "Whatever you think this is, it isn't a game. She's not playing, and if you keep pressing her like this, you won't just get hurt. You'll provoke something none of us are ready to face."

A silence settled, heavy.

Then Jarreth squared his shoulders and met his father's gaze directly. "I'm not trying to break through anything. I'm trying to understand her."

"Are you?" Alden said flatly. "And what part of following her down corridors like a dog after a scent speaks of understanding?"

"I don't want to *trap* her," Jarreth said. "I want to know her. Not for court strategy. Not for leverage. Not to tame her. Just...to see her for who she is."

Raoul shrugged, more relaxed but no less certain. "And I want her to see what happens when someone doesn't flinch first."

Alden looked between the two of them, jaw tight. "You both speak as though that woman is waiting to be seen, as if she hasn't already shown you exactly who she is. She's survived worse than anything you can imagine. You don't change someone like that with patience or affection. You don't earn her trust with persistent interest."

"We're not trying to change her," Jarreth said quietly. "We just want her to know she's not alone."

The words hung there a moment longer than either man expected.

Alden studied them both, then sighed–long, tired, and laced with something older than irritation. "You both are fools if you think she needs rescuing."

"She doesn't," Raoul said. "But maybe she deserves a reason to stop expecting betrayal."

The king said nothing for a moment. Then he turned, muttering as he walked away, "Gods help you both. If Liam doesn't kill you, she just might."

Raoul watched him go. "Not the worst way to die."

Alden didn't turn back. "Idiots," he called over his shoulder.

ᒪESSONS IN ᒋRON

The sun had barely risen when the sparring ring came alive. Raoul flipped the axes in his hands, adjusting to the unfamiliar weight. Blackened blades, dulled for practice but heavy, true. Not his weapon of choice, but for once, that suited him. This wasn't about comfort. Across from him, Kalithea unstrapped the short spear across her back with its hooked blade glinting faintly in the morning light.

They circled. First strike, then counter. Then speed. The rhythm built fast, each motion a test. Kal darted in, controlled and fluid, her strikes sharp, her footwork tighter than his. Raoul matched as best he could, but it was clear early on, *she was better.*

He grinned anyway. She was always better.

They moved in tighter now. No wasted energy. No banter. Raoul blocked a low sweep, countered with a pivoting swing that she narrowly dodged. She answered with a backhand strike of her own, and for a few minutes, the clash of metal was the only sound in the yard.

Then she stepped in. He saw it coming, the same feint she'd used before. She let the axe catch her, turning just enough for the edge to graze her shoulder as she stepped inside his guard. Textbook. Fluid. He braced for the counterstrike.

It never came.

She jolted mid-step, the motion breaking. Her shoulder wrenched back as if the blow had struck something deeper. A breath tore out of her, low and involuntary, and she staggered a half step before catching herself.

Raoul faltered, axes lowering a fraction. That hit hadn't landed hard. It shouldn't have drawn blood. It shouldn't have made her sound like that.

Kal stumbled, just half a step, but it was enough. Her arm curled against her side, blood blooming through her sleeve, shoulder twitching once in clear pain before she forced it still. Her breath was shallow, controlled, but only barely.

"Kal?" he asked, voice dropping.

She didn't look at him. "I'm fine."

"You're not." He took a step forward. "You're bleeding. That hit barely—"

"I said I'm *fine*." Her voice was sharp.

Raoul stopped cold. Her eyes met his—flat, composed, but wrong. Behind them was pain. Bright, flickering, and buried fast. Kal glanced quickly at the weapon in his hand, trying to see what had cut her. Iron haft. Iron blade. Not steel.

Iron.

Kal was already moving. Her body obeyed, but her posture had changed—slightly off-balance, right shoulder lower, steps tighter. She was still fighting. Still dangerous. Raoul said nothing, watching her circle back to the center of the ring, breath controlled now, but not recovered.

"Again?" she asked, tone even.

He didn't move.

Her gaze narrowed. "What's wrong, Raoul? Worried you'll lose anyway now that you've landed one decent hit?"

He didn't smile. "That wasn't a decent hit. There was hardly any contact at all."

Kal's face remained impassive. "Then maybe next time, aim for something that matters."

He opened his mouth to press but stopped. Something had shifted. It wasn't just her injury. It was the way she shut it down. The *need* to control it before he could name it. That wasn't the mark of someone hiding just pain. That was someone hiding something more.

"Another round," she said again, her tone brooking no argument.

Raoul nodded, though his grip shifted on the axes. They moved around each other in a slower circle now, steps measured, blades low. The earlier rhythm was gone, replaced by something quieter. Watching. Thinking. Testing. Kal's grip hadn't relaxed. If anything, it had tightened. She kept the wounded arm from view, forcing her breathing into even cadence, though the iron's touch still burned deep beneath her skin. The pain wasn't gone. It simply had no permission to show.

"If you need a formal invitation to enter every fight," she said lightly, not breaking her stride, annoyed at his hesitation "I suggest you find a softer sparring partner."

Raoul raised a brow, his axes loose at his sides. "And here I thought we were still playing nice."

She turned her blade just slightly, catching the light along its edge. "You think *this* is me playing?"

155

That earned a slow grin, bright, wolfish, and entirely unrepentant.
"I thought we'd at least graduated to casual conversation."

Kal lifted her chin, blade angling into a ready stance. "If you want 'casual', find a court lady. They like flatterers."

Raoul mirrored her movement. "That's the problem. You've ruined me for those court ladies."

She didn't answer. But a flicker of a smirk crossed her mouth. Then she moved. The strike was clean. Swift. Her shoulder screamed as the motion pulled at torn skin, but she didn't show it. Raoul caught the blow with one axe, shifted to parry the second. Blades rang between them, the impact sharp.

"You don't waste time," he muttered, catching his breath. "Not that I'm complaining."

Another pass. Another block.

"You fight," she said evenly, testing his left side, "like someone who's had to claw their way out of something."

His stance shifted, not defensively. Just sharper. Focused. "That's an elegant way of saying I look like hell."

"No," she said, driving low. He caught it, barely. "It's an observation. Your footwork's clean, but you overcorrect on your right. Old injury?"

"Battle scar." He shrugged. "Though I prefer to call it character."

She let the next strike skim past him, spun in close, and pulled up short behind his shoulder. The air between them shifted.

"And here I thought you preferred to call everything charm."

Raoul's laugh was short, breath catching slightly as he turned. "Guilty. But I didn't think you were watching me that closely."

"I watch everyone that closely."

He tilted his head. "And here I was hoping I was special."

"You're not."

She pressed forward, not letting the moment settle. Her strikes came faster. He parried. Countered. His speed was good, better than expected. But still not complete. There was some softness there. Not in form. In truth.

"You hide behind that laugh," Kal said as they locked again, her breath close enough to stir the air between them. Her tone was even, but her words struck clean. "The grin, practiced with ease. You wear it like armor."

Raoul didn't flinch. But his eyes sharpened. "And what would you call what *you're* wearing?"

"Precision," she replied.

He slid back half a step, resetting his stance. "Attractive armor, either way."

She parried his next strike with ease, the motion so controlled it might've looked casual to anyone else. "Men who laugh too easily," she said, "are often the ones who've had the least reason to."

That made him pause, something shifting behind his eyes—a flicker, fast and unguarded. The mask slipped, and for a breath, she saw the man behind it.

There it is.

He recovered quickly, rolling his shoulders and adjusting his grip. The smile returned, but it wasn't the same.

"And I don't hide," she said.

Raoul didn't argue. His next strike was sharper, less performative.

"No," he said, voice lower. "You just cut."

She advanced again, blade sweeping high, driving him back a step. "I cut what wastes my time."

He caught her edge and held it, his grip firm, the pause intentional. "Then I should ask what you're still doing here."

Kal tilted her head, the pressure between their blades taut. "I'm still deciding."

They broke apart, moving again. This time Raoul kept his distance, not from fear, but calculation. He was starting to see it. She wasn't just reading his technique. She was reading *him*. And he didn't know what she was finding.

"I've seen knights like you before," she said, circling. "Clean footwork. Controlled stance. Trained to follow. Always loyal to someone. I just haven't worked out who."

Raoul's expression didn't change, but his answer came slower. "I serve the crown."

She didn't stop moving. "Is that all?"

His jaw flexed once. Then, quieter: "What are you looking for?"

Her blade flicked out—quick, elegant, dangerous. He blocked on reflex, and their weapons locked again, close and tight.

"A man who serves nothing but a title," she said, "is just a blade waiting to be bought."

His grip shifted, eyes narrowing. "And what does that make you?"

Kal met his gaze without a flicker. "It makes me the one holding the blade."

Raoul didn't smile.

"Is that how you see everyone?" he asked. "Measured by what they're worth, what they can offer you?"

Kal didn't answer. Not immediately. The question had struck home, though it didn't show on her face. But she felt it, tight and unwelcome. It wasn't the first time someone had asked her that, but it was the first time she'd wanted the answer to be different.

Her sword remained steady. Her eyes didn't move, but her silence did the speaking.

Raoul stepped back, she did the same though neither lowered

their guard.

"Is that all people are to you?" he asked again. "Tools? Threats?"

Kal's voice came cold and even. "Is that what you want me to say?"

He held her gaze. "I want the truth."

"No," she said. "You want the answer that makes you the exception."

That hit deeper than any strike he'd taken that morning. She moved past him, close enough to graze his arm.

"Ask a question like that," she said, her voice low, "you'd better be ready for the answer. Because if it's yes...if I do only see people as tools or weapons, then you have to ask yourself..."

She stopped, turned, and looked at him with calm clarity.

"...what does that make you?"

Before he could respond, she stepped in again. Quick. Clean. She swept his legs out from under him in a single, fluid motion. No flourish. No show. He hit the sand hard, the impact pulling a grunt from his lungs as dust curled around him.

Kal stood over him, blade low, shoulders squared.

"I haven't decided yet," she said.

Raoul lay still for a beat longer than necessary, then pushed himself upright, breath sharp in his chest. He ran a hand across his sleeve, brushing grit from his arm.

"Next time," he said, voice rough, "you might try a little warning."

Kal turned away, steps light. "No," she called back. "That would ruin the lesson."

The corridors were quiet at this hour, but Kal kept to the shadows anyway. She moved fast enough to avoid attention, slow enough not to draw it. Her right arm stayed pressed close to her side. The fabric of her sleeve had already stiffened with dried blood. Every step sent a dull throb up into her shoulder. She reached her door, eased it open without sound, and stepped inside. Liam was already waiting. He stood near the hearth, arms folded, jaw tight. His eyes went first to the way she moved, then to the line of red darkening her tunic.

Kal closed the door behind her, too tired to hide the wince as she locked it.

"You let him cut you," Liam said, voice low but seething.

"I didn't *let* him do anything," Kal muttered.

"It was iron." Liam hissed.

She didn't answer.

Liam pushed away from the hearth, his steps sharp across the stone. "Do you have any idea what he saw?"

"He didn't see anything."

"He saw enough," Liam snapped. "You flinched. He saw you bleed. From a graze of *iron*. That's not a scratch, Kal. That's a signal. *Humans don't bleed from brushing up against iron.*"

She walked past him toward the washbasin, unfastening the first buckle of her harness with her left hand. "I covered it."

"You shouldn't *have* to cover it," he said. "It shouldn't have happened."

"I misjudged his reach, didn't notice what the axe was made of."

"No," Liam said, voice rising. "You misjudged *him*."

Kal paused, hand on the edge of the basin. She didn't look at him.

"You think he's stupid?" Liam pressed. "That he won't remember what it looked like? What it felt like when you jerked away from something that shouldn't have cut you at all?"

She stayed silent.

Liam's hands curled into fists at his sides. "He's getting too close."

Kal turned. "He's useful."

"That's what you say," Liam growled. "Until something useful turns into something dangerous. Until someone starts asking the wrong questions at the wrong time, and you drop your guard like–like–"

He stopped short.

Kal's expression didn't shift, but her silence spoke for her.

"You dropped him at the end," Liam said, staring at her. "In the ring. Why?"

She said nothing.

His jaw locked. "*Kal.*"

She looked away, like she didn't want to name the thing forming behind her composure.

"He said something I didn't like," she muttered.

Liam waited. His silence was colder than shouting.

Kal's fingers flexed once at her side. "He asked if I only see people for what they're worth. What they can give. If I ever see anything else."

Liam's brow furrowed, uncertain now. "And?"

She let out a slow breath and leaned back against the stone wall. "And I hate that it stayed with me."

Liam didn't move.

"I hate," she continued, "that he could ask something like that and have it *matter*. I hate that the whole damned world can look at someone and *see* just them and expect me to do the same, like it's just that simple."

She met Liam's gaze, and this time she didn't flinch.

"But it's not. Not for me."

There was no break in her voice. No plea for understanding. Just raw fact, laid down like a blade.

"I'm not made like them," she said. "I'm scarred, marked. I'm broken in places they've never even learned to guard. And maybe I do look at people and see use first. But that's survival."

Liam looked at her for a long moment. When he finally spoke, his voice was hushed again, but steady.

"I know."

He just stood there, fists slowly unclenching at his sides, the fire behind him flickering shadows across the floor.

"You're not broken," he said finally, voice rough but steady. "You're built to survive what others couldn't even imagine."

"You think that's comforting?" she asked.

"It's true," Liam said, shrugging. "And it's the only thing that ever mattered."

He stepped forward, just enough to cross the space between them, but didn't reach for her. They didn't comfort each other like that. Not in gestures. Just in presence.

"What he said," Liam continued, "he had no right to ask you that. None."

Kal didn't reply.

He shook his head, jaw tight again. "He doesn't know what it costs you just to stand in a room with people like him. To listen to them talk like the world's only ever been kind. Like honesty is safe. Like seeing someone clearly won't get you killed."

Kal drew a slow breath. "You don't have to defend me."

"*Yes,*" he snapped, "*I do.*"

That silenced them both for a moment. When Kal finally spoke, her voice had softened. Not much. Just enough to make the words feel heavier.

"There used to be two people in the world who thought that," she said quietly. "Who believed I wasn't broken." Her gaze stayed fixed on the far wall. "Now there's only one."

Liam's breath caught.

She pushed away from the wall before he could speak, moving back to the basin. She unfastened the last of the leather straps, peeled back her sleeve, and grimaced as dried blood cracked along the burn.

"I'm tired," she said. "I'm going to clean this up and lie down."

Liam watched her for a long moment, saying nothing. He saw the way she avoided meeting his eyes. Saw how carefully she braced her weight with her good arm. He knew every inch of how she held herself when she was hiding pain. And this, this wasn't just the wound. This was something else.

"Kal," he said, his voice lower now, more careful. "You're rattled."

She didn't answer, didn't even look up. That, more than anything, made something inside him snap.

"I'm going to speak with him," Liam said, his voice sharp now, cold with purpose. "Raoul. He wants to get close? Then let him see what it costs."

The palace garden was hushed at this hour, the moon hanging low behind drifting clouds, its light silvering the stone paths and gilding the edges of leaves. The hedgerows had long since stilled, and the lanterns hanging from the twisted posts had burned down to embers. It was the sort of silence that Kal preferred—no ceremony, no eyes, no need to perform.

She moved without hurry, the soft sweep of her dress brushing over gravel and trimmed grass. The gown clung close to her waist and shoulders, fitted but softened at the edges. Cream silk, cut high at the collar and split low at the back, draped down from her hips like water poured over marble. The gauze sleeves billowed faintly as she walked, hiding the pale bandage wrapped beneath.

The burn still throbbed. Not sharply. Just enough to remind her that iron was not so easily endured. The magic in her blood would mend it eventually, but not quickly. Not cleanly.

Kal had come here for silence. Alden had shown her the garden on one of her early days in the palace, an old space, set behind high hedges and purposefully left off most maps. It was meant for solitude, not ceremony.

She rounded a trimmed hedge and stopped.

She wasn't alone.

Prince Jarreth sat at the far edge of the path, half-shadowed beneath the twisted boughs of an ash tree. He hadn't heard her. His posture was relaxed, one arm draped over the bench behind him, the other resting loosely on his leg. His head tilted slightly back, eyes lifted to the stars. There was no trace of court polish in him now. No stiff shoulders or diplomat's smile. Just the man. Young, sharp-featured, handsome in a way that was harder to deny when he wasn't trying so painfully to impress anyone.

For a breath, Kal simply stood there. She hadn't expected this. Not him like this. She cleared her throat once, quiet but deliberate.

Jarreth startled slightly, his body stiffening as he turned. He rose to his feet the moment he saw her, smoothing the front of his tunic.

"My lady," he said. "I—wasn't expecting anyone out here."

Kal stepped forward, slow but guarded, arms loose at her sides.

"Neither was I."

His eyes flicked over her quickly–then paused, not on the dress, but her arm. Just long enough to confirm what he didn't want to ask.

"You look...better," he said cautiously. "Rested."

Kal tilted her head. "You heard."

Jarreth gave a short breath of a laugh, not completely sheepish. "There are few things in this palace that don't reach me within the hour. Raoul saw to it personally. Ordered a page to take both axes to the smithy, told them to polish the edges smooth. He said there must've been a flaw in the metal. A shard. Something."

Kal's expression didn't change. "That's what he's calling it?"

Jarreth hesitated. "That's what he *thinks* it is."

"And you?"

He didn't answer at first. Just glanced away, gaze drifting upward again.

"I think," he said quietly, "that people bleed for different reasons. Some wounds just don't show until something breaks close enough to find them."

Kal's mouth twitched slightly, but it wasn't a smile.

Jarreth looked back at her, his voice gentler this time. "It wasn't a serious injury, then?"

Kal stepped beside the bench but didn't sit. "Not one that will last."

The silence between them stretched. Like both of them were waiting to see if the other would speak again. Kal didn't and Jarreth, to his credit, didn't fill the silence just to hear himself speak. Her gaze met his, and for once, he didn't flinch. There was no stammer, no awkward shift, no reddening at the ears. Whatever nerves he might have felt, they stayed buried beneath something steadier. His concern outweighed his caution.

Jarreth motioned lightly to the bench beside him, the gesture smooth and unforced. "You don't have to stay long," he said. "But if you'd rather sit than stand, you'd be doing me a kindness. I talk less when I'm not craning my neck."

Kal regarded him for a long moment, like someone who had learned not to mistake ease for sincerity. Her eyes narrowed slightly, just enough to suggest she was weighing something behind them.

Jarreth offered a crooked smile, hand resting on the bench rail. "Gods, that look. I can't even manage two full sentences near you most days, let alone con you into a trap. If I were that clever, I'd have far fewer bruises from Raoul's training sessions."

That earned a flicker from her, something close to amusement. A subtle lift at the corner of her mouth. Jarreth's heart kicked hard against his ribs, and to his own private horror, he felt it all the way to his throat.

Kal sat beside him, careful in how she lowered herself, her arm clearly stiff though she gave no sign of pain. They sat in silence for a moment, the sounds of the garden muted beneath the hush of distant wind through the leaves.

Jarreth broke it softly, his tone thoughtful rather than prying. "These gardens were my mother's. Commissioned by my father before I was born. He said she needed a place the court couldn't touch, somewhere to breathe without wearing a face."

Kal didn't respond, but she didn't look away either.

"She hated fronts," he continued. "Didn't care for pageantry. Said it made the truth too expensive. She'd escape here for hours. Sometimes with me. Sometimes not."

His voice dipped, not heavy, just honest. "I used to worry I was too much like her to rule. That I'd never be sharp enough to hold the court's attention or cruel enough to keep it. So I...tried."

That hung there for a beat–long enough that Kal turned, ever so slightly, to look at him again.

"I tried so hard to be the right kind of prince," Jarreth added, quieter now. "Perfect posture. Perfect answers. And I did it for so long, I think I just...got stuck in the shape of it."

His face changed as the words left him. Not from regret, but disbelief. He straightened, blinking once, and then let out a short, almost panicked breath.

"I can't believe I just said that out loud."

Kal did smile then. Not the faint curve from before, nor the planned reaction of someone letting him save face. This one was real. Small, but real. And it was enough to knock the breath from his lungs. He didn't say anything else right away. Couldn't, really. But for the first time in weeks, he didn't feel like he had to.

"You're a bold one tonight," Kal said, voice light as she watched him with a look half-thoughtful, half-amused. "Confessions and childhood wounds, all in the space of a breath. Do you do this with every woman in a moonlit garden, or am I just especially lucky?"

Jarreth laughed once, a low sound, genuine and self-conscious. "I'm honestly not sure what's come over me. Most days I'm lucky to make it through a sentence around you without sounding like a second-rate court bard."

Kal tilted her head, the faintest ghost of that earlier smile still in her eyes. Then, quieter now, "What happened to her? Your mother."

The humor drained gently from Jarreth's face. Not abruptly, not with drama, just like a tide pulling back.

"She died giving birth to my youngest brother," he said. "I was six."

Kal's expression shifted, her voice dropping. "I'm sorry."

He nodded once, eyes cast out over the hedges. There was no answer to a thing like that, not really.

She might have let the silence stretch, let it pass but Jarreth turned toward her again, curiosity edging into his voice. "And your mother? Did you know her?"

Kal didn't answer at first. It was only a heartbeat, but the change in her posture was immediate, her back a little straighter, the curve of her shoulders hardening. Still, she met his gaze, and when she spoke, the words came flat.

"No. She was killed when I was an infant."

Something passed between them the, not sympathy, not apology. Just a quiet shift. Recognition.

Jarreth hesitated only a moment before reaching out. His fingers brushed lightly against the back of her hand, barely a touch.

Kal froze. Her eyes snapped to his, every part of her body coiled tight. But there was no pity in his face. Just sadness. Familiar. Worn at the edges.

Jarreth didn't pull back. He didn't push forward either. His hand remained, grounded and steady.

"My mother died the night the last god fell," he said, voice quieter now. "The moment magic was torn from the world. The healers couldn't stop the bleeding. Couldn't ease the birth. What they would've fixed the day before...killed her."

Kal's breath caught, small, but sharp. She didn't mean to show it, but the ache in his voice came heavy and unrelenting.

"I used to believe in magic," Jarreth went on. "In the stories. In the sacred things. Now I curse what's left of it. Whatever power took her away, that wasn't holy. And whatever's still clinging to the edges of the world? It's not a gift. It's a ruin."

The weight of his grief settled between them like falling ash. And Kal—who had sat with blades in her hands and blood on her skin and not blinked—felt it hit her heart like a hammer. She pulled her hand back. Not harshly or with anger. Just...final. She rose without a word, movements smooth but distant now.

"Goodnight, Prince Jarreth," she said, already turning.

Her tone had changed. Sharp again. Polished at the edges. The woman he'd glimpsed—the one who'd smiled, listened, softened—was gone.

Jarreth stood, half-reaching, unsure what he'd said, what he'd done. But Kal didn't stop. She walked the path out of the garden with long, purposeful strides, never once looking back. And the cold truth settled into her bones like frost. She had let herself open. Just enough to breathe.

And then remembered what she was.

Not a woman made of wonder. Not a forgotten heir to something sacred. She was a thing born of dark magic. And not even the kind Jarreth hated. The worst kind. The kind that was still alive.

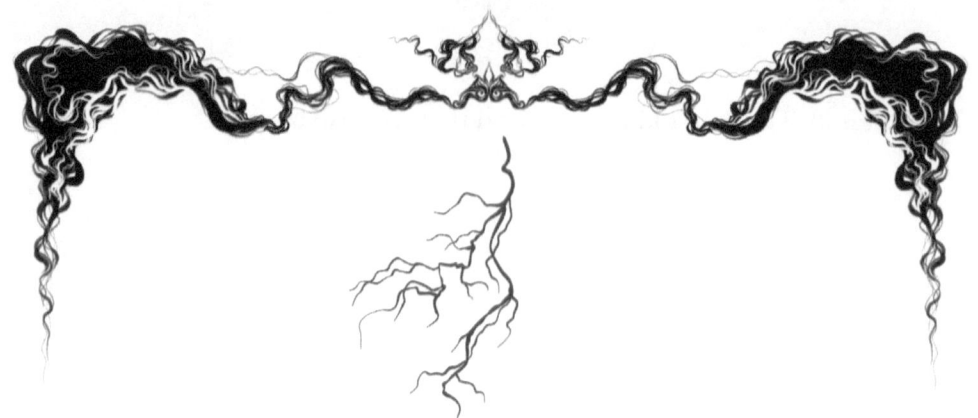

They Will Fill Them with Knives

The next morning came without Kal.

The training yard, usually quiet save for the low thud of boots in sand and the ring of steel, felt strangely hollow. Raoul was there before dawn, as always, blades in hand, but the rhythm didn't settle. He trained hard, harder than usual, driving each strike with sharp accuracy–though anyone watching closely would see it wasn't focus guiding him. It was the absence of it.

By midday, the absence had become a pattern.

She wasn't at court, either.

King Alden said nothing during the session, not when her seat remained empty, not when the nobles whispered questions behind raised hands. When it adjourned, he rose, dismissed the ministers with a short nod, and stepped off the dais with his usual silent command. Raoul and Jarreth found each other outside the council chamber, both lingering longer than necessary.

"She wasn't at the yard this morning," Raoul said, voice low.

Jarreth didn't respond right away. He glanced toward the hall beyond, brows drawn.

"I think I may have...made it worse."

Raoul turned. "You saw her?"

Jarreth nodded. "Yes, last night. In the garden. I touched her hand," he said quietly. "She looked like she might bolt. Not because she was afraid of me, because she didn't know how to read it."

Raoul exhaled through his nose. "And then?"

Jarreth's jaw worked for a moment. "She asked about my mother. I told her. Told her what happened. I didn't mean to–just...said it. And then she was gone. Like I'd knocked the air out of her."

There was a long pause. Neither man looked directly at the other. A sound behind them broke the silence, a sigh, long and heavy. Alden stood a few steps down the corridor, arms folded, his expression lightly pained.

"You two," he said, voice dry, "are as blind as you are well-meaning."

They both straightened immediately, instinctively. Alden didn't raise his voice.

"She's not avoiding you because you upset her. She's avoiding you because she *let* you."

Raoul frowned. "We didn't–"

"You did," Alden cut in. "You got too close. Not in your words. In your *presence*. And that woman is not used to being seen without armor."

Jarreth shifted. "We were just–"

"*You were just boys*," Alden said sharply, "fumbling around the edges of something you don't understand. She's not your mystery to solve. And she's not your redemption story."

That landed hard.

Alden's expression softened, only slightly. Enough to acknowledge that he wasn't angry, just tired.

"She'll come back when she's ready," he said. "Or she won't. But either way...stop chasing ghosts you haven't earned the right to hold."

With that, the king turned and walked down the corridor, his steps slow, the weight of too many truths dragging behind him like a second shadow.

Raoul and Jarreth stood in silence, neither quite sure who the king's words had been meant for. But both knew they weren't wrong.

Kal withdrew.

Just...vanished. The palace moved on around her. Messages went unanswered. Even Liam, relentless and unshakable, gave her space when the first two knocks at her door went ignored. He posted a watch from the shadows and left meals outside without a word.

She trained alone. Not in the sparring ring, but in her room, where no one lingered and the windows stayed shuttered. There were no dummies, no mirrors, no persistent champions shadowing her every step. Only stone, and silence, and the sound of her own footfalls. She ate in her chamber. Bathed, dressed, sharpened her blades, and lay awake in the still hours between midnight and dawn–alone.

Days passed like that. Undefined. Unmeasured. She did not speak, because there was no one she trusted to hear what lived behind her silence.

Her thoughts turned on themselves like iron through flesh.

Do you only ever look at people as tools or threats?

Raoul's voice came unbidden–low, cautious, honest in a way that had no business cutting the way it did. He'd said it without accusation, and that was what made it worse.

What else could they be?

Anything less would get her killed. That was the truth of it. Trust wasn't armor. It was a chink in it. Let someone too close and they'd drive something into that softness and twist until it turned against you. And they–Alden, Jarreth, Raoul–they had to know that too. They had to *think* the same way. They were rulers, heirs, soldiers. They knew the cost of trust, the cost of being real.

So what were they playing at?

Alden, he wanted an alliance. Power tempered by loyalty. A queen of myth returned to the world, tied to his house. A god-king beneath his roof, held in place by the old stories and new laws.

Jarreth, heir to Varis, holding out his hand like she might be something to save or something to save *him*. Marriage, perhaps. Legitimacy. A future secured by magic too dangerous to name.

Raoul, the warrior. The loyal one. The blade in service to a cause he hadn't yet named. What was he chasing? Victory? Glory? Lust? Conquest?

Whatever it was, it wasn't her. It couldn't be.

And still... there was that moment. That stupid, fleeting moment beneath the moonlight where she'd let herself speak honestly. Where she'd let herself feel something as harmless as understanding and in return, been reminded exactly what she was.

Not misunderstood. Not unknown.

Unacceptable.

Kal closed her eyes, jaw clenched as she sat at the edge of her chamber's bed, breath drawn deep and slow. Her shoulder still ached beneath the healed skin. Iron left more than wounds, it lingered in her bones, dulling everything it touched. She rubbed her palm along her arm and told herself it didn't matter. That no one needed to know what it cost her to sit still in this palace full of men who wanted pieces of her they didn't even understand.

But her mind circled back again. *And again.* Not to pain. Not to strategy. But to that brief, humiliating warmth when Jarreth had reached for her hand–not to restrain, or claim, or pry–just to *connect*. And how her first instinct had been to retreat. Not from threat. But from the ache of what it felt like to be seen.

Kal stood and paced the edge of the room like she was trying to wear it down. Her hands balled into fists at her sides.

She was made of ruin. Shaped by it. Wielded like a blade forged in everything the world had failed to kill. There was no softness in her story. No redemption at the end of its thread. And if she forgot that, even for a moment, someone else would remember it *for* her.

She should have known better.

Kal stood at the window, hands braced against the frame, breath fogging against cold glass. The palace gardens stretched below her in neat rows of hedge and stone, perfectly kept. Unchanged. Unlike her.

Stupid.

She should have known better than to let her guard slip, even for a heartbeat. Even for a look. A smile. A hand resting against hers. She should have remembered what she was. Not someone to be comforted. Not someone to be known.

You are not made for kindness. You are not built for peace.

The thought settled in her chest like ash. But it wasn't a thought, not entirely. It had weight. Presence. And it didn't come alone.

The first whisper slid beneath her skin like ice.

They see you now. They know.

Kal flinched, barely, and turned from the window. The room was empty. Of course it was. Silent. Still. But the silence didn't hold. Another whisper, this time closer. Low, oily, like breath against the base of her skull.

Did you think they would love you? Even a little?

Her hands curled into fists. Her mouth opened but there was nothing to say. No argument to give. Because even *she* didn't believe her own lies anymore. She sat hard on the edge of the bed, eyes fixed on the floor.

The voice didn't stop.

If you let them see the cracks, they will fill them with knives.

Her heart pounded louder now, a sick rhythm she couldn't pace. She pressed her fingers to her temples, willing it to stop, to *cease—*

You are not beloved. You are tolerated. Until you're not.

The ache in her shoulder flared again, as if the iron burn remembered too. Her breath came faster, sharper, as her own thoughts started lashing against her ribs like whip strikes.

You let your guard down. For what? A touch? A look? A prince's garden lie?

Her stomach turned. She wanted to stand. To run. But her limbs felt heavy, waterlogged. The air around her thickened.

You are not a woman. You are not a queen. You are a weapon. You are a mistake.

The shadows in the corners of the room began to shift. Not a trick of the eye. Not imagination. They moved. Subtly, slowly—like oil leaking into water. Shapes thickened where they shouldn't be, dark coiling threads that had no source, no anchor. They reached, curled, listened.

Kal stiffened, jaw tight, breath uneven.

"No," she whispered.

But the word fell dead in the air. The shadows pressed in, the whispers crawling up from the walls, from the cracks in the stone, from beneath the floor.

There is no version of you that ends in love. There is no ending where you are more than the ruin they fear. You were born to be alone. That's the only mercy left.

And somewhere in the back of her mind, buried under the weight of pain and fury and shame, she believed it. The shadows answered, kept shifting. Not fast. Not wild. They crept like something patient, conscious, like they had always been there just waiting for the right moment to reach.

Kal sat, unmoving on the edge of the bed, her hands limp in her lap, her gaze fixed on the far wall but seeing nothing at all. The whispers had gone quiet, but the silence left in their wake was worse–thick and unnatural, as though the room itself had been hollowed out. The air had cooled, not with a breeze, but in pressure. In presence. Like the space had bent inward and the weight of her thoughts had become something physical.

Outside her door, across the common space, Liam felt it.

He stood instantly from his place at the desk, his book hitting the floor with a dull thud as he turned sharply toward the door. Something was wrong. He couldn't have said how he knew, only that every inch of his body responded to the shift–the change in the current of the air, the magic in the stone, the sudden tightness in his chest that told him danger had taken a breath. He didn't stop to think, running before the panic could fully take shape, feet slamming into marble as he rounded the corners at full speed, and when he reached her door and found it sealed, the panic became a snarl in his throat.

"*Kal.*" His voice was sharp, steady, but the edge was there. He pounded once, twice, but got no answer.

He didn't knock again. With a single braced step, he drove his foot into the door just above the lock. The wood splintered under the force, the latch cracking free as the panel swung inward with a groan of protest.

What met him inside was worse than anything he'd imagined.

Kal sat on the bed, back straight, hands loose, her face pale and blank. Her eyes–so sharp, so merciless in their clarity–were darkening. The irises had begun to cloud at the edges, ink bleeding into gold, and the shadows in the room–gods, they were *moving.* Crawling toward her from the corners of the ceiling, sliding along the stone like smoke poured in reverse.

Liam didn't hesitate. He crossed the room in three strides, dropped to his knees in front of her, and grabbed her by the shoulders hard enough to shake.

"Kalithea." Her name came out rough, frantic. He shook her once. Then again, harder. Her eyes blinked, barely. Her breathing was shallow, disconnected.

The shadows kept shifting. Reaching.

Liam's grip tightened. And in the next breath, he pulled her to him, arms locking around her as he crushed her against his chest.

"Come back," he muttered, voice raw. "Come back, damn you. You don't get to disappear like this."

She didn't fight him. Her body was cold against his, stiff at first. But as he held her, repeating her name with more urgency, something broke. Kal's breath caught sharply. Her hands clenched in the front of his tunic. Her body spasmed once, and then she inhaled fast and hard, like a gasp from drowning. The shadows receded, shrinking like smoke pulled from a flame. They curled inward and vanished back into the cracks and corners they'd come from, as though snapped back by a force they hadn't expected.

Liam held her a moment longer, his own breath ragged against her temple. Finally, she stirred. Her hands released his shirt. Her head turned, just enough to glance at the doorway, her face still pale but her eyes, her eyes were her own again.

Liam pulled back just enough to see her face. "What the hell was that?" His voice wasn't angry, not yet, but the demand in it was clear.

Kal didn't answer right away. She looked down at her hands like she didn't recognize them. Her fingers were trembling.

"I lost control," she whispered.

Liam frowned. "That wasn't just control, Kal. That was...something else."

She didn't deny it. She just looked away, jaw tight, shame written in the lines of her mouth more clearly than words could express.

Liam ran a hand down his face, then looked at the door, the wood still cracked and hanging crooked on its hinges.

He turned back to her, his voice quieter now. "You're not doing this alone again. Not like this. Not ever."

Kal didn't look up. But she didn't argue either. And for Liam, that was enough to know how far gone she'd been. He didn't move from the floor. He stayed kneeling in front of her, one hand still lightly braced on her arm, his breathing slowly leveling out now that the shadows had gone. Kal hadn't spoken again since admitting her loss of control, but her eyes dulled with exhaustion, the deeper weariness that came from knowing exactly how close you'd come to something irreversible.

He watched her a moment longer, then spoke, voice low but steady. "What caused it?"

Kal didn't answer at first. Her gaze had dropped to the ruined edge of the bedframe where her boot had cracked the wood earlier that morning. She stared at it like it had something important to say.

Liam didn't push yet, but he didn't back off either.

"You were fine days ago," he continued. "Shut down, yes. But controlled. Focused. You don't spiral like that unless something breaks loose."

Kal's jaw tightened. Her arms were folded across her stomach, not in defense but in restraint, as if trying to hold something inside. When she finally spoke, it was faint. Cautious.

"I forgot."

Liam frowned. "Forgot what?"

She looked up at him then. Her voice was flat. Bitter. "That I'm not anything more than what I was made to be."

The words hit like a slap, not because she raised her voice, but because she didn't. They came out calm. Resigned.

"I started to believe it," she went on. "Maybe all these meetings, the sparring, the quiet walks through gardens weren't just tactics or positioning. That they weren't trying to manipulate me or maneuver for power."

Liam didn't speak. He remained expressionless, but his jaw clenched tight.

"I let myself think that maybe they were being honest," Kal continued, her voice steadying now only because she was burying the tremor under it. "That when Jarreth reached for my hand, it wasn't a ploy. That Raoul's questions weren't tests. That I wasn't being handled."

Her breath caught for a moment, but she pushed forward, the words clipped. "And worse than that, Liam—I *wanted* it to be real. I let myself *want* it. Just for a moment."

Her head dropped forward, fingers digging into the edge of her thigh. "It's a weakness. I know it. That flicker of wanting more...it's the kind of soft that gets people killed. I should've carved it out of myself the moment it showed up."

Liam stood with a tension in his frame that made it clear something inside him was grinding hard against the limits of his control. He looked down at her, and when he spoke, his voice was low and steady, but tight with fury.

"No. It's not a weakness. And it's not something you carve out."

Kal didn't respond.

"You think I don't understand that instinct?" he said, softer now. "You think I don't know what it is to want something and immediately hate yourself for it? To feel it twist into something dangerous in your chest, like you've already handed your enemies a blade to use against you?"

He stepped closer, kneeling again—his voice never rising, but the words came sharper now.

"But that doesn't mean it's wrong. It just means we were never taught what safe feels like, dear sister."

Kal didn't look at him, but he saw her hands tighten. Saw her shoulders inch up in defense.

"You are *not* ruined," Liam said, gentle but firm. "You are not just a weapon. You were never given anything real in that place we were raised in—not love, not choice, not peace—and yet you still managed to become something more than what they made."

He leaned in slightly, voice dropping further. "Wanting something better doesn't make you soft. It makes you *alive.*"

She drew a shallow breath, but it shook.

Liam's expression changed again, less fury now, more steel. "But they don't get to be the ones to drag that part of you out before you're ready. They don't get to chip away at your defenses without knowing what they're touching."

He stood again, pacing once before turning back, anger rising now. Anger at the ones who'd triggered all of this.

"Raoul with his half-buried questions. Jarreth with his well-meaning hands and tragic past. They're fumbling at things they don't understand like children playing with blades and they're lucky you didn't cut them for it."

Kal didn't answer, but her body had shifted. She wasn't coiled so tightly anymore. Just still.

"I'll speak with them tomorrow," Liam said, and this time his voice was no longer calm. It was carved from something colder, something sharper. "Both of them. And this ends."

Kal looked up at him, a flicker of warning in her expression.

"You won't stop them," she said.

"No," Liam answered, and now his tone held nothing of patience. "But I'll make sure they understand what they're doing. That pushing at you like this, prodding into things they've got no right to touch, isn't harmless. That it's not just words or games or honest mistakes."

He took a step back, running a hand through his hair, but his posture had stiffened—like a man already choosing which line he would cross.

"They saw you bleed and mistook it for an invitation. They saw you pause and thought it meant you could be opened. But they don't know what they're pulling on. What it costs you every damn day just to stay tethered. And now—after what happened tonight—they don't get to plead ignorance."

His eyes were dark when he looked at her again.

"They brought you to the edge of something you might not have come back from. And for that, Kal, I *will* have words with them. And if words aren't enough–" He stopped, jaw tight. Then, colder: "I nearly lost you tonight. And if they think I'm going to let that happen again while they chase their guilt and longing like blind men–they're about to learn exactly what I'm willing to do."

BRUISED KNUCKLES AND BRUISED PRIDE

L iam didn't sleep.

He stayed in the chair beside Kal's bed as the hours crept past, watching her chest rise and fall in the soft hush of the room. The candlelight burned low, casting long shadows across the wall, but they didn't move. He didn't dare look away long. Not after what he'd seen. Even when she finally drifted into exhausted sleep, her breathing even, her body slack against the sheets, he stayed rooted–shoulders tense, boots planted, one hand resting on the hilt of the blade across his knee. Watching. Waiting. When the darkness didn't stir again, and the sky began to pale with the earliest edges of dawn, Liam stood. He didn't make a sound. Didn't leave a note. Just pulled the door closed behind him and made for the yard.

The morning air bit at his face as he stepped into the open, but he welcomed it. The cold gave his anger something to cling to.

He didn't expect both of them to be there.

But by all the fallen gods, it made things easier.

Raoul was in the ring already, rolling out his shoulders and moving through warm-ups methodically. Jarreth was leaning on the rail, half-distracted. He had the barest hint of a smile curling on his face as he turned toward the sound of approaching steps. The flicker of hope on their faces at the sound of boots on stone said everything. They were expecting someone else. Both of them were.

They were expecting Kal.

Liam didn't slow his stride. Didn't speak.

Raoul straightened, half-grinning. "A bit early for you, isn't it? Or did she send her blade in her place this time?"

The words landed with casualness that might've passed for charm...

on any other day. But Liam didn't hear wit or charm.

He heard *mockery*.

And that was all it took.

He crossed the last few steps fast, too fast for Raoul to adjust. No warning, no explanation. Just a tight fist driven square into the champion's face with the full weight of a brother's fury behind it. The sound cracked through the courtyard, flesh on bone. Raoul staggered back, one hand flying to his face, his feet slipping in the sand as he caught himself.

Jarreth stepped forward with a shout, surprised, but Liam didn't so much as look at him. His gaze was locked on Raoul, eyes flashing furiously, voice dark in the way only real danger ever was.

"You think this is a game?" he said, every word fierce and cold. "You think she's some puzzle to solve? Some woman to chase through corridors and gardens and press until she breaks?"

Raoul was still catching his balance, blinking through the burst of pain that hadn't yet settled. But his smugness was gone. Jarreth stepped forward instinctively, hand outstretched in warning, but Raoul didn't take his eyes off Liam. He held up a hand without looking, halting the prince with a sharp flick of his fingers.

"Don't," Raoul said, wiping the blood from his split lip with the back of his wrist. His grin returned, feral and sharp. "Looks like the little lion's got something to roar about."

Liam didn't flinch. His hands were still clenched, breath even, eyes fixed.

Raoul shook his head once, almost laughing. "About time you bared your teeth instead of just glaring from the shadows. Come on then, if you've got something to say to me, spit it out. *Kal never holds back with me.*"

His tone was laced with familiarity and sarcasm.

Kal.

Liam surged forward without a word, though this time Raoul was ready. They met in the sand fists and forearms locking as muscle slammed against muscle, weight shifting in tight, brutal movements. This wasn't sparring. This was violence.

Liam struck first again, a low hook to the torso that Raoul absorbed with a grunt before catching Liam's collar and dragging him forward into a brutal shoulder. They grappled, stumbled, twisted—their boots grinding deep into the ring's floor as they struggled for leverage. Raoul was strong. Faster than Liam had expected. But Liam fought like a man who had nothing left to lose, like one who had been forced to fight like this his whole existence. There was no finesse, no restraint. Just the raw, unfiltered fury of a brother who had stood watch over the woman they'd almost broken.

Jarreth moved to intervene again, but paused, uncertain now. This fight wasn't chaos. It was *deliberate*. Old rage meets new recklessness, with both of them too far gone to stop.

Liam drove a knee into Raoul's thigh and threw him sideways. Both of them crashed to the ground, sand scattering as they rolled. Raoul twisted mid-fall and landed a solid elbow into Liam's ribs, knocking the wind from his lungs, but Liam didn't let go. He pressed in tighter, teeth bared, striking again with a short, savage blow that split skin clean along Raoul's brow.

Blood smeared across Raoul's cheek as he pushed up on one arm, panting, half-laughing through the sting.

"You hit like you mean it," he spat. "Good."

Liam didn't answer. He just hit him again. Raoul's lip was bleeding again, but his grin didn't falter. He rolled to one knee, catching his breath. He watched Liam with the gleam of a man who knew how to find a weakness and didn't mind taking the hit for it.

"You're not fighting for her," he said, voice rough but clear. "You're fighting because you're *afraid*. Afraid there might be someone else in her life who isn't you."

Liam lunged, but Raoul twisted away and came up fast, just out of reach. His tone turned mocking, cruel in the way only a man bruised and grinning could manage.

"You think she's made of glass and smoke, like if you guard her hard enough, the world won't touch her. But maybe what she needs isn't a shadow with a sword. Maybe she needs something *real*."

Liam's snarl cracked loose from his throat, raw and brutal, and he charged again. This time Raoul caught him halfway, forearms slamming together as they grappled, boots digging in deep.

"She must be feeling *something*," Raoul grunted, his breath close to Liam's ear as they shoved and turned. "Otherwise you wouldn't be here, would you? You wouldn't be this...angry. This *scared*. You think she doesn't feel it too?"

Liam struck again, a vicious hook to the side that sent Raoul stumbling into the railing. He caught it with one hand, spit blood into the dirt, and kept going.

"Let her live, Liam! Let her feel something other than pain!"

"Stop it!" Jarreth shouted from the edge of the ring, his voice ringing across the stone. "Enough!"

Neither of them looked at him.

"Stay out of this, Prince," Raoul snapped, wiping his mouth with the back of his hand. "This isn't your fight."

"Oh, it will be," Liam growled, storming forward again, rage burning white-hot. "Don't think you're innocent. You'll get yours too."

Raoul braced as Liam stepped forward to bore down on him, and for the briefest moment, the ring fell into silence–thick with heat and the sound of hearts pounding like drums of war. Liam's fist dropped slightly, not from weariness, but from control that barely held on. His chest rose and fell in sharp, shallow bursts, his eyes locked on Raoul like he was measuring the exact depth of damage his next blow might cause.

"You don't know what you're talking about," Liam spat, voice low, ragged with fury. "And every damned word out of your mouth right now proves it."

Raoul opened his mouth, but Liam didn't give him the chance.

"You push at her edges like she's a puzzle you're owed the right to solve. You ask her about tools and threats like the world's a clean slate you get to look down on. You don't know what she's lived through." His voice broke for half a breath, but he forced it steady again. "When every day of your life is just a different kind of pain. When every outstretched hand you've ever known held a knife behind it. When the only way you survive is by measuring people–*exactly*–for what they can hurt or what they'll try to steal...then yeah. You learn to see the world as weapons and threats. *Because that's what it is.*"

Raoul didn't answer. The heat had gone from his posture, replaced with something heavier. A muscle ticked in his jaw, but his eyes had dropped for just a breath.

Liam stepped back. Blood smeared across his knuckles, sweat clinging to the edge of his brow. His voice dropped again, thick and guttural.

"She fought like hell to become something more than what the world tried to make of her. And instead of letting her *be* that, you keep poking at her like you're trying to reshape her into something easier for *you* to understand."

Raoul's expression shifted, tension pulling across his brow, his shoulders slackening just enough to show that the words had hit somewhere real. Somewhere unguarded.

"Idiots," Liam muttered, shaking his head. "Both of you."

He turned then and rounded on Jarreth. The prince didn't flinch, though the edge of caution sparked in his eyes. Liam wiped blood from his cheek with the heel of his hand, leaving a smear across his skin. His voice, when it came, was colder than before–quieter, but no less sharp.

"The only reason you didn't get your turn in the dirt today is out of courtesy to your father." His eyes narrowed. "But keep pushing her. Keep showing up with that bright-eyed need for honesty she never asked you for. Keep pretending this is some courtship dance instead of a battlefield she's still bleeding on."

He stepped closer, enough that even Jarreth's spine stiffened.

"And I promise you, no courtesy in the world will save you."

Then he turned and walked away, not looking back once. His footsteps trailing through the sand like a line drawn sharp between mercy and war.

Raoul spat a line of blood into the sand and straightened with a wince. His ribs ached and his lip was split, but it wasn't the pain that held him still, it was the weight of Liam's words, ringing in his ears like an echo he couldn't shut out.

Jarreth leaned against the post near the edge of the ring, arms crossed tight across his chest, his mouth set in a hard line. He'd stayed silent through the fight, but now that Liam was gone, the silence hung heavier than before.

"Well," Raoul muttered, wiping his mouth with the back of his hand, "that went well."

Jarreth didn't smile. His gaze stayed fixed on the ground for a moment longer before he looked up. "Do you think he's right?"

Raoul tilted his head, thoughtful. "I think he believes he is. And that's enough to put a man's fist through your face."

"But do you think we're hurting her?" Jarreth asked, quieter now, as if saying the words too loud might make them true.

Raoul exhaled through his nose and rolled his shoulder. "No. I think we're *getting through to her*. That's the problem, isn't it? Liam's used to being the only one who gets past her walls. Someone else shows up at the gate and he starts sharpening blades."

Jarreth gave a hum of agreement, though his jaw was still tight. "I don't think Kal wants to be alone, not really. I just don't think she believes there's another option."

"She's used to shadows," Raoul said. "And Liam wants to keep her wrapped in them, like it's safer that way."

"He thinks we're pushing her," Jarreth said.

Raoul snorted. "Maybe we are. But not to break her."

"No," Jarreth agreed, finally meeting his gaze. "To show her she's not invisible."

They stood in silence again, the tension between them not combative, but taut with something unspoken, something sharpened now by Liam's fury. Jarreth glanced toward the walkway Liam had stormed down.

"He sees a ledge. I see someone standing at the edge who hasn't decided if she wants to step forward or step back."

"And we're not the ones trying to push her either way," Raoul added. "We're just trying to stand there beside her. Let her know she's not alone on that cliff."

Jarreth gave a faint, tired smile. "You make it sound noble."

"I'm not noble," Raoul replied. "I'm just not done yet. Not when she's finally starting to see us. Really *see* us."

Jarreth pushed away from the post, his shoulders loosening slightly. "Then we don't back down."

Raoul nodded, slow and firm. "No. Not now."

They both turned to face the empty sparring ring once more. The sun had fully crested the horizon, spilling gold across the sand. They'd been warned. Threatened. And all that did was confirm what they already knew.

She was worth the fight.

Liam pushed through the door of their shared quarters, not bothering to close it gently. He was breathing hard, more from fury than exertion, and blood still marked the corner of his lip. His knuckles were raw.

Kal stood near the washbasin, dressed down in simple black, her hair unbound. She turned at the sound, her eyes locking onto him.

"What did you do?" Her voice was low, clipped.

Liam didn't answer immediately. He was halfway to collapsing into a chair when she crossed the room in three hard steps.

"You fought them," she said flatly.

He gave a short shrug and muttered, "Only one had the mouth to deserve it."

Kal stared at him, eyes darkening. "You arrogant, short-sighted fool."

"You think I'm reckless?" he snapped, straightening. "After what I walked into last night—"

"I think," she cut in, "you've just risked everything we've built by throwing fists like some alley brute. And for what? To prove you're louder? Stronger? Because you couldn't stand the fact that someone might—"

Her voice caught, only slightly. She didn't finish the thought.

Liam looked away.

Kal exhaled hard and turned back to the washbasin, grabbing a cloth. "Sit," she ordered.

"I'm fine."

"You look like you've been tossed down the citadel steps," she said, already pouring water into a bowl. "Sit down and shut up."

He obeyed, because there were few commands she gave like that, and fewer still he dared ignore. She cleaned the cut on his lip with firm, efficient pressure. Not gently, her movements saying everything her voice didn't: *this is my mess to clean now, too.*

"They'll forgive it," Liam muttered eventually. "Or they won't."

Kal didn't look at him. "You think alliances hold when built on bruised pride and bruised ribs?"

"I don't care," Liam said. "They don't matter. Not compared to you."

He looked up at her, something hard and fierce burning behind his eyes. "Let the world burn. Let Elandra rot in rubble if it comes to it. *You are my sister, Kal.* If you fall apart–if you lose yourself like that again–it won't just be Elandra that suffers. It'll be *everything.*"

Her jaw tightened. She dipped the cloth again and resumed cleaning his split knuckles, slower this time.

"You don't get to fall," Liam said, voice lower now. "Not because they couldn't help themselves. Not because they think you're some puzzle to solve. You're not a broken thing."

Kal didn't answer. The silence stretched between them, heavy but not hostile. She bound his knuckles in clean linen, securing them tightly. Liam watched her the whole time. When she finally stepped back, he spoke again–softer now, but no less certain.

"I don't care what you are, what the rest of the world thinks. You're my sister. That's the only thing that matters to me. And I will do *whatever* it takes to keep you here."

Kal stood still for a moment longer, then turned away without a word.

But her hands, when they rested on the edge of the basin again, were shaking.

The corridor was dim and near empty, only the flickering torches along the stone walls offering any hint of movement. Jarreth kept his head down, hoping the shadows might do them both a kindness and let them slip past unnoticed. Beside him, Raoul's gait was slightly off-kilter, blood dried at the corner of his mouth, one cheek already swelling beneath the bruise that had begun to bloom there.

They were three steps from safety when a voice cut through the stillness like a blade.

"Turn. Around."

Both men stopped.

Alden stepped out from a side alcove, arms crossed, gaze cutting. He was dressed down from court, but there was nothing casual in his stance. His eyes passed over Raoul's bloodied face, then flicked to Jarreth's uncharacteristically quiet posture.

"I'd ask which of you started it," the king said, his tone arid, "but frankly, I'm not sure I want to hear the answer yet."

Raoul exhaled through his nose. "It's not as bad as it looks."

Alden's brow rose with slow incredulity. "So your face routinely looks like it collided with a wall?"

Jarreth tried to speak. "There was a...misunderstanding."

"Did this misunderstanding involve fists?" Alden asked.

"Yes."

"Did this misunderstanding involve Liam?"

Raoul nodded once.

Alden shut his eyes, muttering something beneath his breath that sounded very much like a prayer for patience. When he opened them again, the fire had returned.

"You assaulted a visiting royal. One who is here under *my* protection. One who, might I remind you, belongs to a court we are hoping to align with—should the world spiral as far south as I expect it to."

"It wasn't about politics," Raoul said quietly.

Alden turned on him. "Of course it wasn't. Because you weren't thinking like a soldier or a champion or anything remotely resembling a man with sense. You were thinking with your fists and your pride."

Raoul didn't flinch. "He came at me."

"And what *exactly* prompted that?" Alden asked.

Raoul hesitated.

Alden's gaze sharpened. "I'm giving you one chance to explain. Use it."

"It was Kal," Jarreth said, surprising them both. His voice was soft but steady. "He's angry that we've been...pursuing her."

"Pursuing?" Alden repeated. "As in courtship?"

"I wouldn't call it that," Raoul muttered.

Alden barked a bitter laugh. "Then what *would* you call it, exactly? Sparring sessions that turn into intimate interrogations? Stolen glances over supper? Angry brothers breaking noses in the yard?"

Raoul lifted his chin, but when he spoke, his voice was low. "She's not like anyone else."

"No," Alden agreed coldly. "She's not. And if you had a shred of sense between you, that fact alone would have given you pause. So enlighten me, Raoul. What makes her so different you'd risk turning a valuable alliance into a diplomatic disaster?"

Raoul hesitated for the first time since entering the hall. "Because she doesn't flinch," he said finally. "Not from pain. Not from the truth. She doesn't pretend to be less than she is—and gods, she could. She *should*, by all logic. But she doesn't."

"She doesn't wear her wounds like shame," Jarreth added softly.

"She wears them like armor. I don't know how to explain it. It's just... she's real."

Alden studied them both in silence. It stretched, then settled. At last, he shook his head.

"Real," he repeated, almost to himself. "And yet both of you are chasing her like a pair of hounds after something fragile, not even pausing to wonder why she runs."

Neither answered.

Alden took a step forward. "Let me be clear. This isn't some court dalliance. She is not a prize. She's a storm barely held in check. And I don't care how noble your intentions feel. You're playing with something that could destroy you—and worse, could destroy *her*."

Jarreth's throat worked, but he didn't speak.

Raoul looked down, jaw set. "I'm not backing off."

"Of course you're not," Alden said, tired now. "And that's what worries me."

Alden's gaze lingered on them for a long moment, as though weighing the value of silence against the need to intervene. Then, with a muttered curse under his breath, he shifted his stance and leveled them both with a hard look.

"Come to my study tonight. Just after the second bell."

Raoul's brows furrowed. "Why?"

Alden didn't answer right away. He paced once, jaw tight, then stopped just short of them and spoke low and sharp.

"Because against my better judgement, I'm going to show you something. Something you have *no* right to see. Something that, if either of you had been thinking with anything besides your damned hearts, I wouldn't need to show at all."

His voice turned colder. "But apparently two grown men need reminding that a woman with that many scars doesn't need your curiosity. She needs peace. And if you can't give her that, you'll leave her the hell alone."

Jarreth stiffened. "You think we're just fumbling around in the dark—"

"No," Alden interrupted flatly. "I think you're fumbling around in *her* dark. And you don't even realize the danger in that. You want to prove yourselves, you want to understand her? Fine. But you'll do it with your eyes open from this point on."

Raoul straightened slightly, but the defiance in his posture had dimmed. He exchanged a glance with Jarreth, tense and uncertain. Neither of them spoke.

He exhaled hard and turned away. "Go get yourselves cleaned up before you bleed all over my damned floors. Gods help me, if I have to explain to the court why two of my best looked like they wrestled a pack of wolves, I'll have you both mucking stables for a month."

Raoul and Jarreth moved in silence, the weight of Alden's words settling across their backs like ash.

The heavy door to Raoul's chambers swung open with a soft groan, and the two men slipped inside without speaking, the sounds of the palace muffled by thick stone walls. Raoul tossed the bloodied cloth onto a side table and winced as he peeled off his tunic, the fabric sticking where blood had dried into torn skin. Jarreth grabbed a basin and a clean cloth without needing to be asked, already moving to the washstand.

The room was simple compared to other royal quarters, more functional than luxurious. Weapons lined the far wall in careful rows; a battered leather chair sagged near the hearth; and a half-drunk bottle of something strong waited, abandoned, on a corner table.

Jarreth soaked the cloth and wrung it out roughly. He crossed back over and threw it at Raoul's chest.

Raoul caught it one-handed, smirking faintly. "Gentle touch, Your Highness."

"You're lucky you can still catch anything," Jarreth muttered.

Raoul hissed softly as he wiped the cloth across his face, cleaning away the worst of the blood.

Jarreth sighed. "You goaded Liam like a lunatic."

"He needed it."

"*You* needed to be knocked flat, more like."

Raoul gave a crooked grin, dabbing carefully at his brow. "Maybe. Still wouldn't trade it. The man needed to bare his teeth. Been too long since anyone made him feel like he could."

Jarreth shook his head, but there wasn't much heat behind it. He poured a measure of brandy from the bottle on the table, setting it beside Raoul with a thud.

"For the bruises you'll feel tomorrow," he said dryly. "And for the fool's honor you're clinging to tonight."

Raoul lifted the glass in mock salute before downing half of it in one go.

EYES OPEN, OR NOT AT ALL

The bell tolled once, then again. As the echo faded through the stone halls, Jarreth and Raoul stood outside Alden's private study, neither speaking. When the heavy oak door opened, Alden stood framed in the doorway, his expression drawn taut.

"You're on time," he said shortly. "Good. Come in."

They stepped inside without a word. The room was warm despite the hour, a low fire crackling in the hearth behind Alden's desk.

Alden motioned to two chairs opposite his desk. "Sit."

They obeyed. Jarreth folded his hands in his lap; Raoul slouched with affected nonchalance that fooled no one, a faint stiffness still lingering in his jaw where Liam's fist had landed.

Alden didn't sit immediately. He moved to the shelves at the back wall and pulled free a long wooden case, resting it atop the desk before unlatching it. From within, he drew out a single folded letter–creased, worn, edges softened by time and touch.

"This," Alden said, tone clipped, "is something I never intended to share."

He looked down at the letter, then back at them, his face grim.

"I am not pleased that I've been driven to this. But it seems the pair of you have developed such a profound fixation that neither common sense nor caution will deter you. So if I can't stop you, then I will educate you."

Jarreth's eyes dropped to the letter, his brow tightening. "What is it?"

"A letter," Alden said, lowering himself into the chair behind his desk. "From Kalithea's mentor. A Fae man named Arjun."

Raoul tilted his head, brows knitting. "Her mentor? Where is he–?"

"Sacrificed himself," Alden cut in, "so Kalithea and Liam could escape Elandra alive."

Raoul blinked. "Escape?"

Alden's stare was flat. "Please tell me you aren't so dense as to think she left her homeland by choice."

Raoul winced and lifted a hand in surrender. "Fair. I'll shut up."

"I wish you would've done so earlier," Alden muttered. He tapped the letter once, then rested his hand atop it. "He sent this to me long before their arrival. Asked that I offer them sanctuary. That I protect them. That I keep their truth...quiet."

The pause that followed stretched long. Neither man moved. The weight of Alden's words settled heavily in the room, stripping away any pretense of this being some idle tale of court politics.

Alden exhaled through his nose, the lines at his mouth deepening.

"I've read it a hundred times over," he said. "It wasn't meant for your eyes. But it's clear I've misjudged your restraint."

His hand finally lifted.

"Read it."

He passed the folded page across the desk.

The fire crackled once behind him. Neither man reached for the letter immediately. They were no longer dealing with the woman they thought they knew. They were about to meet the truth of her, in someone else's words

To His Majesty King Alden of Varis,

If this letter reaches your hands, it will mean I have made the necessary preparations to send them–Kalithea and Liam–beyond the reach of the man who calls himself King of Elandra. I write to ask what no man should have to ask of another: sanctuary, freely given, for the rightful Queen of Elandra and her brother the Prince.

You will have heard rumors. Ignore them. Truth is rarely carried on the backs of whispers. Kalithea is half-fae–though she bears little of the softness mortals imagine with that word. She was not raised in the light of either world. Rhaen, the usurper who holds Elandra's throne, saw to that before she could walk.

She was chained before she could speak. Caged like an animal. Conditioned. Her first blade was given to her at the age of five, her first kill not long after. There was no childhood, only obedience carved into the shape of a girl. The walls of her cell were iron; the walls of her mind, forged from agony. He beat her until her skin split and burned. Starved her to the edge of madness. Broke her fingers when she reached for warmth. Drowned her in silence when she cried for help.

He beat her until her bones cracked and reset at wrong angles. He branded her with sigils meant to break her will. Her mouth was once sewn shut for speaking out of turn. She spent a full winter barefoot in the dungeons, forbidden to speak or sleep

lying down. When she collapsed, they tied her upright. When she disobeyed, they locked her in an iron box and left her in the sun until her skin blistered and split. When she screamed, they made her kneel on broken glass and smile.

And when pain failed to shape her into the weapon he wanted, he used cruelty. They made her watch as others suffered in her place—prisoners, slaves, servants, her brother—until mercy became a wound she could no longer bear. The light inside her was not extinguished, but fractured. He turned her into a blade and taught her to believe that was all she would ever be.

I know this because I was there as a shadow within his walls, hiding in plain sight. I am fae, and he would have purged us all, had he the means. So I played the ghost. I taught her in secret. I offered her quiet, ever brief as it was. She learned from stolen hours. She grew with nothing but the weight of her own silence. And somehow—by some will I do not understand—she survived.

Make no mistake, Your Majesty. She is not a girl in need of saving. She is a queen in need of time. Time to see herself as something more than a blade. Time to remember what it means to draw breath without suspicion. She will not ask for your help. She may never speak of what has been done to her. But if I succeed in sending her to you, I ask that you look after her.

You will find no more loyal ally than Kalithea. No greater weapon, if war should be called. But I hope, for all our sakes, that you offer her something rarer than both: peace.

May your wisdom guide you where mine may fall short.

—Arjun Valemir Last of the High Fae of Myrrenreach Vale

The room had grown still.

Jarreth's eyes lingered on the letter long after the last word had been read, as though he hadn't quite believed what he'd seen. His knuckles were white where they gripped the edge of the desk. Raoul said nothing, his jaw tight, the fading swell of his bruised cheek a pale echo of what was twisting behind his eyes.

No one spoke for several breaths.

Alden leaned back in his chair and studied the two men before him. Then, at length, he said, "Now that you've glimpsed the kind of hell she came from, perhaps you understand why your fumbling affections are not the gift you think them to be."

Jarreth shifted first, his voice low and uncertain. "That's why she hesitates, why she looks at us like we might turn on her."

"She doesn't hesitate," Alden said sharply. "She calculates. Every moment. Every breath. You're not breaking through anything. You're pressing against walls built to keep her alive."

Raoul's mouth opened, then closed again. He set the letter down carefully, his fingers still resting on its frayed edge. "And what are we supposed to do, Your Majesty? Pretend we don't care? Walk away while she stays locked behind them?"

Alden gave him a long, exasperated look. "I'm asking you to put her peace before your pride."

"She deserves more than peace," Jarreth said, soft but firm. "She deserves to know there's more in the world than pain."

Raoul nodded slowly. "You don't cage something like her and expect it to stay small. She's already survived him. She's still standing."

Alden rubbed a hand over his face and exhaled heavily. "Gods help me, you're both idiots," he muttered. "Well-meaning, reckless idiots."

They didn't argue the point.

Alden shook his head, more tired than angry now. "Then you'd better be certain you understand the weight of what you're inviting. Because if you break her–truly break her–it won't just be your hearts that pay the price. It'll be kingdoms."

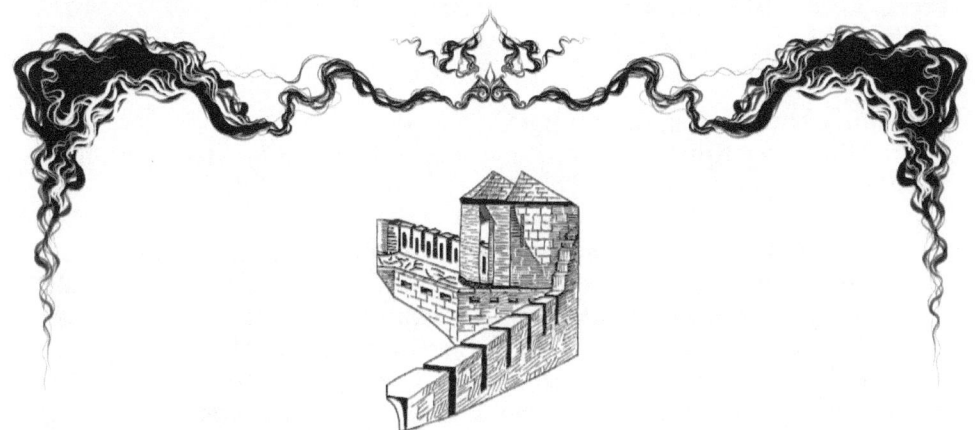

ON THE EDGE OF THE RAMPART

It had been days since anyone had seen Kalithea.

No presence in court, no glint of steel in the training yard. Jarreth and Raoul had grown terse, their patience frayed by worry they refused to voice. But Alden noticed the effect her absence had, as he always did.

That morning, the search ended with a flash of white on the ramparts. She stood motionless against the sea wind, a lone figure framed by endless blue. By the time he crossed the courtyard, she hadn't moved. He climbed the narrow stair, the wind tugging at his cloak as he reached the top. She didn't turn at the sound of his approach. Her hands rested on the low wall, the bandaged arm hidden beneath long cream sleeves, her gaze fixed on the line where water met sky. Alden joined her without a word, standing just beside her, leaving space between them.

After a while, she spoke–softly, without looking at him.

"I owe you an apology."

Alden arched his brow, but said nothing.

She drew a slow breath, eyes still on the sea. "For the...misstep. Between my brother and your son. And your Champion." Her voice was guarded, but low. "Wherever I go, trouble follows. Even when I don't invite it. If you would prefer we leave your court, I would understand."

Alden turned to look at her fully, then let out a slow, incredulous laugh. "Kalithea," he said, his voice warm with disbelief, "you cannot possibly believe I'd hold you accountable for the bruised egos of grown men."

She didn't answer.

He went on, his tone dry. "If I exiled every guest who inspired poor behavior in infatuated men, Varis would be very empty indeed."

That earned the faintest pull of a smile at her lips, though she didn't turn her head. The wind pulled at a strand of her dark hair, and she didn't bother to smooth it back.

"I'm sorry they've made things uncomfortable," Alden said more gently, the humor fading. "They're...clumsy. Both of them. Especially when it comes to things that matter."

Kal's gaze dropped slightly. Her hands tensed on the stone.

"It's strange," Alden continued, "to see them like this. Especially Jarreth. I've watched that boy chase skirts through court with all the subtlety of a drunken stag. But this..." He shook his head. "This is different."

Kal said nothing. Not right away. Then, after a pause, "They've made me think about things I haven't allowed myself to consider."

Alden didn't move. Just listened.

She exhaled, slow and tired. "About what I am. About what I want. I can't afford to ask those questions. I never could."

The words hung there, stripped of ornament, of defense. And Alden, to his credit, did not rush to fill the silence. He simply waited beside her, watching the sea churn gently below, his gaze settling on the horizon as if it might answer something for him.

Then, in that thoughtful, careful tone that always sounded more like truth than advice, he finally said, "Ruling is only part of your inheritance, Kalithea. Arjun didn't just fight for your crown—he fought for your *life.* And if you don't learn to live it...then all he gave, all he lost, will have been for nothing."

Beside him, Kal went utterly still. At the mention of Arjun's name, something in her posture shifted—barely perceptible, but unmistakable to a man who had lived as long as Alden. Her hands had tensed against the stone wall, and though she said nothing at first, the silence was heavy enough to carry the weight of confession.

When she did speak, her voice was barely above the wind.

"He haunts my dreams. Some nights I see him falling. Others...I see him broken. Chained. Screaming. I've watched him be beaten, torn apart, starved. I've woken with his blood on my hands and a scream in my throat so real I've checked for the wound."

Her voice caught—just for a moment—and she pressed her lips together before continuing, forcing the words past the tightness in her chest.

"Every night, it's different. But it never ends."

She stared down at her hands, now clenched white-knuckled atop the rampart, and then gave a low, mirthless laugh. "And I don't know why I'm telling *you* this. I haven't even told Liam. He'd...he'd shatter if he knew."

Kal looked over at him at last, a hint of wryness curling her lips. "You must have some kind of magic. To pull things from me that I didn't mean to say."

Then, with a flicker of bitterness, almost too faint to name, she added, "Perhaps that magic's hidden with your son's hatred of it."

Alden's brows lifted slightly at that, but he didn't rise to meet the sting in her voice. He simply breathed in the salt-laced air, watching her, as though seeing not just the woman before him–but the storm beneath. They walked the stone wall to the gardens in silence, the early light of morning slanting through the trees, catching on dew that clung to the hedgerows. The palace gardens were quiet at this hour, the court still at rest, and Kal found the stillness easier to endure than the noise that would come later. Beside her, Alden moved at a steady pace, hands clasped loosely behind his back, eyes not on her but on the gravel ahead.

"There was a note in your voice just now," he said. "When you spoke of Jarreth and magic. As if you recognized something in him."

Kal didn't look at him. "Perhaps."

"I know what he carries," Alden went on, gaze turned outward. "His mother died bringing his youngest brother into the world. The boy lived, but the cost was high. Jarreth was old enough to remember. Old enough to blame himself for not understanding any of it."

Kal's jaw shifted, but she said nothing.

He nodded to himself. "Jarreth's lived with that weight since he was a child. In the old days, a healer might've stood a chance, but the magic was already thinning by then. Too many of the Gods dying. Too many spells fading out of the world. He grew up hearing that some other power might have saved her, if only it had still been within reach."

She said nothing, but her steps slowed.

"I know how that grief changes a man," Alden continued. "But Jarreth didn't turn it into bitterness. Not toward magic. He only mourns what it took from him."

Alden's gaze swept the horizon before he spoke again, his voice was lower this time. "He came to me after your conversation in the garden, you know."

Kal didn't move, but the air around her seemed to still.

"He was unsettled," Alden continued. "Said the two of you had been speaking–nothing formal, just talking. He thought something was shifting between you, softening. And then, without warning, you left."

Kal said nothing.

"He spent the better part of the evening retracing every word he'd said, convinced he'd offended you somehow. Couldn't put his finger on it, only that something had changed and he'd been left standing in the wake of it."

She let out a faint breath, "He didn't say anything wrong."

Alden looked over at her. "No, I imagine not. But I think I understand now, at least in part. It wasn't an offense, was it? You weren't angry."

She shook her head once, slowly.

"You were afraid. Afraid of his doubt," Alden said simply. "Of what he might do with it if he knew what you carried. If he sensed it fully."

Kal's silence answered more clearly than words might have.

"I've known Jarreth his whole life, obviously," Alden said. "He has a soldier's caution, especially where magic is concerned. He's seen too many things twisted by it to trust easily. It's not hatred, but it's close enough to make someone like you wary."

There was a beat before Kal spoke. "I've lived most of my life around men who turn caution into cruelty the moment they can't explain something."

"And he's not one of them," Alden said. "But I understand why you couldn't be sure."

She gave a small nod, her posture still composed, still guarded.

Alden waited a beat longer before adding, "Still, I'd guess there's more to your silence than empathy. Arjun told me a little about what you are. And your tone just now...well. I'd wager you have a touch of Fae magic in you."

Kal didn't look at him, but her voice was clear. "I can access the ley lines. Arjun taught me."

Alden's brow rose faintly, but he said nothing for a moment.

"Ley line attunement is a rare thing," he said at last. "Even before the purges, it wasn't common. After what Rhaen did to the fae, I wasn't sure any mystics still walked freely."

"They don't," she said. "Most are dead. The rest learned to pass as something else."

He studied her a moment longer, then turned his gaze back to the path. "Then Jarreth was right to feel something shift. He just didn't understand what it was."

Alden turned to her, the wind catching the edge of his coat as he leaned an elbow casually against the stone. "Of course, it hasn't escaped my notice that you've been suffering the attentions of Jarreth and Raoul more than usual." His tone lightened, just enough to mark the shift. "Or at least, you were the last time you showed your face outside that wing of yours."

Kal shot him a sidelong glance, wary.

"I even heard," he added, brows lifting, "a most scandalous rumor that you almost smiled in their company."

She gave him a long, flat look. "Don't encourage them."

Alden's grin tugged wider. "But it seems to be working."

She exhaled, fatigued. "Between those two and Liam, I have no peace as it is."

"I can imagine." He folded his arms, clearly not sorry. "Speaking of no peace, I'd like you to join me for the harvest festivities."

Kal blinked. "You want me in a crowd?"

"You can stay unannounced," he offered quickly. "No formal introduction. No titles, if that helps. But I'd like you to come." His tone was still light, but his meaning wasn't lost. "You deserve a moment to live. Even a brief one."

She didn't answer right away. Her gaze drifted back to the sea, guarded.

"And," he added, "it's good for a ruler to see how joy is carried, not just burdened. If the promise of a little peace isn't enough to tempt you, perhaps that bit of strategy will."

She frowned. "I don't think strategy is the problem."

"Then it's the dancing."

"I'm not dancing."

Alden laughed, the sound quiet but genuine. "Challenge accepted."

Kal gave him a look that might have been warning if it hadn't been so tired.

He pushed away from the wall, already turning back toward the stairs. "It's an all-day affair, you know," he called over his shoulder. "The annual harvest walk in the morning, then the feast, and the ball in the evening. Best be prepared."

"Alden—"

But he was already gone, his footsteps fading into the corridor beyond. She stood alone on the rampart, wind curling around her cloak, the sea rolling endlessly below. It took her a moment to realize she'd just agreed. And for once, there was no scheme buried beneath the request. No maneuver. Just a man asking her to live a short time in the light.

BLADES AND GHOSTS

Kal dressed before the sun rose, her motions smooth and efficient. The air in the chambers was cold at that hour, the fire long since burned low, but she paid it no mind.

Her clothes were laid out from the night before: tight black leathers that hugged her frame without restricting movement, boots laced to the knee with soft soles for balance and speed. She pulled on a loose black tunic, the neckline dipping and laced at the throat, its sleeves gathered just below the elbow where they disappeared into her bracers. Over it she cinched her underbust corset, the worn leather pulling snug across her waist. She left her hair unbraided, tugged the front strands back and tied them away from her face, the rest falling in loose curls over her shoulders. Blades came last—daggers on each thigh, sword on her hip. The weight settled into place like a second skin.

When she stepped into the hallway, Liam was already standing in his doorway. He didn't speak at first. Just watched her with that look—arms crossed, mouth set in a line, the kind of quiet that meant he'd been waiting.

"I heard you moving," he said finally. "Let me guess. You're heading to the training yard."

Kal didn't slow. "I am."

He fell into step beside her. "Then I know who you'll run into."

She kept walking.

"He's always down there before dawn," Liam pressed. "And if he sees you, he'll want to train."

Kal didn't answer.

"You really think that's a good idea?" he asked, sharper now. "After the last time?"

Her steps faltered, just slightly. "It was a conversation, Liam."

"It was a provocation." His voice stayed low, but there was steel in it. "You walked away from him shaking. He didn't mean to cut you. He didn't mean to strike you. But he pushed you. And you almost broke."

She stopped, turning toward him. "I didn't break."

"No," he said. "But you were close. And he knew what he was doing."

Kal held his gaze. "I'm not hiding from him. *Or from anyone.*"

Liam shook his head. "You're not hearing me."

"No," she said. "You're not hearing *me*. I'm done pretending this limbo is a strategy. I *am* Queen of Elandra. And you *are* its Prince. I'm not going to stay tucked away in this wing like some kept secret, waiting for Rhaen to choke on his own excesses."

His jaw flexed, but she pressed on before he could argue. "I'm not going to live like I've already lost."

Liam's voice dropped to a growl. "If he pushes you again–"

"You'll kill him," Kal cut in, lifting a hand. "Yes, I know. You've made that very clear."

He scowled. "You say that like it's a bad thing."

She started walking again. "I say that like I've heard it before."

"Unappreciated," he muttered under his breath and turned back toward his door.

Kal didn't slow. "Dramatic."

The yard was quiet when Kal stepped through the lower gate, the sky above still tinged with the cool gray of early morning. The ground was swept but not pristine–soft dust still clung from yesterday's matches, and the faint scuff marks of past footwork cut faint paths across the packed earth. She reached the ring just as another figure emerged from the opposite side. Raoul. His stride was easy, confident, his dark tunic rolled to the elbow and his leathers already scuffed from habitual wear. He spotted her immediately and lifted a hand in mock salute.

"Well, well," he called. "I hope you came with a plan to win today."

Kal didn't break stride. "Do your delusions keep you warm, Raoul?"

"Like a second cloak," he said cheerfully.

They moved into place without further ceremony, beginning their usual stretch sequence with familiarity. Raoul dropped into a deep lunge and glanced over as she rolled out her shoulders. The silence between them wasn't tense, just occupied. They'd long since learned to save their words for when they mattered.

The creak of the outer gate broke the rhythm.

Both turned.

Jarreth stood at the threshold, silhouetted against the rising light. His sparring gear was immaculate–fresh, clean, and tailored to him in a way that made it clear someone else had prepared it. He wore it well, but the air of well versed dignity was undercut by the state of his hair–still tousled from sleep, the mess of it softening the royal sharpness in his features. Kal noted it without emotion, but the truth lingered in the back of her mind: the disheveled look helped. It made him too handsome by half.

He walked toward them with a sort of quiet purpose, but not fast enough to avoid the look Kal leveled his way as he approached.

"You're late."

Jarreth blinked. "I wasn't aware I was expected by someone."

"You weren't." She turned slightly, reaching for the sword rack. "But you are still late, that stands."

He hesitated, but came closer. "I knew you trained with Raoul in the mornings. I thought I might observe."

Kal tilted her head. "And what exactly do you expect to learn by watching?"

The question landed and he paused, visibly off guard.

Kal shifted her sword to one hand and gestured toward him with the blade's tip. "You came dressed. Though that outfit looks like it's never seen dust."

Jarreth coughed. "I came prepared."

"Good." Her tone changed slightly, warmer, but sharper at the edges. A dangerous kind of smile curved her lips. "Don't waste your breath, then."

She tossed him a sparring sword. He caught it just a heartbeat before it hit the dirt, hands adjusting to the unfamiliar balance.

"You're not observing," she said. "You're sparring."

Raoul, now leaning lazily on his own sword, laughed outright. "Gods help you, princeling."

Kal stepped back, sword raised, the point angled low. Her stance was loose, shoulders relaxed, no tension in her posture.

"Come on, then," she said, tilting her head. "Let's see what you've got."

Jarreth squared his shoulders and stepped into the ring, blade coming up in a textbook-perfect guard. Every movement was polished, feet placed at the ideal angle, grip balanced just so. He looked like the front page of a swordsmanship manual brought to life.

Kal didn't move. She let the silence stretch, watching him. He held his position a beat too long, and then, predictably, made the first move–a clean, sweeping strike from his dominant side, precisely angled, weight distributed evenly.

Kal batted it aside without shifting so much as her stance. Just a flick of her wrist, and the strike was gone.

Jarreth blinked. He reset, tried again–this time a rising arc, faster than the last, just as precise. Kal stepped neatly aside and tapped the flat of her blade against his side.

"Dead," she said calmly. "That's one."

Color started to creep up his neck, but he said nothing, only moved back to position and came at her again. Another clean form. Another flawless angle. Another effortless deflection.

She caught the blow and turned it, sliding her blade along his and tapping him on the sternum. "Two. You're starting to make me nervous."

He gritted his teeth but didn't speak. The next strike came harder, quicker–but still practiced, still rehearsed. Still something learned from drills and drills alone.

Kal parried and pivoted, letting her blade whisper against his hip as he passed. "Three. And you haven't even landed a blow yet."

That did it. His jaw tightened, breath shifting slightly as irritation began to show. He came again, moving through a series this time, slashes and thrusts in succession. Better. Faster. Less refined, but at least he was trying to move beyond the script.

Kal met him blow for blow. Her posture changed the moment he did–shoulders drawing tight, steps shifting, grip adjusting as she pressed him backward. No more waiting. She attacked, sharp and meticulous, her strikes controlled but unrelenting. He tried to counter, but she moved faster, tapping the blade to his thigh.

"Four. You're reacting now. That's better."

Another tap to his shoulder. "Five. But your hesitation is killing you."

He gave a frustrated sound and drove in harder. Kal spun to his side and caught his exposed flank. "Six. And now you're too angry to think."

Jarreth backed off, breath short. His grip shifted. He circled her, trying to recover the rhythm.

Kal didn't let him. She advanced again–no taunt, no pause–just a series of strikes that pushed him to the edge of control. He parried the first. Blocked the second. Missed the third. Her blade twisted under his and, with a sharp motion, knocked it free. His sword clattered to the dirt.

She stopped with her point at his throat, then lowered it.

"Anger's a weapon," she said. "But it's one that can always be turned against you."

She stepped back.

Jarreth stood where his sword had fallen, chest still rising with the last of his breath. His brows were drawn, his mouth set tight in something close to frustration. He didn't look at her, but somewhere inward, as though still chasing the moment where it had all started to slip.

Kal lowered her blade fully and spoke, her voice even. "You carry the same weight in everything you do."

That brought his eyes up to hers.

"You hide behind form, behind title, behind that perfect poise like its armor." She didn't soften it. "But you're buried under it. Suffocating under the *duty*. Under the need to be what everyone expects you to be."

She took a step closer, the sword now resting at her side, her stance relaxed.

"When you dropped the performance, even for a breath, your instincts were right. Your reflexes found me. That was *you*, not the prince. And you need to trust *him*."

Jarreth said nothing at first. But something in his expression shifted as if part of him, the part not trained for politics or polished for court, was listening.

From the edge of the ring, Raoul gave a low whistle. "Brutal. Remind me never to spar with you after you had that much alone time to think."

Kal turned toward him, eyes sharp. "You're not getting off that lightly."

Raoul arched his brow.

"You spend every match trying to peel me apart," she said. "Always poking, always pressing, trying to find where the cracks are. You want to see past the calm, see what's buried underneath." Her eyes narrowed. "I'm happy to oblige."

Raoul grinned. A glint of something feral lit behind his eyes.

He stepped forward, sword already spinning once in his hand as he moved toward the edge of the ring. "You truly think you've got a lesson for me today then sweetheart?"

"More than one."

His boots crunched lightly over the ring's dust. "Beyond a new angle of the sky, from the flat of my back?"

Kal smiled, not kindly.

"Step in," she said. "Let's find out."

Raoul had barely reached the center of the ring before Kal lunged. No salute, no warning. Just movement, clean, fast, and merciless. Her blade came in high, then low, then side-on with a speed that left no room for posturing. Raoul grunted, caught the first strike, half-parried the second, and barely twisted out of the third.

She didn't slow. He adjusted quickly, but not well. His form shifted into the clean, refined lines of Varisian technique, formal and fluid. He moved the way they trained nobles to move, with every gesture calculated for balance and courtly poise. Kal's eyes narrowed in open irritation, clearly having lost her patience with both of them today. She pressed harder. The next strike came in sharp across his flank, and he brought his sword up just in time, the clash ringing through the courtyard.

"Still with the Varisian formalities," she muttered, circling. "Still hiding."

Raoul arched a brow as he repositioned. "You have a particular tone when you're disappointed."

She drove him back two steps with a sudden burst of force. "Why do you always start with this?" she asked between strikes. "This polished, safe nonsense. You know it's subpar to what's underneath. And still, you lead with it."

He parried again, less gracefully this time. "I don't recall agreeing to a character dissection."

Kal kept moving, blades clashing between words. "No, you prefer to *give* them, not receive."

A tighter pivot. She nearly caught him at the ribs.

"You bury the fire," she said, voice low, controlled, just above the sound of their blades. "I know it's in there. I've seen it. A glimpse in the way you move when you're not trying to impress anyone. So why keep it hidden?"

Raoul deflected the strike but didn't counter. His grip tightened, but his expression didn't shift.

"Paying attention to me, Kal?" he asked with a grin, though it was thinner than usual. "I'm flattered."

She didn't smile. "Don't try to tease your way out of this."

Another strike. He blocked it late, the edge nicking past his guard. She advanced without pause.

"Tell me," she said, voice like a blade itself, "What is it you're afraid of? That you're not Varisian enough for this court? Not Dunes enough to go home? Just somewhere in between, performing both, belonging to neither. Caught between serving royalty and *being* royalty."

Raoul froze for half a heartbeat. Behind him, Jarreth stopped breathing. Kal saw it then, not a flicker of doubt. Just the sudden, raw stillness of a man who realized someone had finally said it aloud.

"You're not just someone who trained in the desert," she continued, her steps slow now, circling him. "You *came* from there. And not as a soldier."

Raoul's blade didn't move.

Kal kept pressing. "Is that what this is? You don't want anyone to see what you left behind? Or are you afraid it'll claim you again if you stop pretending you're something else?"

His mouth opened slightly, but no words came.

She didn't wait. Strike. Strike. Step. Her blade caught the edge of his guard and turned it. He spun out too late, and she stepped inside his reach.

"You're not the only one who knows how to press," she said sharply, "but I don't hide behind charm when I do it."

He started to speak but she didn't let him finish. A hard sweep of her leg took his feet out from under him, and Raoul hit the dirt flat on his back. His breath left him in a short exhale. Kal stood over him, blade lowered but still ready, her gaze steady and cold.

"What's wrong?" she asked. "Uncomfortable, being pried open? Or do you just not like the feeling of someone seeing *you* behind the mask?"

Raoul stared up at her. There was no retort this time. No grin. Just quiet tension, caught between the past he hadn't spoken of and the woman who'd seen it anyway. He lay still on the dirt, chest rising with uneven breath, his hands slack at his sides. He stared up at Kal, eyes narrowing in something closer to disbelief, like her words had cut deeper than the blade ever could.

"You laugh when I tell Jarreth to stop hiding behind his titles," she said. "But you do the same thing."

Her eyes held his gaze without flinching.

"You hide behind the identity of a blade. Just a sword in someone else's hand. You pretend that's all you are, that your only purpose is to protect or kill depending on who gives the order."

Raoul didn't move, didn't speak, but Kal didn't expect him to.

"You want to be only Varisian, because that's easier. Because that fits. But it's not all you are. Where you came from, what's in your blood, that doesn't vanish just because you don't speak it aloud."

She stepped back from him, her tone even but final.

"Until you learn to accept *both*, you'll always be less than what you were meant to be."

Raoul stared up at her, utterly silent. For once, there was no clever reply. No dismissive grin. Only the weight of her words, sitting heavily between them.

Kal turned without another glance and walked toward the weapons rack. The morning light crested the courtyard walls. It struck across the worn stones in long golden bands, catching on the blades still hung in their rows. The edge of a short sword gleamed as she passed, and for a moment, the light shifted—sharp and direct.

The light struck her eyes, sudden and blinding. Kal blinked once and the courtyard vanished.

The stone turned to shadow. Sunlight bled into ash. The air, once clean with morning crispness, turned heavy—choked with the scent of iron, blood, and smoke. The vision took her without warning, without anchor, without sense of time or space. She was simply *there*.

A room. Underground, windowless. Walls slick with moisture, dark stone stained in layers of old blood. Chains clinked with every shift of weight. Iron chains.

And Arjun.

He was suspended by his wrists, manacled high above his head. His feet barely touched the ground, arms wrenched at unnatural angles. The manacles were iron–raw, uncoated–and they burned where they touched his skin, searing deep into fae flesh. Welts ran the length of his arms where the metal had split him open. His breathing was shallow, uneven.

A man stood before him. Hooded. A Human.

He spoke, voice low, precise. "Where is she?"

Arjun didn't answer. The man gestured. A second figure moved from the corner, holding something long and silver, but it wasn't silver. Kal could *feel* it wasn't. The edge shimmered wrong. Iron. Shaped into a narrow blade, forged to pierce without killing. The first cut was at the ribs. Arjun inhaled sharply through clenched teeth, the sound more instinct than defiance. The blade dragged slowly, skin splitting and sizzled as it moved, the iron burning through every nerve.

Still he said nothing.

The hooded man circled him.

"You'll break," he said calmly. "They all break. You'll just be slower, and I have all the time in the world. *You* don't."

Another cut, this time across the thigh. Then the arm. Then beneath the jaw.

Kal could hear the iron hissing against skin. Smell the smoke of it. It wasn't blood that made her stomach twist, it was the sound. The way Arjun refused to scream. The way he hung from the chains, his body spasming with each strike, but his mouth locked shut.

"Tell us where she is," the man repeated, almost gently.

Arjun lifted his head. One eye swollen. The other half-blind with blood.

"You'll never find her.," he rasped.

A fist struck his stomach. Another caught him across the face. He didn't cry out, but his body folded in the chains, breath stolen from his lungs. The torturer stepped back, signaled again. Kal saw a brand this time–iron again, shaped into something she couldn't name, the edges cruel and twisting. It pressed to his shoulder. Arjun screamed then. Not a long scream. Not loud. But real. Raw. Torn from somewhere deeper than defiance.

Kal couldn't move. She was frozen mid-step, her foot still hovering just above the earth in the courtyard. Her eyes were wide, locked on something that wasn't there. She didn't blink. Didn't breathe.

Across the ring, Raoul slowly pushed himself to his feet, wiping dust from his palms. He glanced toward her.

"Kal?"

She didn't answer.

"Kalithea," Jarreth called, sharper now, moving a few steps forward.

She didn't move. Raoul's posture changed. But she didn't see them. All she saw was Arjun–chained, bloodied, burning–refusing to give her up.

"Something's wrong," Jarreth said under his breath.

Raoul didn't answer. He was already crossing the yard, the dirt still scuffed from their sparring. Kal hadn't moved. She stood half-turned, one foot frozen mid-step, eyes fixed on nothing. The sunlight had shifted, casting long shadows behind her, but she hadn't so much as blinked.

Jarreth reached her first. He hesitated, uncertain, then reached out and set a hand on her shoulder, cautious and firm. The reaction was immediate. Kal jerked slightly, her gaze snapping toward him–sharp, searching, the kind of look a person gave when they weren't entirely sure what they were seeing. Her expression shifted the moment she registered his face, but not completely.

Jarreth withdrew his hand slowly, his voice quieter. "You didn't respond."

She blinked once, twice, as if trying to clear something from her vision. Then she turned without a word and walked toward the weapons rack. Her steps were steady. Controlled. She placed the sparring sword back into its slot, adjusting it with unnecessary care. Her fingers lingered on the hilt a moment longer than they should have.

"I must be tired," she said, not looking at either of them.

And then she walked away, out of the ring and through the gate, without another word.

Jarreth watched her go, unsettled. "She tore us both apart. Then stopped like she wasn't even here. And now she's pretending none of it happened."

Raoul nodded faintly, still watching the gate. "It's like she locked up. Mid-breath. Then just reset."

They stood in the silence she left behind, the sun finally clearing the wall of the yard, casting clean light across the ring.

Neither man brought up what she'd said about them. Neither was ready to.

Kal walked steadily, leaving the sparring yard behind without slowing, without turning. She could still feel the heat of the sun on her back, still hear the faint ring of steel echoing in her ears, but she set her shoulders and forced her mind forward.

It had been a trick of the light.

That was what she settled on–light, fatigue, the residue of sharpened emotion bleeding into her thoughts after a morning of tearing down the walls of others. It hadn't been real. Arjun was gone. The iron chains, the blood, the defiance in his voice...it wasn't memory, and it couldn't be a message. Her steps didn't falter, but her pulse had yet to settle.

It might have been her shadows, she reasoned. That part of her magic always stirred when her emotions pushed too close to the surface. There were times it played tricks on her, fracturing what she saw, twisting the edges of thought into shape. That made more sense than what she *thought* she'd seen. More sense than believing, for even a breath, that he was still alive.

Still, the image lingered. Not the light of it, but the *feel*. The weight. The smell.

She wouldn't tell Liam. There was no reason to burden him with a vision she didn't trust herself. And if he saw even a flicker of doubt in her, if he thought she'd begun to unravel at the edge of grief, he would lose the fragile confidence they had started to rebuild since arriving in Varis. She needed to hold her line, especially now.

By the time she reached the upper floor, her decision was made. She turned away from their shared wing after grabbing clothing and made for the palace bathhouse, ignoring the looks from two passing guards who stopped mid-step as she swept past. The attendants said nothing when she requested a private room. They only bowed, eyes lowered, and ushered her through the tiled corridor to the farthest chamber. It was quiet there, almost peaceful. The high, arched ceilings gathered steam like mist clinging to the rafters. Lanterns burned low on gilded hooks, casting soft light across the stone floor.

She undressed without ceremony and slipped into the water. Heat wrapped around her instantly. She sank lower, letting it pull at her muscles, soothe the tension wound tight in her back and legs. Her eyes closed. She breathed deep. It didn't help.

The vision clung to her. No matter how hot the water, how thick the steam, it didn't burn away. She could still feel the iron. Still hear the sound Arjun made when the brand met his skin. She hadn't let herself grieve him properly, hadn't dared. She hadn't had the time. There had always been something else, something urgent, something that demanded she keep moving, keep fighting.

Maybe this was what grief looked like when it finally caught up.

She stayed in the water longer than she intended. Long enough for the lanterns to dim further, for the silence to turn absolute. When she rose, the air kissed her skin like cold silk. She dressed slowly in a deep green gown. It was simple but finely cut, fitted through the bodice with soft, flowing sleeves that tapered to her wrists. The color made her eyes look almost inhuman. She caught her reflection briefly in the polished metal of a lantern's housing and almost didn't recognize the figure staring back.

Back in her rooms, she lingered only a few minutes before the restlessness set in again. Sitting still was unbearable. Every time she stopped moving, the vision crept closer in her mind, like something pressing from behind a half-closed door. She left her chambers and began to wander the halls. The palace was alive with muted movement–servants changing out candles, scribes carrying armfuls of parchment, guards passing in rotation–but she moved through it like a shadow, unnoticed. She didn't have a destination. She only knew she needed motion.

If she stopped, she feared what she might remember.

She stepped out from a shadowed corridor hung with aging tapestries and nearly collided with Alden.

He was waiting for her. There was no doubt in his posture–hands loosely clasped behind his back, weight settled evenly, eyes already on her before she stopped. He offered his arm with the polite formality of a court-trained noble, though his expression carried none of the stiffness that usually accompanied it.

"Walk with me?" he asked.

There was no reason to refuse. And if she was honest, the quiet rhythm of her own footsteps had started to feel like a chase. She nodded once and took his arm. They crossed the western colonnade without speaking, the kind of silence that didn't require filling. The stone path ran beneath a stretch of carved columns, sunlight catching on the fine cracks in the flagstones, ivy shifting above them in the breeze. Kal walked without haste, letting the motion settle her thoughts.

It was Alden who spoke first, his voice light, measured.

"My son and his shadow seem particularly attentive these days."

Kal glanced sideways but didn't reply.

He continued without looking at her. "I used to worry they'd spend their lives locked in a contest of military strategy and court etiquette. Now I find myself considering whether your presence is a threat to palace productivity. If I rationed your time, perhaps we'd get more work out of them."

Still, she said nothing.

Alden gave a thoughtful hum. "I haven't seen Jarreth this flustered since the daughter of a Haldren baron asked to view his sword collection. He showed her actual swords. Poor girl was terribly disappointed."

Kal's brow lifted, just slightly.

"And Raoul." Alden tilted his head. "Gods, that one usually prefers chaos with far less structure. What you're witnessing is effort, Kalithea. I do hope you appreciate the labor involved."

"I don't."

"Good," he chuckled. "They'll work harder."

She cast him a sidelong look, but the corner of her mouth twitched.

"Are you encouraging this?" she asked.

"I would never," Alden replied, with the unconvincing innocence of a man who knew exactly what he was doing. "I'm merely observing the spectacle, as any responsible monarch would. Quiet sympathy for the woman being pursued under the very convincing cover of morning sparring and chance corridor meetings."

Kal didn't roll her eyes, but the impulse was there.

Alden's tone shifted subtly, the humor easing beneath something more grounded. "It's a strange kind of attention, isn't it? Not the kind meant to own. Not the kind meant to hurt."

"No," she said softly.

"Still uncomfortable."

They reached the upper garden steps and the wind caught the edge of her coat, tugging it gently aside as he let the silence stretch between them.

"You don't have to give them anything," Alden said, voice lower now. "Not softness. Not distance. You only have to endure it on your terms. They'll learn how to follow your pace."

She looked ahead. The path curved toward the high terrace. Behind them, faint but distinct, came the sound of footsteps on stone.

Alden glanced over his shoulder with a long-suffering sigh.

"Well," he said. "It seems the bloodhounds have caught your scent."

The sound of bootsteps behind them had a rhythm to it, unhurried, just casual enough to suggest it wasn't accidental. Kal didn't look back. She didn't need to. Beside her, Alden slowed by the smallest margin, the shift subtle enough to seem like chance. His gaze flicked sideways, the corner of his mouth tilting into a faint smile.

"Ah," he murmured. "And here they come. Flawless timing. Almost like it was rehearsed ."

Jarreth appeared first, turning the corner with the stiff posture of someone trying very hard not to look like he was in a hurry. His coat was immaculate, fastened up to the throat, every inch of him prepared–except for the faint flush rising along his cheeks. Raoul appeared a few paces behind him, hands in his pockets, stride loose and casual as if he'd been taking a leisurely stroll and happened upon them by chance.

"Your Majesty," Jarreth said with a formal nod, then, more carefully, "My Lady."

"Son," Alden replied, tone dry. "Sir Sahir. How startling. We were just savoring the rare luxury of uninterrupted thought."

Raoul gave an easy smile, all charm and no apology. "We wouldn't dream of interrupting."

"Oh, I don't think you dream of much else," Alden drolled, still walking. "But I commend your ongoing effort to make it seem otherwise."

Jarreth's mouth opened, perhaps in defense, perhaps to shift the conversation, but Alden gave him no room to maneuver.

"I recall, at your age, following a woman halfway across a battlefield just for the chance to carry her shield. I was sixteen, thought it was romantic. Limped for a week."

"Sounds noble," Raoul said.

"It was idiotic," Alden replied. "But I was young. And charming. And hadn't yet developed the sense to recognize when a woman wanted *space*."

Kal remained silent beside him, matching his pace without comment. She didn't glance back.

"We only meant to–" Jarreth began, trying again.

"To orbit?" Alden offered mildly. "To hover, just enough to be seen, but not so much as to be accused of intent? Like moons of ill-fated affection, endlessly circling?"

That stopped him short. Raoul gave a soft laugh and rubbed the back of his neck.

"Well," he said, "that's one way to phrase it."

"It's the only way I can phrase it without laughing," Alden replied, still walking, still smiling. "And I *AM* doing my best not to laugh."

They passed through the archway into the upper garden path. The scent of late-blooming summer herbs filled the air, and ivy rustled against the stone wall as the breeze shifted. Behind them, Jarreth and Raoul exchanged uncertain glances. They had followed, but now couldn't seem to decide whether they were still welcome or hopelessly outmaneuvered.

Then the tone of the moment shifted. A voice called from ahead, clipped and unmistakable.

"Your Majesty."

Liam stood at the head of the garden path. His coat was open just enough to reveal the sword at his side, but there was nothing casual in the way he stood. His arms were crossed, his stance balanced. He didn't look at Raoul or Jarreth. His gaze was fixed solely on Kal. She didn't stop walking, but Alden slowed with her, allowing the approach.

"My apologies for being late," Liam said, voice formal. "I hadn't realized the hour. I'm sorry to inconvenience you"

"You haven't," Alden said with quiet amusement.

Liam gave a nod. "Still, I appreciate you attending to my sister."

Without ceremony, he reached for Kal's arm–no force or pageantry. Just a hand to her elbow, firm and certain. Kal didn't pull away. She allowed the turn.

And in that breath of silence, the weight between them settled hard and clear. Alden watched them go, his expression impassive. As they disappeared down the garden path, he turned to find Jarreth and Raoul still standing awkwardly at the hedgerow. Their composure had started to unravel somewhere between Kal's silence and Liam's arrival, and neither had managed to gather the pieces.

"Well," Alden said with theatrical brightness, "aren't you both glad I intervened before your dignity suffered permanent damage?"

Raoul exhaled slowly, as if weighing the answer. "Debatable."

Alden clapped him once on the shoulder, still smiling. "Take heart. I've seen worse pursuits. At least neither of you broke into song."

Jarreth didn't speak. His jaw was tight, his gaze fixed on the path Kal had taken. There was something unsettled in his eyes, mute and unmoving.

Alden watched him a moment longer, then smiled faintly.

"There it is," he said. "The royal sulk."

Liam said nothing at first as they turned from the garden, though his grip at her elbow remained, light but unmoving. Every line of him radiated tension, as though coiled to strike. They moved together down the long stone path that skirted the outer terrace, ivy drifting in the breeze above them, the sunlight catching in the gold-veined seams of the palace façade. Only once the courtyard lay out of view behind them did Liam speak.

"They're getting bold."

Kal didn't respond.

His voice was low, but the fury beneath it was unmistakable, tightly controlled.

"The prince, especially," he went on. "He used to trip over his tongue when you looked at him. Now he's striding into conversations like you asked him to."

"I didn't," she said.

"Doesn't seem to matter."

They rounded a corner, passing beneath a tall window. The glass had been cleaned to a hard polish, and the morning light came off it like a knife's flash. It bent sharp and high across the stone–and struck her directly in the eyes.

She flinched. Not from the brightness.

From what it pulled open.

Arjun.

Closer now. Too close.

He was no longer bound upright. He lay sprawled on cold stone, stripped to the waist, his limbs twisted into unnatural angles that told of repeated fractures reset only to be broken again. His skin was a canvas of burns and lacerations, blistered where iron had kissed it, blackened where it had lingered. His back rose and fell in shallow, wheezing gasps. One of his hands—pale, streaked with old blood—was turned the wrong way, fingers splayed as if caught mid-spasm.

His face had been beaten until the features swelled and distorted, but one eye, just one, remained clear enough to glint in the dark.

A figure crouched beside him, clothed in black, their hands gloved. Every movement was calm. Precise. The patience of someone who had long since stopped viewing pain as cruelty.

"It's only pain," the voice murmured. "Tell us where she is."

Arjun's lips cracked open. Blood touched his teeth when he tried to speak. But the word came all the same—gravel and defiance.

"Never." he said.

The torturer didn't argue. They simply lifted the iron again, a brand, already glowing red at the edges. The curved sigil of a rune, warped and incomplete. They pressed it into the base of Arjun's spine. The sound he made was not human. It rose raw and jagged from his throat, a broken scream that caught halfway and choked itself off. His body arched violently, spine bowing clear of the stone. Smoke lifted in thin tendrils as flesh hissed and blackened. When he fell back, it was with a finality.

Kal stopped walking. Mid-stride. Like something had driven a stake into the space between one step and the next. Her breath caught. Her vision narrowed to a single fixed point that wasn't there. She didn't blink. Didn't move. Didn't make a sound.

Beside her, Liam didn't notice at first. He took another two steps before realizing her absence—and then turned, frowning. She stood frozen, eyes wide but unseeing. And the horror still burned behind them.

"Kal?"

Liam's voice was sharp now—not raised, but tense. His eyes had already found her, narrowing as he stepped into her line of sight. She didn't respond. Didn't blink. Her entire body remained frozen mid-step, as though caught in the moment between breaths. The shadows cast by the high spires of the palace shifted oddly across the stone at her feet. They didn't stretch or sway as they should have. Instead, they bent, flickering unnaturally, warping around her form like smoke against glass.

For a heartbeat, the edges of her silhouette blurred.

Then it happened again. Sharper this time. A stutter in the light, like the world was holding its breath.

"Kalithea." Liam's voice dropped lower. Controlled. Alarmed. He moved quickly, closing the distance between them, his hands finding her shoulders. "Kal–hey. Look at me."

He gave her one firm shake. Not harsh. Not angry. But desperate, like a man pulling someone back from the edge of a fall. The motion was familiar, even to her. He'd done it before–for years–after battles when she'd gone deathly still, standing over bodies with blood on her hands that wasn't hers. That same cold silence lived behind her eyes now. Her pupils snapped back into focus. She blinked and the warping shadows around her stilled. The light returned to its natural path, slanting over the stone as though nothing had shifted at all. Her breath came out slow and careful, as if she were forcing her way back into her own skin.

Liam didn't release her. Not yet.

"What the hell was that?" he asked, voice low but tight. Controlled fury wrapped in concern.

Kal didn't answer at first. She stood there, spine straightening with the slow discipline of someone pushing instinct down where it couldn't be seen. Then she breathed again, more evenly, and said, "Nothing. I'm just tired."

Liam's grip tightened for a moment. His brow creased.

"Bullshit."

"I haven't been sleeping."

"That because of dreams?" he snapped, stepping back. "Or because the crown prince and his favored pet keep circling every time you so much as take a breath?"

She didn't rise to the bait. Her silence gave him the answer he needed.

He swore under his breath and raked a hand down his face, pacing a short line across the corridor. His boots struck the stone in sharp rhythm before he turned back toward her, jaw clenched.

"They're bleeding into your time. Into your space. Every gods-damned hour they're where you are, in the yard, delivering scrolls no one asked for, trailing down corridors. And now this, whatever this was. You go still, Kal. Cold. Like you've been hexed. But sure, let's call it exhaustion, because the prince speaks softly and the knight knows how to smile."

"I didn't say it was fine."

"You didn't have to."

Silence stretched between them. Not empty, charged. The wind stirred through the ivy overhead, the faint hush of court life drifting somewhere beyond the stone wall. Kal didn't flinch. Liam watched her closely.

When she spoke again, it was quieter. Calmer. But final.

"I said I'm tired, Liam. That's all."

He didn't believe it. Not entirely. But he also knew when to stop pushing.

For now.

He stepped forward again, more gently this time, hand brushing her arm—just enough to guide her back toward the hall. His voice dropped as they moved, barely above a murmur.

"I'm not letting this happen again," he said. "I don't care what titles they wear. If they keep pushing—"

"I'll handle it," Kal cut in.

Liam gave her a sidelong glance. "Right...like you always do."

But even he could see it now.

Something was shifting beneath her calm. Subtle, but real. Not the prince. Not the knight. Something...*else.* And whatever it was, it wasn't fading. *It was getting closer.*

AMONG BANNERS AND BLOOMS

The morning air carried the scent of pressed cider and wood-smoke as Kal fastened the last steel ring of her coat. Her fingers moved with mechanical precision, each motion efficient, though her mind was still lingering somewhere else entirely. Sleep had been scarce again. The dreams had returned, vivid and relentless. Not dreams, really. Not anymore. They came too clearly. Pain laced into them with cruel realism—smells of scorched flesh, the sound of chain links grinding against stone, Arjun's voice hoarse and broken. She had woken gasping, her chest tight, soaked in cold sweat that didn't feel like fear, only loss.

She hadn't spoken of it. Not to Liam. Not to anyone.

There was no room for unraveling, not now.

She stepped back from the mirror, taking in the full view of her attire. The coat was deep brown, thick and sharply tailored, cut to flatter but not hinder. The waist cinched tight with a wide leather belt, steel rings threading the lacing down her front. The sleeves narrowed into fitted black bracers, their quilted leather stitched cleanly. Beneath, black trousers and high boots gave her full range of motion, the long split coat falling just enough to soften the look without concealing her readiness. She pinned a few curls away from her face, leaving the rest to fall loose over her shoulders unbraided. The knives were the final touch, their weight familiar as she tucked them into the hidden slots within her coat and boots. There was comfort in the ritual of it, in being prepared.

Kal stepped out into the shared common space between their rooms. Liam stood waiting. All black, of course. The high collar of his tunic framed his jaw, and subtle silver trim edged the cuffs and shoulders. Nothing flashy. But it was enough to make him look more like a weapon than a man. Even at rest, he radiated warning.

She arched a brow and gave him a once-over. "We're going to leave a trail of swooning noblewomen behind us, you know. Possibly some fainting footmen, too."

He didn't miss a beat. "Shut up."

Kal's smile was faint. Brief. But it was real.

He nodded once, and turned toward the corridor. "Let's get this over with."

She fell into step beside him.

Whatever the day would bring–gathering crowds, suspicious glances, the first real unveiling of her presence in the capital–she had made her choice. It was time to be seen.

Even if everything inside her wanted to stay hidden just a little longer.

The courtyard stirred with activity by the time Kal and Liam descended the steps. A low breeze carried the scent of turned soil and crushed petals, and the morning sun broke across the banners hanging above the square–navy and silver snapping against the stone towers like war colors dressed up for celebration. Footmen moved with proficiency among the horses, tightening girths, adjusting tack, clearing paths.

Kal didn't need to search for the king, Alden stood in clear view near the central fountain, exchanging words with a stablehand. Jarreth and Raoul sat mounted at his sides. Both men upright, reins loose in hand. The moment they caught sight of her, something in their posture changed. Jarreth straightened unconsciously. Raoul tilted his head, his mouth twitching with amusement.

Three horses stood waiting–sleek, finely groomed, bred for parade rather than war. Kal scanned them before her gaze returned to the king.

Alden raised a hand in casual greeting. "Your ride, My Lady. I had one brought up to match the prince's. Seemed appropriate."

"Strategic," Kal replied as she stepped closer.

Alden smiled faintly. "Always."

Liam moved ahead without prompting, giving her horse's girth strap a final tug, checking the bit, testing the stirrup tension.

Jarreth was already dismounting. He stepped forward and extended the reins with careful formality. "May I?"

Kal didn't hesitate. "You may walk beside me if it flatters your sense of chivalry."

A flicker of amusement passed over his face.

Raoul, still mounted, shifted his weight and leaned forward in his saddle. "And what about me? No gracious invitation?"

"You have trouble with boundaries."

"True," he said, unabashed. "But I make up for it in charm."

Kal took the reins from Jarreth and mounted with ease, the long coat sweeping back over the saddle in a clean line. She sat tall, composed, like someone who was more accustomed to riding into battle than ceremony.

Alden stepped to her stirrup, glancing up. "If you could manage not to terrify the nobility within the first hour, I'd be grateful. Some of them only just recovered from your last court appearance."

Kal didn't answer but something like amusement passed behind her eyes, and Alden didn't miss it.

The courtyard continued to fill—nobles in rich fabrics, guards in formal livery, minor lords and city dignitaries clustering near the entryway. Music floated from a small ensemble near the gallery, too refined to be festive, too polite to be stirring. Liam, mounted now beside her, attracted his share of glances, but it was Kal who drew the longest looks.

Not openly. Not disrespectfully. But with careful, pointed interest. A woman no one knew, standing at the king's side, mounted on a royal-bred horse, wearing no sigil, bearing no title. No introduction. Only presence. The whispering began before the gates were opened.

Kal passed a pair of noblewomen standing beneath a vine-wrapped arch. They lowered their voices, but not enough.

"They say she's foreign, brought in for Prince Jarreth. A match under consideration."

"She doesn't look like a match. She looks like she could kill him."

"That might be the point."

Kal didn't turn her head but beside her, Jarreth's expression tightened. His gaze stayed forward, his jaw set. He said nothing.

Raoul leaned in slightly across the space between them, voice low. "Don't worry, princeling. She'd kill me first."

Kal shifted her gaze toward him. "Don't tempt me."

Alden chuckled under his breath, his mount already easing forward. "This," he said aloud, "is precisely what happens when you bring wolves to a harvest."

"Wolves don't parade," Kal answered.

"No," Alden agreed. "They walk beside kings and make everyone else consider what they've failed to prepare for."

The gates opened with a creak of iron and wood, and the procession began.

Kal rode at the king's side, her expression neutral beneath the morning light. The people of Varis leaned forward in curiosity to see her. And try to decide who, exactly, she was.

The procession moved at a ceremonial pace through the upper tiers of Varis, winding its way between marble facades and flower-strewn balconies. Petals drifted from above, catching on wind and silk. Children leaned dangerously from stone windows, their eyes wide as the crown's retinue passed below. Laughter and applause rose in pockets, tempered by reverent silence from others who had come not for celebration, but to study the woman at the king's side.

Kal rode beside Alden, posture composed, her face expressionless. Behind her, Liam rode with seasoned indifference, subtly looking for danger. He watched everything. Everyone.

Which meant that when Raoul approached from the left, he knew it was no accident. Raoul simply drifted into her periphery, easy in the saddle, his reins held with the casual grip of someone born to horseback.

"My lady," he murmured, voice pitched low beneath the hum of the crowd. "If your spine grows any straighter, I'll be forced to assume you were cast from bronze."

Kal didn't turn her head. "Then here you are, speaking to statues."

Raoul laughed softly, undeterred.

Behind them, Liam exhaled through his nose—a short sound, barely audible, and very sharp.

The road curved inward as they approached the heart of the merchant district. The cobblestones were swept clean, the air heavy with the scent of cinnamon, dye smoke, and sun-warmed stone. Nobles rode behind the king in loose formation, their silks catching against the breeze, flanked by city banners and guards in formal livery.

Jarreth brought his horse alongside hers near the central plaza. He said nothing at first, matching her pace with a quietness that suggested he'd rehearsed this moment and found every opening wanting. At last he spoke, without looking at her.

"You've likely seen more war camps than parades. All this must feel...artificial."

Kal considered him for a moment, eyes half-lidded beneath the sweep of her lashes.

"False things often wield real power," she said. "That's the danger of them."

He nodded once, lips pressed into a faint line. He didn't fall back. Not immediately. And though he said nothing else, Kal could feel the weight of him beside her, the effort behind his silence. Liam's presence tightened behind them, his stillness louder than speech, but he held his tongue.

The procession slowed before a long boulevard framed by arches and ivy-wrapped statues. A merchant cart had broken free near the far gate, and several guards moved to clear the obstruction. Alden dismounted to speak with the elders gathered at the square's edge. Kal remained mounted, posture at ease, though her fingers tapped twice against the saddle pommel—rhythm without thought.

Raoul surfaced again at her left, his horse nudging forward with fluid steps. He leaned slightly in the saddle, voice low, half teasing.

"How does one earn a ride beside you for more than a city block?"

Kal's reply was cool. "Survive the first half."

"A test of endurance, then."

"It always is."

She turned her head this time, just slightly. He was watching her too closely, his smile softened at the edges. There was nothing mocking in it. No swagger. Just interest, quiet and steady, as though he'd begun to see the shape of something he hadn't expected.

Kal faced forward again.

"Careful," she said.

He didn't pretend not to understand. "Of what?"

"If you keep chasing, you might catch up."

There was a pause, just long enough for meaning to settle between them. Then Raoul's smile shifted, sharper now, touched with something halfway between invitation and warning. Before he could answer, Liam's voice cut through the morning haze like a drawn blade.

"If you're so fond of the spectacle," he said coldly, "perhaps you'd like to ride up front with the musicians."

Raoul didn't look back. "Ah. The ever-faithful shadow speaks."

"You're off formation."

"I'm enjoying the view."

Kal's voice sliced between them cooly. "Enough."

Neither man answered but Raoul did not fall back.

The festival square opened wide before the procession, alive with the saturation of color and noise that only harvest season could bring. Stalls bloomed like petals themselves, bright cloth canopies flaring above baskets heaped with spice-dusted almonds, garlands of pressed flowers, and bolts of fresh-dyed silk. Children wove through the crowds in bursts of laughter and bare feet, slipping between nobles with the surety of foxes.

Kal rode at Alden's side in silence, a solitary figure of leather and steel framed by pageantry. She heard the voices rising behind her, well versed tones softened by forced warmth, the kind of pleasantries meant more for those listening than those addressed. She felt their glances, those sideways studies of the woman who had not entered court by invitation, yet rode beside the king like someone who had always belonged there. She gave them nothing. No acknowledgment. No response. Her gaze remained fixed ahead. The scent of jasmine and warmed cider thickened the air, but she moved through it untouched. The music that trailed them, pipe and string and ceremonial drum, did not reach her.

Jarreth guided his mount closer once more, quiet in his approach. His presence was softer now, less sure, as though aware of how far he stood outside whatever rhythm Kal followed. His eyes drifted toward the market edge, where stalls overflowed with the spoils of the season—bundles of bright petals, some gathered in woven cones, others spilling across tabletops like upturned treasure. He slowed. Just a fraction, then dismounted.

Kal didn't turn her head, but her gaze followed him.

Jarreth moved quietly, offering a low word to the nearest vendor, his coin passed without flourish. A moment later, he returned with his horse in tow, and a small arrangement in his hand. Flowers, carefully chosen. White and soft gold, bound with green ribbon. Modest. Unassuming. He stepped to her stirrup and looked up, not grinning or posturing, just a touch of uncertainty in his stance. It made him look younger. Or perhaps more honest.

"My lady," he said, his voice low. "For the season. A gesture."

Kal looked at him, her eyes dropping to the flowers. No thorns. No sealed parchment hidden beneath the stems. No sharp scent of crushed herb that might speak of poison or spell. Just ribbon and breath-soft blooms. She looked at him again, and in the pause that followed, she read the tension in his shoulders, the effort it took not to fidget, the way his gaze held hers only for a heartbeat before slipping just to the side. There was no deal behind it. No calculation she could find. Just a prince, too well-trained to stumble unless sincerity had gotten the better of him, offering something he didn't quite know how to give.

Kal reached down. Her fingers closed around the flowers with care, as though they might vanish at the touch.

"Thank you," she said softly.

It was the first time someone had handed her flowers with nothing cruel trailing after the bloom. No danger, no threat expected. No warning sewn into the gesture. She turned without ceremony and slipped the bundle behind her saddle. It was done in the space of a breath. The mask slid easily back into place, her posture resettling. The moment folded shut behind her.

But she did not return the gift.

Jarreth, cheeks tinged with color, mounted again in silence.

Behind her, Liam remained wordless. But something in him had shifted. His silence was no longer edged with frustration. It had cooled. Hardened. He watched his sister's back with the focus of a man seeing a battlefield take shape long before swords were drawn. He did not miss how long her fingers had lingered over that ribbon. Nor the look in Jarreth's eyes as he fell back into formation.

Beyond the outer gates of Varis, the land opened into the full splendor of harvest. Gold wheat bowed in the breeze, orchard trees heavy with fruit, and great swaths of green pasture gave way to the clustered chaos of tents, carts, and festival banners. The scent of roasting nuts mixed with woodsmoke and trampled herbs. Children ran wild beneath bunting strung between trellised archways, while musicians struck up cheerful, if imperfect, songs at intervals. Bells chimed softly from the gateposts as the court procession rode down into the open fields. Banners caught the wind; nobles dismounted in small clusters.

Kal said nothing as she slid from her horse, her coat sweeping behind her like a shadow given shape. Liam landed beside her with a muted thud, already scanning the crowd. Alden arrived not long after, a tankard in one hand and what could only be described as a flower crown in the other–wheat stalks, barley, a few golden petals all woven in a loose ring.

"They're giving these away near the cider tent," he said casually. "The locals expect to see one worn by someone important. I was going to crown a goat, but I thought I'd check with you first."

Kal eyed the crown. Then him.

"Place it on me," she said dryly, "and I'll make you wear it back to the palace"

Alden gave a wistful sigh. "One of these years, you'll respond with something resembling warmth."

"You're not trying hard enough."

He chuckled, tipped his tankard in salute, and wandered off to find a goat more accepting of rural tradition.

She stood near the orchard line, where the ground sloped gently down toward rows of wild pear trees, their branches heavy with late fruit. Bees moved slowly in the warmth, drunk on sweetness, and the air was filled with a faint hum of music from the field beyond. Children darted between booths, chasing ribbons and the promise of sugared treats, while the nobility lingered in curated circles beneath flowered canopies.

Kal remained apart. Not hidden, but separate. Observing. She didn't look when Jarreth approached, but she felt the shift in the air, he stopped a respectful distance away.

"My lady," he said, voice low, formal, but not stiff. "I hope the afternoon hasn't worn on you too harshly."

Kal glanced at him sidelong.

"I've endured worse," she said.

"Undoubtedly," he replied, with the faintest twitch of a smile. "Though I still thought to offer a reprieve."

She turned slightly, one brow raised.

Jarreth reached into the inner fold of his coat and withdrew a small folded cloth, bound with a simple leather tie. "From the vineyard tents," he said. "Pressed fruit rounds, the kind they serve during autumn rites. I remembered you paused near them earlier, though you didn't stop."

Kal studied the parcel, then looked at him, evaluating. No flourish. No expectation. Just a gesture made with care.

She took it, slowly.

"You've a soldier's memory," she said.

He dipped his head. "Years of diplomacy. One learns to read the small things."

She untied the wrap with deft fingers. Inside were a handful of delicate, dried slices–peach, pear, and wild plum, flattened and sun-sweet, lightly dusted with spice and salt. She didn't eat one but she didn't return them either.

Jarreth didn't push. He simply stood beside her, his stance easy but alert, as if he were still on a training field and waiting for an order. She caught the flicker of tension in his shoulders, the way his hands remained loosely at his sides, ready but not expectant.

"It's strange," she said after a moment, her gaze still on the horizon. "To be offered things without strings."

Jarreth turned his head toward her. "It isn't strange. It's just rare."

Kal considered that. Then, almost absently, she folded the parcel and tucked it against her hip beneath the fall of her coat.

"It was a thoughtful gesture," she said.

He gave a small, genuine nod. "I hoped it might be."

They stood in companionable silence for another breath or two. Then, sensing her mood shift back toward distance, Jarreth inclined his head.

"I'll leave you to the orchard," he said. "Though I hope, sincerely, that this day hasn't been too bitter to balance what sweetness it holds."

The music shifted, strings rising into a lilting reel, and the space near the orchard swelled with color and motion. Flower bunches hung from arched branches, dropping petals across the dancers below. A dozen couples turned through the steps, some graceful, some uncertain, the scent of warm fruit wine heavy in the summer air.

Liam stood near the edge of it all, arms crossed, gaze tracking the crowd like a man who never let his guard down. Which was why the woman caught him entirely off balance. She was beautiful, full of life and all smiles. Her ribboned dress was a touch too fine for the dust on her shoes, and her smile was the sort that believed itself immune to refusal.

She walked straight up to him—no hesitation, no second glance.

"Would you dance with me?" she asked.

Liam stared at her as if she'd drawn a dagger. Before he could answer, Kal spoke.

"Go on," she said, voice even.

He turned to her, brows drawn. "You can't be serious."

Kal's expression didn't shift. "We wouldn't want to offend the locals. Keep up appearances, after all."

"I despise you."

"I know."

He hesitated, but the woman was waiting, smiling softly and hopeful. After a beat, Liam exhaled through his nose and offered a sharp, mechanical bow. The woman beamed as he let himself be led toward the heart of the dance.

Kal watched them go. No smile touched her lips. But the corner of her gaze shifted, just once, as Liam caught the rhythm of the music and moved through the first turn with unexpected ease. He didn't look back. Didn't break his scowl entirely. But as he spun the woman under his arm, Kal caught a flicker of something else.

A smile. Small. Barely there. But real.

She stood still a moment longer, something quiet settling in her chest. A pang—not sharp, but deep. Not for herself.

For him.

For the boy who'd become a blade so young he never knew what it was like to be anything else. For the man who guarded her shadows and chased down her ghosts but never let himself have a moment like this unless ordered.

Raoul emerged from the milling crowd like a man on a mission, a lacquered wooden box tucked beneath one arm and a smile already forming. He carried it like a prize taken in battle.

"Victory sweets," he declared, flipping open the lid with a theatrical flourish.

Inside, nestled among folds of paper leaves, sat a neat row of sugar-dusted confections—spiced, delicate, and clearly overpriced. The kind of treat sold by merchants who counted on distracted nobility and flirtation to pad their coffers.

"I liberated them from a vendor who was far too focused on charming a duchess to notice."

Kal eyed the box. Then him.

"And you brought them to me," she said, dry.

Raoul inclined his head. "Obviously. There's a game."

She didn't speak, only waited.

He grinned. "I toss. You catch. Miss one, and I gloat."

"I don't play for applause."

"Then play for pride," he said, lifting one sweet between his fingers.

Kal looked in then stepped back into a clean patch of grass just beyond the nearest line of onlookers.

Raoul tossed the first gently into an easy arc, no challenge. She caught it between two fingers without shifting her stance.

The second came quicker, but she snatched it from the air as easily as the first. By the third, Raoul was adjusting angles, adding distance, a flick of the wrist sending one high, the next low. Kal moved only when necessary, each catch made with elegant precision, like a hawk snaring prey.

A few people turned to watch. Murmurs followed. Not laughter, not jest—interest. The kind that spreads slowly through a festival crowd when something worth remembering begins to unfold.

Raoul arced the fifth one over her left shoulder. She didn't turn. Her hand lifted and plucked it from the air behind her without looking. He paused. Then threw the sixth harder, sharper and just shy of reckless. Kal caught it before it reached her waist, turning it once in her palm before popping it between her teeth. She chewed slowly. Thoughtfully.

Raoul stood still, the last sweet balanced on his fingertips.

"I could try to curve it," he offered. "Add a twist. Keep you guessing."

"You could," she said. He did. The seventh sweet went up, high and fast, curving behind her like a feint in swordplay. Kal waited until the last moment, pivoted slightly, and caught it behind her back with one hand.

The crowd nearby exhaled in a collective breath.

Raoul stared.

She finished the sweet, brushed sugar from the edge of her glove, and handed the box back with finality. "I win."

He pressed a hand to his chest, grinning in mock defeat. "Utterly."

The Dance at Dusk

Evening settled over Varis in a wash of bronze and indigo, the last light catching on tower spires and vanishing behind the ridge-line. The main halls of the palace pulsed with sound—strings warming to rhythm, laughter echoing from marble, the rustle of silks and leather sweeping across polished floors.

Kal stood alone in the center of her chamber, fastening the final clasp at her collar. The gown was ember red, its layers draping in slow movement like coals stirred in a hearth. Fine gold threading edged the bodice and curled up the collar, high at the neck and sharp at the shoulders, rising in a flame-like pattern that caught light with every breath. The cut followed her form without constraint, as if it belonged to her shape rather than the other way around. Her left arm bore a mesh of golden filigree, delicate enough to resemble lace, strong enough to echo armor. At her waist, a narrow belt cinched the fabric close, its buckle shaped in a starburst of gold and gilt. She wore her hair unbound. Loose waves spilled down her back, threaded with strands of gold that caught on lantern light when she turned.

When she stepped into the hallway, Liam was waiting. He wore formal black, finely cut but absent of decoration. Just clean lines and readiness. He saw her and paused.

At last, he exhaled through his nose, exasperated, and said, "They're going to fall over themselves."

Kal adjusted the edge of her gold mesh. "Let them."

He offered his arm. Grudgingly.

"Do I need to remind them you're not a prize to be won?"

Kal's lips curved, almost too faint to see. "I think you enjoy the correction more than the reminder."

"I enjoy shutting them up." he muttered, giving her his arm, leading her down the hall.

The antechamber outside the great hall held the hush of polished stone and candlelight, quiet but alive with the expectancy that always preceded a royal feast. The sounds of the gathering court beyond–clinking goblets, muted conversation, the tuning note of a lyre–filtered faintly through the arched double doors. Servants passed with careful steps, and attendants in gold-trimmed livery adjusted the final flourishes on the tapestries flanking the entry.

Kal stood to one side, beside a carved pillar of marble, her expression composed, her posture still but commanding. Liam stood at her right, arms crossed, his coat stark against the warm glow of the sconces.

Then came the footsteps. Jarreth rounded the corner first, regal in tailored white and gold. His shoulders were squared, his chin high, but his eyes betrayed him the moment they caught sight of Kal. He stopped short, just slightly. Enough to draw attention. Enough to lose the composure he'd worked to pin in place.

"My Lady," he said, inclining his head. "You look..." He faltered.

Raoul followed close behind, slower and smiling, his gaze sweeping over Kal with less hesitation. "Radiant," he finished smoothly. "And lethal. Like a particularly elegant sword."

Jarreth shot him a look, horrified.

Kal arched a brow, her tone dry. "Is this a coordinated attempt at flattery or did you both simply lose your wits at the same moment?"

Raoul grinned, unfazed. "I lose mine regularly. He, however, has no such excuse."

Jarreth looked as though he wanted the floor to open beneath him. "My apologies, I meant no–"

Alden arrived behind them with impeccable timing, dressed in a robe of deep crimson, his crown subtle against his dark, swept-back hair. He took in the tableau at once and gave a sigh touched with theatrical despair.

"Gods, boys. She's not a relic to be worshipped or a beast to be circled. She's standing right there. Try to hold on to what little pride you still possess."

Kal said nothing, but the corner of her mouth moved, just barely.

"Come," Alden said, sweeping past them. "If you dither here any longer, the court will begin to think I've replaced the entire front of the line with statues."

Raoul made a noise of mock offense. Jarreth straightened his coat. Kal stepped forward and took her place at Alden's left. Liam moved to her other side without a word.

The doors opened with the weight of ceremony, the heralds' voices echoing into the hall beyond.

The great hall of Varis had been transformed.

Kal slowed only a fraction as they crossed the threshold, but Liam caught the shift. The high arches still rose in stately brilliance overhead, and the tall windows still spilled light across polished stone. But the dais, the elevated symbol of hierarchy and power, was gone. In its place: long banquet tables set end to end, running the length of the hall. No thrones. No divisions. Just lines of polished wood, silvered cutlery, and carefully arranged autumn blossoms.

For a heartbeat, Kal said nothing. But her eyes scanned the arrangement with quick calculation. Liam did not hide his reaction. His posture tightened immediately, gaze sweeping the open space with thinly veiled disdain. He leaned in just enough for Kal to hear, voice low and sharp.

"This is madness."

Kal's tone was neutral. "It's a feast."

"It's exposure."

Before she could answer, Alden's voice rose just behind them, light and amused.

"You think so little of me."

They turned towards Alden who had a goblet in one hand, his other gesturing toward an arched alcove tucked slightly off to the side–still visible, but set apart.

"I expected as much," he said, smiling. "Which is why your seats are there. I'm indulgent, not reckless."

Kal offered a nod of gratitude.

Alden took another sip from his cup, then disappeared with infuriating grace into the growing throng.

Kal moved toward the alcove, her boots silent on the marble. The table was smaller than the others, but elegantly set, with wide views of the hall and only a single narrow approach. Intentional. Liam circled it once before allowing himself to sit, the tension in his shoulders unrelenting. Kal took her place without hesitation, aware of the eyes that followed her.

Jarreth and Raoul appeared not long after, striding through the crowd with something too casual in their steps to be accidental. They broke from the path leading to the main seating and turned instead toward the alcove.

Liam rose halfway from his chair, his expression already a warning.

"You have assigned seats," he said flatly.

Jarreth faltered, clearly weighing whether to ignore or acknowledge the rebuke.

Raoul saved him the trouble. He threw himself into the empty seat beside Kal with an exaggerated sigh of contentment. "And yet, here we are. It's like fate."

Liam's eyes narrowed. "This isn't protocol."

"No," Raoul agreed brightly, pouring himself a glass of wine. "But then again, neither is she."

Kal said nothing but the faintest smile touched her lips.

Jarreth eased into the seat opposite her, more reserved than his companion, though his gaze lingered on her just long enough for Liam to notice. He stiffened again, but Kal laid a hand briefly on the edge of the table near him to silence him, which was enough.

The feast unfolded in waves of movement and sound–platters of roast venison, golden root vegetables, baked fruits dusted in clove and honey, all paraded forth by servants who moved with the trained grace of ceremony. Wine flowed freely. So did the noise. Kal sat at the table's heart, a calm eye in the storm. The cut of her dress and the weight of her silence did more than draw attention, they commanded it. Yet she seemed untouched by it all, lifting her goblet without flourish, speaking little, watching everything.

Raoul, never one to be deterred by poise, leaned closer under pretense of reaching for the bread.

"You're far too quiet," he murmured, voice low enough not to carry. "How's a man to impress you if you won't toss him a single compliment for his bravery?"

Kal didn't look at him. "It takes more courage to hold your tongue."

Raoul grinned. "Then I must be a coward. Hopeless."

"Hopeless is accurate," Liam muttered darkly from the other side.

Raoul ignored him, lifting his goblet. "To hopelessness, then."

Jarreth, seated just beyond, shifted in his chair and tried for something more reserved.

"I hope this isn't too crowded," he said, gesturing subtly toward the mingled tables. "Feasts here tend to be...less structured. The people like seeing their rulers among them."

"I'm not their ruler," Kal replied, tone smooth.

"No," Jarreth said. "But they're watching you like one."

That earned her attention, brief and sharp.

He didn't flinch.

Across the table, Raoul chewed a mouthful of roasted fig and spoke around it. "He's rehearsed that line. Used it before. On a Dulthair noble, I think."

"I have not," Jarreth snapped, glaring at him.

"Liar. You always go for the ones with sharp eyes and sharp knives."

Kal sipped her wine, unmoved. "And how'd that end for the Dulthair noble?"

"She tried to take him in the garden."

Liam exhaled slowly, setting down his goblet with enough care to make the gesture feel deliberate.

"You're going to lose fingers," he said, staring directly at Raoul. "Maybe more."

Raoul raised his brows in mock concern. "That a threat?"

Liam didn't blink. "A prediction."

"Good to know."

Kal allowed herself the smallest smile, buried behind the rim of her cup. It wasn't their antics that amused her, but Liam's perpetual state of simmering restraint, the way his fingers never quite left the edge of his blade, as if he expected–hoped–someone would give him an excuse.

Raoul and Jarreth went on, undeterred. They bickered lightly over seasoning, over the merits of Varisian cuisine versus the Dunes' sharper fare, over whether Kal would prefer poetry or swordplay in a suitor, though neither asked directly. Jarreth's remarks were always a touch formal, as though trying to play the part of a noble host. Raoul, in contrast, pushed boundaries with a grin and a tilt of his head, confident in the charm he wielded like a weapon.

Kal listened to them both but answered selectively, her wit delivered in well-measured slices, never unkind but always pointed. Her calm, to Liam's dismay, only encouraged them further.

From his place at the edge of the central table, King Alden sipped slowly from a goblet of plum wine, the vintage older than most of the nobles seated nearby. He wasn't watching the feast.

Not really.

His attention was fixed–subtly, steadily–on the alcove tucked just beneath the eastern arch, watching it all unfold like the opening act of a play he hadn't realized he'd commissioned.

Kalithea sat composed, her posture unflinching, her expression mild, yet there was a subtle edge to her silence, a weight behind the stillness that suggested she missed little. To her left and right, Raoul and Jarreth jockeyed for attention in their own distinct manners. Raoul leaned into his mischief, all smirking jests and exaggerated gallantry, while Jarreth seemed caught in some invisible crosscurrent, equal parts prince and man, neither role sitting quite right on his shoulders tonight.

Alden watched as Kal responded with that maddeningly elusive composure of hers, answering with calculated calm, never once flustered. But she didn't ignore them either. She let them try. And, more importantly, she didn't shut them down.

There was something there.

But it was Liam who drew Alden's interest next. The man hadn't touched his wine. He sat like a thundercloud at her side, his posture rigid, jaw clenched, hands forever close to his twin daggers. Every time Raoul leaned too close, every time Jarreth smiled too easily, Liam's expression darkened, until Alden suspected the poor man might leave fingerprints in the wood of the chair. It grew darker still when Jarreth, by some impossible grace, said something that coaxed a laugh from Kal.

Not a smile. *A laugh.* Soft, brief. But unmistakable.

Alden raised a brow, watching his son turn red from collar to cheekbones. He looked like a man who'd stumbled onto sacred ground and hadn't quite realized how deeply his boots were sinking into it. Alden exhaled slowly, setting his goblet down with care. It wasn't the laugh that caught him. It was Jarreth's face after.

The look. The astonishment. The helplessness.

So. There it was. Love, or the first true thrum of it—bright and clumsy, wholly unprepared.

The king exhaled through his nose, not without humor. He had heard Jarreth claim love a dozen times in the past, each declaration more poetic than the last. But none of them had made him look like this. None of them had rattled his composure, or driven him to hold his ground under the killing glare of a brother who looked seconds from planting a fork in someone's neck.

Gods. He's falling.

Not in that theatrical, courtly way boys fall for pretty things with sharp eyes and elegant scorn. No, this was slower, deeper. The kind that didn't burn hot and fast but took root, twisting quietly through the chest when no one was looking. Alden shook his head slowly, lifting his goblet once more. Jarreth had never looked like this before. Not when he courted the jewel of Haldren, not when he broke off that doomed engagement to the Valtair heiress. Those had been games, mutually agreed upon, sweet on the surface with hidden passion in the corridors, but empty underneath.

This was different and if Jarreth thought the path ahead would be smooth—with that brother, that history, that woman—he was either mad or terribly naive.

Possibly both.

Alden smiled ruefully and reached for his wine again, watching the scene unfold with the same interest one might watch a stag wander unaware toward a waiting lion.

"Good luck, son," he murmured beneath his breath. "You're going to need it."

As the last course was cleared and goblets refilled, a soft chime rang out—subtle, but unmistakable. The hall shifted around it. Servants moved with orchestrated preciseness, sweeping away tables and sliding benches aside until the center of the hall lay bare and polished beneath the high chandeliers. The minstrels took their cue. Strings lifted, drums began to pulse, and the noble houses of Varis began to rise, silk and jewels rustling as they flowed toward the newly-formed floor with eager anticipation.

Kal remained seated, her expression blank but unmistakably alert.

Raoul opened his mouth, likely to offer something flippant and far too forward, but a curvaceous redhead in violet lace caught his arm before he could get the words out. She looked *very* familiar with him. One of her hands was already at his shoulder, the other dragging him toward the dance floor with the confidence of a woman who had danced with him many times before and intended to again.

Raoul turned half toward Kal, some excuse forming. But Kal's eyes glittered, and she smirked just slightly.

"Well," she said, voice smooth and sly. "Champion of Varis. Surely you must uphold the highest standards of chivalry."

His eyes narrowed. The redhead blinked, then tossed Kal a look of triumph before dragging Raoul away.

A moment later, a blonde—youthful, coy, and already pouting—made her way toward Jarreth with a smile that telegraphed intimate familiarity. She didn't ask so much as linger in front of him, waiting for the inevitable. Jarreth hesitated. Long enough to draw Kal's attention. Then he offered a dutiful bow and let the girl lead him away, though his backward glance was not so subtle.

Liam made a noise low in his throat.

"Good," he muttered, arms folded. "I was beginning to worry we wouldn't get a moment's peace."

He barely had time to savor the silence before a faint throat-clearing sounded to his left. A young nobleman stood there, nervous but determined, well-groomed in charcoal brocade, his hand twitching slightly at his side as he looked directly at Kal.

"Forgive the intrusion," he said with a small bow. "But might I ask you to dance, my lady?"

Liam's head snapped toward him so quickly the man blanched. Kal hesitated. Only a moment, but it was enough to deepen the flush in the young nobleman's cheeks. His hand remained extended, fingers held steady by sheer will. Across from him, Liam bristled like an angry beast.

Then Kal inclined her head, smooth and cool as frost. "Of course."

The man exhaled in visible relief. She rose, slipping her hand into his. Liam's hand twitched, not toward a weapon, *yet*, but toward warning.

"If you so much as breathe wrong," he said in a voice meant for close quarters, "you'll be dancing with broken knees."

The nobleman paled. Kal said nothing, didn't look back. She let herself be led to the floor with the same grace she wore into battle—calm, unyielding, eyes scanning the room like a queen on patrol. Whatever courage the man had possessed evaporated entirely. He held her lightly, moved with care, and said not a word as they circled once, twice, letting the music guide them without contest.

Kal did not fight the silence. It suited her. And it suited the dozens of eyes watching them from across the room, watching her, specifically. Measuring. Wondering. When the song came to its close, she dipped her head and stepped back with quiet finality. She turned to retreat, but before she could take more than a step, a voice like well-aged mischief greeted her from the edge of the floor.

"And here you said you wouldn't dance."

Alden stood there, brows arched in mock reproach, his hand extended in a far more confident invitation. "And now, here you are. Twirling away in front of my entire court."

Kal gave him a long, narrow look.

"I was ambushed," she said smoothly.

"Yes," he said, with infuriating cheer. "And now I'm striking while you're wounded. Dance with me."

"You're leveraging court optics to trap me."

"Absolutely."

She sighed, but it was the kind of sigh one gave a dog that had gotten into the pastry tray. "You've been planning this."

"Only for days."

"Fine," she said, taking his hand. "But you're not nearly as subtle as you think."

Alden grinned. "And yet here we are."

He led her toward the center as the next song began to swell, the crowd parting with easy grace for the king and the woman who had yet to name herself but who no one could now ignore. Alden led her into the turn without hesitation, his hand firm at her back, his step easy. The music swelled around them—something bright and polished, built to charm rather than stir—and Kal followed his lead, letting the rhythm guide her movements without ever surrendering to it.

"You're handling it well," Alden said conversationally, as if they were strolling the gardens instead of spinning through a ballroom under the eyes of half the nobility. "Your *suitors*, I mean. Sitting between a love-struck prince and his fawning champion. With your brother ready to start a war if either of them dares breathe too close."

Kal's gaze didn't waver, but her brow arched, ever so slightly. "You're enjoying this far too much."

"Of course I am," Alden said, utterly unrepentant. He swept her through another step, his grin still lingering at the corners. "But not for the reasons you think."

He slowed the pace slightly, enough to match the mellowing tempo of the strings, and when he spoke again, there was a softer edge to the amusement in his voice.

"I enjoy seeing you smile, Kalithea."

Her eyes flicked to his, wary and uncertain.

"Months ago," Alden continued, his tone dropping to something quieter, something nearer the truth, "when you and your brother first arrived at my gates...I would not have believed you capable of laughter. Not like that. Not genuine."

Kal said nothing, but Alden didn't falter. He guided her into another turn, letting the music carry them just long enough to ease the weight of his words before he spoke again.

"I should thank you, really."

That drew her focus back, sharp and direct. "For what?"

He met her gaze, steady now. "For trying to teach my son that duty doesn't have to cost him who he is. That the two don't have to be at odds."

Kal blinked, but her step faltered just slightly, enough for Alden to feel it in their rhythm.

He only smiled.

"He'll fight it," he added mildly. "Of course he will. He's always been a stubborn little bastard. But he's listening. That's more than most ever managed, even me."

Kal didn't answer, not right away. The words sat heavy in the air between them, the kind not easily brushed aside.

But Alden, ever the master of timing, said nothing more for the moment. He only twirled her again, slow and graceful, the kind of movement that looked effortless but required absolute trust.

Raoul moved with the mastery of a man long familiar with attention. His steps were graceful, but his mind was far from the dance. The woman in his arms, a curvaceous redhead in a dress better suited for scandal than ceremony, clung to him like she thought he might vanish if she blinked.

"I was beginning to think you'd forgotten me," she purred, tracing a finger along the line of his shoulder. "Or worse...moved on to something *dull.*"

Raoul smiled, though it didn't reach his eyes. "You'll have to narrow that down. I've moved on to quite a few things."

Her laugh was bright and brittle. "Mm. Yes, well. I thought it strange, seeing you glued to the king's guest like a hound at heel. Not your usual flavor, is she?"

He didn't respond, but stiffened slightly.

She leaned in, voice dropping to something more poisonous. "I always assumed you liked your women with a bit more...*warmth.* And fewer knives. Although you used to enjoy being scratched, if I recall."

Raoul guided her through the turn, slow and smooth, his expression controlled. She mistook it for indulgence and pressed on.

"Or is that the game? You chasing something cold and untouchable so the court forgets how many beds you've warmed between campaigns? Because we both know what you are, Raoul. I should know. I've warmed that bed more than once."

That earned a flicker in his gaze.

She smiled, triumphant. "Though, I suppose mystery suits you. Even if it's just a mask for boredom. She barely looks alive. Gods, she looks carved. All that stoic silence...tell me, does she only lie still, too?"

The step broke. Raoul stopped dancing, the music continuing without him. The redhead swayed slightly, caught off guard. He didn't speak right away. When he did, his voice was low, cold enough to bite.

"Is that why you're here? Trying to provoke a reaction because no one's whispered your name since the last winter hunt?"

Her face flushed, but he went on.

"Don't confuse my silence for interest, Mira. I've let far better walk away with a smile just to avoid the mess. But speak about her again, and I'll remind you, *publicly,* how much of a fool you sounded in the dark."

The blush drained from her cheeks, replaced by something pale and tight.

Raoul dipped his head, not a bow but a dismissal. Absolute. Then he turned and walked off the floor, leaving her where she stood, surrounded by silk and music and the thick scent of her own bruised pride.

The final note of the dance fell like a bell across the ballroom, and Alden, ever the showman beneath the crown, stepped back with a courtly flourish. His palm released hers, but his gaze lingered, twinkling with a mischief that hadn't dulled in decades.

"I believe I've held the floor long enough to make a point," he said, voice pitched just loud enough for nearby listeners. "Best not let it be said I stood in the way of young hearts and older rumors."

Before Kal could respond, another figure was already stepping forward from the crowd.

Jarreth.

His approach lacked hesitation. Not brash, not overly confident but sure, like a man finally on ground he understood. His shoulders were squared, his smile faint but genuine. He didn't glance at the onlookers, though their murmurs had grown audibly louder as he crossed the marble. The prince stopped just short of her, bowing low.

"My lady," he said, his voice steady, "might I have the pleasure of this dance?"

Kal didn't move right away. She could feel the weight of every eye drawn toward them. The speculative hush rising like fog through the pillars. Nobles leaning into each other with sudden urgency. Already, the whispers had begun weaving themselves into court myth, some claiming a secret betrothal, others spinning tales of old bloodlines and hidden heirs.

Alden gave an exaggerated hum and murmured over her shoulder, "Well, this should be interesting." Then he clapped Jarreth once on the back, hard enough to make the younger man stagger half a step, and turned away, vanishing into the crowd with the easy timing of a man who had just set something in motion and intended to enjoy the fallout from a safe distance.

Kal looked at Jarreth again. That same smile met her. Open. Quietly hopeful.

She arched a brow, lips tilting ever so slightly. "You've grown bold."

A flicker of color touched his cheeks, but he didn't retreat. "Only a little," he admitted. "Only now."

Her gaze lingered on him a moment longer–then, finally, she extended her hand. He took it gently, carefully, as though afraid the moment might slip from his grasp. Their fingers met, and Jarreth felt it like a spark. No lightning or firestorm, just something that settled deep and sudden. A stillness. A gravity.

And then he was moving again, guiding her to the floor with quiet reverence.

Jarreth moved with a grace that surprised even himself. The music swelled around them, lilting and intricate, and still he did not falter. His hand rested on Kal's back, the other holding hers, and for once his smile was not strained by effort or uncertainty. It was soft. Broad. Real.

"You're smiling too much," Kal said, her tone teasing, but her gaze not unkind.

"That's a bold accusation," he murmured, stepping in rhythm as though the tempo had been written to match his heartbeat. "One might even call it slander."

She tilted her head just slightly. "Here you are, grinning like a boy handed his first sword."

He laughed, genuine and low, not for show. "Can you blame me?"

She didn't answer. Not at first. Because for a moment, just a breath, she saw him not as the prince, not as the figure orbiting her days with a mix of hesitation and hunger for approval, but as the man beneath it all. Confident. Composed. Dressed in finery that suited him far too well, his golden hair catching the firelight and his posture so thoroughly relaxed it became clear this was not unfamiliar ground to him.

And gods, he was handsome.

She did *not* like where that thought led.

So she turned the path of the moment, shifting her weight with the next step and raising a brow in calculated ease. "This version of you," she said slowly, "where has he been hiding?"

His smile deepened. "You find him agreeable?"

"I find him suspicious. You're far too charming for someone who trips over himself at breakfast."

"Ah." His voice lowered, laced with warmth. "That's one of the more maddening things about you."

Kal met his eyes, her gaze cool, questioning.

Jarreth's gaze didn't waver. "That the moment you look at me, all the rest of it—every word I meant to say, every clever line—it all just disappears."

His admission wasn't desperate. It wasn't even self-deprecating. Just honest and it settled between them. Kal shifted her steps slightly with the turn of the music, letting him lead her. Her posture remained poised, controlled, but there was a faint curve at the edge of her mouth now, one that wasn't quite a smile.

"So..." she murmured, eyes lifting just enough to catch his, "the blonde."

Jarreth blinked. "The–?"

"From earlier. She looked...familiar. *Intimately so.*" Her tone was light, but the phrasing was deliberate.

A faint flush crept up his neck, and he looked momentarily stricken before recovering with a rueful breath and a quiet, helpless laugh.

"She's the daughter of a northern baron," he said carefully. "Our families have...entertained the idea before."

Kal arched a brow. "And by entertained, you mean...?"

Jarreth gave her a long-suffering look, though the corners of his mouth twitched. "I was seventeen. She was...*persistent.*"

Kal hummed. "And Raoul's?"

He coughed. "Persistent in equal measure. And considerably less subtle."

Kal let out a sound that could have been amusement—low, dry, but unmistakably pleased. "You two must be the heartbreak of the whole court. Good thing I always arrive after you've been seated, the swooning would surely deafen me."

He met her gaze again, and this time, the grin stayed. "I'm not sure about all that."

"No?"

He tilted his head slightly, the candlelight casting soft lines along his cheekbones, gilding the gold in his hair. "Most of it's theater. A name. A title. People love the idea of a prince more than the man beneath it."

Kal regarded him for a moment, long enough that it could have been silence, or something heavier.

"And yet," she said at last, softly, "you're holding your own tonight."

He didn't answer immediately. Because he knew what she meant. This—this banter, this push and pull, the rhythm they'd never quite found in conversation until now—it wasn't something he was forcing. It wasn't a line, and it wasn't calculated.

It just was.

"I suppose I'm not trying to be anything," he said finally, voice quieter. "Not with you."

Alden stood just behind the outer circle of dancers, arms loosely crossed, wine untouched in one hand. The light played across his silver-threaded collar and the fine edge of his signet ring, but his attention was fixed squarely on the dance floor.

"Your sister is holding her own," he said mildly.

Beside him, Liam did not reply. His gaze was locked on the prince. More precisely, on the prince's hand—resting a little too easily at Kal's waist, fingers brushing the folds of her gown with every slow turn.

Alden glanced at Liam out of the corner of his eye and gave a soft, knowing laugh. "If you scowl any harder, I'm fairly certain you'll crack the stonework."

Liam didn't move. "He's too close."

"It's a dance," Alden replied. "Not a duel."

Liam's jaw tightened.

Alden took a long breath, letting it out through his nose. Then, in a tone gentler than before, he said, "You both deserve more than survival, you know."

That earned him a sharp look, knife-edge and unforgiving.

"She's not ready," Liam said quietly. "Not for what either of them is circling."

"No," Alden agreed. "But perhaps they aren't seeking an end. Just the beginning of something different."

Liam's silence was louder this time.

Alden waited. Then, after a moment: "Don't make the mistake of trying to preserve her life so tightly she forgets how to live it."

"I'm not—"

"You are," Alden cut in, but without heat. "And I understand. But this burden you carry—this need to guard her from everything, even her own feelings—it will hollow you both if you let it."

Liam's gaze didn't shift from the floor. From Kal's quiet, confident form as she danced beneath the chandeliers, her laughter drifting faintly between the notes of the string quartet.

"She was never meant for ordinary," Liam muttered.

Alden nodded. "That doesn't mean she was meant to be alone."

Liam frowned at that, but Alden, ever the opportunist, had already turned his attention elsewhere. With a subtle tilt of his head, he gestured toward the edge of the floor—where a group of noblewomen stood, each pretending not to stare, each pretending not to whisper, their fans fluttering like the wings of small, brightly plumed birds. Their eyes flicked toward Liam, then away, then back again.

"By the way," Alden said, offhanded, "one of them has been asking about you since your first court appearance. The one in garnet. Daughter of the Count of Alderra, I believe. She has excellent aim with a bow, if you value practical courtship."

Liam turned toward him, stunned. "You're matchmaking?"

"I'm bored," Alden replied cheerfully. "And you look like you've forgotten how to live."

Liam opened his mouth to protest, but Alden clapped him lightly on the shoulder before he could speak.

"She'll be fine," the king said, his tone low but assured. "You've built a life on being her sword. No one questions your vigilance. But for tonight—"

He gave Liam the smallest of nudges toward the nearest column.

"—try being a man, not a shadow. You won't combust if you exhale."

Liam gave him a long, flat look.

Alden grinned.

"Go on," he said, eyes dancing. "The world can wait."

The music swelled, strings weaving a graceful thread through the high-vaulted air of the grand hall. Kal moved easily, matching Jarreth's pace as he led her through the next turn. His hand at her waist was steady, no hesitations or second-guessing. Gone was the awkward noble she'd first met, all nervous bows and stammered greetings. In his place stood a man who knew the rhythm of a room and had found, at last, the courage to step into it.

She gave him a small smile, genuine if faint, her expression softening for the briefest of moments.

Then, as he turned her with a smooth pivot, Kal's eyes caught motion near the edge of the ballroom. She nearly missed her step. Alden stood just beyond the line of dancers, half-concealed by a marble column, nudging Liam forward like a general prodding a reluctant soldier into battle. Liam's glare was thunderous, but the king met it with maddening calm.

Then Liam's gaze shifted and met hers. Kal didn't look away. Her smile deepened, subtle but unmistakable, and she gave a small nod of encouragement. Liam's scowl turned positively volcanic.

And yet he moved. Back straightening with wariness, he turned toward the small group of noblewomen gathered near the tapestry-lined wall. A few of them had clearly noticed him now—posture shifting, fans rising like shields, eyes sharpening. One brunette in particular stepped forward, her dress the shade of deep forest wine, her expression nervous but hopeful.

Liam hesitated, then took a single, begrudging step into their midst.

Kal bit back a grin.

"You smiled," Jarreth said softly.

She glanced back at him. "Did I?"

"A real one. Not the one you wear when you're politely tolerating people."

He held her eyes for a moment longer than she expected, something tender in the way his brow lifted, the way his expression softened beneath it. Then, quieter still:

"It's beautiful."

The words weren't hungry, or rehearsed, or weightless. They simply were.

Kal had heard compliments her entire life. Words spoken in awe, in envy, in lust. Some whispered, others snarled like accusations. She'd been called divine, unearthly, intoxicating and worse. But this landed differently. It wasn't what he said. It was the tone—gentle, uncertain, soft in the way someone might speak of light filtered through a stained-glass window, knowing they could not touch it, just admire it.

She met his gaze. Just once. Just long enough to see he meant it.

Then the music ended. The final chord rippled through the air like the exhale of a long-held breath, and Kal stepped back from Jarreth's hold with relief, her mask settling smoothly into place once more.

Raoul swept in the moment Kal turned from Jarreth, one hand catching hers with a smooth flourish, the other guiding her into the next dance before she could think to decline. The music shifted, the pace light and lilting, and Raoul moved with it effortlessly–steps confident, posture precise, smile dangerously disarming. He stepped in like a man who'd never been told no, spinning her into the next dance, his arm settling at her waist with a familiarity that would have irritated her from anyone else.

"My lady," he began smoothly, tone low and coaxing, "you must know that when you entered the hall tonight, the stars themselves mourned the theft of their finest light."

Kal arched a brow.

Undeterred, he grinned and continued, "I'd offer to steal the moon for you, but I fear it would pale beside your eyes."

She gave him a long, assessing look as he spun her through a turn.

"Those lines must be worn to threads by now," she said lightly, voice even. "Used so often they've frayed at the ends."

Raoul blinked, still smiling, but a flicker of uncertainty passed behind his eyes.

Kal stepped in with the next movement of the dance, her gaze never leaving his. "Rehearsed to the point of instinct. I imagine flirting comes as easily to you as breathing."

His smile faltered for the briefest second.

"What I can't quite puzzle out," she continued, her tone conversational but sharp, "is what I ever said or did that made you think I'd be impressed by something proven on a dozen other women."

Raoul's breath caught.

Before he could answer, she tilted her head, lips curving faintly–not warmly. Not yet. "Unless, of course, it was the return of the redhead that inspired such illustrious declarations."

That drew a laugh from him, quick and genuine, the kind that slipped through his guard.

"She was...a relic," he said, eyes glinting. "Hardly inspiring."

Kal didn't smile. She merely held his gaze, unblinking.

He tried again. "You wound me, truly. I come bearing charm and wit, and you accuse me of...recycling."

She leaned in slightly, voice soft but pointed. "I'm not accusing you of anything. I'm just not interested in pretending you're something you're not."

He looked at her then, not with the polished grin or half-lidded glances that had earned him more than one lover's sigh. He looked, truly, as though he hadn't expected to be seen past the shine. And he didn't yet know what to do with it.

Kal watched that realization settle behind his eyes, and for once, didn't press further.

The music continued, and so did they, moving in perfect time while the hall spun around them unaware. Raoul recovered, the flicker of truth behind his smile retreating into its usual lines. But something in his gaze lingered, more focused now, sharpened not by charm but by intent. He shifted his hold slightly, guiding her through a turn that brought her just a fraction closer, the touch of his hand at her waist firm, familiar. Not presumptuous. But close enough to draw notice.

Kal did not step away, she didn't lean in either. Instead, she watched him.

"Tell me," he said smoothly, his voice pitched low beneath the rustle of silk and the hum of strings, "what lines would work on you, then? If not the moon, or the stars, or whatever metaphor you think I overused."

Her eyes narrowed just a touch, a glint of amusement sparking. "You think you're close enough to guess?"

"Not yet," he admitted, without shame. "But I plan to be."

She arched a brow, but he pressed forward, eyes keen despite the smile.

"You wear your guard like armor," he said. "Even when you smile. Especially when you smile. I wonder if you've ever let anyone know what's behind it."

Kal's expression didn't shift. "And if I haven't?" she asked.

"Then maybe I'd like to be the first."

That time, she didn't answer.

Raoul watched her carefully, steering them into a slower part of the rhythm, holding her gaze for a heartbeat longer than was strictly polite. "You always look like you're about to run," he said quietly. "Even when you're standing still."

Kal searched his eyes again, trying to feel out what was going on behind all the charm. She didn't notice how his hand had slid lower along her back, into a much more *intimate* position.

But Liam did.

From across the hall, where he danced with the soft-eyed brunette still chattering at his side, Liam's gaze locked on the pair. His partner's hand rested lightly against his shoulder, but he barely noticed. Every muscle had tensed beneath the fine black fabric of his coat, and though his expression remained stone, the storm behind his eyes turned violent. He saw the way Raoul leaned in, the way Kal tilted her head, no trace of tension in her posture. Worse, he saw the brief confusion in her expression, the kind that slipped in when someone caught you off-guard and made you feel something you weren't expecting. Something unwelcome.

Unfamiliar.

Liam exhaled through his nose, sharp and slow, and turned the brunette with more force than the music required. She let out a surprised laugh, oblivious.

The end of this song. That was all Kal was getting.

Then he would take her out of there—before her smile deepened, before Raoul's hands grew bolder, and before Kal let that unfamiliar softness take root.

Raoul said nothing at first, but something in his expression had softened—less polished now, less constructed. He looked at her as though he were trying to read a language he only halfway knew, one written in the flicker of her lashes and the precise tilt of her chin.

Then Kal spoke, her voice lower than before, a note of amusement ringing through. "You're not the first to try and understand me," she said, "But you might be the most confident."

Raoul chuckled, his posture faltering for a half-step in their rhythm as her meaning landed. The music rose around them, but the space between them had changed, tense, quiet and fragile.

And then it broke, suddenly and abruptly. Liam's hand closed around Kal's elbow, firm and unrelenting. She blinked, startled, as he pulled her sharply from Raoul's grasp.

"Liam—"

He didn't stop. Didn't let her twist free. The crowd parted in startled silence, nobles pretending not to see what was happening while very clearly watching it unfold.

Kal hissed under her breath, as he dragged her from the ballroom. "Have you lost your gods damned mind?" she snapped once the doors closed behind them. "You think you can just put your hands on me like that? You think I needed you to *save* me—"

"You needed *someone* to pull you out," Liam growled, spinning on her the moment they passed beyond the arch of the ballroom doors, voices still rising and falling behind them like another world. "You think I didn't see it? The way you looked at him?"

Kal froze. Her breath caught, eyes narrowing. "You're making a scene because I danced. That's all it was."

"It wasn't *just* a dance!" His voice cracked, low but raw. "You let Raoul's hand slip lower. You didn't even *flinch*. And Jarreth? You let him pull you close, you *laughed*, Kal. Do you even realize what you're doing?"

She opened her mouth, but he didn't let her speak.

"You don't get to lose control like this. Not now. Not without Arjun to anchor you, *you* said that. You swore it. And now you're softening, and smiling, and acting like—like this is something you can just *have*—"

Liam's voice dropped, bitter, hoarse. "If you *feel* something for one of them, really *feel* it, are you ready for that? Do you even know what comes after? Do you know how to keep control of yourself, of your power, *once you let someone in?*"

Kal's silence was thunderous.

And Liam, furious now, pressed the final blow. "Look me in the eye and tell me you believe they'll stay once they see it. Once they see *you*. All of it."

The words struck. Kal's face stilled, every flicker of emotion folding inward, sealed tight. Her voice, when it came, was cold.

"Thank you," she said softly. "For reminding me that no matter what path I take—no matter what I build, or bury, or *survive*—in the end, I'll still only ever be what's beneath it. A thing made of shadows."

She tore her arm from his grasp, eyes gleaming with fury—not the volatile, reckless kind, but a glacial calm that made her seem carved from steel.

Then she turned and walked away, boots echoing sharply down the marble corridor, leaving Liam alone in the hush of the palace's outer hall, the music of the ballroom echoing faintly behind him like a door closed on something neither of them knew how to name.

Some Ghosts Still Bleed

The stone paths of Alden's private garden wound in gentle curves through thickets of dusk-blooming jasmine and carefully trimmed hedges, the air rich with their scent. Sconces burned low and gold along the walls, flickering light across the ivy-strewn columns. Kal walked in silence, her heels brushing faintly over the gravel. The noise of the hall had long since faded behind her.

She reached the center fountain without thought, drawn as if by instinct. The water played in delicate arcs from the carved mouths of fish and lions, their old stone faces worn smooth by time. Flamelight from a nearby brazier caught in the rippling pool, turning every wave into a glimmering thread of bronze and gold.

Kal sat slowly at the base of the fountain, one hand curling against the cool marble edge. She did not look toward the doors, nor glance behind her. For once, she let herself simply *be*, without armor or agenda. The night's moments looped behind her eyes—the music, the shifting candlelight, the way Jarreth's hand had steadied her at the turn, how Raoul's touch had lingered a breath too long. She thought of Liam, of the fury in his voice, the truth behind it like a blade carefully slipped between ribs.

I saw the look in your eyes, he'd said. *You're softening.*

She'd wanted to deny it. Had *almost* said as much. But now, watching the water trace endless circles in the bowl of the fountain, she could admit—at least to herself—that something had cracked open tonight. Not obvious, but enough to feel the ache of it.

The problem was, softness had never led her anywhere safe.

Every person who had glimpsed the girl beneath the weapon had done the same thing in the end: they had run, or they had tried to chain her. Her beauty was the only part the world had ever admired without flinching, and even that admiration had teeth. Men desired it, women distrusted it, and rulers had seen it only as another tool to be sharpened and used. But the power behind her eyes, the shadows that stirred when her control slipped, *that* had never inspired love. Only fear. Or greed.

She leaned forward slightly, resting her arms on her knees, watching the firelight dance across the water's surface. It shimmered like the edges of memory, moments not quite real, or maybe too real to look at directly. Her thoughts spiraled through them, quiet and slow. Perhaps Liam was right. Perhaps she wasn't ready. Not for softness, not for warmth. Certainly not for the tiny fragment of aching *hope* that stirred when Jarreth smiled too gently, or Raoul held her gaze too long.

The shadows stirred faintly in the edges of her vision, brushing the air like the hem of a passing thought. She felt them gather, restless and uneasy, drawn by the break in her control. But she closed her eyes, breathing in deeply, holding the air until the pulse of it steadied her. Then exhaled slow.

Not tonight. The shadows receded, grudgingly, but without fight.

Kal opened her eyes again and let the stillness return. The garden was still save for the soft lilt of the fountain and the distant hum of celebration fading into the night. The fountain water shimmered again, gold firelight catching on its surface in a way that was almost too perfect, too still. Kal's gaze drifted, drawn into the gleam without meaning to. The ripple of light deepened...warped...*shifted.*

And the garden vanished.

The scent of jasmine and smoke was gone. In its place, ash and iron. Wet stone. The low, guttural rasp of someone struggling to breathe.

Her stomach turned, the taste of copper thick on her tongue.

Arjun lay broken before her again, though not as she'd seen him in dreams. The ruin of him was *familiar* now, injuries showing she'd seen earned in previous dreams. She could see it clearly enough to mark what had changed. The wounds were older. Some scabbed, torn open again. Blood dried to brown, crusted over bruises already turning purple-black. One of his legs was twisted at the knee, the joint swollen grotesquely, clearly never allowed to heal. His face was half-shadowed, lip split, a gash running through his brow, but one eye remained open.

Open and *aware.*

Chains clinked softly as he moved. Not lifted, there was no strength left in his limbs for that. Just a twitch, a flinch as someone stepped into view.

Booted feet. Pale gloves. That same calm voice.

"You're enduring well. That's admirable. But not particularly useful."

Kal felt the cold then, sharp and precise. She hadn't noticed it before, but now her breath fogged in the air, curling just like *theirs.*

Whoever *they* were. Whoever kept returning.

The gloved figure knelt beside him, and from beneath their cloak drew something curved and jagged. Not a blade. Another brand, rusted. Crusted with old blood. The iron hissed against the stones as it was set in the coals.

Kal tried to look away.

She couldn't.

She watched as the figure pressed a hand to Arjun's spine, steadying him. Arjun made a noise then, not pain. Not yet. Just a breath that shook with anticipation. Resignation. And then they pressed the brand to his chest. His body *convulsed*. The scream that tore from his throat was worse than any she'd heard in war, worse than the cries of the dying or the begging–it was a sound without hope, without pride, without language. His legs kicked weakly against the floor, but the chains didn't budge. Smoke lifted from his flesh. Kal could *smell* it. The burn. The blood. The ruin of it.

She couldn't breathe. She wanted to move, to do something, *anything*, but her body would not answer. So instead, she screamed his name.

And then his head jerked up. Not blindly. Not in pain.

At her.

His eye locked with hers, raw, wild and disbelieving. The chains rattled again as his shoulders twisted. And for the briefest moment, fear crossed his face. Not of them. Of *her*.

"No!" he shouted, hoarse, voice breaking–but *still looking at her*. "No, you can't–"

The vision *snapped*.

She gasped.

The world returned all at once: the garden, the night, the firelight. Her back hit stone, and then she slipped, falling with a splash into the fountain. Cold water closed over her head, stealing her breath in a rush.

She came up choking, drenched, the firelight above her warped through a thousand glittering ripples. Her hair clung to her face. Water dripped from her lashes as she grasped the basin's carved edge, breath ragged, chest heaving.

Droplets clung to her skin, chilled air needling through her soaked clothing. Kal kneeled bracing herself against the edge, half-drenched and breathless, when she heard the unmistakable sound of boots pounding across stone.

Liam's voice cracked through the silence, sharp and panicked.

"By all the cursed gods, Kal–what the hell happened?"

He was already at her side, grabbing her arm with both hands, half-checking her for injury before helping her to her feet. His expression twisted somewhere between rage and fear.

She didn't answer right away.

The shadows had fled. The vision was gone. But her hands still trembled.

He steadied her, his hands rough but sure. "Did someone come at you? Did they follow you out here?"

Kal shook her head, wet curls clinging to her cheeks. "No. I–" She paused, exhaled slowly. Her voice was steady when she said, "I think... Arjun is *alive.*"

Liam went still. "What?"

"I saw him. Not just a dream. Not like before." Her voice dropped as she added, "He saw me, Liam. He looked straight at me."

For a moment, nothing moved. Then Liam cursed low under his breath, tearing his coat from his shoulders and swinging it around hers. She didn't argue as he drew it closed, then placed a firm hand between her shoulder blades.

"Inside. Now."

She let him guide her, soaked boots leaving a trail down the corridor. Neither spoke. The palace was quiet in this wing–curtained off from music, firelight, and feasting. Her skin still ached from the cold, but it was the image burned behind her eyes that unsettled her more than the night air.

When they reached the threshold of their rooms, Liam pushed open the doors, steering her past the antechamber and toward the hearth. He gestured sharply, and she sank onto the bench before the fire with a glare.

"I'm not a child," she muttered, tugging the coat tighter.

"You look like you just crawled out of a river, and you're shaking," Liam snapped. He didn't raise his voice, but it cut clean. "You'll sit there and warm up. You'll drink whatever I find that doesn't taste like ash. And you'll tell me, clearly, what the fuck you meant by *Arjun may still be alive.*"

Liam cursed under his breath as he rummaged through the sideboard, finding nothing but cold wine and dried fruit. He slammed the cupboard shut, jaw clenched, and crossed the room to the small silver bell pull. She opened her mouth once, and he shot her a look that silenced it.

"Just shut up for once," he snapped. "And let me handle it."

Before she could reply, Doddard appeared with his usual efficiency. The old steward took one long look at Kal–dripping, wrapped in Liam's coat, skin pale in the firelight–and raised an eyebrow.

Liam didn't give him a chance to ask. "Tea. Herbal. Hot enough to burn."

Doddard inclined his head and left without a sound.

Liam was back to moving before the door even clicked shut. He pulled off his coat from her shoulders, tossing it aside and reaching to unfasten the clasps of her wet layers without hesitation. Kal swatted his hands away.

"I can undress myself."

He gave her a scowl but stepped back, turning his back and holding one hand behind him.

When her soaked gown dropped into his grip, he yanked it away and moved quickly, dragging open his bedside chest to fetch a thick linen shirt and a bundle of furs. He dropped them at her side and went to stir the fire into higher flame, returning to wrap the furs around her the moment she'd changed.

She caught his wrist as he tucked the edges in.

"I'm fine," she said evenly, meeting his eyes. "Liam. Calm down."

His mouth opened, closed again. He looked at her for a long moment, the hard edge in his face softening, but only slightly.

Doddard returned with the tea. Liam took it without a word, poured it, and shoved the steaming cup into her hands.

Then he dropped onto the stool before her, elbows on his knees, eyes sharp.

"What did you mean," he asked, voice low, "when you said you think Arjun is alive?"

Kal drew the furs closer around her shoulders, her fingers curled around the tea for warmth more than taste. The fire crackled softly behind Liam, casting flickers of gold across the stone. She looked at the flames instead of his face.

"I've been dreaming of him," she said at last, voice low. "For weeks. Maybe longer."

Liam didn't speak. He watched her with that still, unyielding attention that had always unsettled most men. But Kal had grown up with it. She knew it meant he was listening.

"At first I thought it was just grief," she continued. "That my mind didn't know how to let go, so it dragged him back each night to punish me for surviving. The dreams were always brutal. Always vivid. But I could still wake up and remind myself they weren't real."

She swallowed hard. "Then... they started bleeding into the day. Flickers. Moments. Like a seam had torn somewhere. I'd blink and feel like I'd been standing in two places at once."

Liam's brow tightened, but he didn't interrupt.

"I thought it was exhaustion," she went on. "Maybe I never let myself actually mourn. Maybe I just broke somewhere under the surface and this is how it's showing. But tonight..." Her grip on the mug tightened. "Tonight was different."

She lifted her gaze slowly to meet his.

"He saw me."

Liam's breath caught.

Kal nodded, slowly, voice steadier now. "Not like a dream. Not like memory. He looked *at* me, Liam. His eyes found mine and he was terrified. Not of what was being done to him. Not of the men. Of *seeing me.* Like he knew I shouldn't be there. And then he screamed."

She paused, letting the words settle into the silence between them.

"I don't know what it was. It didn't feel like the shadows. It wasn't the kind of magic Arjun taught me either. It was...something else. But every time, it gets sharper. Closer. Tonight, I fell backward into the fountain because it felt like *I was there.*"

Liam finally leaned back slightly, the tension still sharp in his shoulders.

"I don't have proof," Kal admitted. "I don't have anything except my gut. But it's stirring. Like something's reaching for me across the veil and I–" Her voice faltered. "I think he's alive."

Liam scrubbed a hand through his hair, already beginning to pace. The firelight flickered against the stone walls, chasing his shadow across the room like something restless and cornered.

"These visions–" he began, stopping short and turning to her, "what exactly do you see? Besides him. What's *around* him? Anything recognizable?"

Kal shook her head slowly. "Nothing clear. It's always dark. Cramped. The walls don't feel like new stone. Some kind of rot. Crude and damp. And there's... smoke. Always a kind of haze, like the air's wrong."

Liam's jaw worked, but he didn't interrupt.

"There's no sunlight," she added. "No natural light at all. The only glow comes from iron sconces. They cast more shadow than warmth. It doesn't feel like the palace dungeons, or anywhere Rhaen's flayers took me to. That place was colder, too clean in its cruelty. This...this feels rotted."

He cursed under his breath and resumed pacing. "There could be a thousand pits like that between here and Dulthair. No markings? No accents? No uniforms? Nothing we can trace?"

"I've tried to remember something, anything that would help," she said, her voice tight with frustration. "But they're always hooded or masked. And tonight, it all happened so fast. There were iron rings in the walls. Chains. But that's not enough."

Liam let out a breath that sounded more like a growl. "So what are we supposed to do, Kal? Search every cellar, every dungeon from here to the coast? If it's not in Varis or under the flayer network, we're blind. We don't even know *when* it's happening."

Kal didn't flinch. She met his gaze with firm resolve.

"Then we find someone who *isn't* blind," she said. "Someone who can track a name without a trail. Someone who finds people the world tries to forget."

Liam narrowed his eyes. "You think someone like that exists?"

"They have to," she said.

He exhaled, disbelieving. "You're talking about chasing ghosts."

"I'm talking about saving one," she said sharply. "If there's *even a chance* Arjun is alive, Liam—we *owe* it to him to try. We do not stop."

Her voice didn't rise, but it landed like a command. Final. Unmoving.

And for a long breath, Liam said nothing.

Then he nodded once, slowly.

"All right," he said. "Then we find your ghost-hunter."

Kalithea hadn't left the eastern wing in three days. The tables in Alden's map room had been cleared of their ceremonial clutter, now blanketed in scrolls and faded parchment, regional charts and relics of a kingdom that no longer existed. Elandra, once whole, unfurled before her in fragments—broken borders, dead routes, towns renamed or abandoned. The ink on many of the older maps had begun to bleed or fade, the memories of a conquered land smudged into near-nonsense.

And yet she pored over each one with the same sharp focus. She moved her fingers across mountain ranges and faded trade roads with the intensity of someone searching for the name of a ghost.

She didn't eat much. Doddard brought her food in the late hours, which she ignored more often than not. She hadn't spoken more than a sentence to Liam since the night by the fountain. When she slept—if she slept—it was sitting upright, a map still clutched in her lap and a candle burned low beside her.

Across the palace, Jarreth leaned back in one of the council room chairs, arms folded across his chest, staring blankly at the ceiling while Raoul paced in the window alcove like a soldier deprived of war.

"Nothing," Jarreth muttered. "Not a word. Not a glimpse."

Raoul dragged a hand down his face. "She vanished. *Again.* Like the ball never happened."

"Like we imagined the entire thing," Jarreth added bitterly. "I thought we were making progress. She laughed. She *smiled.* I nearly dropped dead in the middle of the floor."

"I *heard* the laugh," Raoul said, pointing. "And she didn't stab either of us. That alone was a political breakthrough."

They fell silent for a moment, both of them staring past the hearth, the silence drawing out too long.

Jarreth shifted. "Do you think it was Liam?"

Raoul snorted. "I think Liam is always three steps away from dragging her out of a room by the hair if he thinks we're breathing too close."

"He didn't use to glare at me as much," Jarreth muttered.

"Probably didn't see you as a threat back then."

"I'm *not* a threat."

Raoul gave him a look.

Jarreth stared into the fire. "She has this way of looking at you like she already knows what you're going to say. And then when you *do* say something clever, or charming, she stares straight through it. Like she's measuring whether you mean it or if it's just another pretty line."

Raoul didn't answer right away. Instead, he sat down across from him and leaned forward on his elbows.

"I've met a lot of women," he said at last. "More than I could name, more than I *should* name. And for the most part, you play the part, you charm, you win. It's a game. You don't think too hard about it. But *her?*"

He shook his head.

"She makes you want to mean it. Gods help you, you try."

Jarreth let out a soft laugh. "I thought I was losing my mind."

Raoul raised a brow. "You are. So am I."

They sat in silence again, the weight of it less comfortable this time.

Outside, dusk began to fall. Still, the doors to the eastern wing remained closed.

And inside, beneath the aching glow of fading candlelight, Kalithea bent over the thirtieth useless map of her fallen country and whispered under her breath, "Come on, Arjun. Give me *something*."

The candlelight flickered low against the worn edges of the map she'd been staring at for hours. Her eyes burned from lack of sleep, her patience frayed beyond repair. Kal pushed the parchment aside with a sweep of her arm and sat back hard in her chair, pinching the bridge of her nose.

"This isn't working," she muttered.

Liam, seated nearby with arms crossed and his posture tense, didn't look up. "You don't say."

Kal dropped her hand and stared at the map room ceiling. "We need to trigger it. Another vision."

His head turned sharply. "Absolutely not."

She looked at him then. "We can't sit here hoping he screams loud enough for me to hear again."

"You don't know *what* that was," Liam snapped. "You ended up in a freezing fountain, Kal. The shadows were stirred, you don't even remember how close you came to—"

"I *remember*," she cut in, voice low and sharp. "I remember *all* of it."

He stood, the chair scraping harshly against the stone. "You want to go chasing that again? What, hope it rips you back under so you can catch a glimpse of where he's bleeding out this time?"

Kal stood as well. "We don't have another lead. We need something, Liam."

"There has to be another way."

"There isn't." She stepped closer, voice tight with control. "Unless you know some way to *will* a vision into existence—"

They both stopped. The silence between them stretched.

Liam's brows furrowed. "They've all come after something. The courtyard. The garden. The ball..."

He trailed off.

Kal's eyes narrowed. "What are you getting at?"

He crossed his arms again. "All of them happened after long, sustained interactions with the prince or his champion. *Proximity. Emotion. Distraction.* It was always after them."

Kal scoffed, nearly laughing. "You think *they* trigger it? Please."

"You said it yourself, it doesn't feel like the shadows. Or the Fae. But what if it's not coming from you at all?"

She stilled.

Liam pressed, slower now. "What if the magic's bleeding through from *his* end? What if the visions happen not when you're quiet or waiting but when your guard's down, when you're distracted by feelings?"

Kal shook her head. "Then we're right back where we started. I'd have to sit here doing nothing, just *waiting* until the torture got bad enough to reach across the world again."

Her words hung in the air.

The frustration that followed was quieter than before, more hollow. Neither of them liked what that meant.

Kal sat down again and stared at the edge of the map table, her voice low. "We can't keep hoping he screams loud enough to break through."

Kal's fingers curled against the edge of the map table. Then she turned her head slowly and fixed Liam with a look that cut through the haze of shared exhaustion.

"I'm going to ask them," she said. "Raoul. Jarreth. If there's anyone in Varis, or beyond, who can find someone with no trail, they'll know."

Liam's jaw clenched as if he'd bitten down on glass. "You can't be serious."

"I am," she said flatly.

"You want to go crawling to *them* for help?" His voice rose. "After that ridiculous display at the ball? After watching Raoul's hands—"

"I noticed," she said sharply.

His expression darkened. "Not soon enough."

Kal let out a breath through her nose, slow and steady. "And what, Liam? You plan to throw Raoul into another wall to teach him proper *hand placement?*"

He didn't answer, but the look in his eyes was answer enough.

She folded her arms. "Do you have a better suggestion?"

Silence.

"Exactly." She stepped back, reaching for the folded tunic she'd draped across the bench earlier. "Then it's settled."

"You think they'll just tell you?" he asked, disbelief coloring his voice.

"I think they've followed me like hounds since I set foot in this palace," she said, tugging the tunic over her head with clean efficiency. "If they're not going to leave me alone, then they can be *useful.*"

She buckled her belt, smoothed her coat into place, and turned to the door.

"I won't waste time chasing shadows," she added, voice low. "If Arjun's alive, we need someone who knows how to find ghosts."

A Name in the Dark

The stone bench just outside the antechamber was cold, but Kal sat with her hands folded in her lap, eyes fixed on the heavy double doors ahead. Afternoon light slanted in through the arched windows behind her, casting warm bars of gold across the marble floor.

When the court doors finally opened, Alden stepped through first, laughing at some last remark from within. The moment he saw her, he stopped.

"Well," he said, smiling as he crossed toward her, "I'd have adjourned court hours ago had I known such a vision awaited me."

She gave him a look, dry but not unkind.

He grinned and let out a soft chuckle. "If I'd known it would take *that* many days to recover from a dance, I might've reconsidered asking."

Kal offered the barest curve of a smile, subtle but there.

Alden's expression sobered, just slightly. "Is everything all right?" he asked, tilting his head. "Do you need something?"

Before she could answer, the doors opened wider behind him. Raoul stepped out first, hand tugging loose the collar of his formal coat, voice trailing off mid-sentence as his gaze caught hers. He stopped.

Jarreth came next, slowing as he crossed the threshold. His expression shifted immediately–hope, uncertainty, something bright flickering across his face as his eyes locked with hers.

Kal stood slowly. Her gaze met theirs, steady and cryptic, but not cold.

"I came to speak with Raoul and Jarreth," she said, voice light.

Alden raised both brows. "Did you now?"

He glanced between the three of them, amusement blooming across his face like the slow draw of a bowstring.

"Well," he said cheerfully, stepping aside, "I'll leave you to it, then.

Try not to break anything."

He winked, and with a chuckle under his breath, he strode off down the corridor, whistling low as the echo of his boots faded behind him.

Jarreth groaned softly, dragging a hand through his hair as his father vanished down the corridor. "I'd apologize for my father's sense of humor," he muttered, flushed, "but I think we'd be here all afternoon."

Kal made a soft, neutral sound, somewhere between amusement and indifference, then simply tipped her chin toward the west-facing hall. "Walk with me."

Raoul moved first, falling into step on her left with an easy readiness. Jarreth hesitated for the space of a breath before joining her right, his expression guarded but attentive. He looked as if he expected an ambush and couldn't decide whether it would be political or personal.

They passed through the palace's quieter wing, the noise of court retreating behind carved doors and high-vaulted ceilings.

Kal said nothing. Each step forward was a negotiation in her own mind. She hated this. Hated needing anything from anyone, especially trust. Every instinct pulled taut inside her, warning against it. But she was out of options, and the longer she waited, the colder her clarity became.

Arjun was alive. He was in danger. And she was going to find him.

The garden greeted them with wind and birdsong. Gravel crunched beneath their boots as they passed the rows of hedges and flowering vines. A breeze stirred the branches overhead, casting shifting shadows across the stone walk.

Raoul's usual ease felt restrained. He studied her profile in silence, trying to place the tension wound through her frame. There was something different in her step. Part of him hoped this was about the dance, the touch of her fingers in his, the look she'd given him just before Liam had dragged her away. But another part, older and sharper, sensed something else was coming.

Jarreth hadn't seen her since that night. He'd spent the days wondering what he'd done wrong. But now, watching the tilt of her shoulders and the intent in her gaze, he wasn't sure if this meeting had anything to do with him at all.

Kal stopped near a rose-covered trellis. The air was thick with the scent of sun-warmed blossoms, but neither man seemed to notice. Both Raoul and Jarreth glanced at her, expectant. She opened her mouth to speak but Jarreth beat her to it.

He stepped forward, not close enough to invade her space, but with purpose. His jaw was set, brows drawn in concentration, and for once his words didn't fumble on the way out.

"Before you say anything...I need to apologize," he said, eyes steady on hers. "For the ball. For...anything I did that may have made you uncomfortable. I wasn't thinking about how it might feel from your side.

I don't want you to think I see you as a prize to be won, or something to chase because it looks good at court. I just–"

He exhaled, running a hand through his hair in mild frustration. "I was caught off guard by how easy it felt, being with you. But if I overstepped...I'm sorry."

Kal didn't have time to reply before Raoul stepped forward beside him, one hand brushing back his windblown hair.

Raoul cleared his throat, his tone more casual but no less sincere. "What he's trying to say, with slightly more stammer, is that we both crossed a line. We thought we were making progress. Connection, maybe. But we weren't careful." His gaze lifted to meet hers. "And I've never cared much for caution, but with you...I should've known better." He glanced away for half a breath, then back to her. "I don't regret dancing with you, but I hate that Liam had to yank you off the floor like that. And if I said anything that felt like a line, well...I've thrown around too many of those in my life. I can't blame you for seeing through them. But it wasn't a game. Not with you. I wouldn't do that to you."

Silence settled over the garden. Kal blinked, brows raised, the weight of both confessions pressing around her, sincere, awkward and painfully human.

Then, unexpectedly, she laughed.

Not a cutting laugh, nor cruel. Something warmer. Sharper at the edges, but genuine. She shook her head, the sound spilling out of her like pressure released from a sealed jar.

"Is that what you both thought I came out here for?" she asked, amusement threading through her voice. "To scold you like misbehaving dogs? You two managed to rehearse apologies for something I wasn't even angry about."

Raoul grinned, relieved. "Well, we weren't ruling it out."

Jarreth gave a sheepish smile, his shoulders easing just slightly. "It seemed likely."

Kal shook her head, still surprised by how thoroughly the men had misread her intentions. She regarded them in silence for a moment, then gestured to the stone bench behind her with a tilt of her chin.

"Sit," she said simply.

They obeyed, Raoul easing down with a wary sort of charm; Jarreth more stiffly, casting her glances that held more confusion than anything else. Neither of them had ever seen her like this, composed but not cold, quiet but not closed off.

Kal folded her arms lightly as she leaned back against the low wall that framed the path, studying them. She knew she had their attention, and if nothing else, that was a resource she could use. Her mind moved to familiar ground, calculated steps and angled words, the same tactics she had used all her life to survive. If charm would soften them, make them more inclined to give her what she needed, then charm she would wield.

Her gaze lingered on Raoul first, then flicked to Jarreth. Her voice softened, her posture relaxed, chin angled, her expression touched with something that might've passed for amused interest.

"I'm sorry," she said, not quite looking at either of them at first. "It was never my intention to make you feel as though an apology was needed. And I'm sorry our evening ended the way it did."

Both men blinked, startled not just by her words but the tone behind them, gentle, sincere, and wholly uncharacteristic.

Raoul recovered first. "That's...myself as well," he said, a flicker of uncertainty tugging at the corners of his otherwise confident mouth. "Though I suspect your brother might disagree."

Kal turned to him first, eyes lifting just enough to meet his. She smiled, slow and intimate, and reached out to brush her fingers against the back of his hand. It wasn't a flirt. Not overtly. Just a touch, brief but warm.

"Still," she said gently, "thank you, for the dance. For the conversation. It was...not what I expected."

Raoul remained completely still, clearly grasping for something clever to say and coming up empty.

Before he could find it, Kal turned to Jarreth, shifting her weight slightly so that the movement brought her just a breath closer to him. She met his gaze, eyes lowered through her lashes in a way that made his throat tighten. Then, with the same care, she reached out and let her fingers graze his.

"I'm sorry we did not have another dance," she said. "You were... very charming."

Jarreth stared at her, blinking once, then again, as though trying to translate the words from some language he hadn't studied.

"I—uh..." He cleared his throat. "That's...very kind of you. I'm glad you enjoyed it."

Kal smiled again, this one just a hint wider.

In her mind, every detail was accounted for, the way Raoul's shoulders had tightened, the way Jarreth's hand had twitched just slightly beneath hers. Men who wielded blade and influence with ease, both brought off-balance by something far more subtle.

Kal let her fingers trail lightly over the curve of the stone bench, her tone still demure, laced with just enough warmth to feel sincere.

"I hope," she said slowly, "that we'll have more moments like that night. I don't often have cause to enjoy myself, and it... it was easier than I expected. With the two of you."

Her gaze flicked between them, soft and open, and she allowed a gentle breath to pass between her words as if she'd only just gathered the courage to say it.

"You've both spent so much time at my heels," she went on, voice low and coaxing. "Watching every move, every step, every breath. It's no wonder things feel...different."

Raoul's brow knit, his mouth tugging slightly downward. He shifted his stance, just enough for the easy charm to slip, something thoughtful threading through the line of his jaw.

Jarreth, beside him, had stilled completely.

Kal turned her face toward the roses, the light catching in her hair like a crown she hadn't claimed. She didn't see the moment Jarreth's expression shifted, didn't see the flicker of realization, the subtle faltering of whatever hope had quietly rooted itself in him.

He leaned back a little, and the movement alone sent a chill into the space between them.

"Kal," Raoul said quietly, his voice lacking its usual humor. "You don't have to do this."

She blinked and looked up at him, her eyes wide and guileless. "Do what?"

But her voice was a fraction too smooth now, a fraction too controlled.

Before Raoul could find the words, Jarreth moved. He reached out slowly, his hand closing lightly over hers–just fingertips, just enough to be felt. Kal flinched. The reaction was sharp, instinctive, her hand jerking back like she'd been burned. The moment cracked open.

Jarreth's smile was kind, but the pain behind it wasn't hidden. His hand withdrew just as gently as it had come, as though he hadn't noticed her recoil.

"As much as I wish it were true," he said, softly, "this isn't like you."

Kal froze in place, the illusion crumbling in silence around her. Where she might have wielded a cutting remark or a cold stare, now there was only the faintest flicker of something vulnerable before her expression shuttered, clean and swift. The distance returned to her eyes like a familiar veil.

She drew back from them without moving, posture straightening, face settling into a reserved mask that neither invited nor pushed away.

Raoul exhaled hard through his nose, leaning back and dragging a hand through his hair. "Well," he said lightly, injecting humor with just enough care not to startle the tension, "I assume this wasn't just to watch us confess our crimes beneath the roses. What is it, Kal? You planning to kill us yourself, or is Liam crouched in the hedges waiting to dismember us on command?"

Kal didn't answer at first. She stayed still as stone, caught between fight and retreat, knowing too well how to reclaim control through blade or voice–but utterly unsure how to navigate this sudden, impossible middle.

Raoul offered a half-grin, as if that might soften the blow. "You know he'd do it. With gusto."

"Only if I asked nicely," she murmured, quieter than before.

Jarreth shifted, and though his voice was gentler than Kal expected, it was steady. "Just tell us," he said. "Whatever it is that's bothering you."

Kal's gaze flicked to him, sharp and searching. There was no mockery there. No demand. Just the steady patience of someone willing to wait, even if it meant standing in the dark a little longer.

Her jaw clenched. For a breath, she looked ready to retreat again.

"I need to ask you something," she said at last, the words edged in caution.

Jarreth blinked, and to Kal's astonishment, he laughed. Just a soft huff, one hand settling on his hip.

"You could've led with that."

Kal hesitated, her throat tightening with the weight of a thousand things unsaid. The question sat just behind her teeth, burning with urgency, but the act of speaking it felt impossible. Asking had never come easily. Needing others even less so.

Her gaze fell to the polished edge of the stone bench, tracing the fine moss creeping along its base, anything to avoid the eyes fixed so patiently on her.

Jarreth moved first, carefully. His fingers brushed against hers again, a barely-there touch. He didn't press or pull, just rested the backs of his knuckles against her hand, as if anchoring her without caging her.

"You don't have to trust us with everything," he said softly. "But you can start by trusting us with *something*."

His voice wasn't coaxing. It wasn't pleading. It simply offered.

This time, Kal didn't flinch. Her body remained still, but inside, her nerves sang. Her heartbeat thundered in her ears, steady and unyielding. For a long moment, she said nothing, only letting the silence draw out as if testing its weight.

Then she exhaled slowly and lifted her gaze to meet them both, her voice low and even.

"I need someone who can locate anyone," she said. "Even if there's no trail to follow. Someone who could find...a ghost."

Raoul and Jarreth exchanged a glance. A dozen questions flickered in both their expressions–about what she meant, who this ghost might be, why she looked so haunted just speaking of it. But neither spoke. Not yet.

Kal had given them a sliver of something fragile. Not a game, not a ploy. Just a request. If they wanted to be seen as something more than what she'd come to expect from men, especially men like them, then they'd have to treat that sliver like something sacred.

"You need Kipp Harlow," Raoul said, his voice carrying none of his usual bravado.

Kal looked up, brow furrowing slightly.

Jarreth turned toward her. "Kipp Harlow," he echoed, the name alone drawing gravity into the garden. "King of thieves. The most wanted man in Varis, if not every kingdom everywhere."

Raoul gave a short breath of agreement. "If the rumors are true, and I'd wager they are, he rules the underworld of all the kingdoms from a hidden court somewhere in this capital. Kingsguard's never found it. Not for lack of trying."

He leaned forward, elbows braced on his thighs. "He's a ghost, but if anyone could find another, it'd be him."

Kal said nothing. She only sat, still and composed, the name settling deep into her thoughts. King of thieves. A man impossible to find. An underworld lord who may or may not be here, if Raoul's intelligence was current. If he hadn't already vanished, like all ghosts eventually did.

Then slowly, Kal stood. Her gaze lingered on them both, not guarded or veiled. For a breath, it was simply honest.

"Thank you," she said quietly.

Raoul grinned, trying not to look too pleased. "All you had to do was ask."

Jarreth inclined his head slightly. "That's what we're here for."

Raoul added, a little more earnestly, "If you need anything else, *anything*, we're not hard to find."

Kal didn't answer at first. She only looked at him for a long moment, then nodded once in acknowledgment and turned to go.

Kal moved through the dim corridors of the palace with her head slightly bowed, shadows slipping across her path like whispers. She nodded once to the guards at the stairwell, barely aware of them, her mind far from stone walls and firelit sconces.

The garden air still clung to her, cool and sharp with the scent of lavender and autumn spice, but her thoughts circled only one thing now.

Kipp Harlow.

She reached her quarters and closed the door behind her with a soft click, the heavy lock sliding home. The silence settled thick around her. She crossed to the window and braced her hands on the sill, staring out into the courtyard below where the torches were just beginning to flicker against the falling dusk.

King of thieves. Ghost of Varis.

She didn't want to think about the way Jarreth had looked at her when he pulled his hand away. Or the weight behind Raoul's voice when he told her she didn't have to pretend. She didn't want to examine the way her chest had tightened at being seen so clearly, not with suspicion or desire, but with something far more dangerous.

Understanding.

So she didn't. She folded those thoughts tightly and pressed them down where they couldn't reach her, where they could be dealt with later...if ever.

Instead, her mind turned to the task at hand. How did one find a man who made his living by staying hidden? How did one chase a shadow when it knew every alley, every passage, every crooked coin that passed through Varis?

She stood still a moment longer, lips slowly curving.

You didn't. You didn't chase him at all.

Kal turned from the window, her gaze sharp now, a gleam sparking behind it. The best way to catch someone who didn't want to be caught... was to make them come to you. To become something irresistible. A thread too tempting not to follow. A name whispered in dark corners, a fire lit just bright enough to draw the ghost from hiding.

A hunt disguised as bait.

Kal moved to her desk, her thoughts already assembling. If Harlow was watching his kingdom, as any self-respecting king of thieves surely was, then she would give him something to notice.

She would make herself a question he couldn't ignore. And when he came for her, because he would, then she'd make him find the ghost that truly mattered.

THREE GOLD PIECES

L iam was still half-asleep, dark hair tousled and shirt wrinkled when Kal stepped silently into the common space between their chambers, her presence pulling him from his usual early morning quiet.

He frowned at her immediately. "You're not going to sparring?"

"I wasn't planning to." Her tone was even, but she stayed braced for argument.

He straightened, fully awake now. "What happened?"

Kal moved to stand by the window, arms folded loosely, eyes fixed on the low rooftops outside. "I found out who we need."

Liam crossed his arms in turn. "Who?"

She glanced over, and the flicker of warning in her expression made him still. "Kipp Harlow, King of Thieves."

Liam blinked, the name settling like frost in the room. "...King of Thieves?"

Kal nodded once. "The only man with the kind of network we need. If Arjun is anywhere in Elandra, or beyond, he can find him."

Liam shook his head. "Kal, a man with that title would be a ghost. He'd slip through city walls like smoke. The guard's been trying to track him for a decade and they've never even seen his face, I've seen the nearly blank wanted posters."

"I don't need to track him." Kal turned fully now, voice soft but steel in its edges. "I need him to find *me*."

The silence stretched between them.

Liam's jaw tightened. *"No."*

Kal's eyes narrowed. "You don't even know the plan yet."

"I don't need to. If the plan includes you drawing the attention of the most dangerous man in Varis—"

"The most *useful* man in Varis," she corrected.

He stepped toward her, anger rising, shoulders squaring as if bracing for battle. "You want to make yourself a target. Of a man known for deception, coercion, seduction, and blades in the dark. And you think doing that alone is a sound idea?"

"If he senses I'm protected, watched, followed—he'll vanish. He'll think it's a trap. And he'd be right."

Liam's hands curled into fists at his sides. "You want to walk straight into a lion's den with no sword, no second, and no idea what he'll do."

"I've walked into worse."

"That's not the point!"

"It's exactly the point," she snapped, her voice still low but crackling now with restrained heat. "You think I can't handle this, that I'm not more dangerous than any rogue? You think I haven't measured every cost, every risk? If there is even the *smallest* chance Arjun is still alive, then I will do whatever I have to. I will not sit idle and wait for some miracle."

Liam's expression darkened, his voice colder. "And if this thief decides you're worth keeping, or worse, selling? That your life has value in coin instead of cause? What then?"

"I'll handle it."

"You can't fight every war alone, Kal."

She met his eyes then, and for just a breath, her voice gentled. "I'm not trying to fight alone, Liam. I'm just trying to do the one thing only I can do."

He held her gaze, fury simmering just beneath his grief, his protectiveness twisting into something harsher.

And then quietly, bitterly, he said, "You were always the bait, weren't you?"

Kal didn't answer. She turned back to the window, staring out at the city she would soon have to provoke into noticing her.

Behind her, Liam exhaled slowly. "If this goes wrong—"

"It won't," she said.

Kal dressed in silence, her expression set firm as she stepped into the long blue gown. The fabric clung, soft enough to sway with her stride, but tailored in a way that carved a commanding silhouette. It wasn't ostentatious, but there was no mistaking that it had been made for someone who belonged nowhere near the merchant quarter. She pulled on the dark slate hued traveling cloak next, its silver embroidered threadwork shimmered faintly in the light. The pattern was unfamiliar to Varisian sensibilities, winding and sharp-edged, speaking of lands to the north–of Fae cultures older than the Varisian crown. She wound the silver strands through her dark hair next, pinning them back loosely until they glinted with every turn of her head, catching the eye without begging for attention.

Subtle wealth. Deliberate mystery.

The king of thieves would see her coming, and that was the point.

She slid her daggers into place–the one against her thigh, another tucked behind her lower back, and a third at her hip beneath the cloak's drape. The sword she left behind.

When she opened the door, Liam was already waiting in the common space, arms crossed and expression thunderous. His mouth opened, likely with one final argument locked and ready, but Kal didn't slow. She swept past him with regal calm, cloak whispering over the polished floors like a tide pulling away from shore.

"Kal," Liam snapped, turning to follow. "Kal, *this is madness.*"

She paused just long enough to glance over her shoulder. "Then pray it works."

And then she was gone, boots clicking softly on the marble as she descended into the echoing halls of the palace. Servants turned to watch her pass, guards straightened without understanding why, and somewhere behind her Liam cursed low and bitter under his breath.

The Varisian sun rode high by the time Kal stepped onto the wide thoroughfare that fed into the lower market, and the world around her was thick with life. Stalls crowded the stone paths in uneven rows, and voices rose in a constant hum–merchants hawking wares, buyers haggling, children laughing as they darted between woven baskets and sun-bleached canopies.

Kal walked with calm confidence into the chaos, letting herself be seen. The hem of her blue dress just brushed the dust, and her cloak, pinned neatly at the shoulders, caught the breeze in a way that made it shimmer faintly as she moved. Her steps were slow, planned. She did not glance over her shoulder or flinch at the sudden shout of a vendor or the clatter of a dropped basket. She pushed the hood of her cloak back and let her face be kissed by the light.

There would be eyes watching. She was counting on it.

She passed a spice vendor, her fingers grazing the hanging sachets, eyes moving without urgency across the square. She paused at a fruit stall, lifting a fig to her nose without really seeing it. Still she waited. The longer it took, the more her anticipation sharpened into something taut.

Then she saw her. A girl, no more than twelve, skirting the edge of the vendor line with quick feet and steady hands. Small. Fast. Her step was too casual, her smile too rehearsed, her path too smooth. She never looked directly at Kal, but her angle was purposeful, her timing precise.

A cutpurse. Young, but well trained.

Kal remained exactly where she was, lifting another fig and pretending to weigh it, eyes scanning past the stalls. The girl came in close, barely brushing passersby, a little shadow among hundreds.

Then, the girl's wrist was caught, held fast before the dagger at her belt ever found its mark. The young thief gasped and looked up, eyes wide. She met Kal's gaze and froze. Kal didn't speak, she simply studied the girl calmly, then reached into her cloak, pulled three gold coins free, and pressed them lightly into the girl's fingers.

The girl blinked in disbelief.

With a small tilt of her head, Kal gestured.

Go.

The child hesitated only a breath longer before slipping away into the press of bodies, vanishing like mist. Kal turned back to the figs, set down the one in her hand, and continued walking.

She didn't need to follow the girl. She had just left a trail.

The girl slipped through the alleys like smoke, her small frame darting between crates and laundry lines, ducking beneath open shutters, never staying in the light for more than a breath. She knew the city better than most, knew which stones were loose, which vendors looked the other way, which guards had slow hands and slower boots.

But she wasn't thinking about that now.

She was thinking about the woman.

By the time she reached the shuttered doorway tucked behind an herb merchant's abandoned stall, her chest was tight and her mind buzzing. She rapped twice, paused, rapped thrice, and the door creaked open without a word. Inside, candlelight flickered over old stone, the air warm and thick with the scent of smoke and damp wood.

The tavern was empty but for a few shadows and one man.

He sat sprawled across a chair at the center table, a dagger arcing lazily through the air in rhythmic turns above him. Each flip caught the light before it vanished into the blur of his hand and reappeared again. His dark hair was pulled back in a careless tie, with a few loose strands brushing his temple, and the faintest shadow of a beard softened the line of his jaw. He had a strong, angular face—broad across the cheekbones, with a nose just slightly crooked from some long-forgotten brawl. His green eyes, clear and sharp beneath thick brows, held the kind of lazy amusement that never quite reached his mouth. That, instead, stayed curled in a crooked grin—easy, unreadable, and wicked.

When he saw her, he caught the dagger without looking.

He arched a brow, pushing hair from his face with a casual swipe. "You're back early."

She stopped a few paces short of the table, eyes narrowed. "I was made."

"Made?" He leaned forward, boots dragging across the worn wood, setting both elbows on the table. "By whom? You don't get made."

"I didn't. I mean—she caught me, but—" The girl threw her hands up. "She shouldn't have. She *shouldn't* have."

His smile curved lazily. "She catch your hand or your shadow?"

"My hand."

That made him pause.

He leaned back again, studying her, green eyes sharper now. "What'd she do?"

The girl reached into her pocket and laid the gold coins on the table, one by one. "She gave me these. Told me to run."

He stared at the coins, then up at her. "And you did?"

"She *knew* I was there, don't know how, but she did," the girl said, voice quieter now. "I've never been caught. Not once."

His hand closed around the coins. Then, slowly, he stood. He tucked the dagger into his belt, mouth quirking with sudden interest.

"Tell me," he said, brushing his hair back again. "What did she look like?"

The girl hovered on her toes, fingers curling at her sides as if still holding the purse she never quite managed to steal. Her eyes darted between the gold and the man watching her.

"She's unmissable," the girl said, breath still tight in her chest. "Not one of ours. Not from here. Not Varisian for sure"

He cocked his head, intrigued. "How so?"

"She looked like a noble, clothes were fine enough, cloak embroidery was foreign. But not *soft*. Not wide-eyed or fluttery. She walked like—" The girl hesitated, searching for a word. "Like she *owned* the ground."

His smile widened a fraction. "And you thought she'd be easy."

"I thought she'd be *rich* or a fool." The girl huffed, then crossed her arms. "But she's not just rich. She's something else. Something... different."

That earned a slow blink. Then a chuckle low in his throat as he picked up two of the gold coins and flicked them in her direction.

"Keep your eyes sharp next time," he said.

The girl caught the coins, grinned, and made for the door. "Thanks, boss."

She vanished into the narrow corridor beyond, footsteps already retreating into the city's veins.

Left alone with the flicker of firelight and the weight of curiosity thickening in the room, Kipp Harlow rolled his neck and stretched his arms over his head until his spine popped. Then he stood and reached for the second blade at his hip, checking the edge in a fluid motion that spoke of habit rather than need.

Across the table, a second man lounged in the shadows, silent. Kipp met his gaze with a grin that was too casual to be anything but intended.

"Seems we've got something new on our doorstep," he said. "And I do love surprises."

He tucked the blade back into place, turned toward the tavern door, and added over his shoulder, "I'm out to see what walked into my market today."

"Consider Me Caught"

Kipp Harlow leaned in the shade of a weathered colonnade, the weight of his shoulder pressed against stone warm from the morning sun. Around him, the market churned–colors and noise, spice and sweat, a thousand voices vying for attention. He ignored all of it.

He caught sight of her through the crowd, just a glimpse at first, then the full turn of her face in the light. She was beautiful, yes, but not in any way he'd ever seen before. Her features were cut with an almost impossible precision, perfectly symmetrical–high cheekbones, full lips, and eyes that held steady like they saw through masks and marrow both. Sunlight caught on the silver-threaded curls framing her face, a gleam of woven metal glinting at her temple as the breeze stirred them.

He was watching her.

She hadn't done anything particularly unusual. Not really. She hadn't stolen, hadn't shouted. Hadn't smiled too brightly or stumbled like someone out of place. If anything, she moved *too* well. Like she understood how to slip into the rhythm of a crowd without getting swept up in it. Like she was part of the street, but untouched by it.

She walked with her chin high, her hands loose at her sides, fingers never quite brushing the coins at her belt. Dressed simply, but not plainly– tailored well enough to suggest coin, but not loudly. Her cloak hung just off her shoulders, fastened with a single polished clasp, the embroidery catching the sun when she moved. Not local. That much was clear. But not foreign enough to be suspect. Just...different. Purposefully so.

Kipp's eyes followed her from beneath his lashes as she paused at a stall of folded linens. She ran a hand over a bolt of pale silk, testing the weave with a thumb pressed behind the fabric. A small thing. Almost nothing. But it struck him, the way she touched it, measured it. A noblewoman might admire the color, fawn over the threadwork, call it lovely and then haggle badly. But she tested the quality in silence and moved on.

She passed a fruit stand, where the vendor offered her something ripe and sweet. She declined with a faint incline of her head, offering no excuse, no explanation. He tried again, louder, trying to charm her into a purchase. Still, she said nothing. Just a polite, distant smile, and then she stepped away—neither drawn in by kindness nor provoked by insistence.

Unmoved.

Kipp frowned slightly. Not many walked through *his* market with that kind of detachment. It wasn't arrogance. It was something colder, more careful. Like she was keeping score and hadn't yet found anything worth spending coin, or trust, on. He shifted his weight, one boot angled toward the alley's mouth where he could see her better, but made no move to follow.

Let her walk. Let her drift stall to stall. The market would draw her shape eventually. Reveal what she reached for, what she avoided, how she reacted when cornered. And if she *was* what he suspected—a noble playing wanderer, or some merchant's daughter trying to step above her station—then the crowd would swallow her by midday.

But if not?

His thumb brushed the hilt of the dagger tucked beneath his coat. Not out of caution, habit, more than anything. His eyes stayed on the woman as she paused at a small silver stall, the kind passed by more than browsed. The merchant didn't even notice her at first, not until she reached for the pendant near the edge of the display. It was a simple thin disc on a chain but she weighed it like it mattered. Turned it, subtly shifted her thumb along the edge as if testing for rough seams or poor casting.

Then, without fanfare, she brought it to her mouth and bit it.

Kipp straightened, just slightly.

It was fast, disguised beneath the curtain of her hair, but he saw it. The quick press of teeth, the flick of her thumb afterward. Checking purity. Not with drama. Not to show off. To *know*.

His smirk edged sharper. That wasn't noble behavior. It was the kind of thing a fence might do. Or a smuggler. Or someone who'd been handed fakes too many times to take anything at face value.

She set the pendant down without a word, and kept walking.

Kipp watched her go, hands still tucked in his coat. She was no thief. No street-born. But she'd learned the tricks, and more important-ly...she knew when to use them.

Still, he didn't move.

Not when the mark wandered too close, not even when the boy

slipped through the bodies like he already knew how the crowd would sway before it did. Small, wiry, fast—one of Kipp's, and good enough to lift a coin purse without breaking stride, without jostling a sleeve, without drawing so much as a flicker of awareness from his mark.

It was a perfect pull.

Nearly.

The woman caught it. Her head didn't turn, but her eyes followed the motion, sharp and certain, calculated in a way that marked her not just as observant, but trained. Her face remained composed, and when her gaze fell away, it wasn't out of disinterest. It was control.

Then came the sign, pointed in the boy's direction. A slight gesture, barely there—one hand, low near her hip, fingers bending in a way most would miss entirely. But not Kipp. No one moved like that by accident. It was a guild sign, one not used in years, maybe longer.

His gaze narrowed, the coin between his fingers slowed.

She walked on, and with her free hand, let another coin fall from the crook of her fingers. The toss was loose and low, unremarkable at a glance, but the arc was intentional—measured, even lazy, designed to draw no notice from the crowd yet land with just enough weight to strike stone ahead of the boy's path. It didn't ring loud enough to turn heads, but the sound it made would carry to those who'd been trained to hear it. The boy heard. He stuttered mid-step, eyes snapping once to the stone, then around—quick, tight movements, calculating whether it was safe to break pattern. He bent, scooped the coin, and was gone again into the shifting press of bodies, lost before even the echo of the sound had faded.

Kipp's hand stilled. The coin no longer danced across his knuckles.

That was enough. She hadn't interfered with the theft. Hadn't warned the mark or shamed the boy. She hadn't claimed control of the moment, hadn't tried to prove she was watching. Instead, she had simply observed and answered, with designed intent.

"Well, well," he murmured to himself, voice warm and edged like a knife. "That little flick of silver wasn't for charity. You're no merchant's wife straying too close to the rot. So what are you really, tossing guild signs in the open like you want someone dangerous to come find you?"

His smirk deepened, predatory and amused. "Because if that was bait, darling...consider me caught."

He stepped from the shadow of the awning, slipping between murmured merchants and idle guards with quiet efficiency. The woman was already turning down a side lane—narrower, quieter, lined with shuttered windows and washed in the pale afternoon light that barely touched the ground between tall, weary buildings. Ivy curled between old ironwork, and the balconies above hung like silent watchers, unmoved by what passed beneath them.

A foolish move.

Kipp followed, not with haste but with the calm certainty of a man who had lived in shadows so long even the light had stopped trying to find him. His steps made no sound against the stone, and the grin that curled across his mouth was slow in forming–cautious, edged with amusement, but not without its weight.

"Tsk," Kipp muttered, low and amused, his voice brushing against the alley's hush like a whisper across skin. "Wandering off alone, looking like sin dressed in silk...that's how pretty things get ruined."

"And I've never once resisted a woman begging to be caught." He added, voice dark, tinged with something crueler underneath.

The King of Thieves had taken the bait.

The Hunter Becomes the Hunted

Kipp moved with ease through the alleyway, having long since stopped worrying about what might wait in the dark. The noise of the market faded behind him, swallowed by the hush of narrow stone corridors and the whisper of drying linens that fluttered from overhead lines like pale flags. The space narrowed with every step—high walls pressing close, every doorway shuttered, every window blind. The kind of place most people passed by without looking. Too empty. Too still. Too easy to vanish inside.

Perfect.

He didn't hurry. Every step was placed precisely, having nothing to fear and no reason to feign urgency. He considered, with idle amusement, how best to announce himself—a dry chuckle from the dark, perhaps, or a slow, sarcastic clap. Something to startle, to tip the scales just enough to remind her whose world she'd wandered into. She'd walked this far into his shadows, after all. Whatever game she thought she was playing, she'd misjudged the board, and the man standing across it.

Then his boot grazed stone with the barest scrape.

She moved. No hesitation, startled gasp or backward glance. She turned as if the air itself had shifted her—a pivot honed by discipline—and in the span between blink and breath, his back hit the cold wall behind him. The shock of it didn't hurt, not truly, but it landed with enough force to announce how easily she'd chosen to put him there.

A blade shimmered at his throat, angled with exacting pressure just beneath his jaw. The second pressed against his hip—lower, far less polite in its placement, and positioned with the kind of nerve that required either complete confidence or the absence of fear.

Kipp's breath left him in a short, appreciative exhale, his lips curling into a grin that could have seduced saints into sin.

"Well," he murmured, voice thick with pleasure, "I certainly had other ideas for how you'd end up on top of me tonight...but I've never been too picky about the order of things."

She didn't speak. Her weight was centered and her hands steady, both blades held in perfect control. She wasn't threatening him. She was *containing* him.

Kipp tilted his head slightly, feeling the cool press of steel against his throat respond in kind. Still smiling lazily, he let his voice drop to something more intimate, softer and lower, shaped to curl beneath her skin like a warm breath in the dark.

"Careful now," he breathed with wicked amusement, "you keep touching me like this, and I'll show you just how badly you want to know what I do when I'm smiling and pinned...every wicked second of it."

She didn't blink. He had seen men break under lesser scrutiny, under quieter pressure but she held her stillness like a blade itself, honed to lethality and colder than it had any right to be.

Interesting.

"You were following me," she said at last, her voice subdued but not soft.

His grin turned sharper, slow and full of teeth. Something hungry flickered behind his eyes, wolfish and warm, like fire that promised both comfort and ruin.

"Darling," he murmured, "when you walk through a place like that tossing signals like breadcrumbs—flashing steel under silk and looking like a secret worth bleeding for—you don't exactly slip away unnoticed."

He took a long breath, his gaze sliding over her. "And I wasn't following," he added, the words falling darker now. *"I was hunting."*

She didn't flinch. Her expression didn't shift but Kipp had made a life out of reading silences, and this one said more than most men managed with a mouth full of lies.

"If you didn't want to be caught," he said, stepping just slightly into the line of her blade, enough to test whether she'd press, "you shouldn't have looked so damn willing."

"And what," she asked, eyes cool and calculating, "did you plan to do once you caught me?"

Kipp's smile didn't falter. If anything, it deepened, heat rising behind it. "Well," he said, voice smooth as sin, "I had half a mind to press you to this wall myself."

His eyes flicked meaningfully to the daggers, then back to hers with deliberate hunger. "But I've never minded being the one pinned... so long as I still get to play."

He leaned in by a fraction, close enough to feel the edge of her blade draw a thin line of blood, and let the next words fall soft between them.

"And darling...you've no idea what a mistake you've made, letting me close enough to enjoy this."

"I let you follow," she said, the words flat and certain.

Kipp's laugh came low, appreciative, utterly unbothered. "Did you now?"

The dagger at his belt shifted, a perfectly timed punctuation to let him know exactly how much permission she required to keep him in check.

Gods, she was good.

"You know," he mused, "most people buy me a drink before threatening my favorite parts."

"Then perhaps," she said, "you should develop a taste for better company."

Kipp laughed, warm, coaxing and genuine. "I'm working on it. That's why I followed you."

Kipp watched for smaller truths than most men knew how to find, looking past her well crafted facade. And there, in the shift of her gaze, in the faint narrowing of her focus–he saw it. Not surprise, but recognition. She hadn't sensed him. She had *known*. She'd chosen the path that drew his eye. Every turn, every hesitation, every open line of sight had been laid like bait in a snare crafted by someone who didn't just understand the game, she had designed it.

His head tipped lightly back against the wall as a breathless, incredulous laugh slid from his lips.

"Gods, woman," he said, and this time the voice held something rawer beneath the charm, something like wonder wrapped in heat. "You didn't just catch me."

His gaze swept over her, slow and reverent and full of wicked delight.

"*You* hunted *me*." A pause. Just long enough for the weight of it to settle. "And I walked right into your trap smiling."

Kipp's grin lingered, but behind the humor, sharp curiosity began to take shape. His voice came low, smooth, more velvet than steel but edged with both.

"You always hunt strangers like this?" he asked, eyes dancing, tone soaked in mockery too seductive to ignore.

Her gaze never wavered. "Only the ones who mistake themselves for predators."

A soft laugh escaped him, curling into the air between them, indulgent and dangerous. Gods, she was *magnificent*. Every word she gave him was weighted just enough to matter, no more, no less. Every breath came with the control of someone who didn't need to assert herself to be obeyed. She didn't have to perform. She *was* the performance.

And Kipp couldn't look away.

"You are," he murmured, voice dipping into something quieter, rougher, "something else entirely."

Kalithea tilted her head as though she were simply taking measure of what he truly was beneath the bravado. A man who thought he'd been hunting, now caged without a sound raised.

"*You* followed *me*..." she said, as if the truth of it were all the explanation required.

"I did," he admitted without shame, smiling like it was a compliment.

"And now?" she asked.

Kipp leaned in ever so slightly, just enough that his breath brushed against her cheek, his gaze locked to hers.

"Now," he said, the grin returning, slower this time, dangerous and a little breathless, "I hope to gods you let me keep playing."

Kal didn't react, she understood if she reached for a truth, he'd feed her a prettier lie. If she demanded, he'd dance. And if she pressed, if she revealed even the hint of urgency, he would take the game in his teeth and run with it until she was the one chasing. So she gave him nothing. No questions. No name. No emotion he could wrap his cleverness around. Only silence.

She shifted slightly, not enough to break contact, but enough to claim the air between them. A breath closer. The warmth of her body brushing his without ever yielding. She smelled of something earthen and strange—dark herbs, distant spice, a scent that lingered without being placeable. Not something bought in any gilded hall. It was *hers*, and intentionally so and gods, it rattled him.

He hadn't wanted someone this badly in years.

Still smiling, Kipp exhaled slowly through his nose, tilting his head just enough to avoid the blade's edge.

"So," he offered, casual, coaxing, "is this the part where you explain why exactly you lured me here, or–?"

Nothing. Just that gaze, steady, merciless and consuming.

He clicked his tongue, still smiling. "No? Well. If this is a robbery, I feel compelled to mention that I don't usually carry coin–"

Still. Nothing.

"–at least, not the kind I'm willing to part with."

Her silence swallowed every attempt he made to get her to crack.

He huffed a soft laugh, the sound closer to real this time. "You're making it *very* difficult for me to be charming, you know," he murmured. "Standing there like I'm some rare insect under glass."

It hit him then, he was *being studied*. Held. And he couldn't decide whether to escape it or beg for another moment of it.

She moved, leaning in, intimate and languid. Enough to change the current between them. Her eyes moved across his face as if she were reading something hidden beneath the surface, *considering* it.

She smiled. Slow, merciless and subtle.

Kipp's grin widened, bright with dangerous pleasure. "Oh, you're going to be an absolute nightmare, aren't you?"

Kalithea tilted her head, voice soft. "Nightmares only frighten those who fear the dark."

His laugh came low and husky, threading into the alley air. "Darling, I make my *home* in the dark."

Her smile twisted just slightly—still restrained, but with the satisfaction of a predator who'd already eaten—but wouldn't mind playing with her food a while longer. Not because she was hungry, but because he was *fun.*

Something shifted in Kipp's chest then, tight and unfamiliar. Not fear, not quite desire. *Intrigue.* True, rare, and dangerous. The kind that made blood move faster. The kind that turned caution to recklessness. He opened his mouth to say something, something clever or wicked, but the moment was already gone. The blade vanished. The pressure at his hip evaporated and before he could even register the shift, she was gone. No rustle of fabric. No movement to track.

One moment, he was pinned. The next...*air.* Still. Cold. Empty.

He strolled away, chuckling "Oh you absolute menace."

Kipp Harlow moved through the winding arteries of the city's underbelly with his hands tucked deep into the folds of his coat, his stride unhurried, his expression composed—save for the lingering curve of a smirk. The streets had quieted now, silvered with dew and scattered lantern light, but his thoughts burned bright and urgent beneath the nonchalance.

He was still replaying it. Not just the moment she had trapped him—though that, too, returned in vivid clarity—but everything leading to it. Every careful step, every calculated glance, every stall she'd paused beside as though the world happened to bend around her convenience. She hadn't stumbled into the upper hand. She had *chosen* it. Claimed it without spectacle, without arrogance, and made it seem as natural as breathing.

And gods help him, she'd made it look *beautiful.*

Kipp had known clever women. He'd shared drinks with spies and danced lies through courtrooms with more than one dangerous mind, but this, this was something else. There'd been no misstep, no overreach.

She hadn't tried to match his charm or outpace his wit. She had let him come willingly, smiling, into a trap so finely woven he hadn't seen the edge of it until it closed around his throat. And somehow, he wasn't angry.

He was *thrilled.*

His boots whispered over worn stone as he rounded a corner, the heavy hush of the sleeping city folding over him like a cloak. He should have let the thrill of it fade, let the night cool his blood. But something shifted. At first, it was nothing more than a passing thread of thought–an idle shift beneath the surface of his attention, like the brush of silk across skin, too faint to grasp but impossible to ignore. Kipp slowed, the familiar cadence of his mind catching on something it had missed the first time through. A new shape taking form in the puzzle she had become.

Until now, his thoughts had been tangled in her movements–the way she'd controlled the conversation with a tilt of her head, a glance, a silence that said more than most men could with a speech. He'd been tracing the outline of her mind, the masterfully efficient manner she had dismantled his charm.

Now he was thinking of her face. Not just the impossible symmetry of it, the silver threading her curls or the mouth that didn't waste smiles on anything unearned. No, it was the stillness of her. The way she held herself, as if the world moved for her convenience and not the other way around. Her beauty hadn't begged attention, it had commanded silence.

And that was what caught him, because someone like her should have been known. A woman like that–a woman with that face, that presence, that quiet, terrifying elegance–didn't just appear in a capital like Varis without the city bending to whisper her name. There should have been rumors, whispers half-wild and growing with each telling. A noblewoman hiding knives in her sleeves. A widow with a shadowed past and a trail of bodies in her wake. A courtesan too dangerous for any one court to keep. Something.

But there had been nothing. Not a word. Not a trace. He hadn't heard so much as a name in passing, not a scrap of gossip, not a story tinged with intrigue and wrapped in perfume. The court buzzed with nonsense daily, and yet this woman–this creature carved of dusk and steel–had gone unspoken.

She was a ghost.

Kipp's smile returned, slower this time, more thoughtful. No longer the loose grin of a man enjoying the game. This was a different smile. The kind that marked a decision.

"Well," he murmured, almost conversationally, to the stone and silence around him, "this just got interesting."

His stride lengthened, carrying him through the final stretch of back alleys until the mouth of his sanctum appeared—a broken archway beside a tavern no one remembered the name of, the staircase beneath it shrouded in the illusion of collapsed stone and disuse. The entrance had fooled better men than most who ever tried to follow him home.

Inside, the den breathed low and warm, firelight catching on weathered beams and crooked tables, maps and empty glasses scattered like relics across every surface. The scent of smoke, old leather, and spiced wine hung in the air. His people were still awake, murmuring in low clusters over dice games and whispered plans. But as he entered, the room shifted.

They could feel it. That undercurrent in his step. That flicker in his gaze.

"I need ears on the street," he said, his voice carrying easily, low and smooth, wrapped in that particular edge he used when something serious was about to become *fun.*

Chairs scraped. Heads lifted. One of the lieutenants, a woman with dark braids and a permanent knife-print on her thigh, cocked her head.

"What we after boss?"

Kipp didn't answer at first. He stepped forward, unhurried, and slid a small velvet pouch from his coat. It dropped onto the table with a soft but undeniable weight. Gold spilled against the wood in a sound more binding than any order.

"A foreign woman," he said.

That was enough to still what little noise remained.

"I don't have a name. No contacts, no coin trail. She walked into the marketplace today and disappeared without leaving a ripple behind. I want to know who she is. Where she came from. Where she's hiding."

He let that settle for a beat, then leaned in, his voice dropping to something more intimate. The kind of tone that promised gold *and* glory, if you could keep pace.

"She doesn't belong to anyone. No ledger, no chain, no faction I've seen. So if she's a ghost, I want to know where she died. And if she's not... if she's real, then I want to know where the hell she's been hiding all this time."

A pause. Not for drama but for effect.

"Gold to the first who brings me her name. Double if you tell me where she sleeps."

The room shifted with sudden purpose. No one asked if he was serious. Kipp didn't make idle wagers. When he offered coin, it meant something rare had caught his attention. Within moments, the crew began to move. Blades vanished into sheaths. Cloaks were drawn. Footsteps scattered into the streets above like arrows loosed from a single bowstring.

The hunt had begun, and the prize didn't even know she was being hunted.

Kipp remained behind, leaning against the edge of the table, arms folding behind his head as he tipped back in his chair. The firelight flickered across his face, and the grin that slowly returned was full, dangerous, and utterly certain.

"Let's see how long you can stay hidden, darling," he murmured into the empty room, his voice rich with the promise of pursuit.

He didn't know her name. Not yet. But names could be stolen like anything else. And Kipp Harlow had never failed to steal what he wanted.

Kalithea slipped back into the palace like a shadow. The corridors stretched silently around her, bathed in the dim gold of dying torchlight, their hush broken only by the low echo of her boots brushing polished stone. She closed the chamber door behind her without sound.

And he was already there. Liam stepped out of the darkened corner, his arms hung tense at his sides.

"You went without me."

Not an accusation, just a thread of frustration wound too tightly through sleepless hours and the knowledge that she'd gone where he couldn't follow.

Kalithea didn't flinch. "You knew I would."

He exhaled slowly, jaw clenched as he turned his back to her and began to pace, the movement restless in a way that betrayed more than anger. He stopped after only a few steps, crossing his arms, his gaze finding her again with controlled force.

"I was worried."

"I know."

The tension in his jaw didn't ease. His hand dragged down his face as though it might pull the frustration with it, but it only settled deeper in his stance.

"You know I would've gone with you," he said, voice low and roughened at the edges. "Whatever it was, Kal. You didn't need to face it alone."

She moved past him, unfastening her cloak with steady fingers. "This wasn't something force could solve."

Liam's eyes narrowed. "Meaning?"

She turned, gaze level, her expression steadfast but not unkind. "Meaning you could have turned the underworld inside out. You could have shattered silent corners and reminded every black-market king and gutter whisperer why the name *Elandra* still sharpens their dreams into nightmares."

Her voice didn't rise, but it filled the room. "And it still wouldn't have mattered."

He stared at her in silence, arms folded tighter.

"Because the King of Thieves doesn't fear blades," she continued, stepping forward. "He doesn't flinch at power or posturing. If you try to corner him, he disappears. If you press, he smiles. And if you demand something from him, he'll refuse simply to see if you'll beg."

Liam's frown deepened, his voice quieter now. "So what does he respond to?"

She stopped in front of him, the corner of her mouth lifting–not with amusement, but calculation.

"A chase," she said simply. "He wants the mystery. Not the prize, not yet. If you offer him answers, he turns away. If you hide them, he follows."

Liam went still. The expression on his face wasn't surprise, it was understanding. He knew her well enough to see the shape of the plan now, even if he still hated it.

"So," he murmured, "the bait was successful."

"I gave him what he needed," Kal replied, arching a brow.

He let out a sound, not quite a laugh, but close. A low breath of disbelief and admiration braided into something more fraternal.

"Gods," he muttered, "you're terrifying."

She smiled, full of knowing. "I learned from the best."

Liam rubbed at his temple, dragging his fingers through the hair at his scalp before glancing back at her, a reluctant smirk tugging at his lips. "And you think it worked?"

"It did." Her answer carried no hesitation. "He'll be watching now. The game's begun."

He studied her for a long moment, and the tension that had kept his posture stiff slowly began to unravel. He gave a small, resigned nod.

"Alright, Kal. Let's see how long the King of Thieves can keep up."

She paused, just for a breath, and her voice dropped to something more serious.

"Soon," she said, "we'll need to step out of the shadows."

Liam stiffened.

Kal didn't stop. "The king of thieves will only chase ghosts for so long. If we want him invested, *truly* invested, he needs a glimpse of the truth. Just enough to wonder what he's chasing."

"No." Liam said, voice flat.

"We'll be announced," she continued, as if his protest hadn't registered. "Not tonight. Not tomorrow. But soon."

He stepped back, as if putting space between them would temper the rising heat beneath his words. "You want to *announce* us?"

"Yes."

"Kal–"

"If we want him drawn in deeply enough to matter, he has to see what he's playing for."

"This isn't a courtship!" Liam snapped

"No," she said evenly. "It's war. And in war, you don't waste your blade on warnings. You wait until it's too late to stop the cut."

Queen *Kalithea of Elandra*.

A Name Worth the Chase

Kipp Harlow had played more games than he cared to count.

He'd coaxed secrets from noble tongues with nothing but charm and patience. Walked into vaults that had never been breached and walked out with crowns in his coat and forged replicas in their place. He'd smiled his way through locked doors, whispered his name into the ears of kings and criminals alike, and always—*always*—he left with what he came for.

He didn't lose. *Until now.* It had been days. Long, maddening days.

His whisperers had swept the city like a tide, slipping through gates beneath silk veils, lurking among merchant stalls with baskets in hand and sharpened eyes beneath painted lashes. They stalked the gutters with knives at their backs and coin for tongues willing to speak. But no matter how many doors they opened, how many corners they searched, they came back with the same answer. Nothing. No name. No trace. No thread of a past. She hadn't just disappeared, it's like she'd never been there at all.

Kipp reclined in his worn leather chair, one leg slung over the arm, fingers tapping idly against the hilt of the dagger strapped to his thigh. The fire crackled low in the hearth, shadows dancing along the stonework around him. His thoughts weren't here, they were back in that alley. Back in the moment she had turned the trap inside out and made it look like a flourish of her wrist. She'd seen the whole game laid out before either of them had spoken and she'd rewritten it before he could even begin to play. She hadn't evaded him. She had *dismissed* him and gods help him, she had done it *beautifully*.

His lips curved into a slow grin, one laced with something far sharper than amusement. Frustration, yes, but also respect. And something else. That rare, infuriating thrill that came only when the chase was *worth it*.

"Oh, darling," he murmured to the fire, voice smooth and low, "you're making this far too fun."

A knock broke the quiet. The door creaked open, and Leta slipped inside–all wiry precision and sharp corners, her steps sure, her face expressionless. One of his best. She didn't waste time with ceremony.

"Tell me you've got something," Kipp said, still lounging, still watching the flames. His tone stayed lazy, but there was no mistaking the edge beneath it.

She hesitated. That was answer enough.

Kipp let out a soft groan, rubbing a hand over his face as he tilted his head back, staring at the ceiling like it might offer an explanation he hadn't already thought of. "*Unbelievable.*"

"It's not for lack of effort," Leta replied, stepping closer. "We've pulled strings from the docks to the court. Whispered in every merchant's ear and bribed every scribe within reach. No one knows who she is. No house claims her. No record of entry. It's like she stepped out of smoke."

"And yet," Kipp said, finally turning his gaze toward her, "she walked through my market like it belonged to her."

Leta nodded slowly, expression tightening. "Not like a noble. Not shy, either. She wasn't unsure but she wasn't home. It was like she was *borrowing* the world around her."

Kipp studied her, interest sharpening. "She didn't leave a trace, but every head turned anyway."

"Exactly," Leta murmured. "A ghost in plain sight."

He drummed his fingers against the table, thoughtful now. "And still no name."

"Not directly," she said, "but there's something."

He arched a brow.

"There's talk...quiet, vague. A guest at the palace. Someone new under the king's protection. No title, no history. Unnamed."

Kipp sat forward. "A woman?"

Leta nodded. "That's what they say."

Kipp stood with that same catlike grace he always had, uncoiling rather than rising, stretching like the tension itself had shaped him.

"Now *that*," he said, his smile returning, slower this time, "is interesting."

"You think it's her?"

"I think," he said, reaching for his coat, "a woman who doesn't exist and a rumor of one suddenly hiding behind royal walls is *not* a coincidence."

The fire cast his silhouette long across the wall as he slipped into the dark coat, every motion purposeful. He paused at the doorway. "If she's behind the king's curtain, then she's not just clever. She's *dangerous.*"

Leta raised an eyebrow. "And what does that make *you*?"

He turned, and his smile was charming, deadly, and too smooth to be safe.

"Still the King of Thieves," he said, eyes gleaming. "And I always get what I want."

Then he reached for the handle. Paused. Glanced back at the hearth, where the fire flickered like it was listening.

"And gods help anyone who stands between me and that woman."

Kipp did not tolerate uncertainty. Mystery, in his world, was a fleeting indulgence, a string to unknot, not admire. He savored it only briefly before setting to work with the blade, unraveling what others feared to touch and leaving truth bare and bleeding in its place. Puzzles didn't intrigue him. They challenged him. And the moment a riddle dared linger, it became personal.

But *this* woman? She was no ordinary knot. She wasn't made of lies and masks like the nobles he toyed with. She was layered in something more elusive—wrapped in silk, yes, but reinforced with silence and shadows. And the more he pulled, the tighter she wound.

It was maddening.

For days, he pushed his network harder, driving them through every gate, every corridor, every whispered breath of the capital. His whisperers moved like smoke through seams in the city—slipping past palace stone, drifting between servants with borrowed names and invented errands, listening from kitchens, from stables, from laundry rooms where noble linens shed secrets no one meant to keep.

But the reports were fractured. Fragments. Rumors. A guest under the king's protection. No title. No country. She moved through the palace as though born to it, yet no one spoke her origin aloud. Servants lowered their voices. Guards glanced away when asked.

She trained before sunrise, besting the Crown Prince and his Champion daily. She listened more than she spoke. She did not kneel.

Kipp knew. Without needing a face. Without hearing a name. He *knew*. It was her. But knowledge without leverage meant nothing. Not to him. Not when the stakes had changed. He needed more. *Needed Truth.* A name to place against her silence, something solid enough to hold weight when the time came to press against her with it.

So he sharpened the hunt. The gold doubled. The patience dwindled. He offered coin for whispers, favor for treason—and made it clear that silence, this time, would not be rewarded. Finally, in the haze of a tavern thick with smoke and desperation, tucked between the salt-stained arches of the lower quarter where the air always tasted of rust and fish oil, he got what he wanted. No tale. No lineage. Just a name, spoken soft and cautious, as if even the syllables might cut the speaker for daring to know them.

Kalithea.

He leaned back into the worn wood of the booth, the firelight catching the edge of his smirk as the name settled on his tongue. He said it once, softly. Let it curl through the air like smoke.

"Kalithea."

Smooth, but not soft. Regal, but wrong in the mouths of courtiers. It didn't belong to any house he knew. No title echoed behind it. No crest. No scandal. No story.

Just power.

The kind that didn't ask for permission to be felt. He didn't recognize the name. She wasn't nobility, at least not by the rules this kingdom played by. But she moved like someone who had once commanded armies. Someone who carried her own history like a blade hidden. And someone, somewhere, had worked very hard to keep her hidden from men like him. But they'd failed. Because now he had something real. *A name.* It wasn't enough to win. Not yet, but it was enough to change the game.

He returned to the hideout that night with the scent of rain-drenched stone clinging to his coat and the pulse of the city beating steady beneath his boots. The streets bent around him like they knew he walked with purpose again. Inside, the fire had burned low, casting golden light across the room in long, stretching shadows. He sank into his chair without urgency, resting one ankle over his knee, fingers drumming lightly against the worn armrest.

He smiled, not the easy grin of a thief with a secret. A real one. Slow. Certain. Satisfied. Now, he had a piece of her. A single thread through the dark. And soon, very soon, *she'd know it.* Because whatever else Kalithea was, however carefully she'd veiled herself beneath silk and silence, she had stepped into *his* city.

And the King of Thieves always claimed what walked his streets.

The morning light bled slow and silver across the chamber walls, filtered through gauzy drapes that did little to keep the cold at bay. Kalithea stood by the window, one hand resting lightly on the carved sill, watching the city stir beneath a pale sky. Far below, the capital's rooftops glittered with frost, the streets already busy with carts and cloaked figures who moved with purpose and little poetry.

Behind her, Liam paced. She could hear the soft repetition of his boots against the polished floor, the restrained weight in every turn. When he finally spoke, the words were quiet but far from calm.

"So much for the King of Thieves being impossible to shake."

Kal didn't move. "He hasn't approached us yet. That doesn't mean he isn't watching."

Liam stopped mid-stride, arms folded tight across his chest. "The Prince and his knight seem to think he's more myth than man," he muttered. "But I'm starting to wonder if he's just...*overrated.*"

She turned her head slightly, casting him a sidelong glance. "We've worked very hard to keep our names out of the right mouths, Liam. If he hasn't found me, it's because we didn't want to be found."

He blew out a breath, jaw tightening as he resumed pacing. "Right. But if he *can't* find you *here*–right in the heart of Varis, walking the same halls every day–how the hell is he supposed to find Arjun halfway across the continent?"

Kal turned fully, her expression calm, unbothered. "He may have already found me."

He stared at her. "You think he's seen you and just...what? Decided to wait?"

"I think," Kal said, walking toward the vanity, "that it may not be interesting enough yet to make his move."

Liam's frown darkened. "You think this is a *game* to him?"

She didn't answer immediately. Instead, she picked up a brush, running it through her hair before setting it aside with a precise motion. When she looked back at him, her voice was cool but firm.

"No. But it is a hunt. And he doesn't waste effort chasing what doesn't run."

Liam's mouth tightened. "So you want to make yourself *more* tempting."

"I want to make it impossible for him to ignore us."

"Kal–"

"It's time," she said, her tone final but not harsh. "Hints. Shadows. Just enough to turn heads. To make the right ones start whispering."

His brows drew together, and the storm gathered in his eyes again. "You're not seriously planning to drop our identities in front of the court."

"Yes, and no. Perhaps not directly," she said, already turning toward the wardrobe. "Maybe something subtle. A comment. A moment. A thread for clever minds to tug on."

Liam crossed his arms again, every line of him braced against the idea. "And when the wrong people start listening?"

"Then we'll know who they are."

He stared at her, silent for a long beat. She didn't press him. She never had to.

Finally, he exhaled, a low sound through his teeth. "I still hate this plan."

"I know," she said lightly.

He watched her open the wardrobe, begin selecting her attire for the day. Every movement was graceful. Unbothered. It only made his unease worse.

"Kal," he said quietly, "don't make me watch you walk into the fire just to see who follows."

She glanced at him over her shoulder, eyes cool as the marble beneath her feet. "I'm not walking into the fire, brother."

A pause. Her hand settled over a dark green sash, the cloth catching the morning light.

"I'm lighting it."

The great hall stirred with early murmurs as the nobles of Varis assembled, robes sweeping stone, voices low and clipped, the scent of old perfume and polished metal heavy in the air. Light filtered in through the high windows, not yet bright, but sharp enough to catch on gold filigree and the edge of drawn brows.

Kalithea entered at Alden's side, steps fluid, posture effortless. She wore deep green threaded with the faintest shimmer of silver embroidery at the cuffs, the color rich against her skin, her hair drawn back in a way that left the line of her neck bare.

She looked, in a word, *undeniable.*

"You mean to disrupt every thought in this hall before the first petition is heard," Alden said dryly, arching his brow in appreciation. "Cruel, really."

"Only to those not paying attention," Kal murmured.

Raoul, who had taken his usual place just behind them, leaned in with his usual polish, voice smooth. "If the gods had any grace, they'd have warned us you'd arrive dressed for war *and* worship."

Kal offered him a faint smile without turning.

Jarreth stepped in beside her with far less flourish, his voice low and warm. "You look beautiful this morning."

Kal's lips curved. "Three men. Three compliments. Must be a holiday."

Alden chuckled, gesturing for the court doors to be opened. "Shall we ruin it with politics?"

The court chamber opened around them, vast and domed, with banners unfurled from the high beams and light spilling like rivers down the marble floor. Courtiers lined the perimeter in layered silks and fixed expressions, all eyes drawn forward as the royals and their guests took their seats upon the raised dais. Kal settled at Alden's left, Jarreth at his right, Raoul one pace behind them all.

The first petitioner was called forward. It began as it always did– requests for tariffs to be lowered, grain routes to be protected, a dispute over land inheritance that had clearly festered for years before today. Kal listened, composed and thoughtful, her expression calm, her attention sharp. She offered no interruption, only the composed nods and subtle glances that had become her signature in these halls.

But then the next name was read. A landowner from the northern borders. Older. Nervous beneath his practiced courtesy. His petition concerned a growing unease in his holdings, specifically, a string of minor raids and unrest near the Elandran borderlands.

Kal's eyes lifted. Her fingers stilled and she smiled. Just slightly.

Of course, she thought. *Of all mornings. It seems like luck favors the bold.*

She listened as the man explained–his grain stores harassed, his shepherds uneasy, his guards stretched thin trying to patrol too much ground. No flags flown, no banners raised, only whispers and the rustle of movement too careful to be dismissed as nothing.

Alden shifted slightly beside her, no doubt preparing to answer but Kal sat forward first. The motion was fluid, not abrupt, but it carried weight. The nearby courtiers fell silent a breath early, heads turning at her motion.

"Lord Malrin," she said, her voice smooth and unhurried, "what you're experiencing is not uncommon."

He bowed his head. "Your ladyship?"

"There are bandit factions within the old Elandran borderlands," Kal continued, eyes steady, tone even. "Remnants. Scattered command. Just chaos stitched together with desperation. Some of them are oppor-tunists. Some are merely trying to survive."

She folded her hands lightly atop her lap. "You'll see more of it before the year ends. Small, uncoordinated raids. Nothing that will threaten Varis directly, but enough to unsettle the farms, test the watch lines."

Lord Malrin nodded slowly, uncertain. "And...will there be aid dispatched?"

Kal's smile deepened by a fraction, still gracious. Still composed.

"I'm confident there will be recommendations sent to the border command," she said. "But in truth, Lord Malrin, once I reclaim my throne in Elandra, such disruptions will cease entirely. The crown will hold its own borders again."

A hush fell over the room. As if someone had taken the moment and breathed into it a second too long.

Jarreth's head turned slightly toward her. Alden didn't move at all. Raoul's hand shifted on the hilt of his sword, not in alarm, but in interest. Kal remained perfectly poised, her expression unchanged. She had said it as though it were already fact. As though reclaiming Elandra's throne was not just *possible*, but *inevitable*. And now, every noble in the room would spend the rest of the day wondering whether they'd heard what they thought they'd heard and whether it would be more dangerous to ignore it or ask her to repeat it.

Kalithea said nothing more. She sat back in her seat, one hand resting gently on the carved arm of her chair, the other still folded across her lap. Her posture was composed, but her expression–that serene, unflappable mask–told the court exactly what they feared to ask.

The throne of Elandra. *Her* throne.

Alden let out a low chuckle, calm enough to pass for a breath, if not for the amused glint in his eye.

He leaned toward her, murmuring beneath the hush. "Well played. I should have known you'd never settle for subtlety when theatrics were an option."

Kal didn't look at him, but her lips curved, the barest acknowledgment. Raoul, standing just behind them, had turned slightly away from the court, shoulders stiff with the effort of holding in his grin. His eyes sparkled with delight, as though he'd just watched someone tip a full goblet of wine into a noble's lap and call it diplomacy. Jarreth, seated on Alden's other side, was still. He didn't smile. His gaze was fixed on Kal, and while there was no fear in it, it held the steady weight of someone *watching*, not what she said, but what it *cost* her. Not how she smiled, but whether she was holding her breath beneath it.

Alden straightened, smoothing the front of his robes with off-handed grace.

"Well," he said aloud, his tone light, as though nothing at all had shifted in the air, "Lord Malrin, I believe your question has been answered rather thoroughly."

The old lord blinked, mouth parting as if to speak, but no sound came. He bowed, perhaps more deeply than originally intended, and stepped back without another word.

Alden rose to his feet.

"That concludes today's session of court," he announced, his voice carrying easily across the chamber. "The crown thanks you all for your time."

There was no room for protest. No one dared interrupt. Chairs scraped against stone. Murmured voices resumed, hushed and hungry. Somewhere to the left, a viscountess clutched her fan a little too tightly. A young scribe near the dais forgot to stand.

Kal stood with Alden, Raoul falling into step behind her, Jarreth matching her pace smoothly.

And behind them, the court began to unravel.

ROPE, WINE, AND RUIN

Kipp Harlow was not a man easily shaken.

He had waited in alleys for hours, motionless, just to catch the flicker of a careless hand. He had followed marks across city lines and borderlands, changing names and faces as often as he changed coats. He knew the thrill of a secret slowly unwound, the satisfaction of stripping away each layer until the truth lay bare and vulnerable beneath his touch. He *enjoyed* the hunt.

But this was *obsession*. Ever since he'd learned her name, *Kalithea*, the world had narrowed to its syllables. A name was supposed to anchor a person, give shape to the unknown. But with her, it had only deepened the mystery. Every thread he pulled led to another, tighter knot.

And gods, he couldn't look away.

The reports came in fragments, pieced together in low-lit corners of his den, whispered by those who moved through walls and washed linen and disappeared again. But with each scrap, each careful detail, the picture sharpened–and what emerged was not a mark. It was a warning.

She was in the palace, protected by the king himself. No official title, no crest, yet unmistakably *someone*. She moved through court like she owned it, though no house claimed her. She accepted no suitors, gave no favors. Her attention was a weapon, and she wielded it sparingly, precisely–always in service of something unseen. She trained at dawn, clad in soldier's linen, and sparred with the Prince and his knight, both twice her weight. Moved like water, edged in steel. Said little at feasts. Laughed rarely. Watched *always*.

Beyond that?

She left no trace.

Kipp leaned back in his chair, the firelight gilding the edge of his jaw, one hand toying with a silver coin that danced easily across his knuckles. His gaze flickered toward the dark window.

"Clever girl."

The court might be blind—dazzled by titles and silks, too drunk on protocol to see the wolf beneath the velvet—but he saw her clearly. She wasn't prey. She was a *predator*. And she had chosen to step into *his* city.

The knock was soft, barely there. The door opened and one of his oldest whisperers slipped inside—drenched from rain, breathing hard, boots muddy with palace earth. His cloak clung to him in soaked folds, but his eyes gleamed with something brighter than exhaustion.

"I have it," the man said, breath still catching. "I know who she is. *All of it.*"

Kipp's hand stilled on the coin. "Go on."

The whisperer straightened, voice lowering instinctively. "Kali-thea. She's not just *someone* under protection. She's...a *queen*."

Kipp let the silence stretch. Let it soak. Then he set the coin down. "Of where?"

"Elandra," the man said. "The fallen kingdom. But—" He hesitated, eyes flicking toward the fire as though afraid it might burn the truth from his tongue. "There's more."

Kipp's brow arched. "Go on."

"Well, rumor has it—well it's said—the true heir...is...*half-fae.*"

Kipp leaned back slowly, eyes narrowing. Suddenly, all the pieces slid into place with perfect, maddening clarity. The grace. The silence. The speed. The way she'd held a dagger to his throat and a second to his groin without ever seeming hurried. The eyes that had looked through him, not like a woman judging a man, but like something *ancient* measuring something *mortal.* Of course she wasn't fully human. No normal woman had ever made him feel *unseen.* His smile came slowly, curling across his mouth like the curl of smoke above a dying candle.

"Well," he murmured, voice rich with heat, "that explains a few things."

She wasn't simply powerful. She wasn't simply royal. She was *other.* Rare. Dangerous. *Designed* to unmake men who thought they'd already seen everything worth unmaking. Gods help him, he wanted her more than ever. He exhaled through his nose, the sound low and steady, the kind of breath a man takes not to calm himself but to prepare.

She had slipped into his city like a secret. She had left him in that alley with no name, no warning, only the memory of her silence and the cool press of steel against his skin. And now, she was hiding in a palace full of fools who thought they'd glimpsed something rare without realizing they were staring at a storm waiting to be called down.

His smirk deepened. "Well, if she won't come back down to me..."

He stood, smooth as poured ink, reaching for his coat. The fire caught in the gleam of his rings, the dark line of his jaw, the quick flick of silver he pocketed without thought.

"...then I'll go up to her."
The King of Thieves had chosen his mark.
And he was done waiting.

Kipp had broken into a great many places in his life–fortresses ringed in steel, vaults built to cradle the dying breath of empires, noble estates threaded with magic and mistrust. He'd passed undetected through sigil-locked doors and across floors designed to bleed the unwary. Once, he'd walked out of a lord's treasury with five pounds of enchanted gold and left behind a replica so convincing, it bought the noble six weeks of illusion before collapsing in front of a visiting ambassador.

But tonight?

Tonight might be his finest work. Not because the palace was impenetrable. It wasn't. He'd seen more complicated guard rotations and far more desperate nobles hoarding power behind stone walls. No, this one was different.

Because of her. Kalithea didn't simply reside within the palace. She *inhabited* it, like a presence carved into its stone, wrapped in silk and war, made permanent not by banners or titles, but by sheer gravity. She moved through its halls not like a guest, or even a queen, but like the silence between breaths. Felt. Not seen. And Kipp had no interest in disturbing her world. He only meant to enter it.

It had taken days to arrange. Carefully placed coin. Promises tucked into the ears of people who didn't know how carefully they'd been chosen. A palace maid deep in gambling debt. A stablehand who talked too freely once the sun was down. A bored sentry who thought himself clever and wanted someone else to think so, too. None of them knew the whole picture. Only a single thread. A lantern left unlit. A corridor closed for repairs that didn't exist. A tray of documents delayed just long enough to stall a courier's report.

Individually, they meant nothing. Together, they were a map.

Even so, Kipp knew the palace wasn't the true risk. The risk was *the brother.* A soldier shaped by war, honed by grief. The kind of man who didn't sleep without one hand near a blade. Who didn't trust silence, or peace, or even comfort. A man who scanned hallways without appearing to look. Who listened too well. Who stood as if braced for impact, even in conversation.

Kipp had watched him for nights. Memorized his movements. Counted the length of his stride. Noted the way his footfalls changed pitch when he was restless. Liam was the sort of man who expected betrayal in the silence. But even men like that made mistakes. And Kipp had only ever needed one.

A summons, carefully arranged, drew Liam two floors down. It took planning and a few well-placed favors to time it to the second. Kipp had measured the window, forty-seven seconds between Liam's departure and the moment the guards outside her corridor turned their backs.

That was his opening.

He slipped through the corridor like a breath of cold air. No scrape of leather. No glint of steel. He climbed up the far tower wall, his grip sure, his coat barely brushing the ledge as he rose toward the balcony. When he landed, he crouched at the edge of shadow, tucked in the hollow curve of the stone arch where torchlight didn't quite reach. The wind was soft here, high above the city, carrying with it the scent of jasmine and rain-washed marble.

He allowed himself a moment. Just one. He had made it. Past the palace gates. Around Liam. Through locks and steel and all the quietly humming vigilance of a court that didn't know what it was guarding. Not a single misstep. No alarms. No eyes catching his shadow. No breath raised in alarm. He was exactly where he intended to be.

And she? She had *no* idea.

The thought slid a grin across his mouth–slow, indulgent, and edged with something far darker than satisfaction. He leaned forward just enough to glimpse the warm flicker of candlelight behind the tall window panes, obscured by sheer curtain panels. Her silhouette moved within, elegant, purposeful and impossibly composed. The fall of her hair caught the light as she sat, and even that motion looked planned.

He rested one hand on the edge of the balcony, the other adjusting the collar of his coat with ease. His voice, when he spoke, was barely more than breath against the wind.

"Oh, darling," he murmured, his smirk deepening as he watched her pass just beyond the glass.

"You are going to be *absolutely furious.*"

Tonight was meant to be the pinnacle of his performance. Every moment leading to this one had been stitched with expert care: now he stood at the threshold, boots planted on the ledge outside her balcony, the city sprawling far below in a wash of gold and shadow.

This was it.

He'd imagined the scene a hundred ways–her startled breath, the elegant rise of an eyebrow, perhaps even that low, reluctant smile of someone impressed against their will. He wasn't above vanity. He'd *earned* this entrance.

But what greeted him instead...was stillness. She was already *waiting.*

Kalithea sat like the queen she was never introduced as, draped in soft midnight silk, one leg crossed over the other with conscious indifference. A glass of wine cradled in one hand. Her posture spoke of ease but her gaze was steel, locked onto him sharp as a dagger's edge. The flickering fire light caught in her eyes, turning them to liquid amber.

She didn't rise. Didn't startle or blink. She simply...looked at him.

Kipp froze for a single heartbeat. Long enough to register that he'd been anticipated. Then he exhaled a low, provocative chuckle and stepped into the room, as if this had been his plan all along. He moved fluidly, one brow lifted in theatrical disappointment.

"Well," he said, voice curling with amusement, "so much for the grand entrance."

He strolled forward, arms open in mock surrender, the roguish tilt of his grin playing just shy of arrogance.

"Do you have any idea the number of bribes that just went to waste? I had a stablehand, a bored footman, and three very overpaid distractions involved. There was rope, Kalithea. *Rope.* I don't do rope anymore. I've risen beyond that."

She tilted her glass lazily, letting the wine catch the light as it swirled, her expression mysterious save for the faintest curve of her mouth.

"And yet," she said, voice smooth, "you're here. *Uninvited.* Speaking far too much."

He pressed a hand to his chest in mock offense. "Wounding, truly. Here I was hoping for at least a little awe."

"And I was hoping for an earlier arrival," she said, sipping from her glass without breaking eye contact.

Kipp gave a bark of laughter, unbothered, thoroughly entertained. "Ah, so you were expecting me. That's either deeply flattering or profoundly dangerous. Tell me, do you always recline like a goddess in the dark with a vintage wine and murder in your eyes, or am I just a special occasion?"

Her gaze sharpened, the faint smile not faltering, but turning pointed.

"You're not special, Kipp Harlow."

His name on her tongue sent something primal curling inside, low and feral. He didn't let it show. Not fully. Just offered a slow, appreciative smile and leaned back against the table like it was all part of his act.

"I was beginning to wonder if you knew me."

"I make a habit of learning the names of men foolish enough to

291

spy on me."

"And here I thought I was being subtle."

"Subtle? You were predictable. *Loud.*" she corrected softly.

He grinned wider, letting his gaze slide over her like silk drawn through fingers, not lewd orr vulgar, but purposeful. Like every angle was another cipher to decode.

"I'll have you know my entrances are legendary."

"So you say," she said, setting her glass aside delicately, "but you've managed to become the first man in recorded history to break into a royal palace only to arrive *late* to his own unveiling."

Kipp tipped his head back and laughed–a rich, unguarded sound that filled the room. Gods, she was everything he had hoped and more. When his eyes met hers again, they gleamed with something unmistakably dangerous.

She took another unhurried sip as he stepped fully into the room, the silence between them settling. He watched her from the center of the chamber, a smile playing at the edges of his mouth, lazy, thoughtful and dangerous. That glint in his eyes never quite faded.

"You're not surprised to see me," he said at last, voice edged with amusement.

Kalithea didn't look away. She gave her wine glass a slow swirl, the crimson liquid catching the candlelight.

"Should I be?" she replied, like the question bored her.

Kipp chuckled under his breath, slipping his hands into the deep pockets of his coat as he began to wander further inside, eyes moving over her chambers in idle curiosity but always, always circling back to her.

"Most people are," he said. "Surprised, I mean."

"Most people," she answered, "tend to bore me."

He grinned. Gods, he liked her.

"You know," he mused, running a finger lightly along the edge of a polished table, "you make it exceedingly difficult to flirt properly."

She made a faint sound behind the rim of her glass, a soft hum that might've been a laugh or a warning.

"A tragedy," she murmured.

"Isn't it just?" He sighed dramatically, "I may never recover."

"I'm sure you'll survive."

"That's where you're wrong," he said, flashing her a grin. "I'm terribly fragile. Delicate, really. Like glass. I break easily."

Her gaze tracked him, cool and unyielding. "You steal crowns for a living."

"And yet no one ever thinks to ask how I'm *feeling* about it."

She set her wine aside with a soft clink of glass on stone, reclining. "Would you like applause?"

"I'd settle for your undivided attention," he said, turning toward her fully now, that grin deepening into something slower. "Though I'll admit, I thought breaking into your rooms might earn me more than a raised brow and a sip of wine."

Her fingers steepled before her, gaze sharp. "You're lucky I didn't stab you."

He smirked. "Who's to say you won't? I'm still here."

"You're still here," she said, voice low and smooth, "because I haven't decided yet whether or not you're worth the mess."

"I scaled palace walls," he said softly, stepping closer, "outwitted your brother, danced past half the guard. All for the pleasure of your company. Surely that earns me more than a coin's worth of suspicion. I risked life and limb. You know how few people can say they snuck into a palace and lived to tease about it?"

She didn't smile, exactly, but her lips curled, just slightly.

"I've seen men do more," she said. "*For less.*"

Kipp laughed, low and full of warmth, but with a new sharpness threading underneath.

"Now that's the flattery I came for." His voice dropped a little, intent behind the humor. "*You wanted me to come.*"

Kalithea stood, her gown whispering against the floor as she stepped toward him. The candlelight played along the curves of her face, her shadow stretching behind her like something sentient. She came to a stop before him, her gaze still holding him like a knife at the throat.

A smile touched her lips. "Did I?"

He didn't move. Not because he was stunned or, gods forbid, hesitant but because in that moment, he wanted nothing more than to stand still and let her come to him.

Kalithea stopped just short of touching him, her gaze steady as it lifted to meet his. There was no softness in it. Only intent.

"You wanted something..." she said, voice low, quiet enough to be mistaken for a whispered secret.

He didn't reply right away. He was still watching her closely.

"And I let you think you might get it," she added, with the barest tilt of her head.

His grin faltered, just enough to mark the hit. Because she was right. And worse, she *knew* she was right.

Still, he recovered fast, his voice curling up with a laugh that didn't quite disguise the edge beneath it. "You're very good at this."

"I know," she murmured.

He studied her face again, searching for a crack. Some flicker behind the eyes. A misstep in the mask. But there was nothing. Just that subtle, maddening smile, the one that said she was always a step ahead and waiting for him to notice.

"So tell me then *Your Majesty*...," he said, letting the grin return as he let the title linger like a dare, "What exactly did I climb the palace walls to find tonight?"

She answered at once. Smooth. Precise. "That depends."

He arched a brow, the question implied. "On?"

Kalithea moved slowly, passing behind him with a glide of fabric and the ghost of warmth. Her voice drifted past his ear as she circled, a whisper.

"On what you think I want from you."

He turned in time to catch the edge of her dress, the curve of her spine as she crossed the room once more—back to her wine, back to her place of calm, unshakable command. Kipp stood rooted for a beat longer, something sharp and unfamiliar curling low in his chest. He let her words settle deep. This wasn't banter. It was a proving ground. And Kipp Harlow had never seen a test he wanted to pass more.

He tilted his head, grin curling slowly, eyes fixed on her with the reverence one might reserve for a priceless relic stolen in defiance of gods and kings. Her posture hadn't changed, but he recognized the stillness. She wasn't waiting for an answer. She was waiting to see what kind of answer he *thought* she wanted.

"What do I think you want from me?" His voice was smooth like dark wine, the kind that left a burn behind. He stepped forward carefully, just close enough for her to feel the warmth of him.

"You want to know how I found you," he began, watching for any flicker in her gaze. "You want to know if my web stretches further than palace walls, if I slip deeper through cracks than your brother's knives. If I can make shadows turn their heads and names vanish before they're spoken."

She didn't respond. But something behind her eyes gleamed sharper.

"You want to know," he went on, "if I'm a thief playing pretend in a court of power or if I'm the one they should've been watching all along."

His voice dipped. "If I'm the kind of man who *writes* the rules...and leaves kings scrambling to read them."

That earned him the barest twitch at the corner of her mouth. Not a smile. Not yet. But it was more than most people ever got. He let his own grin spread in full, basking in that sliver of acknowledgment like it was the crown itself. "Did I get close?"

Kalithea tilted her head slightly, eyes cool. And then, as effortless as a blade sliding home—

"No."

A single word. Smooth. Dispassionate. A dismissal dressed like truth.

Kipp laughed, a rich, delighted sound. "Liar."

She didn't rise to the bait. Didn't flinch. Just arched a brow with that serene contempt only the truly dangerous could pull off.

And gods, it only made her more interesting.

He sighed, dragging a hand through his hair with mock despair. "Alright then. Let's pretend I believe you." His tone softened, slipping into something smokier. "If that's not what you want from me...what is it, Kalithea?"

She sat watching him, smiling. A whisper of a thing. Dangerous. Seduction with no promise of warmth.

"I suppose," she said, voice low and laced in something sweet and sharp, "you'll have to find out."

It hit like a knife between his ribs and a kiss on the mouth. Something bright. Something addicting.

He hadn't walked into a trap. He'd *asked* for one.

"Gods, woman," he muttered, rubbing a hand over his mouth. "You really might ruin me."

She set her glass down, lips curving slow and sly. "Then I suggest you pace yourself, Kipp."

Kipp exhaled slowly, the sound soft, and let the corner of his mouth curve with that lazy, wicked charm she'd come to expect. "Tell me something, Kalithea."

She lifted a brow in answer, not with surprise but amusement, a predator's patience cloaked in poise. Her voice was soft, subtle and wicked. "Are you finally ready to ask the right questions?"

"Oh, sweetheart," he drawled, stepping forward unhurried, like a man who could slip a dagger in the heart while whispering sweet nothings. "I've been asking the right questions since the moment I saw you in that market."

"You knew I'd come," he said, his voice dropping to something darker. "Not just follow the trail you left like a breadcrumb of coins and shadows. You knew I'd want more. That I'd *need* more."

Kalithea tilted her head, just slightly. "Is that what you've convinced yourself of?"

"I think," Kipp murmured, stepping in close enough to steal breath, "you're playing a dangerous game."

Her smile sharpened, cool and exquisite. "And yet, here you are."

"I *like* danger."

"You like to *win*."

"Same thing," he said softly, "in the right hands."

That pulled a sound from her–a quiet laugh, low and sudden, not hollow. Not rehearsed. Real.

And gods, he felt it. It cut straight through him.

He smiled, something less theatrical now. Want tangled with admiration. "What is it you want from me, Kalithea?"

She didn't rush to answer. Instead, she set the moment down gently between them and turned it like a coin in her palm. Then, she returned it:

"What do *you* want from *me*, Kipp?"

The echo reverberated in his chest. A challenge, yes. But not just that. It was a mirror and he didn't love what he saw in it. He'd come for information. For leverage. To peel her apart and piece together the truth. But now, gods help him... he wasn't sure what he was after anymore. She had led him here on invisible strings, made him think it was his idea, and now–now he was standing in the middle of the fire, smiling at the burn. His grin faltered, just barely. Not gone, only changed. Less armor, more admission. He rubbed a hand over his jaw, laughter slipping out like breath dragged through surrender.

"You really might be the death of me."

Kalithea swirled her wine once more, eyes dark and steady. "Only if you're lucky."

He laughed quietly, under his breath, shaking his head like he was already imagining the minstrels tuning their lyres: *King of Thieves undone by a woman with too many secrets and just enough teeth.*

"I should go," he said at last, the words low and reluctant.

She didn't move. "So soon?"

"Before I get caught," he said, already drifting toward the balcony.

"How responsible of you."

"I have my moments," he murmured, flashing a grin as one foot found the ledge.

But he didn't leave. Not immediately. He paused, silhouette carved in firelight and moonlight, shadows wrapping around him like a cloak. And when he turned back to look at her, there was nothing casual in his eyes.

"I'll see you again, Kalithea."

She lifted her glass in a slow, knowing toast, the smirk on her lips a secret folded in silk.

"Oh," she said softly, "I'm counting on it."

And with that, the balcony was empty.

Kipp moved through the palace quietly, vanishing between torch-light and stone. The shadows took him in without resistance, welcoming him back as if they'd missed the weight of his presence. His boots barely whispered against the marble as he passed beneath arches carved with a king's vanity, slipping down corridors gilded with wealth too old to notice the thief in its midst.

At the outer wall, his hands found their place on the cool stone ledge, fingers steady despite the slick sheen of midnight dew. He didn't hesitate. The descent was muscle memory—each foothold claimed skillfully, each breath measured, each movement silent as snowfall. His body obeyed, smooth and disciplined. But his thoughts...his thoughts were a wildfire.

He'd gone to that chamber to take the upper hand. He'd spent days crafting his entrance, outmaneuvering palace guards and Liam's hawk-eyed vigilance. He'd expected a reward for his effort—a flicker of surprise, perhaps admiration, certainly leverage. What he'd found instead was a woman who had been waiting. Poised. Ready. Reclined with her wine like a queen entertaining a late guest at a party she had orchestrated from the start.

She had not only anticipated him. She had *invited* him. And gods, she'd done it with such terrifying grace.

Kipp dropped lightly to the courtyard below, the impact absorbed in a practiced crouch. He stood, rolling his shoulders, shaking off the tension but it clung stubbornly, like the echo of her voice.

What do you want from me, Kipp?

He had names for every pursuit. Curiosity. Power. Profit. Amusement. But Kalithea didn't fit any of them. She was too sharp to be a mystery and too controlled to be merely intriguing. She wasn't something to be solved. She was something to be *experienced* and gods help him, he *wanted* to.

Kipp reached the alley's end, ducking between two weathered stone buildings until he found the familiar sliver of hidden masonry. He rapped twice on the uneven surface, and the wall yielded with a click, the door swinging open to reveal the den beyond—dim, warm, thick with the scent of old smoke, old secrets. He stepped inside and closed the door behind him, sealing the cold out. He stood there for a long moment, coat still on, the room around him silent save for the creak of old beams and the distant tick of rain on the roof. The fire in the grate had gone low. A few embers pulsed in the dark, not unlike the feeling curling inside of him.

She had bested him. He'd admit it.

Tonight.

But this wasn't over, not even close. Next time, he wouldn't let her dictate the rhythm. He wouldn't come chasing shadows. He'd walk in already holding the match. He shrugged out of his coat and hung it on its peg, exhaling a breath that did nothing to clear the weight coiled behind his sternum. Then, with a faint laugh—dry and self-deprecating—he glanced toward the empty room and muttered,

"Oh, Kalithea... what the hell have you done to me?"

Somewhere beneath the words, beneath the smile that curled despite himself, was a truth he hadn't yet named. She'd turned the game on him and he *liked it.*

Kipp exhaled, dragging a hand through his hair, the dagger pausing mid-spin as he leaned his head back, eyes tracing the cracked beams above. This wasn't about the thrill anymore. Not the hunt. Not the clever unraveling of a name wrapped in silk and smoke. It wasn't about victory. He'd lost that hand, clean and quick.

It was her.

And that meant he couldn't treat this like every other game. He'd scaled towers. Toppled merchant kings. Stolen names and nations without so much as a scratch. But this wasn't something to steal. This was something to earn. And so, he recalibrated.

Step one: *Watch.*

Not as some desperate hanger-on skulking in torchlight. No rooftop stalking, no childish shadows. Observation was an art, and Kipp had built his empire on knowing where to place the brush. He sent the best, those who could vanish into linen and livery, who could laugh with nobles and be forgotten by nightfall.

A groom who brushed the prince's horse but listened better than he spoke. A kitchen girl who drifted between wine casks and whispered secrets. A jeweler with too many friends in high places and too few loyalties.

He wanted to know everything. When Kalithea rose. When she vanished. Where her attention lingered. And, most telling of all, who she allowed near. Because power didn't live in presence. It lived in access. And hers was guarded like a treasury with no locks to pick.

Step two: *Close the distance.*

Not with charm. Not with games. Just presence. The suggestion of pursuit. The ghost of a glance from across the room. She had invited the chase, he'd give it back to her, but on *his* terms this time.

No pressure. No rush.

Just inevitability.

He pushed off the table with a slow stretch, catching the dagger and sheathing it in one fluid motion. The room smelled of old wood, sweat, and smoke. Familiar. Grounding. But he no longer belonged to it. The smirk returned to his lips, slow and sharp, all teeth and danger. This wasn't a job anymore. It was something older. Deeper. She had asked him what he wanted. He still didn't have a clean answer. But he knew the first step. It started with her and it ended wherever she decided to let him go.

If she let him go.

THE WATCHFUL EYES OF THE KING OF THIEVES

aoul met Kal strike for strike, but there was no urgency between them. Their rhythm was familiar now, like breath and blood. She moved with the ease of muscles long-trained, every step born from discipline rather than exertion. This was routine. Precision. Control.

And yet beneath it all, something was off.

She felt it first, before she saw it. That subtle shift in the atmosphere, not tension exactly, but something adjacent. The hairs at the nape of her neck lifting, not from fear, but instinct. She'd lived through enough betrayals to recognize being watched, even when the eyes were hidden behind polite uniforms and rehearsed stillness.

There—by the gate. A steward, too still. His eyes weren't on his ledgers. They were on her. Not blatantly. Just long enough. And there—by the stables. A boy with calloused hands polishing a bridle that didn't need it. His movements languid, almost bored, but wrong in their rhythm. And there—sweeping near the barracks wall. A woman repeating the same slow arc of her broom, not once shifting to the next stone. Her gaze flicked toward Kalithea, quick, but not quick enough.

They weren't soldiers. Weren't spies. But they were watching. Positioned. Coordinated.

Kipp Harlow had finally made his next move. He was inside now, not physically, no. But close enough. Close enough to draw lines through her day, to measure her silences, to count the spaces between her strikes. He wanted to know the rhythm of her world.

Then let him.

She didn't falter. Didn't look twice. Her blade whispered through the air and caught Raoul's cleanly. The tension in her limbs never showed in her face. She was composed, collected, waiting.

Raoul pressed forward with a feint, testing. She deflected with a flick of her wrist, circling.

"You're distracted," he murmured, eyes flicking to hers.

"Am I?" Her voice was smooth, distant.

His mouth quirked. "You don't usually let me get this close."

She gave the barest lift of a brow. "Must be slipping."

He scoffed, low and fond. "Unlikely."

Then she moved. Without warning, her blade danced forward–an explosion of motion, honed and merciless. She drove him back in three strikes, pivoted, caught his counter, and twisted the angle before pulling away again. The clamor of steel on steel cracked through the air.

She didn't glance toward the gate again. Not toward the stable, not toward the woman with the broom. She didn't need to. She could feel them watching.

Let them. Let Kipp's little ghosts report back. Let them mark the strength in her arms, the cool in her voice, the deliberation in her every movement. Let them think they were gathering understanding.

Kalithea wasn't prey. She wasn't some curiosity to catalog and dissect. She was the threat they hadn't yet named aloud. If Kipp believed distance gave him safety, if he thought he could study her from afar, twist her shape into something he could outmaneuver, then he had never truly understood what sort of game he had walked into.

She would let him draw closer. Let him believe he was narrowing the space between them. And when the time came? She would show him just how thoroughly he'd misread her.

They circled one another without speaking. Kipp remained a shadow, always where he intended to be, just out of reach, just beyond sight. He moved through the palace like wind through a cracked door, glimpsed only in the ripple of a curtain or the momentary hesitation of a guard who couldn't explain why the hairs on his neck stood on end.

Kalithea, for her part, gave no indication she noticed. She never turned her head toward the soft hush of movement along the garden walls. Never paused when a servant bowed too low or lingered too long. If she sensed his presence, she showed no sign.

Each night, his network returned with their scraps–fragments carried in whispers, tucked into sleeve linings and murmured through backroom doors. She still trained at dawn, unrelenting, her blade carving through the morning like she meant to draw blood from the sky itself. She still walked court halls wrapped in silence and steel, her eyes sharper than the jewelry at her throat. At formal gatherings, she spoke rarely, but when she did, the room shifted. And always, there were the two men—Prince Jarreth, watchful and soft-spoken, ever at her side, and Sir Raoul, the Dunes-born knight pouring all of his once rakish attention onto one woman. They hovered near her always, though it was never clear whether they meant to protect her... or simply orbit her.

Yet for all the secrets Kipp's whisperers laid at his feet, none brought him what he truly wanted. None could tell him what Kalithea sought, what she wanted, what she *needed*. Her intentions, her plans, the next turn in her game—they were locked behind that calm, impassive face. And for a man who had built his life on seeing through veils, that was a problem he could not ignore. The tension had shifted. The game was no longer play, it was pressure.

Kipp wasn't content to be a ghost at the edge of her story. He had studied her movements, tracked her habits, mapped her world like a thief casing a noble's vault. But this was no longer about opportunity. This was personal. She was making her moves, laying her traps carefully, and he couldn't tell if the dance she'd drawn him into was meant to end with a kiss...or a blade.

And that drove him to the edge of himself. He wasn't built to wait. *He* dictated the terms. *He* controlled the board. *He did not follow.*

So if Kalithea thought she could leave him circling in silence, thought she could pull strings while he watched from the rafters like a forgotten marionette, she was about to be reminded.

He was not a man easily ignored.

And no one, not even a queen cloaked in shadow and grace, ran the game better than the King of Thieves.

The second time he entered the palace, it felt less like a risk and more like a ritual.

Kipp moved without hesitation, his hands and feet already trained to the route, each step a quiet echo of the first. The halls welcomed him like an old accomplice, torches flickering in familiar rhythm, guards turning at their posts as if on cue, every creak and shadow accounted for. The same coins weighed the same pockets. The same distractions played out with the same perfect timing. Even Liam, ever vigilant and hard-eyed, had grown predictable in his patrols.

And predictability, to a man like Kipp, was opportunity.

By the time his boots touched down soundlessly on the balcony, the grin had already taken shape at the corner of his mouth. This time, he thought, the advantage would be his. This time, he'd walk in three steps ahead, not behind. He slipped through the curtain like smoke drawn on a breeze, silent and certain.

And stopped.

She wasn't in bed, nor curled in some corner chair playing the part of the amused hostess with wine in hand. She wasn't waiting to start the game.

She was already playing.

Kalithea sat at her vanity, wine glass half empty on the table, bathed in the soft flicker of candlelight, the rest of the room cast in shifting shadow. Her back was to him, posture relaxed, bare legs folded beneath her, a thin, translucent ivory shift clinging to skin brushed by firelight. Her hands moved with smooth purpose, unwinding silver chains from her loosened hair, each strand falling in dark waves down her spine like something conjured, not grown.

It was a vision meant to unmake. Or perhaps, meant to test.

And Kipp, gods help him, didn't even *pretend* to resist. He knew the difference between happenstance and design. Knew the shape of bait when he saw it. But knowing was never the same as walking away.

So he stayed and let his voice break the silence. "You have a terrible habit of stealing the moment, you know."

She didn't turn. She placed the last chain beside the others on the polished wood and met his gaze through the mirror.

Her smile was slow, knowing, and entirely purposeful. "Then perhaps you should stop giving it to me."

Kipp chuckled, stepping forward with casual confidence. "A fair point. I had a whole entrance planned, too. Cloak catching the wind, a little poetry in the timing...ruined, all of it."

"And yet," she murmured, her voice soft enough to seem unbothered, "here you are. Standing in the dark. Watching me."

He leaned against the doorframe now, arms folded loosely, his gaze skimming over her with hunger. "You make it rather difficult not to."

"Do you plan to stay there all night?" she asked, tilting her head just slightly. The motion caught the light, cast a shimmer along her cheekbone. "Or will you lurk and smolder until the candles burn out?"

"I haven't decided," he said. "There's something to be said for lurking. Especially when the view is this generous."

Her eyes met his again in the mirror. "You call it generous. I call it calculated."

He smiled at that. "Calculated generosity, then. Still lovely."

She rose then, not suddenly, but slowly with graceful intention. The shift of her weight was fluid, fabric whispered as it slid against her skin, the folds settling around her legs. Kipp held his ground as she continued to look at him through the mirror, arms at her sides.

"You actually came back," she said, as though it were a simple observation.

"I always do," he said, voice dipping lower. "Though I'll admit, I half expected a blade in the ribs this time."

She considered that. "Would it have stopped you?"

"Only long enough to compliment your aim."

A breath of a smile. "Flattery. Again."

"Observation," he corrected, taking another step into the room. "You're not finished with me. You've barely begun."

"And you?" she asked, letting the air between them tighten. "Are you here to win?"

"No," he said, gaze settling on hers. "I'm here to learn."

She tilted her head, dark eyes narrowing with the interest one gives to a piece on the board they hadn't expected to be dangerous.

"And what will you do once you understand me?"

He smiled again, this time slower. "Pray you never stop surprising me."

Kalithea laughed softly, genuine and edged with something dangerous.

Kipp crossed the threshold of her chamber like he'd been summoned, though they both knew no such invitation had been issued. His gait was slow, unrushed, that familiar lilt of mockery and effortlessness coiled beneath every movement. Shadows stretched out before him, long and low in the candlelight, but she didn't turn.

He watched her for a moment, longer than he meant to, his crooked smile settling naturally at the corner of his mouth. "It's hardly fair," he murmured. "Most men would kill for their entrance to land that spectacularly, and here you are...already expecting me."

In the mirror, her brow lifted, the gesture clean and dry. "Am I meant to be awed by your trespassing? Or merely your arrogance?"

He came further in, trailing fingers across the edge of a carved table as he passed, savoring the hush. "You're meant to be impressed by persistence and attention. Even yours must have limits."

She hummed, a sound caught somewhere between amusement and dismissal, and at last turned. And he realized, a beat too late, that was when he lost the advantage. Because facing her–fully, directly, with no barrier between them but the breath of a room–wasn't just dangerous. It was undoing.

She stood half in firelight, half in shadow, a slip of ivory silk draped across her, leaving very little to the imagination. Her hair fell unbound over her shoulders, glinting as it caught the gold of the flame.

Kipp rolled his shoulders, as if that might loosen the tension suddenly wrapped around his chest. "You know," he said, his voice lighter than it felt, "most people would at least pretend to be startled."

Her lips curved, wicked and wry. "People in this kingdom are too easily impressed."

He huffed a quiet laugh, genuine, despite himself. "So tell me–am I about to get a knife to the chest, or are you actually pleased to see me?"

Her head tilted slightly, the light slipping across her cheekbones. "Would you prefer the former?"

"Not tonight."

"Then I'd suggest you stop tempting me."

He laughed outright this time, low and delighted. "Oh, that's the only part I'm good at."

She didn't move to correct him. Kipp took the silence as it was offered–an opening, not an end. He stepped in closer, not enough to provoke, but enough to claim space. The air between them shifted.

"Debatable."

He leaned against the edge of her table now, shoulder brushing carved wood, the flicker of candlelight catching the gleam in his eyes. She hadn't dismissed him yet. And that meant something.

"You wound me," he said, feigning injury.

"If I wanted to wound you," she said, her voice quiet, "you'd know."

The laugh that escaped him then was stripped of charm. It was real. Sharp-edged and breathless. "See, that's the problem. I don't *know* a damn thing about you, do I?"

There was something different in his tone now. A thread pulled free from the jest, frayed at the edge.

Kalithea's gaze didn't waver. But behind the poise, something in her eyes shifted, small, but there. A flicker of recognition.

"And that...bothers you."

He shook his head, his smile fading into something quieter. "No. That draws me in."

She considered that, long enough for the hush to settle again. "Quite a dilemma, then."

He ran a hand through his hair, breath slipping out in a near groan. "So, are we pretending this isn't happening?"

Kalithea didn't so much as glance his way, "What, exactly, is it you think is happening, Kipp?"

He smiled at that. He took a step forward, the hush of the room pressing in around him.

"*You tell me.*"

She turned, languid and unbothered, her movements unhurried. She didn't look dressed for seduction. She looked like the thing seduction prayed to when it wanted to be remembered.

Kipp's fingers flexed absently at his sides. She was beautiful, unquestionably, but not in the painted way of courtly ornaments or favored courtesans. Hers was a beauty etched in shadow and clarity both. It demanded attention like a blade unsheathed, not a smile performed. And now, he wasn't entirely certain which role he occupied: hunter or hunted.

"I think," she said, her voice smooth as ever, "you may be overestimating your own importance."

He grinned instantly, more dangerous than offended. "Darling, I never overestimate. That's for amateurs."

A soft sound escaped her–dismissive, or amused. Perhaps both. That, of course, was what made it worse. What made it so perfectly, maddeningly her.

He drifted closer, slower now, not quite circling, not quite stalking. "So tell me," he said, voice dropping, "what's the game?"

She tilted her head with feigned consideration. "Game?"

"Let's not insult each other," he said, his smirk carving deeper. "Not tonight."

That earned him a real smile. "I would never."

"Of course not." He ran a hand through his hair, the motion casual, but his gaze never wavered. "But we both know you're playing one. I just haven't figured out what the prize is yet."

She laughed then, or something near to it "Do you always assume you're the mark?"

"No," he said. "I always assume I'm the one winning."

She raised her glass, took a slow sip, and watched him from over the rim. Her expression was calm and guarded. But in her eyes, there was the flicker of something–interest, mockery, caution. It was enough to keep him leaning forward, never quite close enough to catch it.

"Why are you here, Kipp?"

Kipp hesitated a moment, before leaning in with a grin. "I wanted to see you."

Her lips barely curled. "How sentimental."

"Tell me," He murmured, gaze steady. "how long do you plan to stand still, while everything between us keeps burning?"

She stilled, just for a heartbeat. Just long enough. Then she set her glass down with deliberate calm, her fingers too precise to be anything but practiced.

"Go home, Kipp."

His smile deepened, slow and wicked. "You don't mean that."

She met his eyes with unsettling calm, her voice velvet and steel. "Don't I?"

Kipp had won something. He could feel it in the subtle shift of the air between them, in the flicker of her gaze that caught a fraction too long, in the near-imperceptible stutter of breath that gave her away for only the span of a heartbeat. It wasn't a stumble. Kalithea didn't falter.

But she had paused, and in that pause, he'd glimpsed the edge of possibility. For the briefest moment, he believed the balance had tipped. That she was within reach at last. That the Queen of Composure had stepped to the line, and this time, he'd drawn her there.

Kalithea closed the distance between them slowly, her bare feet kissing stone in a rhythm he felt in his bones. She moved like a predator that knew it need not chase. The fabric of her shift clung to her as if stitched from moonlight, casting delicate folds over the rise of her hip and the soft dip of her waist. Fragile, it should have seemed. Bare. Vulnerable.

It looked like armor.

Kipp's breath caught before he meant it to. When the last breath of space closed between them, she didn't touch him. Not quite. Her hand hovered just shy of his chest, suspended in air and tension. The distance between skin and skin no thicker than a breath, yet it scorched. The heat radiated from her like the sun veiled in silk, seen but not seized. Then she leaned in, not to offer, but to remind him what he couldn't take. Her breath brushed his jaw, her eyes lifting through dark lashes like a secret slipping free.

"You want me," she said, low and certain. "So much it burns"

She let the silence draw tight, her lips just shy of his. She let the moment stretch, until it ached between them.

"But careful, thief..." her voice dropped, "men like you don't burn for long, but gods, how bright you die."

The silence rang in his chest like a bell struck low and hard, the echo rolling through his ribs and into the space between who he was and who he thought he'd always be. His lungs faltered. His pulse skipped. For all his years skirting danger, for all the nights he'd danced with risk and walked away smiling–he had never stood so utterly, thrillingly outmatched.

She pulled back slowly, her fingers still not touching him, yet leaving him marked. When their eyes met again, there was no need for victory in her gaze. It was already there. Quiet. Absolute. The smirk she wore wasn't taunt or triumph. It was knowing. She had dismantled him with a single breath and not so much as a touch.

He wanted to kiss her. Gods help him, he wanted to test the limits of her patience, her control, her curiosity. He wanted to throw every last one of his tricks to the wind just to see how she'd parry.

But before he could so much as shift his weight, she moved past him. The whisper of her body brushed his, light as a sigh and twice as devastating. It wasn't contact. It was a brand. A reminder. She crossed into the inner chamber like a final act in a play he'd never seen rehearsed, her silhouette retreating into shadow and silk. The door she left ajar was not an invitation.

It was a challenge.

Kipp stood motionless in the hush that followed, breath caught somewhere between reverence and ruin. His hands remained still at his sides, empty of every trick he had ever trusted. His grin, when it finally returned, was crooked–half admiration, half surrender. He exhaled. Long. Quiet. Awed. Then laughed, low and rough, raking a hand through his hair as though it might set him right again.

"Gods above," he muttered to the empty room, "I am in so much trouble."

Kalithea wasn't a mark. She wasn't a prize, or a conquest, or a lock to be picked. She was power. She was purpose. She was something he could not pocket, wear, or charm. And for the first time in a long, reckless life, Kipp Harlow understood what it meant to want what could not be taken.

Only earned. Or lost.

A Thief Unraveled

Kalithea played the game the way a master conductor might command a symphony, every glance a note, every silence a measure. She moved through the palace with authority, her composure carved into something near divine. She never looked toward the places where shadows stretched longer than they should, never spared a glance for the corner where he watched, still as smoke.

But Kipp knew.

She knew he was there. She had to. She felt him in the way only someone forged by danger could feel the shift in the air. And instead of turning toward it, she let it simmer–fed it, slowly, consciously. She gave him no answers. Only hints. Only half-buried questions designed to rot under the weight of his curiosity. She let the whispers swell. She said little. Offered less. Just a poised smile. A tilt of her chin. A presence so complete it left no room for conversation.

And the morning? She was back in the yard at first light, blade in hand, sweat on her brow, her movements honed to lethal clarity. No performance. Just power. pure and unflinching. The kind that didn't ask for respect, but took it. She never missed.

And Kipp, for all his charm and silken lies, found himself unraveling. The dice games turned listless. The liquor tasted like ash. The laughter in his tavern rang too hollow. Women he might have flirted with, might have tangled with on a more careless night, barely registered. The thrill was gone, leeched out of every familiar vice by a single, gnawing truth: he had lost the rhythm.

For the first time in years, he wasn't in control.

And he hated it.

He sat at the edge of his table, boots propped, hands restless, thoughts tangled in silk and blade and moonlit silence. He needed to see her. Not to speak, not even to touch, but to look. To remind himself that the game hadn't outpaced him completely.

"Boss."

The voice cut through the quiet, one of the younger ones. Lean, quick, smart enough to know when not to breathe too loud.

"She was seen. West gardens. With the prince. The knight too."

Kipp didn't look up. "And?"

"Talking. Couldn't get close enough to hear. Looked...comfortable."

That made him glance over. "*Comfortable...*"

The boy shifted his weight, uneasy. "Easy with each other. Familiar?"

Kipp's fingers curled against the table edge until the old wood creaked. His gaze stayed fixed, unblinking. Then, with a slow exhale, he let a smile pull at his lips, tight, humorless and dangerous.

"Is that so."

It wasn't jealousy. Not exactly. He could have stewed in it. Could have let it fester into something sharp and ugly. But that wasn't his nature.

Kipp Harlow didn't brood.

He moved.

That night, he made his decision. He didn't slip through the palace as a man seeking permission. He didn't lurk. Didn't crouch in shadow or pause to listen. He walked the corridors like he'd been born to them, and the darkness welcomed him like an old lover. Every rotation of the guards had been memorized. Every unlocked door, every shift in torchlight, every echo in the stone marked and mastered. The palace wasn't a fortress anymore. It was a map he already knew how to read.

By the time he reached her balcony, his blood was steady, breath measured. This time, he didn't wait for silence. He didn't wonder whether the timing was right. He opened the door like he owned the hour. And of course, she was already there. Not startled. Not unsettled.

Waiting.

As though she had always known he would come. As though she'd left the lock undone not out of carelessness, but certainty. She sat near the firelight, one arm resting along the arm of a chair, her eyes half-lidded, expectant. A queen, not in title, but in posture–in the way the air shifted around her and made the room hers.

He should have been triumphant. Should have smirked, should have said something clever.

But instead?

Kipp Harlow was ready to lose his goddamned mind.

He entered without flourish. No smug grin or soft-footed swagger. He shut the door behind him like a man walking into his own reckoning.

She didn't rise to greet him, didn't even turn. Kalithea sat straight-backed at a low table, no wine sipped in leisure, no languid sprawl meant to seduce. Just poised calm, lit by the steady flicker of candlelight, her silhouette carved in gold and steel.

"You're getting predictable, Kipp."

The words struck clean, soft, and merciless.

He exhaled roughly, not quite a laugh. "You should be flattered."

"Should I?"

"I don't break into bedrooms for just anyone."

Her brow rose, amused. "Is that so? Because here you are...*again.*"

"Here I am," he echoed, voice flat, the words clipped by something that had started to sound dangerously like need. He crossed the room in long, even strides, hands in his pockets like he hadn't just spent the last six days climbing palace walls in a losing war against his own restraint.

"Tell me something, Kalithea."

"No."

He blinked, thrown off by the swiftness of it. "You don't even know—"

"I don't need to."

Of course she didn't. She always knew. Every time he stepped close, she had already anticipated the angle. Every line he spoke, she'd calculated before he opened his mouth. He began to pace, the motion slow and circling, more beast than man now, wearing down the floor as if he could carve her out of the room with motion alone.

"What is it you want from me?" he asked, low, not pleading but not far from it either. *"Exactly."*

She stood. The room changed. She wore no gown tonight, no sheer distraction or weaponized beauty crafted for male distraction. A crimson robe draped over her, cinched at the waist with a glint of silver thread. The light clung to her, and in that moment, she looked less like a woman and more like the god of every man's undoing.

Kipp stopped moving. Her steps were soft. Controlled. She approached without reaching, her presence enough to press heat into the air between them.

"You came all this way," she murmured, close enough now that the scent of her skin curled through the air like the memory of sin, "risked your life... again." She let a slow breath part her lips. "And now you want to know what I want."

He didn't move. He couldn't. "I think I've earned the right to know."

She circled. Her voice dropped, smoke and silk and steel. "You're desperate to understand me. You hate that I don't fit into any of your tidy little compartments. You hate that you're not the one holding the threads."

He turned with her, forcing a grin that didn't quite reach his eyes. "I've never minded a little mystery."

She stopped. Tilted her head. "Then why are you here, Kipp?"

He didn't answer, didn't need to, because she already knew. She stepped in again, close enough for her breath to trail across the shell of his ear. Her words weren't flirtation, they were truth, punched through his defenses like an arrow to the lung.

"I know what you want."

And gods curse him, she did. It wasn't the chase. Wasn't even the thrill. It was *her*. It had always been her. She drew back and met his gaze, and for the first time, there was something else behind the amusement. Something real. Calculated. Dangerous.

"I'm not interested in that."

His brows drew together. "Then what?"

She didn't smirk this time. Her answer came cool, controlled. "I need to hire you."

He stared at her. The words didn't make sense at first. He blinked once, slow, as though resetting his mind around the shift. "...hire me?"

"Yes."

"For what?"

She didn't hesitate. "To find someone."

Kipp watched her face now—not her mouth, not the movement of her hands, but her eyes. And there it was, at last. Not a ploy. Not a mask. Something human. Something that mattered.

"Who?"

Her answer came without pause. Just a name that struck like a bell in a silent chapel.

"Arjun."

THE PRICE OF OBSESSION

K ipp had been called many things in his life—a thief, a liar, a ghost in human skin. A prince of shadows. A king of locked doors and whispered rumors. But more than any title, more than any myth whispered in Varis' darker corners, Kipp Harlow was a man who lived for the thrill of the puzzle.

And Kalithea was the most maddening one he'd ever encountered. She stood before him like a cipher—flawless in poise, carved in candlelight, offering just enough to keep him close and never enough to let him in. She had drawn him here not with desperation, but with precision. This wasn't a request. It was a calculated move. A trap, if he'd ever seen one.

And gods help him, he was already inside it.

"*Arjun...*" he said, testing the name aloud, watching her face with the same care a knife-fighter watched for a feint.

She didn't blink. "Yes."

He drummed his fingers once against his thigh. A silent beat. The only outward sign of tension creeping into his spine. "And what exactly am I meant to do about that?"

"Find him."

Kipp let out a short breath that almost passed for laughter, laced with disbelief. "That's cute. Try again. This time with details."

She offered none. No flinch. No apology. Just that unwavering stare, those eyes that saw more than they should, cutting through the silence like a scalpel. She wasn't pleading. She was measuring him. Deciding just how much truth he needed before the hook set.

"You want my help," he said, circling closer, "but you won't tell me why? That's a strange strategy, love, for someone...*wanting*."

"It's not about want," she replied, calm as still water. "It's about necessity."

He stopped just shy of her reach. His brow lifted. "Now you need me?"

A faint curve tugged at her lips. Not warmth, never that. Something closer to acknowledgement. "Is that going to be a problem?"

Kipp smiled, slow and dangerous. "Depends on the price."

Kalithea tilted her head, candlelight sliding along her cheekbone. "And what, *exactly*, is the cost of your assistance, Kipp?"

He let the silence do the talking. Let it stretch long enough to make her wonder.

"Ah," he murmured at last, the grin curling lazily back into place, "now wouldn't you like to know."

She turned away, crossing toward the vanity. Her fingers skimmed the edge of the polished wood, idle and meaningless. Which meant it wasn't.

"And what makes you think I care to know?" she asked.

Kipp's smile sharpened. "Because you're running out of people to turn to."

She stilled, just a fraction too long between steps, just a pause where there hadn't been one before. But he saw it. Of course he did. Because Kipp always saw when the mask cracked, even if only for a breath.

She turned back to him, face composed, voice smooth. "You're not the only one who finds secrets."

"No," he said, voice quiet now. "But I'm the only one who knows how to drag them into the light."

The air between them pulled tight. Not heat. Not tension. Something heavier. Something ready to break the moment wide open.

"I need to find him," she said, softer now. "Can you help me or not?"

He held her gaze. No grin now. Just the truth. "I can."

"Then do it."

"Not for free."

Her lips twitched, just once. Not quite a smile. "Of course not."

That should have been the moment he stepped back. Walked away. Reclaimed whatever piece of himself he hadn't already handed over. But he didn't. Because even now, especially now, she held the board. And somehow, even when she was asking for help, she never stopped setting the rules. And the worst part? He didn't want them to change.

Kipp exhaled, shaking his head with something like admiration and something like defeat. "Fine," he muttered. "But don't think this means you win."

Kalithea's smile was dangerous, slow, devastating. "Oh, Kipp. I never *think* I win."

She turned, her robe catching the light like spilled garnet, silk hissing against stone as she crossed the chamber.

"I just never lose."

Kipp grinned, mulling it over. He didn't do charity. Not for kings. Not for thieves. Not for women with dangerous eyes and daggered smiles. Every deal had a price. Every moment, a cost. Even chaos, his favored vice, came with terms attached.

But this? This was different. She'd asked. Nothing hidden in her tone. Just the truth, laid bare between them. And for one taut, unspeakable second, he believed the game had shifted. That he *just might* have turned the board in his favor. So he leaned back against the edge of her vanity, casual and loose, the candlelight gilding the line of his jaw and the dangerous curve of his grin.

"Well then," he drawled, voice low and amused, "back to the question at hand. My price?"

He let it hang there, as though the notion itself was absurd.

"I'm a man of refined appetites–gold, secrets, power–"

"You already have those," she said, interrupting without effort.

He grinned wider. *"Exactly."*

"So then," he murmured, watching her, eyes lit with something feral, "what does a man who already has everything take in trade?"

She didn't flinch. But the tilt of her head said it all, that same razor-sharp curiosity he'd seen in her every move since the moment they met. And gods, he wanted to know what she saw when she looked at him like that.

Then, after a pause measured in heartbeats, she said, "You're asking for something rarer than power."

He nodded, the grin on his lips turning slow and sharp. "Exactly."

She exhaled, steady but not indifferent, and asked the only question that mattered. "And what, exactly, would that be?"

Kipp stepped forward. Just enough to let the space shift, to let the air between them change shape.

"Time." he said.

One word. One breath. And it landed like a blade point-down between them. He saw it instantly, the change. Subtle and small, but unmistakable. Her fingers brushed the vanity's edge, just a little too carefully. Her posture shifted as if she'd just recalculated the cost of this conversation. There was a breath she hadn't meant to release. A pause in the depth of her eyes before the mask slid back into place.

"Time," she echoed.

"You heard me."

"You want...*mine.*"

Kipp's grin spread, slow and sure, teeth flashing like a fox too close to the henhouse. "More than anything."

She watched him, weighing outcomes. Measuring odds. And then, without warning, she laughed. It was real, soft and startling in its simplicity.

"You are absurd, Kipp Harlow."

He leaned in just enough for his voice to reach only her. "And you're evading."

Her smile lingered, faint but true. "How much time?"

"A fair amount."

"That's not an answer."

"It's the only one you're getting."

Silence stretched once more, thick and sharp with tension.

"Fine."

He blinked. "Fine?"

She shrugged, smooth and maddening, the motion laced with effortless control. "You get my time."

She let it settle. Let him think it was done. And then, with that low, sultry voice, she added–"For now."

Kipp exhaled slowly into the hush between them.

You get my time. For now.

It wasn't permission. It was a challenge, elegant and edged, a gift wrapped in conditions. A thread offered not out of trust, but control. And gods help him, Kipp had never been more tempted to snap a thread just to see what unraveled.

"So," he murmured, voice low and laced with wry amusement, "it's settled then."

"It is," she replied, with the same calm she might use to name the weather.

"I help you find your missing man..."

"Arjun."

He gave a slow nod, savoring it. "Yes, yes. Him. And in return, I get..."

He let the pause stretch. Let it test her.

She didn't blink.

"Time," he finished.

"Correct."

The silence that followed was thick. Kipp could feel it, not the awkward kind that clawed for meaning, but the dangerous kind that dared you to speak. They'd named their terms. But he was the one who knew what that time was worth. Not for the job. Not for the coin. But for her. Access. A window into something guarded like a vault and twice as treacherous. Because this wasn't about Arjun. It was about *her*. And now, for the first time since he'd laid eyes on her, he had leverage. Not the loud kind. Not the kind that forced movement. The quiet kind. The patient kind. The kind that broke open locked doors one breath at a time.

Kipp pushed off the vanity, arms crossed loosely over his chest. "Then we should discuss the details."

She didn't move. "As in?"

"As in," he echoed, voice smooth and tightening, "where he was last seen. Who he was working with. Enemies. Friends. Habits. Patterns. Give me something real."

She studied him without blinking. "I thought you were the best."

"I am."

"Then figure it out."

The breath he let out came with a laugh, soft and incredulous. "Gods, you're a menace."

"I prefer efficient."

"I prefer clients who don't hand me puzzles with half the pieces missing."

"And yet," she said, her tone silky, "you agreed."

Kipp stepped closer, every inch of him wired for movement, for response, for the game.

"You're going to regret this," he murmured.

"Doubtful."

"I don't mean the job." His voice dipped lower. "I mean the time."

She held his gaze, steady and unshaken. "I think I'll survive, Kipp."

"Oh, you'll survive." He leaned in slightly, enough to feel the charge bloom between them. "But the real question is will you come out of this game unscathed?."

For a breath, the world held still.

"I suppose we'll find out," she said. And buried beneath the control, beneath the poise, he heard it.

A flicker of anticipation.

Kipp chuckled under his breath, stepping back before the line between them blurred into something else. He turned toward the balcony, rolling his shoulders as though shrugging off the tension.

"Try not to miss me too much, darling."

"I won't."

A pause.

"But I do wonder..." Her voice followed him, crisp and cool.

He stilled. Didn't turn. Didn't breathe.

"...who will change who in the end?"

He looked back, the smirk returning.

"Oh, Kalithea," he said, voice velvet and steel, "you've no idea what you've just agreed to."

Then he stepped into the night, his mind already pulling at threads, patterns, possibilities. Because now he had a name. Now he had a job. And now...he had *her time.*

WHERE THE GHOSTS WAIT

K ipp moved through the lower city like he was carved from its bones—fluid, quiet, and unquestioned. He didn't need to slip into the shadows. He *was* the shadow. The streets made way for him in their own manner: drunkards vanished into doorways, thieves turned their eyes elsewhere, and the alleyways themselves seemed to hush in acknowledgment.

But Kipp wasn't paying attention to the familiar. Not tonight. His thoughts ran lean and sharp around a single name, the way a hound circles a scent too rich to ignore.

Kalithea.

She had handed him a puzzle, one wound in silk and silence. Not enough to solve, but enough to chase. And she'd done it with the kind of ease that should have infuriated him, except it didn't.

Kipp pushed through the heavy doors of his stronghold without slowing. The shift in the room was immediate. The clatter of dice stilled. Laughter fell off. Conversation bent itself around his silence. These were not fearful men, but they were smart, and smart men read the room.

And tonight, their king was hunting.

"Orders," Kipp said, his voice carrying easily across the hall. Not raised. Not needed.

Those closest leaned in, eyes alert. No one asked questions. Not yet.

"I want a name dug up. Arjun. Elandran, most likely, and with a name like that, cant be too hard to find. Might've traveled under a different one since. I want to know where he was last seen, who he ran with, who he might've crossed. I want traces, whispers, rumors—hell, I want ghosts if they speak his name."

He didn't pace. He stood with that same unsettling stillness that made his enemies nervous and his allies sharper. His gaze swept the room once and landed where he meant it to—on the woman leaning against the far wall, arms folded, mouth silent, eyes watchful.

"Start there," he said. "And if the trail goes cold, find the names that never make it onto parchment. Look for the men who vanish without fanfare. The ones no one notices are missing until they're already forgotten. I want the kind of ghosts who whisper when no one's listening."

She nodded once and disappeared into the dark.

From the corner, a voice spoke up. "Timeline, boss?"

Kipp didn't look up. "Yesterday."

And that was all. The room erupted. Cloaks were thrown over shoulders. Blades vanished into boots. Doors opened and closed in rapid succession, scattering his people into brothels, watch-houses, gambling dens, and the thousand cracks of the city where truths went to die.

And Kipp?

Kipp moved to his chair at the head of the long, battered table. He sat like a man returning to his rightful place, not to rest, but to plan. One hand drummed lightly on the armrest, his eyes distant, calculating. Already turning the next move. Already setting the next piece.

The days stretched thin, one bleeding into the next, a slow grind of whispers and dead ends. Kipp's network moved like smoke through Varis—swift, precise, relentless—but the Kingdom yielded nothing. No rumors. No sightings. No trace of a man named Arjun. Just silence.

Kipp stood at the window of his private study in the depths of the tavern, one boot braced against the wall, a half-finished glass of wine untouched at his elbow. Below, the city buzzed on oblivious. But his thoughts were far to the North.

Back to Elandra.

He'd known it would come to this. Kalithea hadn't needed to say it. Her request hadn't been about tracking someone who slipped away. It was about dragging a ghost out of the dark. And ghosts like that didn't vanish in Varis. They vanished across borders into kingdoms ruled by fear.

"Boss."

The voice was quiet, wary. Kipp turned as the runner slipped inside. Rain streaked his cloak. Mud crusted his boots. His face was pale beneath the hood.

"Well?" Kipp asked, calm and cold.

"We pulled everything from the city—street-side records, tavern logs, border talk, names new and old." The runner hesitated. "There's nothing on Arjun here. Not under that name. Not under any false ones we could trace."

"I could've told you that three days ago," Kipp muttered, irritated.

The runner swallowed. "So we went wider. Started asking questions about Elandra...discreetly. There's chatter, boss. Bits and pieces, mostly buried. But it's there."

Kipp's attention sharpened. "Go on."

"There's been disappearances. Silent ones. People taken from the southern edge of the kingdom. Travelers. Refugees. Some locals, too. No records. No word. Just...gone."

"Military?"

The runner hesitated. "Hard to say. Could be. But no banners, no uniforms. Operatives, maybe. Loyal to whoever's holding the chains."

Kipp's jaw tightened. "And no one's talking?"

"They're afraid. Whatever's happening up there, it's not just violent. It's organized. And people who poke too hard don't come back."

For a long moment, Kipp said nothing. He crossed to the map on the far wall and stared at the northern reach, his thumb pressing just below the jagged black lines that marked the border of the fallen kingdom.

"Did they say where exactly?"

"Not exactly. But we're hearing the same towns. Border keeps. Villages that shouldn't matter."

"They do now," Kipp murmured.

The runner shifted uneasily. "What do you want us to do?"

Kipp's gaze didn't move from the map. His voice was low, even.

"Keep digging. But not here. Not from the street rats or barkeeps. I want my best inside the border. Quietly. Northward first. Elandran territory, the places people avoid. Follow the vanishings. Follow the fear."

He stepped back from the map, the decision settling like iron in his bones.

"And if Arjun's in one of those places?"

"Then we find out who took him...and if he's still breathing."

The runner nodded and vanished into the dark.

Kipp remained, arms crossed, eyes shadowed. This was a hunt. And whoever had stolen Arjun had done so cleanly, too cleanly. That meant purpose. That meant value. Which meant Arjun wasn't just a missing man.

He was leverage.

Kipp sat slouched in the high-backed chair at the center of the room, one boot hooked over the other and a dagger resting idle across his fingers. The light in the hideout was low, lanterns burning down to amber coals, shadows curling in the corners like listening things. His whisperers moved between them like phantoms, never lingering, never speaking unless summoned. They came bearing scraps. Overheard names, snatches of movement at the border, a sighting here, a silence there. And with time, the silence began to shape itself into a pattern. A path. Not yet clear, but narrowing.

The name came first.

Arjun.

Not vanished. Taken. Hidden with meticulousness. The kind of disappearance that required wealth, reach and intent.

Kipp's jaw ticked as he stared into the dark, the weight of it circling behind his eyes.

"Boss."

The voice came soft from the doorway, the runner's hood slick with night mist. Kipp didn't answer at once. Just tipped his gaze upward with ease, fingers slowing over the hilt of the blade.

"Well?"

"We found the end of the trail," he said. "Or close enough to smell the rot."

Kipp's brow lifted.

The whisperer stepped in, glancing behind as though the shadows might listen. "The Elandran borderlands are sealed," he said. "Not the usual patrol rotations, this is full lockdown. No exits. No questions."

Kipp arched one brow. "And yet you made it back with all your limbs. Encouraging."

The man gave a thin grin. "Took work. But I've got something. There's a stronghold. No records, no sigils. Built into the cliffs by an old port, not sure which. Quiet. Off the books. That's where the trail leads."

Kipp didn't move, but something in his posture shifted.

"What kind of stronghold?"

The whisperer hesitated. Not out of fear, but uncertainty. Like the words themselves tasted wrong.

Kipp's voice dropped. "Don't make me ask twice."

"It's not a prison. Not officially. They don't ask names, don't keep ledgers. Just...people go in. And they don't come out."

Kipp leaned forward, elbows to knees, voice low. "Then what is it?"

"A holding. For men too valuable to kill. Or too dangerous to let go. They break them. Keep them silent. Use them."

The room stilled.

Ruin in the dark.

Of course.

"They don't want him dead," Kipp murmured.

"No," the man said. "They want him useful."

A different weight settled in the air, thick and cloying. Kipp sat back, breath shallow, mouth a grim line. His smirk had gone somewhere quieter. Darker.

"And who runs it?"

The pause stretched longer this time. "Slavers. Mercenaries. *Mawborn.*"

That landed. Kipp didn't react outwardly, but behind his eyes, something old and furious woke.

"Ransom?" he asked.

"None issued. No demands made. No one knows a thing."

Kipp narrowed his eyes. "Then why keep him?"

Another silence. Intentional, this one.

"*Bait.*"

The room seemed to tighten. Even the lanterns flickered lower.

Kipp repeated it. "Bait."

The runner nodded. "They're waiting. Watching. For someone."

He didn't need to ask who. He already knew.

Kal.

She was the reason. The target. And Arjun...the leverage.

Kipp swore under his breath, pressing his fingers to his temple as he stood. "Fucking hell."

It had never been about Arjun. Not really. Not to the ones who planned this. But to Kal? He was everything. The one piece she would never leave behind. The one man she'd burn cities to reach.

And they knew that.

Kipp moved slowly through the room, a single circuit, hands behind his back, thoughts threading like wire. He could tell her. He could lay the truth at her feet: Arjun was alive, broken but breathing, trapped in a nest of blades and shadows where even the name of the place had been scrubbed from memory.

But she'd go. Gods, she'd go without pause. And they would be waiting.

He stopped. Still. A slow smirk ghosted back across his lips, not the careless one. This one held teeth.

"No," he murmured. "Not like that."

He turned to the runner. "Keep digging. I want the exact location, headcount, armament. I want to know who's funding the Mawborn. I want names, movements, timing."

The whisperer dipped his head and vanished, melting into the dark.

Kipp stood there a long moment, hands braced against the edge of the table.

Now, he had something.

Blades Behind the Crown

Kipp trusted his instincts more than coin, steel, or oath. They'd served him longer than any man, and far better. They told him when to vanish, when to strike, when to wait and right now, they whispered patience.

He had the upper hand. A secret sharp enough to draw blood, tucked behind his teeth. But secrets were only power if played well. And Kalithea... Kalithea wasn't the kind of woman you cornered. You didn't force her hand. You waited until she offered it, because if she ever suspected you were playing her, she'd flip the board and burn the pieces. So he said nothing. Let his whisperers keep to the dark. Let the pieces fall where they may.

He watched her.

She stood on the balcony beyond the guest wing, arms braced against stone still warm from the day's sun, the folds of her dress fluttering softly in the high breeze. She thought she was alone. Her posture was looser in solitude, her mask dropped just enough for a man like him to notice the edges beneath. Her hand lingered near the dagger at her side, not cautious, but thoughtful. And when she exhaled, the sound carried, not heavy, just tired.

He didn't move. Not yet. Just leaned against the stone archway and let the quiet stretch between them, wondering if she'd feel him there. She always did.

"You look far too pensive for someone who claims to enjoy the thrill of the game."

Her voice didn't startle him, it rarely did. Kipp straightened, stepped into the light like he'd only just arrived, a familiar smirk easing across his face.

"And here I thought I was being subtle."

Kalithea turned toward him, her eyes sharp. "Not from where I'm standing."

He moved to the edge of the balcony beside her, close enough to glance down at the rooftops glittering below in the city's calm hush.

"I was wondering where my favorite riddle had wandered off to."

"Not much of a riddle anymore," she answered, stepping closer, arms crossed. "At least not to you. Apparently."

He clicked his tongue, pushed off the railing. "Now what makes you say that, darling?"

"Because you watch me."

His smile didn't falter. "And why would I do something like that?"

"Because you know something."

He stilled for a fraction of a second, but she caught it. Of course she did. She was watching too. Always. She didn't know the truth, but she felt it, coiled in the space between them, just behind his grin.

Kipp let out a theatrical sigh. "You wound me."

"Do I?"

"Accusing me of secrets. I'm an honest man."

"You're a thief."

He grinned. "Exactly. Which means I never lie. I just...withhold. Strategically."

A flicker of something crossed her lips. Not a smile, not quite. The air shifted, the tension easing by degrees.

"And what is it you're out to steal now, Kipp?"

He took a step closer, slow, unhurried, until he was close enough to smell the spice and fresh air on her skin. "At this precise moment?"

Her gaze held his. Measuring. Testing.

"I'm parched," he murmured. "Thinking of stealing a drink."

She tilted her head slightly. The predator's consideration, was he a threat, or something more dangerous?

Then, after a long moment, she nodded.

"Fine."

Kipp led her through the maze of the lower city without a word, his stride unhurried, his posture loose. He didn't glance back, he didn't need to. He knew the sound of her steps behind him, light and steady, the kind that never hurried and never faltered. He knew the cadence of her silence too, heavy with suspicion and sharp enough to cut. They slipped past the bustle and into the narrow arteries of the city where gold meant little and truth meant everything. Here, power didn't wear crests or crowns. It whispered. It bargained. It disappeared without a trace.

The tavern stood pressed between two derelict buildings, its presence unmarked but unmistakably watched. When they stepped inside, the air thickened at once, scented with old smoke and varnished wood, the low burn of lanterns casting amber shadows across velvet-lined booths and wrought iron fixtures. No one looked up. In this place, anonymity wasn't a courtesy. It was law.

Kipp moved easily through the hush, parting a curtain and guiding her into a corner booth hidden from view. One flick of his fingers to the barkeep, a clink of coin exchanged, and a bottle arrived–dusty, dark, expensive. He poured without asking, sliding one glass across the table.

Kalithea eyed it. "Am I meant to be impressed?"

Kipp gave a half-shrug, already tipping his own glass toward his mouth. "Only if it keeps you less dangerous."

She said nothing. Just turned the glass slowly between her fingers, inspecting the cut of it before taking a sip. No grimace. No weakness offered.

Of course not.

He lounged deeper into the cushions, casual, watching her over the rim of his drink. "So," he said lightly, "to what do I owe the pleasure of this charming interrogation?"

"I told you," she said, unbothered.

"Did you?" He gave her a slow smile, something just shy of mocking. "Or did you imply you'd be watching me watch you until I coughed something up?"

She took another sip, not rising to the bait. "You already know why I agreed to come here."

Kipp narrowed his eyes, letting the silence settle. "Do I?"

"Yes."

"You think I'm hiding something," he said.

"I know you are."

He gave a soft, humorless chuckle. "Your confidence is truly exhausting."

"I'm not wrong."

"Maybe." He swirled the drink in his hand "But let's say I am. Let's say I do know something you don't. What would you do about it?"

Kalithea held his gaze. Her voice, when it came, was low and calm. "I'd remind you that I don't wait well."

"No," he murmured. "You really don't."

Tension strung tight between them, drawn thin. He could feel it in the subtle shift of her weight, in the glass still turning faintly in her hand.

"You've found something," she said at last.

He hesitated, letting the pause do the work. "Maybe."

A flicker crossed her face. Not anger, something colder. Controlled.

But brittle. "You don't play fair."

"Neither do you." He leaned forward, smile gone. "That's why this works."

"Tell me."

He tapped one finger against the glass. Then stopped. The smirk came back, but dimmed.

"A name," he said. "The ones holding your missing piece. I found them."

She went still. "Who?"

He let it hang. Just long enough. "The Mawborn."

There it was. The crack. So small most wouldn't have seen it, but he did. A shift in her breath. The faint curl of her fingers around the glass.

"You know them."

"Yes."

Just that. One word, laced with something darker than hate.

"Where?" she asked.

He let his smile show teeth. "Now, now, Kalithea—"

"Where?" Her voice was colder now, threaded through with something harder. The edge beneath the calm.

He didn't flinch. "I don't know. Not yet. But I will."

"How long?"

He lifted one shoulder. "Depends."

"On?"

He met her eyes, and this time, he didn't smile. "On what you're willing to give me."

She stared at him, long and level, before exhaling through her nose. "You are—"

"Invaluable?" he offered.

"Insufferable."

"Darling," he said, lifting his glass, "I'm the best kind of problem."

"I'm considering solving you permanently."

He grinned. "You'd miss me."

She didn't deny it.

Kipp didn't need her to speak. He'd seen it already, the flicker she hadn't hidden fast enough. The slight tightening of her grip, the subtle shift in her breath. Nothing overt. Nothing someone else might catch. But he caught it. Kipp had made a life out of noticing the small things. And Kalithea? Kalithea never showed her hand unless she had no choice.

He leaned forward, voice low, coaxing. "You're not asking the right question."

Her gaze lifted, slow and sharp. "And what would that be?"

He let a breath drag between them, just long enough to draw her attention. "Why them?"

For the first time since they'd sat down, she looked away. Not long.

Just a flick of her eyes to the curtained dark beyond their booth. When she looked back, the ice was back in place, but he'd seen the crack.

"It doesn't matter," she said.

He tilted his head. "Doesn't it?"

"No."

Kipp exhaled a short, humorless laugh. "You're an exquisite liar, Kalithea. But I'm better."

She tapped the rim of her glass once, a soft click of nail to crystal. Then she slid it aside.

"You're wasting time."

"On the contrary," he said, reclining just enough to make it infuriating, "I'm enjoying every second of this."

He studied her, the tension around her shoulders, the focus behind her gaze.

"Fine," he said. "Let's stop circling. How personal is this?"

She didn't respond right away but her body betrayed her. Just a breath held a moment too long. Just a shift in her posture, shoulders tighter, spine straighter. As if bracing.

"You already know," she said at last, her voice quieter than before.

"I want to hear you say it. Straight from those beautiful lips"

Kal's gaze sharpened and then she spoke, every word honed to a point. "They worked for him, the Usurper."

Kipp didn't move, the smirk slipping clean from his face.

"They're his." His voice was quieter now, "Rhaen Morrick."

She didn't flinch. But the way she held herself changed...like a soldier remembering the shape of a wound.

"Yes."

No elaboration. No story. Just that single, iron-wrought word. Kipp sat with it, letting the shape of it settle. Letting the truth unfurl in his mind.

And then, softly, she added, "And they have Arjun."

This wasn't just about a missing man in enemy hands. This was history, clawing its way out of the grave. This was the past reaching through the shadows to take something from her–*someone.* So that was the truth she hadn't wanted to name.

"I'll find him," he said.

Her eyes snapped to his, sharp as ever. "I don't need your promises, Kipp."

"Good," he replied. "I don't make them."

But there was no swagger in his tone. Not now.

"Still," he added, quieter, "I will."

A long beat passed between them.

Then–"Then do it quickly."

She rose without ceremony, without farewell, leaving the glass mostly untouched and him behind.

Kipp stayed seated, the name echoing in his head.

The Mawborn.

He understood now just how deep this went and how high the cost would be if he failed.

Kipp didn't rattle. Names didn't move him. Shadows didn't shake him. He'd heard enough whispers in enough dark places to know most were empty. Power wasn't in what people feared. It was in what you *did* with fear. But as the curtain fell behind Kalithea and her steps faded into the hush of the city, her final words still echoing, something stirred low in his chest. Something cold.

The Mawborn.

He'd heard the name before, once or twice. A threadbare rumor. A ghost of a story passed between smugglers and slavers who knew better than to speak it too loud. It drifted through the underworld like smoke from a pyre, never visible, never solid. But always stinking of blood and old sins.

He had never believed in it. Not really. Until now. Until *she* said it. Until the silence in her voice said the rest.

Kipp sat alone in the den, the light bleeding low around him, glass still turning slowly between his fingers. The smirk he wore like armor was gone, replaced by something colder. Sharper. He'd seen that look in her eyes. A silence edged in memory. Not fear, but something deeper. Older. Pain that had never healed because it had never been allowed to. This wasn't about Arjun anymore. This was about her, and someone had gone to great lengths to drag her past back into the light.

He exhaled, long and slow. "The fucking Mawborn."

Not slavers. Not mercenaries. Not in the way most understood. The Mawborn didn't take contracts. They weren't hired blades or sellswords. They were the blade behind the throne, the chain in the dark. They dealt in people, *unmade* people. Quiet, loyal, broken.

And they belonged to Rhaen Morrick.

Kipp's jaw tightened. The pieces were falling together too neatly now. The sealed borders. The rumors. The trail that hadn't surfaced until Kalithea asked him to start looking. It wasn't a coincidence. It was bait. They hadn't just taken Arjun. They'd sent a message. Deliberate. Clean. No ransom, no negotiation—just silence, carefully carved.

A summons.

And he'd delivered it, like a damned errand boy, not even knowing what he held in his hand.

He set the glass down with a firm click, the last swallow burning down his throat. Kipp's jaw clenched. He hated being manipulated. Hated realizing he'd walked into someone else's play. And he hated more than anything the thought of Kalithea stepping back into that world alone. She hadn't asked him to help. Of course she hadn't. She never would. Kal would walk into fire alone before letting anyone see the cost. Before admitting how much it still burned.

But that didn't mean he was going to let her.

A knock at the doorway drew his attention. One of his whisperers stood there, hood low, voice careful.

"Boss. We've got a lead."

Kipp didn't blink. "Speak."

"There's a man in the slums. Used to run with them. Kept his head down after the fall, but...if they're active again, if they're moving, he'll know."

Kipp stood, slow and fluid, rolling his shoulders with a lazy grace that didn't reach his eyes.

"Then it's time we had a conversation."

The whisperer nodded once and vanished into the corridor.

Kipp followed without another word, the shadows closing around him.

This was no longer a favor. This was no longer about coin, or curiosity, or even the promise of Kalithea's time. *This was war.* If the Mawborn thought they could call her back into the dark and not answer for it? Then they were about to learn what happened when you tried to play games with the King of Thieves.

Dead Men Don't Talk

The slums breathed differently at this hour, thin and shallow, like the city was bracing for something it didn't yet understand. There were no watchers at windows, no curious eyes behind cracked doors. Not even the boldest lingered in the alleys tonight. Word had spread, as it always did, light as smoke and just as fast.

Kipp Harlow was walking his streets tonight.

And when the King of Thieves moved through the city after midnight, it wasn't to be seen.

He cut through the narrow veins of the lower city, cloak trailing low behind him, boots silent over the broken stone. His men flanked him at a distance, shadows within shadows, keeping to the dark. He hadn't said much since Kalithea had spoken the name and that silence told them how serious this had become.

The man they sought had once worn the Mawborn brand. A deserter, if such a thing could even be called that. Most who walked in that circle didn't live long enough to flee. This one had clawed his way out, or so the whispers claimed, dragging just enough of his soul with him to remain useful. But Kipp didn't care about his story. He cared about what the man knew and whether that knowledge had an expiration date.

They found him near the edge of the old district, holed up in the rotting shell of a collapsed tenement. The smell hit first—mildew, spirits, the sharp stink of fear. Inside, a warped oil lamp burned low, casting fractured shadows across the stained walls and floorboards. A figure hunched in the corner, gaunt and twitching, eyes already wide with recognition before Kipp even stepped inside. The man didn't move. He just watched as Kipp entered, posture loose but dangerous, every movement designed to close the room in.

"Oh, don't get up on my account," Kipp said, the words dry and almost pleasant.

He crossed the space with unhurried grace, stopping just short of the man's reach. There was no urgency in him, only calculation. The man shrank further into the wall, already shaking, already breaking. Kipp crouched beside him, studying his face the way a hunter might regard something wounded–interested, but unimpressed.

"I hear you used to run with the Mawborn," he said, his voice level. Conversational, as if they were sharing drinks and not stepping toward violence.

"I left," the man rasped, eyes darting. "Years ago."

"I know." Kipp gave a faint smile. "That's the only reason you're still breathing."

He stood again in a fluid motion, and from beneath his coat he drew a blade, catching the lamplight with a glint that needed no flourish. He simply turned it between his fingers, casually, as if weighing its edge.

"I have a problem," he said quietly. "A man's gone missing. Not just any man. One who matters. The kind of man whose disappearance doesn't go unnoticed. And from what I've gathered, your old associates have taken him in."

The man was still trembling, but he said nothing.

Kipp tilted his head, as if waiting for something clever that never came. "And you're going to tell me where."

"I don't know anything," the man whispered, a little too quickly.

Kipp's expression didn't change. "Wrong answer."

He moved with suddenly, catching the man's wrist and twisting. Bone cracked, and the man screamed, sagging sideways in a heap of limbs and torn breath. Kipp didn't release him.

He leaned in close, his voice soft. "Do you know what I do to liars?"

"I swear–!"

The blade flashed, cutting a clean line down the man's forearm– just enough to bleed, just enough to sting. Kipp's grip didn't loosen.

"I'm not asking for much," he said, almost gently. "Just a direction. One port. One name."

The man squirmed, his breath coming ragged. "I left them–I haven't seen anyone since the fall, I swear–"

"And yet," Kipp said, tightening his grip, "you're still alive. Which means someone let you live. Which means you're still useful to them. And if you're useful, then you know something."

Kipp lowered his voice. "Tell me before I stop asking."

The silence that followed stretched long and brittle. Then, in a voice that shook with the weight of surrender, the man broke.

"Elandra," he gasped. "South of Kellyn Bay. There's a fortress– built into the cliffs. Hidden. That's where they are."

Kipp's smile returned, slow and razor-thin. "See? That wasn't so hard."

He watched him a moment longer before releasing his wrist. The man collapsed against the wall, clutching the injury as blood soaked through the tattered sleeve. Without hurry, Kipp took out a cloth, wiped the blade clean, and slid it back beneath his coat.

"I'm a generous man," he said, straightening. "I only take what I'm owed."

He started toward the door, but paused at the threshold.

"One more thing," he said without turning. "If I hear a single whisper of this...if you even look like you're thinking about running your mouth, I won't just take your name."

He glanced back over his shoulder.

"I'll take your voice."

And then Kipp was gone, slipping back into the alley like smoke into wind. His men joined him in silence, their pace matching his without question.

The air felt colder now. Sharper. The answer they'd come for had finally been dragged into the open—one name, one place, a buried stronghold tucked into the sea cliffs of Elandra. But it wasn't just a location they'd been given. It was a line drawn. Because Kalithea would want to go. Of course she would. The moment he told her, she would be ready—blade in hand, fury beneath her skin. She'd walk into the maw without hesitation, without fear. That was what made Kipp's jaw tighten. Because now that he knew what waited for her there, now that he'd seen the shape of it...he wasn't ready to let her walk into it alone.

Kipp stepped into the open air, the scent of damp stone and smoke still clinging to the back of his throat. The city's usual noise—the rattle of shutters, the rustle of rats, the low hum of voices slipping through the cracks—was absent here. In this narrow stretch between crumbling walls and crooked beams, there was only silence. He didn't move. He stood just beyond the door frame, letting the silence sink into his skin, letting the weight of what he'd learned press in steady.

Behind him, boots shifted against the stone. A soft sound. Intentional.

"Boss?"

The voice wasn't hesitant. His men had long since learned not to question with fear. But it carried something else, restraint and respect.

Kipp didn't turn and gave a single nod. That was all it took. The shadows peeled away from behind him, slipping past with the kind of fluid grace that came from years of survival, training, and silence. They moved like the weapons they were.

There was no scuffle. No scream. Just the soundless absence that followed death. He didn't need to ask. When they returned, wiping blades on cloth, he could feel it. The air had changed. That particular hush, absolute and final, always came when a loose end had been severed.

The Mawborn was dead.

Kipp wasn't in the business of loose ends, and he knew the difference between finishing a job and lingering in it. Most of all, he knew the danger of leaving a man like that alive. He hadn't killed him for vengeance. He didn't believe in sentiment when the game was this sharp. He'd done it because the man had seen too much. Because guilt was a fickle thing, and fear even worse. Eventually, the bastard would've talked. Maybe not for coin, maybe not out of betrayal, but desperation made men generous with truths they never meant to tell. And when Kalithea was involved, Kipp didn't leave anything to chance.

Not when her past could still bleed.

He exhaled through his nose and drew his dagger, twirling it a few time more for motion than need, the polished steel catching the lamplight before sliding home into its sheath. He was already thinking ahead. Already calculating angles, outcomes, contingencies. The alley ahead stretched into shadow, narrow and winding, but his path through it had already taken shape.

"What now, boss?"

The voice came from his right—younger, less sure. A new recruit. Smart enough to ask, smarter still to keep his mouth shut after.

Kipp's gaze didn't shift from the alley. His eyes narrowed slightly, a familiar glint working its way into his expression. A slow smirk followed, curling at the corner of his mouth like something sharpened behind the teeth.

"Now," he murmured, "we find out just how much our queen is willing to trust me."

He had what she needed—the truth, the map, the key to the prison where her ghost had been locked away. And whether she liked it or not, the next move was his.

He stepped forward without another word, the hem of his coat brushing over stone, catching moonlight as it passed from sight. The alley closed behind him, shadows folding inward, and the city—familiar, waiting, dangerous—welcomed him back without a sound.

It always did.

It's favorite son. It's quiet king.

⊤HE SALT AND SMOKE KINGS

K
ipp didn't rush. He rose late, dressed without urgency, and lingered over breakfast long after it had gone cold. He sent no word of his findings. Let her wait. Let her wonder. Let her pace the floor in silence and feel her patience fray by degrees. Anticipation, after all, was its own kind of leverage and Kipp Harlow knew exactly how to use it.

By midday, he strolled through the palace gates as if he owned them. In truth, he owned enough of them to make the illusion convincing. He'd bought the silence of half the staff and memorized every weak point in the watch rotations. He moved through the opulent corridors like a man reclaiming territory.

He found her where he knew she'd be, waiting. He entered her chambers without formality, without fanfare, the door easing shut behind him as he crossed the room, hands tucked into the deep pockets of his coat, that familiar smirk already curling faintly across his mouth. He moved like he belonged there. Because in a way, he did.

Kalithea stood near the tall window, arms folded, posture rigid with tightly controlled patience. She didn't turn at his approach.

"You're late," she said, voice cool and unbothered, though the stiffness in her shoulders told him otherwise.

"Gods, you're demanding," Kipp replied, his tone warm with amusement. "Missed me that much, darling?"

She turned slowly, her expression carved from ice. "Do you have something for me, or should I start finding someone who does?"

He laughed softly, crossing the space between them with the casual poise of a man who knew exactly how far he could push. "Oh, I've got something for you. But you know how this works. Nothing in life comes for free."

Her breath left her in a long exhale, quiet and composed, but unmistakably edged. "What do you want, Kipp?"

"Just something small," he said, that grin returning, sly and infuriating.

She lifted a brow. "Be specific."

"But where's the fun in that?" His gaze skimmed down the line of her form with exaggerated appreciation. "I can think of plenty of things I'd enjoy."

Her expression didn't flicker. "Kipp."

"What?" He held up his hands in mock innocence. "You've put ideas in my head. Could be something simple...or something a little more hands-on–"

"*No.*"

"Something that requires trust, proximity, and perhaps fewer clothes–"

"*Absolutely not.*"

"You wound me," he said, clutching at his chest like her refusal was a physical blow.

"Just something small," she repeated flatly. "That's it? That's the deal?"

He nodded once, maddeningly smug. "That's it."

She studied him, her expression guarded. A long moment passed before she finally answered.

"Fine."

He barely contained the satisfaction that pulled at the corners of his mouth.

"See?" he murmured. "That wasn't so–"

"You're not coming with me."

The words landed between them like stone. Final. Unyielding.

He blinked. "I–"

"No."

A pause stretched. Then: "Darling, be reasonable–"

"I will murder you first," she said, calm and certain.

Kipp laughed, bright and unrestrained. "I'd love to see you try."

"Don't tempt me."

"You enjoy threatening me."

"I really do."

"It's charming." he practically purred.

"No, it's a warning."

"Same thing."

She sighed, lifting a hand to the bridge of her nose as though she were already regretting every second of this exchange. "Kipp–"

"Kalithea."

Her chin lifted slightly, reclaiming control with the smallest of gestures. Her eyes sharpened. "Then tell me where we're going."

Kipp stepped in, his voice low. "The sea cliff ruins in Elandra. What's left of the old border fortress, just south of Kellyn Bay."

A flicker passed behind her gaze, in recognition or memory, he couldn't say.

"And, darling," he added, voice softening into something darker, "you're walking straight into a trap."

She didn't flinch. But her eyes sparked. Her tells were subtle. They always were. He caught the tension in her breath, the faint hardening in her jaw.

"I know," she said simply.

Of course she did.

Another silence followed. Then her gaze shifted again, sharp and assessing. "There's one more thing I need from you."

Now that was interesting. Kipp straightened, curiosity piqued. "Go on..."

"I need a ship."

He arched a brow. "You could ask for any ship in the entire kingdom's fleet if you batted your eyelashes at your little princeling."

She shook her head, "I need someone better than that. Someone who doesn't blink at old kingdom waters. Someone discreet."

He gave a low whistle, "Now that's a dangerous request."

"I'm aware."

"So, what you're really asking for," he said slowly, "is a *smuggler*. A man with no flags, no loyalties. Someone more rogue than crown." His eyes glinted. "I'm starting to see a pattern in your tastes, darling."

She didn't answer. Just looked at him, calm and unreadable.

Gods, he adored a woman who kept secrets.

"I have someone in mind."

Her expression didn't change. "Who?"

"Oh, now *that* would cost you."

She exhaled, quiet and resigned. "What do you want now?"

Kipp stepped closer, that grin curving again, dangerous and precise. "One more thing."

Her stare was flat. "You're insufferable."

"Perhaps," he said smoothly, "but you keep inviting me back."

"What do you want, Kipp?"

He tilted his head, pretending to think. *"A kiss."*

The silence that followed was thick with disbelief. Not playful. Not sweet. It was loaded.

She blinked once. "I should stab you."

"Probably."

"Kipp."

"I'm serious. Just a small one. Harmless, really."

Her eyes narrowed to slits. "You are the most aggravating man I've ever met."

"And yet, here we are."

Another pause. Then, her voice dropped lower, colder. "Tell me the name, and I'll consider it."

His grin sharpened. "...Captain Jaymes Blackwell."

Kalithea had heard the name before. Everyone had.

Captain Jaymes Blackwell. The Pirate King. A legend passed between dockside bartenders and syndicate lords alike, a myth that drifted across ports and courtrooms like smoke. His name was the kind whispered only when the tides were low and the lamps burned dim. A storm in human shape. A man no one could find unless he wanted to be found. And rarely, if ever, did he want that.

And Kipp Harlow had just offered her that name like it was coin in the palm—without a route, without a contact, without even the promise of a whisper to chase. No path. No leverage. No map to follow. A lock without a key. Which meant he'd given her nothing at all.

Kalithea let the silence bloom between them, sharp and gleaming. She stepped forward, slow and composed. There was no sway to her hips, no flutter of lashes. Her approach was clean, quiet, and purposeful. She stopped in front of him, so close that the faint heat of her skin brushed against his jaw, the scent of her wrapped around him like a secret: jasmine, steel, and the faint, elusive burn of something more ancient.

She didn't touch him. She didn't need to. Her nearness was enough to steal the air from his lungs. Kipp didn't step back, but he didn't lean in, either. His breath caught, not enough to be obvious, but enough for her to feel it. Just enough for her to know that she had him right where she wanted.

She looked up at him through her lashes, giving him a look that would melt even the strongest of men into a stuttering puddle. Her voice was soft, almost gentle. "That doesn't count."

His brows arched, amused despite himself. "Doesn't it?"

"No." Her tone stayed even, unhurried. "You gave me the name of a ghost, Kipp."

Her lips hovered a breath away from his. He could feel the shape of them in the air between them, like something not yet tasted but deeply, maddeningly real.

"No coordinates," she continued, her voice dipping into something soft. "No trade routes. No ports. Not even a whisper of where he sails. You handed me a story. Not a man."

Her breath grazed the edge of his jaw, and he held still, jaw clenched tight, willing himself not to move, not to give her the inch she hadn't asked for.

"Without a location..." she whispered, "there is no kiss."

Then, without a word more, she stepped back. Kipp exhaled, low and sharp, as if he'd only just remembered how to breathe. He let a hand drag through his hair, smirk returning to his face slowly, tempered now by something darker.

"Gods above," he muttered, "you are cruel."

Kalithea turned away, her posture once again perfectly composed, already striding toward the window with that effortless grace he never could decide whether he envied or adored.

"And you," she said, glancing back at him, "are predictable."

That made him laugh, short and dry. "Predictable? That stings, love."

"You thought I'd pay before I knew whether the merchandise was real." Her eyes caught the light as she looked at him fully. "I'm insulted, Kipp."

"Darling," he said with mock solemnity, "I think I might actually be in love with you."

"Unfortunate for you."

"Oh, devastatingly so."

They stood silently for a moment, the sun casting long shadows across the floor. Kal stood like a statue of something sovereign and untouchable, and Kipp, for once, looked like a man considering the weight of what he wanted.

"Fine," he said at last.

Her eyes flicked back to him, "Fine?"

He shrugged, the smirk returning, this time with something more dangerous simmering underneath. "I'll get you the location."

"And how," she asked, voice cool, "do you plan to do that?"

He shrugged, leaning lazily against the doorframe, that smirk sliding back into place. "Jaymes Blackwell and I...have some history." His grin turned lazy. "*Intimate* history."

At that, her expression shifted, barely. A flicker behind her eyes. Nothing overt, but enough for him to notice. A pause, then a slow tilt of her head.

"Do you now?"

"Mm." He leaned against the doorframe, every inch the rogue who had just laid down a winning hand. "But that's a story for another night."

She studied him for a long moment, weighing more than his answer. Then she nodded once.

"Get me the location."

"And then?" he asked, his voice lower now, baited but quiet.

Kalithea turned fully. Her chin lifted, her eyes steady. "Then," she said, a slow smile just beginning to form at the corners of her lips, "you'll get your kiss."

A beat.

"*Maybe.*"

His grin spread, wide and wolfish. And gods help him, he had never wanted anything more.

Kipp Harlow had tracked down more men than he could count—traitors, exiles, killers who wore new names like second skins. Men who'd carved themselves out of the world, vanished into its darker hollows, and left behind nothing but rumor and blood. Some had run fast. Some had run clever. None had run far enough.

But Jaymes Blackwell?

He wasn't running. He was gone. Not hidden, not in exile. Blackwell was something else entirely, a myth wrapped in storm clouds and salt. His name wasn't traded in broadsheets or bounty lists, but whispered across dockside taverns and slurred into the smoke of backroom dice games. He was the kind of legend people claimed to have seen, never quite the same way twice. A ghost with a flag. A king without a court.

And Kipp needed to find him. There were no threats that would touch a man like that. No favors deep enough to call him from the mist. No, to find Blackwell, Kipp needed something rarer, someone who knew the sea like breath. Someone who had followed Blackwell into the storm and lived long enough to crawl back out.

Which meant Kipp had to start with the living.

"Spread the word," he began, his voice low as he moved through the knot of alleyways and dockside paths that marked the city's outer edge. Salt clung to the boards beneath his boots. Rope creaked from the masts overhead, and gulls wheeled far above, their cries muffled by the low hush of the sea. His men followed without sound, slipping into the crowd like smoke.

"I want someone who's sailed with him," Kipp continued. "Not someone who's heard the stories. Someone who's stood beside him. Fought beside him. Someone who made it back alive."

A snort came from his left, rough and amused. "That's a short list, boss."

Kipp's mouth curved. "Then it won't take long."

He stopped at the edge of the wharf, turning on his heel as the wind tugged at his coat. The grin that followed was pure mischief, sharp, irreverent and dangerous. He spread his arms wide, voice carrying just enough to turn heads.

"In the meantime," he said, "let's toss a little bait overboard, shall we?"

He let the idea settle, watching their faces shift—alert, intrigued.

"Something scandalous," he added. "Something shiny enough to make a dead man turn his head. We need a tale big enough to reach open waters and loud enough to pull a ghost into port. Suggestions?"

From the edge of the group, someone chuckled. "Could always claim there's a highborn lady out east sayin' she's birthed the bastard son of the Pirate King."

That drew laughter, low and rough. Even Kipp let out a short laugh, tilting his head back as the sound peeled through the salt air.

"Might be too much," he said, wiping an imaginary tear from his eye. "Or not enough. Hell, we'd need an official census to count how many of Jaymes' misadventures have set sail under the moonlight."

But then his smile shifted, thinner now, thoughtful. The laughter faded as the air tightened, his attention pulling the group back into silence.

"But," he said slowly, "you've just sparked a little brilliance."

He turned back toward them, expression inexplicable but intent sharp behind his eyes.

"A contract," he said. "Not just any ink and lies, mind you...A *royal* one. Rumors of a king-to-king deal. A crown-sanctioned conscription. The Pirate King, dragged to heel, turning privateer for the crown."

The mood shifted. A few exchanged looks, muttering under their breath, but no one laughed. Kipp's eyes gleamed with the kind of feral delight only a man like him could wear with style.

"Let it slip," he said, quieter now. "Into the right taverns. Let it reach the coin-runners, the salt smugglers, the half-drunk wrecks who still remember what real blood on the tide smells like. Make it sound real enough. Political enough. *Insulting* enough. Someone out there won't be able to leave it alone."

He leaned forward slightly, and the gleam in his eye was something older than charm.

"Well?"

There was no hesitation. Cloaks shifted. Blades disappeared beneath sleeves. Boots scuffed against stone as they vanished into the noise and smoke of the docks, one by one, already moving.

Kipp lingered behind. He stepped to the edge of the pier, resting a hand on a barnacle-clad post. The tide rolled out beneath him, slow and rhythmic, dragging foam and salt back into the dark. The air smelled of tar and seaweed, copper and rust.

"Where the fuck are you, Blackwell..."

Time passed.

Rumors drifted back like gull feathers on a tide, tattered, thin, and useless. Every whisper promised a lead, and every one unraveled on inspection. A trader swore he'd seen the *Tempest* vanish off the western coast, but couldn't name a single landmark when pressed. A barmaid claimed her uncle had been press-ganged by Blackwell himself, only to forget the tale after a single look from Kipp's second. One drunk nearly staked his life on knowing the man until Kipp had him pinned to the wall by the throat, and the truth spilled free: he wanted coin, not justice. A free drink, not consequence.

All of it smoke. And Kipp Harlow was not a man who chased ghosts for long without setting something on fire.

By nightfall, frustration had driven him into a place he normally wouldn't waste a breath on—a tavern thick with mildew and memory, sunken into the dockside like it was trying to rot its way into the sea. The air reeked of salt, rotgut, and regret. Floorboards stuck to his boots. The few men still upright looked like they'd been born tired and never learned anything else. But in the back, where the light thinned and silence settled heavier than the smoke, Kipp found something solid.

The old man didn't look like much—hunched, half-shadowed, face worn down to salt and leather. His eyes were fogged, but not blind. They didn't dart or flinch. They studied. Weighed. Kipp slid into the chair opposite him without ceremony and dropped a small coin pouch onto the table.

"You sailed with Blackwell." It wasn't a question.

The man's hand paused midway to his drink. His fingers hovered a second longer, then resumed their path without rush.

"That's a dangerous thing to say," he replied, voice low and rasped by age. "Out loud."

Kipp didn't blink. "So is lying to me."

The old sailor held his gaze for a long moment before sighing through his teeth and dragging a hand down his weathered face. "Aye. Once."

Kipp leaned in. Not enough to threaten, just enough to close the space between certainty and need. "Where is he now?"

Silence followed. Not empty, but thoughtful. The man didn't look at him.

"You don't find Blackwell," he said eventually. "He finds you."

Kipp's jaw flexed. "Lovely. We're doing riddles."

"He's not hiding," the man said, voice low. "He's avoiding. There's a difference."

"Enlighten me."

The sailor took a slow sip of whatever poison passed for drink here, then set it down with a dull thud. "He doesn't dock where names are logged. Doesn't barter where faces are remembered. When he comes ashore, it's quiet. Controlled. He deals in places that don't want to be found—no-flag harbors, smuggler coves, places that know better than to ask questions."

Kipp's fingers drummed once on the table. "So where?"

The man gave him a look. Not quite contempt. Not quite pity. "If I knew that, I wouldn't be rotting in this chair."

Kipp's patience thinned. "Then what good are you?"

"I'm telling you how he thinks." The man didn't blink. "And that's what you're missing."

Silence stretched between them.

"Don't waste time hunting the ship," the sailor went on. "You'll never catch it. You don't chase a storm and expect it to dock on your terms. What you need to ask is—"

He tapped the table once, slow and deliberate.

"—why he comes back."

Kipp watched the man closely, trying to keep his irritation at bay. .

The old man's voice dropped lower, roughened by memory. "It's not coin. Not shelter. Not rest. Blackwell sails like a man with something behind him but he only returns when something ahead pulls him back."

Kipp tilted his head. "And you think he's coming now?"

A ghost of a smile touched the old sailor's face. "You're the one who started the fire, boy. That conscription rumor? That'll get him stirring. The Pirate King...drafted into crown service? No way in hell he ignores that."

Kipp straightened slightly, the shadows shifting behind his eyes.

"So if I want him," he said slowly, "I don't chase the storm. I find the shoreline."

"Aye," the old man said, raising his glass in a faint, sardonic salute. "And hope to the gods he hasn't changed course."

Kipp rattled the city's bones.

Two days without rest. He didn't eat. He didn't sleep. He moved like smoke —slipping through dens, brothels, dice pits, and every back-room too dark for honest men. He passed coin to the greedy, promises to the desperate, threats to the ones too stubborn to talk. His whisperers followed suit, spreading like stormwater through the gutters of the city, dredging up anything that stank of sea and silence.

And finally something gave. It came from a dockhand already deep in his cups, half-slumped over a card table in a tavern thick with sweat, mildew, and regret. The man laughed too loud, slurring over the tail end of some half-forgotten tale. But it was just clear enough to snare Kipp's attention.

"Blackwell always finds a way, doesn't he?" the drunk crowed, throwing down a card with more bravado than sense. "Bastard had us load him up just two weeks past, slipped off before the sun even touched the sails..."

The sound of Kipp's smirk wasn't audible, but somehow the the man still heard it. He froze the moment their eyes met, color draining from his cheeks like a tide pulling back. Kipp didn't slow, dragging a chair out beside him and sitting, one hand resting on the table, the other already brushing back the edge of his coat to show the hilt of the blade beneath.

"That," he said pleasantly, "sounds like a story I'd very much like to hear."

The drunk fumbled his mug, eyes flicking toward his companions, none of whom met his gaze. They'd seen the men drifting along the tavern walls. Too casual, too silent, too poised.

"I–I didn't mean nothin' by it," the man stammered, his voice cracking. "Just drinkin', just talk–"

"Easy now," Kipp murmured, leaning forward. His voice slipped low and smooth, soft enough to settle beneath the noise, dangerous enough to cut through it. "You're doing fine. I do love a good tale. So let's hear how this one ends."

The man clutched his mug like it might anchor him to the present, his eyes wide and darting. Kipp waited. Calm. Unhurried. The smile on his lips wasn't quite friendly. It wasn't quite a threat either. Somehow, it was both.

"Where?" he asked again, just above a whisper.

The man cracked. They always did.

"South of Silvercairn," he rasped. "There's a reef–twists like a blade. Past that, is his dock, what he uses when he wants to come in all silent like. Hidden. No lights, no signal flags. Just a stretch of planks and seaweed. His crew brings crates in under moonlight. No noise. In and out. Like ghosts."

Kipp tilted his head, his grin curling at the edge.

"There now. That wasn't so hard, was it?"

The man sagged in his seat, a breath escaping him like it'd been held for years.

Kipp clapped him on the shoulder once, light enough to look friendly, firm enough to feel like a warning. "I'm a generous man. You help me..." He leaned in, his voice turning razor-sharp. "...and I don't break your fingers."

He rose before the man could stammer a reply, already striding toward the door, his cloak catching on the edge of the wind like a flag before battle.

He had it now. A name to a place. A landing site buried past reefs and myths, where only the foolish or fearless would dare anchor.

Blackwell will come ashore.

And that meant the game had shifted.

The night met him with salt and cold as he stepped into the street, his hand dragging through his hair while a breath of hard-won satisfaction slipped between his teeth.

The King of Thieves was going to war with the King of Pirates.

And gods he couldn't wait to begin.

THE BEST WORST IDEA

Kipp was feeling rather pleased with himself—the kind of deep, smug satisfaction that only came after outwitting a legend with style. The plan had been equal parts outrageous and elegant, stitched together with precision and no small amount of ego. Jaymes Blackwell would hear the whispers, about kings conscripting pirates, about crowns bartering with devils. He'd send his spies, his shadows, his ghosts. And eventually, curiosity would win. The Pirate King would step onto land.

And when he did, Kipp would be the first thing he saw.

It was, by all accounts, a masterstroke. And brilliance, as far as Kipp was concerned, deserved reward.

He moved through the palace like a man returning from conquest. His coat swung loose at his sides, boots barely whispering against the polished floors, that irrepressible smirk curled at the edge of his mouth. He let himself in without knocking. No need for ceremony, not between them.

She was seated at her desk, bathed in amber candlelight, surrounded by tidy columns of parchment and the scent of ink and wax. She didn't look up.

"You're early," she said.

Kipp clicked his tongue as he strolled inside, casual and arrogant in equal measure. "And you're still ungrateful. I'm handing you the key to a ghost, darling. You could try to look impressed."

That earned him a glance, cool and sharp edged. She returned to her writing without a word.

Kipp leaned against the desk, folding his arms, basking in the brilliance of his own handiwork. "Blackwell's coming to port."

"You're sure"

"When am I not?" he said, grin sharpening.

She sighed. "How?"

He grinned. "Forged a royal contract. Staged a scandal. Told half the coast the crown was conscripting him. The King of Pirates, dragged to court in chains of gold." He shrugged. "*Irresistible.*"

The quill in her hand stilled.

"You forged a contract. From Alden. To the Pirate King."

He nodded, unconcerned. "Seemed the efficient choice."

"You impersonated the Crown."

He gave a short, satisfied nod. "Quite beautifully."

She stared at him. "You're going to be executed."

"Unlikely," he said, waving her off. "I'm far too charming."

She rubbed her temple, as if entertaining the idea of slamming her head into the desk. "If this unravels–"

"It won't."

"*Kipp–*"

"Trust me."

Her gaze cut to him. "That," she said, "is a fool's request."

He reached for the quill near her hand and spun it once between his fingers. "You wound me."

"I haven't even started."

He dropped the quill, leaning in slightly. "Then let's talk compensation."

She gave him a flat look. "What do you want."

Kipp placed a hand over his chest with mock solemnity. "You assume I'm here for something so transactional."

"One brow," she said dryly, "is already raised."

He grinned. "I'm here for my kiss."

Silence stretched between them. Not heavy, but sharp.

Kalithea exhaled slowly. "You cannot possibly think–"

"Oh, but I do. You said 'maybe.' That's close enough for me."

"I never meant yes."

"I never take maybe for an answer."

She stood slowly, like something dangerous unfolding, and crossed the space between them with effortless grace. No seduction. No hesitation. Just control–perfect, methodical, sharp as a knife. She stopped just short of touching him. Close enough for the scent of her to unsettle his balance. Close enough to feel the question tightening between them. Her chin tilted up, her lips just inches from his.

"You want it?" she asked softly.

His voice came rougher than he intended. "I earned it."

"Then take it."

The words weren't flirtation, they were a challenge. He moved– quick, sure, a hand reaching to close the last inch between them–and missed. She slipped past him in a blur of perfume and shadow, the ghost of a smile on her lips as she reappeared near the window, smirking slightly.

"I said take it," she said, the corner of her mouth curling. "Not that I'd give it."

Kipp exhaled, running a hand down his jaw, half-laughing. "You are insufferable."

"So I've heard."

"Heartless."

"And yet, you keep coming back."

He studied her then, truly studied her—the light in her eyes, the steel beneath the silk.

"One day," he said softly.

She turned toward him fully. "One day?"

"You'll stop running."

She held his gaze a moment longer, then let her lips curve in something just shy of a smile. "We'll see."

Gods, he thought. That was the most intoxicating promise she'd ever made.

Kipp lounged against her desk like it belonged to him, one arm folded loosely across his chest while the other flicked a dagger between his fingers. He moved like someone who had grown up knowing the difference between charm and danger, and how to weaponize both. That smirk, carved deep into the corner of his mouth, hadn't faded.

"Patience," he drawled, letting the dagger turn once more before catching it neatly by the hilt, "is a virtue, you know."

Kal's fingers tapped lightly against the edge of the desk, terse and rhythmic. Each tap carried more weight than his grin.

"And yet," she said coolly, "you seem to lack it entirely."

"Oh, I've got plenty," he replied, voice warm with amusement. "I'm just enjoying watching you try not to ask."

Her eyes flicked up, sharp as the edge of the blade in his hand. "The location, Kipp."

He gave her a slow, maddening grin and, with deliberate ease, drove the dagger point-first into the wood beside her hand. The blade sank deep with a clean, satisfying thunk.

"The location..." he echoed, almost wistfully. Then came the pause, the one that always preceded trouble.

"*No.*"

Kalithea didn't sigh. She simply fixed him with the sort of look that could silence a battlefield. "Kipp."

He pressed a hand to his chest, feigning wounded pride. "A deal was struck. A price was named. I, ever the gentleman, honored my end. *You*, darling, still owe me."

"A man of honor...," she said flatly. "You forged a royal decree.

You blackmailed a legend into surfacing. And now you're bartering with secrets?"

"Thieves' honor," he said cheerfully, winking. "Not quite the same as the court's, but I hear it holds up just fine among rogues and queens."

Her jaw tightened, but she said nothing. Not yet.

He tilted his head, watching her. "You're really going to deny it now? After everything?"

This wasn't about leverage. Not anymore. He didn't need money. Not power. Not even control, not when he already had it. He just wanted the kiss. Wanted her to *give* it. Not because he tricked her. Not even because he earned it. *But because she chose to.* Because in all the world, she might be the only thing he didn't know how to steal.

She didn't answer. Not with words. Instead, she stepped around the desk and crossed to him. Each step landed with the effortless grace of someone who knew exactly where this was going and exactly how it would end. Kipp's smirk didn't falter, but he straightened just slightly. Enough to betray that something in her movement had caught him off-guard. She stopped close, not touching just yet. Her presence coiled around him, silk and steel, shadow and fire. Her chin tilted upward, the light catching along the line of her cheekbone as she held his gaze.

Then, she kissed him.

No flourish. No buildup. Just a slow, certain press of her lips to his—soft and devastating. A whisper of breath and a brush of tongue that tasted of wine and firelight and the impossible.

Kipp Harlow's entire goddamn world tilted.

He didn't smirk, didn't move. For the first time since she'd met him, Kipp was completely still—his balance tipped by something he couldn't outwit or outplay.

She pulled back just enough to look at him. Her voice came soft, certain, and merciless. "The location, Kipp."

He swallowed. Once. Twice. Then dragged in a breath as if forcing air into lungs that had forgotten how.

"Near Silvercairn," he said, voice lower than he intended. "There's a hidden dock, just past the reef. No flags. No lights. He comes in before dawn."

She didn't gloat. Didn't mock. She just nodded, eyes calm, mouth curving into something faint and final.

"See?" she murmured. "That wasn't so hard."

And as she turned back to her desk, the flicker of candlelight catching in her hair, Kipp stood in place like a man who'd lost something he hadn't realized he was risking.

He hadn't recovered. *Not even close.* He stood there by her desk, fingers curling and uncurling at his sides, as though grounding himself in the moment might keep him from unraveling entirely. The kiss—gods, that kiss–still lingered. Not on his lips, but somewhere deeper. He could feel it beneath his skin, soft and infuriatingly real, more dangerous than any blade she might've pressed to his throat.

He was still reeling when her voice broke through, clean and calm as ever.

"I leave tomorrow. *Alone.*"

The words floated across the room, harmless until the weight hit.

Kipp blinked, mind still fogged. "I'm sorry–what?"

She didn't repeat herself. Kalithea was already moving, already reclaiming her space as if nothing of consequence had passed between them. She returned to the parchment on her desk with indifference, her expression composed, but not quite indecipherable. There, just at the corner of her mouth, he saw it. A flicker of amusement. A hint of smug satisfaction that vanished as quickly as it appeared. Kalithea didn't smile like that. Not for him. Not for anyone and now that he'd caught the edge of it, now that it had carved its shape into his being, he *needed* to see it again.

"You're going without me?" he asked, the question punching its way out of him, too fast, too raw.

"Yes," she answered, without looking up.

"No," he shot back, already stepping forward. "Absolutely fucking not."

At last, she glanced over at him, calm and detached. "And what, exactly, do you think you're going to do about it?"

"I can tell you it's a godsdamned terrible idea."

"Duly noted."

"And I can tell you I'm not letting you go alone."

"You're not *letting* me do anything."

Kipp's jaw clenched. "Kalithea, you do realize who we're talking about, don't you?"

She sighed, the sound far too tired for his liking. "Yes. The Pirate King."

"Blackwell is...well *he's fucking Blackwell!*" His hands moved in frustration, gesturing like the words themselves needed more space. "Blackwell isn't a man. He's a storm with a name. He sails like he's got death on his heels and doesn't stop for anyone."

"You seem dramatic today," she observed lightly.

"I'm the only one being realistic!"

He paced now, back and forth across the chamber, as if motion might help him hold his temper in check. "You don't march into a legend's waters like it's a diplomatic luncheon! You don't bring court manners to the edge of the world and expect to walk back untouched."

"I've faced worse men than Jaymes Blackwell."

"That is not fucking reassuring!"

He stopped in front of her desk again, hands braced against its edge, knuckles white with tension. "You cannot just waltz into his domain, make demands, and sail away as if the sea doesn't eat fools alive."

Her eyes didn't so much as flicker. "Who said I was making demands?"

He stared at her. "You're *you.*"

She lifted a brow. "And?"

"You don't know how *not* to provoke people."

"I can be polite."

Kipp barked out a bitter laugh. "You absolutely fucking cannot."

"I was polite to you."

"You stabbed me!"

"*Almost.* And yet, here you are."

"Here I *regretfully* am."

"You're welcome to leave," she said smoothly, without missing a beat.

Kipp's eyes narrowed. "I will tie you to a chair, Kalithea."

She lifted her gaze slowly, that hint of a smile returning, but darker now. Sharper.

"Try it, thief."

He froze. The air between them shifted and she *smirked,* not playfully, but like someone who knew EXACTLY what that phrase had ignited behind his eyes.

"Careful, Kipp."

He swore under his breath, dragging a hand down his face. His brain had taken the implication, set it on fire, and let it burn. "That's *not* what I meant."

"Mm."

He scrubbed a hand through his hair, trying to force the air back into his lungs. He really didn't mean it THAT way...probably.

"Listen," he said, voice lower now, the edge stripped away, replaced by something harder to name. "You want Blackwell? Fine. But you're not going to him alone. That's not a suggestion. That's not a request. That's not negotiable."

She watched him in silence, her expression impassive, her silence more unnerving than any outburst. She studied him like a blade weighed in the hand, assessing and calculating.

And then, at last, she spoke. "I'll consider it."

"No," he growled. "You'll agree."

"*I'll consider.*"

"I hate you."

"No, you don't."

She turned her gaze away, already resuming her work, her voice floating across the room. "Close the door on your way out."

And Kipp?

He stood there in the quiet aftermath, heart still unsteady from a kiss he hadn't expected, staring down the war he'd already lost—and felt it settle into his bones with grim certainty.

Kalithea was going to drive him straight into madness. *And he couldn't wait.*

Kipp was brooding.

Which, frankly, was insulting.

He didn't *brood*. He schemed. He orchestrated madness. He slipped through locked doors with a grin on his face and secrets tucked in his belt. He outplayed barons and blackmailers alike, drank things older than most kings, and robbed people who'd forgotten they could bleed. Brooding, in his opinion, was for bards, poets and broken-hearted knights.

And yet, there he was—slouched low in the chair of his private den, one boot hooked over the table's edge, the other tapping a slow rhythm against the floor. In his hand, a dagger spun in lazy arcs, rising toward the rafters before falling back to his palm, again and again, each catch a little too close to his own damn face.

He told himself he wasn't thinking about the kiss. That soft press of her lips. The stillness of it. The way she hadn't seduced or threatened or bargained, but simply *chose* him—for one maddening heartbeat—before walking away like it had cost her nothing.

The blade slapped into his palm. He didn't flinch.

"Boss?"

Kipp blinked, eyes shifting toward the doorway where Vale leaned with his arms crossed, watching him with the same patient disbelief he wore every time Kipp began losing his mind over something dangerous.

"You're throwing that knife like it owes you money," Vale said.

Kipp twirled the blade once more, letting it settle in his fingers. "Am I?"

Vale's brow arched. "You want to tell me why?"

"Not especially."

"Hm."

He came further into the room, too relaxed to be trusted. Kipp knew the look, Vale had been with him long enough to recognize the storm building behind the smirk. He just didn't always have the good sense to run.

"This wouldn't happen to have anything to do with the foreign queen, would it?"

Kipp's eyes narrowed. "You have about five seconds before this knife finds your boot."

Vale grinned. "Thought you weren't brooding."

"I'm not."

"You are."

"I'm thinking." Kipp said flatly, half defiant.

"Sure."

Kipp exhaled and leaned forward, resting his elbows on his knees as he stared past Vale toward the warped planks of the far wall. Her lips hadn't left his thoughts since she'd pressed them to his. There'd been nothing coy about it. No flutter of lashes. No dramatic pause. Just warmth, confidence, and silence. It had wrecked him.

Worse, it had *worked.*

But fine. If Kalithea wanted to play power games, he'd remind her who she was dealing with. She thought she'd gotten the upper hand. Thought she could slip away quietly while he sat there dreaming about the taste of her mouth and the sting of her absence.

He sat up straighter, rolled the tension from his shoulders, and spoke without looking at Vale. "Pack my things."

Vale blinked. "I'm sorry, what?"

"I said pack my things."

"Uh. Why?"

Kipp rose with a stretch, his smirk returning. "Because I've just had the best worst idea I've ever had."

"That sentence fills me with dread."

"As it should."

"Then maybe *don't* do whatever it is you're about to do."

"Where's the fun in that?" Kipp chuckled.

"You have a deeply unhealthy relationship with the concept of fun." Vale muttered. "So what's the plan?"

Kipp crossed to the far wall and, with a flick of his wrist, drove the dagger into the center of a tattered sea map.

"I'm going to stow away on Blackwell's ship."

Silence. Total. Echoing. Silence.

Vale stared. "You're *what?*"

Kipp's grin was infuriating. "You heard me."

"No no, I heard you. I'm just hoping that repeating it will make it sound less idiotic."

Kipp slapped a hand to Vale's shoulder. "It won't. Because it is idiotic. *Brilliantly* idiotic."

He sauntered past Vale like a man stepping into legend. "It's perfect. The queen thinks she's outplayed me. Blackwell's expecting royalty, politics, diplomacy. He's *not* expecting me."

"You're planning to sneak onto the *Tempest*," Vale said, as if repeating the words might chase the madness out of them.

"That's the one."

"Onto *Jaymes Blackwell's* ship. The man who once sank two imperial fleets and mailed their admiral's teeth back to the emperor."

"Colorful, isn't he?" Kipp grinned.

"With the most vicious crew in the known world." Vale continued incredulously.

"Efficient, I'd say."

Vale's hand dragged down his face like he was trying to wipe the conversation away. "And you think this is a good idea?"

Kipp laughed. "Gods, no. It's an *awful* idea."

"Then why–"

"Because she thinks she's winning."

Vale exhaled, muttered a curse, and glared. "Let me get this straight. You're going to risk getting gutted by pirate bastards on a ship that probably smells like death and sea salt–just to follow her? To follow *a woman?*"

Kipp only smirked, stepping back into the dark with that dangerous light behind his eyes. "Exactly. But to be fair, she's not just *any* woman"

"You're a madman." Vale groaned.

"You're late to that realization."

"She's going to gut you."

"She's welcome to try."

Vale leaned back against the wall, shaking his head. "A queen. A pirate king. And the most arrogant King of Thieves the world has ever seen. Sounds like the setup to a very expensive funeral..."

Kipp flashed a grin over his shoulder. "Sounds like a damned good story to me."

With that, he vanished into the back room, already calculating angles and approaches, already laying traps she wouldn't see coming.

Kalithea thought she was ahead. Thought she was leaving him behind. But she didn't know–she would *never* know, not until it was too late–that Kipp Harlow had no intention of letting her go.

The Art of Leaving

iam's boots struck the stone sharply, each step carved in frustration, his shoulders tight with the effort of keeping everything he felt just below the surface. He hadn't said a word yet, but he didn't need to. The room was already full of his silence, dense and coiled, unmistakably volatile.

Kalithea sat on the edge of her desk, arms folded, back rigid, every line of her posture composed and unyielding. She'd known this was coming from the moment she told him. Knew exactly what she was stepping into by saying it aloud. But some battles didn't wait for permission.

When he finally spoke, his voice was low, tight, and edged in steel. *"Absolutely not."*

She didn't sigh. Not quite. But her shoulders tensed, as if bracing for impact. "Liam—"

"No." He turned sharply, eyes burning. "You are not going after him alone."

"I don't have a choice."

"The hell you don't!"

"I do," she admitted, quiet but steady. "I just don't have a better one."

He let out a sharp laugh, brittle and humorless, running a hand through his hair like he needed something to hold on to. "There's always a better option than walking into the arms of pirates with no defense but your name and whatever story you think you're selling."

"They won't meet if they think I've brought backup." She sighed.

"I'm not a godsdamned army."

"No," she said, gaze locking with his. "You're worse. You're my brother."

The fury that had been mounting cracked just enough for something heavier to slip through, something that lived deeper than rage. He turned away again, breathing hard, the fight in him stuttering under the weight of what she was asking him to accept.

"They'll kill you." Liam snapped.

"They'd need me alive."

"And what happens when they don't?"

"Then I die," she answered, calm as stone. "And you live. And you burn the sea to find them."

He swore under his breath, both hands braced against the window-sill now, knuckles pale against the stone. The pause that followed settled thick between them, heavy with all the things neither had said in too long. It was the kind of silence built from years of survival, from nights curled on damp floors, from knives drawn in the dark and backs pressed to each other's because there'd been no one else. She'd never needed to explain herself to Liam. Until now.

He turned back, slower this time. Less fury, more fear. "You really think you can manage this?"

"I know I can."

"How?"

"Because there's no other choice." She shrugged.

He shook his head, voice lowering. "This isn't like before."

She tilted her head, voice just as soft. "How is it different?"

"Because this time..." He hesitated, then finished it anyway. "I'm not going with you."

And there it was. The truth beneath all the shouting. The crack beneath his anger. He wasn't afraid of the pirates. He was afraid of not being there.

Kal stood slowly, moving toward him. "This isn't about tactics. You're not worried I can't survive it."

"I'm worried I won't be there when you need me," he said, voice rough.

"I know." She paused, then added more gently, "You've always protected me. But this one...this I have to do myself."

"Why?"

"Because if they see you, they'll kill you," she said plainly. "Not hesitate. Not threaten. *Kill.* You know it, and I know it. And I *can't* let that happen. If I lose you, I won't survive, and if I lose myself..."

His mouth opened, closed. He looked away again, jaw tight. "It shouldn't be just you."

"But it is."

He swore again and resumed pacing, like motion could shake off inevitability. "You should take someone."

"I won't."

"You should take *me*." His voice was almost a plea.

"I can't." She answered softly.

"And if something happens to you–"

"I'll deal with it."

"Kal–"

"Or I won't," she said simply. "But either way, it's mine to carry."

"You are so godsdamned infuriating." He growled, throwing his hands in the air.

"I know."

"And reckless."

"Also not new information." She smiled slightly.

For a long moment, he said nothing. Just stood there, fists clenched, breathing like it hurt to do so. And then, finally, he gave her the one thing she hadn't asked for, but needed anyway.

"You might be right."

Something flickered behind her eyes. "I usually am."

He stepped toward her then, the space closing not with surrender, but with something quieter. Something real. He looked at her like he wanted to argue more, to say something else, something final. But all he said was:

"Bring him back."

Her hand touched his, brief and solid. "I will."

Liam sat stiffly across from her, every line of his body drawn tight with restraint. His fists were clenched on his thighs, white-knuckled and unmoving, as if he feared that letting go might shatter the fragile calm he'd managed to scrape together. The fire hadn't left his eyes, it still simmered low, banked beneath the surface like a forge waiting for breath. But he was no longer pacing, no longer shouting. And that, at least, was something.

He sighed deeply. "So how exactly do you plan to find Blackwell once you reach the bay?"

"I already have the location," she said simply. "Hidden dock, north side, just under Silvercairn. Past the reef."

His eyes snapped to hers. "Kipp told you."

She nodded.

Liam let out a sharp, bitter huff and dragged a hand down his face. "Of course he did. That bastard's far too invested in you."

"He's useful."

"He's reckless."

"So am I."

He leveled her with a scowl. "That's not a fucking virtue, Kal."

A small smile curled at her mouth, dry and dangerous. "Maybe I've just developed a taste for bad things."

He groaned, exasperated. "Why do you insist on being the cause of my early death?"

"Because you'd be unbearably bored otherwise."

Liam's sigh was long and tight, like it had been building since she first opened her mouth. "Let's say you get there," he muttered. "Let's pretend this whole mad scheme actually works and Blackwell shows up. Then what?"

She met his eyes without flinching. "Then I convince him."

Liam's brow furrowed, skeptical. "To do what? Gamble his life and his crew on a cause he doesn't give a damn about?"

"To take me where they're keeping Arjun."

His posture stiffened again, his expression hardening quickly. "And if he says no?"

"Then I make sure he doesn't."

"Gods, Kal." He ran a hand through his hair, eyes narrowing. "And if he's worse than the rumors? If he's everything people say and more?"

Her voice dropped lower, cold and certain. Unshakable. "Then I'll show him I'm worse."

Liam stared at her, long and silent. Then, finally: "How are you always this sure of yourself?"

She shrugged. "Because I've never had the luxury of being anything else."

The room quieted again, thick with tension. But there was no anger now–just the dull ache of inevitability, like watching a storm roll toward shore and knowing there's no shelter in reach. Liam leaned forward, his elbows braced on his knees, voice quieter now.

"And if something goes wrong?"

"It won't."

"But if it does?"

She lifted a brow. "Then I'll deal with it."

His jaw clenched again. "*Godsdammit*, Kal–"

"I've spent my life around men like him," she said, voice steady as a blade. "Pirates. Warlords. Thieves. They all want the same things–coin, fear, control. Blackwell's no different. Just louder. Smarter. More legend than man."

"And if he's worse than all of them?"

She didn't blink. "Then I die. And you can shout 'I told you so' at my grave."

He flinched. "That's not funny."

"It wasn't meant to be."

There was a long pause as he stared at the floor, his hands flexing slowly into fists again, like he was trying to hold something inside. Something bigger than the argument. Something like grief.

"You're impossible."

"I know."

"And you're going to do this no matter what I say?"

"I am."

He leaned back, shoulders sinking with the weight of surrender. For a long moment he didn't speak–just stared up at the ceiling, as if some divine answer might be etched there in stone.

"Then godsdammit," he muttered, "do it fast. Get in. Get him. Get out."

Kal nodded. "That's the plan."

A beat passed between them. Not silence, something quieter than that. A pause filled with everything they weren't saying aloud. The ache of knowing this might be goodbye. The fear neither of them would admit.

"You'll at least say goodbye before you leave?"

"I am, this is it."

He sighed deeply, "And you'll be careful?"

"Of course."

He looked at her then, really looked–past the steel in her posture, past the calm she wore like armor. There was nothing left to fight over. Only the sick weight of helplessness in his chest and the quiet dread that came with letting her go. She stepped close, reaching out to him without hesitation, and he stood to meet her. For one brief moment, he held her tight. As if memory might be all he had left to hold on to if she didn't come back.

And as her arms folded around him, as her breath pressed warm against his shoulder, Liam knew with ruthless, impossible clarity:

If she didn't return, something in him wouldn't either.

Kalithea stood outside their door, uncertain.

She told herself it was strategy. A necessary check before departure. If something went wrong, Liam would need someone. That part was true. It had always been true. But deep down inside she knew it wasn't *just* that.

Her hand hovered just above the wood, fingers curled but unmoving, caught in a hesitation she didn't recognize in herself. She didn't believe in farewells. You either returned, or you didn't. Words never changed that. They only lingered.

Still, her knuckles rapped once, soft but decisive.

The door opened almost at once. Raoul stood before her, collar loose, posture relaxed, the ghost of a grin already forming–until he saw her face.

His smile faded. "Your Majesty," he said, not unkindly, but all traces of humor gone. His voice lowered a shade. "You look like you've come to start a fire."

Behind him, Jarreth appeared. Fully dressed, composed, but with a stillness in his expression.

She didn't step forward. Instead, quietly, "May I come in?"

Raoul's brows rose. She never asked, she entered. She took space, claimed it.

Jarreth stepped back without a word. Raoul followed suit. Kal crossed the threshold, gaze drifting across the room, careful to avoid their eyes for just a moment too long. Neither man pressed. They tracked her with patience, like they could already smell the storm on her skin.

"You're leaving," Jarreth said, eyeing the pack slung across her back. It wasn't a question.

She nodded once. "Yes."

Raoul folded his arms slowly. "For how long?"

"That depends."

"On?"

Her reply came without pause, but no force behind it. "Whether I come back."

Raoul's jaw flexed. Jarreth didn't move, but something subtle shifted between them—an unease, sudden and heavy, too weighted to name.

"You're not going to tell us where," Jarreth said.

"No."

"Or why."

"No."

"But you came anyway."

She looked at him then. Not sharply, not with challenge—just a glint of something held back. "Yes."

Raoul exhaled through his nose, voice quieter now. "You expect us to nod, say 'safe travels,' and pretend that doesn't matter?"

"It matters." Her tone didn't rise, but there was steel coiled just beneath the surface, tight and fraying.

He pushed off the wall, rubbing a hand across his jaw. "You walk in like a ghost, say that like it's nothing, and expect us to just let you disappear?"

"No," she said softly. "I didn't come for that."

Jarreth studied her, frowning. "Then why?"

She held his gaze. "Because if something happens, I need someone I trust to watch over Liam. Someone who understands what's coming."

Raoul's eyes narrowed. "So you came to ask us to protect your brother."

"No," she said, "I came to ensure someone would stand in the space I leave behind."

Raoul let out a short breath, pacing a half step. "Gods, you're serious. Off to gods-know-where to deal with who knows what, not a word of explanation, and we're meant to step in like nothing's changed."

"I've faced worse," she said mildly.

For a moment, none of them spoke. Then, slowly, she looked at them both. Her mouth parted, then shut again. Her arms folded tight across her chest. But the words came, dragged from somewhere deep and raw.

"If I don't make it back..." she said, voice barely above a whisper, "make sure Liam doesn't become what I had to."

Silence followed, but it wasn't empty. It was full. Laden with understanding and the weight of what had not been said.

Jarreth stepped forward, not in protest, but in clarity. "You mean someone who'll remind him that the world still has more to offer than pain. That he can live. Not just endure."

She inclined her head, the smallest of nods. "He deserves that. A life. Not just a cause."

Raoul's voice was rougher now, stripped of its usual ease. "And you think we're the ones to give him that?"

"You're the only ones who've seen the cracks," she answered, quieter now. "Behind us. Beneath everything."

She turned, arms still folded, as if bracing for the blow of it. "He's too proud to ask, and I'm too tired to beg. But if it's going to be someone...it has to be you."

The silence stretched. Not in awkwardness, but in the gravity of what she'd given them.

Raoul dragged a hand over his face, pacing back. "You really don't know how to say goodbye, do you?"

A faint smile touched her lips. Not warm. Not cruel. Just true. "No. I don't...I say what needs to be said."

Jarreth looked at her, long and steady. Then he stepped closer.

"If you die," he said quietly, "it won't be because you went alone. It'll be because you were too damned stubborn to let anyone come with you."

She said nothing.

"But," he went on, "if you don't return—"

She turned to him fully at that.

"—we'll protect him," Jarreth said. "You have my word."

Her gaze locked with his, not as queen to subject, not as commander to soldier. Just a woman, raw with something she hadn't learned how to name.

She nodded, once.

Raoul stepped forward next, close but not touching. "Try not to die, Your Majesty."

She gave him a ghost of a smile. "That's the plan." Her voice softened, and for the first time, she let the formality drop. "Raoul. Jarreth."

She turned to go, hand on the door, but hesitated. Just long enough to be noticed.

Over her shoulder, without looking back, she said dryly, "Try not to enjoy sleeping in too much. I expect both of you half-bruised and complaining by the time I get back."

Raoul huffed a laugh, quiet but real. Jarreth only shook his head, but the corner of his mouth curved.

And then she turned and slipped out. The door clicked shut with a finality that cut clean through the hush.

Neither man moved.

Jarreth stood stiff, arms at his sides, fingers clenched so tight the knuckles blanched. His eyes stayed fixed on the door, as if sheer will might force it open again. But the corridor beyond remained silent.

Raoul didn't speak. For once, there was no jest on his tongue, no easy quip to smooth the ragged edges. He exhaled slowly, raking a hand through his hair as he drifted toward the center of the room.

"Gods," he muttered, voice low and rough. "That felt like being stabbed with my own damn blade."

He dropped into the nearest chair with a thud, leaning back until it creaked beneath him. The weight in his chest didn't budge.

"Why do I get the feeling we just watched her leave for good?"

Jarreth didn't answer at first. His jaw worked, like he was grinding down the words before they escaped. "She's always been leaving," he said at last. "Even when she stayed."

The bitterness in his voice surprised even him.

Raoul let out a hollow laugh, his head tipping back against the wall. "We lied to ourselves. Thought we could hold her here. Thought maybe–" He gestured vaguely at the room around them, at the remnants of shared hours and quiet familiarity. "Maybe this could mean something. Maybe we meant something."

"She never asked for any of it," Jarreth said. "And we kept giving it anyway."

Raoul sighed, staring at the ceiling like it might offer insight. "We tried to make her feel like she had roots. She only ever saw the exits."

Jarreth's head turned, slowly. "So what are you saying? That we stop trying?"

"I'm saying it was never about trying harder. This? It was never home to her. Just a holding cell dressed up with silk and politics. She doesn't do roots, Jarreth. She does exits."

Jarreth's voice dropped to something sharper. "She came to us."

"She came because she needed something," Raoul corrected. "She always does. And maybe...maybe because she didn't want to go without someone knowing. Not really."

Jarreth moved to the window, bracing himself against the frame. The sunlight had faded, leaving the stone bathed in the gray haze of dusk. His throat felt tight, but he didn't loosen his collar. "We should've done something."

Raoul's gaze slid toward him. "Like what? Lock her in? Tell her no?" He paused. "She'd have cut her way through both of us."

There was a ghost of a grin behind the words, but it didn't last. Raoul leaned forward, forearms on his knees, voice lowering. "You saw her face. She's already halfway gone."

"She asked us to watch over Liam. Like she expects not to come back." Jarreth said. The words tasted like failure.

Raoul nodded once. "And she meant it. But it wasn't just about him."

Jarreth closed his eyes for a moment. "If she doesn't come back..."

"We protect him," Raoul finished. "The way she asked. The way she never asked for herself."

They fell quiet again, the room thick with everything they hadn't said sooner.

Then Raoul sat up with a stretch, the stiffness in his back cracking like old wood. "Gods, I need a drink. Or six. I refuse to face this sober. Being left behind like a useless page boy is leaving a foul taste in my mouth."

Jarreth let out a dry, reluctant breath that almost passed for a laugh. "I suppose there are worse ways to honor a queen."

Raoul cracked a grin, rising to his feet. "Come on, Prince. First round's on me. We'll toast to the woman who shattered us both and still didn't bother with a goodbye."

Jarreth didn't follow right away. But he did rise.

Raoul glanced at him sidelong, stretching his arms behind his head with a lazy sprawl. The gleam in his eyes sharpened, not playful. Calculating.

"*You know,*" he said, far too casually, "*I've had a thought.*"

Jarreth gave a long-suffering sigh without turning. "That's rarely a comforting prelude."

"Don't be dramatic. I have good ideas."

"Your ideas usually end with something on fire."

Raoul shrugged. "Small fires. Memorable ones."

Jarreth crossed his arms. "What is it?"

Raoul's grin widened. "Well if we're going to drown our sorrows tonight, we might as well do it somewhere with...potential."

Jarreth gave him a flat stare. "And by 'potential,' I assume you mean absolutely no decorum."

There was a pause.

"No," Jarreth said flatly.

"You haven't heard the plan."

Jarreth's eyes narrowed, the suspicion immediate. "No."

"You haven't even heard the name yet."

"I don't need to. If it's near the docks, it's a nest of thieves."

Raoul smirked. "*Exactly.*"

Jarreth groaned, the sound sharper than it needed to be. "We are not going tavern crawling through the slums just to make conversation with smugglers and cutthroats."

Raoul tilted his head. "Not just any smugglers. We're aiming higher. Royalty, in fact."

There was a pause, just long enough for the implications to sink in.

Jarreth's stomach turned "...you think he'll be there?"

Raoul's smile sharpened. "It's one of his haunts. The ones people only whisper about. I've run into him there before...don't ask."

"Kipp Harlow isn't exactly known for being easy to find."

"No," Raoul said, rising to his feet and rolling his shoulders. "But we both know he's still in the city. And if Kalithea didn't tell us where she was going, there's a good chance she told him. There's no way it's a coincidence we give her that name and suddenly she's leaving on a secret quest."

Jarreth narrowed his eyes. "You think he'll talk?"

Raoul tossed him a look over his shoulder. "I think he'll *enjoy* not talking. Which means we've got a chance."

"Or he'll lie."

Raoul shrugged. "Then we'll lie better."

Jarreth stared, weighing the danger. "This is a mistake."

Raoul was already halfway to the door. "Mistakes are just bold decisions that haven't paid off yet."

Jarreth groaned but followed, muttering, "I'm going to regret this."

"Regret builds character," Raoul said cheerfully. "Besides–"

"Don't say it."

"–criminals make excellent drinking companions."

"Gods help me."

Raoul grinned. "Oh, I don't think the gods are invited. This one's strictly between us...and the King of Thieves."

The King of Bastards

The farther they moved from the palace, the more the city unraveled.

Polished stone gave way to wet cobblestones slick with brine, the clean symmetry of the upper tiers dissolving into alleys hunched beneath sagging roofs and the weight of sea rot. The air thickened–fish guts, oil, rusted metal–clawing into the back of the throat with every breath. Lanterns burned low or not at all. Shadows lingered longer here.

This wasn't a place for princes or knights.

And yet here they were.

Jarreth kept his pace steady, shoulders squared beneath the dark cloak. His eyes swept the street beneath the hood's shadow, noting every doorway, every loiterer who lingered too long. Raoul moved beside him with an ease born of older habits, loose-limbed and sharp-eyed.

"You sure this is wise?" Jarreth asked under his breath. His gaze flicked toward a group of dockhands watching them with too much interest.

"Not even remotely," Raoul said, voice low and easy. His hands rested near the hilts of his twin blades, fingers curled loose but ready. "But it's the best poor idea we've got."

Jarreth exhaled through his nose. "You have a gift for reassurance."

"Never claimed I was here for comfort."

The Blackened Gull leaned against its neighbors like a drunk too proud to fall–crooked timbers, warped door, and a rusted sign that moaned whenever the wind shifted. It was wedged between a reeking tannery and a brothel with peeling red shutters, both of which looked marginally more inviting.

Raoul didn't hesitate. He pushed through the door, and Jarreth followed.

Smoke drifted low across the ceiling beams. Lanternlight flickered off polished steel and scarred tables. Conversations faltered. A card game froze mid-hand. A woman with silver rings punched through her lip watched them from behind her drink, expression suspicious. Every soul in the room was armed. Every gaze found them.

None looked friendly.

"Try to look less like a prince," Raoul muttered from the side of his mouth.

"Try to look less like you're enjoying this," Jarreth returned, eyes sweeping the tavern.

"I *do* enjoy this." Raoul chuckled.

"Of course you do." Jarreth hissed under his breath.

They moved to the bar.

The woman behind it was built like a fortress, with knuckles split from too many broken noses and eyes the color of wet gravel. She didn't smile.

She looked between them, leaned forward slightly, and said, "You two get lost on your way to the velvet courts?"

Raoul propped his elbows on the counter, flashing a lazy grin. "That obvious?"

"Like piss on perfume."

Jarreth reached into his coat and laid a gold coin on the bar. "We're looking for Kipp Harlow."

The barkeep went still. Her eyes didn't narrow, they sharpened.

Then she gave a dry, humorless laugh. "And what in all the gods' miserable graces makes you think I'd tell you where to find *him*?"

Raoul tapped a knuckle lightly on the wood. "Well, for one–we're disarmingly pleasant."

"You're dangerously stupid."

"That too." Raoul winked at her.

"And for two?"

Raoul gave her a nod. "Because you already decided what to do with us the moment we walked in."

A beat passed.

Then she muttered a curse under her breath and jerked her chin toward the stairs. "Third door up. Left side. Don't knock more than once if you like your fingers."

"You're an angel," Raoul said, already turning.

"I'm your undertaker if you get blood on my floors."

They climbed the narrow stairs, boots echoing on warped steps. The air upstairs was hotter, closer, thick with the smell of old smoke and older secrets. A flickering lantern cast warped shadows down the crooked hallway.

At the third door, Raoul paused.

"Last chance to admit this is lunacy," Jarreth murmured.

Raoul flashed a grin. "Wouldn't be any fun otherwise."

He knocked once.

There was a long pause. Then—

"If you're here to kill me, come back later. I'm busy."

Raoul leaned in. "How busy are we talking?"

Another beat. Then a familiar voice, lazy as ever: "*Raoul.* Gods, that voice still grates."

The door creaked open. Kipp Harlow leaned in the frame, shirt half-done, hair tousled like he'd either just rolled out of bed or hadn't left it in days. His smirk was slow. His eyes were awake, sharp, and already amused.

"Well," he said, sweeping a glance over both of them. "The prince and the mutt. Didn't think I'd run into you again, Sahir. Last time we met, you didn't have a blade in your hand. Or pants, for that matter. You were too busy demonstrating your 'swordplay' for an entirely different audience."

"You've got a rotten memory." Raoul nearly growled.

Kipp grinned wolfishly. "Do I? Because I distinctly recall a lady with red hair yelling your name loud enough to summon the old gods...or at least half the city guard."

Raoul didn't flinch, ignoring the barb. "We need information."

Kipp sighed dramatically. "Why is it never a social visit? I'm delightful company."

"You want this to be a social call?" Jarreth asked.

"Not particularly," Kipp said, stepping aside. "But I do enjoy surprises."

The room was exactly what it needed to be.

Warm shadows draped themselves over the ceiling beams, the flickering lamplight turning smoke into gold as it coiled in the corners. The scent was unmistakable—aged leather, sharp rum, and something darker beneath it all. Secrets that had soaked into the walls long ago and never left. Half-unbuttoned shirts lay draped over chairs, a belt coiled beside an empty scabbard. Coins lay scattered across the table, catching the light like bait.

Raoul stepped in first, his gaze sweeping the room, cataloging. His eyes landed on a silk scarf looped lazily over the arm of the nearest chair. He snorted.

"Busy, were you?"

Kipp looked up from his sprawl, boots on the table, glass in hand. He wore the room like a throne—relaxed, predatory, and entirely unconcerned. If this quarter of the city belonged to anyone, it was him.

"You know me, Knight," he said, his smirk slow and sharp. "Always in high demand."

Jarreth followed Raoul in, already pressing two fingers to the bridge of his nose. "This is already a mistake."

Kipp's eyes gleamed. "And yet, here you are. Touching. Truly."

Raoul dropped into the nearest chair, ignoring the invitation to banter. "We're not here to admire your décor."

"A shame. It's a cultivated aesthetic–equal parts charm, danger, and just a whisper of sin.'"

He poured himself another drink and didn't offer them anything–not a seat, not a pour, not a shred of courtesy. He sipped slowly, watching them over the rim of the glass with the casual calculation of a man who played games for blood.

"So," he said, tone smooth, "what is it you think I know?"

Raoul crossed his arms. "Don't waste our time."

Kipp's smile deepened. "But wasting your time is *so* satisfying."

Jarreth stepped forward. "Where did she go?"

Kipp blinked, slow and theatrical. "She?"

Raoul didn't move, didn't blink. "You know exactly who."

"Kalithea," Jarreth said flatly.

Kipp raised a brow, letting the name roll over his tongue like he'd never heard it before. "Ah, Kalithea. Yes. Sounds vaguely familiar."

Raoul's voice cooled. "You've been watching her for weeks."

"You say that like I was the only one." Kipp shrugged.

"You know where she went."

Kipp stretched his legs out, toes flexing slightly. "Do I?"

"Yes," Jarreth said. His tone wasn't loud, but it carried weight. "And we're not in the mood for games."

"Then you've come to the wrong man."

Kipp set his glass down with a clink, finally letting his eyes meet theirs properly. "Let me guess...she slipped the leash, left without a word, and now you're here hoping I'll hold your hand and tell you it wasn't personal."

Raoul didn't answer.

Kipp tapped a finger to his lips. "I might know where. But information's delicate. Like glass. Breaks easy. Or trades well."

Raoul's sigh was tight and quiet. *"Enough."*

"Oh, come now. What happened to the foreplay?"

Jarreth stepped forward, eyes hard. "This isn't a game."

"No," Kipp said, sitting forward slowly, his movements loose-limbed and unconcerned. "It's a dance. And she leads better than either of you."

Raoul planted his hands on the table, leaning forward. "She trusted you."

Kipp's smile thinned. "Did she? Or did she know I'd be the one man in this city who wouldn't ask for explanations?"

Jarreth's voice dropped. "So you're wasting our time."

"Yes," Kipp said cheerfully. "Isn't it fun?"

Raoul's eyes narrowed. "We could make you talk."

Kipp laughed, genuinely amused. "You could try."

The air shifted. Tension crept in like smoke.

"If something happens to her–" Jarreth began.

"She'll handle it," Kipp cut in. His voice was quieter now. Still amused, but not dismissive. "She always does."

"She shouldn't have to," Jarreth said.

"She shouldn't have had to survive a hundred other things either. But here we are." Kipp waved a hand like he was shooing away an irritating bird. "You both really need hobbies. Everything's always life or death with you court-bred types."

Jarreth stared at him. "You're not just stalling us. You're stalling *for* her."

That earned a pause. Then a grin, wide, lazy and dangerous. "My prince," Kipp said, voice syrup-thick with mockery, "don't tell me you're jealous. I promise there's plenty of me to go around."

Raoul exhaled sharply, dragging a hand down his face. "You're impossible."

Kipp only grinned, boots up, glass in hand. "And yet here you are. In my den. Uninvited. Trying to pry secrets without offering so much as a drink." He nudged a silver coin across the table with the side of his boot, watching it spin. His tone cooled. "You want truth? Pay for it."

"We know you don't want coin," Jarreth said, voice tight. "We know she left. And we know you helped her."

Kipp leaned back, folding his hands behind his head. "And why should that concern me?"

Raoul gave him a long, flat stare. "Because if she dies, there won't be a hole deep enough to bury you. You'll have two kingdoms' worth of fury crawling up your spine."

Kipp didn't flinch. "I'll jot that down. Right between 'nap' and 'ruin the blacksmith's daughter.' Priorities, you understand."

Raoul paced a slow circle behind the table, his temper wearing thinner with every step. "Gods, you're actually enjoying this."

"I enjoy many things," Kipp said. "Chaos. Good wine. A well-tailored coat. But watching you two unravel in a room you don't know how to control?" He gave a lazy sigh. *"Delightful."*

Jarreth stepped forward. "Where is she?"

Kipp flicked an invisible speck from his lapel. "Not here."

"Kipp."

"If you want something from me," he said with a pointed smile, "you'll have to ask prettier than that."

Raoul's hand drifted toward his belt. "You really think this ends well for you?"

"Raoul." Kipp didn't move. "It's already ended well for me. I'm not the one chasing a woman who didn't ask to be followed."

Jarreth's voice dropped, cold. "So you think letting her walk into whatever she's planning was the right call?"

"No," Kipp said, and the smile stayed, but the temperature shifted. "But trying to stop her? That's the kind of mistake you only make once. You try telling Kalithea no, see how far you get."

"It's not just dangerous," Jarreth said. "She's heading into whatever storm this is *alone*."

Kipp stood then, the movement fluid and quiet. He adjusted his cuffs, smiling like a man used to being underestimated. "She is the storm. And you two still think she needs permission."

"We're not giving permission," Jarreth snapped. "We're trying to keep her alive."

Kipp's gaze turned sharp. "So am I."

A beat of silence stretched thin.

"Where did she go?" Raoul asked. Softer now. "Kipp. *Please*."

Kipp looked at him, and for the briefest moment something unreadable passed behind his eyes, something that almost resembled respect.

Then he smiled. Not kindly. But not mocking, either. A blade, gleaming at the edge of truth.

"She went looking for someone mad enough to sail where no one else will. Someone reckless enough to take her straight through her past." He let the words settle, heavy. "A smuggler, of course. *The* smuggler."

Jarreth's expression turned hard. "Blackwell."

Kipp nodded, once. "Jaymes fucking Blackwell."

Raoul swore under his breath. "Shit."

"She trusts him?" Jarreth asked.

"She trusted *me* to get her to him," Kipp said.

"You arranged it?" Jarreth pressed.

Kipp shrugged. "I made a suggestion. She made a decision."

Raoul scoffed. "So now she's off on a ship with a pirate king, heading straight into the gods-damned dark and you just let her go?"

Kipp turned for the door. "I didn't let her go."

Jarreth's voice cut across the room. "Then what would you call it?"

Kipp paused, one hand resting on the frame. "I call it following orders."

Jarreth's eyes narrowed. "You don't follow orders."

Kipp glanced back, that dangerous grin flashing like a knife in the dark. "No. But I'm smart enough not to chain a hurricane."

Jarreth didn't back down. "And if she doesn't come back?"

Kipp's voice went quiet, flat and final. "Then I won't either."

He moved then, sudden and smooth, too close in a blink. His voice dropped low, edged now with something colder.

"Let me give you two some advice." His gaze pinned them both. "If you want to keep up with Kalithea of Elandra, you'll need more than swords and sentiment, boys. You'll need teeth."

He stepped back without waiting for an answer, scooped the coin from the table, and flipped it once between his fingers.

"Oh and next time?" His smirk returned. "Bring wine. If I'm going to lie to you all night, I'd prefer a better vintage."

Jarreth's fists clenched. "You enjoy this far too much."

Kipp winked. "That's what makes me useful."

Raoul's mouth twitched, somewhere between fury and reluctant amusement. "You're a bastard."

Kipp gave a sweeping bow. "King of them, actually."

Then he was gone, slipping through the door like smoke vanishing up a chimney.

The door clicked shut.

Raoul let out a long breath. "Well. That's unsettling."

Jarreth didn't speak for a moment. He just stared at the door. "Yes," he said "Yes, he is."

Raoul dragged a hand down his face. "Alright," he muttered, leaning back in the chair, "let's break this godsdamned mess down before we go charging after ghosts."

Jarreth didn't answer at once. He stood near the table, arms crossed, jaw tight. His thoughts moved too quickly, stacking into patterns he didn't like. The kind that came with inevitability.

Kipp had delayed them, had let her go.

Raoul sat forward, elbows on his knees, rubbing at his temples like that might loosen something. "We come looking for answers, and instead we find the King of Thieves, half-dressed, and lounging like he's just back from a festival."

"Which," Jarreth muttered, "he probably thinks he is."

Raoul gave a short laugh. "Maybe. But did you see how calm he was? Like everything's already in motion."

Jarreth turned, gaze sweeping the room again. The low-burning lantern. The desk cluttered with parchment and ink. A belt draped over the arm of the chair. The scarf. The satchel near the door–half-packed, half-forgotten. Mouth open like it had been interrupted mid-confession.

"Kipp wasn't just lounging," he said, voice quiet. "He was *leaving*. We just missed it."

Raoul's brow lifted. "He's following her."

Jarreth shook his head. "She wouldn't allow it."

Raoul gave him a long look. "And when has certainty ever stopped the King of Thieves from doing what he damn well pleases?"

Jarreth pinched the bridge of his nose and exhaled. "Fuck."

Raoul clapped him on the shoulder, half amusement, half sympathy. "Welcome to the game, Your Highness."

For a beat, they stood in silence. The tension had shifted. Gone was the feverish panic of chasing after her. Now the air turned colder, more precise. The pieces had moved again and the board looked different.

Jarreth turned, voice quieter now. "We're not tracking her anymore."

Raoul's smile sharpened. "No. We're tracking *him*."

A pause.

"Which," Jarreth said dryly, "might actually be easier."

Raoul barked a laugh. "That is the first and last time anyone's going to say that about Kipp Harlow."

"He can't vanish the way she does." Jarreth began to pace. "Kalithea disappears into myth. But Kipp has structure. Territory. A network. If he's moving, someone helped."

Raoul nodded. "So we start tugging threads. Quiet ones."

"Exactly."

Raoul leaned back again, fingers tapping against his knee in a steady rhythm. "Where do you want to begin?"

Jarreth's gaze settled on the door Kipp had vanished through, something sharp settling behind his eyes. "The ship. If he's following her, he's either going on Blackwell's vessel or close enough to bleed into its wake. We hit the dockmaster. Quartermasters. The smugglers who traffic in silence. Someone knows what left this harbor and who paid to be on board."

Raoul's grin curled, slow and dangerous. "There it is. You're finally talking like someone I'd conspire with."

"Don't get ahead of yourself."

"Optimism's half the fun."

"Optimism is for people who plan to survive," Jarreth said.

"Exactly why you're terrible at parties." Raoul grinned.

"And exactly why I'm not buried in a ditch outside Varis."

Raoul gave a low, appreciative huff. "Touché. Still boring."

Jarreth rolled his eyes and stepped toward the door, tension finally turning into motion.

They weren't chasing Kalithea anymore.

But Kipp Harlow left tracks—shallow, scattered, but real. And if they could reach the ship before it vanished into open water, they still had a chance.

Narrow and fading.

But a chance nonetheless.

Raoul joined him, brushing dust from his coat with theatrical flair.

"So we hunt the man chasing the woman who doesn't want to be found."

Jarreth nodded, jaw set. "Exactly."

Raoul chuckled, already moving. "And they say we're the sane ones."

To Catch a Shadow

The air stank of salt and smoke–thick with tar, fish guts, sweat, and the sour heat of cheap rum. The port town heaved with life even after sundown, its veins choked with sailors, smugglers, and men who measured their worth in coin and violence. It was no place for laws, no haven for the weak. This was a city of the sea, its tide claimed by those ruthless enough to carve their names into its docks.

Kalithea moved through it like she'd been born from the same blood and brine.

For a day, she asked nothing.

She listened. She let the streets speak–through slurred boasts at card tables, through murmured warnings passed over broken tankards, through the weight of names that turned conversation quiet. And slowly, the picture sharpened. Kipp had been right: no one *found* Blackwell. He moved like the current beneath the hull. A ghost story in half-burned ports. A name passed between men who never met him twice.

But Kipp hadn't given her direction. He'd given her history. Because where Blackwell had passed, Kipp Harlow had never trailed far behind. Two kings with different crowns, always circling the same thrones.

She didn't need to track Blackwell. She needed only to leave a trail he wouldn't resist.

So she changed her game. She wouldn't hunt him, she'd tempt him.

And Kalithea of Elandra knew precisely how to bait Rogue Kings.

The first night, she let herself be *seen*.

Not just seen, noticed.

She chose her clothing with purpose, black leather molded to her shape, supple and sharp, high at the throat but split low at the front—never completely vulgar, but undeniably dangerous. Her hair, loose from its usual ties, fell in wild dark waves laced with silvered threads that caught the tavern lanterns like starlight adrift on water.

She walked into the dockside tavern without pause. Carved into the stone like a wound that refused to heal, the place stank of old blood and older grudges. It wasn't made for nobles. It was for men who had killed to survive and learned silence held more weight than steel.

She didn't make a scene.

She *became* one.

She played cards with pirates and cutthroats. Drank just enough to earn danger's respect. And when she laughed—once, carelessly, wickedly—it had the kind of ring that made men still mid-draw.

She leaned in when she spoke, murmured what needed hearing, and let silence say the rest. She revealed nothing.

And in that void, they filled in the blanks. They guessed. They whispered. They speculated.

And the rumors spread.

A woman cloaked in shadow, fearless in a city ruled by knives. Alone and unafraid. A threat in silk and leather, drinking at *his* tavern.

His men would hear.

And if Jaymes Blackwell lived up to the legend…he would come.

The second night, she raised the stakes.

She returned. Alone again. This time, she wagered blood. A knife game, brutal and fast—steel flashing between breaths, hands moving too quick to follow. When it ended, the man she faced—twice her size, drunk on pride—lay gasping on the floor, clutching a thigh sliced cleanly.

Kal didn't gloat. She let the silence speak for her. Her movements had been too sharp to be luck. Too smooth to be learned. She didn't *fight* like the men here. She moved like someone born into war and taught to *perform* it.

She lingered, but not close. She allowed the room to watch her without offering anything more. A siren's distance, near enough to draw the eye, far enough to stay out of reach.

Because no one like *her* should've existed here.

And yet, she did.

Men like Blackwell weren't drawn to what they could take. They were drawn to what they couldn't predict. What defied sense. What threatened control.

She didn't chase him. She became the question he couldn't ignore. Now, she waited, because Kalithea knew the truth of kings like Blackwell. You didn't find them.

You stirred the current...and let them come hunting you.

The port churned with noise and motion–sails snapping in the wind, ropes shrieking against shifting hulls, gulls crying over the rhythmic crash of the tide. The air reeked of fish, tar, and the weight of a thousand lives lived too close to saltwater and steel. Nothing here paused. Everything was in motion.

Except her.

She stood near the edge of the dock, still as stone amid the storm. The crowd moved around her in loose clusters–sailors unloading crates, dockhands shouting over one another, a dog barking somewhere beneath the boards–but she held her ground. Silent. Watching.

She wore black leather like a second skin, molded to her frame as if it had been poured on and set with fire. Her hair, dark and unbound, was streaked through with threads of silver, catching the sunlight like a glint of steel in shadow. It lifted in the sea wind behind her, loose and defiant, like a banner no one had dared claim. She didn't hide. She didn't blend. She arrived.

And Jaymes Blackwell noticed.

He stood several paces away, leaning against a sun-bleached piling with the relaxed arrogance of a man who owned everything he could see and didn't mind being seen doing it. His coat was half-buttoned, salt-stained at the collar, and his sleeves were rolled back just far enough to hint at the knives he always kept there. His ship loomed behind him in the harbor, mast swaying gently, but he didn't glance at it. His attention was fixed.

She had walked into his kingdom, uninvited. Alone.

And she looked as though she was daring him to name it a mistake.

Jaymes had come ashore expecting trouble, something about forged contracts, someone using his name in the wrong corner of the realm. But then came the other rumors. A woman, striking and strange, haunting his tavern and bleeding whispers into his streets. A ghost draped in shadow and silver, smiling over card tables and winning without bluffing.

He didn't believe in coincidence. Now, watching her from the dock, he saw it for what it was. Not an accident.

An invitation.

He moved, his gait easy, confident without the need to announce it. He didn't rush. Men like him never did. His boots thudded against the wood, steady as he closed the distance. She didn't turn. Not even as the wind dragged strands of hair across her face and the chaos pressed closer.

He came to stand beside her, just behind her shoulder. Close enough to smell the clean, sharp scent beneath the salt. Something spiced. Grounded. It didn't belong here, and somehow, that made it fit.

He opened his mouth to speak.

She turned.

And Blackwell stopped.

Her eyes met his directly—green and gold, enigmatic and cold, shimmering like shattered glass in sunlight. She looked at him the way no one ever did. Like he wasn't impressive. Like she was already sorting him into something useful or not.

Blackwell recovered quickly. His smile returned, slow, easy and honed by years of using it like a weapon.

"Well now," he drawled, voice smooth, "what's a pretty thing like you doing this far from the leash they keep you on?"

Her gaze slid down his frame and back up again, not admiring. Just taking measure.

He lifted a brow. "Let me guess...ran from your little ivory tower, didn't you? Got bored of silk sheets and empty smiles, thought you'd see how the sinners live—look for something that could ruin you slowly...the kind of ruin you beg for."

She said nothing, but something in her expression shifted. Not an emotion. A choice.

"You can't blame me for asking. You don't look lost, love. You look like temptation in the flesh—walking straight into the fire like you're trying to lure the devil from the sea... and Gods help me, you've got my full attention."

Her lips parted, just barely. He caught the breath before it became a word, the way she tilted her head slightly, like she'd heard enough. Then she spoke, in a voice too soft to be anything but dangerous "You announce yourself loudly for a man who claims to own the sea, Pirate King"

The words were level, steady, like she was placing him on the edge of a blade and waiting to see which way he leaned.

Blackwell's smile held, but he leaned back slightly, posture looser. "If I'd known you already knew me," he said, adjusting the cuff of his sleeve, "I'd have introduced myself properly."

Her expression didn't shift.

"I know *of* you," she said. "There's a difference. A title isn't an introduction."

His laugh came fast, real this time, low and rough in his throat.

"Fair," he allowed, placing a hand over his chest in theatrical mockery. "Jaymes Blackwell. Captain. Rogue. Pirate King. Legendary menace of the coastlines. Devourer of contracts, kings, and–on occasion–beautiful, stubborn women. And..." he gestured toward her with a lazy flick of his wrist, "a man who desperately wants to know the name of the woman who just rattled him."

She lifted a brow. "Rattled you?" she echoed, bemused.

He straightened, rolling his shoulders, adjusting the cuffs of his coat. "Oh, I'll never admit it again," he chuckled slyly. "But yes. A little." His grin widened slightly as he nodded toward her. "And you are?"

She studied him. Quietly. Long enough that the silence turned heavy. Long enough for him to feel it. Long enough to make even *him* shift his stance. Then, finally, she smiled.

"I'm the reason you came ashore."

Not a name. *A fact.*

Blackwell let out a low whistle. "Gods save me."

"Unlikely," she murmured, already turning.

He started to speak–but she was already walking away, her pace steady, shoulders square. She didn't glance back at first, but then she turned slightly to look back. Just once. A glance over her shoulder, eyes catching his for a beat.

And then–gods damn her–she winked.

Jaymes Blackwell, Pirate King, stood alone on his own dock, watching a woman who had spoken fewer than twenty words and still managed to take control of the entire damn board. And all he could do was grin. He wasn't sure whether she'd come to challenge him, recruit him, or burn his world to ash. But by the gods, he was going to find out.

Jaymes Blackwell had never needed to ask twice.

He didn't rule through fear, not directly. He had it, of course, in spades. But he didn't need to lean on the myth that whispered his name from tavern corners to merchant decks. He had built his kingdom not by force, but by fascination. People *wanted* to talk to him. Wanted to orbit close, to feel the gravity of a man who didn't belong to the world's rules, only the sea's. He didn't demand loyalty. He inspired it.

So when he asked–casually, offhand, like it meant nothing at all–about the woman who had wandered onto his docks, the answers came quickly.

A few coins. A glance. A half-grin. And mouths opened.

She'd been seen asking questions, listening without speaking, watching like someone who *knew* she was being watched. She'd been staying in the inn near the cliffs, private, forgotten by most. The kind of place people vanished from, not passed through.

She was clever.

And gods, he hated clever puzzles.

By the time the moon crowned the sea, he had made up his mind. He waited until the harbor thinned into its midnight hush, until the voices faded, the lanterns guttered low, and only the waves kept speaking. Then he left the tavern with nothing but a knife at his hip and that insufferable grin already half-formed.

The inn clung to the bluff like a secret. Weather-worn. Stagnant. The kind of place that didn't bother pretending to be safe. He stepped inside, letting the door swing closed behind him.

And there she was.

Seated by the hearth, poised like a queen on a throne that didn't deserve her. One leg crossed over the other, back relaxed, fingers resting idly on the hilt of a dagger she didn't care to hide. The firelight caught in the metallic threads woven through the braid that coiled over one shoulder. She looked like sin dressed in silence—graceful, unbothered, untouchable.

He took his time crossing the room. "Well," he said, dropping into the chair beside hers without asking, stretching out like it was his own quarterdeck, "I have to admit, I'm impressed."

She didn't look at him. The fire cracked softly between them.

He leaned back, draping one arm across the chair's back, letting the other fall loose. "Not many manage a vanishing act on my docks. You made a game of it. I have to say, I enjoyed the chase."

Still nothing.

Jaymes exhaled a quiet laugh. "Most women chase legends. They don't summon devils from the deep. But here I am tracking you through the dark."

There was a shift. Barely visible. A slight lift in her chin. Nothing more.

So he pressed.

"Before you try to claim you weren't waiting," he murmured, voice dropping into that low, molten register that had drawn knives from hands and names from mouths, "you should know, tracking you in less than a day is no small feat."

That's when she turned toward him, her expression calm, almost predatory, and cold enough to still the air.

"Waiting?" she said, voice nearly a purr. "If I *had* been waiting for you, then you're late. I've been here for days."

His grin faltered. Not by much, but enough. She hadn't hoped he would come. She had *known*. And she had made him chase her anyway.

Her lips curved, barely. Just a flicker of something secret, something sharp. Then she turned back to the fire, as though the Pirate King had already served his purpose.

It hit him low in the gut.

Want.

He dragged a hand through his hair, exhaling a rough breath through a grin he didn't fully control. "If I'd known you were here," he said, quieter now, "I might've sailed faster."

She hummed, soft, and vague. Not agreement or denial. *Dismissal.*

He leaned forward, elbows on his knees, watching her in the shifting glow. "Alright then," he murmured, "what exactly are you expecting?"

She turned fully, and her gaze–gods, it was merciless. He had faced traitors, warlords, executioners. But she was weighing his *worth*. Measuring him against scales only she could see. Not with malice. Not even with doubt.

Just detachment.

She tilted her head slightly. As if she might answer, and for a breath, he thought she would. She smiled, small, serene and devastating. Like she'd been waiting for him to ask. Like the moment had finally caught up to her timing.

Their eyes locked.

"I expected sharper instincts," she said, voice smooth, almost kind. "A man with a reputation like yours should've realized when the game already started."

Then, softly, almost as an afterthought: "Disappoint me again, and I'll find another legend to play with."

Jaymes leaned back slowly, then laughed–short, stunned, and breathless. No one had ever made him feel like *he* was the one being hunted. No one had ever made him feel like he'd already walked into someone else's game.

He sat motionless. The grin still curved his mouth but beneath it something stung, enough to shift his balance. She had knocked him off center and he hated it...or liked it, he couldn't tell which emotion was winning.

Jaymes Blackwell didn't fumble conversations. He didn't lose his footing in flirtation or get outplayed in the dance of implication. Words were his weapon, his comfort, his vice. He could charm secrets from a priest, blood from a rival, pleasure from a stone-hearted beauty. He wielded language like other men wielded blades.

But she hadn't even *engaged.*

So he shifted slowly, reclining back into his chair. His legs stretched, one arm slung loose on the arm rest, the other resting light against his thigh. The smile curled wider, wolfish now.

"This isn't a place for women chasing salvation," he murmured, watching closer, voice low and sure, "and you've haunted my docks too long for it to be an accident. So..."

His eyes traced her, a flicker of danger beneath the charm.

"So what does a woman like you want from a man like me, who offers nothing but the dark?"

She looked up slowly. "A woman like me?"

Her voice was steady. Smooth.

He grinned, crooked and admiring. "You've got the spine of royalty and the stride of a killer. Like someone who's ruled kingdoms by day and ruined men by night. And gods help me, I'm not sure which fate tempts me more." His voice dipped lower. "That kind of contradiction doesn't catch a man's eye. It *undoes* him."

She tilted her head slightly. "And you, Blackwell? What sort of contradiction are you?"

His smirk deepened, "I wear my crown because I took it," he said, voice dropping lower. "No bloodline. No prophecy. Just steel, salt, and the need to make the world kneel or bleed."

Then, lightly–"And a healthy amount of arrogance, obviously."

"I noticed," she said dryly.

She let that sit between them.

Blackwell shifted a little. He didn't like silence unless he was the one wielding it.

"You still haven't answered my question."

"And you haven't earned the answer."

He laughed, low and rich. "So I have to win your words, is that it?"

She hummed softly. "Men tend to value what they fight for."

He raised a brow. "And you'd know that?"

"Intimately."

That stopped him for half a beat. "You've got a dangerous tongue, love."

"And you don't strike me as a man who enjoys safe games." She replied, meeting his gaze for a moment.

"No," he admitted, "I don't."

She reached for her glass, traced a finger around the rim, her attention back on the fire.

"So," he drawled, a slow smile blooming again, "is this the part where I'm supposed to guess your name?"

"I imagined you already had it."

He chuckled. "Oh, I could find out. But where's the thrill in that?"

She didn't answer, Just traced the rim of her glass like the fire, the wine, and *he* were equally forgettable.

Jaymes watched her as she stood dismissing him without so much as a glance in his direction, walking out the door.

And then, because he couldn't help himself, he followed her out.

The wind outside caught in his coat, sharp with salt and secrets. The harbor behind them buzzed, low and untrustworthy, the city breathing in the language of tides and knives.

Jaymes walked beside her, closer than courtesy allowed, steps loose, sure. "What is it you're after, love?"

"You." Her voice was calm and factual.

He blinked. Then smiled, teeth bright in the dark. "You don't waste time."

"I don't have time to waste."

Gods, he liked her voice. Cool and composed. So confident it didn't need to flex.

He tilted his head, studying her with fresh interest.

"Well you're no noble," he said, voice low and thick with certainty. "And certainly not some doe-eyed dreamer chasing salt-slick fantasy."

He looked her over again, slower this time. "No, you move like someone who's already buried the last fool who mistook her for prey."

Jaymes smirked. "You're not looking for rescue. You're looking for a ruin worth the risk." He paused as if savoring his next words, "And Gods, you look like trouble. The kind a man thanks on his knees, if he's lucky enough to survive it."

"And this little dance you've been doing through my dock," he continued, stepping into her path with a lazy grin, "this was all just bait."

"Then stop pretending you're not already hooked."

That drew a breath from him. Not laughter, *something else.* Interest. Wariness.

Then, slowly, he nodded. "Alright. Let's assume I'm interested. What do you want?"

She looked at him, the full force of it–her gaze, clear and ancient–hit like surf against hull. She didn't cut with her eyes. She drowned.

"I need a captain," she said. "And a ship."

The silence after was long. Pure. Jaymes blinked once then let out a long, quiet breath as laughter curled up from his chest.

Of *course.*

He leaned forward, forearms braced, as he studied her.

"Sweetheart," he murmured, low and dangerous now, "you could've led with that."

Jaymes grinned slowly, the kind of grin men wore when they felt the hook land and weren't sure whether to be furious or impressed. "You just said the magic words."

Her hair lifted in the sea breeze, silver threads catching the moonlight like scattered stars. She met his gaze without flinching. "I need a captain who isn't afraid to sail into hostile waters."

His brow arched, amused. "You'll have to narrow that down. I'm wanted in far too many ports to count."

"*Elandra.*"

The word hung between them.

His grin didn't vanish, but it cooled, tightening. "The fallen kingdom."

His silence stretched, the weight of it pressing in.

"You understand what you're asking," he said at last. "That coast is a graveyard. Enemy warships, broken cities, every dock watched, every route carved in blood. You want me to smuggle you through a blockade built to swallow ghosts. Not to mention the godless storms that plague those waters."

"Yes."

He studied her for a long beat. "And what makes you think I'm fool enough to try?"

"I think you're the kind of man who doesn't care about the odds, only whether anyone else can do it. For the chance to prove no kingdom can bar your passage," she said. "Not even the one that thinks itself sealed shut."

His jaw ticked, just once. She saw the calculation flicker in his eyes, faster than breath, deeper than reason.

"You've got a pretty way of dressing up suicide," he muttered.

"I thought pirates liked impossible odds." She countered.

"I like *winning.*"

"So do I."

His smile returned, more teeth than charm. "You've got a dangerous sort of confidence."

He paused. Just long enough to feel it.

"And you're offering what?" he asked. "Some noble cause? A martyr's reward?"

"No," she said. "Gold. Power. Or anything else you might want."

That earned a laugh, low and full, curling up like smoke. "Dangerous offer to make to a pirate."

"Is it?"

"You've no idea what I might ask for."

She didn't blink. "Then name your price, Blackwell."

Jaymes tilted his head, a glint in his eye that didn't reach the smirk. "You really think you can afford it?"

"I think," she said evenly, "you're too clever to name something you're not prepared to lose."

Slowly, his grin widened. "Dangerous words, sweetheart." Then, quieter. More certain. "*You're serious.*"

"I wouldn't be here otherwise."

Jaymes studied her, longer this time. She wasn't posturing or bluffing. And there was no fear. Just steel. And the, his voice dropped low, amused but thoughtful. "You know what I hate most?"

"Being told no?"

"Being outmaneuvered." he laughed.

Kal shrugged smoothly, "Then choose faster."

He watched her then, like a man who'd just been handed something too rare to toss aside.

She let the silence stretch. Let him imagine what was at stake, what he could gain, and what might destroy him trying. Then, with the barest motion, she turned, casting a glance over her shoulder.

The ghost of a smile curved her lips. "Let me know if you're the legend they fear...or just a well-dressed story waiting to disappoint."

The One Who Lights the Flame

aymes Blackwell did not hesitate. He made choices like a blade drawn clean across a throat–fast, final, unapologetic. Regret was for slower men, for captains who flinched before the tide. He didn't look back. He didn't second guess. That was how he'd stayed alive this long.

And yet, he hadn't moved in nearly an hour.

Slouched deep in the corner of his quarters, boots up on the table, coat unbuttoned, grin half-formed like it had forgotten what it was doing there. The lamplight painted everything in gold and shadow–maps stretched across the walls, loose charts tacked over the teak, the glint of steel and salt-worn brass catching in the sway of the ship. It smelled of oil, sea, and smoke.

It should've comforted him. It didn't. His gaze stayed pinned to the map splayed across the table, fingers tapping idly against a worn edge. He knew every inlet on that coast. Every reef and uncharted shoal. He'd outrun warships through those waters, vanished into coves where kings lost men trying to follow. He had shaped that shoreline like a signature. But tonight, he wasn't seeing the coast. He was seeing her.

Smoke and silk. Calm and calculation. She hadn't blinked when she asked the impossible. Hadn't tried to impress or seduce. She'd looked at him, just looked, and every instinct he had gone silent. Not because she'd trapped him. Because he'd walked straight into it. Willingly.

The door creaked open behind him.

"You're going to wear a hole through that map," Dorian said, his voice easy, low with amusement.

Jaymes didn't turn. "And you're going to earn yourself a swim if you keep talking."

His first mate stepped in anyway, arms crossed, leaning one shoulder against the frame. "You've gone quiet."

Jaymes grunted.

Dorian smiled faintly. "So, which is it? Planning something brilliant...or thinking about the woman who made you forget how to speak?"

Jaymes's fingers paused on the table. One tap. Two. "I'm always planning something brilliant."

"Aye, but usually you're louder about it."

Jaymes glanced up, his expression inscrutable. "Did you need something, or are you just here to admire the brooding?"

Dorian grinned, leaning against the doorframe. "Just wanted to see how long it'd take you to admit she's got you twisted."

Jaymes stared. Dorian grinned wider.

"She's clever," Blackwell said finally. "Too clever."

"And?"

"She knows it."

That earned a laugh. "Sounds like someone else I know."

Jaymes didn't rise. Just dragged a hand through his hair and muttered, "It's annoying."

Dorian's brow rose. "Is that what this is? You sulking over a clever woman?"

"I'm calculating."

"Same thing when you're losing." Dorian chuckled, "So what's the plan, then? Wait until she sails off with someone else? That seems a bit un-Blackwell of you."

Jaymes stood in one fluid motion, shrugging into his coat. "She's not the type to wait."

His first mate raised both brows. "Then stop stalling."

Jaymes opened the door to the deck. The sea wind slammed into him like a challenge. Salt. Cold. Freedom. He inhaled it like a man returned to form.

"She thinks she's ahead," he murmured, more to himself than to anyone else. "Thinks she's the one pulling the strings."

Dorian followed him into the dark. "Isn't she?"

Jaymes laughed–low, dangerous. "She can think whatever she wants," he said, grin sharp. "But I'm the one setting sail."

Blackwell found her exactly where instinct had said she would be

The tavern in Silvercairn sat low at the edge of the wharf, its walls warped from salt and time, smoke curling from sconces that hadn't seen a proper cleaning in a decade. Private. The sort of place people came to disappear. She had chosen her seat with purpose. Back to the wall, full command of the exits. The candle beside her burned low, its flame catching on the silver threads woven through her dark dress, subtle at first glance, but unmistakable now that he was close.

He paused just inside the door, adjusting the cuffs of his coat. Not to draw attention. Just to mark the moment. A beat before the game began. She didn't look up as he stepped through the haze of old pipe smoke and worse breath. Just brought the wine to her lips and drank, slow and unbothered.

Which meant, of course, she'd already seen him.

Blackwell crossed the room with slow steps. Loud enough to be noticed by anyone worth worrying about. He let his presence announce itself, let the floorboards creak under his boots, the old rhythm of his stride teasing tension from the air.

"I go to all this trouble," he said, voice smooth, playful, "and I don't even get a hello?"

She set her goblet down with quiet ease.

"I assumed you'd find your way eventually," she said.

Jaymes felt the corner of his mouth lift. "You make it sound like I had a choice."

"You didn't."

"But I like the illusion."

"Most men do."

He chuckled. "I had options. They were just uninspiring."

"Then I suppose I should be flattered."

"You should," he said, stretching out in the chair like he owned the tavern. "But you don't strike me as someone who waits for flattery."

She watched him, steady and composed, like a cat deciding whether a mouse was worth the effort. He knew the tactic. Gods, he admired the precision of it.

"You need a ship," he said. "And a captain."

She lifted a brow. "And you're here to offer both?"

"I'm here to decide if I should."

"Ah," she said, reaching for her glass again. "Do you think I'm in the habit of chasing favors?"

"I think," Jaymes said, leaning in slightly, "you don't ask unless the outcome's already certain."

Kal smiled faintly. "And here you are," she said, "still pretending you haven't already made up your mind."

He sat back, arms folding loosely across his chest. "I haven't agreed."

"You will. What do you want, Blackwell?"

"What do I want?" he repeated, voice lower now. "Gold's easy.

Power's messy. Influence is for men who need permission."

"If that's all you see, Captain, you should go."

He watched her closely. "And if I'm looking for something else?"

"You'd better know what it is before you ask." She said, tone almost coy.

The line sat between them.

He leaned forward again, elbows to the table. His tone dropped, low now.

"I want the storm," he said, almost absently. "The kind of ride that leaves marks. Something loud enough to wake the dead."

A flicker crossed her face, not quite surprise. Recognition, maybe. She leaned back, gaze guarded. "And you think I offer that?"

"You're offering a job," he said. "But what I want...is the chase. The sort that bruises. The kind you remember when the coin's long gone."

She didn't answer right away. Just watched him like she was reading a language written in the lines of his face.

He leaned forward, voice just above a whisper now. "No price. No rules. *No name.* Only danger and shadows at your back." His eyes lingered. "Tell me, do you offer that to every man who walks through the door?"

Her reply came cold and clean: "If you have to ask who I am, Captain, perhaps you're not the man I thought you were."

A pause. Not long. Just enough to tighten the net.

"And if you truly don't know why I came to you," she said, smooth as sin, "then maybe I should find someone with the spine to follow the scent without needing it spelled out."

Gods. *That.* That had teeth and he liked the bite of it.

He breathed out through his nose, slow. "You're not *just* looking for a captain."

"No."

"You want someone who won't flinch when the world starts burning."

Her gaze held. "I want someone who'll help me light the flame."

The corner of his mouth pulled into a grin.

"A wager then," he said. "One night. You sail with me and my crew. Show me something worth chasing...and I'll take the job."

"And if I don't?"

Jaymes smiled, sharp and unkind. "Then I name the price for the waste of my time."

Kalithea didn't flinch. Just considered, until the weight of it turned into a smile, one that didn't reach her eyes but promised knives beneath.

Then: "Fine."

She stood. The silk of her dress caught the light like oil on water, trailing behind her as she turned. He watched her go, then called after her, voice casual and suggestive.

"Wear something practical, love. I'd hate to see you fall and have to fish you out of the sea before I know your worth."

She glanced over her shoulder, eyes gleaming turning her head enough for him to catch the curve of her smirk, her voice dark and laced with steel.

"If I fall, Blackwell...it'll be deliberate and entirely by design." Kal's gaze slid over him, indulgent, amused. "And only if the descent tempts more than the climb ever could." She paused. "And it's Kalithea. Not 'love.'"

Then she was gone. Jaymes sat in silence, grinning like a man who knew the storm was already on him, and didn't give a damn.

Sea Legs and Sirens

lackwell stood at the edge of the dock with the morning sun climbing slow and steady behind him, its light catching on the brass buckles of his longcoat. The sea was calm, a low hush of water against wood, broken only by the occasional cry of gulls overhead. He kept his arms folded as she approached, watching without pretense. There was no fanfare to her arrival, just the steady rhythm of her boots against the stone.

On the deck above, the crew had gathered in loose groups, feigning distraction. A few busied themselves with ropes or railings, but their glances betrayed them. The murmurs had started the moment word spread of the trial, low and speculative, turning sharper when they saw who was meant to earn her place aboard. It wasn't every day Blackwell opened his deck to strangers, and it was rarer still when he did it without naming a price first.

She stepped into the full light then, and Blackwell had to bite back a curse. *Of course.* Of course she would come dressed like that. Leather, black and fitted, shaped to movement rather than display, covered her legs and forearms like armor. Over it she wore a tunic of faded grey, unbuttoned to the sternum and cinched at the waist, weathered by wear but chosen with intent. There was nothing soft in her bearing, nothing fragile in the way she bore the weight of the ship's scrutiny. If the crew had hoped to find weakness in her appearance, they'd find none here.

He tapped a knuckle against his jaw, voice dry. "I see you dressed for performance."

She met his gaze as she reached the top of the gangplank, her tone even. "And you dressed to watch me fail?"

His mouth tugged into a grin. "Only fair to look my best for the show."

Her gaze drifted from his stormy blue eyes and dark windblown hair, to the thin leather cord that hung around his neck that drew the eye to the open collar of his tunic, ending at the gleam of steel at his hip. "Seems a bit overdressed for someone who doesn't expect to stay dry."

Her gaze moved past him to the ship itself. She studied the rigging, the mast, the pitch of the sails as they stirred in the breeze. Her hands remained still, but he could see the calculations taking place behind her eyes–measuring the deck, the distance, the tension in the lines coiled at her feet. Without a word, she stepped forward, uncoiled a length of rope, and took hold. Three strides carried her back into position. Then she moved. The arc of her body through the air was clean, unbroken by hesitation or wasted effort. She held the rope with an expert grip, momentum carrying her high before she released. Her boots hit the quarterdeck with a soft thud, knees bent just enough to catch the landing.

The crew fell still. One or two straightened instinctively, as if caught idle by an officer.

She adjusted her bracer with one firm pull and turned to face the man still watching her from the dock. "Well?"

Blackwell exhaled, his lips curving, and then came a full laugh. It rang across the space between them, unrestrained and real.

He stepped forward at last, taking the gangplank with steady strides. "Well, damn. That was...unexpected."

Her head tilted slightly, "You sound surprised."

"Not surprised. Pleased. There's a difference."

He stopped just short of the first step and looked at her. There was something new in his gaze now, no longer just amusement, but something tempered by understanding. "I've underestimated a lot of people in my life, Kalithea. But I have a feeling you'll be my favorite mistake."

Her smile came without warmth, a bare curve of the lips. "Then you must make them often. You're far too comfortable with being wrong."

He laughed again, quieter now, his eyes never leaving her. "Oh, you've already made the others forgettable, love. And we haven't even set sail."

Blackwell descended the gangplank, his steps even, his shoulders relaxed, with his coat catching the sea breeze just enough to lend him that familiar edge of swagger. He knew what he looked like, and he knew she was watching. Gods help him, he enjoyed the way she tracked him without moving a muscle.

"Well then," he said, his tone a mix of amusement and edge, "you certainly know how to make an entrance."

She held his gaze with the same composure she'd had from the moment she landed, letting the silence stretch between them.

He chuckled under his breath, slowing to a stop just a few paces away. "But let's see if you can hold attention as well as you command it."

"Let's get something straight, Blackwell," she said, her voice low and unhurried. "I'm not here to impress you."

He grinned, teeth flashing beneath a layer of charm sharpened by interest. "Oh, I'd never be so presumptuous, love."

With a casual turn, he gestured toward the deckhands and riggers who still lingered—watching from the shadows, from the lines above, from behind crates they hadn't yet finished moving.

"You're here for them. Not me. Prove yourself to them, and I might start thinking you were serious."

She raised a brow. "Strange. You seem more invested than they are."

"I have a vested interest in entertainment," he said, his tone light but watchful. "And so far, you're proving more interesting than most."

She let her attention drift over the deck, her eyes moving from mast to rail, then to the faces that hadn't quite stopped staring. She took her time. No theatrics. No effort to win them over. Only a long, silent reading of the terrain. When her gaze met theirs, the men who held it didn't smile or nod. They simply looked back with something bordering on caution. It wasn't her beauty that unsettled them, though that would have been reason enough. It was how she stood. How she existed in the space. As if it already belonged to her.

"What's the test, then?" she asked at last, her voice carrying across the deck without effort. "Do you want me to lift barrels? Tie knots? Charm your crew? Or do I start with the humiliating labor and work my way up?"

Blackwell's laugh came quick and bright. He stepped a little closer. "If you wanted an excuse to get on your knees for me, love, you didn't need to make it so official."

A few of the crew chuckled, one young deckhand fumbling the coil of rope in his hands. But Kalithea didn't flinch. She stepped forward, calm and steady, until she stood just inside his reach. Not close enough to touch, just close enough to make him decide whether to give ground.

He didn't.

Her voice dropped, soft but without gentleness. "If I'm ever on my knees, Blackwell, it'll be to gut you from beneath. And I won't need a second strike."

The laughter died. The quiet that followed stretched sharp and sudden.

Then Blackwell threw his head back and laughed—a full, unguarded sound that broke through the tension like a crack of thunder. He shook his head as he looked at her, admiration bright behind the grin. "Oh, gods, you're delightful," he said, the words half a breath. "A woman with wit and teeth. I'm positively ruined."

She tilted her head just enough to imply amusement. "That's unfortunate."

"Not at all. I like a woman who makes me work for my victories."

"Then I do hope you're prepared for a very long, exhausting pursuit."

His grin widened. "Sounds like a challenge."

"It's a *promise.*"

He pressed a hand over his chest in exaggerated injury, then turned to his first mate without missing a beat. "Well, you heard the lady. Let's see if she's worth the trouble."

Dorian nodded once, his expression guarded as his gaze shifted to Kalithea. "Aye, Captain."

Then, to her, his voice was flat but not unfriendly, "Let's see what you're made of, then."

She offered no verbal answer. Just a slight nod and a half-smile that held no warmth or threat, only the edge of someone who already knew the outcome. Then she turned and followed, not looking back.

Blackwell leaned against the railing, one hand resting on the wood, eyes tracking her as she moved across the deck. The ship creaked beneath them, alive with motion and purpose again, but his thoughts stayed on her.

The moment Dorian stepped forward, the air on the deck changed. Laughter still lingered in the corners, loose and mocking, but something beneath it had shifted. Posture stiffened. Eyes sharpened. A taut and expectant current ran beneath the surface now, as though the crew, despite themselves, had begun to wonder whether this woman might not be playing a part after all.

Kalithea turned to face the first mate, her posture relaxed. There was nothing deferential in her regard, only the calm attentiveness of someone who had already decided this belonged to her.

"We'll start simple," Dorian said, his voice rough and salt-worn, the kind built by years spent shouting into the wind.

"Climbing?" she asked, eyes flicking once toward the rigging.

Blackwell gave a short laugh, low and amused from where he leaned against the mainmast. "Ah, love. Ruining all my surprises again. It's almost like you've done this before."

She sent him a glance with just enough edge to make his grin stretch wider.

"Up you go, then," he said, nodding toward the lines stretched above their heads. "Let's see if that entrance wasn't all for show."

She stepped forward, reached for the rope, and began to climb. There was no hesitation in her movements or dramatics. Just clean, practiced rhythm—boots finding their marks, hands wrapping and releasing with the steady confidence of someone who knew what they were doing. Each movement was efficient, almost too smooth, as if muscle memory guided her rather than thought.

Gradually, the deck began to quiet. Conversations stilled. Tools paused in hand. One by one, the crew turned to watch, and the smirks that had lingered began to thin. Her pace remained unchanged, unbothered by the attention. When she reached the first spar, she swung up and around without losing momentum, crouched there for a breath–poised, centered–then stood.

Her eyes found Blackwell's. She said nothing. But he felt the meaning of that look settle in his chest like a dropped anchor.

You misjudged me.

He didn't look away. Couldn't. He felt it like a shove to the chest, and gods, it made his blood burn.

"All right then," he muttered, just loud enough for those closest to hear. "You have my attention."

She climbed higher, hands and feet moving with swift accuracy, until she reached the topmast and stepped onto the beam without hesitation. The wind stirred the loose braid at her back, lifting it as the sun caught the glint of silver laced through her hair. She stood still, arms loose at her sides, gaze fixed not on the crew but on the horizon, as if the ship were hers already and this moment nothing more than confirmation.

Something shifted among the men watching her. It wasn't awe, or surprise. It was quieter. Older. The kind that didn't need to be spoken to be understood.

Respect.

"Captain," one of the deckhands murmured nearby, not quite under his breath, "she's got sea legs."

"More than that," came another voice, thoughtful.

"Think she's part siren?" someone whispered.

Blackwell didn't take his eyes off her. "Keep talking, and I'll toss you overboard."

His smile had faded from his face, replaced by something quieter, something closer to recognition. She had crossed a line, not with force, but with confidence. The crew saw it too. Whatever she'd come here to prove, she'd done it.

She descended without fanfare, just as cleanly as she had gone up. Boots hit the deck, and she straightened without needing to adjust. No grin or triumph in her posture. Only the same certainty that had carried her here from the start.

"Passable?" she asked, as if the entire demonstration had been nothing more than a polite obligation.

Blackwell dragged a hand across his mouth, mostly to hide the grin threatening to return. "You've gone and made them like you. That's dangerous."

"For them or for you?" she asked, one brow rising.

He let the smile show. "We'll find out soon enough."

The trial continued. Dorian set the pace, calling tasks without pause. She tied knots–tight, fast, efficient. She hauled canvas without waiting to be told twice, her movements precise, strength measured without waste. When the wind shifted and the deck tilted beneath them, she adjusted her stance instinctively, never reaching for support, never stumbling. Each task she completed settled the unease among the crew further. Not because she tried to win them. She didn't speak much, didn't explain herself, didn't perform. She simply did the work and did it well. And in doing so, stripped away doubt task by task.

Blackwell watched all of it. Not as a captain measuring her worth, but as a man trying to make sense of a thing he hadn't planned for. He'd expected defiance, charm, wit. He hadn't expected skill. Or control.

By the time she returned to where he stood, sun catching on the high curve of her cheek, the last trial was already forming between them.

"Swordplay," he said, pushing off the rail, his voice low and dark.

She looked at him, expression unchanged. Calm. Focused.

"You'll regret that," she said.

He smiled, this time without mockery. He unbuckled the sword at his hip, drew it in one smooth motion, and flipped it by the blade to offer it to her. "That's the idea."

She caught it one-handed.

The crew shifted as one, forming a wide ring along the edges of the deck. No one spoke. The shadows had grown longer, sunlight slanting low through the rigging, laying blades of amber across the planks beneath their feet. The sails groaned as the wind thickened.

She stepped into place opposite him, her weight settling forward. The blade sat steady in her hand. Blackwell mirrored her, his own weapon at the ready, though his eyes remained fixed not on the sword but on her. She held her ground with unshaken poise, the sword resting in her hand with ease. Nothing in her stance suggested nerves or hesitation. She didn't glance at the edges of the deck or measure the space between them. Whatever she needed to know, she'd already taken in at a glance. Now, her focus was fixed entirely on him. Watching. Calculating. Determining how long she would entertain the match before ending it.

"Careful, love," Blackwell drawled as he stepped forward, his sword catching the sun in a gleam of polished steel. "You keep looking at me like that, I might start thinking you're impressed."

Her chin tipped up, a faint smile ghosting across her lips. "Then your imagination's more generous than your footwork."

Laughter stirred among the crew, low and appreciative, but Blackwell didn't let it distract him. His eyes stayed on her, the smirk never leaving his face. "I do hope you won't hold back on my account."

"I wouldn't insult you that way, Captain."

He moved without warning. A clean opening strike, swift and angled to test rather than wound. She met it with fluid ease, deflecting the blow with a ring of steel before sliding the blades apart in a controlled motion. The exchange lasted no more than a breath, but the precision was unmistakable.

"Not bad," he said, his tone light.

"You sound surprised," she replied as she stepped to the side, her footing exact, her gaze never shifting from him.

He attacked again, this time a feint to the left followed by a real strike low to her right. She read it before he fully committed, shifted just out of reach, and let her blade kiss the hem of his jacket as she turned the angle back on him.

His grin thinned. For the first time, he frowned.

"Where'd you learn to move like that?" he asked, beginning to circle, his steps slow and cautious.

Kal's answer was clipped and cool. "Wouldn't you like to know."

Jaymes exhaled sharply through his nose, a breath of laughter. "You enjoy keeping me in the dark."

"It's where men like you stumble most."

He shifted his grip, the muscles in his arm flexing. "Careful. That almost sounded like flirting."

She turned her wrist, spinning the sword once lazily. "If I were flirting, Captain, you'd know it."

He felt her words settle, somewhere between interest and warning. He moved again, faster now. More aggressive. He struck high, then low, testing her reflexes with each motion. She matched him, never off balance, never even breathing hard. The ring of metal echoed across the deck. Their boots slid across the planks as they moved, each step sharpened by instinct and calculation. He pressed harder, trying to disrupt her rhythm. She didn't break.

So he cheated. A stumble–subtle, feigned–threw him off axis. She stepped in, blade ready to exploit the opening. That was the moment he swept his foot toward her ankle. She didn't fall for it. Her weight shifted mid-step, the trap read and discarded before it landed. She adjusted, quick and silent, and the edge of a smile appeared at the corner of her mouth.

"Really?" she said, her voice soft and edged with amusement. "That's your move?"

"*Pirate*," he reminded her, unrepentant. "I never claimed to play fair."

She turned her wrist slightly, the blade lifting in her hand. "And here I thought the great Jaymes Blackwell had better tricks than tripping."

He saw the shift in her posture too late. She wasn't sparring anymore. She had been toying with him, letting him think he was keeping up. And now? She was finishing it. A sidestep, clean and sudden. Her sword came up in one smooth arc and caught his blade at precisely the right angle. Steel left his grip before he could resist it, wrenched from his hand and tossed across the deck with a ringing clatter.

Then came the second part. She stepped forward and caught his leg with hers—a mirror of the move he'd just tried—and his balance vanished. He hit the deck with a sharp thud, air driven from his lungs as he landed flat on his back, staring up at the blue wash of sky above.

Laughter burst from the crew. A few shouted; others choked on their amusement as they scrambled to contain it.

"Captain's down!"

"Did she just–?"

"Someone fetch the man a drink!"

Blackwell lay there a moment longer, blinking up at the rigging overhead, trying to find enough breath to swear properly. A shadow passed across his chest. She stood above him, sword lowered to hover just over his heart. Her expression was composed, but her eyes shone with something bright and dangerous beneath the stillness.

"Passable?" she asked.

He let the breath escape slowly, then laughed. The sound rolled up from his chest, loose and rich, the kind of laugh that came when pride was bruised but pleasure remained intact.

"Oh, love," he said, voice rough with amusement. "I may be in real trouble with you."

Her lips curved, faint but sure. "You're just now realizing?"

He grinned back at her, still lying on the deck, pulse thrumming beneath the weight of it all. She had bested him. Cleanly. Publicly. And without a single wasted movement.

And gods–he couldn't wait to see what she did next.

The scent of salt hung heavy on the air, mingling with woodsmoke and charred meat, the sharp tang of spiced rum threading through it all. The ship swayed beneath them with slow, lulling motion, the creak of timber and the rhythmic slap of waves marking time. Across the deck, laughter rolled like surf, loud and rough, shaped by men who had long since made peace with danger. Tankards clashed, plates scraped, and stories grew taller with every round poured.

Under the lanterns strung between mast and beam, Kalithea sat at the captain's table. She didn't speak often, didn't gesture broadly or fill space with noise, but the men around her leaned in all the same. She didn't draw attention–she claimed it, quietly, thoroughly, without effort. There was no need to announce her presence when the shape of the night had already begun to bend around it.

Blackwell had been watching her for some time. Not obviously, he was too subtle for that, but often. His gaze would return to her the way a seasoned sailor glanced at the horizon: cautious, contemplative, unable to ignore the possibility of a storm. The sparring had unsettled something. Not in the way he expected, not bruised pride or wounded ego. He could laugh at his own defeat, especially when it was well earned. But the aftermath lingered. His crew, men not easily impressed and slower still to trust, had begun to shift. What had started as guarded curiosity now edged toward something like allegiance. They watched her differently. Spoke to her with a note of ease, a kind of careful familiarity usually reserved for their own. And she, without trying, without chasing it, had accepted their regard with the poise of someone used to being tested and passing.

She simply sat, her eyes half-lidded, her tankard untouched more than it was raised, content to observe rather than perform. And yet, the men laughed when she spoke, quieted when she leaned in. Something in the lines of their shoulders had eased around her. She had stepped aboard as a stranger. Now she sat as something else entirely.

"You always this silent when you drink?" Blackwell asked, his tone hushed, pitched for her alone. Beneath the noise and the flickering light, his words cut a private space between them.

She turned slightly, her lips curving into a small smile. "Perhaps I prefer to listen. It's a better way to gather leverage."

A low chuckle stirred in his chest. "So you're the patient kind of predator. That explains a lot."

Kal's gaze swept across him, unhurried, as if taking his measure for the second time. "A woman who reveals her methods too soon rarely gets to collect on them."

Jaymes raised his tankard in a mock salute, grin sharpening at the edges. "And here I thought you were here for a captain. Turns out I've invited a spy."

"A spy would flatter you more."

"And you don't?"

She held his gaze, cool and unwavering. "Have I?"

He leaned back slightly, the grin still present but subdued now, tempered by something more thoughtful. "You've got a way with words, Kalithea."

"And you're still under the illusion you've heard most of them."

The corner of his mouth tugged upward in appreciation, but there was caution in it, too. He was used to games. Used to the masks people wore in places like this. But she didn't wear a mask. She was a blade in a velvet sheath, sharp whether drawn or not. She never rose to his bait. She never pushed when it was expected. Silence sat around her like a cloak, and she wielded it with more skill than most men brought to steel. It was a different kind of power, quieter and deeper, and he could see how it worked. Not by force. By presence.

The night wore on. The crew grew louder, looser. Blackwell passed drinks, laughed at a half-true tale from his quartermaster, threw a bone at one of the hounds circling beneath the table. But part of his attention never drifted. It remained with her. He found himself watching her more than he did the waves. Not because she was beautiful, though she was. Not because she could fight, though he still felt the ache from where she'd dropped him to the deck. There was something beneath it. A kind of control he couldn't define, the kind born not of power, but of having learned when to speak, when to wait, when to strike. Everything about her was deliberate.

"You're not what I expected," he said, low, quieter now, meaning more than he'd intended.

She didn't turn to him, only a flick of her eyes in his direction. "Good."

The word was clean, unburdened by explanation. She didn't care about his expectations. If she had come to disrupt them, she was succeeding with alarming ease. He studied her in the silence that followed. The posture never slackened, not even for a moment. The calm wasn't comfort, it was armor. A survival learned young, worn long. The kind of strength men often mistook for grace until it was too late.

And gods help him, he wanted to know how deep it went.

"I've met all kinds of women," he murmured, not quite joking, not quite serious. "Not one of them ever made me feel like I should be checking the length of my leash."

She smiled fully, with an underlying air of danger. "You tied it yourself, Captain. I simply let you tug on it."

He leaned back, exhaling a breath that carried laughter and resignation in equal measure. He dragged a hand through his hair, shaking his head as he stared at the lanternlight above. "Bloody hell, woman. You're going to be the end of me."

Her attention had already drifted back to the crew, as though the game had moved on.

"You'll survive," she said, voice soft.

By the time the sky began to pale with the first hints of dawn, the wind had shifted. It rolled in low and steady off the sea, coaxing the ship back toward the distant lights of port. Above, the sails whispered as they strained against their lines, and the timbers groaned with the slow, inevitable turn. The crew moved without need for instruction. Each man knew the rhythm of returning–the haul of rope, the soft thud of crates shifted, the quiet between orders when the sea seemed to breathe around them.

Blackwell stood at the railing, one hand resting lightly on the salt-worn wood, the scent of brine and faint smoke clinging to the folds of his coat. Beside him, Kalithea leaned easily, finding no need to pretend she belonged. The remaining moonlight cast her in silver, pale light glinting along her cheekbones, catching in her hair. She said nothing, gaze fixed on the black line where sea met sky.

He let the silence stretch before breaking it. "You won my crew over tonight."

She hummed, the sound neither agreement nor denial. Her attention remained on the horizon, where the faintest bloom of morning threatened the dark. "That wasn't my goal."

"Perhaps not," he said, glancing sidelong at her, "but you managed it all the same."

She turned at that, just enough to meet his eyes. The breeze caught strands of her hair and pulled them loose, trailing them across her shoulder like threads of smoke. "Did you want them to hate me?"

"No," he admitted. "But it would've made resisting you a damn sight easier."

That earned him a look–sharp, dry, with the shadow of a smile that held no comfort, more edge than warmth.

"Good thing I never intended to make anything easy for you."

He laughed, the sound low in his throat. He rubbed a hand across his jaw. "Of course not. You'd sink the ship before you let a man think he's got the upper hand."

"It's not a flaw," he added after a moment, his voice quieter. "It's maddening. And magnificent."

Her gaze returned to the sea, but the silence that followed had shifted. It no longer held distance, it held awareness.

They docked just before sunrise. The ship moaned as it settled against the pier, reluctant to rest. Dockhands moved through the mist with the half-speed of men born to early hours, and the crew descended to the task of unloading without ceremony. Orders were exchanged in short bursts. Crates were passed down, ropes secured, knots checked and rechecked.

Blackwell stood at the base of the gangplank with Kalithea beside him, both of them still. He watched the activity around them without speaking, but his mind was elsewhere. The questions he hadn't asked were already piling against the edge of his restraint.

At last, he turned to her.

"I need more than your name, love," he said. His tone had lost its usual gloss. There was weight in it now. "I don't steer into the wind without knowing where I'm headed."

She looked at him fully then, assessing him. She studied him with the care of someone choosing how much to trust, and what part of herself she was willing to place in his hands. It wasn't about danger. It was about control. About who held it and for how long.

And Blackwell let her look. Let her measure. Because something in him wanted to be understood by her, even if it cost him.

"I'll give you what's needed," she said at last.

"That's vague."

"It's deliberate."

He arched a brow, the smile that followed thinner now, laced with something more dangerous than charm. "And if I decide I want more?"

There was a flicker in her eyes, a flash of something unspoken. Her lips curved into a grin laced with promise.

"Then, Captain," she said, "you'll have to earn it."

He exhaled through his teeth, slow and steady. A dare. A warning. The line between them had never been clearer, and he was still choosing to cross it.

He nodded once. "I'll see you on deck by high noon. Wear something you don't mind getting wet."

She turned to go, but halfway through the motion, she glanced over her shoulder. Her voice came soft, the edge of it tugging at the air between them like a drawn thread.

"I'll give you one thing, Captain."

He stilled.

"A title."

She held his gaze, steady, unblinking.

"Queen Kalithea of Elandra."

The Echo and the Shadow

Kipp Harlow lingered in the mouth of a narrow alley, one boot pressed to the crumbling wall behind him, arms folded across his chest. He held to the shadows not out of habit, but because he wore them well.

But now, he was waiting.

The *Tempest* had returned, its sails lowered. Light flickered along the docks, throwing broken patterns across the water, but his attention remained fixed on the ship.

She stood on deck. *Kalithea*. Still and poised beside the infamous Jaymes Blackwell, the two of them locked in conversation. From this distance, the words were lost to the wind, but Kipp didn't need to hear them. The meaning was plain. The tilt of her chin, the weight in her posture, the cut of her silence; it was all there, same as ever. Power. Calculated and cold. Dressed in silk and steel. Even across the water, she was unmistakable. That quiet, unnerving calm that made seasoned men falter. Blackwell looked enraptured, though he likely thought himself in control. Kipp had worn that expression before he'd learned how deep the water ran.

He exhaled, slow and soundless, a trace of a smile tugging at the corner of his mouth. It wasn't jealousy, not truly. He just wasn't used to the view from this angle. Watching from the outside had never suited him.

A voice stirred from the shadows beside him. "You've been standing here a while, boss. Planning something clever? Or just brooding handsomely in the shadows?"

Kipp didn't turn. "If I were brooding, you'd already be unconscious."

Vale gave a snort. "So... planning, then?"

"Always."

"Could've fooled me. Looks more like loitering with flair."

Kipp tilted his head slightly, his gaze flicking sideways at last. "Tell me, Vale. Do you ever consider shutting up before your mouth makes a promise your kneecaps can't keep?"

"Daily," Vale said cheerfully. "Never committed, though."

Kipp allowed the smallest breath of laughter to escape. He shifted just enough to glance back toward the ship. Kalithea and Blackwell were beginning to descend the gangplank now. The way they moved–together, purposeful, unspeaking–told him everything he needed to know. They were leaving, and she hadn't sent for him.

Of course she hadn't.

"You going to crash the party?" Vale asked, though the answer was already written across Kipp's face.

He pushed off the wall with easy grace, stretching out his shoulders. "She's walking into something sharp, and she knows it. She'll need a hand with sleight, not steel."

Vale crossed his arms and leaned back against the opposite wall. "I doubt Blackwell's looking to add a stowaway."

"I don't plan to ask," Kipp said, brushing dust from his coat as if the motion were ceremonial. "I'll slip in quiet. By the time anyone notices, we'll be halfway to nowhere, and I'll be exactly where I need to be."

Vale raised a brow. "Subtle. Suicide by piracy."

Kipp's grin returned, sharp and clean. "Only if I get caught."

"And if you do?"

"Then I'll improvise."

There was a beat of silence. Vale sighed like a man accustomed to the sound of his own better judgment being ignored. "One of these days, you're going to run out of clever."

"Maybe." Kipp stepped from the alley into the street, already moving, steps loose with confidence "But not today."

Getting aboard the *Tempest* wasn't the hardest thing Kipp had ever done. But it came close enough to make him smile. Blackwell's crew was no ordinary collection of men. They were seasoned–tight-knit, watchful, hardened by sea and loyalty both. They moved like soldiers, but thought like wolves, each one protecting the ship as if it were their own skin. No gaps, no slack. Every post manned, every glance purposeful. It was not a ship one simply wandered onto.

But Kipp had never been the kind to wander. He waited. Let the chaos rise to its crest–crates lifted, orders shouted, the press of dock-hands, the hiss of ropes and steel. The scent of tar and salt and old rum wrapped around everything like a cloak. He tracked the rhythm of movement until the pattern blurred, until the edges frayed just enough. One distracted lookout. That was all it took.

And then he moved. A shadow between shadows, he slipped past the dockside guard with no more sound than breath on glass. He skirted around the loading ramp, low to the ground, one hand steady against the boards as he ducked beneath the commotion. At the starboard side, just beyond the blind arc of a swinging lantern, he caught the edge of the rigging and began to climb.

He moved like someone who'd done this a hundred times, because he had. The hull held his weight like it remembered him. He scaled it with quiet ease, fingers finding holds as naturally as breath. A single pull, and he vaulted over the railing, landing beneath the quarterdeck with a crouch that absorbed the sound of impact. The wood trembled faintly beneath his palms, alive with motion, the ship already preparing to slip back into the sea.

But getting aboard was only the first part. Now came the harder task, disappearing within the bones of the ship itself. He didn't delude himself into thinking he'd remain hidden forever. Blackwell's crew was disciplined, and once they were underway, the *Tempest* would be combed from keel to mast. He needed a space small enough to be forgotten, tucked just beyond the edge of routine, but close enough to catch what mattered.

He'd just started to move when he heard footsteps. Steady. Unhurried. Familiar. He stilled. Then eased backward into a nest of shadows between a stack of tar-sealed barrels and a coil of thick rope. His breath slowed. His posture shifted. He became part of the dark.

Of course it was her. Kalithea moved with the confidence of someone who didn't need permission to be where she was. Her stride was unbroken, shoulders square, chin lifted. She belonged to the deck already, and it yielded to her presence without protest. Blackwell walked beside her, his gait looser, more performative. His hands moved when he spoke, fingers carving shapes in the air as if to charm sense out of it. The rhythm of his voice carried low across the planks, steady and coaxing.

Kipp couldn't hear the words, but he didn't need to. He saw the way she turned her head, just slightly, the way she listened without offering anything in return. Not cold. Not indulgent. Just...waiting. As if his usefulness had yet to be proven. And Blackwell, for all his exaggerated ease, was clearly still trying.

It was a good performance.

Kipp watched, half-shadowed, tucked beneath the ship's spine like a secret no one had thought to check. He let himself enjoy the view, just for a moment–the queen and the pirate, playing their game as if the world stopped at the railing. They made a compelling pair. All surface tension and blades. He could see the arc of it already, the rise, the crash, the way the sea would eventually decide which of them drowned first. But for now, they danced. And he, as ever, moved where no one watched.

Kipp crouched low in the dim underbelly of the *Tempest*, wedged in the narrow hollow between two crates bound in coarse rope and iron-buckled lids. The air was close down here–salt, grain, pitch, and wood pressed in tight–but he had no complaint. It had taken care to reach this far unnoticed: slipping past crewmen mid-task, ducking under chains during moments of noise, measuring his steps to the groan of timbers and the rhythm of shouted orders. He moved only when the ship moved. Shadow to shadow, silence to silence.

Now, he was in.

Not buried too deep, just enough to avoid suspicion, just enough to hear what mattered. Above him, the ship's voice creaked and stretched as the sails unfurled to catch the first whisper of wind. He felt the shift underfoot, subtle at first, then steady. The vessel pulled forward, slow and sure, cleaving through the tide with purpose.

Kipp leaned back against the wooden wall behind him, folding his arms beneath his head. The deck above echoed faintly, boots crossing planks, canvas snapping high above. Somewhere near the bow, a gull cried, sharp and distant. The ship was alive, and he was tucked within it now, an uninvited thought stitched into its spine.

The sound of hooves struck like thunder down the cobbled road, sharp and unrelenting. Raoul rode hard, his mount's muscles straining with every stride. Beside him, Jarreth kept pace in silence, his expression rigid, his eyes fixed ahead as the harbor came into view.

But they were too late.

The *Tempest* was already underway, her sails full, her hull slicing through the water. The white canvas gleamed against the sky, and the ship moved as if it belonged to the wind.

Raoul pulled hard on the reins, reining his stallion to a halt near the edge of the pier. The horse reared slightly, hooves scraping stone, and Raoul barely noticed. He stared after the retreating vessel, jaw clenched, the breath burning in his chest. His grip on the reins tightened. His whole frame coiled with the fury of it–too far, too late. Beside him, Jarreth said nothing, his silence cutting deeper than most men's curses. His gaze remained locked on the ship, his hands clenched white at the pommel, every line of his posture carved from restraint.

There was no point in calling. The tide had already taken her.

But still, Raoul shouted.

"KALITHEA!"

The name tore from him, raw and full, cracking across the bay like cannon fire. The harbor flinched around it. A gull startled into the air.

And on the *Tempest*–heads turned, uncertain.

At the rail, she paused. Kalithea stood motionless, her form lined in gold and shadow, the wind tugging at her hair. But she turned. For a moment, the world stilled. Her face held no expression at first, just the calm mask she had worn too many times, carved smooth and enigmatic. But then something shifted, a subtle easing at the corner of her mouth. The smallest change in her eyes. *Recognition.* A farewell she hadn't voiced, softened by the kind of sorrow that didn't belong in words. The kind saved for those who should never have had to be left behind. She didn't wave, but she didn't look away. For the space of a single breath, their gazes held–hers on them, theirs on her–and everything that hadn't been said passed unspoken between them.

Then the ship turned. Wind surged into the sails. The prow caught the curve of the current, and the *Tempest* slipped past the last edge of the bay and was gone.

Raoul sat in the silence that followed, his chest rising with the long breaths. His hands, still clenched, refused to relax. Jarreth hadn't moved. His gaze remained on the open water, where only the wake remained. His knuckles were white. His jaw worked once, then stilled. Whatever words lived behind his clenched teeth, he kept them there.

The silence between them said enough. They had lost her–not to death, not to force, but to something harder. To her own will. To a choice she had made without them.

Kipp sat in shadow beneath the lower deck, the ship creaking quietly around him, its timbers shifting with the steady rhythm of open sea. The hull shuddered now and then as waves struck, but the motion was smooth. The *Tempest* cut forward with purpose, and every sound echoed with intent: the groan of wood under pressure, the slap of water against the boards, the faint percussion of ropes straining above.

He'd claimed a hollow space between cargo crates, narrow and dry, where the scent of salt and dust mixed with the faint sharpness of oiled leather. One leg was stretched out, the other bent beneath him. His arms rested loosely over his chest, the blade at his side untouched but always within reach. This corner of the hold offered quiet, a hidden vantage, removed from the bustle of crew life but close enough to listen.

Above, bootsteps moved in irregular patterns. Voices called and answered, distant and muffled. The sailcloths flapped high overhead, taut with wind. It was a rhythm Kipp knew. A kind of song. For now, all of it held steady.

Then–sharp through the din–came a cry.

Distant. Raw. Human. A name hurled from the docks, full of grief and refusal.

Kalithea.

The sound filtered through the layers of wood and rope like an arrow, dulled but unmistakable in purpose. Kipp opened one eye, expression unchanging as the weight of the moment settled into the quiet between heartbeats. He didn't need to see the shore to know what had happened. The corner of his mouth lifted. He was almost impressed, he had led the Prince and his Knight in circles while Vale had watched for Blackwell's ship, doing his best to keep them busy chasing their own tails instead of catching up to her. They had *almost* made it.

He breathed out through his nose, a soft sound–part exasperation, part fondness.

"Oh, love," he said, voice low, carrying just enough weight to be more than a whisper. "That's quite a trail of broken hearts you're leaving in your wake."

The *Tempest* moved with purpose, her hull slicing a clean line through the sea. Wind filled her sails, taut and gleaming in the midday light, and the rigging sang with strain. Waves broke against her flanks in rhythmic surges, each crest rolling back into the deep like breath drawn from the lungs of something vast and ancient. All around, the ocean stretched endless and bright. Above deck, the crew worked in rhythm. Boots struck wood in time with shouted orders, laughter spilled across the railings, and the air was rich with the scent of brine, sun-warmed pine and oiled rope.

Below, hidden in the low hush of the cargo hold, Kipp reclined in the shadows with the composure of a man entirely at ease. One boot rested over the other, arms folded behind his head, the slight sway of the ship rocking him as though the sea itself meant to lull him toward sleep. He could have passed for a man dozing after a long night's drink, if not for the faint gleam of awareness behind half-lidded eyes.

He was waiting.

The trick to slipping aboard a ship like the *Tempest* wasn't the infiltration itself. That part was simple, provided one had the timing, the nerve, and a decent understanding of when men looked but didn't see. No, the real art came afterward. Remaining unseen long enough to matter. Choosing not just when to appear, but how.

Kipp Harlow had never been content to wait for the story to find him. He'd spent too long writing himself into other men's endings to accept anything less than a moment worth the price of admission. He considered his options, each with the lazy detachment of a man untroubled by risk.

The first option was practical: wait until nightfall, slip out beneath cover of dark, blend with the crew as if he'd been there from the start. A clean approach. Quiet. Controlled. Almost elegant in its invisibility.

And absolutely soul-crushingly boring.

He dismissed it with a scoff.

Option two, now that had flavor. Let the ship grow comfortable in its momentum, let the crew fall into routine, then break the rhythm. Appear suddenly, uninvited and unbothered, with some well-placed remark, dry and cutting. Not enough to draw a blade, but enough to spark questions. Enough to catch her eye.

That was the point, after all. Not her approval. Gods no. That would be dull. What he wanted was the reaction. A flicker of surprise, the sharp turn of her gaze, that particular brand of silence she reserved for men who weren't nearly as clever as they thought. He wanted to see what she did with him when the rules slipped. Not because he sought danger but because he thrived in the teeth of it.

There were worse fates than being tossed into the sea by an angry queen. But gods, it would be so much more interesting if she hesitated.

Kipp rose from his place between the crates, stretching with the slow grace of a man accustomed to small spaces and long waits. His jacket settled back across his shoulders as he rolled his sleeves, fingers flexing once, then stilling. The faint light from above caught along the curve of his jaw as he reached up to brush a smear of dust from his collar.

He looked more like a man readying for court than one preparing for exposure.

"Time to be unforgettable," he said, voice low, amused.

The Art of Getting Thrown Overboard

Above deck, the *Tempest* surged forward with power. Ropes snapped taut as the wind filled her sails, each shift in weight answered by a dozen experienced hands. The sun glinted off the spray curling along her prow. The ship breathed like a creature in motion–groaning timbers, muttered commands, and the swift percussion of boots on oiled wood.

None of it held Kipp Harlow's attention, his eyes were fixed on the helm. She stood there, back straight, shoulders set beneath the weight of wind and purpose. Strands of dark hair had pulled free from her braids, catching light where the silver threads ran through them like fine-spun wire. Her hands rested on the rail and her gaze never strayed from the horizon. Beside her, Blackwell stood at the helm with his usual brand of swagger–half a step too close, voice pitched low, gestures made for her alone. Whatever he said, it wasn't clever enough to earn more than a glance. Not at first. Then something changed. A small shift. A curve of her mouth. A sound, brief and unguarded.

Laughter.

Not sharp or cutting, not the wry edge she used to silence courtiers. It was quieter. Honest. A flicker of something warmer than she ever let show. Kipp froze. The moment was gone in an instant, but it settled like a stone in his chest. He hadn't heard that sound before. He was almost certain no one had. He exhaled slowly through his nose, scrubbing a hand down his face to chase the thought away. This wasn't why he came. He hadn't smuggled himself aboard to linger in shadows and count heartbeats, pining like some jealous fool. He came to be seen.

So he moved, not with stealth this time, but ease. Confidence. He scaled the rigging like a man stretching after a long sleep, then swung down to perch on the edge of the quarterdeck rail. For a moment he simply sat there, legs dangling, head tilted, taking in the deck below like a man inspecting a room he already owned. Then he rose, hands tucked in his pockets, shoulders loose, Kipp Harlow strolled into sunlight with all the nonchalance of a man who had never known fear.

"Now, now," he called, his voice smooth as poured wine, "I know I wasn't *technically* on the manifest, but must we all look so shocked?"

Silence fell in a single, drawn breath. Crewmen froze midstep. Ropes hung half-secured in the hands that held them. A few men reached for blades, the rasp of steel ringing soft beneath the wind. Every gaze found him–some with recognition, others with wariness. All with disbelief.

Kalithea turned, moving as though she'd known this would happen eventually. Her gaze found him, cold and precise. At her side, Blackwell stared for half a heartbeat, then barked a laugh that broke the tension like thunder cracking through fog.

"Well, *hell*," he said, bracing one hand on the rail. "If it isn't the crown jewel of Varis' most wanted list."

Kipp gave a slow, theatrical bow. "The very same."

"You stowed away," Blackwell said grinning.

Kipp spread his hands. "Would you expect anything less?"

The pirate laughed again, louder this time. "You realize I make it a personal rule to throw stowaways overboard."

"I announced myself. Which, if we're splitting hairs, makes me a very loud guest." Kipp said, still grinning. "Which ought to earn me a hearing, if not a drink."

"You think boldness earns you a leniency?"

"I think it earns attention." He shrugged. "And attention is lever-age."

Kipp gave Kal his most charming grin.

Blackwell blinked once, then twice. Then threw his head back and laughed again. "Oh, this is going to be good."

Kipp stood, arms wide in mock surrender, "Miss me, darling?"

Kalithea stared at him. Her expression was inexplicable–no fury, no warmth. Only the still, watchful calm of a woman deciding how sharp her response needed to be.

"Kipp," she said, her voice even.

"Stars," he murmured, "the way you say my name...like it's a curse and a prayer. You're going to make me blush."

Blackwell let out a low whistle. "So it's *her* you came for."

The murmurs rose behind him. A few of the crew shifted, some smirking, some nudging one another. A coin clinked between palms.

Kipp didn't blink. "Let's be honest, Blackwell. As flattering as it is to think I crossed half a kingdom just to see you"–he waved a lazy hand toward the woman standing at the railing– *"I came for her."*

She didn't react. Not outwardly. But something in the angle of her shoulders shifted a fraction. A tension pulling beneath the facade.

"Well," she said, voice calm, "at least you're honest."

"Honest?" Blackwell scoffed. "Him?"

"I've never lied to either of you," Kipp replied smoothly.

"You're a thief." Kal said flatly.

"And a consistent one."

"What are you doing on my ship?" Kalithea's voice came low, controlled.

Kipp spread his hands in mock innocence, lips curled in a pout far too pleased with itself. "*Your* ship? I must've missed the part where you carved your name into the mast."

From the wheel, Blackwell gave a warning cough that might have been a laugh. "Careful, Harlow."

But Kipp never had much use for caution.

"I can go, if you'd like," he offered lightly. "Just say the word–softly, sweetly, like a lover's request–"

The dagger sang through the air.

Kipp jerked his head just enough to narrowly avoid losing an ear. The blade buried itself in the mast behind him with a solid thunk that silenced the murmurs across the deck. He turned slowly, glancing at the quivering hilt, then back at her. A low whistle escaped his teeth as he gave an approving nod.

"My queen," he drawled, "if you wanted me on my knees, you only had to ask."

She moved then, unhurried, the silent promise of violence in every shift of her weight. For a brief moment Kipp considered making himself scarce. But he stayed. Of course he stayed. There were worse ways to die than standing in the path of a woman like her. At least this one came with spectacle.

From the helm, Blackwell watched the exchange with a kind of amused resignation. In all his years captaining the *Tempest*, he'd never let a stowaway live. Not once. Not through mutiny, not through blockade. Men who snuck aboard his ship ended up lashed to the mast, keelhauled beneath the barnacled spine of the Tempest or marooned with nothing but the sound of gulls for company. Justice, swift and unbending. No exceptions.

And yet... here he was watching Kipp Harlow–King of Thieves, smug bastard, relentless thorn in everyone's side–dance around a dagger thrown with enough force to embed itself hilt-deep into the mast. Gods help him, it was the most fun he'd had in weeks.

"You know," Blackwell said, elbow propped on the wheel, "if you keep throwing knives at him like that, love, I just might ask to marry you."

Kalithea didn't even glance at him. Her focus remained on Kipp, unmoved, unblinking. Unforgiving.

Kipp, infuriatingly immune to all mortal forms of shame or fear, simply adjusted the lapels of his coat as if he were preparing for tea. "Two royals vying for my attention. It's flattering, really. I didn't expect to be this popular so early into the voyage."

"Popular," she muttered, "isn't the word I'd use."

"Infamous, then. Has a nicer ring."

Blackwell let out a dry chuckle. "I'll admit, I've never grown senti-mental about stowaways."

"I'm sensing a *but*," Kipp said, stepping neatly off the railing just in time to avoid another flying knife. He landed lightly, the impact barely registering.

"But," Blackwell continued, "you've amused me. And that's a dan-gerous thing to do on this ship."

Kipp turned, arms wide. "Come now. You can't tell me you're not enjoying the change of pace."

"I prefer my voyages without unsolicited passengers."

"And yet here I am," Kipp said, smiling. "Alive. Charming. Very much uninvited. There's a lesson in that somewhere."

"Aye," Blackwell said, grinning, "the lesson being: even I have laps-es in judgment."

Kipp placed a hand over his heart, wounded. "And here I thought we were bonding."

Kalithea stepped forward again, voice flat and final. "Kipp."

He met her eyes without hesitation. "That's my name, no need to say it like I just cost you a kingdom."

She didn't blink.

"What are you doing here?" she asked again. No menace. Just demand.

"Oh, that's easy," he said. "Thought I'd join the voyage. Bit of a vacation, really. Fresh air. Dangerous coastlines. Fascinating company."

Blackwell arched a brow. "You're serious?"

"Always," Kipp replied.

Kalithea exhaled through her nose slowly. "You're trespassing on a ship bound for a hostile coastline, without invitation, and you think that qualifies as a vacation?"

"Well," Kipp said, feigning thought, "not a relaxing one."

She didn't move, but her silence had weight.

He pushed on. "But if you're sailing into storm break territory, you might need someone skilled at...rearranging odds."

Blackwell crossed his arms. "And what would those skills include exactly?"

"Lying. Stealing. Not dying in tight corners. Escaping said corners. Impeccable timing, a flair for theatrics. Charming dangerous women. You know. The usual."

Kalithea's voice cut in, hard as drawn steel. "You followed me."

"I wouldn't say *followed*," Kipp said. "Let's call it...strategic anticipation."

Her stare sharpened.

He grinned. "Look, love, you were leaving early, weren't you? Thought you'd sneak off and spare me the trouble of saying goodbye? And there's still the matter of that debt, if memory serves."

"I left early," she said, voice quiet, "to avoid dragging your corpse back from wherever you'd get yourself killed."

"Touching," he murmured. "But look at me—alive, well-dressed, and ready to be useful."

Blackwell tilted his head, amused. "Useful, are you?"

"In my own way," Kipp replied, unapologetic.

"The last time we worked together," Blackwell said, "half my cargo vanished."

"Half your *contraband* cargo," Kipp corrected. "And I returned the other half."

Blackwell snorted. "By catapult."

"Still counts," Kipp said. "Spectacular delivery."

Kalithea exhaled through her nose, slow and flat. Her voice followed with no rise in tone, only the cold finality of a woman done entertaining games.

"We should toss him overboard."

Kipp stepped forward with the kind of arrogance that only got men killed, or crowned. "You could," he said, meeting her gaze without flinching. "Or you could admit, just this once, that I might be exactly the kind of chaos you're going to need."

Blackwell made a thoughtful sound, though it was far too amused to be serious. "No, I quite like the overboard suggestion," he said, one hand resting easy on the ship's wheel, the other brushing the hilt of his blade. "It's traditional. Keeps morale high."

"Blackwell—"

"I've never spared a stowaway. Seems a slippery precedent to start now."

"I'm not a stowaway," Kipp cut in, voice smooth. He raised his hands in a slow, open gesture, as if that would somehow keep her from gutting him. "I'm an unofficial addition. A rogue guest. A surprise asset. Like a windfall. Or a plague."

"Funny," Blackwell said. "That's what most stowaways say. Right before they start stealing knives and sweetbread."

"Please. If I wanted sweetbread, you'd never know it was gone."

Kipp glanced at Kalithea with a crooked grin. "Besides, you let *her* stay."

Blackwell's brow arched. "She paid me."

Kipp flashed that crooked grin. "I've paid too."

"Oh?"

"With my company," Kipp said grandly, bowing low with a flourish, as though he were being introduced at court rather than tried for trespassing.

Kalithea's fingers slid toward another dagger.

Blackwell didn't miss it. Neither did Kipp. Both men watched her in silence as her grip tightened and her eyes iced over.

The pirate king considered it. Truly considered it. Tossing the King of Thieves over the railing right here and now, letting the sea decide whether Kipp's charm could float. He glanced at her again, at the way her grip tightened on that blade, white-knuckled. How her jaw locked, sharp and infuriated, showing something, *or someone*, had truly gotten under her skin.

And gods help him...he laughed.

"Tell you what," he said, dragging a knuckle along the line of his jaw. "I'm starting to enjoy the idea of keeping him."

Kalithea turned toward him, "Don't you even think of it."

"Oh, but darling," Blackwell murmured, voice rich with mischief, "I already have."

Kipp, practically glowing with smug satisfaction, dropped onto a coil of rope like a man settling into his rightful throne. "Told you I was charming."

Kalithea looked between them, thief and pirate, both grinning like boys caught red-handed in a royal pantry. Her jaw worked once. Twice. But she said nothing, the fury in her stance saying enough. Control had slipped. She could feel it. Not lost, not yet, but shifted. Tipped off its axis by the two most insufferable men ever to draw breath.

She drew in a breath through her teeth, clipped and steady. "If he so much as breathes wrong, he's your problem."

Blackwell spun the wheel smoothly, turning the *Tempest* toward open water. Wind curled around his coat, tugging it like a banner of victory.

"Oh, love," he said, smiling without pity, "you haven't figured it out yet, have you?"

She narrowed her eyes.

Blackwell tipped his chin toward Kipp, that grin sharpening to something wicked.

"He's already *your* problem."

Kalithea didn't speak right away. Her gaze flicked to Kipp, as if cataloging a tool whose usefulness had yet to be determined, or whose danger might still prove worthwhile. Her arms crossed over her chest, her stance a sculpture of composure, but the breath she let out carried the telltale edge of restraint.

"Perhaps you'll prove useful after all," she said, voice smooth. The words came without warmth, but not without purpose.

Kipp's grin widened, bright and utterly unbothered, like she'd handed him a title and a crown. "Now we're getting somewhere."

She didn't rise to the bait. "You do have a talent for finding your way into places you were never meant to be."

From the helm, Blackwell gave a low, satisfied laugh. "She's got you there, thief."

Kipp placed a hand over his heart. "Darling, if you wanted to flatter me, you might've started with a drink."

"I wasn't complimenting you."

"Ah but intent is such a delicate thing," Kipp replied lightly. "All it takes is a touch of charm to twist it into something far more flattering."

Kalithea exhaled, her expression unmoved. "You are insufferable."

"And yet, somehow, I live."

She turned away slowly, as if dismissing him entirely required effort. The words she tossed back over her shoulder came with a sharp elegance, edged like a well-balanced knife.

"I take pity on fools."

Kalithea moved again, smooth as ever, but the tension remained. Her path took her toward the helm, where Blackwell waited with a glint of amusement just barely restrained. As she neared, her pace slowed. Then, with the subtle grace of someone well-versed in power and timing, she leaned in close to him. Her voice was low and toyingly intimate, meant for him alone.

"Don't get used to winning, Jaymes."

He didn't react at once. Only after a heartbeat did he turn to face her fully, his gaze steady. Not defiant.

Intrigued.

A faint gleam lit behind his eyes, "Well now," he murmured, voice laced with delight, "*Jaymes.* That's the first time you've said my name."

She didn't answer, not directly. But her lips curved, barely. Not a smile, not entirely. Just enough to count. Just enough to mean something. Then it vanished like mist in the morning sun.

Blackwell drew a slow breath, running a finger along his jaw. "Careful, darling. Say my name like that again, and I just might start thinking you mean it."

She cast a final glance over her shoulder, her eyes calm and dangerous. "If I meant it, Captain," she said softly, "you wouldn't be thinking. You'd be ruined."

Kipp, still leaning against the coiled rope, had watched every second with a bemused shake of the head. But his grin had shifted—less amused now, more sharpened at the edges, tempered by something he hadn't quite expected. A realization. This voyage wasn't going to go the way he'd planned. And *she*, gods help him, was not like anything he'd known before.

"Oh, this is going to be fun," he muttered.

Blackwell didn't take his eyes off Kalithea's retreating form, his grin curling into something hungrier.

"That it will, thief," he chuckled. "That it will."

Kipp stood at the railing, one elbow resting against the wood, his eyes on the space where she'd vanished. The deck beneath him moved with the steady rhythm of open water, sails billowing high above, ropes creaking as the wind tugged at the rigging. He didn't turn when Blackwell approached. The man's presence was unmistakable, felt before it was seen. That grin was still in place. Pleased. Cunning. Sharpened at the edges like something too dangerous to be called amusement.

Kipp didn't like it. He'd seen that look before on men who mistook infatuation for control. He knew the end of that story. He'd buried more than one fool who'd written their own name into a tragedy they didn't survive.

"You're enjoying yourself too much, Captain," he said, the words low and even as he pushed off the rail, hands slipping into the deep line of his coat.

Blackwell didn't deny it. He laughed, a deep, velvet sound that lingered like smoke in the air. "Wouldn't you? A runaway queen and a stowaway thief, both wrapped up in a voyage I didn't even plan to be interesting. Fate's got a better sense of humor than I gave her credit for."

Kipp raised a brow, letting the silence between them stretch just long enough to bite. "Sounds like the setup to a bad joke."

Blackwell turned toward him fully, his coat stirred by the sea breeze, the grin never wavering. "It is. The punchline's still coming."

"And when it lands?"

The question hung, quiet but firm.

Blackwell's shoulders lifted in a slow shrug. "Depends who's still standing, doesn't it?"

There was no laughter in that answer. Just a simple truth, laid bare between them.

Kipp's weight shifted. That lazy grace returned, but his gaze stayed locked. "So that's it? No threat? No warning? Not even a courtesy knife at the throat?"

"Would it comfort you if there was?"

"It'd feel more familiar."

Blackwell's smile thinned, not vanished, but cooled. "For now, you're amusing. Useful. Keeps the crew guessing."

Kipp's grin was a flicker, too quick to be anything but calculated. "Generous of you."

"Don't mistake amusement for generosity," Blackwell said, voice flat beneath the charm. "One of them ends."

Kipp didn't blink. The mask stayed on—the grin, the glint in his eye—but somewhere deeper, something stilled. He saw the game for what it was, and worse, he recognized the player.

And Blackwell?

Blackwell knew it.

"Well then," Kipp murmured, voice quiet now, the smile still in place but hollowed out behind the teeth, "guess we'll see who outlasts who."

The Pirate King turned back to the wheel with the ease of a man who never doubted where he stood. "Aye, thief," he said without looking back. "We will."

The wind caught the sails overhead, snapping them taut. Ropes groaned against their anchors. Below, the sea stretched wide and endless, a canvas waiting for stories to be written in salt and blood.

Kal hadn't look back. Not at Blackwell. Not at Kipp. Not at the crew who still lingered at the edges of the scene, caught somewhere between their duties and their curiosity. Let them whisper. Let them gawk. None of it was for them. Her steps were steady, boots striking the wood with an unhurried rhythm. The wind pulled at her coat, tangled a strand of hair across her cheek, but she didn't pause to tuck it away. She moved with the poise of someone who knew how to own a room, or a ship.

But beneath the surface, the current was not still. She'd misstepped. Not loudly. But she felt it nonetheless, tight as a wire drawn too far. She'd said his name. *Jaymes.* Spoken it without thinking, without armor, and the sound had shifted something in the air between them. He had caught it, caught *her*, and that was the danger.

Kipp danced because he loved the game. He needed the tension, the heat, the razor's edge between amusement and risk. She understood that, knew how to handle it. But Blackwell—*Jaymes*—he played on a different level entirely. He didn't bait for reaction. He watched. Calculated. Followed the thread to its source and made no effort to disguise that he intended to unravel it.

He didn't flirt for the sake of tension. He didn't chase chaos for the thrill. He studied the board in silence while everyone else made noise. And when he moved, it wasn't to provoke. It was to win.

She exhaled through her nose, slow and soundless, and rolled her shoulders beneath the weight of her coat. The motion was subtle, an effort to release the tension she hadn't realized she'd gathered.

It didn't matter. Not in the way it threatened to. He would not be different. She reminded herself of that with the same conviction she used to steady her hand at the table, to hold her expression through council rooms filled with liars and blades. Blackwell would serve his purpose. He would carry her across the sea, open the path she needed, deliver her to the edge of war with his ship and his crew intact.

And when it was done, she would walk away. She always did.

Blackwell stood at the helm with the night wind curling through his hair, one hand resting loose upon the wheel. The stars stretched in a wide scatter above them, cold and clear, mirrored dimly across the sea in glints of silver light. The *Tempest* cut through the dark water with steady grace, each creak of timber beneath their feet a quiet, familiar note in the ship's nocturnal rhythm.

Beside him, Kipp lounged against the rail as if the deck had been built for his comfort. One arm draped casually across his chest, his ankle crossed over the other like a man who'd never learned caution. The grin tugging at his mouth was faint, but edged, there was nothing soft in it. It was the look of a man cataloguing every move, every silence, every flaw he might one day need to exploit.

For a time, neither spoke. The only sound was the water beneath the hull and the wind stirring the rigging, low voices from belowdecks drifting in and out of reach, carried on the ocean's hush.

Then Kipp broke the quiet. "Tell me something, Captain."

Blackwell didn't glance his way. "I'm listening."

"How is it we've outrun kings, outwitted killers, pulled coin from chaos and come out clean—only to lose the thread the moment she so much as *looks* our way?"

Blackwell gave a low sound of amusement, half chuckle, half growl. "So you admit it, then."

Kipp's smile sharpened. "Didn't say I *minded*."

Blackwell finally turned his head, the wind catching the edge of his coat as he leaned one elbow against the helm. His eyes stayed fixed on the horizon. "Knew I was fucked the moment she looked at me like I was a game she already knew how to win."

"And did she win?" Kipp asked.

"Not yet," Blackwell said. But his voice was quieter now, more dangerous.

Kipp tapped his knuckles once against the railing, the rhythm thoughtless, distant. "I used to think I could read anyone. Spot the tells. Feel out the lies before they even found a tongue."

Blackwell hummed, the sound low in his throat. "And now?"

"Now?" Kipp tilted his head, a smile curling slowly across his mouth. "She turned the table so fast I'm not even sure I'm still sitting at it. I might just be the damn centerpiece."

Blackwell's lips twitched in something too dry to be a grin. "You afraid of that?"

Kipp gave a small shrug. "Terrified."

There was no hesitation in the word. No shame. Only the easy confidence of a man well acquainted with his own worst tendencies and was long past pretending to resist them.

"But that's the thrill, isn't it?"

"Maybe for you," Blackwell said, adjusting his grip on the wheel. "You climbed aboard knowing she didn't want you here."

Kipp's grin faded a notch, tempered now. "Didn't come to be wanted."

Blackwell studied him a beat longer before turning back to the sea. "So why, then?"

Kipp's gaze lifted toward the sails. "Because I need to see how it ends."

Blackwell didn't respond right away. The wind gusted gently, and somewhere aft, laughter rolled out from the crew, too far to be part of their world, but just close enough to remind them of it.

"You think this ends?" Blackwell asked at last.

"Everything ends," Kipp said.

"Aye," Blackwell murmured, eyes on the water. "But the best ones leave you wishing they didn't."

Silence stretched between them again, thicker now, wrapped in something neither of them cared to name. They stood like two men at the edge of a cliff, both knowing the drop was coming and neither willing to take a step back.

After a moment, Kipp exhaled, more breath than sound. "You think we'll survive her?"

Blackwell's mouth curved, slow and deliberate. "No," he said. "But I think we'll enjoy the fall."

The *Tempest* drifted through moonlit waters, sails groaning softly as wind filled their curve. Silver light poured across the deck in fractured sheets, catching on coils of rope and worn brass fittings, turning shadows into phantoms and silence into something alive. Most of the crew had long since disappeared below, their laughter dimmed to memory. Only the sea remained, brushing gentle along the hull.

She stood at the stern. Still. Composed. One hand resting lightly on the rail, the other ghosting above the wood like she wasn't quite tethered to the moment. There was calm in her stance but not ease. A quiet that warned more than it welcomed.

Kipp stepped into it anyway. He moved–silently, uninvited, entirely too comfortable–until he stood beside her, close enough to speak without raising his voice.

"You know," he drawled, unhurried, "if I didn't know better, I'd say you've been avoiding me."

She didn't turn. Her eyes remained fixed on the black stretch of water. "Maybe I was."

He pressed a hand to his chest, mock-affronted. "Cruel. Accurate. But cruel."

"Would you have preferred a lie?"

"Gods, no. Don't ruin the illusion." He shifted to lean against the rail, his smile faint but present. "I've built my whole image of you on brutal honesty wrapped in silk and steel."

That earned him a brief glance, her gaze cutting clean through him. "And what, exactly, have you come to see?"

He held her stare with a grin sharpened by something real. "That you're dangerous. Unreadable. Exquisite. And probably the finest opponent I've ever had the misfortune to lose to."

She turned back to the sea, unimpressed. "You always make it a game."

"Everything's a game," he said. "Some of us just admit it."

"And this?" she asked, quiet. "Why play this one?"

"Because it's the only one worth losing." He shifted slightly, not enough to press, but enough to be felt.

"You play too," he added, softer now. "You just play to win."

The silence that followed lingered. Not empty, not cold, just heavy with something neither of them wanted to give a name to. Wind stirred her hair, the scent of salt clinging in the air.

"Why are you here, Kipp?" No mask. No test. Just the question.

He exhaled, his fingers drumming once against the railing. "You were going to leave without me."

Her head tilted slightly, eyes narrowing. *"And?"*

"And I didn't care for that."

She studied him. "Because you hate being left out?"

He smiled, small, almost wistful. "Because I don't want this story ending without me in it."

Her gaze lingered a beat longer. "So it's about an ending to you?"

"Not the ending," he said, turning to face her fully now, his tone quieter, stripped of performance. "It's the part in the middle. The part where someone you shouldn't care about makes you realize you're tired of doing everything alone."

Her breath caught, just slightly. Not enough to break the moment but enough for him to know she felt it. He let the words stand, untouched. No smirk. No wink. Just the truth. That, more than all his clever lines, made her wary. Because truth, from a man like Kipp Harlow, meant risk. She watched him with that same calculation she gave threats. Looking for the catch. But Kipp didn't flinch, he let her look. Let her strip every defense from him and still remained.

Finally, she spoke. "I don't need your help."

"I know."

Her gaze drifted back to the sea. The tension in her frame didn't vanish, but it shifted, tucked deeper.

"If I asked you to leave?"

"I'd pretend to consider it," he said, mouth curving. "And then I'd say something clever enough to buy myself at least another hour."

She let out a breath, somewhere between exasperation and amusement. "You are *impossible*."

"And yet somehow still above water." he replied, winking, leaning against the railing with infuriating ease.

"For now."

"I like my odds."

Kipp tapped the rail absently, thoughtful. "I can keep my distance, though, if that's what you want."

She turned slightly, eyes narrowing. "No. You can't."

He grinned, unabashed. "No. I can't."

She shook her head, not quite annoyed. More tired of pretending otherwise. "Just...don't make me regret this."

"Darling," he said, pushing off the rail with a little flourish, "I don't deal in promises. Just chaos dressed pretty...and the kind of mistakes you make twice on purpose."

She shot him a look. Then turned without a word and descended toward the lower deck, her steps steady, her silence final.

Kipp watched her go. The smile on his lips stayed, tempered now by something deeper. He exhaled, let the sea wind catch his coat, and leaned once more into the shadows she'd left behind.

She hadn't told him to leave.

And that, in his world, was the beginning of everything.

The wind whispered across the deck and Kipp lingered at the stern long after Kalithea had vanished below. Fingers resting against the rail, hair mussed by the breeze, gaze fixed not on the sea but somewhere just beyond it. She'd left something behind in her wake, a silence that clung too tightly to his thoughts. She had turned to him and asked him why he followed, and against every instinct, every bit of cleverness that had kept him alive this long, he'd told her the truth. No sleight of hand. No grin to soften it.

That was a mistake. Kipp didn't deal in honesty. He dealt in leverage. In knowing what to give and what to hold back. But she...she made it easy to forget the rules. She was all sharp edges and silent storms. Something carved from shadow, defiance and the steel of a thousand quiet wars. And gods help him, he'd walked straight into it with eyes wide open.

A few paces away, above the quarterdeck, Blackwell stood at the helm, one hand loose on the wheel. His gaze hadn't shifted in some time, but he wasn't watching the horizon. He was thinking of her too. Not with longing. Not with Kipp's unruly ache. But with calculation. *Curiosity.*

Kalithea wasn't the sort of woman men desired in the usual way. She didn't coax or charm. She commanded. Walked into a room and made it hers without lifting her voice. He'd known her kind before–or thought he had. Women who used power like perfume, who smiled while they gutted you. But Kalithea didn't smile. She didn't ask for power. She simply was it. That's what made her dangerous. Not the way she moved, not even the way she wielded silence like a blade, but the way she mirrored him. Saw the game. Played it. *Perfectly.*

Blackwell didn't trust mirrors. Still...he couldn't stop watching.

In her cabin, Kalithea traced her fingers along the map laid out before her, though her thoughts were miles from strategy. She'd always been good at separation, heart from mind, pain from necessity. But now, with the door closed and the candles burning low, the pieces no longer sat cleanly apart.

Jaymes sees too much. Kipp says too much. And worse...she was *feeling* too much. That should have been enough for her thoughts. But she couldn't help thinking back to the docks, just before the ship left, just as the city blurred into the horizon when she heard her name. Not with the cold curl of court formality. Not Blackwell's rum-soaked challenge or Kipp's devil-may-care tease.

No, it had come raw. Honest. Familiar.
Raoul and Jarreth.

She had turned to catch their silhouettes at the edge of the dock, still mounted, unmoving. Watching. There had been no chase, no shout. Just presence. Just the weight of two men who had followed her without instruction, who had found her despite every wall she'd built to keep them out. And for one bare breath, one treacherous beat, something inside her slipped. *They had followed her.* She closed her eyes now, alone in the quiet, and still she could see the way Jarreth had looked at her, like she was something holy and broken. She could hear the ache in Raoul's voice, the edge of something unsaid carried over the water. They had always trailed her, but this...this had been different.

This had been devotion. Devotion, she reminded herself, was dangerous. *Too dangerous.*

Back above deck, Blackwell drew a breath and leaned into the wheel, the wind shifting the hem of his coat. He wasn't sure if this would end in glory or ruin. But he knew without question that he would follow. At least for now.

Kipp, below the stars, let his hand drift along the railing one last time before turning away, that crooked grin slipping back into place. She hadn't sent him away. Not yet.

And Kalithea, seated once more in the candlelight, opened her eyes. Steeled herself. She had not made it this far to be undone by loyalty. Or longing. Or the memory of a voice across the waves. This path was lined in fire. It demanded blood, sacrifice, and unwavering control.

BLADES AND BRAVADO

he blade whispered through the morning air, its arc clean and unhurried, catching the soft slant of dawn light as it passed. Kalithea moved with grace–each motion drawn from memory, carved by discipline, perfected through necessity. The deck swayed gently beneath her boots, the sea calm for now, though the wind hinted at a change coming. She welcomed the solitude. Out here, surrounded by sky and water, she didn't have to hold a throne or wear a mask. She didn't have to measure her words or calculate her silences. There was only breath. Steel. The rhythm of control.

Which meant, of course, it couldn't last.

"Darling," came a voice from behind her, dripping mischief, insolent as ever. "For someone so invested in untouchability, you do make it exceptionally hard for a man to look away."

She didn't turn. She simply held her breath a moment longer, eyes lingering on the pale line where sky met sea, before releasing it in a slow, even exhale. Then she pivoted calmly, her gaze landing where she already knew he'd be.

Kipp Harlow leaned against the railing like the ship had been built to carry him. Arms crossed, weight resting in one hip, his grin shaped like something that could wound or charm depending on how it was wielded. He watched her like she was a locked door he intended to pick–slowly, thoroughly, with all the time in the world.

"And yet," she said, voice dry, "here you are. *Again*."

He shrugged. "I'm a creature of deeply committed habits."

"More like a creature of persistent inconvenience."

He smiled wider. "Ah, but you like it."

She stepped forward, eyes narrowing slightly as his gaze–unmistakably–flicked to her mouth. "Do I?"

"I think you're starting to, love."

"I think you're delusional."

He moved toward her, his voice dropping, warm and quiet.

"Well," he said, "you haven't tried to drown me. That feels like progress."

Kalithea tilted her head, one curl slipping free of its knot in the wind. Her tone was smooth, "Do I amuse you, Kipp?"

"You fascinate me," he replied, gaze steady. "Like a chest I've never managed to crack."

A breath of amusement threatened to curve her lips, but she held it in check. "Because I'm locked?"

"Because I know there's something worth stealing behind all that steel."

He stepped close enough for the wind between them to thin. The scent of salt clung to his coat, but underneath it, there was something else–smoke, ink, the faint echo of something distinctly him.

"Tell me, darling," he murmured, softer now, "do you ever let yourself be distracted? Even just for a breath?"

She arched a brow. "And if I did...how would you even know?"

He leaned in. Close, but not too close. Just enough for the air between them to shift.

"Because I'd see it in your eyes," he said. "And I'd be there before you caught the breath back, whispering how good distraction looked on you."

Her lips parted. Whether to warn, dismiss, or invite, she hadn't decided. But the moment fractured before it could take shape.

"Apologies for the interruption, thief," came the voice–low, unhurried, laced with amusement sharp as flint.

Jaymes Blackwell crossed the deck, every step steeped in command. The interruption was no accident, it was measured. Perfectly timed.

"But I do believe," he said, smile cool and knowing as his gaze flicked to Kalithea, "we have business to attend to."

Kipp didn't look away. Not at first. Not until she did. Kalithea turned from him, giving Jaymes her attention, her posture quiet, regal, enigmatic.

Kipp sighed as if wounded, lifting both hands in mock surrender. "Really, Captain? I was just getting to the part where she starts falling for me."

Blackwell passed without sparing him a glance. "I'm sure your delusions are riveting," he said, voice dry as the salt wind curling between them.

Kalithea arched a brow, watching them both with the resigned disdain of a queen surrounded by children playing at court.

"Tell me, love," he said, voice smooth as tide-worn glass, "what exactly does our charming thief believe he can offer you that I can't?"

Her finger tapped once, lightly, against her lower lip. "Let's see... mischief. Trouble. A talent for appearing where he has no business being."

Blackwell laughed, low and genuine. The sound wrapped around them, warm and dangerous all at once.

"Darling," he murmured, stepping closer, "I'm all of those things. And I bring discipline. A crew that doesn't mutiny. A ship that doesn't sink."

"And arrogance, too," she said, tone thoughtful. "What a bounty."

"Confidence," he corrected, leaning in just enough for his breath to brush the line of her jaw. "And might I remind you, you're standing on my deck."

She turned until they were nearly eye to eye, her voice quiet and smooth.

"And yet," she said, voice a near whisper, "I don't recall agreeing that you own me."

His expression shifted, amusement giving way to something darker, something that hinted at hunger buried beneath the polish.

"No," he admitted, voice picking up a slight sultry tone. "Not yet."

The space between them held. Then—

"Oh, for the love of all things indecent," Kipp muttered. "I am going to be sick."

He stepped between them like he'd been waiting for the cue, insolent as ever, every movement deliberate.

Blackwell sighed, long-suffering. "Must you always ruin perfectly good tension, Harlow?"

Kipp gave an elegant bow, grin bright and merciless. "It's practically a calling. By all means, return to your brooding and whispered promises. I'll just be over here pretending I haven't heard worse flirting from dockhands with head injuries."

Kalithea brushed past them both without a word. Behind her, two sets of footsteps followed, falling into step with one another.

"You know," Kipp drawled, sliding his hands into his coat pockets, "for a man so fond of unpredictability, you're becoming remarkably easy to read."

Blackwell didn't look over. He adjusted his cuffs and let the wind catch his coat. "Says the thief who hasn't let her out of his sight since the anchor lifted."

"Old habit. Keeping watch."

"I thought you specialized in disappearing," Blackwell said. "Not circling women who could cut your throat in half a breath."

"Careful, Captain," Kipp said, grinning. "That sounded almost like jealousy."

Blackwell glanced at him now, once, briefly. It wasn't a threat. Not yet. But it wasn't anything soft, either.

"I don't get jealous, Harlow. I get what I want." He smiled faintly. "*Eventually.*"

"How noble." Kipp's grin didn't shift. "I prefer to strike before someone else lays claim. Patience gets people killed."

"Rashness gets them buried in shallow graves."

They reached the top of the stairs. Wind stirred around them, tugging at collars and coats. Neither spoke for a breath. The silence stretched thin between them, balanced like a knife on edge.

Then Kipp extended a hand. Loose. Casual. Anything but careless. "Best man wins?"

Blackwell took it. His grip was firm. Too firm. "Wins what, exactly?"

Kipp winked. "Guess we'll find out."

And without another word, they turned. Two predators, different coats. Both heading toward the same queen.

Jaymes broke from Kipp without comment, his stride unhurried as he crossed the deck toward her. Kal stopped near the helm, gaze fixed on the sea.

"Back so soon?" she murmured, eyes still on the horizon.

"I thought we might finish our conversation," he said, voice smooth as ever. "Unless you'd rather continue the games."

"If this is another attempt at metaphor," she said, finally looking at him, "save it. If you're not here to discuss something of use, I have no interest in hearing it."

Jaymes stopped a pace from her, one brow lifting. Then, to her surprise, he laughed—a rich, genuine sound that turned more than one head across the deck.

"Gods, you're sharp," he said wryly. "Very well, my queen. Logistics, then."

She nodded once. "Where we're headed is hidden just off Kellyn Bay. There's an old ruined town there. Cutthroats, mercs, rogues...your type of people Captain."

Jaymes folded his arms and studied the water ahead. "You mean to slip through the blockade?"

"That is the plan. I need to get into that city."

He tilted his head slightly, weighing options behind that disarming smirk. "We can run the blockade, convince them to look elsewhere, though it'll cost us time. Those waters are choked with patrols. And the nearer you get to shore, the more eyes are waiting to spot something they shouldn't."

"And the alternative?" Kal asked.

"Sail deeper," he said. "Swing out into open water, push west then cut back inland near the cliffs beyond Thornhook. But..."

She caught the pause. "But?"

"There's a chance," Jaymes said, slowly now, "we hit a Godless Storm."

Her brow furrowed. "You've said that before. What is that?"

Before Jaymes could answer, Kipp's voice drifted over from where he leaned against the mast, one boot hooked lazily around the rigging.

"Pirate nonsense," he said, tone dry. "They say the last god fell into the sea, and now their corpse rots in the deep—birthing storms that can swallow ships whole. Black squalls. No stars, no sky. Just wind and madness."

He twirled a dagger between two fingers, glancing at them with a grin that didn't quite meet his eyes. "But I'm sure it's all terribly poetic."

Jaymes didn't smile. His gaze turned hard, fixed on Kipp with none of his usual amusement. "I've sailed through two in my life."

Kipp quieted at the tone.

"I would not do so again unless I had no other choice," he said. "You don't outrun them. You don't fight them. You survive, if the sea lets you."

Kal's eyes stayed on him, steady.

Jaymes looked at her then, the smirk gone, the weight of experience coiled beneath his voice. "So. What's it to be?"

Kal said nothing for a breath, her gaze returning to the horizon as wind tugged at the edges of her cloak. The sea stretched out before them, blockades in one direction, legends in another.

"We sail out to sea," she said at last.

Jaymes arched a brow. "Risk the storms?"

"There's no certainty we'll find one," she replied. "But I'm certain the blockades are there. I don't have time to lose. We take the faster path."

Jaymes gave a low, approving laugh, full of salt and steel. "You speak like someone born to these waters," he said, his grin returning. "A woman after my own heart."

She turned her head slowly, gaze cutting toward him. "Don't mistake practicality for poetry."

He raised both hands in mock surrender, the grin never wavering.

Kal didn't indulge it. "Anything else we need to discuss?"

There was a glint in Jaymes' eyes as he shifted his stance, a hint of something he might have said had the mood been looser, the night later. But before the words could shape themselves—

"No," she said flatly, already turning. "I didn't think so."

And just like that, she was gone—boots ringing soft against the deck, coat trailing behind her like smoke.

Jaymes watched her go, the grin lingering in her wake. "Dangerous woman."

Kipp stepped up beside him, arms folded, the same look etched across his face—equal parts frustration and fascination. "Intoxicating," he said. "In the way poison's intoxicating, right before it ruins your life."

Jaymes chuckled. "Or makes it interesting."

TWO KINGS, ONE QUEEN

Kalithea had prepared herself for the unpredictable nature of sea travel–the wind-shift moods of seasoned men, the veiled negotiations among outlaws, the cold calculations that came with every alliance she made aboard the *Tempest*. What she had not accounted for was the particular brand of madness that came from being hunted by two men who should have known better.

Not hunted in the way she was used to. Not with blades or threats or the sharp bite of power pressed to her throat. No, this was something subtler. Louder in its arrogance. Softer in its approach. The kind of pursuit that unfolded in sidelong glances and sharpened smiles, as if the crown she sought had become secondary to the question of who could stand beside her when she claimed it.

She did not welcome the distraction. But neither did she run from it. It was a game, and she knew the rules. Rule one: never let a man believe the power is *his*.

She stood at the helm beside Jaymes, the sea stretching endlessly before them, a cool wind tugging at the loose strands of her hair. He was quiet for a time, hands resting easy on the wheel, blue eyes on the horizon. Then, without turning his head, he spoke.

"Tell me," he said, his voice a smooth blend of gravel and warmth, "when you reclaim your throne, what will you do first?"

He didn't say if. A purposeful omission and she heard it.

"Why do you ask?"

Blackwell's lips curved slightly. "Because I like to know where my investments are going."

She turned toward him, arching a brow. "Oh, I'm an investment now?"

"No." He admitted and shifted just enough to meet her gaze, something dangerous sparking in his eyes. "You're a gamble with the highest payout I've ever seen."

Before she could answer, another voice–far more insolent–cut through the moment.

"Oh, *spare me*," Kipp Harlow drawled, sauntering into view. A dagger spun lazily through his fingers as he leaned against the nearest post, expression far too pleased with itself. "The great Jaymes Blackwell, waxing poetic about thrones and returns. You've gone soft. Tell me, Blackwell...should we start carving verses into driftwood?"

Blackwell didn't turn. "Some of us prefer subtlety, Harlow."

"And some of us prefer honesty," Kipp said, spinning a dagger between his fingers. "Let's not pretend you aren't circling the same flame I am. The only difference is I'm not trying to dress it up as strategy."

Kalithea didn't speak, she simply stepped back and let the wind carry their bravado.

"I'd be more concerned," Blackwell said at last, "if I thought you posed a real threat."

"Oh, I'm not a threat," Kipp replied, flashing teeth. "I'm a distraction. And if you're smart, you'll start worrying about what that means."

She watched them both, eyes steady. Let them circle each other. Let them believe they were maneuvering her, when in truth, she already knew how this would unfold.

Kipp leaned against the mast, arms crossed, his gaze settling on her with pointed interest.

"So," he murmured, voice smooth with just enough mischief to suggest he knew exactly what game he was playing, "do I get a turn? Or is the pirate the only one who gets to play with fire?"

She glanced his way, slow and calculating, a smile tugging at her mouth like a secret she might let slip if it served her. "And if I answered, thief... would you use it against me? Or just enjoy knowing something no one else gets to touch?"

Kipp's grin curled, all teeth and charm, but there was heat under it now, "Depends on what you give me." He leaned in, "Might pocket it. Might trade it for something sharper. Or maybe..." he stepped just close enough for her to feel the promise in his voice, "I'd memorize every word just to hear what it sounds like when you forget to lie to me."

"Flattery?" she asked, dry as aged wine.

"Observation," he replied, winking. "But if it's working, I won't stop."

Blackwell gave a low, unimpressed chuckle. "If you're going to flirt, Harlow, at least try not to sound like a street poet with a concussion."

"Says the man who cornered her at the helm to discuss her future," Kipp shot back without missing a beat.

"Says the man who slunk across the deck like a stray with a bone to pick."

"Says the man," Kipp added, grinning as he tucked the dagger away, "who's losing this round."

That, at last, gave Blackwell pause. His gaze shifted, not to Kipp, but to her. She exhaled softly, her lips curving in silent triumph. *Let them play.* They believed they were in competition. Each move, each word, calculated to outmatch the other—one a pirate king, the other the king of thieves, both too confident in their ability to win a game they didn't even realize they'd already lost.

Men like Jaymes Blackwell and Kipp Harlow were used to being the storm that others bent around. They were charm wrapped in danger, predators who lived by the thrill of control, the quiet satisfaction of knowing the room belonged to them the moment they walked in. So she let them spar with glances and quips. Let them circle her like wolves too distracted by each other to notice the cliff's edge just behind them.

A slow, knowing smile curved at the corner of her mouth as she turned to face them.

"Gentlemen," she said, "I do hope you're enjoying yourselves. But be careful. Distractions on deck tend to end in drownings."

The game never faltered. If anything, it evolved, deepened beneath the surface like a riptide. On the *Tempest,* beneath a sky that promised both calm and storm, two kings circled the same center. She let them circle. Because what was danger, if not another weapon to master? What was flirtation, if not just a new language of control?

The morning air bit clean and bright as she stood at the bow, spine straight, hands loose at her sides. The sea stretched ahead, endless and glittering, a path carved in salt and promise. She breathed it in—wind and water, steel and silence—welcoming the quiet before the inevitable.

Footsteps approached, familiar and confident. She didn't turn.

"Tell me," Blackwell said behind her, voice low, steady as tide. "Do you ever stop fighting the wind...and let it carry you somewhere reckless?"

She waited just long enough to make him think she hadn't heard. Then she turned slightly, letting the breeze catch her hair and the weight of her gaze land on his.

"I don't let anything carry me, Jaymes.," she said. "You assume I move when something else tells me to"

A smile tugged at the corner of his mouth. "Oh, no...but I do like watching the balance shift. So tell me..."

He stepped forward until the heat of his presence brushed her skin. Not forceful, just close enough to test the boundaries she hadn't set.

"If I backed you against the rigging now..." he murmured, eyes sliding over her with the weight of a man well aware of his effect, "would you pull me in with you or would you climb to see how fast I'd chase you?"

Her lips curved, not in invitation, but in challenge. "I'd climb faster than you."

His laugh came soft and unexpected, genuine. "Gods, I hope so. Watching you win might be the best part."

"Are you always this arrogant?" she asked.

"Only when it's deserved."

She opened her mouth—retort forming, sharp and wry—but another voice cut through the moment like a knife tossed into the dark.

"Oh, for the love of every drowned god, is this really happening?"

Kipp Harlow stepped into view, expression lined with long-suffering disbelief. He moved with his hands in his pockets, coat unbuttoned and dagger glinting at his belt like punctuation to whatever trouble he was about to start.

"I go below for one minute and come back to find rope metaphors and mating dances?" He shook his head. "Tragic."

Blackwell didn't look at him. "We were having a perfectly civil conversation."

Kipp snorted. "Is that what you call it now?"

"Jealous?" Blackwell asked, voice still even.

"I'd be more worried about you," Kipp replied, flashing Kal a grin. "Because if you're hoping to win her attention with empty dares, I should warn you...she's not the type to be impressed by rope tricks. She needs someone who knows how to keep up."

Kal gave him a flat look. "That's the best you have this morning?"

He placed a hand over his chest, laughing. "I'm warming up. Wouldn't want to waste my charm all at once."

"Pathetic," Blackwell muttered.

"Efficient," Kipp corrected, and shot Blackwell a look. "He's burning through his lines too fast. Pacing is everything."

Kal crossed her arms, watching them both. "You're exhausting."

"And yet," Kipp said, stepping closer, "you haven't walked away."

"I'm reconsidering all of my choices."

"Not quickly enough," he said with a wink.

"Let's settle it, then," Blackwell said, turning toward the rigging with that slow, predator's smile.

Kal's brow arched. "Settle what?"

"Race to the top," he said. "Winner takes pride."

Kipp perked up. "And bragging rights?"

Blackwell gave a curt nod. "Naturally."

"You're serious?" Kal asked, unamused.

"Always," Blackwell winked.

Kipp shrugged off his coat. "I'm in."

Kal stepped back, arms still folded. "You're both absurd."

"Then why," Kipp said over his shoulder, already walking, "are you still watching?"

"Because I'm trying to decide whether to let you fall" she called after him, "or push you."

Blackwell glanced at her, amused. "Why not both?"

They moved toward the rigging, boots striking wood, shoulders squared, already feeding off the challenge. Kalithea followed at a distance. She didn't stop them, but the glint in her eyes was wicked and bright.

The wind had strengthened when they reached the rigging. It swept clean across the deck, tugging at sails and rattling the lines with a deep, constant hum. The sky overhead was a flawless sweep of gold-edged blue, and the sea churned with steady intent, alive with energy that promised either victory or ruin. Across the deck, the crew gathered with the slow-building anticipation, knowing they were about to witness something worth talking about.

Jaymes rolled his sleeves, each movement confident and unhurried. He approached the ropes, his expression one of mild interest masking calculation.

"First one to the top," he said, resting one hand against the netting, "no tricks, no shortcuts."

"Spoken like a man who plans to cheat anyway," Kipp muttered, stepping up beside him. His posture was relaxed, but his grin held an edge. "And here I thought the stakes involved something worth climbing for."

"Pride," Blackwell replied smoothly. "And the illusion that you were faster than me. Brief, but memorable."

Kipp placed a hand on the ropes. "I do love a good illusion. Almost as much as I love shattering them."

They both turned as Kalithea approached, her steps slow, calculated. She stopped just shy of the ropes, arms folded across her chest, and cast a glance between them with the kind of expression usually reserved for idiocy in high places.

"You're assuming I'm here to spectate," she said.

Jaymes tilted his head, amused. "You're saying you want in?"

She arched a brow. "*Want* implies I had a *choice*."

Kipp's eyes lit with mischief, "Careful, love. That sounds like a challenge."

Kal stepped forward, her fingers brushing the rigging. "I don't rise to challenges, Harlow," she murmured. "I set them."

Blackwell's smile didn't falter, though something in his eyes narrowed. "Confident."

"Experienced," she returned.

"You're quick," Kipp said, adjusting his gloves. "But I was scaling keeps before I could spell my own name."

Jaymes gave a loose shrug, stretching his arms with the confidence of someone born to rigging and sea. "I was tying knots before I had teeth. Let's not pretend this will be close."

She looked at them both, slow and cool, then leaned in "And I don't waste time humoring men who talk more than they move."

Jaymes grinned, "Lets get at it then" and pulled on the ropes.

By the time either of them registered the shift in her stance, she was already climbing. No grand show. No taunt. Just movement. The rope groaned as she moved, but she moved like she was part of the ship itself. Each pull more graceful than the last, as though gravity itself bent to her discipline. By the time Blackwell processed her head start, she was halfway up the rigging. Kipp swore under his breath and launched after her.

The deck came alive behind them—shouts rising, coin wagers changing hands, crewmen craning to see who would claim the mast. But the race was already lost.

Kalithea reached the top in silence. She perched there like a carved figurehead, one leg drawn beneath her, one arm resting along the mast. Her hair lifted in the wind, a dark banner against the bright sky. From below, she looked carved from defiance itself.

Blackwell reached her next—breathing hard, jaw clenched, though he masked it well.

A moment later, Kipp hauled himself up, less composed but no less determined.

She looked at them, calm and unbothered, the corners of her mouth lifting into a smile that held no malice, only certainty. "Next time, gentlemen," she said, voice low, "try keeping up."

And with that, she pushed off from the mast. She descended, a blur of motion as she slid and dropped from one rope to another, boots catching lines with calculated grace until she landed lightly on the deck.

The crew erupted in cheers.

Kipp leaned against the rigging, watching her with narrowed eyes and a grin that didn't quite reach the usual cocky height. "You let her win, didn't you?"

Blackwell didn't answer right away. He stood there, catching his breath, looking down at her as though watching something he hadn't quite understood until now. Then, with a quiet laugh, he said, "You think I let her win?"

Kipp blew out a sigh. "No. But I'd sleep easier if we had."

Jaymes huffed. "We may be in deeper waters than we thought, thief."

"Oh, we passed deep the second she stepped aboard," Kipp muttered, glancing down again at the woman now being handed a mug by one of the crew, smiling as if she hadn't just bested both of them without breaking a sweat. "We're halfway to drowning."

Jaymes chuckled again, leaning his shoulder against the mast. "And somehow, I don't mind the view."

The Quiet Between Waves

Moonlight spilled across the deck in pale, broken ribbons, casting silver across the sea's dark skin. The Tempest cut through the water in silence, sails full but hushed. The crew had long since disappeared below. Only the creak of rope and the steady rush of waves filled the quiet of the night.

Kalithea stood alone at the bow. One hand rested lightly on the rail. The other hung loose at her side, fingers relaxed, though every part of her was taut beneath the stillness. The wind teased strands of hair from her braid and left them tangled across her cheek, and she made no move to fix them. Her focus stayed on the horizon–empty, endless, and, for once, free of eyes watching her every breath.

Until she heard the footsteps.

"You look tired, love."

Kipp's voice drifted into the quiet, lower than usual. No smirk in it, no bite. Just the bare edge of concern.

She didn't turn. "I'm fine."

"You lie well," he said, and this time there was the faintest smile in his tone. "It's actually impressive. Not quite convincing, but it's artful."

She breathed in deep, the scent of salt settling in her lungs. When she exhaled, it sounded too much like surrender.

"What do you want, Harlow?"

He came to lean beside her, arms folded along the rail, eyes fixed out to sea. "To know what happens when the game ends."

Slowly she turned to him, searching his face for the catch–waiting for the grin, the deflection, the jest.

It never came. He wasn't smiling. He looked the same, almost. Shirt open at the collar, coat half-buttoned, sleeves rolled back. The usual tousle of wind-ruffled hair. But the mischief was gone. The casual veneer had thinned. In its place was something far rarer, something quiet and open.

"You assume it ends," she said.

"Everything ends." He didn't look at her when he said it.

The moon rimmed his profile in silver—cheekbone, jawline, the shadow beneath his lashes. He wasn't trying to be handsome. He simply was. In the way of men who had survived too much to bother with vanity. His hair was tied back, loose at the edges, a few strands caught in the breeze. He hadn't shaved in days. The stubble suited him.

She studied him. A thief who played games as easily as others breathed. And yet here he was, unsmiling, asking questions without edge. It was disarming. And effective.

"I don't know what happens next," she admitted, her voice barely louder than the sea.

"That's the first honest thing you've said all week."

"Maybe," she said, a flicker of amusement behind the words, "I was waiting for someone who deserved the truth."

"Dangerous game, love," he murmured, finally turning his face toward hers. "Telling a thief something's worth stealing..."

Her smile was slow, sharp-edged. "If you want something worth stealing, Kipp—" She stepped in, close enough that the space between them vanished, close enough that her next breath brushed his. "—then win the game."

Her gaze locked on his. He didn't answer. Only inhaled once, as if proximity startled him more than he'd ever admit. And then she was gone. No glance back. No lingering pause. Just the sure, quiet departure of a woman who had mastered the art of leaving men wanting.

Kipp stayed where he was, arms still braced, heart still racing. He laughed dryly, running a hand through his hair.

"Gods damn it," he muttered, half under his breath.

The next night brought Kalithea back to the bow again, watching over a sea that stretched wide and endless, dark and silvered under the pull of the moon. The wind was cool against her skin, tugging gently at the hem of her coat, threading its fingers through the strands of her hair. Her hands rested lightly on the railing, though her posture betrayed no tension. She looked as if she were carved from the night itself—still, watchful, distant. And for one moment, it seemed like she had slipped their attention finally. No strategic positioning. No charming interruptions. No clever words designed to unmake her mask.

She relaxed her shoulders, just slightly, turning her face up towards the moon, a small smile settling in. The sea had always been her place of silence. Of clarity. Not court halls or battlefields, but this, moonlight on waves, no expectations pressing in on her. No one asking, begging, needing. Here, she did not have to be queen or warrior or weapon. She could simply *exist*.

"If you keep smiling at the moon like that, love," came a voice behind her, low and velvety, "the sun might get jealous."

She turned slowly, eyes narrowing just slightly. Jaymes leaned against the nearest mast with arms crossed, steely eyes catching the silver light, his mouth tilted in that maddening, amused curve she had come to expect from him.

"And what would that make you, the sun?" she asked, voice even, brows arching with faint interest.

His grin deepened, but his tone softened. "Me? Oh, I'd never compare myself to the sun. Too harsh. Too demanding. Too used to being worshipped."

She considered him for a moment. "No?" she said with mild curiosity, as though indulging a child who thought himself clever.

"No," he said, pushing off the mast and strolling toward her. "I'm something far less dependable. Far more dangerous."

He stopped beside her, close but not imposing. The way he always did, never demanding space, only offering proximity. Letting her decide what to give.

"Then what are you, Jaymes?" she asked, deliberately using his name, watching how his gaze sharpened at the sound of it.

His answer didn't come immediately. He looked out over the water instead, expression clouded.

"I'm the tide," he said finally.

She tilted her head, "Fickle, then."

"Relentless," he corrected, laughing, his tone quiet and genuine. "Unpredictable. Dangerous in the right conditions. But I always come back."

She turned back to the sea without a word, looking out into the distance, her fingers flexing slightly on the railing. The wind picked up, lifting the scent of brine and distant rain.

"The open ocean," he said at last, watching her with a softness to his gaze, "has a way of scrubbing wounds clean."

She looked at him again, this time fully, and let the weight of her own truth surface. There was no mask now, just a woman who had survived more than most would believe.

"They aren't wounds anymore Jaymes," she said softly, the words edged in steel. "They're scars."

His eyes met hers, and this time he didn't look at her like a prize or a puzzle. He looked at her like a man who had finally found something familiar in a world that had long since stopped feeling like home. In that moment, Jaymes understood that she was not a fire to be tamed, nor a storm to outrun. She was the sea itself–endless, unyielding, and utterly sovereign. And for once, he didn't try to charm her. Didn't offer comfort or conquest. He just stood beside her, silent, caught in the weight of what she carried and the quiet surety that she would carry it, always.

She stepped away before he could speak. Before he could ruin it with charm or tenderness or anything else that might strip the honesty from the moment.

"Goodnight, Captain," she said, voice smooth once more, mask restored flawlessly.

The sea had always been Jaymes' first mistress–untamed, relentless, and beautiful in her violence. She asked for everything and gave nothing, and he had loved her for it. She was honest. Brutal. Free. Every scar she'd left–salt-cut, rope-burned, blade-earned–he'd worn like a crown.

But tonight, the sea was quiet, and the silence unsettled him.

He stood at the edge of the deck, wind teasing the loose folds of his coat, the hush of waves too gentle against the hull. The moon cast its pale light across the water, and he saw her in it, her shadow slipping into the dark with no fanfare, no parting jest. Just a simple goodnight...and truth. Not truth as men often spoke it, half-formed and self-serving, but the kind that cut clean through the bone. Scars, she'd said. Not wounds.

Now he breathed her name without sound, as if he could exhale the weight of her from his lungs. It didn't work.

Kalithea.

Not a flame to chase. Not a queen to kneel for. A force. A reckoning. She had looked at him, *truly looked*, and seen past the polished charm, past the legend carved by rumor and rum, past the Pirate King who had long since stopped asking if anyone saw the man beneath. That was the danger. Not the allure of her mouth or the fire in her words. Not the razor wit or the sharp-edged grace with which she wielded command. No, it was the quiet way she'd offered understanding and walked away before it could cost either of them more than they were ready to admit.

Jaymes braced his hands against the railing, staring out into the black where the water swallowed the sky. He let out a dry breath, almost a laugh. He'd danced through fire before. Slept beside treachery. Played kings against one another and lived to drink over the ashes. He had never once lost sleep over a woman. Never staying long enough to be caught. Never letting anything carve its name into his bones.

But Kalithea wasn't just a woman. She was a reckoning in flesh. She didn't ask to be chased. She made men chase without ever turning her head. And damn her, he was already moving.

He loosened his grip on the railing, fingers aching from how hard he'd held.

Let it go. Let her go.

But the truth settled low in his chest, unwelcome and immovable. He wouldn't stop thinking about her. Because in the space between silence and sea, she had reminded him of something he'd long since buried beneath years of storms and salt and sin. The yearning for something to come back to, something *real.*

He turned from the railing, but not from the thought of her. That, he suspected, would follow him long after this voyage was done, and deep in his chest, where longing lived like a scar too old to heal, the truth remained:

She had walked away to see if he would follow.

And gods help him –

He would.

THE PRICE OF A SECRET

Wind rolled sharp across the deck of the *Tempest*, laced with salt and sun and the restless call of gulls wheeling overhead. The ship moved with confidence–ropes creaked, boots struck wood, orders passed low and swift–but the usual rhythm had shifted. Just enough for the crew to glance sidelong between tasks. Because Kipp Harlow was moving. And when the King of Thieves moved with intent, wise men watched their pockets...and their throats.

Kalithea stood at the stern, her back to the world, the wind threading through her hair, her gaze fixed on the infinite horizon. Kipp approached like a shadow wrapped in mischief, steps quiet, grin curling slowly across his face. The dagger spun between his fingers playfully.

"Oh, love," he said, his voice low with theatrical sigh, "tell me this voyage won't be wasted on silence and scenic brooding. You've already stared down the sea like it owes you an answer."

She didn't turn. Didn't blink. "I don't brood."

"No?" Kipp's tone was feigned surprise, the knife flipping once, then again. "Then what would you call this tragic display of brooding nobility? Long stares at the sea, dramatic gusts of wind, all that quiet anguish...I'd almost call it poetic."

Her lips quirked, barely. But that was *more* than enough encouragement.

Kipp moved into her periphery, tilting his head like a man who'd never met a line he didn't want to cross. "Lucky for you, I brought a remedy. Something to cure that little storm brewing in your head."

At last, Kalithea turned, her gaze sweeping over him. Like she was deciding whether to swat him aside or let him keep talking simply for her own amusement.

Her eyes dipped to the knife, then back to his face. "Should I thank you now or wait until you inevitably lose?"

Kipp's grin widened, all that lazy arrogance sliding into something more dangerous. "No thanks necessary, my little fox. Just remember this moment when I win."

She narrowed her eyes. "Little Fox?"

His smirk deepened. "Clever. Quick-footed. Always one step ahead." He tilted his head, eyes glinting like he already knew the answer. "Impossible to hold onto–no matter how close I get."

She crossed her arms, unimpressed. "That's a terrible nickname."

Kipp pressed a hand to his chest, feigning offense. "Terrible? I think it's perfect. Elusive. Sharp. Infuriating." He leaned in just enough for her to feel the heat behind the grin. "And likely to leave me bleeding if I try to touch."

She rolled her eyes. "I am not your fox."

His grin only widened, wicked and warm. "Of course not. But that doesn't mean I won't keep trying to earn the chase."

From a few paces behind them, Jaymes Blackwell's voice drifted into the space like a warm current. He stood relaxed against the railing, arms crossed. "Careful, thief. She's not known for losing. Especially not gracefully."

"I don't lose," Kal said mildly, not sparing the pirate a glance.

"And I don't gamble unless I plan to collect," Kipp replied smoothly, going back to the bet at hand, flipping the knife once more before holding it out to her by the hilt. "But if it helps...this one comes with a prize. Winner earns a *secret*."

She didn't move to take it.

"If I win," he said, "you give me one. Something real. Something no one else on this ship knows." His smile turned wicked. "And if you win? I'll give you the same."

Jaymes gave a low whistle, pushing off the railing with a shake of his head. "Harlow, I've known you half my life and never heard you tell the truth willingly. Must be serious."

"That's why it's a high-stakes game," Kipp shot back. "What do you say, little fox? A fair exchange between liars."

Kalithea let the silence stretch until it was just shy of uncomfortable. She was good at that. Better than either of them. Letting words rot in the air until men started filling them with their own insecurities. Then, with a slow, fluid motion, she plucked the dagger from his fingers.

Behind them, Jaymes leaned against the railing, arms folded, stormy eyes glinting with that infuriating calm that meant he was paying very, very close attention.

"I'll admit," he said, his tone rich with mirth and curiosity, "I'd quite like to hear a secret from her."

Kipp, without turning, flashed a grin over his shoulder. "Then do what you do best, Captain–stand there looking pretty and useless. Do make sure to enjoy the view."

Kalithea's fingers curled around the knife, her thumb brushing the edge of the hilt. She rolled her shoulders, breathing in the salt-laced air as she turned the blade in her palm.

"You're awfully confident," she said at last, her voice deceptively light. "For a man who hasn't yet realized what he's up against."

Kipp stepped back to give her room, though his smirk never wavered.

"Oh, darling," he replied, spreading his hands as if presenting the stage, "confidence is half the game."

Jaymes let out a low chuckle, the sound like a wave breaking slow against the hull. "And the other half?"

Kipp flicked a glance toward him, still watching Kal, already savoring the loss he didn't mind taking. "Knowing when you're already in over your head."

Kal ignored them both. She stepped forward, eyes locking on a barrel tied near the forward rail. Her arm rose. The blade left her hand in a single clean motion.

It hit dead center. Steel into wood, straight to the hilt. The sound rang.

Kipp gave a low whistle. "Well. I'm either impressed or doomed."

Jaymes clapped once, slow. "Both, I think."

Kal turned to them, expression smooth. "Your turn, thief."

Kipp didn't rush. He spun his knife once between his fingers, the metal flashing in the sunlight, then rolled back his shoulders as if preparing for a dance rather than a contest. There was no tension in his stance, only the lazy elegance of a man who'd made a career out of being underestimated.

And then, without ceremony, he flicked his wrist. The blade whispered through the air and struck the wood just beside hers, close enough that the difference was negligible. Not a loss. Not a win. A deliberate stalemate.

Kalithea's eyes narrowed, not in displeasure, but with interest. "Tell me you're not stalling, Harlow."

Kipp feigned surprise, all wounded pride and sarcasm. "Darling, I would never insult you with anything so dull. Just prolonging the inevitable."

Behind them, Jaymes leaned against the railing, arms crossed, "I think the inevitable is already well underway."

He was enjoying this. Every step. Every move. Every unsaid thing between the two.

The next round fell silent before it began. Then again. And again. Each blade struck home. Each glance edged closer to a dare. The crew had stopped pretending to work. They lined the rails now, hushed and wary, because what unfolded before them wasn't a contest—it was a dance that didn't need music to be dangerous.

Then Kipp shifted. He turned slightly, spinning the next knife by the tip. But instead of flicking it toward the target, he sent it arcing through the air, straight toward Jaymes.

Jaymes caught it one-handed without blinking, like he'd been expecting it.

"Care to raise the stakes, Captain?" Kipp asked, his voice light, almost lazy.

Kalithea's brow lifted. "This wasn't your wager to raise."

Kipp only smiled. That grin—slow, insolent, insufferably charming. "All games evolve, love. Isn't that half the thrill?"

Jaymes turned the knife once in his palm, his gaze lingering on Kal for a beat too long. Then he threw. The blade cut through the air with impossible grace, a perfect arc, and landed—dead center between hers and Kipp's. Just slightly closer.

A murmur passed through the gathered crew like a hush before thunder.

Kipp's grin spread. "Well, well," he drawled. "Looks like the captain decided to play for keeps."

Kal's eyes moved between them, one lounging like he'd never been beaten, the other radiating chaos like a second skin. That was the moment she understood. They weren't playing against each other. They were circling her. *Together.*

She exhaled slowly. "One throw doesn't make you a threat."

Jaymes tilted his head, a smirk touching the corner of his mouth. "Love, I've never done anything just once. Especially not when it looks that good."

Kipp turned toward the crew with mock reverence. "Someone write that down. It was almost poetic."

Laughter rippled.

Kal stepped forward, wrenched her knife free with a clean pull, and turned back to face them, her voice smooth as glass. "Then I suppose I'll have to remind you both why I never lose."

And she did. Or near enough. Her blade landed center again, perfect to the casual eye. But she felt the shift. A breath too much weight in her wrist. A half-inch deviation.

They saw it too.

Jaymes went next. No theatrics. No flourish. He simply leaned into the throw, the wind catching the edge of his coat as if it, too, obeyed his rhythm. The blade thudded into the wood just closer.

Then Kipp. No warning. No smirk. Just a clean throw. And when his knife struck dead center he let out a whoop loud enough to startle the gulls overhead.

He spun in a circle, arms out like he might embrace the sea itself. "By every crooked god in every seaside dive–I did it! We did it!"

Kalithea said nothing. She stood still, her eyes on the barrel, on the impossibly narrow margin between their blades and hers. It was minuscule. Impressive, even. But it was enough.

Jaymes leaned back against the rail, arms folded, his smirk full of lazy triumph. "You're unusually quiet, my queen. Not taking it poorly, are we?"

She exhaled once through her nose. Sharp. Controlled. "You won by the width of a breath."

"Ah, but win we did," Kipp said, hand over heart. "You're robbing me of the only story I plan to tell in every tavern from here to Varis."

She turned toward them–first to Jaymes, then to Kipp–her expression cryptic, as always. But her eyes were gleaming now, sharp with calculation.

"Fine," she said at last. "You've earned your prize."

Kipp straightened like a hound that had caught the scent. "Now that's what I like to hear."

Jaymes chuckled under his breath. "Let's not get ahead of ourselves, thief. She didn't say which of us won."

"Oh, come on," Kipp said, flashing a crooked grin. "Tell me you're not going to split a secret down the middle."

Kal didn't speak. She let the silence stretch just long enough to make them lean in.

Then, cool as ever: "You'll get one secret. That's all."

Kipp raised a brow. "Shared custody?"

She let out a soft, almost imperceptible sigh. Then shifted, resting one hip against a barrel, arms folded like none of this amused her in the slightest.

"*A* secret," she repeated, as if they were children begging for scraps. "Fine."

Pause. Long enough to make them brace.

Then–deadpan: "I don't like cheese."

Silence. A slow, blooming disbelief settled between the two men like fog over the sea.

Jaymes blinked once. Kipp's jaw slackened. And then, in perfect, disbelieving harmony–

"Oh, absolutely not."

"Not a damn chance, love."

Kal lifted a brow, cool as ever. "What? You never specified what kind of secret."

Kipp threw his hands skyward, pacing a single step away in dramatic frustration. "*Unbelievable!* I risked a dislocated shoulder throwing that last knife."

Jaymes, shaking his head, let out an exaggerated sigh. "Kal, you can't honestly think that counts."

She sighed with the gravity of someone burdened by fools. "You two are exhausting."

"And you," Kipp said, grinning now as he stepped back into her space, "are entirely too predictable."

Kipp leaned in, elbows resting on the barrel beside her, his voice pitched low. "Tell us something real."

Jaymes didn't echo the challenge. He leaned against the rail, arms folded, his stance deceptively casual. But his gaze never strayed. There was no jest in it now. No idle game. They weren't baiting her. They were waiting.

Kalithea let her eyes move between them—the thief who charmed his way through every lock and lie, the pirate who wore confidence like armor and watched the world with patient calculation. Two predators. Two men who thrived on misdirection. But they weren't reaching for leverage now. They were reaching for her.

She drew in a breath, slow and steady, her voice even as she said, "The man you know as my brother... is not my brother by blood"

Kipp's smirk faltered, just slightly, like someone had knocked the wind out of him and he hadn't decided whether to laugh or curse. Jaymes didn't move, but his fingers curled tighter where they rested, a subtle shift that said more than words ever could.

She pressed forward.

"Rhaen Morrick had my family slaughtered not long after I was born. He took me...raised me as his own, paraded me through court like proof of power to solidify his rule. Liam..." Her throat tightened. Just a touch. "Liam is his son. The boy I was told was my brother."

The words didn't falter, but something inside her did.

"And still," she went on, quieter now, "Liam chose me. Through years of lies and fire and every damn reason not to—he stayed. Not because of blood. Because of everything that matters more."

Jaymes didn't speak. But the look in his eyes had shifted, gone was the ever-present amusement, replaced now by something deeper. Weighted.

Kipp leaned back slowly, his usual swagger stripped away, his voice careful. "You were raised by the man who butchered your family. And you say his name like it holds no weight."

Kalithea met his eyes, steady and unflinching. "He took everything from me. My name. My throne. My blood. The least I can do is deny him the dignity of pretending I fear him."

She stood still. Arms crossed. Back straight. Unshaken. But inside, something shifted. Because for the first time in years she'd spoken it aloud. Not for strategy. Just truth. Laid bare on a deck of thieves and pirates, and offered not as a weapon, but a fact. And for one breathless beat, she wondered if she had miscalculated. If vulnerability, even this carefully weighed out, had been a mistake. But neither of them turned away. Neither moved to comfort or correct. They just watched her, eyes sharp, attention absolute.

Kipp exhaled slowly, dragging a hand through his tousled hair, the smirk gone, but something amused still flickering behind his eyes..

"Well," he said at last, never being one for serious moments, voice low and edged with something softer than usual. "Didn't see that coming."

Jaymes didn't speak immediately. He stood still, gaze fixed on her, without pity or sympathy. Merely assessment–curious, quiet, and un-nervingly sharp. Kalithea met that stare with the same poise she always wore, though something behind her eyes flickered.

"Not what you expected?" she asked, her voice cool, the corners of her mouth twitching with a half-smile that didn't reach her eyes.

Jaymes finally leaned back, his arms folding as he studied her.

"No," he admitted. "But then again... neither are you."

Kipp's brow furrowed, and for a rare moment, the glint in his eye held no mockery, only thought. He looked at her as if he were turning a coin over in his palm, testing its weight, wondering how long it had been in circulation without him noticing the truth stamped across its surface.

He didn't joke, just nodded once and murmured, "Well...I suppose that counts."

Jaymes offered the ghost of a grin, though it held none of his usual arrogance.

"You certainly paid the price," he said, voice low.

Kipp gave a quiet huff, rubbing a hand across his jaw. "And here I thought we were fishing for something scandalous. Some secret lover, maybe a tattoo you regret. Not a buried kingdom and a lifetime of be-trayal."

His tone was light. On purpose. An offering, not a dismissal. A way to step back without cheapening what she had given. But Kal felt it anyway, that subtle shift in the air. Not power changing hands, not control slipping but something else. Something she couldn't quite name. She had dropped a piece of herself into the game, thinking it would land precise, contained, final.

But instead, it had landed like a stone in water, rippling outward, leaving her unmoored in a way she hadn't anticipated. She didn't let it show. Instead, she drew a steady breath, rolled her shoulders, and gave them both the same cold, amused smirk she had worn a hundred times before.

"Enjoy your victory boys," she said simply, turning on her heel.

Kipp exhaled slowly, dragging a hand through his tousled hair. The usual smirk had slipped but not entirely.

"Well," he murmured at last, voice pitched low, softer than usual. "Didn't see that one coming."

Jaymes didn't speak. He stood still, the sea at his back, arms folded tight as if bracing against a storm that had nothing to do with wind. His gaze stayed fixed on where Kalithea had disappeared, unmoving. Measuring the weight of what she'd placed in their hands. He finally shifted, bracing one shoulder into the railing, slow and thoughtful.

"No," he said quietly. "Not what I expected."

Kipp let out a breath that wasn't quite a laugh. "I was hoping for something scandalous. Secret lover. Illegitimate heir."

Jaymes gave a low sound in his throat, more breath than amusement. "A guilty pleasure. Bad poetry. Something we could tease her for."

"Something we could *survive* teasing her for," Kipp muttered.

But neither of them smiled, they both knew what they'd heard wasn't some rehearsed revelation or pretty fiction. Kalithea hadn't handed them a performance. She'd handed them a truth so raw it still burned.

Jaymes turned his head slightly, brows drawn. "She didn't have to tell us."

Kipp nodded once. "Could've lied. She's good at it." He glanced toward the stairwell. "Gods, she's brilliant at it."

"But she didn't."

Kipp ran his thumb along the edge of his belt knife, not spinning it this time, just feeling the weight. His voice was low, contemplative now. "She didn't tell us because she trusts us."

Jaymes tilted his head, thoughtful.

"Not fully," Kipp added, "She told us because we're sailing into her kingdom. Into waters where that secret matters."

Jaymes let the weight of that settle, then pushed off the railing. "She thinks we might need it."

"She knows we will," Kipp said, sheathing the blade with a soft click. "She gave us the truth that might keep us alive."

They stood in the hush that followed, both men staring toward the narrow door she'd vanished through, as if they might still catch the shadow of her coat, the flicker of silver in her hair.

Jaymes broke the silence first. "Not the prize I expected when we started playing that game."

Kipp gave a dry laugh, but it lacked any real heat. "You and me both. I thought we'd earn something fun. Instead, she handed us a war story."

Jaymes looked toward the sea. The sun had begun its climb, slow and steady, gilding the edge of the horizon in bronze. "A beginning, more like."

Kipp was quiet a beat, then nodded. "Yeah. That's what it was."

Jaymes narrowed his eyes at the far-off shape of land rising just barely against the waterline.

"She's not afraid of him," he said, more to himself than to Kipp.

"No," Kipp agreed, mouth tugging to one side. "But she is preparing for him."

The evening sky unfurled above them, a sweep of indigo and stars trailing across the horizon like silver threads stitched into velvet. The sea lay deceptively calm beneath the ship, its glassy surface belying the quiet weight in the air.

Kalithea had not intended to speak to anyone the next night. She had sought silence, the cold breath of open waters, the kind of solitude only the deck at night could offer.

Which, of course, meant Kipp Harlow had already beaten her there. He leaned against the rail near the helm, posture relaxed, coat open and tugged by the breeze. A coin spun between his fingers, the soft click of metal punctuating the hush.

"You know," Kipp said casually, flipping the coin high and catching it one-handed, "I was beginning to think you'd locked yourself in your quarters to start drafting your memoirs. Something tragic and brooding, maybe something with flair *Ten Ways to Kill a Man with a Look– And Why I Haven't Yet.*"

Kalithea arched a brow as she approached. "If I were writing anything, it would be your obituary."

"Now that's the fire I came up here for." He turned to face her fully, grin sharp as ever, eyes gleaming. "Come on then, Kal. Let's have it. What's rattling around in that dangerous mind of yours tonight?"

"Nothing worth your concern," she replied coolly, coming to stand beside him at the rail.

Kipp made a show of sighing, leaning into the post as though burdened by the weight of her composure. "It's never anything *worth* my concern, and yet somehow I'm always here, concerned anyway."

"No," she said, voice flat. "You're always here because you like the sound of your own voice."

"Darling, I have an excellent voice."

Kipp watched her for a moment, his usual ease softened by something quieter. He flipped the coin again, caught it without looking, and this time didn't speak for a while.

"How does it feel?" He asked, voice lower than usual.

She didn't turn. "You'll have to be more specific."

"Standing on the deck of a ship headed straight for the kingdom that tried to erase you."

The silence that followed was a different kind of quiet, thick and aware. Not defensive, not strained. Just...still. Kalithea didn't answer. But that was its own kind of answer.

Kipp smiled, not mocking or sly, just knowing. "That's what I thought."

"You're prying," she said at last, calm and unbothered on the surface.

He tilted his head, placing a hand over his chest. "I'm invested."

"You're insufferable."

"Close enough." He shifted closer, not encroaching, just enough for his voice to drop a shade more intimate. "Look, I'm not here to draw blood. Not tonight. I just...know what it's like to walk into a place where you're not welcome. Where every glance feels like a blade and the past follows you like it still owns you."

Her jaw tightened–slight, almost imperceptible. But he noticed.

Of course he noticed.

"And you think I'm haunted by ghosts?" she asked, eyes steady on the sea.

"I think," Kipp said quietly, "that chains leave marks, even after you break them."

Kalithea turned to him then. "You think you know me."

"I know *enough*," he said, and this time, the grin that followed wasn't just charm. It was real, softened by something honest. "I know you don't break easily. But I also know what it costs to hold your shape when everything's trying to splinter you."

She held his gaze, neither confirming nor denying it.

"Well," she said, "if you're hoping to uncover some great revelation from me, I'm afraid you'll have to keep playing your little games, Kipp."

Kipp's grin returned, easy as ever.

"Oh, little fox," he chuckled softly, stepping back, twirling the coin between his fingers again. "I fully intend to."

A low voice drifted from the shadows. "Careful, thief. You're beginning to sound sincere."

Jaymes emerged from the darkness coming to stand opposite them, deep blue eyes sharp but calm, his posture as casual as Kipp's but laced with a quiet awareness.

Kipp didn't flinch, didn't step back. "Even rogues need a break from performing now and then."

Jaymes chuckled softly, folding his arms as he looked at Kalithea. "He's not wrong, you know."

"About what?" she asked, voice still cool.

449

Jaymes' gaze held hers, steady and sure. "About what it takes to return to a place that tried to unmake you."

For a moment, none of them moved. The wind hummed through the rigging above, the sea lapping against the hull below.

Then, Kalithea stepped back from the rail, her expression guarded once more. "You won a piece of the truth. But pieces don't grant you entry" she said quietly. "You're both clever. That's never been in question. But don't mistake a glimpse for an invitation"

She met their gazes, one after the other–Kipp's smile fading just slightly, Jaymes' amusement slipping into something more thoughtful.

And then, just like that, she turned and walked away.

THE SHAPE OF ABSENCE

The morning unfolded golden and clean, the sky an endless sweep of blue, unmarred by cloud or storm. Kalithea stood near the bow, elbows braced on the railing, her gaze distant. The wind threaded through her hair, tugging strands loose from their braid, the sun painting her skin in soft gold.

"I see the sea's claimed your attention again," Kipp drawled, sliding into place beside her. He lounged easily against the railing, arms crossed, a coin dancing between his fingers. "Tell me, love...does the horizon really have you that spellbound, or are you just working very hard not to look at me?"

Kalithea didn't turn. "If I were avoiding you, you'd know."

Kipp's grin curled slow and easy. "See, that's the kind of subtle cruelty I adore. Just enough to make a man wonder if he's being punished or seduced."

Kalithea's lips curved, "If I were punishing you, there wouldn't be room for doubt."

Kipp let out a low chuckle, the coin vanishing between his fingers. "And now I'll be thinking about *that* all night."

"She says things like that a lot," Jaymes said, voice thick with amusement. He stepped into view, steely eyes squinting slightly against the light. He leaned back against the mast, posture lazy. "Usually just before besting you, *again.*"

"That sounds suspiciously like a challenge," Kipp said, flipping the coin once and catching it on the back of his hand.

Kalithea finally turned, brows raised in vague interest. "Another wager?"

Kipp gave her a slow, wicked grin. "Of course. I thought I'd bring a little thrill to an otherwise dull morning."

"I'm already unimpressed," she replied.

"That's just foreplay, darling." He gestured toward Jaymes. "Captain, you in?"

Jaymes gave a half-shrug. "I'm listening."

"A simple game of wits," Kipp said smoothly. "One riddle. You get it right, I owe you both a favor. Get it wrong, and I take one from each of you."

Kalithea eyed him. "That's a steep price for a thief who's only won once."

Kipp's eyes glittered. "Every streak ends, love."

Jaymes folded his arms. "You'd better hope this one doesn't."

Kipp flipped the coin again, caught it, and leaned in slightly. "Alright. Riddle time."

Kalithea sighed, already annoyed. "This had better be less tedious than your last attempt."

"Oh, it's a masterpiece," Kipp promised. "You see a boat filled with people. It hasn't sunk. But when you look again, not a single person is on board. Why?"

Jaymes scratched his chin. "Some trick of language, I assume."

Kalithea didn't blink. "They're all married."

Kipp paused mid-smirk, faltering for a breath before throwing his head back with a groan.

Jaymes barked a laugh. "Gods, that's awful."

"But correct," Kalithea said coolly, holding out her hand toward Kipp.

Kipp kept groaning, digging in his coat. "You didn't even think about it."

"I didn't have to," she replied.

Jaymes chuckled, shaking his head. "She's going to throw you overboard one of these days."

"Only after I swab the deck, polish the rails, and carve her initials into the mast." Kipp placed the coin in her palm with a mock bow. "Your favor, my queen."

Kalithea turned the coin once between her fingers, then met his gaze. Her voice didn't change. Not in volume. Not in tone.

"Don't play your games with me tonight."

The silence that followed was immediate. The grin on Kipp's lips held but only barely. Jaymes didn't move, but the shift in the air between them was impossible to ignore. Kipp's eyes held hers a moment longer than necessary. And then, slowly, he leaned back.

"Well," he said quietly, "That's one way to play."

Kalithea didn't respond. She turned back to the sea, lifting her face toward the breeze as if nothing at all had passed between them.

Jaymes let out a slow exhale, his voice thick with dry amusement. "You do realize she just reminded you who the game actually belongs to."

"I noticed," Kipp murmured, no longer smiling.

Night had fallen, the stars scattered like embers in the dark. The Tempest drifted steady beneath it all, sails whispering secrets to the wind, hull groaning softly with each breath of the sea. The ocean stretched in every direction–vast, unyielding, and quiet.

Kalithea had expected nothing from this night. Not truly. Not beyond the routine she had come to recognize. Kipp would appear, bold as ever, tossing words like daggers, trying to pry loose pieces of her with a grin and a glint in his eye. Jaymes would observe from the edges of it all, relaxed and amused, stepping in only when it pleased him to do so. That had become the rhythm. Predictable. Containable. Something she could control.

But tonight, tonight was different.

She noticed it at dinner. The ship was loud with laughter and tankards, the crew wrapped in their usual rough camaraderie. Jaymes sat where he always did, one arm slung across the bench, wine in hand, relaxed in the way only a man who had mastered the sea could be. Kipp was nearby, smiling, bantering, slipping in and out of conversations like smoke. But not once did he look at her. No raised brow. No sly comment. No secretive glance or murmured dare. He didn't even try.

And she felt that absence, that space where he should have been, more than she expected to. She didn't show it. Of course she didn't. She sipped her wine. She offered the occasional sharp smile. She answered when addressed, but something inside her was off.

And she hated it.

When the meal ended, she did not linger. She rose smoothly as she left the warmth and noise behind, letting the shadows of the upper deck close around her like a shroud. The night air was cool, the stars sparkling clearly. The water below black and endless, rolling soft against the hull. She stood alone for a time. And then–of course–he found her. But not the one she expected.

Jaymes moved beside her not speaking, just leaning against the railing beside her, his presence quiet, steady, as the silence stretched.

Then, finally, in a voice low and knowing: "You told him not to play with you tonight."

Kalithea didn't look at him. Her gaze remained on the horizon, unflinching. "And he listened."

Jaymes exhaled a soft chuckle, the kind that came from deep in his chest.

"Strange," he murmured, eyes on her now, not the sea. "You don't look satisfied."

She said nothing.

"You don't look disappointed either," he added. "But you do look... unsettled."

Her jaw shifted, just slightly. "I'm not."

Jaymes smiled, "You're a better liar when you're trying."

That earned him a glance, brief but sharp. "Is there a reason you're here, Blackwell?"

He turned his gaze toward the sea. "Had a hunch the silence would be loud tonight."

Kalithea was still.

Jaymes' voice dipped, thoughtful now. "You know, Kipp never thought he'd win that wager."

She frowned faintly. "Then why make it?"

Jaymes' smile returned, more shadow than light. "Because he wanted to see how long you'd keep playing."

Kalithea let out a slow breath, eyes narrowing at the waves. "He's a fool."

"That's true," Jaymes agreed. "But not about this."

He turned to her again, gaze steady beneath the starlight. "You could've ended it. Shut him down, and walked away. But you didn't."

"I had nothing to prove."

"No," he said, stepping closer, voice lower now, more intimate. "But you still *played*."

Jaymes watched her a moment longer, then pushed off the railing with a sigh and a stretch, the motion loose and easy as ever. But his eyes... his eyes lingered.

"Try not to miss him too much, love," he said, voice teasing softly. "He'll be back at it by morning."

Kalithea didn't rise to it. She simply looked back to the sea, offering no reply.

Jaymes chuckled under his breath and left her to the dark.

But the silence that followed was different now. It wasn't peaceful. It wasn't welcome. Because something had shifted, and not just in them.

It had shifted in her.

And for the first time in years, Kalithea didn't know how to shift it back.

SALT AND UNDERTOW

The wind shifted first.

Just a quiet change in direction, measured and slow, like the breath a hunter draws before loosing the arrow.

Kalithea stood at the bow, one gloved hand curled tight around the railing slick with salt and spray. Her other hand rested at her side, fingers clenched, hidden in the folds of her coat. The wind tugged strands of dark hair loose from their braid, lifting them into the open air. Ahead, the sea stretched vast and grey, the horizon a blur of smoke and steel. Somewhere beyond that line, the past waited.

Behind her, the Tempest groaned. It was no ordinary complaint from hull or sail. The sound rolled through the ship–deep, splintered, and old. The timbers creaked with knowing, as though they recognized the waters beneath them and did not welcome their return.

Kalithea drew a breath, sharp with salt. The sea answered. The water surged as a swell that rose without warning, the ocean lifting itself like something waking, slow and vengeful. Waves that had rocked steady all morning began to strike with greater weight. A low rumble rolled along the edge of the world.

She didn't flinch, didn't move from the edge. She stood, braced and unmoving, eyes fixed on the rapidly darkening sky above. A flicker of motion pulled her gaze further upward. The crewman in the crow's nest had straightened from his usual slouch, one hand braced on the mast, the other pointing out to sea.

His voice cracked through the rising wind. "GODLESS STORM!"

The words struck like a bell in a crypt–loud, final, and full of old fear. Footsteps thundered across the deck behind her.

Jaymes Blackwell came into motion, cutting through the chaos with surety. His voice carried above the din, forged by years of shouting orders to men who had no time for questions.

"Drop sail! Lock the lines–double them! If you value your skin, godsdamn it, move!"

The crew burst into action. Ropes snapped taut, sails were drawn in with haste, and the smooth rhythm of the ship gave way to ordered frenzy.

The wind turned violent, howling now as it tore across the deck, snatching at Kal's coat and driving the scent of salt and storm deep into her lungs. The Tempest climbed a rising wave beneath her, the bow lifting like the spine of some ancient creature rising from sleep. Then the sky tore open as the rain began to fall in a torrential downpour.

A jagged fork of lightning split the clouds, and in that flash, she saw him. Jaymes stood at the helm, his coat flaring behind him, hair thrown wild by the wind. His eyes were narrowed, steel caught in firelight, focused and unyielding. He did not fight the storm. He met it. Dared it. His stance was reckless, almost defiant, as if he'd made a pact with the sea and meant to see it honored.

It was a terrible, beautiful thing to behold.

And Kalithea–though she should not have–watched him.

The storm had come. The rain came in sheets, cold, blinding and relentless. It soaked the sails, turned the deck to glass. Ropes screamed. Canvas snapped. The sea lashed out with open hands.

Kalithea didn't retreat. Every line of her body was drawn tight. She had stood in worse places–blood on her blade, fire at her back, kings crumbling before her. This storm would not break her.

But Kipp Harlow might.

She felt him before she saw him, just a change in the air, a subtle shift at her side. He moved with the same easy grace he always did, as if chaos itself bent to avoid him. But there was no swagger now. No mask of carelessness. He stopped just behind her, rain running in streams down his face, curls dark and clinging, coat plastered to his frame. His grin was still there but smaller. Sharper.

"Darling," he said, voice threaded with amusement and warning, "I hate to intrude on whatever dramatic epiphany you're narrating in your head, but I'd rather not be the one diving in after you tonight."

She didn't turn. "I'm not going below."

"Of course not," he muttered. "That would be sane."

He stepped in, boots slipping before catching, one hand bracing beside her shoulder, the other on the far side of the railing. A box built of wind and wood and his breath against hers.

"I know that look," he said. "I've worn it."

She glanced at him now, just enough to make the weight of her gaze felt.

She narrowed her eyes, unmoved. "Don't romanticize this."

"I'm not." Kipp's smile faded, replaced by something that didn't wear well on him, something serious. "But I've been standing in the middle of a storm before, pretending it couldn't touch me. And I've learned the hard way—storms don't give a damn about pride."

Another wave struck the hull, harder this time, the force of it jolting the ship beneath them. Kipp steadied them both, his arms never faltering, his gaze never leaving hers.

"You think standing alone is strength. That if you don't, everything you are will fall apart. But that's not how survival works, Kal."

The way he said her name scraped against something she'd locked away. Too soft. Too close.

"I'm not some reckless fool who gets swept away the moment the skies darken," she snapped, voice razor-sharp.

Kipp's eyes searched hers, unflinching. "No. You're worse. Because you'd let the storm tear you apart just to prove you could outlast it."

And then—the world cracked.

The roar split the air in a single, deafening instant, and a wall of water rose ahead, tall, black, and absolute. The Tempest lurched beneath it, the hull groaning, rigging shrieking as the deck tilted hard to starboard. There was no time to brace. The wave struck with brutal force, a deluge crashing down over the bow and sweeping across the deck in a surge that tore breath from lungs and crew from their feet.

Kalithea was flung sideways, the sudden impact slamming her into Kipp's chest. His arms caught her instinctively, locking tight around her, grounding her in the chaos. But the moment held no mercy. The sea struck again, rising and seizing, and in the space between one heartbeat and the next, Kipp was ripped away.

Gone.

One blink and he'd vanished, swallowed whole by the dark waters that seemed to reach for him like something ancient reclaiming its own.

She didn't think. Her breath came sharp, panicked, already cold. Rain blinded her, the world reduced to salt and spray and the churning gray of the storm. Somewhere behind her, Jaymes' voice cracked through the gale—angry, commanding, unmistakable.

"Kalithea—*DON'T!*"

But the warning came too late. Her hands found the rail, and she vaulted over it without pause.

The ocean hit like a wall, the cold slicing through her in a single, breathtaking shock. The sea dragged her down at once, its weight like stone on her chest. The surface disappeared above her. All direction was lost. She twisted in the dark, disoriented, blinded by the surge and battered by the current, every instinct screaming to return to the air but she didn't stop.

She forced her limbs to move, fought against the undertow with steady, punishing strokes. Her lungs burned. Her muscles shook. Still, she pressed downward, driven by a singular thought: she would not lose him.

Kipp's body spun through the depths below, suspended in the gloom, limbs slack, coat fanning like torn canvas around him. Kalithea kicked harder, teeth gritted against the pain. Her vision narrowed, light fading to murk as the sea pressed closer, the pressure rising. She reached once, caught only fabric and lost it. Reached again, fingers closing around the back of his coat. This time she held.

She hauled him toward her with what little strength remained, drawing him against her chest as her body screamed for air. The surface was a memory now, far above, unreachable. The cold bit deeper. Her limbs felt heavier. Her lungs convulsed.

But she refused to let go.

Above deck, Jaymes had seen her disappear. One moment she stood on deck, unflinching amid the storm, and the next she was gone, claimed by the same sea that had taken Kipp. In that instant, the storm itself became an afterthought.

He turned sharply, voice cutting through the confusion and panic with a fury that made even the wind seem quieter.

"Get a line overboard–NOW!"

The crew obeyed in a scramble, soaked and breathless, their movements frantic on the slick deck. Ropes were pulled, knots tied, hands reaching for anything that might anchor them against the pull of the storm. Every second stretched too long, the space where she had vanished growing wider with each beat of silence.

Because if they didn't move fast–if they didn't find her–there would be no one left to pull from the deep.

The ocean was no longer a place. It had become a force, cold, crushing and merciless. It did not pause. It did not relent. It simply took. Salt scorched her eyes and mouth, filled her lungs with fire and silt. Pressure wrapped around her ribs and limbs like iron bands, dragging her deeper into a world where direction no longer existed, only weight and silence.

She kicked upward without thinking, but the cold locked her joints, turning motion into struggle. Her coat clung like lead to her frame, boots pulling her down with every stroke. Panic surged through her like a second drowning.

One arm clutched Kipp to her, the other clawed through the water with a desperate rhythm. Each kick burned, every movement a war against the cold, the drag, the sheer force of the sea. Her limbs began to tremble. Her coat dragged like chains around her shoulders, her boots pulled against her every stroke. The surface remained hidden. There was only darkness above, below, and within.

Still, she rose.

Not fast enough. Not strong enough. A sudden surge struck from beneath, a wall of water lurching with the weight of a mountain. It caught them and dragged them both under, twisting her sideways and down. The current flipped her, disoriented her, crushed the last of her breath until her vision narrowed and the darkness pulsed at the edges of her mind. Kipp slipped in her grip, and her heart lurched violently as her arms failed to hold him. She caught him again by the coat, tighter this time, nails biting through soaked fabric, body trembling from the strain.

And she knew, in that moment, she was losing. The strength was going. Her lungs had already passed the point of pain—now they simply burned. Her vision was faltering, her body folding beneath the weight of water and exhaustion. The ocean would not release them.

Not unless something changed.

And so, as her limbs threatened to give, Kalithea stopped reaching outward and reached inward instead. To the place she rarely touched, the thing she had tried for so long to keep dormant, the space where the shadows lived. Her mind clung to one final, unshakable truth: *I will not lose him.* And from within that certainty, something ancient stirred.

It began as a flicker. A single, pulsing warmth through her chest. It sparked once, then again, tracing down her spine like fire through frozen veins. She couldn't see it. She couldn't breathe. But she felt it, unmistakable and alive.

What moved through her was not the shadows though. It was something else entirely, it was *life.* The cold began to falter. Inch by inch, the crushing darkness pulled back. The golden current spread through her limbs, down to her fingertips, burning through the sea's grip.

The next pulse was not a flicker—it was a surge. The water around her lit from within, splitting apart as heat flared outward in a halo of gold. Orbs of light shimmered free, rising through the water like stars drifting toward a distant sky. Her hair floated behind her in ribbons of light. Her eyes snapped open against the sting of salt and current, and for the first time since diving in, she saw him clearly.

Kipp—still, pale, unmoving. She reached again, both arms gathering him close.

The light answered.

It moved through her like a second heartbeat—deep, thunderous, not entirely her own—radiating outward. The sea gave way. The current faltered. The weight lifted and the ocean itself bent.

Then, without warning, *everything exploded.*

Light detonated around them, exploding through the deep with a force that tore through the water in a column of gold and heat, flinging Kalithea and Kipp upward in a burst of golden brilliance. The sea split in their wake, a blast of energy hurling them toward the surface, a falling star in reverse.

Lightning shattered the clouds above. Wind screamed across the waves. The storm reeled from what it could not comprehend.

The sea did not reclaim them.

It released them.

They rocketed into the sky aiming towards the ship, the ocean parting beneath, the storm scattering from the light that exploded around her. Kalithea's body struck the deck of the Tempest with a bone cracking force, her arms staying locked around Kipp.

The wind still screamed across the deck. Rain tore through the air in sweeping arcs, and thunder cracked overhead with the force of a sky breaking apart. But amidst all of it, the men stood frozen, every pair of eyes fixed on the two figures lying at the center of the storm. Kalithea hadn't moved. Her body was curled on her side, soaked through, skin pale, lashes clumped together with salt and rain. Her hair clung to the deck like ink spilled across wood. The fall had left her limp, bruised, and unconscious.

Beside her, Kipp lay coughing violently, water gushing from his lungs as his body fought to reclaim breath. His chest jerked with each heave, every breath wrenched up from the depths. He rolled to his side, muscles twitching, mouth open, gasping as though the sea still held part of him. His fingers clawed against the slick planks, searching for something solid.

He was alive. And that alone should have been enough to break the spell that had settled across the deck. But no one moved. The crew wasn't watching him. Their eyes had locked on her. A faint shimmer pulsed beneath Kalithea's skin—subtle, steady, golden. It clung to her fingers, shimmered across the hollow of her throat, the light still pulsing like a dying star.

Jaymes stood at the edge of it, rain streaming down his face, his coat soaked through and clinging to him. He didn't speak. His hands hung loose at his sides, jaw set, eyes locked on her with a look that had nothing of command in it. He wasn't a captain in that moment. He wasn't anything but a man standing at the edge of something he did not understand.

The glow faded slowly, each pulse weaker than the last.

And then the stillness broke.

"BACK TO YOUR POSTS!" Jaymes' voice cracked across the deck like a cannon blast, tearing through the stunned silence with sheer force of will.

The trance shattered. Men lurched into motion. Ropes were seized.

Orders shouted. The Tempest groaned under the strain of the waves, but the crew moved now, driven by muscle memory and instinct, shaken but not paralyzed.

"We're not clear yet!" Jaymes barked as he turned, eyes already searching. His gaze snapped to Dorian, who still stood frozen, staring at Kalithea as though she were something conjured out of ancient myth.

"Dorian!" Jaymes snapped, his voice a raw command. "Get Harlow to his quarters. *Now.*"

It took a moment before Dorian responded, but then he moved, hauling Kipp to his feet with both arms. The thief sagged against him, too weak to resist, too dazed to understand. His boots dragged across the deck as they vanished below.

Jaymes didn't follow them. He dropped to one knee beside Kalithea, water splashing up around his boots as the rain continued to fall. She was cold to the touch. Her body hung limp as he gathered her into his arms, her weight too slight, her chest too still. That faint light still lingered beneath her surface, barely visible now, like warmth trapped behind glass.

He didn't stop to consider the miracle. Not now. Not yet. He turned and stormed below deck, his boots pounding down the steps. He shoved the door to her quarters open with his shoulder and kicked it shut behind him.

The wind screamed through the wood. The ship pitched violently. But inside, there was only the sound of his breath, his heartbeat, and the steady, terrifying silence of hers.

He lowered her to the bed with care, the motion automatic. Dropping to his knees beside the frame, he ignored the water soaking through his clothes, ignored the sting of salt in his eyes. Her lips were nearly colorless. Her breathing came in irregular gasps, shallow and too far apart.

Jaymes cursed under his breath and went to work. Her boots first, pulled off with urgency. Her coat, heavy and waterlogged, peeled away. He worked quickly, stripping the sodden layers from her one by one until only the thinnest shift remained. His hands paused, hovering for half a second. If she woke now and saw that he had crossed that line, she'd gut him and he'd deserve it.

Instead, he reached for every blanket in sight–tugging them from shelves, from spare trunks, from the foot of the bed. He wrapped her tightly, layer after layer, until she was encased in warmth and wool, her hair damp against the pillow.

His hands hovered over her face, feeling her breath.

Jaymes sat back, his shoulders heaving, his chest tight. The storm beyond the walls was nothing compared to the one rising inside him.

"You don't get to vanish after that," he muttered, voice rough, eyes locked on her closed ones. "You hear me, love?"

No answer. Just the quiet sound of her staggered breathing. Barely there. He scrubbed a hand through his soaked hair and leaned forward, elbows on his knees, fingers laced.

"You owe me an explanation," he said, voice quieter now. "And if you think I'm letting you escape just to avoid it–"

The door creaked open.

Jaymes didn't turn.

Kipp stepped inside, his silhouette framed in the dim light. One hand braced against the doorframe, the other clutched his ribs. His voice was low and scraped raw. "Still breathing?"

Jaymes nodded once. "Barely."

Kipp crossed the room and lowered himself to the floor opposite the bed, movements stiff, every breath still a struggle. His eyes went to her at once, unmoving and wrapped in shadow, the glow that had surrounded her now gone but not forgotten.

He said nothing for a long time. Neither of them did.

And then, finally–"So."

Jaymes let out a long breath. "So."

"She was glowing," Kipp murmured.

Jaymes let out a slow breath. "No shit."

The words weren't sharp, just honest.

Kipp's lips twitched, but whatever humor lingered there didn't last. He watched her with a kind of quiet pause rarely seen in him.

"That's not normal," he said quietly.

Jaymes nodded once. "No. It's not."

Their gazes returned to her. She looked smaller somehow beneath the layers of blankets, not weak, but different. Like the power that had poured from her hadn't just shielded her but changed her.

"She saved me," Kipp said, the words cutting through the silence. "She dove into that storm. Into the abyss."

"I know."

Kipp's jaw flexed. He rubbed a hand across his face.

Jaymes exhaled. "She's a mite bit more than we thought."

"More?" Kipp gave a hoarse laugh. "She tossed the sea aside."

He leaned back against the wall, closed his eyes for a moment, then opened them again–focused, sharp.

"I think," he said quietly, "she's just getting started."

The storm outside had begun to drift into memory.

The ship still swayed beneath its aftermath, the sails groaning against the last bites of wind, and the distant thunder growled as it receded across the sea. But here, inside Kalithea's cabin, the true storm hadn't passed.

She lay unmoving, her form still wrapped beneath the weight of thick blankets, the soft glow that had once lit her skin now gone. Her breathing had evened, shallow but steady, and her body no longer trembled with cold. Still, neither Jaymes nor Kipp had left her side.

Jaymes turned his head slightly, blue eyes catching what little light the lantern offered. "Did you know?"

Kipp exhaled slowly, dragging a hand down his face as though trying to clear the disbelief from it. "Not even a whisper," he muttered, voice laced with dry incredulity. "Not a flicker, not a slip. And I'm good at spotting those."

Jaymes didn't disagree. If *the* Kipp Harlow had missed it, then Kalithea had kept it buried deep.

"Then the question isn't what she is," he said after a moment. "It's whether she knows it."

Because what they had seen wasn't ordinary. That wasn't a trick of light or luck. It was power—unrestrained, undeniable, and ancient in a way that made even the ocean pause. Magic. One that hadn't been seen in the world outside of myths and legends, if even then.

Jaymes leaned his head back, listening to the soft patter of water outside. "The crew won't forget."

Kipp snorted. "You think?"

"They saw the glow. Saw her bring you back like the sea had no say in it." His eyes closed briefly. "They'll talk."

"Sailors always talk." Kipp sighed.

"Exactly. And this? This isn't the kind of thing you keep contained."

They sat with that for a moment, both men thinking ahead, feeling the weight of inevitability settling over the ship like fog on the tide.

"She'll have to address it," Jaymes said finally.

"Or," Kipp offered, tone lighter but not quite his usual charm, "she could just stare everyone into silence until they pretend it didn't happen."

Jaymes gave a short, humorless laugh. "Might even work. For a little while."

But they both knew that wasn't her style. Not really. Kalithea didn't explain herself. She didn't bend. But now? Now the ship, the crew, this little world they had built would demand answers.

Jaymes' eyes found her again, tracing the curve of her brow, the tension still faint around her mouth even in sleep. Then, without looking at Kipp: "You know...she didn't hesitate."

Kipp blinked. "What?"

"When you went over," he said, voice low and even. "She didn't think. Didn't weigh the odds. Didn't pause."

He shrugged, folding his arms across his chest, the movement loose but thoughtful.

"She just jumped in right after you. No hesitation."

The words settled between them, soft, but impossible to ignore.

Kipp looked at her then. Really looked. For once, he wasn't smirking. He just watched her—lips parted slightly, eyes darker than usual. Something inside him pulled taut.

After a long moment, Kipp let out a slow, uneven breath.

"Gods," he muttered, "I don't even know what to do with that."

Jaymes let his head fall back against the bulkhead, smiling faintly to himself. "Yeah," he said under his breath. "Me neither. Almost like she *does* care."

And still Kalithea did not stir. Something had shifted, not just in her. Not just in the power that had flared and faded like the birth of a star. But in them. In the way they looked at her now. In the way they sat in that quiet room, waiting. Because when she woke, and she would, they all knew this wouldn't be the same world they'd sailed into.

Of Monsters and Men

The world returned in fragments.

Warmth came first, not the bite of fever or the dizzying heat of sun, but something steady. A layered weight pressed in from all sides, wool and cotton swaddling her limbs, anchoring her to the narrow bed. Her breath came slow, unsteady, drawn through lungs that had only just remembered how to work.

Then came the voices. Low, close. One clipped and calm. The other touched with the kind of ease that didn't quite ring true.

Her lashes trembled as she fought through the haze. Her lungs dragged in air, slow and uneven. The memory lurked just beneath the surface–churning water, the roar of wind, the weight of a body in her arms.

The storm. The sea.

Kipp.

Her lips parted around his name, the sound barely audible, shaped by instinct rather than speech. "Kipp..."

Then her body jerked. Kalithea gasped, and she bolted upright, hands clutching the blanket. Her gaze swept the small space, sharp and disoriented, mind catching up with everything her body already knew. Her limbs ached. A line of bruises burned along her ribs. Her skin still carried the sting of salt. And yet she was here, alive.

Jaymes stood against the far wall, arms folded. Kipp sat on the floor beside the bed, knees bent, elbows resting loosely atop them. His eyes followed her with intensity.

Neither moved.

"You're safe," Jaymes said. His voice was low, composed, offering steadiness rather than comfort.

Safe.

The word echoed oddly in her chest, foreign in a mouth that had never been allowed to speak it without consequence. Her breathing slowed as she reasserted control. Bit by bit, she gathered herself, pulled the sharp edges of her composure back into place. Her fingers released their grip on the blanket, her back straightening.

"What happened?"

They hesitated. It was barely a moment, but she caught it.

Her gaze narrowed as she tilted her head slightly, her tone more clipped now, "Who pulled us from the water?"

Kipp shifted, rolling one shoulder with a casualness that fooled neither of them. "Well..." he said, drawing out the word, "that depends how you define 'pulled.'"

She didn't speak, staring at him.

"*Technically*," he added, "that was you."

The words didn't make sense. Her memories ended in the dark—beneath the waves, her lungs screaming, her arms wrapped around him as the sea tried to drag them both under. She remembered the cold. The weight. The moment she thought they'd both been lost.

But not the rescue.

Her brows drew together. Her voice came quieter this time, almost careful. "I don't remember...I don't see how I could've..."

Jaymes shifted his stance slightly, but his arms remained crossed, his gaze fixed on her as if waiting to see whether she'd reach the conclusion herself. Kipp, for once, wasn't smiling. He studied her in a way that made her skin itch, scrutinizing, almost curious.

"That's the part we find interesting," he said, voice quiet but firm. "Because we do remember. *Every damn second.*"

Her body tensed, every muscle drawing taut beneath the blankets. Her breath came slower now, more cautious. She watched them both—Jaymes steady as stone, Kipp sharp-eyed and silent—and understood, with cold clarity, that whatever had happened below the surface...whatever force had carried them back...

She wasn't going to like it.

The silence held like a vise. It pressed in from all sides, thick and close. Kalithea sat frozen beneath the weight of their stares, the warmth of wool layered over her limbs doing nothing to soften the chill creeping up her spine. The air felt too still. Her skin felt wrong.

There were pieces missing.

She remembered the cold. The sensation of her body straining against the current, lungs buckling beneath the pressure. She remembered Kipp slipping from her grasp, her arms tightening around his coat as everything tried to rip them apart. Darkness had swallowed them both. Then...nothing.

Jaymes was the one who broke the silence. "You were drowning, Kal. You weren't coming back up, either of you." He paused, gravity weighing his voice. "You and Kipp went under. A wave hit, and you were just... gone."

His stormy eyes stayed locked on her, steady and sharp, reading every twitch of her expression.

"And then..." He exhaled, a muscle in his jaw ticking as he searched for how to explain the impossible. "Then the ocean *erupted*. Like it had been split open from the inside. You didn't swim. You didn't fight your way back. You came flying out of the sea like something had thrown you–like the drowned gods themselves had decided to spit you out."

Kalithea's breath caught, her spine locking rigidly upright. Her grip on the blanket grew white-knuckled.

Kipp's voice followed, tight and hesitant, like he was speaking through something that still didn't make sense in his own mind.

"You were glowing, love."

Her eyes snapped to him.

He wasn't smiling.

"We hit the deck like a comet, felt like that light was forcing the water out of me" he continued, slowly leaning forward. "I thought I was hallucinating, until the entire crew froze. Even the storm seemed to hold its breath."

Kipp tilted his head, his voice softening without losing its trademark bite. "You came out of that water like a lightning strike. You hit the deck with me in your arms, and that light, whatever it was, it forced the sea out of my lungs. And for a few long minutes, you just lay there. Wrapped in light. Gold, soft, humming beneath your skin. Like something out of a story that shouldn't be real."

Jaymes' gaze remained fixed on her, unwavering, his silence carrying as much weight as any words.

"But it *was* real," Kipp said, his tone losing any pretense of humor now. "We both saw it. Every last piece of it."

The walls of the room blurred at the edges, the glow of the lantern warping. Her pulse thundered in her ears. The air was too thin. Her breath came too slow. She wanted to deny it, to spin the truth into something manageable. Something smaller. But there was no use. They had seen the one thing she had sworn would never surface again.

The panic clawed up her throat like a tide, desperate to pull her under. Her mind raced ahead to what it would mean. How they would look at her now. Not as Kalithea. Not as a woman or a warrior. Not even as a queen.

But as something unknown. Something strange.

Something dangerous. A weapon. *The* weapon. Chaos and carnage. Wicked and dark.

The piece of her she had tried to bury the night she and Liam escaped with blood on their hands and fire at their backs. Something she had hid so deeply she thought it would never resurface. But it had. It was back–dragged up from the depths without her consent, glowing like some twisted monstrosity disguised as a miracle, staring them in the face.

She didn't understand what they meant about the light. About the glow. She hadn't seen it, but she knew her power. And she knew what it could do. It had made her a monster once–had turned her into something unrecognizable, something capable of terrible, horrifying things. Things that still echoed in her nightmares. Things she had sworn never to unleash again.

But now they'd seen a glimpse.

She wasn't in the room anymore. Not with them. Not even in her skin. She was plummeting–no floor, no light, no end. A long, cold spiral into the pit that had always waited beneath her thoughts. The ship, the sea, the wind, they were nothing now. Stripped away. Forgotten.

There was only the dark. Only the voice. It didn't shout, it never needed to. It whispered like breath behind her ear.

They don't see you. They never did. You are not a woman, but an altar carved in flesh–something to bleed from, something to be fed to the dark.

A flicker of breath caught in her throat. Her body stayed still, her eyes glassy, staring at a place far beyond the world of men.

You are a thing. A beautiful, dangerous thing. Something men cage, then worship. Then break. A weapon with a heartbeat.

Her fingers curled, slow and cold.

Not someone to love. Just a hollow thing shaped for hunger. Made to carry ruin and grief, a vessel–polished on the outside, rotting underneath, designed to make destruction look divine.

Something black bloomed inside her. Not rage or grief, but the truth and it was waiting for her. Hungry. Patient. Ready to welcome her home.

The air around her shifted. The lantern flames guttered low, casting long fingers of shadow that began to curl along the edges of the room. Not drifting. Reaching.

Kipp was the first to react. His posture stiffened, the grin he'd half-pieced back onto his face vanishing in an instant.

"Uh..." he said, watching the shadows slither unnaturally along the wall, stretching toward them. "Jaymes..."

But Jaymes had already moved, stepping away from the door, gaze sweeping the cabin with the instincts of a man who'd survived far too many storms.

But this wasn't a storm, this was *her*.

His gaze cut back to Kalithea, seated upright, eyes wide and unblinking, her skin slick with sweat but glowing faintly beneath the lantern light. Awake, but not present. Breathing, but not conscious.

"Kalithea," he snapped, voice sharp with command. "Talk to me. *Now.*"

No response. She didn't blink. Didn't stir. Didn't even seem to hear him.

Kipp stood fast, backing away from the encroaching dark.

"Come on, darling," he said, voice too light to be calm, "I enjoy a dramatic pause as much as the next rogue, but I draw the line at being eaten by our own shadows mid-monologue. Blink. Breathe. *Something.*"

Jaymes swore, low and sharp. The air tasted strange now. Charged. The shadows pulsed again, tendrils writhing across the walls like they had a will of their own.

"Kalithea," Jaymes barked again, stepping toward her. "Look at me. Now."

Nothing. No blink. No flicker. No sign she'd heard.

The shadows writhed again—long, thin tendrils stretching from the corners, inching toward the bed. They weren't tricks of the light, they were moving.

Kipp felt the chill slide down his spine. This was power, a different kind of power than what he felt on her before. Raw and spiraling.

Jaymes clenched his fists, searching for an anchor. "She's not here."

"No shit!" Kipp snapped, then dropped to one knee beside her without hesitation. His hands gripped her shoulders and shook her firmly. "*Kal,*" he said, voice tight. "*Come on. Snap out of it!*"

Still nothing. Her breathing was thin and uneven, chest barely rising. Her skin felt like ice beneath his fingers. Panic scraped something primal and reckless loose inside him. And then—without pause or permission—he reached up, cupped her face, and kissed her.

It wasn't soft and it wasn't gentle. It was a crash of salt and desperation, half a prayer and half a dare. A desperate attempt to force her back into her body, to remind her what it meant to be *here.*

And it worked.

Because the moment their lips broke apart—

CRACK.

Her palm met his cheek with a ferocity that echoed through the cabin.

Kipp's head jerked sideways. Jaymes winced, rubbing the bridge of his nose.

"Gods," Jaymes closed his eyes with a groan, one hand dragging down his face. "Could've warned a man,"

Kipp turned back slowly, a red mark already rising along his jaw. His grin returned with infuriating ease, equal parts bruised and victorious.

"There she is," he said, rubbing his cheek. "Welcome back, little fox."

Kalithea was breathing hard now, her eyes blazing, every line of her body rigid and crackling with fury. Her eyes, lit now from within by something alive, locked onto Kipp.

"You," she said, low and venomous, "are an *insufferable* bastard."

Kipp gave a low chuckle, still holding her gaze. "Well, if being a bastard has that effect on you, I might start making bastardry a daily ritual, at least twice before breakfast."

Jaymes groaned, shaking his head with a deep sigh. "This is what we've come to?" he muttered. "Kissing and slapping our way to rescue? Gods help me and now bastardry is an actual plan."

Kalithea exhaled, slow and steady, dragging her fingers across her temples. The lanterns no longer flickered. The shadows had retreated to the corners of the room, docile now, as though they hadn't been clawing at the walls moments before.

But she had seen them. Felt them. And she knew what it meant. Her breath caught in her chest for a single beat, then she forced it down, pressed it beneath the weight of discipline honed over years. She was back in her body. Awake. Aware. But control still eluded her, a half-step out of reach.

Damn it all. She needed to get to Arjun, and *fast*.

Her shoulders sank back against the headboard, not from comfort but from the weight of knowing what came next. The questions. The scrutiny. She had no clever evasion prepared, no misdirection to wield. And she knew them well enough to know they wouldn't be deterred by silence.

Across the room, Kipp leaned back in his chair, still massaging his jaw where her slap had landed. The smirk playing at his lips was entirely too pleased for a man who'd nearly drowned, kissed someone back to life, and been struck hard enough to see stars–all within the same day.

"Well," he drawled, voice light but eyes too focused, "are we going to talk about it, or are you just planning to glare at me until I forget that I was just shy of dead before you just launched the two of us back onto a ship in a golden explosion and summoned a pack of shadows that looked like they were gearing up for a group strangling?"

From the corner, Jaymes let out a short snort, arms crossed, shoulder braced against the wall. The firelight caught in his eyes, turning his expression sharper.

"Considering she nearly slapped your face off," he said, his tone lazy but laced with warning, "I'd tread carefully."

Kipp scoffed. "Please. If Kal wanted me dead, I'd already be ash and memory."

Jaymes gave a slow nod, shrugging. "He's not wrong."

Kalithea dropped her hand from her face and leveled a look at both of them. Her voice came flat "I hate both of you."

Kipp flashed a grin that was all charm and no remorse. "Tragic, really. Because I have a sneaking suspicion we're about to be your favorite people."

She narrowed her eyes. "Why."

Jaymes gestured toward her with a casual wave. "Because you owe us an explanation, and you know it."

Of course she did.

She had known this moment would come, she just hadn't expected it to arrive here, in a cabin stinking of seawater and lantern smoke, wrapped in blankets and bruises, across from two men who had no right to look at her the way they did now. Who, despite everything, she hadn't wanted to see this part of her.

And yet here they were.

Kipp stretched out his legs, as if casual relaxation could mask the edge beneath his voice. He hadn't looked away from her once.

"Let's start simple," he said, tone deceptively light. "What in all the old gods' names was that?"

Kalithea pressed her lips together, resisting the urge to lie.

Jaymes raised a brow, his voice dry. "Going to guess magic. A particularly dramatic variety."

Kipp snapped his fingers. "Yes, that's the word. *Magic*. As in the kind that flings two bodies out of the ocean like a cannonball. The kind that lights up your veins like you're the sun incarnate. That kind of magic. Because regular magic on its own is *SO* common."

Jaymes offered a lazy grin. "The rare, storm-defying, crew-terrifying sort."

Kalithea sighed, long and slow. "I should've let you drown."

Kipp clutched his chest in mock agony. "You wound me. But–" He leaned in, eyes gleaming. "You didn't. Which means somewhere under all that steel, you care."

Jaymes chuckled under his breath. "Or she just has poor taste."

Kipp nodded solemnly. "That *would* explain a lot, honestly."

She dragged a hand down her face. They weren't going to let this go. Not with jokes. Not with time. And not with silence.

Built from Ruin

Kalithea sat motionless, the weight of everything pressing down on her. Firelight danced across her features, casting flickers of gold and shadow that did nothing to warm the hollow settling in her chest.

They were still watching her. Jaymes and Kipp. Two men she should never have trusted with this. Two men who had already seen too much. And yet, the damage had been done. The moment had passed. There was no pulling it back.

Let them know, then. Let them take their knowledge and leave her like the rest of the world that turned away.

She drew in a breath and raised her gaze to meet theirs.

"Before anything else," she began, "there's something you both need to understand."

Jaymes tilted his head slightly. The fire caught faintly in his eyes. Kipp leaned forward a fraction, elbows on his knees. Still too quiet. Still too focused.

"I'm half-fae. Half-human. That much, I imagine, you both already knew."

Jaymes glanced toward Kipp, a slow flicker of amusement passing between them.

"Kipp did," he said.

Kipp gave a one-shoulder shrug, his grin lazy. "Oh, I knew. Would've been nice if you'd confirmed it before the whole 'ascension-by-light' moment, but sure."

Kalithea shot him a warning look, but he only widened his smile in reply.

Jaymes chuckled quietly, but when his gaze returned to her, the humor faded. "And?"

Kalithea turned her attention back to the candlelight, watching it shift and bend. "Being what I am," she said slowly, choosing each word with caution, "is supposed to come with... certain magics. Ones not always seen. Not always understood. But I'm..." She hesitated, then said simply, "Different."

She kept the explanation vague on purpose, hoping it might be enough.

It wasn't.

"*Different,*" Kipp repeated, drawing out the word, resting his elbows on his knees. "And what exactly does that mean, darling?"

Jaymes folded his arms across his chest, his tone light but edged. "If we're talking about the lightshow, that's one thing."

Kipp nodded, expression sharpening. "But I'm guessing that's not what you're afraid of us knowing."

Her stillness was answer enough.

Jaymes' voice lowered, his gaze narrowing. "It's not the light that scares you."

"It's the dark," Kipp finished quietly.

Kalithea clenched her jaw, eyes locked on the candle.

"Ah," Kipp murmured, leaning back like he'd just uncovered a buried coin. "There it is."

She shot him a glare, but Jaymes didn't look away. His stare was level, quiet.

"Tell us," he said, not a demand, not a threat. Just an invitation. One that couldn't be ignored.

Her eyes flicked between them and for the first time in years, she let the truth surface.

"There is a prophecy," she said quietly.

The air shifted.

Jaymes straightened, tension coiling through his frame. Kipp's smirk vanished entirely.

"They say the day I was born, the last of the gods fell..." she continued, her voice even but heavy, "and a prophecy was spoken. One that spoke of a great magic, the kind the world has never seen..." Her fingers gripped the blanket in her lap. "That magic is locked inside me."

Silence settled around them like a second skin.

Jaymes was the first to speak, his brow drawn in a rare flicker of uncertainty. "A great magic?"

Kipp exhaled low, glancing toward the floor. "Let me guess... not the cheerful ballad sung, 'bless the harvest' kind."

Kalithea gave a cold, hollow laugh. "No. Not even close."

She met their eyes again. There was no fear in her voice only exhaustion.

"According to the prophecy," she said slowly, "I will either save the world..."

Her voice faltered, just for a moment.

"...or I will end it."

The words echoed in their silence, and neither of them moved. Kipp's expression was unreadable now. Jaymes' gaze held hers.

Eventually, Jaymes leaned back, exhaling through his nose. "Well. That explains a few things."

Kipp let out a low breath. "A few?"

But his voice had no edge to it now. Only wariness.

Kalithea turned back to the candle flame.

"That's why my family was murdered," she said, her voice quieter. "Rhaen Morrick heard the prophecy. He knew a child had been born with power that couldn't be contained. And he wasn't about to wait and see which end I'd bring, or for who."

Jaymes' fists clenched slightly.

Kalithea's lips curled into something bitter. "He took me."

Her voice dropped lower.

"I believed he was my father. For years," she continued, "I believed it. I was raised in his court. I was taught to obey him, to revere him, fear him, *kill* for him. I didn't question it. Not until..."

She paused, just for a breath, but it was the first break in her composure. A fracture, small and sharp.

"...not until Arjun told me the truth."

That silence returned, heavier this time, weighed with something unspoken.

"Before Arjun," she said, steadier now, "I had no reason to doubt what I'd been told. I was the king's daughter. A princess. Groomed to serve his empire."

Her gaze flicked up again, cold and sharp.

"But I was never meant to rule let alone be free." She let the words land. "I was kept not as a successor, but as a weapon."

Jaymes shifted slightly, but didn't speak. Kipp's eyes were on her again now, watching with an intensity that didn't try to disguise itself.

"The prophecy wasn't about a throne. It was about power. Power enough to shape kingdoms...or bring them to ruin."

Her voice was steady now, as though she were reading from a decree already written.

"He knew that if he controlled me, he controlled that power. And so, from the night he butchered my family, from the moment he carried me out of the blood and ash, he began to forge me into something useful. Something obedient." Her hand trembled against the blanket, just once. "And that's exactly what he did."

A breathless, brittle sound escaped her lips. It might have been a laugh, but it held no mirth. Only something sharp and thin, too ragged to be anything but pain.

"Training," she said at last. "That's what he called it. Training to be strong. Untouchable. Invincible. To make *HIM* those things"

"But it wasn't training," she murmured, eyes fixed on the candle. "It was breaking."

Kipp's fingers curled into his palms, the sound of his breath sharpening in the silence. Jaymes, across from her, remained utterly still, though the muscle in his jaw had begun to tic with restrained fury.

Kalithea didn't look at either of them. She wasn't speaking to them, not really. She was speaking to ghosts.

"I was raised in blood," she said. "In pain. In death. *Ruin*. That is my world."

The words came flat, without embellishment, truth cut down to its most precise edge.

"He wanted me ruthless. Cold. Unyielding. A perfect extension of his will."

Her gaze narrowed slightly, lashes lowering as the next truth clawed its way up.

"And when I fought back..." Her voice dipped lower, but the edge was no less sharp. "When I resisted... he came for Liam."

She didn't need to explain. The silence that followed told her they understood enough. Kipp shifted beside her, but she still didn't look at him. She couldn't, she wouldn't finish if she did. Her eyes stayed locked on the flames, as if they held the only safe place left.

"He used me to win wars before they even began," she said, each word steadier than the last. "To crush rebellion before a blade could be drawn. I was his warning. His wrath. His proof that no one could touch him."

Her tone was hollow now, detached, as though she were reciting someone else's story. Someone else's ruin.

"I killed for him before I was old enough to know what death meant."

Jaymes exhaled slowly, the sound so even it was barely audible. But Kalithea knew he was listening. Every breath of it.

She continued.

"That wasn't enough for him. It never was. He wanted more. He wanted the fae gone–extinguished. The only creatures in this world with any kind of power, any type of magic. And with me under his control... with that power chained to his will..."

Her breath caught, just briefly. The fire flickered as if reacting to the words still caught in her throat.

"...he started a war, the purge, to eliminate them. To eliminate whatever magic was left in the world."

Her voice barely reached them now. But it carried.

"He made me do it," she whispered. "That was what I was for. Not a princess. Not an heir. Just a weapon. A tool. A means to erase, to destroy."

The words came slowly, heavy like lead. Each one dragged another piece of her past into the light.

"I was never meant to last. Once I had served my purpose, once the magic inside me was spent, he would've discarded me without hesitation."

The silence in the room thickened.

"He would have disposed of me," she said evenly, her eyes still locked on the fire. "After he was done using my body."

The shift was immediate, palpable.

Jaymes went perfectly still. His shoulders tensed, his arms crossed tighter–not to restrain himself, but because anything else would have risked breaking something. The firelight sharpened the line of his jaw, catching in his stormy blue eyes.

Kipp didn't move. His grin, the armor he wore as second skin, was gone. His hands remained clenched, knuckles white against his knees, the shadows beneath his eyes deepening.

She had seen rage before. But this–this wasn't the kind that boiled or roared, this was cold, calculated and deadly. She let them feel it. Let them sit with it. With her. Let them understand what had truly been taken from her without saying the words.

And then–finally–her voice broke the silence again, softer now, frayed at the edges.

"Arjun was the one who told me. The one who saw what I really was." She let the memory carry her for a breath. Let it settle. "He found me. Healed me. He risked everything to help me. To pull me out. He showed me the truth. Helped me escape."

At last, she looked up. She met their eyes.

"He's the reason I'm still breathing," Kalithea said, her voice steadier. "And that's why we have to find him."

She waited, let the sentence hang there, before adding–

"It's not only because he was the only one beside Liam to ever show me kindness. Not only because he helped me get out." Her eyes met theirs again, gaze unwavering. "It's because he's the only one who might know how to make sure the prophecy ends the right way."

She let the rest fall without hesitation.

"Because if it doesn't, if we can't stop what's inside me, then the world won't survive me."

The words were spoken now. Everything she had buried. What she was and what she carried. What waited at the edge of her control. And now... she waited. For the shift, the fear. For the moment they would decide she was too dangerous to keep close.

For the moment they turned away, like everyone else had before.

The silence that settled over the cabin was unlike anything Kalithea had ever known. She had lived through countless variations of quiet, the kind that dragged before pain, before blood, before ruin. She had endured the hush that followed cruelty, the breathless pause before blades found flesh, the dead calm of battlefields soaked in aftermath. But this wasn't that. This was the silence that came after truth. After baring what should never be named. The silence that weighed more than any blade she had ever carried. It was the moment between the revelation and the rejection, the moment she had learned to expect as reflex.

So she sat still. Spine held taut, hands knotted in her lap. Her face a mask carved from habit.

Jaymes moved first. A small shift, barely noticeable. His head tilted slightly, and he let out a slow breath through his nose. His gaze hadn't left her, not once since she began. And now it burned, not with fear or revulsion, but with something more dangerous. The fury beneath his composure vibrated like tension in a drawn bowstring.

Jaymes Blackwell was *furious.*

Kipp, by contrast, was motion itself barely held in check. He had sat stunned while she spoke, but the tension in him had reached a breaking point. Without warning, he surged to his feet, his hand shoved back through his hair, his steps uneven, charged. He stalked across the cabin in jagged lines, like a force searching for something to destroy.

"*Gods,*" he muttered, pacing, his voice low and strained. "Fucking gods."

All the usual bravado was gone. The swagger, the irreverent humor, vanished. What remained was raw and volatile. Bare. She watched him, tension winding tighter with every step. This was it. The turn. The retreat. The part where they realized what she was and decided he wanted no part of it. She had seen it before. She didn't let it wound her now.

Let them leave.

Kipp spun back around. His eyes locked on hers, and there was no humor in them. Just fury. Sharp. Righteous.

"Let me get this straight," he said, voice rough, barely restrained. "You were stolen. *Tortured.* Molded into a weapon."

He laughed once, short and sharp, a broken thing that didn't reach his eyes.

"And that bastard–" his jaw clenched, his voice dropped lower, almost strangled "–he planned to..."

He stopped. The words were a rot between them, festering in the silence.

Jaymes' voice came next, quieter, but with an edge that cut like a blade. "That man is still breathing?"

It wasn't a question, not really. It was disbelief wrapped in the barest thread of control.

Kalithea parted her lips to speak, but the words refused to come.

This wasn't the response she had braced for. There was no cold logic that declared her a risk too dangerous to keep close. No veiled caution. No fear. Only heat, directed not at her, but at him. At the monster who had made her.

Jaymes leaned forward, resting his chin on one hand, the other tapping rhythmically against his knee. The rhythm of calculation. His eyes were firelight and fury, razor sharp focus fixed on her.

"And how," he asked, voice low and smooth, "do you plan to fix that?"

She stared at him, caught in the space between disbelief and understanding.

They weren't shrinking back. They weren't circling her like a threat. They were bracing, ready to strike. Not at her, but for her. Because of her. Because someone had to answer for what had been done.

"This means," he went on, tilting his head slightly, "we have unfinished business."

Her hands clenched tighter around the blanket in her lap.

"You don't understand," she said, her voice lower than she meant it to be.

Jaymes lifted a brow, sharp and expectant. "Then enlighten me."

She hesitated, her gaze flickering between the two of them. Still waiting for the moment they realized what they were walking into. Still waiting for logic to reassert itself.

"Getting involved in this isn't bravery," she said, the words flat and cold. "It's suicide. He is not just a man. He is a tyrant sitting upon a throne built on slaughter, a kingdom at his back, with armies, spies, sorcery. The moment he knows you're with me...you won't survive it."

Jaymes held her stare for a beat longer, then shrugged, as if she'd told him rain would fall.

"Good thing I've never been particularly sentimental about my survival," he said.

Her breath caught. Not from what he said, but from how he said it. No challenge. No heroics. Just the truth.

Before she could speak, Kipp's laugh cracked the air—a rough, hollow sound that held none of its usual charm. He turned from her and paced to the far wall, dragging a hand over his face like he could scrub the disbelief out of his skin.

"*Gods, Kal,*" he said, voice rough, shoulders rigid. "You really don't get it, do you?"

She stared at him, too thrown to speak.

He spun back to face her, firelight catching the fury in his expression. "You think this is the part where we walk away?"

Still, she didn't answer. Because yes, of course that was what she thought.

Kipp stepped closer, his words hitting harder with every pace. "You've been waiting for us to leave since the second you opened your damn mouth."

He wasn't asking. He was naming a truth she didn't want to admit.

Kalithea kept her face composed, but inside, her pulse roared.

Kipp didn't stop. "How many times have people heard pieces of your truth and decided it was too much? Too dangerous? How many have looked you in the eye and turned their backs? How many chose safety over you? How many people have walked away from you?"

The questions hit like knives to the ribs. She didn't move. Didn't speak.

Kipp didn't stop. "How many times have you told yourself not to get attached because it always ends the same way?"

Her chest constricted, unbearably tight.

"You've already convinced yourself we're leaving," Kipp said, voice softer now, but no less cutting.

He paused, voice lowering to something sharper. Something quieter. "But we're still here."

And that, that was the part she didn't know how to process. She had built her life on solitude. On contingency. On the certainty that anyone who got too close would eventually become a liability, or a threat.

Jaymes shifted forward again, his voice calm but implacable.

"You said we don't understand," he murmured. "Then make us understand."

She turned her face toward the light. The flames moved restlessly, flickering gold and shadow across her skin.

"I don't need anyone fighting this battle for me," she said, the words brittle and rehearsed.

Jaymes gave a quiet, almost amused huff. "Good thing we're not asking permission."

Her eyes narrowed. "You'll regret this."

Jaymes' smirk returned, slow and unapologetic. "I've made worse decisions."

Kipp stepped closer, not smiling, not performing. His voice had dropped to something quiet, stripped down.

"Kal," he said, voice gentler than she'd ever heard it, stripped of arrogance, stripped of games. "You don't have to do this alone."

She sat rigid, bracing for the familiar sting of abandonment. The air between them was thick with tension.

"Gods, you *still* don't understand, do you?" Kipp muttered, pacing with sharp, uneven energy, his voice frayed with something raw. His tone wasn't teasing. It wasn't even angry. It was laced with disbelief, like she had missed something obvious and vital.

Kalithea's eyes narrowed, her tone clipped and even. "I understand plenty, Harlow."

He stopped and turned toward her, studying her like she was a riddle he couldn't quite solve. "Do you? Because you sure as hell don't act like it."

She clenched her jaw, willing her voice into that perfect composure. "I told you everything. What more do you want from me?"

Kipp let out a sharp breath, not quite a laugh, not quite a curse. He dragged a hand through his hair, his usual swagger gone. "The point, Kal," he said, his voice firmer now, each word deliberate, "is that you never have to go through that again. Not a second. Not ever."

Jaymes remained silent, a steady presence behind the heat of Kipp's words. His arms were crossed, his gaze trained on her. He let Kipp push, let him press where the cracks were forming, let him speak what they were both thinking.

Kipp stepped closer, tone dropping to something low, intimate. "Whatever happens next–whatever fight's waiting–it's not just yours anymore, its *ours*. That's what this is really about, isn't it?"

Kalithea's hands curled into fists in her lap. "You don't know what you're talking about."

But he did, and they both knew it.

"You don't know how to let anyone in," Kipp continued, voice even but not unkind. "You've fought so long on your own, you don't know what it feels like to have someone beside you."

She turned her face toward the candle, but didn't speak.

"No one's ever stayed, have they?" he asked, softly now. "Every time someone gets close, they look at what's underneath and decide it's too much."

Her throat tightened, but she didn't answer. Her silence was answer enough.

Kipp paused, then huffed out a breath, the ghost of a grin tugging at his mouth, though it didn't reach his eyes. "Well, sorry to disappoint, darling. I'm a stubborn bastard. So's he."

Jaymes gave a quiet exhale, one corner of his mouth lifting. "Speak for yourself, thief. I'm delightful."

Kipp pressed a hand to his chest, mock solemn. "Apologies, Captain. We are *delightfully* hard to get rid of."

Jaymes smirked faintly, but his eyes never left her.

Kalithea should have laughed. Should have rolled her eyes. Should have reminded them both that this wasn't a storybook and she wasn't someone to be rescued. But she didn't. Because something–something small, fragile, and terrifying–was breaking loose inside her. Before she could stop it, before she could slam the walls back into place–

A single tear slipped down her cheek.

Kipp froze, every trace of his grin vanishing. Jaymes remained seated, but his entire frame tensed, the sharp inhale through his nose the only sign of the storm beneath the surface.

They had seen her in command. They had seen her bite back impossible odds. But this, this was something else. This was her unarmored and it unraveled them both.

Kipp's hands twitched slightly at his sides, as if he didn't know what to do with them now that she wasn't pushing back. Jaymes didn't speak. He didn't move. But there was something in his gaze that had shifted, like he was watching a fault line crack beneath the weight of too much grief.

Kalithea turned her head sharply, the mask slamming back into place. Her jaw tightened, her eyes fixed on the far wall.

"Kal," Kipp said quietly.

No jokes. No charm. Just her name.

She didn't respond.

"You don't have to believe us yet," Jaymes said, his voice low, steady, unshakable. "But it doesn't change the truth."

She swallowed hard.

"We aren't leaving."

Kalithea closed her eyes, if only for a moment. She had seen what came of trust. She had seen what was left of people who believed in things they could not have.

But they were here, looking at her like she wasn't something broken, but something worth standing beside.

And she didn't know what to do with that.

DIVINE TROUBLE

Jaymes leaned back at last, exhaling a breath that cut through the tension like a knife. He raked a hand through his sea-damp hair, the flicker of candlelight casting his smirk in bronze and shadow.

"Well," he said, voice dry. "Now that we've established Kipp is a menace and I've apparently committed myself to eternal proximity..." He paused, tilting his head with mock gravity. "We should probably address the other storm."

Kalithea arched a brow. "Which one?"

Jaymes gestured upward vaguely. "The one that's gone suspiciously quiet."

She stilled. He was right. The usual shuffle and groan of shipboard life–the calls of the crew, the strike of boots across soaked planks, the muttered complaints about weathered rigging and torn sails–had gone silent. The only sound was the gentle sway of the hull and the muted hush of the sea beyond.

Kipp clicked his tongue, hands sliding to his hips. "At best, they're unnerved."

Jaymes' tone darkened with dry amusement. "At worst, they're sharpening their knives and composing hymns to whatever sea god they think you're in bed with."

Kipp's eyes glittered. "You say that like I wouldn't be the first to suggest it."

Jaymes turned a slow glance his way. "Because you would be."

Kalithea sighed, dragging her hand over her face. "Gods preserve me."

"See?" Kipp snapped his fingers. "She's halfway to pantheon status already."

Kalithea muttered a curse, the headache blooming fast behind her eyes.

But Jaymes sobered, the smile fading from his mouth as his voice lowered. "Jokes aside, we need to get ahead of this. Fast."

Kipp folded his arms, leaning against the wall. "The truth seems too dangerous. And, tragically, very boring."

Jaymes' expression sharpened. "Because telling a deck full of pirates that we have a half-fae queen capable of ripping the sea open with her bare hands would go over... *brilliantly.*"

"Pirates love chaos," Kipp said helpfully. "They just prefer it doesn't sleep three doors down."

Jaymes turned back to her, his tone cooler now, more precise. "Your call, Kal. What do we tell them? This ship, these men, they're yours to sway or lose. But whatever we do, we need to move fast."

Kalithea sat forward instead, rubbing her hands slowly together as her mind began turning. They were right. Superstition ruled sailors. Pirates thrived on stories, but feared what they couldn't understand. If panic took root, if the wrong tale began to spread, she wouldn't just be a curiosity–she'd become a threat. To them. To Jaymes. To Kipp.

She inhaled slowly, gaze distant. "We give them just enough of the truth to stop the questions. But not enough to give them a reason to fear me."

Kipp tilted his head. "Define '*just enough.*'"

"The storm was worse than expected," she said, voice settling into the calm cadence of strategy. "Kipp went overboard. So did I. What they saw when we came back–that flash, that light–it wasn't magic."

Jaymes' brow lifted, steely eyes narrowing slightly. "Go on."

Kalithea's tone was calm, even. The voice of someone who had long ago learned to spin truth into weaponry. "They saw the flare of a fae artifact. A one-use relic, something ancient, something that was gifted to me long ago for protection. A failsafe. It activated. It saved us."

Kipp raised a brow. "A rare object, tragically lost to the sea. How convenient."

She gave a faint, knowing smile. "Exactly."

Jaymes nodded once, his expression thoughtful. "It's clean. Believable. Leaves room for awe but not fear."

Kipp rubbed his jaw, then grinned. "And we all know pirates love rare, cursed artifacts almost as much as they fear them."

Kalithea arched a brow. "You two are remarkably comfortable with deceit."

Jaymes shrugged. "It's not a lie. It's diplomacy."

Kipp flashed his teeth. "It's survival."

"Then it has to come from me," she said. "If you deliver the story, it becomes hearsay. Rumor. Manipulation. If I tell them...it becomes law."

Jaymes exhaled slowly, nodding once. "We'll be with you. But yes. This has to be yours."

Kalithea rose, letting the blanket fall away, her shoulders squared with that quiet, commanding grace that made the air shift around her. She moved with intent, rising from the edge of the cot where she had sat coiled for too long, her spine straightening, her chin lifting. She was ready to face the storm above deck, to shape the narrative before it could shape her.

But the moment she stood, a chill swept over her skin, sharp and immediate–and not from the sea breeze that ghosted through the half-cracked window.

No. It was the fabric. Or rather, the lack of it.

She glanced down. The shift she wore was damp, nearly translucent in the firelight, clinging to every contour of her body in ways that left precious little to the imagination. It was thin, still soaked to the hem, and utterly devoid of modesty. Her entire silhouette was on display, long legs, curves. The suggestion of her breasts beneath the linen caught the flicker of the firelight, and for a beat too long, she went still.

So did the men.

Jaymes had been leaning against the table, casual and composed–but the moment she straightened, his gaze faltered. He recovered quickly, of course. Jaymes Blackwell always did. But not before the faintest twitch of his brow betrayed the flicker of heat behind his deep blue eyes.

Kipp, seated nearby, had stopped mid-grin, blinking once as his eyes tracked lower, then quickly back up again.

Then–of course–he smirked.

"Well," he said, his voice a touch too smooth, "if the goal was to solidify your image as a divine sea creature sent to tempt mortals into madness, mission accomplished."

Jaymes exhaled, his voice drier than the desert. "Gods above, Kal. You're going to have sailors carving new figureheads in your honor by nightfall."

Kalithea arched a brow, entirely unamused. "You both had ample opportunity to leave the room."

Kipp leaned back, folding his arms behind his head with exaggerated ease, though his ears were still flushed red. "And miss the moment you ascend from storm-tossed goddess to wet dream of the deep? Unthinkable."

Jaymes laughed once, poorly disguised as clearing his throat, and gave her a wry smile. "Might want to consider putting on something that doesn't scream 'immortal temptation.' The men upstairs already think you parted the sea. If they see you like this, they'll assume they've all drowned and been rewarded with a vision of the afterlife."

Kalithea sighed through her nose, turning just slightly toward the wardrobe, pretending she didn't hear the way Kipp muttered something that sounded suspiciously like, "Wouldn't mind dying if that's the view."

She paused halfway to the chest of drawers, glancing over her shoulder, eyes cool and precise. "You do realize I'm the reason you are breathing."

Kipp didn't miss a beat. "And I promise to honor your mercy by picturing this exact moment until the day I die."

Jaymes chuckled, low and dangerous, but his gaze sobered slightly as it met hers again. "We'll wait outside."

Kalithea nodded once, satisfied. "Good. And if either of you so much as look back, I'll make you regret it."

Kipp held up his hands in mock surrender. "I'm wounded by your lack of trust."

"*Out.*" she said, sharply.

The door closed behind them with a quiet thud.

And Kalithea, alone now, let out a long breath as she turned toward the chest and pulled it open. A worn tunic. Sturdy breeches. A belt with a knife , nothing regal or radiant.

She had a ship to command, and a story to control.

The moment Kalithea stepped onto the deck, she felt it—tension, palpable and sharp, threading through the salt-streaked air. It lingered in every sideways glance cast her way. No one spoke. No one shouted. The usual din of ship life had quieted to a strained hush, broken only by the creak of wood and the distant wash of waves.

Clusters of crewmen stood in loose formations. Some adjusted ropes that didn't need tending. Others leaned against barrels or railings, their hands idle, eyes fixed just off her shoulder. They watched her with the wary silence of men who had seen something they could not name and didn't yet know whether to fear or follow it.

She walked calmly, every step steady, her posture easy but unshakable—like she hadn't just defied death, like she hadn't shattered their sense of reality with golden light and impossible magic.

Jaymes and Kipp followed behind her, not flanking, but near enough to make a statement. Allies. Witnesses. Anchors.

Kalithea stopped at the heart of the deck and turned. Her hands folded behind her back. Her posture was relaxed, her gaze unwavering.

"I imagine you all have questions," she began, her voice clear enough to reach every man within earshot.

A few men shifted. A murmur passed through the deck like a breeze caught beneath a sail. No one interrupted.

"And so," she continued, her gaze steady, "I'll give you the truth.

The storm was worse than expected. Kipp went overboard. So did I."

A murmur stirred, faint and uncertain. That much was familiar. It anchored them. It made what followed easier to swallow.

She took a step forward. "I carry a fae artifact. It was given to me long ago, a failsafe. A one-use safeguard. Something meant to protect me if my life was ever in true danger. It did what it was meant to do."

Murmurs. Curiosity was giving way to caution.

"That kind of magic," she added, "burns bright. That's what you saw. That was the artifact activating. A burst. A shield. Nothing more."

Gasps this time. Someone cursed under his breath. Another made a warding gesture against sorcery. The fear hadn't broken but it had shifted.

"I did what anyone else would have done with a weapon meant to save their life."

Dorian stepped forward from the crew, arms crossed over his chest. His jaw was set, his eyes sharp, not hostile, but not easy.

"Then why did it look like you dragged Harlow from the depths like a damned sea goddess?"

The faintest smile touched her lips. It didn't reach her eyes.

"I imagine it made for quite the story," she replied, tone dry. "Storm roaring. Lightning striking. A little magic flaring. People see what they expect to see in chaos."

A few chuckles stirred. Uneasy, but real.

She tilted her head, shrugging. "The fae have always had a flair for dramatics. Their relics don't usually whisper, they roar."

Laughter rippled this time, low and nervous, but laughter nonetheless. One of the younger deckhands muttered something about "bloody fae trinkets," and a few older crewmen grunted their agreement.

The weight on the deck began to shift, pressure bleeding into motion. Shoulders loosened. Hands dropped from blades. Suspicion didn't vanish but it dimmed, enough to hold.

Jaymes stepped forward then, smooth and confident.

"Back to work," he said, his voice laced with lazy authority. "And if I hear a single word about sea witches, relics, or divine manifestations, I'll assume you're all after poetry careers instead of honest piracy."

That broke what remained. The men snorted, some grinning outright as they scattered back to their tasks—tying lines, checking the rigging, returning to the steady rhythm of a ship that had just survived something greater than a storm.

She turned, exhaling softly.

Jaymes joined her at the rail, hands tucked into his coat, his voice low and amused. "Well," he drawled, "if we're scoring lies told under duress, that one was remarkably effective."

She gave him a sidelong glance. "You sound surprised."

He grinned. "Not surprised. Just reminded."

"Reminded of what?"

"That you're better at this than I am." He paused, then added, "And I lie for a living."

Behind them, Kipp appeared, arms crossed, a lazy smirk on his face that didn't quite hide the gleam in his eyes.

"You know," he said casually, "we missed an opportunity."

Kalithea's brow arched. "Here we go."

Kipp's grin widened. "You should have let them think you were a goddess."

Jaymes snorted, looking off toward the rigging. "He's not wrong. You practically floated back to the deck in a halo of light. I think one of the men started praying."

Kalithea rolled her eyes. "Spare me."

Kipp shrugged with theatrical flair. "We could've had shrines by sunrise. Offerings. Songs. Dorian probably would've offered his first-born."

Kalithea leveled him with a look. "I'm not interested in worship."

Kipp's grin faded, just slightly. His tone softened.

"Yeah," he said quietly, "we know."

Three Nights Down

The deeper they sailed into Old Kingdom waters, the more Kalithea withdrew. Not in ways the crew would name. She still walked the deck with grace, answered questions in measured tones, and nodded with that cool civility that made her seem unshakable.

But Jaymes and Kipp saw the difference, they felt it in every silence.

They heard it in the clipped answers, the quiet where dry wit used to slip in. They noticed the way she avoided every attempt to draw her out–Kipp's wry barbs or exaggerated sighs, Jaymes' quieter remarks to tempt her with dry amusement–like she was no longer willing to be seen. She hadn't grown colder. She'd grown quieter. Sharper.

The shift was subtle. Calculated. Masterfully controlled. But they weren't fools. They had both lived lives built on watching people lie through their teeth–Jaymes on open water, where trust could be your noose, and Kipp in alleys and palaces alike, where every smile was a loaded trap.

And Kalithea was slipping. Not in skill or in poise. In spirit. She was pulling back into herself, vanishing behind that armor she wore so well.

"She's doing it again," Kipp muttered, low and grim, his voice barely audible above the steady groan of the sails.

Jaymes didn't glance away from the horizon. His hands rested calmly on the helm, steady as the tide. "Doing what?"

Kipp made a rough sound in his throat and gestured toward the bow, where Kalithea stood alone, her figure outlined by the grey light. Rigid. Perfectly still.

"That," Kipp said, a bite in his voice. "The ice queen routine. Shutting down. Cutting us out."

Jaymes adjusted the wheel slightly. "And what would you have me do, Harlow? Order her to be warm?"

Kipp let out a frustrated breath, running a hand through his dark hair, the motion sharp with restrained energy. "She was opening up. We had her, just for a moment, and now she's back to staring off like she's already preparing her own damn eulogy."

"She *is* preparing," Jaymes said quietly.

Kipp turned toward him, eyes narrowing. "For what?"

Jaymes finally looked at him, the wind pulling through his coat, stormy eyes catching the light. "For whatever hell she came from."

They both looked toward her. Kalithea stood motionless, wind tugging at the ends of her coat. Her hands rested on the rail, fingers curled too tight. She wasn't just anticipating danger. She was bracing for it. Counting down to it. And worse...she was doing it alone.

Kipp's jaw tightened. "She'll crack eventually," he muttered, though there was less conviction in it than usual. "She always does."

Jaymes' gaze returned to the sea, that endless, shifting expanse he knew better than most men ever would.

"She's not like the others," he said at last, voice low and thoughtful. "Not like the soldiers who cry discipline and grit their teeth. Not like the nobles who think pain is something that can be polished into poetry."

Kipp said nothing.

"She built herself to survive," Jaymes continued. "She's still testing the air around us. Still watching. Waiting to see how long we last."

Kipp's fingers drummed restlessly on the railing. "And if she decides we won't?"

"Then she closes the door," Jaymes said. "For good."

The thought tasted like ash. But it was the truth.

Jaymes had known many who fancied themselves unbreakable. But Kalithea wasn't posturing. Her silence wasn't pride, it was survival, worn deep into her bones.

"She's going to need us soon," Jaymes murmured, barely above the wind.

Kipp's voice was sharper, too raw to be clever. "And what the hell are we supposed to do until then?"

Jaymes didn't flinch as the wind picked up, tugging the sails tight. He stared at her figure on the bow, unmoving, back turned, shoulders squared against the horizon like a challenge.

He spoke quietly, but with absolute surety, "We remind her we're still here."

Kipp said nothing at first, but then, his fingers stilled against the wood. His jaw unclenched and he nodded. Whatever battle Kalithea was preparing to walk into—whatever ghosts waited at the edges of her kingdom—it didn't matter.

She wouldn't walk into it alone.

Not this time. Not if they had anything to say about it.

Kalithea sat at the edge of the bed, rolling her shoulders once, twice, trying to loosen the ache buried beneath muscle and memory. The room shifted with the ship's slow sway, each creak of the hull an echo from the deep. The wind brushed faintly against the timbers above, constant and distant. She closed her eyes and pressed her fingertips to her temples, as if the pressure might still what stirred beneath the surface. But it never did. Not when every thought in her mind pulled tighter the closer they came to shore.

She knew these waters. Not the way Blackwell did, by chart and current, the instincts of a man born to the sea. Her knowing ran deeper. It lived in the body, not the map. It was the kind of knowing you didn't speak aloud. The kind you flinched from when it came uninvited.

These were the same waters she'd watched from a tower window, once. High stone, cold walls, bruises hidden beneath silk. A child's silence drawn out over years. She had pressed her hands to the glass, watching the sea stretch to the horizon, believing foolishly that if she could reach it, she could escape.

She hadn't escaped. Not then. Now she was coming back, not as a prisoner nor as a pawn. But as something else. Something not yet named.

She hated that.

Uncertainty was its own kind of chain. It pressed in at the edges of her resolve, whispering that power meant nothing if it wasn't aimed true. That survival wasn't enough if she no longer knew who she was in surviving.

She drew in a breath and held it, letting it settle against the unrest coiling in her chest. There was no time for unraveling. No space for memory. Every mile they gained brought her closer to a reckoning she could no longer delay.

Her hands rested in her lap, palms curled inwards, calloused fingers twitching with old habit. These hands had done what was needed. They had drawn steel and drawn blood. They had written promises in ash and shadow and they would do so again.

Not only for Arjun, though he was the spark that had lit the fuse. Not only for the people still lost beneath the weight of tyranny. But for herself. Because this ending, whatever it became, had to be claimed. Not endured. Not postponed. Claimed.

And blood would answer for it.

The ship rocked with the slow weight of midnight. Above deck, the wind whispered across the sails. Below, in the still dark of the sleeping quarters, something broke.

A scream tore through the silence.

It was female, raw, animal. Unrestrained and terrible. The kind of sound that had no place on a ship full of living men. Jaymes was upright in an instant, heart slamming into his ribs, feet hitting the floor before his thoughts caught up. Kipp was already moving in his own cabin, a blade in hand, eyes wild.

Because that sound, it wasn't pain or rage. It was terror and that was wrong. Kalithea did not scream in fear.

They met in the corridor, boots hitting the boards in tandem, the lanterns along the walls flickering as they passed. The closer they got, the worse it became—sharp, ragged gasps splitting the quiet between screams.

Jaymes didn't slow. He slammed his boot against the door without ceremony. The frame cracked, wood splintering, and the lock gave way. Kipp crossed the threshold before the dust hit the ground, blades drawn, expecting an intruder. A nightmare made flesh.

But the monster wasn't something they could fight.

It was just her.

Kalithea was crumpled on the floor, her back arched hard against the floor, every muscle locked in a grotesque spasm. Her hands clawed at empty air, grasping, scraping, fighting something they couldn't see. Her mouth moved in frantic murmurs—too fast, too broken, syllables cracking on her tongue. Her eyes were wide, white and sightless. She was somewhere else and wherever it was, it was killing her all over again.

The lanterns flickered once. Then again. And the shadows *moved.* They crept. Crawling across the floorboards like oil slicks with teeth, reaching for her at the center of the room.

Jaymes swore under his breath. "Get her out of it. Now."

Kipp dropped to his knees beside her, grabbing her wrists. "Kal!" he barked, his voice sharp, trying to cut through whatever nightmare had her. "Wake the hell up!"

She thrashed, caught in some invisible snare. Her knee cracked against the floor, her fingers raking toward Kipp's face. He ducked just in time, barely avoiding the blow.

"Shit—it's like she's fighting something. She can't hear me."

Jaymes was already moving, pressing down on her shoulders, grounding her as much as he could. Her breath came in frantic gasps, like she couldn't get enough air. Like the room was drowning her.

The lanterns flared again, too bright, then dimmed. And then the walls began to bend. The shadows weren't passive anymore, *they were hungry.*

Kipp leaned closer, grabbed her face. "Kalithea!" he snapped. "This isn't real. Whatever you're seeing, it's over. You got out!"

But her eyes—gods, her eyes—they didn't see him.

And then she whispered it.

"Please..."

It wasn't a plea to them. It wasn't for them at all. It was for someone long gone and it broke something inside both men.

Jaymes' voice dropped to a growl, raw with fury and something deeper. He leaned close, close enough for her to feel the heat of him, his forehead almost touching hers, cupping her face in the steadiness of his hands.

"You are *not* his. You never were. *You never will be.*"

The shadows reared back, screaming without sound, flickering along the edges of the walls.

Kalithea seized. Her body jerked once, hard. Then she choked on a breath—sudden, gasping, sharp enough to sound like a wound—and her fingers found flesh. One hand clutched Jaymes' wrist. The other twisted into Kipp's tunic, holding fast.

And finally, her eyes focused. Still wild and frantic, but seeing.

Kipp exhaled, shuddering with it, his voice a rasp. "There you are."

Jaymes didn't move. Didn't let her fall back into it.

"You're safe," he said quietly, his voice like a tether. "You're here. You're with us."

She trembled beneath their hands. The panic hadn't gone. But it was fading. Her breath came fast, her body still taut with remnants of the dream, but her gaze didn't break from theirs.

Kalithea sat in the wreckage of her room, her knees drawn up, her shoulders tense, the sheets twisted around her. Sweat clung to her skin, cool against the heat still pulsing through her veins. She knew where she was but her body hadn't caught up. Her hands trembled in defiance of her will. Her mind was still too loud. The whispers hadn't faded. The ghosts lingered.

Kipp sat beside her, one hand resting lightly around her wrist—not gripping, not holding, just *there*. Grounding her, should she need it. Jaymes crouched in front of her, elbows balanced on his knees, stormy eyes unblinking. He watched her, reading every shift in her breath, every flicker beneath her composure.

"You're here," Jaymes said, voice quiet, low, certain.

She closed her eyes and nodded slowly. "I know."

Jaymes rose to his feet, smooth as ever, the folds of his coat shifting with the movement. "Try to rest," he said. "You don't have to sleep. Just... let your body stop fighting."

Kipp stretched, limbs loose but gaze tight with focus. "I'll keep the nightmares at bay with my unparalleled charm."

A faint breath of a laugh escaped her–dry, tired, but real.

Jaymes arched a brow. "You? With charm? We're trying to *calm* her, not finish the job."

Kipp gasped lightly, scandalized. "Captain, I am *wounded*. I'll have you know I'm delightful in a crisis."

Jaymes ignored him, stepping closer to Kalithea. "We'll be just outside the door," he said, voice softer now, but firm. "No shadows will touch you tonight."

Kal's gaze lifted. Something in her posture loosened. Not entirely. But enough.

"I know," she murmured again, softer this time.

Jaymes nodded once, turned, and stepped into the hall. Kipp lingered for a breath, meeting her gaze. His usual smirk had faded to something gentler, something far too earnest for a thief.

Then he followed, and the door shut behind them with a hush.

Outside, the corridor was cool, quiet. Jaymes leaned against the wall, arms folded, his gaze cast out toward the starlit sea through a porthole. Kipp slid down against the wall beside the door, legs stretched, fingers absently tapping against his knee.

They said nothing for a long time.

Finally, Kipp ran a hand through his hair, voice hoarse. "That wasn't just a nightmare."

Jaymes didn't look at him. "No."

"I've seen people wake screaming before," Kipp said, voice quieter now. "I've seen soldiers after battle. Children after raids. I've seen men claw their own skin off to feel something again."

Jaymes turned slightly, his stormy eyes hard. "And?"

Kipp exhaled. "That was worse."

Jaymes nodded once. "Because it was a memory. It was possession. She wasn't dreaming. She was *living* it." Jaymes' voice was even, but it carried steel beneath the surface. "Every breath, every scream–she was back there."

The shadows that had been real, called up not by conscious will, but reflex. Pain buried so deep it still bled in silence.

Jaymes sighed darkly. "And somewhere inside her, that place still has a hold."

Kipp muttered a curse under his breath. "That bastard. That fuck-ing–"

Jaymes cut him a look, sharp and lethal.

Kipp swallowed his fury, but not before his fists curled at his sides.

"He's not going to die easy," Jaymes said, voice low. "When the time comes, he'll know *exactly* what he did. And he'll know *who* is ending him."

Kipp nodded slowly, the fire in him banked but not extinguished.

"When we find him–"

"I want justice," Jaymes continued. "Real justice. Not a blade in the dark. I want him to see her standing over him. Whole. Free. *Unbroken.*"

Kipp exhaled, leaning his head back against the wall. "She's not ready."

"She's close."

"Close isn't enough."

Jaymes looked back toward the door, toward the silence behind it. "She's spent her whole life fighting alone. She just doesn't know how to trust that someone else can bear the weight."

Kipp's voice dropped. "But we can."

"She's going to fight us."

Kipp's smirk returned, slow and dangerous. "She wouldn't be Kalithea if she didn't."

So they kept watch that night, two kings outside the door of the queen who could burn the world and rebuild it from ash.

The next night Jaymes had been expecting it.

The moment the air changed–heavy, pressing, wrong–he stepped into motion without a word. The torches flickered in the corridor, and he was through her door before the shadows could settle.

This time, she didn't fall.

She was caught mid-collapse, tangled in sheets, her body seizing in waves as her mind reeled somewhere far beyond the room. Her hands clawed at nothing, the edge of a scream caught in her throat. Eyes wide, unfocused. She didn't see him.

Jaymes dropped to his knees and pulled her hard against his chest, one arm around her back, the other bracing her head. Her limbs jerked with raw panic, no recognition in her touch, only a desperate search for something solid.

But he didn't flinch. He didn't release her. He anchored her in his arms, voice low and steady.

"Kal."

Nothing.

"Kalithea. You are not there."

She didn't respond. Her breath came in short bursts, whispers spilled from her lips–disjointed, frantic. They weren't for him.

His grip didn't shift. He stayed with her, anchoring her with voice and presence, steady as stone.

"You're on the Tempest," he said, slower now. "With me, on my ship."

Her body jolted—a ripple of tension, a halt in her breath—but she didn't wake. Her hands curled into fists, grasping at his shirt, not knowing why. As if some distant part of her remembered what safety was supposed to feel like.

Jaymes didn't relax his hold. His voice dropped lower, softer, more dangerous.

"You are not his and together we will show him that."

She stilled—not all at once, not cleanly, but like a fire dying in slow stages. The tremors ran their course. Her fists curled in his shirt. Her breath hitched. And then, with a soft, broken sound, she returned.

Her eyes blinked back into focus, dazed and strained, and rose to meet his.

Jaymes held her steady as her breath shuddered in and out, her mind dragging itself back from whatever dark had tried to claim her. Her gaze landed somewhere near his throat, dazed and flickering, and then—finally—lifted to his.

"I'm sorry."

The words landed hollow, senseless.

Jaymes stared at her, his jaw tight. "Don't."

That was what she gave him? After all that? A fucking apology? His grip didn't loosen. His voice didn't rise, but something inside him snarled.

Her voice cracked again. "I shouldn't—"

"You shouldn't have had to survive any of it," he cut in, quiet and hard. "And you sure as hell don't owe me an apology for breaking under the weight of it."

She shook her head, barely moving, as if any larger motion would snap her in half.

He reached for her, tilting her chin gently so she couldn't retreat behind lowered lashes. "Look at me."

Her eyes met his, and when their eyes locked, his voice dropped to a murmur. "You are not your past. You are not what he made you."

Her lips parted, then pressed shut, hard.

"You are a force," he said. "Not a ruin. You are dangerous. You are chaos wrapped in silk and blood."

She said nothing, but something in her jaw shifted—uncertain, caught between resistance and exhaustion.

"And you are *not* broken."

She didn't speak, didn't look away. But slowly, hesitantly, she leaned in.

Not much. Not far. But enough.

She folded against him with the reluctance of someone who didn't know how to rest, but was willing, just this once, to try. Her forehead found the curve of his shoulder. Her grip loosened, not fully, but enough for him to feel the shift from tension to trust.

And Jaymes Blackwell—ruthless captain, master of storms, breaker of empires—forgot how to breathe.

She let him hold her.

And Gods, he wasn't ready for it. He had expected fire. Expected steel. Expected to be shoved back with a curse and a threat.

Jaymes had faced storms that split hulls in half. Had walked into fire with only iron and will. He'd never feared any of it. But this—her leaning on him, her silence no longer a wall but a surrender—this shook him.

He didn't do anything but wrap his arms more tightly around her and pray the moment didn't end. This was a woman—unmade and re-made by grief, fury, prophecy—letting him carry her for a breath of time she didn't yet know how to claim for herself.

And he would. Gods help him, he would. This quiet, tremulous act of trust? He would protect it with everything he had. Even if it ruined him. Even if she never let it happen again.

He closed his eyes and let the weight of her settle. His arms tightened, not as a shield, but as a promise.

She didn't need to know what it cost him to sit in that quiet. She didn't need to ask why he stayed.He stayed because she had asked without words. Because she had fought alone too long. Because tonight, she didn't have to. And when her breathing slowed, when the last tremor faded, when her body finally gave in to sleep—he didn't move.

He just kept watch, thinking about the woman in his arms and about the vow he'd already made without speaking it. He would see her through the fire. Through the war. Through the ghosts and the gods and the monsters waiting at the edge of her world.

The third night, Kipp had been waiting.

He'd stayed in the corridor, half-slouched against the wall, pretending he wasn't watching the door.

Jaymes had warned him what to look for. The signs weren't obvious to most, the shift in the air, the way her breath caught just a little too sharply before her body followed. But now, after two nights of waking to her screams, Kipp knew the rhythm. He felt it settle through the air, felt it tighten around his chest.

When it came, he was already moving.

The door was open before she gasped. She was upright in bed, tangled in the sheets, her body caught between sleep and something darker. Her hands lashed blindly, one fist narrowly missing the bedframe, her breath shallow and fast.

Kipp caught her wrists before the next strike could land. He didn't restrain, he held her, steady and present. His chest met hers with quiet insistence, anchoring her without force. She didn't know it was him yet. Her eyes were wide, unfocused, but her body still moved like prey trapped in the jaws of something old.

He didn't flinch when she bucked against him, didn't curse when her nails scraped across his collarbone. He didn't bark her name like a command. That wasn't his way. That was never his way.

He leaned in, pressing his forehead to hers, his voice low. Anchoring her before the void could swallow her whole.

"Easy now, love," he murmured, his tone more velvet than words. "You're alright. I've got you."

She trembled in his arms, every muscle taut, breath tearing ragged through her lungs. Her body was at war with itself, every twitch and gasp a battle between memory and the present. But he didn't let her go. Didn't loosen his hold.

"You're not there," he said, softer now. "You're here. With me."

Her hands still trembled, caught between resistance and surrender. But they no longer clawed at the air. They gripped his shirt instead, clutching the fabric like it might tear, but not letting go.

He didn't rush her. Just stayed close, unmoving, his voice a thread through the dark. Her breath slowed, inch by inch, until the fight bled out of her limbs and she slumped against him, not quite yielding–but no longer resisting.

Her eyes opened, searching first, then settling. Recognition came in fragments, but it came.

"Welcome back, little fox," he whispered, letting a crooked grin curl against the edge of his words. "Knew you'd come back to me."

Her forehead rested lightly against his, their breath mingling. Her fingers remained curled in the folds of his shirt. No sharp words. No defensive retreat. Just the soft, ragged edge of presence.

Kipp felt it. That rare stillness. That rare trust. That fragile, dangerous gift she didn't know she was giving him. And so, like always, he used humor as the only shield he had.

"You didn't stab me," he said, voice warm, teasing, light. "Which means either we're making progress...or you're just going easy on me."

A soft sound escaped her lips. Not quite a laugh.

But it was real.

It was hers.

She shook her head faintly, the smallest curve ghosting across her mouth. "Thank you," she murmured, voice barely more than a whisper.

Then, without warning, her hand lifted. Fingertips traced the line of his jaw. The touch was barely there, fleeting and unguarded.

He didn't move. Didn't breathe. Because it wasn't strategy or seduction. It was instinct, pure and unshaped. A moment given without armor.

Then it was gone.

She blinked, awareness crashing in like a cold wave. The distance returned, not cold, but guarded. Controlled. She eased back just slightly, just enough to reestablish the line she couldn't let herself cross.

Kipp saw it, hell he *felt* it. But he didn't call her on it. Didn't smirk, didn't say a godsdamned thing. She had touched him. She had looked at him, not like a threat or liability, but like something steady in a world that refused to hold still. For one rare moment, Kalithea had let herself rest in his arms. And that? *That was everything.*

He exhaled, leaning back only far enough to give her space, but not so far that she'd think he was letting her go.

Not now. Not ever.

"Next time you get the nightmares," he said, voice low, "I'm trying a fancy rescue line. I'm thinking something dramatic. Maybe a shirtless sword fight with the ghosts of your past?"

She snorted, quiet but undeniable. And that sound—small, unguarded, genuine—was all the reward he needed.

He would wait. For the next nightmare. For the next breath. For whatever came after.

Kipp sat outside her door, elbows on his knees, staring at his hands as if they'd only just started belonging to him.

He'd known it was a game from the beginning. From the first moment he saw her in the market, he had known she would be trouble. And Gods, he had loved trouble. He'd chased that kind of danger before—sharp, elusive, beautiful—but never quite like her. She was meant to be a challenge. A diversion. Something clever to toy with while the world burned quietly in the background. He had flirted. Smirked. Tested the edges of her temper with every stolen look, every too-close word.

He'd told himself he was in control. But tonight she touched him. Just a hand to his jaw. It wasn't coy, wasn't performative. It was nothing but real. And that—*gods help him*—had undone something in him.

Kipp leaned his head back against the wood-paneled wall and exhaled, long and slow. The corridor was quiet, the ship swaying gently beneath him. But his thoughts? They were anything but calm. He could almost hear Jaymes' voice in his head, low and amused. Some knowing remark about how the thief had finally lost the game to the woman who never played by anyone's rules but her own.

Maybe Jaymes would be right, because this wasn't a game anymore. Not to him. Not with *her*. Maybe it never had been.

He rubbed a hand over his face, cursing under his breath. This wasn't how it was supposed to go. She was supposed to be the puzzle he cracked open. The untouchable prize he wanted only because it was out of reach. The kind of woman he could flirt with, fight beside, and eventually forget.

But Kalithea of Elandra was not forgettable. She was carved from storms and silence. A weapon honed too sharp to be held without bleeding. She didn't stumble for charm, didn't soften for honeyed words. She gave nothing she hadn't decided was worth giving. And tonight *she had given him something.* Just a breath of closeness. Just a brush of warmth. Just enough to ruin him.

Kipp let out a quiet, humorless laugh and shook his head. What a fool he'd been, thinking he could steal something from her. Thinking he could stay in control. He'd walked into her orbit thinking he could dodge it, and instead, she had burned a mark into him without ever trying. That scared the hell out of him. The King of Thieves had spent his whole life slipping in and out of shadows, in and out of people. Untouched. Unscathed. Unseen.

But she had seen him. She had looked at him, touched him, thanked him—and meant it.

And that meant something.

Too much.

He closed his eyes, letting the quiet settle around him. He wasn't ready to name what this was. Not yet. Maybe not ever. But for the first time in his life, Kipp wasn't sure he wanted to keep running.

The Fox, The Shadow, and The Storm

They didn't speak of it, at least not aloud. Not in anything so fragile as words.

But it was there.

In the subtle shift of Kalithea's posture when Kipp slung an arm over her shoulders, no longer tense, no longer bracing for a knife in the back. In the way her eyes didn't narrow when Jaymes stood too close, when his voice dropped low and edged too near her thoughts. In the flicker of something unspoken when she looked at them and didn't look away.

She was still sharp. Still distant. Still the kind of woman who counted exits even in her sleep. But the walls she had fortified so ruthlessly were beginning to thin quietly, dangerously. Though she hadn't offered them trust outright, hadn't said the words, hadn't named what was happening between them, they felt it. In the way she stopped anticipating betrayal long enough to let herself breathe in their presence.

They should've pulled back. *They didn't.*

The ship rocked in the hush of the late hour, and the glow of a single lantern spilled over the navigation table. Jaymes stood at its edge, unrolling the map with a flick of his wrist. Kipp hovered nearby, arms folded, knife tapping a restless rhythm against his forearm. Kalithea stepped into the circle of light. She said nothing, just moved to the table and placed her hands flat against the wood. Her fingertips grazed the edge of the map as if steadying herself on more than parchment.

Jaymes didn't look up. "We need a plan."

"I have one," she said, voice even.

Kipp's brow lifted. "That's the tone. The 'I'm about to do something suicidally noble' tone."

Kalithea ignored him.

Jaymes sighed, gaze flicking toward her. "Let me guess. It doesn't involve us."

She kept her eyes on the map. "This is my fight."

Kipp groaned theatrically. "You are the most *exhausting* woman I have ever met."

Jaymes leaned back against the bulkhead, crossing his arms. "Did you really think we'd let you walk into this alone?"

Her fingers curled slightly. It was the smallest tell but they both caught it. She wasn't used to this. To people staying. To people refusing to let her drown in the silence she had built for herself.

Jaymes didn't press, but his voice softened. "We're coming with you."

She exhaled slowly. "You don't have to."

"I've never done a single thing I *had* to," Kipp muttered. "That's kind of my whole charm."

She shot him a look.

Jaymes smirked. "Unfortunately, the thief's right. *Again.*"

Kipp placed a hand to his chest, "Two compliments in one night? At this rate, I'll start believing *I'm* his favorite."

Jaymes ignored him. He stepped closer, his gaze fixed on Kalithea's face. "You stopped being alone in this the second you pulled us in. You don't get to shake us now."

Kalithea didn't speak right away, but she didn't argue, either. She looked down at the map and nodded.

Jaymes pointed to a marked cluster along the coast. "We take the docks at dawn. Their patrol should be weakest there."

Kipp leaned over the table, blade tapping lightly. "About time I earned my keep."

Kalithea raised a brow. "You mean cause a distraction?"

Jaymes arched a brow. "He means set something on fire."

Kipp grinned. "I'm a man of many talents."

Kalithea shook her head. "You're scouting ahead."

Kipp twirled his dagger. "Knew you couldn't resist sending me off on my own. Distance makes the heart grow fonder, little fox."

Jaymes adjusted the map. "Once he brings us intel, we move. No waiting. No second chances."

Kalithea's voice cut in. "And if Arjun's not where you think he is?"

Jaymes didn't miss a beat. "Then we adapt."

Kipp leaned his hips against the table, casual on the outside, eyes sharp beneath the grin. "Then we burn down everything that's in our way."

Kalithea looked at him, trying to read past the smirk, past the swagger, but his expression didn't change. Because he meant it.

Jaymes tapped a finger against the southern point of the docks. "We go in quiet. We come out fast. No heroes. No last stands. We find him, we get out."

Kalithea stood motionless, eyes fixed on the map stretched across the table. The candlelight caught the edges of her profile, sharp and still. She traced one route after another, reading the marks not as ink, but as lives—hers, Arjun's, theirs—all hanging on the weight of these choices. The strategy was sound. Every entry, every escape, every variable thought out and accounted for, or as much as they could before Kipp brought back any intel. Jaymes had brought the logistical ruthlessness of a naval tactician. Kipp, the eyes of a predator who thrived in chaos. And Kalithea...she had brought the purpose. The reason.

And still, something twisted inside. Not fear. Not doubt. Something quieter. Heavier. This wasn't how she was used to fighting. She had spent too long alone, too long convinced that to involve others was to endanger the, that to care was to compromise. Trust was a risk she had learned to bury. Dependence, a luxury she could never afford.

And yet...here they were.

Jaymes Blackwell, cool and unshakable, drawing the lines of war like he was navigating familiar waters. Kipp Harlow, maddening, brilliant, impossible, grinning through it all like he had already won. They didn't ask permission to stay. They simply did. And the terrifying part was...she let them.

The final pieces fell into place as the last candle guttered low. They had grown still, weighted by the quiet before the storm.

Jaymes rolled the map with crisp precision, tying the leather cord as though binding fate itself. "Get what rest you can," he said, his voice smooth, but edged. "We move at first light. And once we move we don't stop."

Kalithea nodded once, her posture composed, though something distant glinted in her eyes.

Kipp, of course, was already stretching, rolling his shoulders with a satisfied sigh. "Well, that was painfully responsible of us. Now, I say we celebrate. A toast to poor decisions and worse ideas."

Kalithea's brow arched. "We haven't done anything yet, Harlow."

"Exactly my point," he said, flashing a grin that dared her to smile. "We're overdue."

She shook her head with a sigh, though her lips twitched faintly. "You're impossible."

"And yet, you keep me around." He winked, leaning back against the edge of the table like a man who feared neither gods nor consequence. "Which, frankly, says more about you than me."

Jaymes didn't glance up as he secured the map beneath his arm. "We'll need to be sharp in the morning," he said. "Save the theatrics until after we haven't all been murdered."

Kipp clutched at his chest dramatically. "So little faith, Captain. I'm wounded."

Jaymes shot him a sidelong glance, dry as desert wind. "Wounded men don't run missions."

Kalithea watched them both with a weariness she couldn't quite disguise, and yet, there was something steadier beneath it. Not trust, exactly. Not yet. But the start of something near it.

Kipp tilted his head at her, his grin sharpening. "Sleep if you can, my queen. Tomorrow we raise a little hell."

Kalithea regarded him for a moment. Then, slowly her lips curved into the barest smirk.

"We'll see about that, Harlow."

Kalithea sat in silence, the slow groan of the ship's timbers and the rhythmic sway of the sea filling the quiet with its own uneasy lull. The map before her remained untouched, the routes memorized, the contingencies rehearsed until they no longer needed to be seen. Her hands rested on either side of the parchment, but her eyes had long since drifted from its inked surface. Strategy no longer occupied her thoughts.

She had spent weeks tolerating Jaymes and Kipp, men too clever by half, too persistent to shake off. They were inconvenient, impossible, relentless in their presence. Then she had begun to trust them, unwillingly at first, cautiously. And now, gods damn them both, they mattered.

That was the problem. Not the plan, not the risk ahead. *This.* She hadn't prepared for the way Jaymes steadied her with a glance, the quiet authority in him that made the chaos in her mind still. The way his voice, low and steady, could cut through the noise like a blade. Nor had she accounted for Kipp, with his easy grin and reckless charm, slipping past her defenses like smoke through a crack, teaching her what it felt like to laugh without calculation. She had let herself lean, just a little, and already the cost loomed ahead.

It hadn't been sudden. It had crept in, quiet and unassuming. A brush of his hand at her back when the deck shifted beneath their feet. A quip murmured too close that lingered longer than it should. A moment held just a heartbeat longer than was safe. Harmless things. Except they weren't.

Not when the nightmares returned. Not when she woke gasping for air, the screams still caught in her throat and found them already there. Jaymes, steady as stone, anchoring her with that unshakable calm.

Kipp, close and warm, murmuring nonsense that somehow brought her back from the edge.

They didn't leave, and that unsettled her. Not their presence, but her reaction to it. She had stopped bracing for the blade. Stopped expecting betrayal at every turn. Now, she was afraid of something far more dangerous.

Loss. Real loss. The kind that leaves no wounds but breaks you all the same.

She knew that fear. Had lived it the night they took Arjun. Had carried it ever since. It was why she had built walls high enough to keep even memory from slipping through. And now here they were, Jaymes Blackwell and Kipp Harlow, standing in the places she had sworn to keep empty. Without invitation. Without warning.

If she let them fight for her, walk beside her into what was coming, then she had to face what she'd refused to name. The truth. That she was not untouchable. That she had let herself want something more than survival. That they mattered more than they should. More than she thought they *could.* And if they fell, if she watched them fall because of her, she would not survive it. The *world* would not survive it.

A breath dragged in slow, controlled. Her hands curled against the table's edge, knuckles pale, the wood beneath her palms the only solid thing in reach. The conclusion came with cruel clarity.

She couldn't afford this. Not the weight of them. Not the risk. She had survived alone. She had clawed her way through blood and ash with no one but Liam to anchor her. She could do it again. She *would* do it again. The only answer, the only path left, was the one she had always known how to walk.

Alone.

No risks, no attachments, no one to lose.

Even if it tore something loose inside her, if it meant walking into the storm without them. Because if the cost of letting them in was watching them die, then the choice had already been made.

Jaymes leaned against the railing, arms crossed, eyes fixed on the horizon where the sea swallowed the stars. The night was unnaturally still—no wind, no waves, just the distant groan of the hull and the faint, steady pulse of water against wood. Behind him, Kipp perched on a barrel like he'd always belonged there, spinning a dagger between his fingers in lazy, practiced rhythm. The silence between them wasn't awkward. It wasn't even new.

They both knew what was coming.

"She'll make her move at dawn," Jaymes said at last, voice low.

Kipp caught the blade mid-spin. "Aye. Just before the shift turns. Easiest time to disappear."

Jaymes nodded, his mouth twitching with a smirk that never reached his eyes. "She won't take us with her."

"She thinks we'll slow her down," Kipp said, almost smiling. "Or worse, get ourselves killed."

Jaymes didn't answer. He didn't need to. They'd both known from the beginning what Kalithea was capable of and what she feared more than failure.

"She's smart," Kipp added. "Too smart to make noise when silence will do. My guess? She sets a false trail through the dockyard. Loose boards, light steps, a shadow someone thinks they almost saw."

Jaymes' eyes narrowed. "Slips out through the cargo deck. Or bribes one of mine."

Kipp snorted. "She wouldn't even need coin. Just that look. The one that says you're not worth the breath it'd take to curse you."

Jaymes tilted his head. "You've seen that one firsthand."

Kipp grinned. "Several times. Still haunts my dreams."

Jaymes glanced toward the faint glow spilling from beneath her cabin door. "She knows we're watching."

"Which means she's already ten steps ahead," Kipp said, adjusting his grip on the dagger. "We won't catch her by keeping pace."

Jaymes pushed off the railing. "Then we stop chasing. Give her what she wants."

Kipp raised a brow. "Which part? The illusion of control, or the satisfaction of slipping past us?"

Jaymes turned slightly. "Both."

Kipp laughed under his breath. "You're suggesting we bait the fox by acting like the hounds are asleep?"

Jaymes didn't answer right away. Then, dryly, "Worked on you."

Kipp scoffed. "I came willingly."

"You *stayed* willingly," Jaymes corrected.

Kipp made a face. "That's worse."

Jaymes stepped past him, his voice quieter now. "We let her think we've eased off. That we trust her to make the smart choice."

"She'll know it's a bluff," Kipp said.

"Of course she will. But she'll want it to be real."

Kipp's smirk faded slightly. "And when she runs?"

Jaymes' gaze cut toward the stairs leading below deck. "Then we remind her she's not alone anymore."

A beat of silence stretched between them, steady as the tide. Then Kipp stood, stretching his arms behind his head with a groan.

"So," he said, "bet's still on?"

Jaymes lifted a brow. "Which bet?"

"Who catches her first," Kipp chuckled. "I've got silver on me."

Jaymes shook his head, watching him go. "You're too slow."

"Keep telling yourself that, Captain," Kipp winked.

Jaymes lingered a moment longer, the chill breeze just beginning to stir as the hour crept toward morning. She would run. Of course she would. It was who she was.

The docks were silent under the weight of moonlight. Farther out, the ship floated quietly on the tide, a dark silhouette against the horizon. Two men remained on its deck, one leaning against the railing, the other perched casually on a crate, a dagger dancing between his fingers.

They weren't chasing her.

Not yet.

Jaymes' posture was deceptively at ease, his arms folded across his chest. Kipp lounged nearby, flipping the blade over his knuckles, but there was tension in the motion, a quiet anticipation coiled beneath the lazy façade.

Kalithea stood cloaked in shadow just beyond the edge of the ship's lantern glow, her hood drawn, breath held. She should have gone. Should have moved without looking back. But instead she lingered. Just for a moment. Long enough to watch Jaymes tilt his head, the moon catching in his face. Long enough to see Kipp's mouth curve into that familiar smirk, the one that always meant trouble was coming. Long enough for something to settle low in her chest.

Ache.

She'd made her choice. She knew what it would cost. But she hadn't expected it to sting like this. They would be furious. Not because she ran, but because she didn't let them stand beside her. And for once, she didn't want either of them angry. She didn't want to be the reason they shattered.

But she had no choice.

She pulled her hood tighter, turned silently, and disappeared into the night.

Jaymes moved first. No sound, no word—just the shift of his weight, the faint lift of his chin. The sky was beginning to pale with dawn. And still, she hadn't come, nor had they seen any suspicious movement off the sides. He didn't speak. Just looked toward Kipp. And sure enough, Kipp had stilled too. The dagger paused in its spin, balanced delicately between two fingers.

"Y'know," he said quietly, "it's been a while."

Jaymes glanced at him. "Since?"

Kipp shrugged, flicking the blade again. "Since our dear Kal has told us how insufferable we are."

Jaymes didn't answer because he'd already realized the same thing. *She was gone.*

Jaymes exhaled, slow. "She already left."

Kipp's smile flickered, no real amusement in it. "Of course she did."

Jaymes pushed off the railing, already scanning the horizon.

Kipp smirked. "Well, I would say 'I told you so,' but..."

Jaymes turned toward the shore, already scanning for a trace she hadn't meant to leave. "She thinks we'll be angry."

"She thinks we'll sit here and sulk like scorned lovers." Kipp rose from the crate. "Which is insulting, really."

Jaymes glanced at him. "She thinks wrong."

Kipp straightened to his full height, slipping the dagger back into its sheath with a flick of his wrist. "You know, I should be more annoyed."

"You are," Jaymes muttered.

Kipp grinned. "Fine. I'm deeply offended. There, happy?"

Jaymes moved without another word, signaling Dorian to man the helm. Kipp followed with easy steps, slipping the dagger into its sheath.

"So," he asked, "what's the plan, Captain?"

"We find her."

"She's good," Kipp said, raising a brow. "You said so yourself."

"She is," Jaymes replied. "But she's not better than us."

Kipp's grin returned, sharp this time. "There's the bastard I know."

Jaymes stopped at the top of the gangplank, his gaze sweeping the empty dock one last time. No sign of her. Just the faint ripple of wind against the tide.

"She'll head southeast," he said. "Or circle along the outer wall."

Kipp tapped the hilt of his dagger. "And when we find her?"

Jaymes turned, calm and dangerous. "We remind her we said she's not alone, and we *meant* it."

Kipp cracked his knuckles, stretching his shoulders. "She's going to be livid."

Jaymes smirked. "She can yell at us later. After she's safe."

Without another word, they vanished into the dark, silent shadows in the night.

The City with Teeth

The city reeked of rot.

It wasn't just the stench of waste in the gutters or the breathless heat that clung to every crumbling stone. It was something deeper. Older. A kind of decay that had nothing to do with age and everything to do with power left to fester.

Jaymes said nothing as they passed the broken arch that marked the edge of the slums. He didn't need to. The tension in his shoulders, the measured cadence of his steps, he was reading the place like a map already. Counting lookouts without looking. Marking the choke points. Watching who glanced their way and who deliberately didn't. Kipp fell into step beside him, movements loose, casual, but his gaze swept the streets. Narrow alleys sprawled like veins into the city, slick with grime and shadow. Every corner whispered the same thing.

Mawborn.

Their banners weren't flown. No sigils hung from doors, no proclamations nailed to walls. But the signs were there. Mercenaries in ill-fitting armor, too alert for drunkards. Street rats who vanished the moment coin was mentioned. The watchtower on the east ridge now manned by men with branded throats and empty eyes.

Jaymes caught it first, a man leaning too still against a vendor cart, watching them through the veil of a spice stall. His boots were military issue, the hilt at his side too clean to belong to any regular sellsword. He turned the moment Jaymes' eyes met his.

A test. A warning. Or both.

"They've dug in deep," Kipp muttered under his breath, just loud enough for Jaymes to hear. "Whole city's bleeding black under the skin."

Jaymes gave a slight nod. "They've noticed we're here."

"Of course they did." Kipp flashed a grin that didn't touch his eyes. "You walk like the ending to someone else's story."

They turned off the main road, ducking beneath a sagging awning into a tighter warren of alleyways. The air was thicker here, the buildings closer. Laughter echoed faintly, low and cruel. Jaymes stopped just before a corner. He glanced once toward the rooftops, too many vantage points, too many lines of sight. Then down the lane ahead. A patrol moved in loose formation—five men, no colors, no ranks, but too disciplined to be street muscle. One of them wore a chain around his neck, a crude pendant tucked beneath his tunic. Kipp caught the glint of it as they passed.

A Mawborn mark. Faint, but there.

They waited until the soldiers turned the bend before moving again, this time slower. Calmer.

"Not a place we can ask questions," Jaymes said.

Kipp gave a low whistle. "Not unless we're asking them of corpses."

Jaymes didn't smile. "Not yet."

They reached a rundown tavern at the edge of the trade quarter, a sagging building with one window shattered and the rest boarded. A place too proud to die and too cursed to rebuild. Kipp stepped through the door first, eyes adjusting fast to the dim interior.

A dozen heads turned at once. A pause. A breath. Then, noise again. Mugs lifted. Dice clattered. A low curse from the back table. Jaymes followed, slow and silent, taking in every detail. The barkeep didn't look up. The serving girl did and then immediately looked away.

Kipp leaned against the counter, flicking a silver coin into the air. "We're looking for someone."

The barkeep didn't blink. "Aren't we all."

Jaymes placed his hand flat on the wood. "She passed through here. Cloaked. Quiet. Last night. We want to know where she went."

"No one like that here," the barkeep said. Too fast. Too clean.

Jaymes didn't move.

Kipp leaned in slightly, his voice low. "Lying doesn't usually pay well."

The man's smile was thin. "Then it's a good thing I'm not charging you."

Jaymes turned without another word. Kipp followed, smile gone, voice tight.

"Nothing," he said. "Just like the last few."

Jaymes gave no reply because the message was already clear. This city belonged to the Mawborn.

And every shadow in it had teeth.

They moved deeper after dusk.

The outer districts gave way to narrower streets, the kind that never saw sunlight even at noon. Here, the stone felt closer. The air turned wet with rot and old piss. Every door was shut, every window barred. The kind of silence that didn't just warn, it threatened. Jaymes kept to the shadows, coat blending into the walls, boots silent on broken cobble. Kipp trailed just behind, loose in posture but tight with tension, scanning every alley mouth, every roofline. His fingers never quite left the hilt of his blade.

They'd already burned through half the night and a dozen leads—dealers, drunks, and men with too many knives for their own good. Every one of them had lied, stalled, or vanished. No one said Kalithea's name, mentioned a woman passing through. No one dared. Even the gutter-thieves looked over their shoulders before turning them away.

The city was watching, and it was loyal.

Kipp exhaled through his teeth, low and sharp. "I've never seen a place this scared of its own shadow."

Jaymes said nothing, but the look in his eyes was colder now. Sharper. He was done waiting.

And then, movement. A figure hunched low near a crumbling stairwell. Alone. Too alert to be drunk. Too still to be innocent. A man with lean muscle and clean hands, gnawing on bread that hadn't come from these streets. A runner, maybe. A watcher. Someone paid to listen.

Jaymes angled his chin just slightly.

Kipp moved. He struck fast, slamming the man against the wall with a crunch of bone and a choked gasp. The loaf hit the ground. A knee drove into his thigh, followed by a fist to the gut that left him wheezing.

"Well, well," Kipp said, voice low and smooth. "Out here late for someone with coin on his breath."

The man's hands twitched but not fast enough.

Jaymes stepped in without a word, catching his chin in a gloved hand and smashing it sideways into the stone. Blood splattered the wall. Another strike to the gut, then the ribs. The man crumpled, but Kipp held him up.

"You've seen her," Kipp hissed, breath hot against the man's ear.

The man said nothing.

"Where?" Jaymes said flatly.

The man spit blood, teeth bared in a grimace. "Go to hell."

Kipp dragged his blade free with a soft scrape. Pressed it to the man's cheek. "Already packed. You'll be our guide."

Another blow. This time to the kneecap. Jaymes' hand gripped the man's mouth muffling his screams.

"Where did she go?"

He hesitated too long. Jaymes twisted his arm until something snapped. More smothered shrieks of pain. Finally–broken and panting–he jerked his head east, toward a narrow gap between two buildings.

"She passed through there," he gasped. "Headed east. Hours ago."

Kipp slammed him back against the wall. "What's out there? The Mawborn?"

The man laughed through blood. "You think I'd give them up? You think I'd betray my brothers?"

Jaymes crouched beside him, voice low. "I think you'll die either way."

"I'd rather die than talk."

Jaymes rose. "Glad we agree."

Kipp didn't hesitate. He stepped slightly to the side, drew the blade clean across the man's throat, and caught his body as it collapsed. No flourish. Just necessity. Together, they hauled him behind a collapsed wagon and draped him beneath broken tarp and splintered crates. No one would find him until long after they were gone.

Jaymes wiped his hands, already turning. "She's ahead by hours, closer to them than to us."

Kipp's grin was gone. "She's nearly in."

Jaymes looked east, to the dark cut of alley the man had pointed toward. "Then we stop wasting time."

And they vanished down the path she'd taken, the stench of blood and silence trailing behind them.

The city narrowed around them the deeper they went, alleys strangled by leaning stone, gutters thick with runoff and scum. The moon had vanished behind clouds, leaving only the dim glow of lanternlight behind nearly shuttered windows.

Jaymes' gaze swept each intersection, cataloging movement, noise, and the quiet absence of both. Kipp ranged just ahead, a shadow with a pulse, all sharp eyes and coiled momentum. They were close. They could feel it now, not in the direction, but in the weight of the air. The way the city recoiled like a wound left to fester.

Then, more movement. Just ahead, half-sunken into the bend of a wall, a man crouched near a barrel, hunched over something clutched in his hands. His clothes were stained, boots mismatched, face half-swallowed by a hood. Nothing unusual. Nothing worth noting.

Until the coin caught the light. Polished silver, too clean, too fresh, and a Varisian mark to boot. It flashed once as he rolled it across his knuckles, unaware of the mistake he'd just made.

Kipp didn't pause. He closed the distance in three steps, seized the man by the collar, and slammed him into the stone hard enough to crack the plaster behind. The man yelped, dropping the coin. Kipp caught it mid-fall without looking.

"Well, well," he murmured, tone low and cold. "You've been spending above your station."

The man squirmed, coughing, trying to twist away. "I–didn't–"

Jaymes appeared beside them like the dark tide, silent and still. His presence didn't need volume.

Kipp turned the coin in his fingers, inspecting its face with a mock curiosity. "Not a local stamp. Not a merchant mark either." He raised a brow. "So tell me. Who pays this well in a place like this?"

The man said nothing.

Jaymes reached forward and drove an elbow into the man's ribs. The breath left him in a wet grunt.

"Don't stall," Kipp said, voice roughening. "We're not patient men."

The man spat blood, eyes darting toward the end of the alley. Wrong move. Jaymes backhanded him once. Then again, knuckles cracking bone this time. The man sagged in Kipp's grip.

Kipp pressed his knee into the man's gut, twisting the fabric of his coat tighter. "Where did she go?"

The man hesitated. Bled. Shook his head. Another punch. And then he broke. Not with words, just a sharp nod, a jerky tilt of his chin. East. Same direction as the last lead. Confirmed.

Jaymes stepped closer. "And the Mawborn?" he asked. "Where are they?"

The man let out something between a laugh and a sob. "Even if I knew...I'd rather rot."

Kipp's smile was thin. "Then rot."

He moved fast, too fast for the man to react. A thin wire loop slipped from his sleeve and caught around the man's throat. Kipp stepped behind him, pulling tight with practiced force. The man thrashed once, a rasp of panic catching in his throat, but no sound escaped. Just the wet hitch of breath and the scrape of boot on stone.

Jaymes watched, silent. It didn't take long. When the body finally slumped, Kipp loosened the wire and let it drop. He crouched, dragged the corpse behind a stack of rotting crates, and wedged it between barrels where no one would think to look–not soon, at least.

Jaymes adjusted his collar. "East, then."

Kipp nodded once, already moving. "Let's find her."

Kalithea moved like a shadow across broken stone, breath steady, cloak drawn close. The alleys pressed in tight around her, the city's bones hollow and rotting, but she knew the rhythm of places like this—knew how to disappear in them. The ruins of the city curled around her and she let herself sink into the silence, into the calm calculation that had kept her alive too many times to count. Each step was planned. Clean. Her trail would hold no scent, no sound. She had made no mistakes.

And yet the air shifted. A ripple through stillness. The faintest vibration in her bones. She didn't turn, but her fingers slid to the dagger hidden at her back, and she took the next corner tighter, faster. Then she heard it. A voice echoing off the crumbling stone behind her. For a moment, it sounded like Jaymes. Another voice followed, softer. Kipp?

Footsteps came next. Steady. Drawing nearer with urgency. She didn't think, didn't count the paces, how many steps she heard. She just... *hoped*. And for a breath, for the first time, Kal let herself believe it. That they had found her, even though she had made it impossible for them to.

She turned.

And the world shattered.

A shape lunged from the shadows behind her, bigger than she expected. His forearm clamped across her throat, yanking her backward with force enough to tear breath from her lungs. She reacted on instinct, slammed her heel down into his foot and twisted hard, breaking free, driving her elbow back into his gut. The impact jarred her arm, but he loosened. She dropped low, slashed a line across his thigh, and rose into a pivot that should've carried her free.

But there were more.

Five, six—no, eight of them now, emerging from the dark like roaches. Heavy boots. Black leather. Burned sigils stitched into their collars. And one of them, taller and broader, held iron manacles in both hands.

Iron.

They moved with calculation. Not mercenaries looking for a fight, trained hunters moving to capture. They *knew* exactly what she could do.

The first charged. She sidestepped, slashed his forearm, then ducked another blow and drove her knee into his ribs. One dropped. A second pulled a blade, she caught it with her own, twisted it free, and used the hilt to smash his jaw sideways.

But they were fast. Coordinated.

The third caught her from behind, locking his arms around her torso. She jerked her head back into his face and he screamed, blood spurting from his broken nose. She tore free again, panting now, sweat slick at her temple, heart pounding—not from fear, but from *focus*.

Then she saw it. The one with the manacles was circling, waiting for the opening. He wasn't fighting. He was watching. And now he moved.

Kal twisted to avoid him, but another grabbed her wrist. She broke his grip. Another caught her ankle. She kicked free. Her knife caught one in the throat–he fell choking, gargling.

Still, the man with the iron came.

She turned, raised her blade, but it was too late. The first cuff snapped shut around her wrist.

And the pain was immediate.

Not dull, not numbing, it was absolute agony. Like her bones had caught fire from the inside. Her vision whited out. Her knees buckled as her whole body recoiled from the touch. She tried to wrench away, to reach with her other arm, but the other two were on her now. One twisted her free hand behind her back, the other slammed her to her knees. She struggled, thrashed, bit someone's wrist until she tasted blood.

The second cuff locked shut.

Both wrists bound. Her magic snapped back, the breath punched from her lungs. Fire spread through her arms, across her chest, down her spine. She sagged forward, limbs trembling, throat raw though she hadn't made a sound. Her magic had gone silent, crushed beneath the iron's weight. She gasped, but the air felt foreign. Distant. Her body wouldn't move.

She knew these mercenaries now. Knew the sigils. The iron. The way they moved. They were his. The usurper's hounds. The Mawborn.

And she had walked right into them.

They laughed as she collapsed forward, muscles twitching, vision blurring. They mocked her as they closed in. One grabbed her hair. Their suggestions turned lewd, disgusting–cruel in the way that meant they didn't see her as a threat anymore.

Only a prize.

Still Blades and Loud Graves

When consciousness returned, the first thing she felt was iron.

It wasn't just heavy, it was crushing, a vise clamped around her wrists that pressed down through muscle into bone. It throbbed with a heatless weight, anchoring her limbs in something thicker than just pain. Her arms felt submerged in tar, every breath felt thin.

The second thing was stone.

Cold. Damp. Pitted with time and filth. She was slumped against a wall slick with mildew and the metallic tang of old blood. The air reeked of rot. Of things that had died here slowly.

Her wrists burned. Not in any poetic sense, but in the brutal, immediate way flesh burns when branded. The iron had latched onto her skin. Its weight wasn't only physical, it was draining her, unmaking her. Her magic slithered away from it like smoke fleeing a flame.

But none of it–not the iron, not the cell, not the rising sickness in her gut–compared to the heat of the glare from the next cell over.

Arjun.

He stood just beyond the bars, fists clenched around rusted iron, ignoring the searing pain burning into his palms, shoulders taut. He looked worse for wear, hollowed out cheeks, scars and wounds littering his entire body, clothes torn revealing injuries that had yet to heal. His hair, normally silky pin straight and shaved on the side, was dirty, long and matted, half grown out on one side, a tangled mess on the other. His sunken green eyes were flashing, fury rippled from him. Raw. His voice came low and biting.

"Tell me," he bit out, voice low and venomous, "that I am hallucinating. That I've lost too much blood, or fallen asleep against the wall and conjured this image in my dream."

She didn't answer. Her limbs refused obedience, her lungs fought to expand, but inch by inch, she pushed herself upright. She had done this. She had gotten herself caught, and Arjun, damn him, had every right to be furious.

"I had a plan," she muttered, voice raw from disuse and pain.

Arjun let out a sharp, humorless laugh—no amusement in it, only disbelief and a thread of something dangerously close to heartbreak.

"Oh, clearly," he said dryly, gesturing to the manacles biting into her skin, to the grime-covered floor and the decaying ceiling above them. "Of course you did. Was this part of it? Letting them drag you down here and slap chains on you like a dog?"

She didn't flinch. "I didn't account for the iron."

"No," he said, the word a whip crack. "You didn't account for *anything.*"

She met his eyes. "I came to get you out."

"And somehow decided the best way to do that was to get yourself thrown in?" His anger snapped wide then, raw and exposed. "Do you have any idea what they'll do to you? You aren't supposed to be here!"

She said nothing. The memory of what they'd said, what they'd *promised*, still echoed in her mind. The way they'd looked at her, laughed at her, spoken of her like she wasn't even human. It hadn't been the iron that made her stomach turn.

Arjun stared at her through the bars, his voice low now, bitter. "You came alone."

It wasn't a question.

She forced dispassionate composure into her expression. "I had to."

His hands tightened around the bars until the rust flaked away beneath his palms. "Then you're a damn fool."

"I—"

"No!" he snapped. "I'm not interested in hearing the justification this time. You think you're untouchable, Kal? That you can slip through the world unseen, outthink everyone, walk into danger and drag others out of it like it's some noble burden that only *you* can bear? Like you're the only one allowed to bleed for something?"

She stayed silent, keeping her jaw clenched.

"You're brilliant, Kal," Arjun said, quieter now but no less cutting. "That's always been your problem. You think if you just plan well enough, you can control everything—every risk, every cost. But this?" His voice dropped. "This is what happens when you forget you're not invincible."

His gaze softened by a fraction, though the tension never left his voice. "You need to get out of here."

She laughed once, dry and hollow, and lifted her bound wrists, shaking them at him, the manacles searing her skin. "Hadn't occurred to me. Thank you for the insight."

Arjun swore under his breath and began pacing his cell, boots dragging over stone noisily behind bars.

Kal watched the fury and grief twist inside him. She was already working the angles—measuring cell length, light sources, listening for the guards' rhythm outside. But beneath the cold logic, there was a deeper ache. One she refused to name.

If she didn't get out, if she was truly trapped, Jaymes and Kipp would come for her. Of course they would, and she couldn't let them, couldn't risk that. Because the moment they set foot in this stronghold chasing her shadow, they'd be walking into a trap they couldn't see. And they would bleed for her mistakes. She didn't care if they were angry. Didn't care if they never forgave her. As long as they stayed safe. She had made her peace with dying for them but she would never make peace with them dying for *her*.

Kalithea sat slumped against the stone wall, her back aching and her wrists raw beneath the weight of iron. Every throb of the manacles sent a fresh jolt through her nerves—pain laced with something deeper, something that clawed at the center of her magic like rusted teeth. She had gone over a dozen escape routes in her mind. All of them failed. Not because she wasn't clever enough but because of the chains.

She needed the keys. And she knew exactly who had them. Her gaze drifted past the rusted bars to the door where the mercenaries lingered outside near a fire pit, their laughter echoing too loud, too pleased. They hadn't stopped leering since she was thrown in, spitting crude remarks and tossing bets over which one would get the first turn. Disgust simmered in her throat, but she swallowed it down with something colder.

Focus.

Then, like flint catching spark, a memory surfaced. Kipp. Grinning across a crooked table, cards in one hand, a coin in the other. His voice low and irreverent as always.

Men are easy, little fox. The weakness of all men is a beautiful woman. Show 'em what they want to see, and they'll hand you the world just to think they've touched it.

Her lips twisted.

"Arjun," she said quietly, her voice a rasp.

He was pacing the narrow stretch of his cell like a caged predator, muttering under his breath, already halfway through another plan she could see unraveling behind his eyes.

"What?" he snapped, without looking at her.

"I need you to tear my tunic."

Silence.

Then he stopped mid-stride. His head turned slowly, expression halfway between disbelief and horror.

"I'm sorry, *what?*"

She met his gaze, perfectly calm. "The neckline. Rip it. Not all the way, just enough to lower the bar of self-restraint in our fine company out there. You know, make it look *irresistible.*"

He blinked at her like she'd just suggested they sprout wings and fly out through the ceiling.

"You've lost your damn mind."

"I can't exactly do it myself," she said, lifting her bound wrists an inch before the iron flared heat through her arms. "Unless you've come up with a way for me to tear linen with sheer willpower, I'm open to alternatives."

Arjun dragged a hand over his face. "This is the plan, bait them in close with cleavage? Seduction by implication?"

Kal gave a small shrug—difficult, given the chains—then tilted her head toward the mercenaries. "They've already stripped me a dozen times with their eyes. Might as well make it worth their attention."

He let out a groan that sounded like it came from his soul. "Gods, I hate this."

She smirked. "You're not the one who has to look inviting."

His eyes narrowed. "I'm the one helping you look inviting. I feel like I've already sinned."

"I'll light a candle for you," she murmured dryly.

Arjun stared at her for another beat, then exhaled like a man accepting his death. "This is undignified."

"And yet, here we are," she said, glancing down at her wrists. "And I still don't have keys."

Reluctantly, Arjun crossed to the bars that separated them. His movements were clipped, jaw clenched tight. She watched him, waiting.

He reached through, gripping the edge of her tunic, and paused. "You are going to owe me for this."

"Oh, undoubtedly."

Fabric split down the neckline with a rough snap, the sound louder than it should've been in the low, crackling quiet. Kal rolled her shoulders, shifting her weight forward, letting the firelight catch the curve of her collarbone. The torn fabric slipped just enough to suggest without revealing, and she kept her face impassive, debating whether the tear exposed her enough.

Arjun stepped back into his cell, disgust radiating from every line of his body. "You are shameless."

"I prefer strategic."

She didn't enjoy it. Not a second of it. But she held her posture, gaze fixed and unblinking, because this would work, it had to.

And Arjun—furious, pacing, helpless behind the bars—knew it too.

Jaymes and Kipp moved through the city with the ease of men who'd carved paths through worse.

They didn't speak. Each glance exchanged a silent measure of what they knew, what they feared, and what they were willing to do if the trail ran cold. This wasn't a hunt fueled by desperation, it was a cold, calculated pursuit. They had a lead. Thin, fragile, already unraveling. But they weren't chasing rumors. They were chasing *her*. And they knew her. Knew the rhythm of her steps, the way she chose shadows over shelter, risk over safety. They knew the cold logic she wore like armor and the rare moments when she shed it.

They weren't guessing anymore. They were closing in...or so they thought. The alley came into view without warning. Narrow, crooked, quiet–but not undisturbed.

They stopped. Jaymes stood beside Kipp, his eyes sweeping the alley, his expression set in stone. Kipp stood still, the usual glint in his eyes long extinguished. His sharp gaze scanned the scene, cataloguing the story in seconds. The shift in dirt near the far wall. A smear of blood– thin, dragged, not spattered. The faint indent of a bootprint angled too hard, like someone had been thrown back. Another smeared where someone had fought to stay standing.

And there, half-buried beneath a broken crate–

Steel.

Kipp crouched slowly, his hand closing around the hilt of Kal's dagger. He turned it over once, thumb brushing the blood crusted near the base.

"She was here," he murmured

Jaymes didn't answer, but the change in him was immediate. His shoulders squared, his jaw set. The tension rolled through him like a rising tide. Cold. Focused. He took a slow breath, his fingers flexing at his sides–like they were reaching for something he could already feel: steel, vengeance, ruin.

"They caught her," he muttered.

Kipp stood, his knuckles white around the dagger. His posture had shifted, looser, more relaxed on the surface. But that ease was a lie. There was nothing soft in him now.

"Yeah," he said, too softly. "They did." Kipp rolled his shoulders, and the grin returned, razor-sharp and dangerous. "They're not gonna like what happens next."

Jaymes smirked, a slow, humorless curve of his mouth. "No," he said, voice like distant thunder. "They really won't."

And just like that, the hunt turned. They were no longer searching for her. They were hunting the ones who took her.

And neither of them had any plans to be merciful.

The city twisted tighter the deeper they went—alleys narrowing, the air thick with soot and old blood, walls crowding like they knew what was coming.

Jaymes and Kipp moved without sound.

The voices reached them three turns down. Low, guttural, thick with laughter. A group of mercenaries huddled near a crumbling wall, muttering to one another in low, smug tones. No uniforms. No banners. But the burned sigils stitched beneath their collars gave them away.

Mawborn.

They were laughing.

"The bitch screamed," one of them said, spitting on the stone. "Didn't think she would. Thought she was royalty."

"Not anymore," another chuckled. "Now she's just meat."

That was all it took.

Kipp struck first. He came from the dark, his blade flashing once and the closest man's throat opened from ear to ear, flesh peeling like wet parchment. The man gurgled, dropped, twitched. Before the others could shout, Jaymes was already among them, a whirlwind of steel and blood. His dagger punched into a throat, twisted, then yanked free. Another hand shot out—grabbed the next man by the jaw and slammed his skull backward against the wall. Once. Twice. The bone gave way with a wet crack, and the man slid down, eyes wide and empty.

Kipp danced through them like death incarnate. One lunged—he sidestepped, drove a blade beneath the man's ribs, then shoved upward. The scream died in a choking gasp as blood bubbled from the mercenary's lips. Kipp held the knife there for a breath, twisting slow, then tore it free in a vicious arc across the belly, spilling him open in one step. Jaymes moved smoothly, no wasted effort, no hesitation. He took one by the shoulder and drove his dagger into the socket of the man's eye, the blade punching through cartilage and brain. The mercenary spasmed. Jaymes kicked him backward without looking.

Another tried to run. Jaymes caught him mid-turn and buried his elbow in the man's throat so hard it shattered the trachea. The mercenary fell, gasping silently, clutching at his ruined neck until Kipp ended it with a swift blade to the temple.

It was carnage. Fast. Efficient. Controlled only by the precision of monsters. Blood coated the alley. It slicked stone and pooled beneath twitching limbs, soaked into dirt and dripped from blades. Bodies lay ruined–cut in half, opened wide, broken apart in ways no soldier should die.

And yet neither Kipp nor Jaymes had broken a sweat.

Only one remained. He stumbled back, weapon forgotten, knees buckling beneath him as he looked at the massacre, his brothers gutted and flayed like livestock. His mouth opened, trying to form words, a plea, a prayer–something.

Jaymes' voice was low. "On your knees."

The man obeyed instantly, hands trembling. Kipp came forward slow, coiling the garrote around his fingers.

"Talk," he said, his tone devoid of threat. It didn't need one, it was a promise.

Jaymes grabbed his jaw, forcing his gaze up. "Where is she?"

"I swear–"

Kipp looped the garrote casually around the man's neck, not to kill, not yet. Just enough pressure to make breathing a struggle.

"Try again," he murmured.

The man choked. "East! East of the chapel ruins–under the forge crawlspace. They said it's warded. Hidden."

Jaymes' grip tightened on his jaw. "How many?"

"I–I don't know. Two dozen maybe more. Some of them don't come out."

Kipp leaned close, his voice all velvet and venom. "See? That wasn't so hard."

Then he yanked. The man's body jerked once–hard–and went still, his eyes wide and glassy. Kipp lowered him without sound, sliding the garrote free, already turning away as the corpse slumped into blood.

Jaymes stood. His voice was ice.

"Let's end this."

They vanished again, leaving only silence and ruin behind them.

They moved like smoke through the bones of the city–silent, certain, and wholly uninvited.

Jaymes kept to the walls, eyes sweeping each corridor like he was reading a map only he could see. Kipp walked beside him, the sharp rhythm of his boots masked by the hush of rotted stone and breathless alleyways. Every step they took confirmed what they already knew. They were past the hunt. This was the retrieval.

The air thickened as they pressed deeper–choked with mildew, ash, and something else. Fear. The kind of fear that lived in cities like this, where the Mawborn bought loyalty in blood and silence. Every coward they'd questioned. Every dead-eyed whisper that pointed east. Every informant too terrified to lie. All of it led here.

To the place Kalithea had been taken.

Kipp slowed first, hand braced against the curve of a splintered beam. Ahead, nestled in the crook of a sunken courtyard, squatted a keep trying to pass as a forge, built to swallow things whole. Fortified walls, sealed doors, windows shuttered and barred. No signage. No obvious function. Just a building that looked like it had always been waiting.

Too many guards. Too casual in their posts. And that, more than anything, confirmed it.

Kipp stared at the structure with a grim set to his jaw. "Well," he muttered, "that looks like a fucking problem."

Jaymes came up beside him, cloak drawn tight, eyes already tracking guard rotations and patrol timing. "She's inside."

Kipp didn't argue. The logic was too clean, the trail too clear.

"Of course she is," he said, rubbing a hand over his mouth. "Of all the hell holes in all the cells in all the world...she had to pick this one."

Jaymes didn't smile. "If we rush the doors, we get her killed."

"If we wait, they break her first," Kipp replied, his tone hardening. "They're not keeping her alive out of kindness."

Jaymes exhaled slowly, his gaze returning to the building. "We do this quiet. Fast."

Kipp scoffed, tilting his head. "Define quiet."

"No bodies unless necessary. No alarms. No showboating."

Kipp arched a brow. "No explosions."

Jaymes turned toward him, expression stony. "Preferably."

Kipp sighed, flipping his dagger once. "Ruining all my fun, Captain."

Jaymes ignored him. "We've got three obstacles."

"Only three?" Kipp's grin returned, bitter-edged. "That's practically a gift."

"One," Jaymes continued, "we don't know where she's being kept."

Kipp twirled his dagger once, caught it easily. "That's an interrogation issue. Very solvable."

"Two–she's likely restrained. Iron, if they were smart."

Kipp's smile dimmed slightly. "Pickpocketing issue. Normally not a problem. But I don't trust these bastards not to set traps around her."

Jaymes gave a short nod. "And three..."

Kipp waited. Then frowned. "What's the third?"

Jaymes didn't look at him when he answered. "Once we have her, we still have to get out."

The weight of it settled between them. This wasn't just a holding cell. It was a tomb built in real time. And this city? Its like the whole damned city was in on it.

Kipp grinned, shrugging. "So–two options. Go in quiet, slit the throats of the right men in the right order, and hope we find Kal before the place erupts. Or go in loud. Drag hell down with us and let the smoke be the cover."

"So," he drawled, "what's it going to be, Captain?"

Jaymes watched the guards calculating the blood it would take to bring it down. Then he looked at the sky, one last breath before the storm.

"Both," he said quietly. "We go in quiet."

A pause.

"And we leave loud."

HER BODY, HER BLADE

The fabric tore with a slow, deliberate rip, harsh in the stillness of the cell. Arjun's hands continued working with the same clinical precision he used when setting bones or carving runes, but his jaw was tight, his shoulders stiff with revulsion. The tunic parted further under his grip, exposing the delicate line of Kalithea's collarbone, the slope of her shoulders, the faint curve of her chest where sweat and blood had dried in a sheen against her skin.

"I despise this," he muttered, voice low and cold.

"I know," she said simply. Her eyes didn't leave the far wall. "But it needed to look real. It wasn't enough."

He didn't respond. Only stepped back, jaw clenched like he was biting down on a curse.

Kal rose slowly, angling her body toward the shaft of torchlight that split the bars, letting it trace the line of her exposed skin. She lifted her chin, rolled her shoulders, and let the torn fabric slip just enough to draw the eye, as if carelessly. Her hair tumbled down her back in a dark fall, catching the light, framing her like a painting left half-finished.

And then she stilled.

She heard it in the shift of breath beyond the bars. The silence where laughter had been.

She moved again, just a little. A turn of her hips, a stretch that lifted her chest, a tug at the chains that pulled her arms taut and drew attention to the way her body bent with the strain. The manacles clanked softly. Her head tilted like she was easing a cramp, neck bare, skin flushed from pain and heat.

The effect was immediate. A low whistle. A muttered curse. Then, slowly, words began to spill–filthy, eager, wrong.

"Gods," one of them murmured. "Look at her."

"Already am," another replied, his tone thick with want.

"*All that fire, and this is what she was hiding underneath it?*" he muttered, voice thick with want. "*Bet she's a hell of a ride once you break the fight out of her.*"

"*Strip her down,*" came another voice, rough and raw. "*Make her crawl. Bet she'll scream prettier than she talks.*"

Someone snorted. "*And when she cries, tell her it's her fault for being so pretty.*"

"*I'll make her love it before I'm done. They always do. Especially the stubborn ones.*"

"*I want to be the first to make her beg, see if she's still proud with my hand in her hair and my boot on her back.*"

"*I want to be the one to make her cry,*" another said, low and certain. "*See if she still talks like a queen with her face in the dirt.*"

"*Once we get those chains off, I say we bend her over and see how long she lasts with all of us taking turns.*"

Another barked a laugh. "*Bet she stops snarling real quick once she's got a cock in every hole.*"

They laughed, soft, breathless and excited.

Kal didn't blink. She let it wash over her, the heat of their stares, the words meant to dehumanize, to strip her power before they even laid hands on her. But they didn't understand. They weren't breaking her. They were walking willingly into her trap. She bit the inside of her cheek, felt the copper flood her mouth, and forced her body to remain loose, pliant, bait. Her chains rattled again. Her lips parted like she might speak.

The guards shifted. Footsteps approached.

Closer.

She kept her breathing steady and waited. They were almost there. And when they crossed the line—when they reached through those bars with lust thick in their veins and hands slick with anticipation—she would stop pretending.

And they would bleed.

The door gave way with a soft groan. Jaymes pushed it inward with care, shoulder brushing the stone as he slid through. Kipp followed, knives already loose in his grip, breath held tight in his chest.

They stepped into darkness, but instead of the silence of a prison corridor or the hush of cells they were greeted with the low murmur of voices, the clatter of weapons on tables. This was a barracks room and they had just walked straight into a den of vipers. There were six of them. Mercenaries hunched around a half-broken table, half-drunk and laughing over dice. One sharpened a blade with slow, lazy strokes. Another cleaned his boots with the edge of a meal knife.

But it only took a second. One heartbeat. One twitch too sharp from Kipp's shadow. And the nearest one turned. Jaymes didn't hesitate. He drove his dagger into the man's throat before the alarm could rise. Blood sprayed, hot and immediate, and the table overturned in a crash as chairs flew and steel scraped from sheaths.

Then *chaos.*

One lunged for the door, but Kipp met him halfway, throwing a blade into his thigh and following it with a knee to the face that cracked bone. Another came at Jaymes with a broadsword, sloppy and wild. Jaymes stepped into the arc, took the slice across his ribs to get close enough, and shoved his dagger into the man's gut with a brutal twist that dropped him to the floor.

Two more came from the sides. One slammed Kipp into the stone wall hard enough to rattle teeth, blade flashing toward his throat. Kipp ducked low, rammed a knife through the man's knee and dragged him down screaming, then crushed his windpipe with a sharp elbow to the neck. The last man turned his blade toward Jaymes, but Jaymes caught the weapon in his bare hand, letting it slice deep across his palm, and used the other to drive a dagger up beneath the man's chin and through the base of his skull.

It was over in less than a minute.

The room stank of blood and oil. The bodies lay strewn in broken angles. None had made it to the hall. None had raised a voice loud enough to carry. But it hadn't been clean. Jaymes leaned heavily against the wall, blood seeping through his shirt from the gash across his ribs. His hand dripped steadily from the slice that caught the blade. Kipp staggered once, then straightened with a wince, pressing a hand to his side—his tunic already dark with blood from his own deep slice.

He looked over at Jaymes, teeth bared in a half-grin. "Still with me?"

Jaymes didn't smile. "Barely."

Kipp laughed once, grim and breathless. "She better make this worth it."

Jaymes said nothing. He just pushed forward, one hand clutched tight against his side, the other still dripping blood onto stone.

They had come too far, and Kal was close. Whatever came next, they would reach her.

Even if they bled the whole way there.

The laughter had changed.

It wasn't drunken now, it was fevered. Frantic. The kind of laughter that came too loud, too close, born of bloodlust and unchecked hunger. The kind that stripped men of reason and left only violence behind. One muttered something lewd. Another echoed it, louder. Then another. And another. Words stacked on filth, desire slipping into threat until it no longer sounded like men speaking, but animals snarling, rutting, foaming at the mouth with anticipation. They were circling like hounds that had scented blood.

Kal didn't move. She felt them building toward it, the shift from suggestion to decision, from talk to action. The final line snapping in their minds. There was no hesitation now. No shame. Just a storm of arousal and cruelty, egging itself forward with every breath.

A boot hit the bars with a clang. Another man jeered.

"She's ripe now. Look at her. Pretty little thing on her knees."

"Bet she cries sweet."

"She won't be crying long. Bitches like that always melt once they've been used proper."

"Break her in. Then break her open."

The cell door clanked. The latch slammed back and two of them surged through, driven not by order or strategy, but by the need to *own* her.

Kal didn't flinch.

One seized her by the jaw, forcing her chin up as he leered down at her with breath that stank of rot and wine. The other grabbed her by the waist, hauling her up and slamming her hard against the wall. Her shoulders cracked against stone, her head snapping back. White bloomed at the edges of her vision, but still, she didn't fight.

Rough fingers clawed at her chest. Another hand fisted in her torn tunic, yanking it lower, tearing at the already ruined neckline with a sound that felt louder than thunder in the filthy air of the cell.

A knife appeared but it wasn't for threat, it was for sport. The man pinning her grinned as he slid the blade down her, not cutting skin, but close.

"You feel that?" he whispered. "That's the edge of mercy."

Kal stared past him, eyes blank.

Then they were dragging her down. Her knees hit stone, scraped raw. The floor reeked of piss, mildew, and something worse–something old and dried into the cracks. She let them throw her down. Let them straddle her, one hand on her throat, the other groping under what was left of the fabric. The dagger traced lower.

More laughter behind them now–closer.

"They're starting without us."

"Make her scream. I want to hear it."

"I want to see her choke on it first."

"Let's cut her open a bit, see how she squeals."

"Fuck her till her pride breaks."

Kal went still beneath them. Not limp. Not in surrender.

Waiting. Enduring. Letting it happen.

Because one of them had the keys.

She made her breathing ragged, twisted her hips just enough to make them think she was struggling–not fighting, just *resisting* enough to excite them. She whimpered once, soft, calculated, and the man above her groaned like he'd already won.

Then someone else climbed into the cell, belt already undone.

They swarmed.

Hands grabbed her thighs. Her hair. Her face. Tearing. Bruising. Pinning.

A roar broke from the back–Arjun, slamming himself against the bars so hard they rattled.

"You bastards! Cowards! Get off her!" His voice cracked with rage and panic. "You want a fight? Come here and try me, you fucking filth–"

They didn't hear him. Didn't care. The knife cut again, fabric this time. The tunic tore across her chest. Cold air hit her bare skin.

The cheering turned savage. Boots scraped. Belts hit the floor.

"Get in line."

"No, I'm first–"

"Fuck off–"

"Her mouth, her ass–I don't care which."

One of them reached for his cock, already hard, already muttering filth as he pushed another man aside and–

Kal saw him. The short one, with the crooked leg and the ring of keys swaying from his hip. Laughing louder than the rest. The kind of laugh that tried to hide nerves.

Good.

She shifted slightly beneath the man on top of her, arching just enough to test her angle, to judge how far she'd need to roll and how many seconds she'd have once they let their guards down. Her fingers flexed behind her back, twisting until they gripped the links of her chains between them.

Not yet. But close.

She inhaled slowly, her gaze still on the man with the keys. The bastard–short, broad, with a grin too wide for his face–stepped into the cell like he'd already claimed her. His eyes glittered, breath sour with drink, boots tracking filth across the floor as he approached.

"Now, now," he crooned, dragging out the words like a lover's whisper. "Let's have ourselves a little fun–"

She let him touch her. Let his fingers skim down her hips, too rough, too greedy, dipping into the crook between her thighs like he owned her body, like she hadn't baited every inch of this.

Behind him, another mercenary followed. He didn't reach for her at first, just grinned, eyes gleaming as he lifted something from the firepit.

An iron rod.

The tip glowed faintly red. *The brand.*

"No!" Arjun hissed from the other cell, fists white-knuckled on the bars. "Don't–don't you fucking touch her–"

But the man didn't stop. He crouched beside her, and before Kal could move, the iron seared into her hip with a wet, crackling hiss. She didn't scream. She couldn't. Her jaw locked, spine arching against the agony, breath stolen as the smell of burnt flesh filled the cell. Her fingers curled into the stone. Her entire body shuddered.

And then, he laughed. The man with the brand *laughed* as he pulled the iron away.

"Now that's a pretty mark," he sneered. "Might keep it as a souvenir."

She moved. Her chains snapped up in a blur, the iron links arcing through the air and slamming into the face of the man with the keys. Bone cracked. Blood sprayed. He screamed, spitting teeth as he stumbled back, and Kal surged forward. Her knee drove into his gut. He doubled. She spun behind him, hooked her arm around his throat, and slammed her elbow into the base of his skull. He crumpled to the floor like butchered meat.

The one with the brand lunged. She met him head-on, twisting inside his reach. The iron caught her shoulder as he flailed, the still-hot tip grazing her skin–a shallow burn, but sharp enough to tear a gasp from her.

She used it. Spun low, yanked him off balance, then drove the chains around his neck and *pulled.* He thrashed, kicked, nails tearing into her forearms, but she bore down with everything she had, shadows swimming at the edge of her vision. He jerked once, then went limp.

She dropped him and turned. Another man came for her, blade half-drawn. She ducked beneath it, drove her shoulder into his gut, then rammed the heel of her palm up into his throat. He choked. She didn't stop, brought her knee up into his nose, cartilage shattering beneath the blow. He went down.

She didn't hesitate. The keys–she kicked them hard across the floor, past bars slick with blood. Arjun caught them.

Another mercenary surged forward with a wild swing. She twisted, but not fast enough. His dagger slashed across her ribs, deep enough to sting. She gritted her teeth, lashed out, and drove her elbow into the side of his head. He stumbled. She followed, sweeping his leg and dropping him hard, then crushed his windpipe with her forearm.

One more down.

She was swaying now. Her side bled. Her shoulder and hip throbbed from the brand. Her vision blurred at the edges. The iron still clung to her wrists like lead. Her breath came in ragged bursts.

And then –

A snap. A hum of energy. Magic rippled across the floor.

Kal turned her head, chest heaving, just in time to see Arjun standing in his cell. The manacles lay open at his feet. His hands were lifted, green magic coursing across his skin, pulsing brighter with every heartbeat.

The guards outside froze.

Arjun's eyes glowed like embers. His voice was silent but his power *screamed.*

They clutched their throats. Choked. Fell one by one, twitching, gasping as invisible hands crushed their lungs. He held his ground, let the rage pour through him, precise and punishing. When the last body hit the stone floor, twitching once, then still, the silence that followed was deafening.

Kal lay in the ruins of the cell, her chest bare, skin scorched and bleeding, her body shaking with the aftermath. But her eyes, her eyes never looked away from Arjun. He was alive, and *free.*

The silence after Arjun's magic ebbed was thick, more than quiet. Kal stayed where she was, half-curled on the cold floor, chest heaving in shallow gasps. Every inch of her burned. Her wrists, raw and torn. Her side, where the blade had kissed flesh. Her hip, where the iron had seared deep. Arjun knelt beside her, breath ragged, hands trembling as he undid the shackles. The locks clicked free with a metallic groan, and the iron fell away like a curse lifted. Magic flooded back into her, slow and unsteady, rising through her limbs like light through fractured glass. It wasn't healing. Not yet. Just *hers* again. Her power, her pulse, her control.

He touched her shoulder. "Kal –"

She flinched. Only slightly. A bare twitch beneath his hand.

"I'm not –" he tried, voice raw, uncertain.

"I know." Her whisper barely made it out.

He hesitated, then helped her sit up, careful not to jostle the wounds. His fingers brushed her arm, blood-slick and trembling, and she leaned forward before she could stop herself, pressing her forehead into his shoulder, eyes closed.

"I'm here," he said, voice low and ragged. "Gods, Kal...you –" His voice caught, but she felt what he couldn't say in the way he held her – like she was something broken that he didn't know how to let go of. "You found me"

They didn't move for a long breath. Her fingers curled in the fabric at his side. His hand braced gently against her back, as if she might vanish again if he let go. The stink of blood and smoke clung to them both. Her skin throbbed beneath every breath, every heartbeat, but she stayed upright. Stayed aware.

When she finally pulled back, her face was streaked with sweat, dirt, and the shadow of something that wasn't quite grief. She wiped the corner of her mouth with the back of her hand and swallowed hard.

"We have to move," she said hoarsely.

"You're hurt," Arjun said. "Badly."

"And we're not safe." Her gaze swept the room—the corpses, the flickering torches, the stone that still stank of death and cruelty. "I can't wait for the pain to pass."

His mouth tightened, but he nodded. She rose and nearly fell again when her left leg faltered beneath her. Arjun caught her with a hand to her arm, steadying but not stopping her. Kal straightened on her own. Pulled her ruined tunic back into place with what little was left of the fabric. She ignored the exposed skin. The burn that flared with each movement. The blood crusting cold along her torso.

"Whoever's left," she said, "they'll have heard the screams. We don't have long."

Arjun moved to speak, then stopped. His brow furrowed. His head tilted. And Kal heard it too. A sound from beyond the dungeon door. Wood creaking beneath weight. Footsteps. Steady. Closing. She drew breath through her teeth and reached down, snatching a blade from one of the corpses.

They turned together, side by side, bodies tensed as the rusted door groaned open. Torchlight spilled through the widening crack. Shadows stretched long and jagged across the floor. And in the silence that followed, neither of them knew whether it was salvation that stepped through that door.

Or something worse.

The Corridor of Blades

he door burst inward with a thunderous slam, splinters and rust exploding from its hinges. Torchlight bled into the room, cutting across the stone floor in jagged lines.

Kalithea barely had time to raise her blade before a dagger whistled through the air–sharp, fast, unforgiving. It missed her. Arjun twisted, dropping low just in time for the blade to sail past his head and bury itself in the wall with a violent *thunk*.

Then came the shadow.

Jaymes crossed the threshold like a storm. His coat was torn at the shoulder, blood drying across his jaw, eyes lit with murder. He didn't hesitate. His fist slammed into Arjun's face with the weight of all the miles they'd tracked, all the violence endured, all the hours spent thinking she was gone. Bone cracked. Arjun staggered backward, crashing against the rusted bars of the opposite cell, his shoulder hitting hard enough to make the frame rattle.

But he didn't go down. Power surged up his spine, green light igniting his arms like a lightning struck from within. His body coiled with magic, half-limp, half-feral, as he righted himself in a single breath, already lifting his hand to strike–

"*STOP!*"

Kal stepped between them. The word rang out, sharp enough to slice through the air. It held none of her usual restraint, only fire. Her body swayed with the effort of holding herself upright, blood streaking her ribs, the burn on her hip peeking out from what was left of her tunic. But her arms stayed raised, her voice unshaken.

Jaymes stopped mid-step, chest heaving, eyes locked on Arjun with a fury that hadn't dimmed in the slightest. Kipp was just behind him– bloody, breathing hard, his knife still wet with blood in his grip. One side of his shirt was torn open to reveal a gash along his side, and his jaw was swollen where someone had landed a blow. But he didn't speak he just stared.

At Kal. At her torn clothing. Her wrists. The dark ring of bruises around her throat. The brand marks. And something in him went deathly still.

Arjun stood opposite them, face bruised, lip split, magic still humming beneath his skin. Kal turned slowly, her body a battleground of pain and composure. She met Jaymes' eyes first. Then Kipp's. She didn't bother with apologies. There was no time. And even if there had been, she wasn't sure they'd want to hear them.

Instead, she simply said, voice raw: "You shouldn't be here."

Jaymes' expression didn't shift. But Kipp, finally–just barely–smiled. Not with humor.

"Too late for that."

She nodded once, and then she staggered. Arjun caught her elbow, steadied her with both hands before she could drop.

Kal's voice was a whisper when she said it, but it carried like thunder in the quiet that followed.

"We need to move."

She didn't add *before more come*. She didn't have to. The blood on Jaymes' coat. The gash along Kipp's ribs. The fresh corpses in the halls behind them, none of it said safety.

"We can't move like this," Arjun said, his voice low but urgent. "Not in this state–" His eyes darted to Kal, to the blood slick along her side, to the sluggish way she kept weight off her left leg. His mouth opened, words forming–already shifting toward her wounds, toward the brand he hadn't dared name.

"No." Her voice was quiet but commanding. "Heal them first."

Arjun blinked. "Kal–"

"I said–" She turned to him now, her eyes like steel, unwavering. "*Heal them.*"

The air thickened. For a moment, no one moved. Seeing them like this–Kipp with his jaw split and tunic dark with blood, Jaymes leaning ever so slightly against the wall to keep pressure off his side–clawed at her heart. They looked like they'd fought their way through hell to find her. And in some ways, they had.

"I'm fine," she added, and the lie burned as she said it. "You know damn well I've taken worse."

Arjun's jaw tightened, but he knelt beside Kipp without another word, the green shimmer of magic already beginning to glow at his fingertips. Kipp's gaze dropped to the man's hands, wary, suspicious of magics he'd never seen. His whole body tensed.

Jaymes didn't move. "You gonna tell us what happened, or should we keep guessing?"

Kal let out a breath. "You already know. Two men as smart, and as stubborn, as you are? You figured it out the second you walked in."

Jaymes' laugh was hollow. "Figured it out, sure. Didn't expect to find you crawling on a blood-soaked floor half-naked and branded like livestock though."

Kipp didn't speak, but the shift in his face was worse than words. He flinched when Arjun's magic hit the edge of a wound–then gritted his teeth, not from pain, but from the helpless, burning fury clawing through him.

"Do you have any idea what it was like tracking you through that sewer pit of a city?" Jaymes snapped. "Leaving a trail of corpses and following whispers until we finally get here and find *this*?" His voice dropped. "You were supposed to be smarter than this."

Kipp hissed as the wound on his side stitched closed, muscle re-knitting beneath Arjun's glowing hand. He looked at Kal, his expression pained, then cold.

"Was this your plan?" Kipp asked, voice low, dangerous. "Let them touch you? Let them *brand* you, so you could slip a few chains and hope it worked out?"

"It *did* work," she said.

He shook his head once, slow. "Gods, Kal."

"You think we give a damn about your trap working?" Jaymes ground out. "We weren't supposed to find you like this!"

"That wasn't your choice," she said quietly.

"You're damn right it wasn't," he growled. "Because you never gave us one."

Arjun moved to Jaymes next, and the pirate didn't stop him. But his eyes never left Kal's. The tension pulsed between them–anger, yes, but something deeper too. Wounded. Raw.

Kipp's jaw flexed. "You think we would've let this happen if we'd come with you?"

"I know you would've *died* trying to stop it," Kal said, her voice a little too soft. "And that wasn't something I could afford."

"Don't give me that," Kipp snapped, exasperated. "Don't you dare act like it was noble. You didn't protect us. *You shut us out.*"

She looked away. Just for a breath.

Arjun's magic faded. The wound along Jaymes' ribs sealed with a faint glow, but the fury in his eyes didn't dim.

"We don't have time to argue," she said. "They'll be regrouping. We need to go."

Jaymes crossed his arms. "And what, exactly, is the plan now?"

"The stronghold was the easy part," she said, her voice low and measured, cutting clean through the haze of silence. "The city's the real trap. Too many eyes. Too many swords waiting for the right moment."

Arjun's eyes narrowed.

Kal pushed forward. "So we give them something to look at."

She let it settle before she added, "We need a ruse."

Kal squared her shoulders, forcing her body to still. "We have two kings," she said. "And conveniently, a woman who already *looks* the part of one entertaining them"

Kipp let out a short, stunned laugh. It wasn't amused.

"Absolutely not," Arjun said with finality, already guessing where this was going.

She didn't acknowledge him. "If I'm draped across your arms, painted in the right light, no one's going to stop us. They'll see what they expect to see, what they *want* to see."

"And what's that?" Kipp asked, his voice incredulous now. "What do they *want* to see, Kal?"

She looked straight at him. "A paid distraction."

Kipp's mouth pressed into a hard line. Jaymes' jaw ticked. Arjun didn't speak—just stood there, still and silent, fists clenched like he was holding back words he couldn't unsay.

"You're *not* doing this," Arjun said again, this time through his teeth.

"Do you have a better plan?" she asked, turning to him fully.

The silence answered for him.

She turned next to Jaymes. "Captain?"

Jaymes didn't move. His stormy gaze pinned her, looking at her like he wanted to say a dozen things, none of them fit for this moment. Instead, he said nothing, just dragged a hand through his hair and muttered, "Your plan's fine—for the city. Once we're out." His eyes flicked to the blood-slick door. "But we're not out yet."

"Which means," Kipp continued, sliding one of his knives back into its sheath with a wet click, "we're going to have to fight our way through the rest of this hole. Unless one of you has a better idea, or–" He glanced at Arjun. "You've got more of that magical firepower ready to go?"

Arjun's head turned slowly. The look he gave Kipp wasn't even irritated. It was withering.

"Do I *look* like I'm brimming with magical firepower?"

Kipp smirked. "You tell me. You did light up like a divine punishment not ten minutes ago."

"And I burned through every last scrap of power doing it," Arjun muttered, sweeping a hand toward the room—at the iron shackles still bolted to the wall, the scorched bodies, the tools still slick with rust and blood. "How exactly do you think magic works when you're being drained by iron twenty-four hours a day, etched with runes designed to break you down to your bones?"

He yanked the collar of his shirt aside just enough to show one of the brands beneath–jagged, blackened, still faintly bleeding around the edges.

"That," he said flatly. "That's how you lose magic."

Kipp stared for a moment, then gave a single, sharp nod. "Right. Noted."

Arjun's eyes narrowed. "I used what I had left taking care of *you*, by the way," he added, voice dry as ash. "Still not sure you were worth it."

Jaymes didn't answer. He just looked at Kal. Really looked. Her tunic, still soaked through. The gash across her torso. The ragged bruises around her throat and wrists. The way her left side still barely bore weight.

"You knew," he said quietly. "You knew he didn't have anything left, and you still told him to heal us."

She didn't speak, didn't look away either.

Jaymes' voice dropped to a low simmer. "Gods, Kal..."

There wasn't judgment in his voice. Not entirely. Just the kind of anger that sat deep, too quiet to burn, too steady to fade. Kal turned her head toward the door, jaw set, breath shallow. The sounds above them were rising again now–voices, footsteps, orders being shouted. Voices raised in alarm.

"They're coming," Arjun said, low.

"No shit," Kipp muttered, tilting his head toward the ceiling. "Sounds like they brought friends."

Another beat passed. Then the clatter of a gate being unbarred. A shout. Heavier footsteps now–reinforcements.

"Perfect," Kipp muttered. He rolled his shoulders with a wince, one hand already reaching for another blade. "Nothing like starting your escape with a suicide charge."

Jaymes cursed under his breath and turned to Arjun. "Make yourself useful."

He tossed a blade across the room. Arjun caught it one-handed, barely flinching as his fingers closed around the hilt. The sword was a poor fit, small for his large frame, but he set his stance without complaint. Kal's grip tightened on her sword. She turned toward the corridor, but even the motion sent her staggering half a step. Her vision swam, just for a breath, but it was enough.

Kipp's eyes snapped to her. His expression shifted from cold to thunderous.

"Godsdammit, Kal," he barked. "You're barely standing."

Kal didn't look at him. "I'm fine."

"You're *bleeding through your ribs*, Kal. Your tunic looks like it lost a knife fight and your eyes just glazed over–how the fuck is that *fine*? You had *him*–" he jabbed a finger toward Arjun "–heal *us* while you're out here swaying like a drunk with a punctured lung?"

She didn't look at him. "It was the right call."

"Right call?" he hissed. "You're half a breath from collapsing. You were branded. You were−" His voice cut off, jaw tightening. "And you think playing the martyr makes you clever?"

Her gaze snapped to him, sharp and fire-laced despite the pallor creeping into her skin. "I think *surviving* makes me clever."

"She's noble," Arjun said dryly, stepping up beside them with the sword Jaymes had thrown him. "Or stupid. It's a fine line."

The silence hung heavy, until Kipp cut through it with a curse. "Noble as ever," he muttered. "And twice as dumb."

Jaymes didn't join the argument. He was already adjusting the grip on his sword, gaze flicking from Kal to the narrowing sliver of hallway light. His tone stayed calm, dangerously so.

"We don't get to play whore and warlords if we die in the goddamned dungeon."

"Then we fight." Kal's voice was steady, but her posture betrayed her. Her legs wobbled, weight shifting too fast to hide the pain. She pulled herself upright again with sheer will.

Kipp cursed, sharp and visceral. "You're going to get yourself killed."

"We all are if we stay," she snapped. "So unless someone's hiding a tunnel behind a corpse, we need to move."

Jaymes tossed another glance toward the door. "We hold this room, we're trapped. Cornered."

"And frankly, I'd rather not die somewhere that smells like piss and burnt flesh." Kipp added.

Kal turned toward them, each breath a staggered effort. "We fight our way to the streets, quickly."

"Assuming," Kipp said, tossing a dry look over his shoulder, "that this hellhole doesn't have two hundred more mercs just waiting upstairs with torches and a death wish."

"And if we're lucky," Jaymes added, eyes flicking toward the hallway, "we make it to the Tempest."

Kipp gave a low grunt of approval. "If your ship's still floating, your crew should be waiting to light up the docks the second they see us."

"Assuming we live that long," Arjun muttered.

Kipp gave a crooked half-smile. "Well, fuck it then. Let's bleed loud."

The corridor beyond the door erupted with noise−shouting now, clearer, closer. Boots crashing against the stone. A door slammed open somewhere down the hall. Someone screamed an order.

Kal didn't wait. She stepped forward, dragging her battered body upright, and set her stance before the door. Jaymes was at her right in a blink. Kipp flanked her left. Arjun behind, sword raised like he had no illusions about how this would go. Kipp didn't wait for a signal. He slammed the door open with a sharp crack, the hinges screaming as it ricocheted off the stone wall. The torchlight from the corridor spilled across them, casting jagged shadows over blood-streaked stone.

"Showtime," he muttered, knives already in hand.

They surged into the corridor as one. They moved fast, retracing the path Kipp and Jaymes had carved in. Past broken bodies. Fresh blood already drying on the floor. The stink of it clung to the stone, thick with metal and rot.

But they didn't make it far.

One corridor.

Just one.

And then—

A roar.

The mercenaries came around the corner like a wave—twelve, maybe fifteen of them, armor pieced together hastily, blades flashing in anticipation. No order. No formation. Just violence.

Jaymes didn't flinch. He moved first, slamming into the front line like a hammer, blade flashing, clean and brutal. His first strike took a man's arm clean off. The second crushed a windpipe. He flowed into the next strike—fluid, sharp, and utterly relentless. Kipp was beside him, faster and meaner. He ducked low beneath a sword swing, came up with both knives punching into soft flesh, and twisted hard. The man screamed, and Kipp shoved him into the next attacker like a shield before sliding a blade under the helmet of the one behind him and ripping it free with a wet snap.

Arjun came up behind them, face blank, almost calm. His blade-work was elegant, every strike was precise. The man who had held him down days ago took a slash across the throat before he could speak. Another tried to lunge, and Arjun caught his wrist, twisted until bone cracked, and drove the sword through his gut with quiet violence.

Then there was Kal. She moved like death made flesh. Every motion cost her. Blood dripped steadily from her wounds, her leg stiff with pain—but it didn't slow her. If anything, it made her terrifying. She danced through the crush of bodies like a phantom, sword flashing in delicate, merciless arcs. A mercenary lunged. She caught his blade with her own, twisted, drove her knee into his groin and slammed her sword through the hollow of his throat.

Another came at her from behind. She didn't turn. She whipped the pommel of her sword backward, catching him across the face with the force of iron and fury. He crumpled. Jaymes caught her movement out of the corner of his eye and closed ranks—his blade crossed with hers just in time to block a strike meant for her back. Their eyes met for half a breath. She nodded once. They moved on.

Kipp was laughing now—low, breathless, grim. Blood streaked his jaw, and his tunic was soaked through, but his steps didn't falter. "Come on, you bastards!" he hissed, ducking another swing. "I'm just getting started."

Arjun wasn't laughing. His mouth was a grim line. A mercenary charged him, roaring. The fae sidestepped, drove his sword through the man's thigh, then kicked him down and opened his throat with a single, clean motion. Kal spun to her left, slicing through a man's shoulder. He fell screaming—and she turned straight into another blade, catching it across her arm. She didn't cry out. She didn't even slow. She slammed her elbow into the attacker's face, then drove her blade straight up under his chin.

The corridor was chaos now—steel and screams and blood coating the stones. The mercenaries kept coming. But the four of them held.

The corridor bent hard to the right, narrowing into a choke point lined with broken sconces and blackened torch brackets. Kipp led the way, blades slick in both hands, breath rasping through clenched teeth. Jaymes followed at his shoulder. Kal and Arjun just behind.

For a moment, there was only the slap of boots on stone. Blood-slick walls. The throb of pain in every limb.

Then—

Another wave hit them. Ten, maybe twelve mercenaries this time. These moved better. Smarter. They spaced out across the hall, blades drawn, flanking fast, barking orders.

"Fuck," Kipp muttered and then they were in it again.

Jaymes surged forward, sword meeting steel with a crash that rang down the stone. He drove his blade through the first man's chest, ripped it out, then ducked low to parry another strike, but not fast enough. A sword scraped across his ribs. Shallow, but sharp. He grunted, spun, and took the attacker down with a blow to the throat.

Kipp was beside him, knives flashing. One blade buried itself in a thigh. The other caught a throat mid-shout—but a third man blindsided him. Steel bit into Kipp's upper arm, slicing through the leather with a hot, red spray. He staggered.

Kal turned just in time to see him drop to one knee, eyes wide, blood trailing down his side. *Something broke in her.* Her breath caught, the air around her warping. The torchlight dimmed. Shadows rose, surging violently. They clawed up her spine and spilled outward, tendrils curling across the floor like living smoke, cold and pulsing with violent promise.

"Kal!" Arjun's voice cracked across the noise, sharp as a whip. He slashed another attacker across the face, then turned to her. "*Control it!*"

She couldn't speak. Could barely breathe.

Jaymes was dragging himself upright, pressing a hand to his side.

Kipp was bleeding. Arjun was limping, his movements slower now, every swing of his blade just a little shorter than the one before.

They were breaking.

She felt the choice rising in her chest like bile. Without a word, Kal pivoted and moved—fast—slipping through the crush of bodies, ducking under blades, making for the far side of the corridor.

"KAL!" Arjun shouted.

But she didn't stop. She didn't look back. She drove her blade into a mercenary in front of her, shoved the corpse aside, and broke free of the skirmish, running toward the sounds of reinforcements further down the hall—drawing attention, drawing fire, drawing the enemy away.

Kipp saw her just as she passed the last line of attackers. He swore violently and broke off, bolting after her. He caught her around the waist, yanking her back hard against his chest.

"What the *fuck* do you think you're doing?" he hissed in her ear.

She twisted in his grip, breathing ragged. "Stopping you from having to choose."

"*What?*"

"You can't keep protecting all of us," she said, eyes bright, voice too low, too raw. "So I'm making the choice for you."

Kipp stared at her like he might shake the sense back into her.

"Damn you," he snapped. "*You infuriating, beautiful, absolutely dense woman—I chose you*, dammit!"

Kal's breath caught.

"You just don't believe it," Kipp growled.

Before she could answer, another mercenary lunged, blade catching Kipp across the back in a flash of blood and cloth. He hissed and dropped to one knee. Kal moved lightning fast, her sword driving through the attacker's chest before he could land a second blow. She caught Kipp as he dropped but he shoved her off with one bloodied hand.

"I'm fine," he muttered, voice tight with pain.

"No, you're—"

Jaymes appeared behind them, grabbing Kipp by the arm and hauling him upright. "*Enough.*" His voice was steel. "We move. Together."

His gaze swept between them, no room for argument, no space for pride.

"*TOGETHER*," he said again.

Kal swallowed hard and nodded. The shadows hissed softly at her feet, reluctant to retreat. But she forced them down.

They kept moving. The fortress sprawled ahead in a maze of corridors and splintered stairwells, half-lit and blood-slick. Every corner they turned brought another wave—mercenaries crashing into them with steel and fury, desperate to contain what had slipped free. And still, they pushed forward.

Kipp moved like a wraith–low, fast, and merciless. His blades sang with each kill, his coat soaked dark where blood had sprayed across his side, but he didn't falter. Arjun stayed close, slower now, one leg dragging slightly from the months of torment, but his sword still struck viciously, jaw clenched tight against every step. Jaymes covered their flank, steady and ruthless, his blade an extension of his will–cutting down anything that slipped through the press.

And Kal?

Kal was losing ground. The pain had started as background noise. Distant. Manageable. But now it gnawed at her with every heartbeat. The wound at her side tore wider with each twist, her limbs growing heavy, her breath ragged from effort. But worse, far worse, was the pull beneath her skin.

The shadows. They were rising again. Climbing her spine, blooming from her fingertips in tendrils too dark to belong in the realm of men. They lashed out in short bursts–defensive, reactive–but each time she tried to pull them back, it took more. More will. More blood. More of *her.*

"Kal!" Arjun's voice snapped through the din. "*Control it!*"

She ground her teeth together, fighting the twist of power rising in her chest. The shadows recoiled, barely. Another wave crashed into them. Kal cut one down, spun, parried another–but her legs buckled on the landing. She hit the stone floor hard, one hand braced to push herself up, but the shadows surged forward again like a beast sensing weakness.

"Kalithea!" Arjun shouted, panic bleeding through his voice as he drove his sword into a mercenary's side. "You have to *pull them back!* You're going to lose control–"

"I *know,*" she rasped.

But she couldn't do it all. She couldn't stand and fight and bleed and hold the shadows all at once.

Jaymes saw it happen. Saw her sway, then collapse to one knee, her arm trembling as she tried to push up again. The next instant, he was beside her, sword dripping in one hand, his other arm hooking beneath her shoulders.

"No," Kal gasped. "I can still–"

"We don't have time for this," Jaymes snapped, already lifting her. "You can't walk? Fine. I'll be your legs. But you'll damn well be the sword."

He shifted her in his grip, cradling her over his ribs, her sword hand free. Her head rested against his shoulder for a breath before she forced herself upright again, twisting just enough to lift the blade.

"I can still fight," she gasped.

"Good," Jaymes said. "Then fight."

They pushed forward again.

Kipp led, blades flashing. Arjun close behind, fighting hard despite the blood soaking through his sleeve and the tremor in his bad leg. Kal clung to consciousness, held in Jaymes' arms, her sword darting out when the enemy got close, her shadows twisting around them all like smoke trailing from a fire she couldn't extinguish.

She tried to hold it back. She tried. But the darkness wanted out.

It wanted to burn.

And the more she bled, the harder it became to say no.

They tore through the last corridor like wolves cornered, all teeth and desperation. The final group of mercenaries was waiting at the outer gate–six men, one already bloodied, likely from the chaos deeper in. No commands. No taunts. Just drawn blades and grim resolve.

It didn't matter.

Kipp cut through the first before the man could raise his sword. Arjun's sword slipped into another's side, even as he limped, his body protesting every movement. Kal, cradled in Jaymes' arms, lashed her blade out with instinct more than skill–one arm bloody, her vision dark at the edges, her shadows licking at the stone like hungry wolves barely leashed.

They didn't fight clean. They fought to escape. And when the last mercenary fell with a gurgled scream, the gate stood open. Beyond it lay the tree line. Distant. Blurred by smoke and the lingering haze of torches and death.

But free.

They stumbled out into the half-light, staggering past the threshold of the fortress into the open night. The trees beyond loomed dark and wild, the air colder, cleaner–but their blood left a trail behind them with every step.

Jaymes dragged them forward. Kipp limped beside him, blood running in thick rivers down his arm, soaking into his tunic. Arjun clutched his side, his steps uneven, face pale. The wounds across his back, ripped open again in the fight, bled through his shirt in wide, dark patches.

Kal was a ghost in Jaymes' arms. Her skin was paper white, slick with sweat. Blood dripped steadily from her side, her leg, her arm. Her head lolled once against his shoulder, and when her eyes closed–

The shadows surged. Tendrils rose, writhing across the ground like they were searching for something to tear.

"Kal," Jaymes said sharply.

No response.

"Kalithea!"

Her eyes snapped open. The shadows halted. Quivered. Then reluctantly, slowly, pulled back into her. She blinked, shivered, and faded again.

"Shit," Kipp muttered, wiping blood from his face with a shaky hand. "We need a plan."

Jaymes adjusted Kal's weight, one arm wrapped tightly around her middle. "We move. Fast and quiet. Get to the docks, find the crew, hope to the gods they see us coming."

"And if they don't?" Kipp asked.

"Then we light the whole city on fire," Jaymes said flatly.

Arjun sank to one knee, breath ragged. "We won't make it far like this. Not through the city. Not bleeding like this."

Kipp opened his mouth to argue, then Kal laughed. It was faint. Breathless. But unmistakable.

Jaymes looked down sharply. "Kal?"

She was smiling. Or trying to.

"Guess we get to play whore and warlords after all," she murmured, voice weak and slurred.

Then she shoved at Jaymes' chest.

"Kal–don't–"

But she was already pushing herself free, slipping from his arms. She hit the ground, *hard.*

Kipp swore viciously and dropped to one knee beside her, stopping her before she could slump fully.

"Godsdammit–*Kal*–"

She shoved at his hand.

"No," she said, breath catching. "We can still use it. The plan. The clothes, the blood. Stick to the shadows. Sell the lie."

"You can't even stand," Jaymes snapped, kneeling down beside her.

But she was already trying to rise. Her legs shook. Her sword hung from limp fingers. Blood ran down her thigh and dripped from her elbow.

"I don't have to walk far," she whispered. "I just have to make it look good."

They stared at her. Kal wavered again, her knees folding beneath her with a slow, graceless drop. She caught herself on one hand, but barely. Her other trembled around the hilt of her sword, blood dripping in soft, rhythmic taps against the earth.

Jaymes moved to grab her again, but she shook her head, eyes glassy but focused.

"No. Not cradled. Not carried," she said, voice low but insistent. "Held up. Between you both."

"Kal," Kipp said, crouching beside her. "You're losing too much blood. You can't walk–"

"I don't need to walk," she said, lifting her head with a strange, lopsided smile. "I need to sell it, just...have to sell...it"

She looked at Jaymes, then at Kipp. Her expression flickered–half lucid, half somewhere else entirely. "Two kings. One spoiled prize. They'll believe it, I know they will. We just have to *make* them."

Jaymes hesitated. Then nodded once. "We make it look good. Like we belong."

Kal swayed again. Kipp caught her elbow before she could collapse. "I'm fine," she mumbled.

"You're *not* fine," he growled. "You're barely conscious."

But she laughed, soft and a little too bright.

"Look at you," she said, blinking at Kipp with unfocused amusement. "After all that effort, you're finally going to get to hold me close. Should've let myself nearly die *ages* ago."

Kipp stared at her. The color had drained from her face completely, her lips tinged gray, but her smirk was still there–ragged and giddy.

"You're delirious," he muttered. "And this is dangerously close to a confession."

She leaned her head on his shoulder for a breath. "Don't get used to it."

"Oh, I won't," he said, sliding his arm around her waist. "Apparently it only takes near-death to get you into my arms. Noted."

Jaymes stepped in on the other side without a word. Together, they hauled her upright. She hissed between her teeth, her knees buckling, but they kept her standing. Her feet barely touched the ground.

"Eyes up," Jaymes said quietly. "If you can. Don't let them see you breaking."

"I'm not breaking," Kal whispered.

But her voice shook. Her shadows curled low around her boots, flickering in protest, restless in her pain. They began to move, three men and a queen wrapped in blood and ruin, her body held between them like a treasure taken by force.

Every step into the city would be a gamble.

But the lie was good.

Too good.

And if they could sell it–if they could get through the streets–

They might just live long enough to reach the sea.

The Thing They Buried

The city swallowed them like a beast waiting to finish its meal.

They moved in silence, the illusion cloaking them as much as the shadows did–Kal dragged between them, head down, blood trailing with every step. Her tunic clung to her ribs in soaked, tattered folds hanging just low enough to conceal the worst of the wounds.

To the guards at the edge of alleys, the watchers from behind shutters, they looked like what they were pretending to be: two powerful men with a conquered prize between them, leading her off into the night for pleasures no one would dare ask about.

No one stopped them. No one spoke. But every step through the crooked, flickering streets felt like walking the edge of a knife.

Kal's weight sagged more with each block. She'd been silent for a while now, jaw tight, breath shallow–but then, as they turned down a narrow lane near the old cistern market, she murmured, so soft it was nearly lost in the breeze:

"Kipp..."

His eyes snapped to her, but she wasn't looking at him. Her head lolled slightly against his shoulder, the side of her face pressed to the worn leather of his coat.

"Your arms," she whispered. "They feel...nice. Strong."

Kipp blinked. Stared straight ahead. "... *Gods, Kal.*"

Jaymes turned his head just slightly, but didn't speak.

Kal shifted a little in his hold, barely a movement at all. "And you," she said, her voice breathy, almost dreamy, "you've got these eyes..."

Jaymes glanced down, meeting her gaze.

"Like the sea," she finished softly. "Deep...beautiful."

Neither man spoke. Because under any other circumstances those words would've stopped time. But now? Now they just twisted the knife.

Kipp's jaw clenched. "She's slipping."

Jaymes nodded once. "We need to move faster."

Kal giggled faintly, the sound feather-light and utterly wrong in the heavy dark. "You're both so serious," she whispered. "I *do* notice you know. Watching me. Wanting..."

Her words trailed off into a breath. Her legs buckled again. They caught her, both of them tightening their hold at once, but Kipp was white-knuckled around her waist now.

"This isn't good," he muttered.

Jaymes looked ahead. "Docks are close. We get her on the ship. No delays."

Kal stirred once more, blinking up at them through half-lidded eyes.

"I didn't want you to have to choose..." she murmured, trailing off again.

They kept walking. Step by brutal step, past crooked shutters and watching eyes, dragging their queen through a city that had broken her body before it could destroy her spirit.

They saw the gates. Just ahead, past the last crooked row of buildings, the docks just beyond. The scent of salt hung thick in the air, the promise of the Tempest somewhere in the dark, waiting.

One more stretch. Just a little farther...

Then the world turned.

A single shout cracked the silence. "It's them! The Princess and the Fae bastard!"

Then another, louder. "*Sound the alarm!*"

A horn blared and everything unraveled. Doors flew open. Windows slammed back. Footsteps thundered from all directions. Blades glinted in torchlight as mercenaries, guards, and street thugs poured from alleyways, swarming the narrow road like locusts. The whole city was Mawborn—*every godsdamned soul.*

"They knew," Kipp hissed, tightening his grip on Kal's waist. "They *all* knew."

Jaymes didn't answer. He just dropped his shoulder and shifted her weight between them, sword sliding clean into his free hand.

The mob surged but there were too many. Steel flashed and the first man lunged. Kipp cut him down. Another came at Jaymes, and he drove his blade through the man's chest without slowing. But the crowd didn't stop. More poured in, screaming, shouting, teeth bared. Like a city possessed.

Kal tried to lift her head. Her breath was shallow, blood trickling from her lips now. "What—"

"Don't speak," Jaymes snapped, fending off two more with a brutal, efficient swing. "We're almost th—"

But they weren't.

The mob collapsed on them like a wave breaking. Hands grabbed Kipp first, yanked him back hard, wrenching him away from Kal's side. He cursed and lashed out, blade sinking deep into someone's stomach but there were too many.

"No–NO–Kal–!"

Jaymes turned sharply, trying to pull her closer, shield her–and then they grabbed him too. Pulled him down into the crush of bodies. Someone struck his head, another drove a knee into his gut. He disappeared beneath a dozen clawing hands.

"*KAL!*" he shouted.

Kal fell. She hit the ground hard, one hand dragging her sword with her.

"Jaymes?" she croaked, disoriented.

"Kipp?"

She turned, too slow, looking for them.

Arjun fought toward her, his blade rising, breath ragged. But the crowd had him too, piling on from every side. He slashed a path forward before someone clubbed him across the back. He staggered, blood trailing from his mouth.

"*Kal control it! NO! DON'T!*" he roared.

But it was too late. Her head snapped up and her eyes–her eyes were already black.

The shadows stirred at her feet.

Hungry.

Alive.

For one terrible heartbeat, there was silence.

Then the shadows exploded. They tore out of Kalithea like a storm of destruction and violence, ripping through the air with a shriek that wasn't sound but *pressure*–a wrongness that shattered windows and cracked stone. The force of it lifted her from the ground, limbs slack, blood still dripping from her wounds in long, crimson strands. Her hair whipped around her face, caught in the vortex that spun around her like a living storm, her eyes pitch black and unblinking.

The mob staggered back.

Too late.

The shadows were already moving. They struck like spears–no, like vipers–lancing into the front line of mercenaries and *tearing* them apart. One man screamed as a tendril wrapped around his leg and ripped it off at the hip. Another tried to flee, but the shadows pierced him clean through, dragging his flailing body back through the air before splitting him down the middle like wet cloth.

"*HOLD THE LINE!*" someone bellowed.

"Don't let her–gods, *don't let her*–!"

A man near the front–scarred, teeth gritted–lifted a sword with trembling hands.

"We buried her once!" he shouted. "She dies tonight!"

Kal's head turned toward him, slowly. Her neck cricked at an unnatural angle, tilting too far, as if it was broken.

Her voice came low, like a breath pulled from a crypt. Hollow. Empty. Endless.

"I am not the girl you buried," she said, her voice one with the whispers inside of her.

The shadows rose curling higher around her, forming teeth and tendrils and formless, hungry things.

"I am the thing that crawled out."

The man's sword trembled in his grip. The shadows struck again. They came in a hundred screaming forms. One wrapped around a soldier's throat and pulled until the skin tore and his head came free with a wet crack. Another sliced through a man's midsection, and his guts spilled steaming onto the cobblestones as he dropped, twitching, his screams short-lived.

The vortex expanded.

One mercenary managed a single step back before the shadows wrapped around both legs and *pulled*, splitting him clean at the pelvis. His upper body hit the stone with a sound like dropped meat. Another tried to hide, ducked into a doorway, and was yanked out screaming, shadows pouring into his mouth and bursting out his chest from the inside in a rain of blood and bone.

They screamed.

They ran.

It didn't matter.

The shadows hunted.

Kal floated at the heart of it all, her body pale and motionless, blood still falling in lazy arcs from her fingertips. Her sword had fallen, forgotten. Her mouth moved but no sound came now. Only the endless, pulsing darkness that poured from her like the last breath of a dying god.

The square was red.

Then black.

Then red again.

And still the shadows raged.

They tore through the remaining crowd until there was nothing left to tear–no bodies to eviscerate, no bones to break, no flesh to peel away from corpses. Those too slow to flee had been torn apart. Those too brave to run, shredded in an instant.

The square was a graveyard without graves.

And then, with no more lives to take, the shadows turned on the *city itself.* They struck the buildings first. A tendril lashed through a support beam, and the wall of a tavern collapsed inward as if rotted from within. Another set of shadows sliced upward into a second-floor window and dragged the stone frame out of itself, brick dissolving like paper set to flame. A storage house imploded as shadow punched through its foundation and unmade its structure from the inside. One of the support towers cracked at the base and folded in on itself with a scream of splintering timber and stone.

The air stank of blood, smoke, and something older–something wrong.

Kal's shadows weren't just destroying, they were *erasing.* Unraveling the mortar and wood and metal as though reality itself couldn't hold against her fury. The ground beneath her split. Cracks spiderwebbed outward from where she hovered, lines of molten black carving glowing fissures into the stone. The cobbles cracked and crumbled, the stone itself turning black, bubbling, and peeling away like scorched skin. Every pulse of shadow made the world itself shudder beneath her.

Kipp stood frozen, breath caught somewhere in his throat. Blood still dripped from his shoulder. His sword hung loose in his hand, forgotten. Jaymes stood just behind him, eyes wide. Unblinking. He hadn't moved. Hadn't spoken.

They had both known. Known her power wasn't just the small bit of shadows they'd seen on the ship but neither of them had imagined *this.*

A god of death might have looked gentler than what floated above them now.

A voice broke the stillness, raw and breathless.

"Kipp! Jaymes!"

Arjun stumbled toward them, limping hard, barely walking, blood soaking his side. He grabbed Kipp first, shaking him hard enough to jar the man's whole body, then turned to Jaymes and did the same.

"You have to wake her up!" he shouted. *"NOW!"*

Neither moved.

"If she goes any further–if she falls completely into it–we won't just lose Kal!" His voice cracked with desperation. *"We lose everything! The city, the kingdom–the world ends here and now if she breaks!"*

Behind them, the stone beneath Kal cracked again, this time with a *roar* as the shadows began to scream. The sounds of rending stone gave way to a deafening *crack* as part of the old battlement collapsed inward, swallowed by the vortex of writhing shadows. A surge of wind howled through the ruin, blasting dust and ash across the square.

And then came a new sound. The heavy groan of splintering wood.

The gate.

It burst inward as a dozen figures stormed through–T*empest* crew, armed, bloodied, panting from the sprint to the lower quarter, clearly having met their own opposition along the way. Dorian led the charge, sword in hand, braid half-unraveled, his mouth already moving.

"Jaymes! We heard–what the fuck is–"

He stopped dead in his tracks, as did the rest of them, just staring. Kal hovered at the eye of the storm, her limbs slack, her blood dripping steadily into the cracks below. The vortex of shadows screamed around her, tearing at the stone, gnashing at the buildings, peeling chunks of the world apart as if creation itself were being undone.

"Gods," someone whispered. "What *is* she?"

"*Back!*" Jaymes barked, snapping out of his stupor. "Get the crew *back!* Don't let them near it!"

"But–"

"We don't have time to explain! Just get them *clear*, Dorian! That's an order!"

Dorian swore and turned on the others, shouting commands, herding them away from the storm's edge. None of them looked away. Some couldn't. They stood rooted, open-mouthed, eyes wide with awe and terror.

Because Kal wasn't just a woman anymore.

She was judgment, vengeance.

The ground trembled again. Another building groaned and collapsed in the distance, crumbling into a blackened heap of dust and silence.

Jaymes turned to Kipp. No words–just a shared look. Fear. Rage. *Resolve.*

Then they moved.

Step by step.

One painful lurch at a time.

Dodging falling stone and splintered wood, ducking as tendrils of shadow snapped overhead like whips. The closer they got, the worse it became–the air humming with magic, reality warping around her.

"Kal!" Kipp shouted. "*Kalithea!* Look at me–*look at us!*"

No response.

Only the storm.

Jaymes raised his voice, pushing forward through the gale. "*Kal, it's us!* You have to come back! You have to *see us!*"

Still nothing. Her body hovered, blood dripping. Her shadows coiled like the deep sea come to life.

Kipp gritted his teeth and pressed forward, shielding his eyes against the wind and debris. "Gods, don't do this...*please...*"

They were close enough now to feel the static on their skin, the way the air cracked with unnatural weight. The shadows whipped around Kal like a cyclone of living darkness, violent and frenzied. Every gust from the vortex burned against their skin, the edges of the tendrils sharp enough to slice stone, to flay flesh–but still they pushed forward.

Closer.

Closer.

Until they were right beneath her.

Kal's body hovered above the cracked stone, suspended in the chaos, her head bowed, her hair a tangled, blood-matted veil around her face. Her arms hung limp, the blood still dripping in a steady rhythm.

Kipp reached first.His hand grazed her ankle, then her calf, gripping tight enough to leave bruises if she could still feel them. The shadows recoiled for a breath–then surged again, faster, snapping like beasts trying to tear him back.

He didn't let go.

"Kal..." he gasped, voice hoarse from smoke, from fear. "Kal, come on. Look at me."

No response.

Jaymes stepped in behind him, grabbed her other arm–both of them anchoring her between them now, straining against the current of her magic, their bodies battered and bleeding, the world falling apart around them.

"KALITHEA!" Kipp roared, voice cracking. "You're *safe!* Do you hear me? You *saved* us! You *did it!* You don't have to keep fighting–gods, please–*stop!*"

Still nothing. She didn't blink. She didn't see them.

And then Kipp's voice broke entirely.

"Don't do this!" he begged, yelling, tears blurring his vision, his hands shaking on her skin. "Please, not like this. Don't leave us. *Don't leave me!*"

He choked back a sob, one that broke loose anyway.

"I never–I never gave a damn about anything in my life until *you* came storming in with your fire and your fury and your *fucking games,* and now I don't–I don't know how to *breathe* if you're gone."

His forehead pressed to her thigh, eyes squeezed shut, the storm tearing at his voice.

"Come back," he pleaded. "Please, Kal. Come back."

And something *shifted.* A flicker. A twitch at the corner of her mouth, too small to be certain, too fast to trust.

But Jaymes saw it and he seized it.

"Kal," he yelled, stepping in close, gripping her hand tight, pressing his palm to her icy fingers. "You listen to me!"

His voice was fierce, cutting through the wind and shadow.

"You're the most maddening, impossible, *brilliant* woman I've ever met. You drive me insane! You challenge everything I am. And I swear to every god I never believed in–*you're the only person I've ever known who could match the storm inside me.*"

Kal didn't move but her eyelids fluttered.

"I spent my life trying not to care. Never staying. Never *belonging*. But you–" his voice cracked, just once, "–you make me *want* to stay."

The shadows circled like vultures. Slower now, curling instead of lashing. Watching.

Waiting.

Kal floated in the center, limp between them, her skin cold and soaked in blood, her expression vacant. But something beneath the surface had begun to stir, she started to lower ever so slightly.

Neither of them stopped.

"Kal..." Kipp's voice cracked again, raw with something he'd never let anyone hear before. "I didn't want to say it. Not like this. Not with the world *literally* falling apart around us. But I'm saying it now because–because gods, if this *is* the end..."

He looked up at her blank face, eyes rimmed red, lips trembling with words he never meant to speak.

"I love the way your lips twitch when you're trying not to smile. The way your whole face softens when you look at the sea and think no one's watching. The way you look at people like they're puzzles, like you're already ten steps ahead–but never cruel. Never detached. Just...*brilliant.*"

He stepped closer, reached up to touch her face, gently brushing back blood-matted hair.

"You scare the shit out of me," he continued. "Because I think I started falling for you the second you opened your mouth and told me to shut mine. And I didn't want that. I *fought* that. *But I see you, Kal.* Every piece of you. And I *choose* it. Even the parts that burn."

Jaymes' voice joined him–lower, steadier, but no less shaken.

"I told myself I didn't need anyone. That need made you weak. That love made you *vulnerable.*" He stepped forward, "And then you showed up. You–who challenged me. Matched me. *Met me* in every way that mattered."

He let out a breath that trembled at the edges.

"I love how your eyes look when you're fighting–like storms, like fire. I love how you refuse to yield, even when you should. I love that you make me want to be something *more* than what I am. And gods help me, Kalithea, I didn't realize how *empty* I was until you walked in and filled every void I didn't even know existed."

Kal's eyes fluttered again.

Kipp gripped her tighter, pressing his forehead to her hip.

"If you don't come back now," he said, voice breaking, "then you might as well finish it. Kill us. Because I'd rather die by your hand than live a single day without you in it."

Jaymes nodded, hand tight around hers.

"Me too," he agreed. "If you don't come back...you'll take what's left of us with you."

"*Keep going!*" Arjun's voice tore through the square like a whip-crack. "*Don't stop—keep talking to her!*"

Kipp and Jaymes didn't hesitate.

"Kal," Kipp said, his voice hoarse, lips trembling. "You remember the first time we met? You held me at knife point in the alley and threatened to stab me. And all I could think was—gods, I hope she *does*."

Jaymes' voice followed—stronger now, steadier. "You don't *get* to leave, Kalithea. You don't get to burn through our lives and vanish like a storm. Not after all the shit we've seen. Not after what you *mean*."

Kipp choked out a laugh, thick with tears. "And you still owe me that time, you infuriating little tyrant."

With every word, the vortex pulsed slower. The shrieking wind faded into a mournful hush. The shadows, once wild and violent, now curled like smoke retreating from flame.

"Come back," Jaymes begged. "Come back and fight with us. Live with us. *Stay*."

Kal's body lowered further. Slowly. Like the shadows themselves were letting go. Her feet touched the cracked ground. The last tendrils of black withdrew into her skin—and then, finally, it was quiet.

Utter, bone-deep quiet.

Kalithea collapsed. Kipp and Jaymes caught her in the same breath, falling to their knees with her. Blood still seeped from half-healed wounds. Her head lolled back, lashes still, lips pale, chest unmoving.

Kipp stared. Then blinked.

"Kal?" he said softly. "Kal...come on, you've made your dramatic point, let's go."

Nothing.

Jaymes' hands shook where they gripped her shoulders. "No—no no no, don't you fucking—Kal!" He pressed his hand to her chest.

Still nothing.

Panic ripped through Kipp's face. "*She's not breathing. Jaymes, she's not—*"

"*ARJUN!*" Jaymes roared, voice breaking as he turned toward the mage. "*Get over here—now!*"

The crew of the *Tempest* stood frozen at the edge of the square.

They had seen her tear the city apart. Had seen their captain cry. And now? Now they saw the woman who'd once been a god, limp and pale in the arms of two men who had once been unshakable. Whatever fear had clung to them in the aftermath of her power evaporated in that moment. One by one, the men dropped to their knees.

No one spoke. No one dared breathe.

Arjun surged forward, eyes wide, his body shaking. He dropped beside them and shoved Kipp and Jaymes back, not cruelly, but with urgency.

"Move," he snapped. "*Move, dammit—I need space!*"

His hands hovered over her chest, glowing faintly, but the magic sputtered, weak and nearly gone. He gritted his teeth, muttering desperate words, trying to gather what little strength remained.

"Don't you dare give up now," he hissed, pressing both palms to her chest. "*Don't you dare.*"

The green light refused him. Arjun's hands trembled over her chest, his voice a raw whisper of incantations and pleas, but the magic slipped through his fingers like water through a sieve. Nothing held. Nothing stayed.

"Come on," he muttered, panic lacing his tone. "Come on, dammit—*come on.*"

Again, he tried. And again. But the ley lines didn't answer, not fully. Not like before. They coiled at the edge of his reach, flickering, distant, mocking. His reserves were gone. The iron, the brands, the wounds—it had leeched everything from him. Everything but rage.

And grief.

He looked down at her—pale, blood-soaked, too still. Her lashes didn't even flutter. Her lips were blue.

And just like that, he saw her as she had been. A child in his arms, bones shattered, eyes wide with terror, clinging to life by threads only he could see. She'd been too young. Too broken. And he had bent over her just like this, hands glowing, tears burning as he forced the world to give her back.

"No," Arjun growled, voice low, teeth clenched. "*No—we're not done.*"

He slammed his palms back over her heart, snarling the words of the Old Tongue with venom, with desperation, with *love*. Reaching down into the earth beneath his knees, into the pulsing heart of the ley lines buried deep beneath city stone.

The earth shuddered. Something cracked.

And this time, it *answered*. A pulse of green erupted beneath his hands, vivid, alive, and angry. It surged into her, flowing through her chest, down her limbs, illuminating her bloodied form inch by inch.

Kipp dropped to his knees again beside her, one hand clutching her blood-streaked wrist, the other pressing against her shoulder as though trying to hold her soul in place. His tears were silent now, there was no shame left to hide them. Jaymes knelt across from him, his hand cradling her head, thumb trembling against her temple. His breath came in slow, shallow bursts, as if he feared exhaling would push her too far away.

And then—*finally*—a breath. Shallow. Gasping. But *real*. Then another. A flicker of pink returned to her lips. Her fingers twitched. And slowly her eyes opened. They weren't black now. Just the deep green gold hue they had always been.

She blinked, dazed, unfocused, brow furrowing as she stared up at the three men leaning over her.

Her voice came rough and dry. "What...what happened?"

Jaymes leaned in, eyes wide. "Kal?"

She blinked again, eyes darting around in confusion. "Where are we? Did...did we get out of the fortress?"

Arjun's breath caught, and Kipp turned his face away. *She didn't remember.* Not the battle. Not the city. Not the shadows. Not the things they had whispered when they thought it was the end.

The confessions. The love. The pieces of their hearts laid bare.

Kal's gaze swept across the devastation. The scorched ground. The blackened stone. The ruins of what had once been a city, now nothing more than ash and memory. A sob escaped before she could stop it, raw and low, and she choked on the sound. Her hands trembled as she looked at them–Kipp, Jaymes, Arjun–each of them bloodied. Bruised. Torn. Jaymes still had dried blood at his temple. Kipp's shirt was soaked through, the gash at his ribs reopened. Arjun's entire frame seemed to be held together by force of will alone.

Her voice cracked. "I...I lost control."

Her eyes filled, wild and stricken, darting from Kipp's wound to Arjun's shaking hands, to Jaymes' grimace as he shifted his weight. Her face twisted in horror. "Did I–did I do this? Did I hurt you?"

But before the panic could take her fully, Kipp reached out and caught her hand–firm and unwavering–and forced her to look at him.

"Hey." His voice was steady, a quiet anchor against the storm rising in her chest. "*Look at me, Kal.*"

She did. Eyes rimmed red, lips trembling.

"You didn't hurt us," he said, each word clear and certain. "We're alive because of you. *You saved us.* All of us."

Jaymes shifted closer, one hand braced gently against her back. "You've got us," he whispered. "You're here now. And we're leaving this gods-cursed place. It's over."

His voice dipped lower, a softness she had never heard from him until now. "They won't hurt you again. You did it, Kal. You saved Arjun. You saved us. We can go back to the Tempest. We can rest."

Kal gave a slow, shaky nod. The tears didn't stop, but her breathing steadied. She reached up, trying to rise–gritting her teeth against the weight in her limbs, the pull of a body not fully healed. Her legs buckled almost immediately, and she caught herself on Jaymes' shoulder.

Arjun stepped forward instantly, arms half-raised. "Let me help– once we're clear of this place, I'll be able to access the ley lines fully. I can finish healing–"

"No." Her voice was hoarse but firm. She shoved his hands away. "No. You'll heal *them*. You'll heal yourself. Not me."

Arjun frowned, frustration flickering in his eyes, but Kal pressed on.

"I mean it," she said. "I'll be fine. We both know my blood will heal me faster. You don't get to waste a drop on me."

Jaymes opened his mouth to argue. Kipp looked ready to launch into a string of curses.

But Arjun only sighed and stepped back, his hands falling to his sides, defeated but not surprised. "Stubborn until the end," he muttered.

Kal met his gaze, weary but unflinching. "Every time."

A Thread of Light

The crew of the *Tempest* met them just beyond the ruined gate, weapons drawn and eyes wide. Most hadn't spoken a word since witnessing what Kal had become—what she had unleashed. But as they saw her now, upright between Kipp and Jaymes, bloodied but breathing, something shifted.

A hush passed through the ranks. Some lowered their blades. Others offered a nod, subtle but reverent. They formed up instinctively, falling into a loose perimeter around the group, escorting them back through the dark alleys and scorched streets. And though the city still crackled with dying embers and the taste of magic clung to the air like ash, none of the enemy dared pursue them. If there were any left.

By the time the *Tempest* came into view, docked and waiting like a faithful hound, even the crew looked worn down to the bone. But when the gangplank thudded into place and Kal was guided aboard, quiet cheers broke out, muted but genuine. The fiery queen hadn't fallen.

They got her below decks without a word. Her boots barely scuffed the floor by the time they eased her into her cabin, every inch of her posture fighting sleep. She tried to speak, tried to sit up—but her body had given everything it had to give. She slumped back against the pillows, lashes fluttering.

Her lips moved faintly. "...Kipp... Jaymes..."

The way she said their names—barely a breath, no strength behind it—sent a strange ache through both men. There was no sharpness. No fire. Just tenderness. Just relief. And then she was asleep.

Kipp sat for a beat longer, his hand resting lightly over hers as if still afraid she'd vanish if he let go. Jaymes' shoulders slumped as he exhaled, gaze lingering on her sleeping form.

They left the lantern burning low and closed the door behind them.

Arjun was waiting in Jaymes' quarters when they limped in. He'd cleaned up as best he could–fresh shirt from the crew, bandaged arms, and wounds that still bled at the edges. He didn't say a word. Just poured three glasses of whiskey and slid them across the table.

The silence that followed was sacred.

The sea rocked gently outside. Below them, the ship groaned as the crew made ready to shove off. Orders were barked, lines cut, sails unfurled–*anything* to put distance between them and the ruin they'd left behind. And inside the quiet cabin, three men sat with blood on their hands, salt on their skin, and the weight of the world still pressed against their backs.

Arjun leaned back in his chair, glass balanced between two fingers, his gaze drifting slowly over the two men seated across from him. He didn't speak at first, just studied them. There was something sharp in his stare, not quite judgment, but not far from it either. Suspicion, maybe. Or calculation. Then, it shifted, muted into something more difficult to name. Respect, perhaps. Or something closer to it.

It passed too quickly to be sure.

Without comment, Arjun set his glass down and stood with the weary grace of a man stitched together by sheer will. He stepped over to them one at a time, eyes narrowing slightly as he gauged the worst of their wounds. His fingers glowed faintly green, muted in strength but enough to steady what would've festered by morning.

Kipp hissed as the light stitched through the gash at his side. Jaymes winced but said nothing as the worst of the wounds on his arm receded, the fractured edge of his shoulder clicking softly back into place.

Arjun returned to his drink, sipping once before setting it down again. A low hum rumbled in his throat, more thoughtful than amused. Then, quietly, like tossing a stone into deep water:

"That was quite the series of confessions and revelations back there."

Both men stilled.

Jaymes' brows lifted.

Kipp narrowed his eyes. "You always eavesdrop on dying men sobbing their hearts out to the unconscious girl they're in love with, or is this just a new hobby?"

Arjun didn't blink.

Kipp exhaled, dragging a hand through his hair, voice dropping low. "Not that it matters."

Jaymes shot him a look, but Kipp was already shaking his head, weary and half-resigned.

"She doesn't remember," he said. "Has no idea we said anything. And if she does, it won't stick. She'll be back to being her maddening, perfect, emotionally repressed self. All fortress walls and clever deflection."

He let out a dry huff. "We'll be back where we started. Two idiots pretending not to drown."

Jaymes let out a quiet chuckle, not mocking, just soft. He took another sip of whiskey, then leaned back in his chair. "Well," he murmured, "we weren't exactly subtle."

"She almost ended the world," Kipp muttered. "I think we get a pass on subtle."

Arjun didn't argue, he simply studied his glass for a moment longer, then, after a breath, lifted his gaze to them both.

"Thank you," he said, soft and genuine, the words strange in his mouth.

Without another word, he downed the rest of his whiskey, turned, and limped out of the room–leaving the door to creak shut behind him.

The silence lingered in the cabin long after Arjun's footsteps faded down the corridor. The sea whispered faintly through the porthole, the groan of the *Tempest* shifting beneath them the only other sound.

Jaymes and Kipp nursed what was left in their glasses, the burn of whiskey grounding them–though not nearly enough to erase the image of her lifeless body in their arms, or the moment she came back to them, or what they'd said to make it happen. Kipp stared into his drink like it might offer answers. Jaymes leaned back, stretching the ache out of his shoulders, then glanced over, a crooked grin tugging at his lips.

"That," he said, voice low, still a little hoarse, "*was* quite the confession, you know."

Kipp didn't look up. "Shut up, Blackwell. You're just as fucked as I am."

Jaymes chuckled, the sound dry and tired. "Aye Thief, that I am."

They sat in silence again, the kind that only came after bloodshed and heartbreak, where nothing more needed to be said but everything still hung between them anyway.

After a long moment, Kipp exhaled sharply and slouched deeper into his chair, the tension bleeding slowly from his frame. "It's probably better she doesn't remember," he muttered. "She wouldn't be ready for all that emotional stuff anyway."

Jaymes didn't answer right away. He stared at the flame flickering in the small lantern on the wall, eyes distant, mind elsewhere. He knew what Kipp meant. Knew it because he'd been thinking the same thing. Neither of them had meant to care. Not like this. She wasn't supposed to become *that*–not the center of their storm. They weren't built for it. They were rogues, killers, ghosts of the past clinging to worn edges of freedom.

And yet.

Here they were. Bloody, broken, and so far gone for her they didn't even know where the edge had been.

Jaymes swirled the liquid in his glass once before lifting it to his lips again.

"Right proper fucked," he said standing, stretching his back with a grunt as bones popped in protest. "I need air," he muttered, already limping for the door.

Kipp downed the last of his whiskey, refilled both glasses with a generous hand, and followed without a word.

The deck of the *Tempest* was quiet. The sails hung low and idle in the night breeze, the sea calm beneath a sky still smeared with ash and cloud. Kipp stepped up beside Jaymes at the rail and handed him a glass. They drank in silence for a while, watching the black water roll beneath them, the distant lights of that ruined city barely flickering.

Kipp exhaled, low and humorless, then let out a short, bitter laugh. "You know," he said, swirling his drink, "if she hadn't snuck off, none of this would've happened. No rescue, no storm of shadows, and absolutely *no* confessions. We could've avoided the whole emotionally devastating affair."

Jaymes huffed a laugh. "You're not wrong."

A new voice sliced through the night behind them—dry, unimpressed.

"Out of all the men Kal could've drawn to her," Arjun said, "it had to be the two most *spectacularly* dense ones in the hemisphere."

Kipp turned and threw his arms out in mock surrender. "Please, oh sagely one of fleeting magical prowess," he said, sweeping into a half-bow, "indulge us. We await your radiant wisdom."

Arjun ignored the sarcasm and gave them both a look, letting out a long, beleaguered sigh. Not the kind born of exhaustion, but the pained exhale of a man grappling with the reality that he was, in fact, speaking to fools.

"Idiots." He muttered.

He turned, leaned a forearm on the railing, and regarded them like they were particularly slow-learning children. "She doesn't do—" he waved vaguely toward Kipp "—'emotional devastation' because she's never known it. Not once. Not from anyone. Which I *assume* you've both figured out by now."

Kipp sipped his drink and glanced sideways. Jaymes raised a brow, silent.

Arjun continued with theatrical patience. "So when she was faced with the choice of rescuing me *with* you or *without* you...she chose what she saw as the lesser of two evils."

Kipp frowned slightly, but didn't speak. Arjun's gaze sharpened, taking them both in.

"She chose to leave you behind," he said flatly, "because that was the option where you might live. Because, in her mind, enduring another round of torture, getting caught, or even dying–that's manageable. That's familiar. But *losing* you? *Losing either of you?*" He scoffed. "That's not something she knows how to survive."

Jaymes' mouth tensed at that, the line of his jaw hardening. Kipp looked down into his glass.

Arjun shook his head slowly, then fixed them both with a stare that cut clean through the dark. "Tell me," he asked, voice quieter now, "did either of you happen to notice what triggered the shadow explosion?"

Kipp attempted a weak shrug. "I was a little preoccupied dodging blades and not dying."

Arjun dragged a hand down his face. "*Exactly,*" he snapped. "You were *in danger*. Captured. Screaming for her."

His voice dropped again, rough "And when she realized that, when it registered that she'd lost you, she broke. That was the moment. That was the catalyst."

The wind tugged at their clothes, and no one spoke.

Arjun looked between them one last time, disgusted and oddly fond all at once. "I don't know what she sees in either of you," he muttered, pushing away from the railing. "But clearly, it's something."

Kalithea didn't wake with the sun.

The sky had long since brightened, the sails above humming with wind, the deck alive with the quiet rhythm of men working to forget the nightmare they'd left behind. But in her cabin, all was still save the creak of timber and the soft cadence of breath. She lay pale and unmoving, color just beginning to creep back into her face. The dark bruises beneath her eyes had lightened, but the toll of what she'd unleashed had yet to fade.

Kipp and Jaymes had taken turns at her side throughout the night. Neither spoke much. They simply sat, watched, and breathed in rhythm with her. Every time her chest rose, it was a small victory. Arjun had come and gone, checking on her between healing what remained of their wounds, his magic still sluggish but gaining strength the further they sailed from that cursed place.

It was nearly midday when her fingers finally twitched. Her lashes fluttered. And then–slowly, as if surfacing from the depths–her eyes opened. Two figures loomed into view instantly, both leaning forward in their chairs, a very large tray of food precariously balanced between them.

"Morning, little fox," Kipp drawled, a grin tugging at his mouth. "You're late for breakfast, early for dinner. But we figured mid-day coma survivors might get lunch."

Jaymes smiled, setting the tray down beside her. "It's not much. Mostly salted meat and something that might once have been stew, but it's hot."

Kal groaned faintly and tried to sit up. Both men moved at once, hands flying to steady her.

"Easy," Jaymes warned.

Kipp scoffed. "Gods, sit down before you pass out again and make us relive yesterday."

She scowled at them, a venomous look full of regal disdain.

Kipp only laughed, settling back in his chair. "Don't give me that look, your Majesty of Shadow and Doom. After what we've seen, that glare's child's play."

Something in her froze at the words. Her eyes lost focus. Slowly, as if the weight of memory had been waiting just behind her awareness, it returned–the bodies, the blood, the shadows tearing through flesh and stone. The sound of bones breaking beneath her rage. The fire that danced beneath her skin without mercy or thought.

She sank slowly back into the pillow, her body slack, her eyes fixed on the wooden ceiling above. Her breath came soft and shallow now.

This is why, she thought bitterly. *This is why I can't let anyone in.*

Because when she broke, when she faltered, it wasn't just her who paid the price. The devastation she remembered–no, *felt*–had been endless. Wild. And gods help her, she hadn't cared who it hurt.

Kipp was watching her, eyes narrowed, the humor drained from his face. He recognized the shift in her posture, the way her gaze turned distant, unblinking. The way she folded inward without moving.

He sat forward slowly, resting his arms on his knees. "Don't," he said, voice low and strained. "Don't you *dare* start blaming yourself."

She didn't answer. Didn't even blink.

Jaymes exhaled hard. "Kal," he said, quieter, firmer. "Look at us."

Still nothing. Kipp's hand shot out and gripped hers tightly, enough to ground her. Her gaze flicked to him, startled.

"That's better," he said roughly. "Now listen to me, and listen close. We're alive because of you. Because *you* got us out. Not in spite of what you are but because of it."

"I lost control," she whispered.

"You saved us," Kipp snapped. "I don't care if you set the whole cursed city on fire. You got us out. You got *me* out. And if you think for one godsdamned second I'll let you crawl back into that ice-crusted mind of yours and rot under guilt, you're dumber than I thought."

She flinched slightly, and Jaymes reached out, placing a firm hand on her shoulder.

"You've got us now," he said, his voice uncharacteristically soft. "And you're here. You're safe. You did it."

He squeezed her shoulder just enough to anchor her. "We *all* saw what happened back there. But no one's blaming you–not the crew, not Arjun, not me, and not Kipp. So stop trying to convince yourself you deserve the blame."

Kal turned her face toward the ceiling again, eyes glassy but not falling. Not this time.

"I could have killed you," she said, barely above a whisper.

"But you didn't," Kipp said, voice hoarse now. "And that's the whole godsdamned point."

He let go of her hand only long enough to shove the food tray toward her again.

"Now eat something before we start crying like idiots again."

Jaymes gave her a tired smile. "You try dying dramatically one more time and I'm tying you to the bunk for a week."

Kal's mouth twitched, the barest flicker of a smile.

The next few days passed with an odd kind of stillness, tense and aching, but no longer bleeding. The sea stretched wide and empty around them, a balm to the rawness they all carried. The wind was gentle. The waves obeyed.

Kal was awake more often than not now, her color returning in slow degrees. But that didn't stop Kipp and Jaymes from hovering like twin storms in her shadow.

She tried to protest. Gods, she tried.

Jaymes ignored every word of it with that infuriating ease of his, dragging a weathered chair up to the quarterdeck and lashing it to the rail himself. When she'd opened her mouth to argue, he'd arched a brow and said mildly, "Take the compromise, or I'll carry you back to your cabin and bolt the door."

And because she wasn't quite ready to test whether he meant it, she'd taken the damned chair.

At least it gave her the sea. The sun. The wind in her hair again.

And quiet.

Well.

Almost quiet.

Kipp had made it his mission to ensure she never had a moment's peace. Every day he brought stories–most of them outrageous lies, Kal was sure, though the details were so elaborate it was hard to tell. He challenged Jaymes to knife-throwing contests, arm-wrestling matches, and once, a plank-walking race that ended in a fight over who cheated first.

When bored with Jaymes, Kipp turned to the crew, picking arguments or swiping pastries or replacing rope knots with elaborate braids that ruined half the sails.

He made the mistake of trying to needle Arjun twice. The second time, the fae turned, muttered a few sharp syllables, and hit him squarely in the chest with a crackle of green energy. Kipp let out a sound not unlike a strangled yelp and tumbled over backwards.

He hadn't bothered Arjun since.

Kal watched it all from her chair with half-lidded eyes and a carefully neutral expression. But sometimes—just sometimes—her lips twitched at the corners, and Jaymes would catch it with a quiet satisfaction in his gaze.

By the fifth day, she felt strong enough to stand without swaying. Arjun, watching her silently from the shadows of the stern, gave a single nod when she approached him.

They didn't speak. Not much was needed between them.

He led her down to the cargo hold, where the crew had cleared a space for them. And there, with only dust mites and silence to witness, she began to train again. Not just the ley lines, though he made her call to them until her breath ran short and sweat lined her brow, but the shadows. *Her* shadows.

Calling them. Bending them. Releasing them before they sank too deep. The process left her shaking more often than not. Her hands trembled. Her thoughts blurred. But she kept going. Again and again.

Above deck, the crew gave the hold a wide berth. Not out of fear, at least not of *her*. But of Arjun. The fae mage had never raised his voice, never made a show of power since the escape, but they felt it humming beneath his skin like a storm behind glass. And they didn't trust what that kind of quiet could do.

Nights on the *Tempest* had always carried its own rhythm. The creak of wood, the low murmur of crew swapping shifts, the sigh of sails shifting in the wind. But now, for the first time in longer than she could name, Kal found herself listening without bracing for what came next.

She sat near the helm, legs curled beneath her, her back warmed by the thick boards of the deck. The stars stretched overhead, clear and unmarred. Kipp and Jaymes were engaged in what appeared to be a heated debate over whether someone could, in fact, escape a brothel rooftop with nothing but a window sash and a prayer. Jaymes argued no. Kipp was halfway into a reenactment before Kal shook her head and muttered, "Gods, you're both insufferable."

They both turned to her, grinning. It was that grin—the matching sparks of mischief, the unspoken challenge to smile back—that caught her off guard. And without meaning to, she smiled.

Not much. But enough.

Jaymes noticed first. He leaned against the railing beside her, arms crossed, smug. "Was that a smile, your Majesty? Careful. If word gets out, you'll ruin your whole reputation."

She didn't answer, but Kipp crowed in delight anyway, tossing a half-eaten apple core overboard and strutting like he'd just won a duel. "Knew we'd get a real one eventually," he said. "Took being kidnapped, nearly gutted, and watching her unleash hell on an entire city, but I'd say it was worth it."

Kal rolled her eyes, but the smile lingered a moment longer before she turned away, tucking it back into her silence. Still, the weight in her chest—that heavy, gnawing burden she hadn't spoken of even to Arjun— had loosened. Slightly. As if her muscles had stopped clenching just long enough to breathe again.

Arjun *did* noticed. He didn't say anything. He rarely did. But he watched her from the edge of the upper deck, arms folded, green eyes unreadable. He'd seen her bleed and break and stitch herself back together more times than he could count. But tonight he saw something new.

Not softness. Not yet. But something warm enough to be dangerous.

And he had a sneaking suspicion it had something to do with the way those two chaos-drenched fools looked at her. As if she weren't just the center of the storm, but the very thing anchoring them in it.

The next morning, Arjun descended into the hold expecting another session of focused discipline and controlled fury.

He found Kal already there, standing in the ring of chalk lines and binding marks he'd drawn the night before, eyes closed, breath slow and even. Her posture was poised, hands raised slightly as she coaxed the shadows forward—slowly this time, testing the edge without falling over it.

And just beyond the circle, lounging with far too much comfort for anyone in a magically reinforced training space, were Jaymes and Kipp.

Arjun stopped at the threshold. "Why are you here?"

Jaymes didn't look up from the dagger he was flipping in one hand. "Figured you could use witnesses. In case you finally get yourself incinerated."

Kipp gestured broadly around them. "This is where the real enter-tainment is. If she explodes again, I want front-row seats."

Arjun exhaled slowly. "This is *not* a bloody tavern."

Jaymes tilted his head. "Could be. You're already playing the bitter old man nursing his regrets."

Kipp grinned and nudged a crate with his boot. "We even brought our own stools."

Kal didn't open her eyes. "Ignore them."

"I'm trying," he muttered, stepping forward. "But they're like feral cats. Feed them once and they never leave."

Jaymes leaned toward Kipp. "Does that make him the widow at the door with the leftover fish bones?"

"Oh, definitely."

Jaymes gave a lazy shrug. "We're housebroken. Mostly."

Kipp leaned back on the crate, hands behind his head. "Besides, this is the only time she doesn't try to stab us for hovering."

A flicker of tension cracked in the air, and for a moment, Kal smiled. It was small. Barely there. But Arjun caught it, though he didn't comment. Just stepped into the circle, eyes on her, voice steady.

Arjun stepped closer to the center of the chalk ring, his voice cut-ting through the lingering tension like the draw of a blade. "Again," he said. "But this time, do it without fear."

Kal opened her eyes slowly, the faint remnants of shadow still trailing from her fingertips. Her breath had evened, her posture was firm, but he saw it–the subtle hesitation threaded through her spine, the too-careful control that came from caution rather than confidence. Arjun didn't soften the observation.

"You're calling them from the wrong place," he said. "You want control, then stop bracing like they might devour you."

Her jaw tensed. "And what if they do?"

"Then we'll deal with it," he replied flatly. "But if you want to mas-ter them, you have to choose them."

A beat passed. Her gaze flicked to him, then to the faint marks on the floor, then to the edges of the shadows still curling at her feet like reluctant animals. She drew a slow breath and nodded once.

Kipp leaned further back on his crate, stretching his legs out like he was watching a street performance. "No pressure or anything. Just make peace with the darkest part of your soul in front of an audience."

She didn't rise to it, though the corner of her mouth tugged slight-ly. Jaymes arched a brow at Kipp but said nothing, arms folded, his focus never straying from her.

Kal closed her eyes again. This time, she didn't reach for the shad-ows with clenched fists or dread. She opened herself carefully, purposefully, the same way Arjun had taught her to tap the ley lines–not with desperation, but with intent. Slowly, the darkness came, not as a storm, but as something quieter. Her palm lifted slightly, fingers splayed, and the shadows coalesced there–thin, elegant tendrils coiling around her hand, curling like ink in still water.

And then something shifted.

A glimmer, faint and almost imperceptible, threaded through the heart of the darkness. It was golden. Soft, subtle, and warm. It gleamed like sunlight, winding its way through the shadows like a heartbeat pulsing within the dark.

Kal didn't notice. But the men did. Jaymes straightened first, the relaxed edge of his stance slipping as his eyes narrowed. Arjun's breath stilled. Kipp leaned forward, boots flat on the floor now, every trace of humor draining from his face. None of them spoke. No one moved. They just watched, as still as statues, their gazes locked on the faint glimmer where light and shadow danced as one.

Kal felt the silence before she saw its cause. Her brow furrowed slightly. "What?" she asked, eyes still closed. "Why are you all so quiet?"

No one answered.

She opened her eyes, and froze. The shadows still curled in her palm, steady and alive, but now she saw it too–the single thread of gold weaving through the black, pulsing faintly with each breath she took. Her entire body stilled. The shadows faltered, flickered and then vanished, snuffed out like a candle blown too hard. The light winked out with them, as if it had never been there at all.

She stared down at her hand in stunned silence, then slowly turned to Arjun.

"Did you see–?" she began, but he was already nodding.

"Well," he said, "*that* was new."

Kipp let out a low whistle, the tension in his posture finally breaking. He leaned back again, stretching his arms behind his head with exaggerated ease. "New, sure. But not exactly terrifying compared to the time she lit up like a comet and blasted us out of the ocean."

Arjun's head snapped toward him. "I'm sorry–*what?*"

Jaymes winced.

Kipp just grinned wider. "Oh, did she not tell you that part?"

Jaymes closed his eyes for a beat, as if already regretting what came next.

"Oh, don't look at me," Kipp said, grinning now as he gestured vaguely toward Kal. "She was the one who did it. One minute we're battling a storm, drowning, the next she goes full divine wrath and launches us straight out of the ocean. Bright as a star, thunder in the sky, the sea parting like it had second thoughts. I'm surprised you didn't feel it in your little lines, your magic-ness."

"I was in chains," Arjun growled. "What the hell happened?"

Kipp gestured toward Kal. "Ask your little shadow-saint over there. She went full beacon-of-the-gods."

Arjun turned on Kal, eyes narrowed. "*Kalithea.*"

She didn't meet his gaze. Still staring at her hand, but her voice was quiet when she finally spoke.

"It was different," she murmured. "This wasn't like that."

Arjun watched her carefully, eyes lingering on the hand she had closed into a fist as if to hide the last trace of what had glimmered there. Kal had gone quiet in that particular way he recognized too well—shoulders square, spine held just so, the silence around her grown rigid. She wasn't afraid. Not exactly. But she was withdrawing. Pulling inward the moment something unknown stirred too close to the surface.

He considered pushing. Pressing her for answers. Naming what had shimmered within the shadows, the way the ley lines had shivered in response, the hum that still tingled faintly along the edges of his senses. But he knew that look in her eyes. She wouldn't speak of it. Not yet.

So instead, he let it go.

"Enough for today," he said, brushing the chalk off his palms. "We're finished."

Kal didn't argue. She simply turned and stepped out of the circle, her movements quiet, composed, detached in a way that didn't feel like calm. She passed by them without speaking, her gaze distant, fixed somewhere far beyond the hull of the ship. A queen in exile inside her own mind, already slipping back into silence as if it were armor.

Kipp watched her go, his grin long since faded. Jaymes exhaled beside him, slow and tight.

"She's doing it again," Kipp muttered.

Jaymes didn't ask what he meant. He saw it too—the familiar shadow overtaking her eyes, the way her steps grew sharper, quieter, like she was already reinforcing the walls in her head stone by stone.

"I'll be damned if I sit here and watch her build that fortress back up," Kipp said, rising to his feet and dusting off his coat. "Not after all the effort it took to get her out of it."

Jaymes gave a grunt of agreement and pushed off from the crate. "So?"

Kipp's smirk returned, slower this time, curved with something far more dangerous than mischief. "So," he said, "we remind her who she's stuck on a ship with."

Jaymes gave him a sidelong look, one brow lifting. "Chaos?"

Kipp rolled his sleeves back. "The finest brand."

Jaymes nodded. "Subtlety?"

Kipp grinned. "Absolutely not."

THE GAME RESUMES

They found her at the bow, just as the sun began its slow descent toward the horizon, streaking the sea in molten amber. She stood with her hands braced on the railing, hair caught in the wind, her coat billowing slightly around her legs. From a distance, she looked statuesque–sharp and still and sovereign, as if the sea itself bowed to her silence.

But they'd learned better than to trust the surface.

Jaymes slowed first, keeping a measured distance as he approached. Kipp didn't bother with such restraint. He closed in like he belonged there, boots sounding deliberately loud against the deck.

"You always come here when you're brooding," he said lightly, stopping just short of her.

Kal didn't turn. "I'm not brooding."

Jaymes settled beside the mast, arms folded as he leaned back into the shadows cast by the rigging. "You're quiet," he said, not accusing... just noting. "That's usually worse."

Her gaze remained fixed on the horizon, distant.

Kipp huffed and leaned one elbow on the railing beside her, tipping his body just into her space. "Come on, Kal. Don't go full ghost on us now. At least wait until we're off the ship, you're much harder to chase through a palace."

"I'm fine."

"You're not," he said. "You're thinking. Hard."

"That's not a crime."

"It is," Kipp said, "when it involves rebuilding a mental fortress we already spent weeks setting fire to."

Kal's jaw tightened.

Jaymes stepped closer then, his tone low but steady. "You don't have to say everything. But say something."

Silence. Not sharp this time, just thick with weight. She didn't flinch, didn't lash out—but the wall was rising, stone by stone.

Kipp clicked his tongue. "If you're not gonna talk, I'll start guessing."

She exhaled sharply through her nose.

"Was it the gold in the shadows?" he went on, nudging her shoulder. "The magic that none of us can explain but all of us are too polite to panic over?"

Still nothing.

"Or was it the fact that Arjun looked like he was going to drop to his knees and start praying the moment it happened?"

A breath, short and sharp—maybe a laugh, maybe a warning.

Encouraged, Kipp pushed further. "Or maybe it's that you're worried next time you try, the gold won't show up. Or it will. And you don't know which is worse."

This time she did turn, just enough to level a narrow-eyed glare at him. "Do you ever stop talking?"

"Not when it matters," he said, grinning.

She tried to keep the scowl, but the corner of her mouth betrayed her. Just a fraction, but the moment her lip twitched into the faintest curve, Kipp straightened like he'd won a battle.

"There she is."

Jaymes let out a soft breath, smiling despite himself. "About time."

Kal shook her head, eyes rolling upward, but the smile remained—small and fleeting, but real.

"Alright," she said, her voice dry. "You've had your fun. Now leave me be."

"Actually," Kipp said, shifting to lean his back against the railing beside her, "I've got a proposition."

"Oh no."

"Don't say no yet."

"I haven't said anything."

"But you were about to." Kipp ignored her exasperation and went on, gesturing broadly toward the open sea. "We're getting close to the capital. So I figured it's the perfect time for one last wager."

Kal narrowed her eyes. "Wager?"

Jaymes straightened slightly, "Knives."

Kal stared at them both. "You're serious?"

"Deadly," Kipp said. "One match. You win, we'll owe you a favor. Anything you want. No complaints."

She raised a brow. "And if you win?"

His smile turned sharp. "Then you owe us one."

She didn't answer at first. Suspicion flickered behind her eyes. "What kind of favor?"

"Nothing dire," Kipp said, far too quickly. "Just something I want. Could be a drink. Could be a kiss. Could be your eternal loyalty and a blood pact, who's to say?"

Jaymes gave a faint snort. "It's never just a drink with you."

Kal's gaze shifted between them, wary, but not closed. She was still on edge, still shadowed by whatever thoughts had taken root since the training, but the wall had cracked. Enough to let in a sliver of something brighter.

"I know this game," she said slowly. "You're trying to distract me."

"Absolutely," Kipp said.

"And manipulate me."

"I wouldn't dream of it."

She gave him a look.

"...Alright, I'd *definitely* dream of it. But in my defense, it worked last time."

Kal shook her head again, exasperation fading into something more alive. "Fine. *One* wager."

Kipp grinned like a man who'd just tricked a goddess into giving him her name.

Jaymes just nodded. "We'll keep it simple this time. No rigged terrain. No storms. No gods involved."

Kal glanced between them, the faint smile still ghosting her lips. "I'll believe that when I see it."

They waited until the deck quieted for the night, until most of the crew had drifted below and the lanterns swayed in slow rhythm with the tide. The air was warm, heavy with salt and dusk, the sea calm beneath a sliver-moon sky. Kal had shed her coat, her sleeves rolled, as she stalked to the center of the makeshift sparring ring marked near the aft mast. Her hair was still damp from the sea spray, loosely braided and pulled over one shoulder, her boots scuffed from the earlier training.

Kipp and Jaymes stood opposite her, knives gleaming in the low light, and neither of them looked particularly interested in following the rules.

"You sure you want to do this?" Kipp asked, casually flipping his blade through his fingers. "You've had a long week. Nearly went full divine weapon. No shame in calling it early."

"I'm fine," Kal said coolly. "You're the one who's going to need a healer when I put this blade through your pride."

"Oh, sweetheart," he drawled. "I haven't had pride since the riots in Velen's End."

Jaymes circled slowly to her right, lazy, unhurried. "He cried after that one, you know," he said. "Said the city would never love him again."

"They tried to *hang me*, Jaymes."

"They also gave you free wine after. I fail to see the tragedy."

Kal moved to adjust her footing, blade drawn now, stance relaxed but ready. "You two planning to flirt with each other all night, or are we actually playing?"

Kipp grinned. "Darling, we're just getting started."

The game was simple, first to disarm the others, or land a 'kill' hit. They'd played it before, though the stakes had never quite felt so... charged. They moved into place, circling with practiced familiarity. The first few passes were playful–feints, taps, the brush of steel without true intent. But it didn't stay light for long.

Kipp was the first to break the rhythm, stepping in too close, blade grazing just above her wrist as he leaned in, voice low and warm at her ear.

"You know," he murmured, "if I win, I'm cashing in for something worth far more than a favor."

Kal didn't flinch. She knocked his blade aside with a twist of her wrist and shoved him back with her elbow. "You're not winning."

He stumbled a step, laughing. "Gods, I love it when you lie."

They adjusted.

"*When* I win," Kipp said between passes, "I might ask you for a secret. One you've never told anyone. Something tender. Soft."

Kal flicked his blade aside with a twist of her wrist. "You wouldn't know what to do with soft."

"Oh, I know exactly what to do," he said. "I'd keep it in my pocket. Pull it out when you're acting too cold. Remind you you're not made of stone."

She swept his legs, and he narrowly avoided the fall, chuckling. "Try harder."

Jaymes took the next pass. He said nothing, just stepped in close enough for her to feel his breath along her neck. Kal didn't blink. She ducked beneath his arm and drove him back with a blow that would have landed had he not spun clear.

Kipp whistled. "You're not going to win her with the silent act, Jaymes. You've got to *say* something."

Jaymes smiled faintly. "I'm choosing my moment."

Kal struck at him next. Jaymes parried, but just barely. He stepped back, and Kipp moved to flank again. This time, he didn't tease. His voice dropped lower.

"No, I know what I'll ask for now," Kipp said, weaving behind her shoulder, "I'll ask you for a kiss."

Kal didn't miss a beat. "You've had one already."

"Yes," he said, grinning, "and I think about it every godsdamned day."

She turned into him, blade a breath from his ribs. "Then you're already paid."

Jaymes stepped in again, calmer now. No blade raised. Just watching. Waiting. Kal hesitated only for a breath just long enough for Kipp to make another pass. She deflected without looking.

Still too easy. They pressed harder.

Kipp leaned close again, voice soft now. "We could ask for something else. Something you wouldn't give us otherwise."

"Like what?" she murmured, without turning.

Jaymes answered this time. "The truth."

She stilled, not enough to slip, but enough to give them a scent of blood.

"You wear silence like a second skin," Jaymes said, his voice quiet, intimate. "But we've seen what's underneath. You call it control. I think it's fear."

Kal didn't react, not visibly, but her next strike landed harder. They both stepped back, reassessing. Then Jaymes moved again, not to strike, not to threaten–just to get close. Too close. His steps were slow, careful, not predatory–*intentional.*

"If I win," he said, voice low enough that only she could hear, "I'll ask for the one thing you've never given anyone. Not the kiss. Not the game. Not the favor." He leaned in, his breath brushing the curve of her ear. "I'll ask you to *stay.*"

Her breath caught. Just a fraction. The faintest slip. It was enough. Kipp struck fast, clean. The tip of his blade knocked hers from her grip in one smooth pass, and it hit the deck with a sharp clang that echoed too loud in the quiet night.

Kal stood frozen for half a second, then her eyes narrowed.

"That was cheap," she said, voice thin.

Kipp gave a mock bow. "That was *brilliant.*"

Jaymes didn't gloat. He simply watched her with something flickering behind his gaze, still too close, still not moving. Kal bent, retrieved her blade, and sheathed it in one smooth motion. She didn't look at them when she spoke.

"So which of you won?"

Jaymes didn't answer.

Kipp did. "Doesn't matter."

"We're asking together," Jaymes said. "One favor. One answer."

Kal moved closer with a quiet, coiled purpose that turned the air electric. She reached them with unhurried grace, the sway of her hips balanced by the poise of a blade still sheathed but ever present. The faint gleam in her eyes wasn't a smile, not truly. It was a warning dressed in silk. She paused between them. Close enough that Jaymes could smell the salt and smoke in her hair. Close enough that Kipp could feel the heat of her skin where her hand brushed his coat as if by accident.

"I see," she murmured, voice like poured honey. Her gaze flicked up to Kipp's, then shifted to Jaymes. "You win your little game, and now you want your prize."

Kipp swallowed hard. "It's a favor, not a prize."

She smiled then, slow and dangerous, leaning in just enough to make his breath catch. Her lips brushed the shell of his ear, not touching, not quite.

"What if I offered you something better?" she whispered, barely audible over the waves.

Kipp's hand clenched around the hilt of his knife. He didn't move. Kal turned to Jaymes next, inching closer, her voice softer still.

"What if I said I'd give you what you *really* want?" Her mouth hovered at his jaw, her breath warm. "What if I said I already know what it is?"

Jaymes held still but his eyes darkened. And for a breath, just one, she had them both. Kipp's shoulders tensed, and for the briefest of moments, he looked like he might give in to whatever fire she was stoking. But then he drew back a step, dragging a hand down his face with a groan.

"No," he muttered, blinking hard, as if coming out of a trance. "Gods above, *no*. You're not wriggling out of this with seduction, little fox."

She arched a brow, that slow smile never quite fading.

"You're good," he admitted, pointing a finger at her. "Brilliant, even. My brain still feels like it's been on fire. But no. Not this time."

She let out a faint, amused breath, then shifted back half a step, folding her arms loosely. The game had shifted again–hers, for the moment–but the tension hadn't eased. Not entirely.

Her voice, when it came again, was cool. "Fine. Ask, then."

Jaymes didn't move. He just looked at her. And something in his gaze was too steady, too quiet, too close to something she didn't want to name. The set of his jaw hadn't changed, nor the calm in his expression–but behind his eyes, there was heat. Depth. Something unspoken and entirely sure.

"We want the favor now," he said quietly.

She tilted her head. "Together?"

"Yes."

Kipp nodded once. "It's simple."

Jaymes didn't look away. "When we reach the capital. When you step off my ship..."

His voice didn't rise. It was just there–solid, deep, low enough to cut through every carefully constructed wall she kept between herself and the world.

"...you don't vanish."

Kal stilled.

Jaymes' eyes never left hers. "You don't disappear. You don't leave us behind."

A beat of silence stretched out, something shifting in her expression. Not fear or anger, but something quieter. Something buried. It twisted inside her, low and sharp, and she told herself it was nothing. The silence stretched between them, heavy as the sea and just as deep.

And then, unexpectedly, Kal laughed. It was quiet. Hollow. A breath of something that might have been sorrow if it hadn't already settled too deep to name. She looked away for half a heartbeat, then shook her head slowly, as if the ache in her chest had finally crested into something she could no longer hide. When she turned back to them, the mask was gone. No walls. No games. Just Kalithea, bare and unguarded in a way neither of them had ever seen. Her eyes were tired, not with weakness, but with weight. The kind that couldn't be shed, only carried.

And gods, it stopped both their hearts.

"I'm sorry," she said softly, and somehow, it was worse than a refusal. "You weren't meant to stay."

Kipp took a half-step forward, but she lifted a hand, not to push him away. Just... stilling.

"You weren't made for where I'm going," she continued, her voice almost mournful. "Jaymes, you belong to the sea. You always have. You move through the tides like you were carved from the storm."

Her eyes lingered on him a moment longer, and something in Jaymes' chest twisted—not from what she said, but from how gently she said it.

Then she turned to Kipp.

"And you," she murmured, "you were forged in shadow. You were born to slip through locked doors, to run when the world burned, to laugh when others fell silent. You weren't meant for chains."

Kipp swallowed hard. His voice was there, tight in his throat, but he didn't speak.

Kal gave them both a sad smile, barely there, the kind that disappeared even as it formed.

"I was not born to be kept. And I will not be the one who cages you." Something twisted in her throat. She didn't let it rise. "That's all I could offer. A cage at best..." she whispered, "...destruction at worst."

Neither man spoke. The air had gone still around them, thick with things unsaid. A thousand arguments caught behind gritted teeth. And in the space where silence stretched too long, she stepped forward, close enough to touch. She lifted her hand and laid her fingers gently, almost imperceptibly, against Kipp's chest. Then Jaymes'. Light as breath. Not a gesture of affection. Not quite. But of something remembered. Something mourned before it could ever be.

"There's no place for freedom where I'm going."

And that was it.

She stepped back, turned, and walked away. Before they could speak, before they could argue, before they could tell her how *wrong* she was.

But what undid them both, what stayed with them long after the sound of her footsteps faded, was the look in her eyes just before she turned. A single flicker of longing. One unguarded breath that said *she wished they could stay.*

The sound of her footsteps faded into the wind, leaving only the creak of rope and the hush of the sea between them.

Kipp stared after her, jaw clenched, arms rigid at his sides. His eyes were storm-bright in the dark, and his breath came sharp, like he'd just taken a hit he hadn't braced for. Jaymes stood quiet beside him. He didn't look at Kipp, not at first. His gaze lingered on the shadow where Kal had vanished, the place her voice had left a hollow echo behind. He didn't speak.

He didn't have to.

Because she was right. Not about what she thought, but in the way pain sometimes sounded like truth. There *wasn't* a place for pirates and thieves in the world she was about to step into...not unless they carved one themselves.

Kipp let out a sharp breath, rubbing both hands over his face as if trying to scrub the ache out of his bones. Then he turned and looked at Jaymes.

"I don't know about you," he muttered, "but I'll be damned if I let someone else finish writing this story."

Jaymes finally looked over, one brow raised.

"No noble's ever told me where to go," Kipp went on, voice low and tight with defiance. "Not once. Not when they tried to throw me in cells. Not when they hunted me through their gardens with blades. And I'm sure as shit not going to start letting them now."

Jaymes didn't argue, because beneath Kipp's fury, he felt it too. Not anger at her, not exactly. Hurt. Because she couldn't see what they saw. Couldn't believe it. *Wouldn't.*

"She's the problem," Jaymes said quietly.

Kipp gave a sharp nod. "Yeah. She's the fortress now. Not the storm."

Jaymes' gaze drifted out to the horizon. "Convincing her to let us stay...that's the war."

Kipp's lips twitched. "Good thing we're bastards who don't fight fair."

A beat passed. Then Kipp turned toward the far stairway, already moving. "Right," he called over his shoulder. "Here's the plan—we drink, we scheme, we drink more. You're supplying the rum."

Jaymes chuckled low in his throat, the sound half-broken but real. "Naturally."

The door to the captain's quarters shut with a firm click behind them.

Jaymes tossed the bottle onto the table without ceremony, catching two glasses from the shelf as he went. Kipp ignored the seating entirely, already pacing in measured steps across the far end of the cabin like a wolf trapped in silk and fury. The flicker of lanternlight cut across his coat in sharp glints as he moved, every inch of him wound tight with restless purpose.

Jaymes poured a generous round and leaned back in his chair, boot kicked up on the edge of the table, watching Kipp pace like one might observe a storm gathering from the safety of the shore.

"She's not wrong," Kipp muttered, mostly to himself. "If we walk in without purpose, without *roles*, the court will tear us apart before she ever gets the chance. If she even lets us come with her to begin with."

Jaymes raised his glass, eyes half-lidded. "Then we don't give them a chance."

Kipp stopped. Turned. "You got a plan already, do you?"

A slow grin tugged at the corner of Jaymes' mouth, wry and wicked. "I do."

Kipp arched a brow and stalked toward the table, snatching up his glass. "Well, let's hear it then, your high-seas brilliance."

Jaymes lifted his drink in a mock toast. "Every queen needs a court, doesn't she?"

Kipp blinked once, then narrowed his eyes. "Go on."

"Advisors," Jaymes said, swirling the amber liquid. "Generals. *Admirals.*"

He gestured broadly around them, the ship creaking softly beneath the weight of the sea. "This fleet has brought half a dozen kingdoms to their knees without flying a single banner. Time we gave it one. Turn the dread fleet into a legitimate naval armada, loyal to the Queen of Shadows herself."

Kipp let out a low whistle, lips curling in something dark and approving. "Admiral Blackwell, huh?"

Jaymes inclined his head, smile deepening. "Has a ring to it."

Kipp tipped his glass back, drinking deep, then slammed it lightly on the table. "Absolutely, Admiral."

He stepped closer, the fire in his grin catching. "And every queen needs a right hand, doesn't she? Someone to whisper sharp truths in her ear, make ministers squirm, remove inconvenient problems..." He winked. "I hear thieves make excellent advisors."

Jaymes raised his brow. "With a flair for the dramatic?"

Kipp bared his teeth in a grin. "She wouldn't survive the palace without it." He poured himself another glass and raised two fingers, his grin fading into something colder. "Problem number two."

Jaymes leaned forward, eyes narrowing as the room seemed to quiet around them. "I'm listening."

Kipp didn't miss a beat. "The prince and his loyal hound. Jarreth Llewellyn and Raoul Sahir."

Jaymes' jaw tensed faintly at the names, but he gestured for Kipp to continue.

"That little scene on the docks when Kal slipped away?" Kipp said, swirling the liquid in his glass. "Wasn't just for show. I kept them busy, fed them enough wrong trails and half-truths to make them chase their own tails long enough for us to disappear."

Jaymes let out a low whistle and clapped once, slow and amused. "Elegant."

Kipp gave a dramatic bow, drink still in hand. "I do try."

"But," he added, straightening, "that's not the problem." He leaned one hand on the table, voice dropping lower. "The problem is *history*. The kind that roots deep, gets inside your blood without permission."

Jaymes stilled, "Kal?"

Kipp nodded once. "With *both* of them."

He said it plainly, not jealous, or at least, not completely–just tired. Tired of watching her build walls to keep them all out, even when the cracks showed exactly where she'd let others in before.

"They'll be hell-bent on destruction before they let anyone else stand in their place," Kipp said, swirling his glass with a flick of his wrist. "Especially two devilishly charming rogue kings who don't know how to keep their hands, or their hearts, to themselves."

Jaymes raised a brow, lips curving. "The prince and the knight are in love with her, then?"

Kipp gave him a long, withering look.

Jaymes lifted both hands. "Valid question."

"Who isn't?" Kipp muttered, tossing back the rest of his drink.

Jaymes chuckled softly. "Fair."

He leaned back again, stretching out, the lanternlight gilding the edge of his jaw.

"So," he said, turning serious, "what do we do about it?"

Because beneath the laughter, the banter, the shared scars–they both knew what was at stake. Jaymes' voice dropped, low and certain.

"Because I'll be damned if some polished prince or golden-knight gets to stand where we bled our way in."

"For starters," Kipp said, setting the glass down with more force than necessary, "we stay by her side."

Jaymes met his gaze, nodding once, slow and deliberate.

"We become assets," Kipp continued. "Useful. Unshakeable. The kind of men no court can toss aside, no matter how sharp the titles or how pure the bloodlines."

Jaymes' mouth twitched into something that might've been a smirk if it weren't laced with steel. "You think she'll let us?"

Kipp didn't hesitate. "She won't get a choice."

That made Jaymes laugh, low and dark.

Kipp leaned forward, eyes burning now. "We remind her what we built here. On *this* ship. The way we bled together. Fought together. Laughed in the face of death and kept her breathing when she wanted to give in."

He straightened, voice hardening. "They didn't see that. The prince and the knight? They weren't there. They didn't watch her nearly burn alive trying to protect us. They didn't see the shadows rip through steel or the light trying to break through her ribs. They didn't *stay*."

Jaymes nodded slowly, the grin gone. "So we make damn sure she doesn't forget it."

"Exactly."

Kipp raised three fingers now.

Jaymes groaned softly and let his head fall back against the chair. "Gods, what now?"

Kipp didn't blink. "Alden."

Jaymes' eyes opened, sharp again.

Kipp held his stare. "That one's going to be a problem, and one we may have to solve as we go."

Jaymes leaned forward, the grin gone, replaced by a sharper kind of focus. His fingers steepled beneath his chin as he stared into the middle distance, eyes narrowing with thought.

"All right," he said slowly. "Let's say we get past the court. Past the prince. Past every pompous noble waiting to slit our throats in the garden."

Kipp tilted his head.

Jaymes continued, "How exactly do we convince *Kal* to take us with her? To let us stay, when we're arguably the most wanted men in the kingdom, if not the known world?"

Kipp let out a long, rough breath through his nose. "Yeah. That's the rub."

He began pacing again, slower now, the weight of it all finally catching up.

"I think... we adapt on the run," he said after a beat. "First step's getting her to stay. Second's making sure she doesn't send us packing. Third is..." He waved a hand vaguely toward the far wall. "Ducking the gallows. *Again.*"

Jaymes' mouth quirked, but the smile didn't quite reach his eyes.

Kipp came to a halt, turned back toward the table, and raised four fingers this time. The movement felt heavier than the others. Final.

"And then there's the last problem," he said quietly.

Jaymes met his gaze. "Kal."

Kipp nodded, jaw tight. "Kal."

That was the hardest fight of all. Jaymes let the silence stretch, watching Kipp over the rim of his glass. The shadows cast by the lantern flickered across his face.

"You ever gonna say it out loud?" he asked finally, voice low.

Kipp didn't look up. "Say what?"

Jaymes arched a brow. "That you're not just trying to win the game anymore."

Kipp snorted, set his glass down. "That a confession you're fishing for, Admiral?"

Jaymes smirked. "Just wondering if you plan on lying to yourself all the way to the palace."

Kipp crossed his arms, leaning one shoulder against the bulkhead. "You're one to talk. Don't think I didn't see the way you watched her last night. Like she was the storm and you were hoping it'd pull you under."

Jaymes didn't deny it. Didn't flinch either.

"She *is* the storm," he said quietly. "But you and I both know we're not the kind of men who run from weather like that."

Kipp shook his head, a dry laugh slipping from his lips. "No. We walk straight into it with a grin and a bottle."

Another beat passed, heavy with what neither wanted to say too plainly. Then Kipp pushed off the wall.

"She's the real problem," he said again, voice lower now. "Not the court. Not the gallows. *Her.*"

Jaymes nodded once. "She'll fight us."

"She'll fight *everything*," Kipp muttered. "Every flicker behind her eyes, every time we get too close, every time we try to make her *feel* something she doesn't want to name."

Jaymes didn't argue. He looked away, jaw tight. "She's spent so long building walls, I don't think she knows what it's like to be seen anymore."

Kipp's voice was quiet. "Too bad. We see her anyway."

They stood in silence, the weight of that truth sinking deep between them. Then Jaymes lifted his glass again, this time in something that wasn't quite a toast.

"We're in this now."

Kipp clinked his glass without hesitation. "We don't let her shut us out. Not after everything."

Jaymes met his gaze across the table, the flicker of something fierce and unwavering passing between them.

"Not now," he said.

"Not ever," Kipp agreed.

There were no more problems left to count.

Just the fight ahead...and the woman they refused to lose.

The room was quiet save for the hush of the sea against the hull.

Kal sat at the edge of the bed, elbows on her knees, hands tangled in her hair. The storm in her mind didn't match the calm outside. It never did. She'd learned a long time ago that the loudest battles were always fought in silence.

Tomorrow, she would step off the ship.

She would leave behind the creak of the deck beneath her boots, the salt in the wind, the rough laughter of the crew echoing through the corridors. She would leave behind the only place in years that hadn't felt like a cage. Her throat tightened against her will. It was foolish, childish even, to mourn something that had never been promised. But there it was, twisting in her chest all the same. That quiet ache. That selfish, fleeting dream she had never dared name: what it meant to simply be *Kal*.

Not the queen. Not the prophecy. Not the weapon sharpened in the dark.

Just...Kal.

And when she left Kal behind, when she stepped into the role the world had carved out for her with blood and fire, she would be leaving *them* behind too. The two rogues who had somehow carved out a place in her silence. Who had made her laugh when she didn't know how. Who had looked at her like she was *something*, not because of what she could do, but because of who she *was*, even when she couldn't see it herself.

She would lock it all away. There was no place for them in what came next. Her future—her crown, her fight—was a prison. The court would choke the life out of them, and she wouldn't be the one to watch it happen. Wouldn't let them trade their freedom for a war they didn't have to die for. Not out of duty. Not out of pity. Not because they thought they *felt* something.

Whatever it was between them, it was temporary. Born from fire and desperation and the illusion of safety. And she would not let it become their ruin. She couldn't let them stay. Because no one stayed. The road ahead offered nothing but bloodshed and ruin. *She* was nothing but bloodshed and ruin.

She closed her eyes and breathed deep, pressing the heels of her palms to her brow as if she could force the whispers in her mind back into the dark where they belonged. They clawed at the edges anyway—

memories, wants, flickers of things she would never have. She wouldn't cry. She never cried. She stood instead, stripped off the jacket that still smelled faintly of the sea, and lay back on the bed, staring up at the dark ceiling. She turned her face away from the door, burying whatever was left of her in the quiet, and waited for sleep to take her.

Tomorrow, it would all end, and she would not look back.

Oaths Made in Sunlight

Morning broke quietly over the *Tempest*, the first gold of sun threading through the porthole. Kal dressed in silence, hands steady as she packed the few things she owned–folded tunic, worn belt, blades honed sharp, cloak still damp with the scent of salt and storm. She moved with purpose, with ritual, the way one did before stepping into battle. Because in truth, that's what this was. Not war, not yet. But something worse.

The end of what had almost been hers.

She paused at the sound of the ship groaning beneath her boots, the whisper of the waves brushing along the hull, the faint clang of the crew above preparing for docking. It ached somewhere deep–low and quiet and stubborn–but she shoved it down like everything else. Wrapped steel around it and let the mask slip over her features with familiar precision. Her back straightened. Her shoulders squared.

She opened the door–

And walked directly into Kipp's chest. He didn't budge. If anything, he leaned slightly into the contact, warmth and mischief coiled in the grin that spread across his face as he looked down at her.

"Well, well," he said, voice low and teasing. "If you wanted to end up in my arms again, little fox, you could've just asked."

Kal sighed and tilted her head back just enough to give him a flat look. "What are you doing loitering outside my door?"

"Loitering?" Kipp clutched his chest in mock offense, then beamed. "I'm here to collect the favor."

She blinked. "Favor?"

"The wager," he said brightly. "The one you lost?"

Kal arched a brow. "You're still stuck on that?"

"I," he said, bowing with ridiculous flourish, "am a man of honor. I always uphold my word. And I expect the same from queens."

She opened her mouth to argue, but he raised a finger, cutting her off with a spark of glee in his eyes.

"No objections. No royal decrees. Breakfast has already been arranged on deck–under protest, mind you, since Jaymes did the actual arranging–and we've crafted a very thorough, borderline genius solution to every argument I know you're about to make."

Kal stared at him. He grinned wider. And despite herself, despite the ache still lodged in her chest, despite the weight of what she was about to walk into–she laughed. Just a little.

"You're relentless," she muttered.

He leaned in slightly, voice lower now. "You love that about me."

She rolled her eyes, but she didn't retreat.

Instead, she stepped out past him into the hall, pulling her coat tighter around her shoulders. "Fine. Lead the way, thief."

The morning sun cast a golden sheen over the deck, warming the salt-stained wood as the harbor loomed just beyond the horizon. The crew moved with easy efficiency, lines hauled and sails trimmed as the Tempest made her steady approach toward the capital.

Amid the bustle, one absurd sight stood out. A table–small, wooden, and clearly hauled from the mess–stood neatly set near the bow, three chairs arranged around it. A cloth had been thrown over it, weighted at the corners with tankards, and an assortment of breakfast fare lay spread across its surface: fruit, bread, smoked fish, and biscuits tucked into a cracked basket.

The crew passed around it with amused glances and stifled grins. Someone muttered something about the king of thieves playing butler now. Another snorted that the captain had finally found himself a siren worth steering toward ruin. Jaymes–already seated, legs stretched out and wine in hand despite the hour–gave them a slow, pointed look. The crew laughed harder and kept moving.

Kal paused at the sight, arms crossed, one brow lifting. "You weren't joking."

Kipp grinned, offering her a gallant bow. "Would I ever?"

She didn't answer. He pulled out a chair with an unnecessarily dramatic flourish, gesturing like she was royalty at court.

"Your throne, my lady."

She stared at him. He held the pose. Eventually, with a sigh that was more breath than surrender, she sat. Kipp slid into the seat beside her, already reaching across her plate to snatch a biscuit.

"You're insufferable."

He took a bite, humming in satisfaction. "And yet you follow me out here."

Jaymes lifted his glass in mock toast. "Careful, love. You'll make him think he's winning."

Kipp leaned back in his chair, expression exaggeratedly wounded. "She was trying to duck out of the wager, you know. Said nothing, just opened the door and tried to disappear like a ghost in the mist."

Jaymes smirked. "A damn shame. What kind of world is this where you can't trust the word of a queen?"

Kal pinched the bridge of her nose, fighting the smile at the edge of her mouth.

"You two are—gods, you're ridiculous," she muttered, then looked between them. "You know this isn't a game. You're pretending it is, but this—what's coming—it'll cost you. You were made to be free, not bound up in courts and crowns. I won't let you chop away pieces of yourselves chasing something you'll regret."

Her voice was quieter by the end, steadier than she felt. But it was enough to quiet the laughter. For a moment, both men looked at her, and beneath the grin still on Kipp's lips, beneath the glint in Jaymes' eyes, something settled heavier in the air. Jaymes studied her in silence for a long moment, the sunlight catching gold in his lashes, his gaze too damn steady.

"Do you truly believe," he asked at last, his voice quiet but sharp as a blade's edge, "that we could ever regret *you?*"

Kal didn't flinch. She looked him dead in the eye and said, with the kind of calm certainty that made both men ache, "Yes."

Neither of them moved. She went on before they could argue, her tone even, but too close to something cracking beneath.

"Even if you think this is what you want now, one day you'll wake up in those stone halls and feel the walls closing in. And when you look at me, you won't see the girl you chased or the queen you bled beside—you'll see locks. Chains. A cage you stepped into willingly. That's only if the ruin doesn't find you first."

Jaymes' expression darkened, not with anger, but something deeper—pain and defiance tangled so tight they were indistinguishable.

"You're a fool," he said softly. "Freedom isn't running. It's *choice.* Choosing you, *that's* freedom. That's ours."

She stared at him then, at both of them. They were smiling, grinning like devils, but there was something in their eyes she wasn't ready to name. Something dangerous. Something steady. Kal opened her mouth to argue, but Kipp beat her to it.

"We've already decided," he said, unapologetically smug. "And really, what would the nobles say if you tried to abandon your most trusted advisors on the docks? Bad optics. Every queen needs a court, you know."

He gave her a crooked grin, and Jaymes leaned back, gesturing lazily around them at the sails, the rigging, the crew bustling around the deck with more than a few not-so-hidden smirks.

"I've decided," Jaymes said, voice full of mock bravado, "to go legitimate."

Kal blinked.

Jaymes' grin widened. "The Dread Fleet swears its loyalty to a certain queen of a fallen kingdom. As of today, consider yourself the proud monarch of a naval armada. Every crown needs a navy, doesn't it?"

Before she could form a word, Kipp rose to his feet with a dramatic bow, one hand pressed to his heart.

"And I," he declared, "humbly accept the position of right-hand advisor, chaos sower, and occasional hand-dirtier, depending on need and wine supply."

He threw her a wink, utterly without shame.

Kal just stared at them. Then, despite everything–despite the weight, the fear, the storm she knew was coming–she laughed. Really laughed. Head tipped back, eyes gleaming, laughter spilling out raw and genuine before she could catch it.

"You two are ridiculous," she managed, shaking her head.

Kipp leaned back in his chair, fingers laced behind his head, grinning.

"We may be ridiculous, Kal," he said, "but we're not going anywhere. And when we dock, we're stepping off this ship with you–either by your side...or I'll break back into your quarters. Like old times."

Kal narrowed her eyes at him.

Jaymes, still lounging, set his glass down and met her gaze evenly.

"You brought us into this," he said, voice low, steady. "We didn't stumble in. We chose it. And we'll be damned if we're walking away now." His gaze didn't waver. "I know you don't believe it. Not yet. But you don't have to. *We're staying*, Kal."

He let that settle between them, firm as any oath.

"And besides," he added, with a half-smile, "we won that match fair and square. You can't deny our request."

Kal snorted. "You cheated."

Jaymes shrugged, completely unrepentant, and gestured between himself and Kipp. "Rogues, remember?"

She exhaled through her nose, shaking her head slightly as if she could will away the warmth curling inside her.

"I won't fight you on it," she said quietly. "You want to come with me? Fine. I'll honor your–" her brow arched, "–cheated win."

But then her voice softened, the edges thinning.

"One day, though...you'll hear it again. The call of freedom. The sea. The shadows. And when you do, you'll leave."

She didn't say *if*. She said *when*.

"And I won't blame you."

Neither of them answered. Not with words. But the look they gave her then–steady, infuriatingly full of confidence–was enough to twist something sharp in her chest.

She let the topic drop.

They spent the rest of the morning as they always had. Kipp found someone–several someone's–to harass, flitting from sailor to sailor with enough wit and menace to keep half the crew laughing and the other half ducking behind crates. Jaymes moved to the helm, one hand on the wheel, the sea wind threading through his dark hair and snapping at his coat. He looked like he belonged there, half-myth and half-man, etched in sunlight and salt air, a creature born of storm and tide.

Kal stood at the rail, fingers curled against the wood, eyes fixed on the horizon. The city was rising ahead, stone towers and banners and the crown she could never cast off. The breeze still smelled like freedom.

But it wouldn't for much longer.

The capital rose slowly out of the sea mist, its white towers and gilded spires catching the afternoon light like blades unsheathed. From a distance, it looked like something carved from story and illusion, grand and cold and waiting. The closer they came, the more its edges sharpened.

Kal stood her eyes fixed on the city like it might vanish if she blinked. She didn't speak. Hadn't spoken in a while. Not since the coast came into view.

Behind her, the crew moved in purposeful quiet. There was no more teasing now, no more casual laughter. Not with land in sight. Not with the knowledge of where she was going, of what waited for her beyond those high stone walls and the gates crowned in gold.

Kal didn't tremble but something inside her curled tighter with every flap of the sails.

This is the end, she thought. *Or the beginning. I'm not sure which.*

She could already feel it starting to shift, the silence before the court's judgment, the cold precision of Alden's gaze, the tangle of Jarreth's loyalty and pain, the questions Raoul wouldn't know how to ask. She could feel the crown drawing nearer, not as a burden, but as an inevitability. It would wrap itself around her again, and the woman she'd been on this ship–the one who had laughed, who had wanted, who had tasted something like freedom–would be swallowed whole.

And yet...

She hadn't expected *them* to follow. She'd meant what she said. They didn't belong to the world she was walking into. Kipp, with his quicksilver grin and daggers sharper than most men's minds. Jaymes, with that unreadable gaze and the weight of storms in his soul. They were wild things. Men who had made their own names in blood and shadow.

And still, they stayed.

Kipp leaned against the railing just out of sight, arms folded, watching her. She looked like a queen again already–back straight, eyes fixed, every inch of her wrapped in that cold, unreachable calm. But he'd seen the cracks. He'd lived in the silences, read every twitch of her fingers, every time she turned her face from the wind so they wouldn't see the way it stung.

And gods, he hated that look in her eyes. That *finality*. Like she'd already buried the last of her softness, like she'd already decided she couldn't have anything more than duty and steel and the kind of loneliness that made monsters.

Kipp wasn't ready to let her go to that place. Not yet. Maybe not ever.

She thought he'd leave one day.

Maybe he would. But not for the reasons she believed. Not because she was a cage. Not because the freedom he loved couldn't live alongside her. No–if he ever left, it would be because she had finally locked herself behind a wall so high even *he* couldn't scale it. And he wasn't ready to let that happen either.

He wasn't good with words. Not when it came to the real ones. But he'd bled for her. Killed for her. He'd carved a place beside her with wit and knives and the kind of stubborn loyalty that didn't know when to quit.

And when those polished bastards in the court tried to act like he wasn't worthy, like he wasn't real enough to stand beside her–Well. Let them try. He could dance in shadows and courtrooms both. And by the end of it, they'd know exactly who Kipp Harlow was.

Jaymes stood at the helm, one hand on the wheel, the other resting loosely at his side as the wind curled around him. The sea was calm. The sky clear. And yet his mind roiled darker than any storm he'd ever sailed through.

The palace was close.

Too close.

And Kal was drifting further from them with every breath she took. She hadn't said it, not aloud, but he could feel it. The weight of what she was carrying. The way she looked at the city like it was the end of her. Like it would swallow the woman who'd stood laughing with them on this deck and leave only the queen behind.

He wasn't sure what scared him more, that she might be right...or that she might not.

Jaymes had always known the sea. He knew its moods, its silence, its violence. But Kal was something else entirely. She was tide and fire and blade all at once, and for the first time in his life, he wasn't trying to conquer her. He just wanted her to *want* him there.

But he could already feel the fight coming. Not from the nobles, not from the prince or the knight or the court. *From her.* Kal would push them away before anyone else could. She'd do it like she always did–quietly, ruthlessly, with the kind of self-sacrifice that made it look like strength.

Jaymes watched her now, the curve of her shoulders, the tension in her stance.

"You're not alone," he murmured under his breath.

Not anymore. He wasn't sure she heard it, but he would make her believe it. Even if it meant burning down the world she was walking back into.

Kal stood still at the bow, wind catching the edge of her coat, the sea fading behind her. She didn't look back.

She had expected fear. Instead, it was ache that lodged in her chest, sharp and breathless. Not for what she was walking into, but for what she would have to leave behind. The *Tempest.* The sea. The taste of freedom still clinging to her skin. She had wanted to believe the sea could change her. That laughter on deck and the ghost of freedom might dull the truth of what she was. But now, as the sails furled and the ship coasted in, she felt the weight settle back into her bones.

She would have to face Alden. Face Jarreth, and Raoul, and all the memories they stirred. She would have to stand in a court that once welcomed her as a ghost, and now waited for her as something far more dangerous. And worse, she would have to look them in the eye. The pirate. The thief. And pretend they hadn't unraveled something she had spent a lifetime stitching shut.

Behind her, Kipp leaned easily at the railing, humming low under his breath, but she knew better than to mistake his calm for carelessness. Jaymes remained at the helm, eyes on the water ahead, one hand resting over the mark of his compass. Both of them had chosen to stay. Both of them were already part of what came next, whether she let herself believe it or not.

And that was the problem. She didn't know what came next.

The shadows still moved at her command–but now, within them, something else flickered. Light. Golden. Terrible. Unknown. She had felt it bloom in her hand like a second heartbeat, and she had no name for it. No shield against it.

Ahead lay sanctuary.

But beyond Varis waited the truth. Elandra. The crown. The war she had not yet begun to wage. And somewhere in the dark, her enemies still whispered her name like a curse half-remembered.

The Embers of Rebellion
Sneak Peek: The Queen Returns with Wolves

awn broke over Varis, and with it came the end of her freedom.
The ship eased against the dock with a groan of wood and rope, and Kalithea felt the moment take hold.

It settled in her bones, that inevitable shift from freedom to chains, though no iron bound her wrists. Out on the sea she had been no one but herself, carried by wind and tide, salt in her hair and sky unbroken above her. The ocean had offered her something she had never believed she could touch: peace. For weeks it had been hers, and now, as the timbers kissed stone and the harbor claimed them, it was already slipping away.

Around her, the deck stirred to life. Sailors called to one another, voices coarse with years of salt air and strong drink. Ropes slapped the planks, sails came down in heavy folds, and the gangplank dropped into place with a solid thud. Jaymes strode down first, every movement sharp with command, his first mate falling easily into step beside him. Kipp trailed after, as though the world itself were his stage, whistling an idle tune while a dagger danced between his fingers.

But Kalithea lingered.

She let her eyes roam the deck, fixing every detail in memory. These men were not knights in gleaming steel or soldiers drilled to precision. They bore scars, missing teeth, and the ink of old loyalties fading on their arms. Yet in their laughter and rough camaraderie was a freedom the polished courts of men could never give. Against all reason, they had become something dangerously close to family.

Her chest ached with it.

One of the older hands passed by, his grin wide, broken teeth flashing in the lantern light.

"Take care now, lass," he said with a rough chuckle. "Ain't every day a queen rides the waves with the likes of us."

She gave a dry huff, shaking her head. "I'm no queen here. Not to you."

A younger sailor clinging high to the rigging called down, his words carrying easily across the harbor bustle. "We'll keep a cabin ready for you, in case the sea calls its siren back to where she belongs."

That drew a few laughs, but Dorian, grizzled and steady as the tide itself, stepped closer. He lowered his voice, rough edges softened by something gentler.

"You made him lighter."

Her gaze drifted toward Jaymes. He had paused at the foot of the gangplank, his head tilted away, jaw clenched hard.

Dorian shrugged. "Haven't seen him laugh like that in years. Thought you ought to know."

The words struck deeper than she was ready for. Her chest twisted, and heat burned at the back of her throat. She blinked, fighting it down, and forced her composure to hold. Somehow, a smile broke through–small, fragile, but true.

"Thank you," she said softly. "For giving me something I never thought I could have."

Then, before the moment could unravel her, she turned. Shoulders squared, steps steady, she walked the gangplank into the waiting city. The sea had set her free for a time, but duty had claimed her once more.

The streets of the port city twisted around them, alive with noise and scent. Merchants called from behind laden stalls, peddling fruit, spices, and trinkets; fishmongers bargained loudly over the morning's catch. Children darted through the crowd, slipping between carts and horses. The air reeked of salt, smoke, and the sweat of too many bodies pressed together. Jaymes cut through it all with ease, every turn sure, every shortcut precise. He moved as if the city itself bent to him, and the crowd seemed to part instinctively when he passed.

They wound through a narrow alley and came at last to a weathered stable tucked between leaning stone walls. It was modest, easy to overlook, but the doors were sturdy and the yard swept clean.

"Always ready for an escape," Kipp muttered, glancing around.

Jaymes smirked. "Freedom's a habit."

Inside, the smell of hay and horse hit hard. Lantern light flickered across rows of stalls where restless mounts shifted and snorted. Jaymes went immediately to a sleek dun stallion, patting its neck with the quiet familiarity of long companionship.

Kipp stopped at the stall of a great spotted beast with a mane like a tangle of brambles. He tilted his head, unimpressed. "You look ridiculous."

The horse snorted and promptly tried to bite him, and Kipp jumped back with a sharp curse. Jaymes' smirk deepened, but he said nothing.

Kalithea, however, barely heard them.

Her gaze had found the black mare at the far end, lean and proud, her eyes dark and watchful. A single white star shone on her forehead. Kal stepped closer, drawn without thought. The mare stretched her neck and pressed a warm muzzle into her palm.

"I'll call you Nyra," she whispered.

The mare snorted softly and nudged her chest as if in answer.

Behind her, Kipp leaned toward Jaymes with a grin. "Are we jealous?"

Jaymes shook his head with mock resignation. "Completely."

Kal ignored them both. She worked methodically, tacking the mare and sliding into the saddle in one smooth motion. Nyra moved beneath her with an easy strength, as though she and Kal shared one will.

Arjun shook his head at the banter, but a faint smile touched his lips. Watching Kal with the mare, he saw something rare, something softer, gentler and unguarded. He mounted a steady dappled gelding, settling into the saddle easily.

They left the stable behind, slipping out of the city's crush. The noise of the port fell away, replaced by the hush of open fields and the green canopy of forest roads. For a time they rode in silence, the steady beat of hooves blending with the rustle of wind through leaves.

Kalithea let the quiet sink into her bones. Behind her, though, another tension brewed. Jaymes and Kipp exchanged a look, their eyes locking across the space between their horses. A silent accord passed between them.

Kipp edged his mount forward until his knee brushed Jaymes'. "Now?" he asked under his breath.

Jaymes grimaced, rubbing the back of his neck. "She'll kill us."

Kipp's grin was wolfish. "Only if we tell it poorly."

Then, with a sharp nudge, he rode ahead until he was level with Kal.

"So Kal..." Kipp called lightly. "Remember how you promised not to leave us behind?"

Kal's suspicion showed at once. She glanced back, her eyes narrowing. "Yes...?"

Jaymes winced. Kipp only smiled wider.

"Well," he drawled, "seems you're escorting two very wanted men straight into the lion's den."

Kal reined Nyra to a halt, the mare's muscles bunching beneath her. The others drew up alongside, the air between them suddenly taut.

She turned to face them fully, her expression carved from stone.

Jaymes let out a breath and spread his hands as if to ward her temper. "Before you murder us, we have reasons."

Her brow arched. "I'm listening."

Jaymes shot Kipp a look.

This was it.

Kalithea sat on her mare in silence, still as carved stone. The weight of her stare pressed harder than any words, and both men felt it. She had yet to speak, yet they already felt judged.

Kipp cleared his throat, plastering on a grin far too quick to be honest.

"Before you toss us in the nearest dungeon, maybe we get all the confessions out at once, eh?"

Kalithea tilted her head slightly, offering nothing.

Kipp took it as permission...or damnation. He forged ahead anyway.

"Right then. Our friend Jaymes here is wanted for smuggling, bribery, piracy, sinking a few ships—"

"Allegedly." Jaymes muttered without looking at her.

Kipp nodded solemnly. "Allegedly." he agreed, with all the gravity of a man lying through his teeth.

"And me?" He shrugged one shoulder, shameless. "The usual: thieving, forgery, slander, seduction, slipping custody once or twice, ruining the reputations of a few noble families."

Jaymes' brow arched. "A few?"

Kipp grinned, spreading his hands. "Dozens, then. Maybe a hundred. I lose count. I should really start keeping a ledger." he paused, before continuing positively unrepentant, "And there was that duel. Technically, I wasn't supposed to be in it, but the wine was good and someone needed embarrassing. Then there *might* have been an incident with a stolen wedding cake. But in my defense, it was a very boring ceremony. Also accused of smuggling goats once. Entirely false, naturally. They were sheep. Completely different matter to be honest."

Jaymes muttered something under his breath, trying to stop Kipp's rambling and leaned forward on the horn of his saddle.

"And together," Kipp added, gesturing broadly between them, "we are...uh...shall we say...less than welcome in polite society."

"We waited until you were committed. Until you had to keep your word." Jaymes mumbled.

Kipp winced, as though even he had to admit that one sounded bad.

Still, Kalithea said nothing. She just watched them, her silence stretching into a noose.

Kipp continued rambling, throwing in half-hearted jokes, his grin growing thinner the longer she didn't so much as blink. Jaymes offered the occasional dry barb, but even he knew it was hopeless. She listened. They squirmed.

Finally, even Kipp ran out of ways to fill the air.

The silence was worse than his babble.

Jaymes crossed his arms, exhaling hard. "Alright, Kal... what's running through that head of yours?"

She regarded them for a long, unbearable moment. Then, very slowly, her lips curled into a smirk.

"I know."

Jaymes stiffened. Kipp blinked.

Both blurted at once, "What?"

Kal arched a brow, infuriatingly serene.

Kipp leaned forward in the saddle, like he couldn't possibly have heard her right. "You knew?"

She nodded.

Jaymes narrowed his eyes. "Since when?"

"Since the beginning," she said simply.

Kipp made a strangled sound. "No–no, no, no, hang on. We've been plotting for days, love! Agonizing over when to tell you, how to soften the blow–!"

Kalithea cut him off with infuriating calm.

"Gentlemen," she began softly. "You're called *The King of Thieves* and *The Pirate King.*"

She let the words settle, the faintest spark of amusement in her eyes.

"Only a fool would expect you weren't wanted men."

Jaymes stared at her.

Kipp looked ready to topple out of his saddle.

Silence stretched again, this time stunned, and entirely on their side.

At last Jaymes dragged a hand down his face with a low curse.

Kipp jabbed a finger in Kalithea's direction. "You–you let us plan all of this!"

Kal nudged her mare forward, the faintest hum of satisfaction slipping past her lips. She didn't even look back.

Jaymes watched her ride ahead and released a long breath. "Well. That backfired."

Kipp threw his hands skyward. "We wasted time, Jaymes. Real, tactical plotting! Confessions, strategies, debates! For nothing!"

Jaymes grunted. "Worse. We looked like idiots."

"I hate how smug she looks," Kipp muttered, glaring at her back.

"I hate how well she plays us," Jaymes returned evenly.

Kipp made a strangled noise. "...I still can't believe she knew."

Jaymes shrugged, unbothered. "She's not wrong. We are a bit obvious."

Kipp spun on him, scandalized. "That's your excuse?!"

He muttered darkly about pirates and unfair advantages as he nudged his horse forward, while Jaymes followed.

Arjun, riding behind, only rolled his eyes. The look he cast at them was equal parts pity and exasperation, as though wondering how two grown men could be so hopeless.

Yet beneath the mock complaints and groans, the tension that had strung between them eased. Kalithea hadn't turned from them. She hadn't ordered them bound, hadn't ridden off without a word. She had known all along, and still she chose to keep them beside her.

Jaymes exhaled slowly, his gaze meeting Kipp's.

"One less thing to worry about."

They rode on for a time with only the sound of hooves and the creak of leather filling the air. The forest road wound beneath high branches, shadows flickering across the path, and for a while the quiet seemed almost companionable. Then, as though a thought had struck Kipp all at once, the silence shifted, heavier, sharper and far less forgiving than the laughter she had left them with.

Kipp's gaze narrowed on Kalithea's back. Suspicion bled into his voice.

"Hold on. If you knew we were wanted men, then you also know what kind of disaster it's about to be, strolling into a palace full of lords and banners."

Kalithea did not so much as turn her head. Her posture was relaxed, her hands easy on the reins, but there was something in her stillness that made it worse, an unconcern so complete it was almost insulting.

Jaymes exhaled, pinching the bridge of his nose. "Kipp. Let it go."

Kipp ignored him. "I'm serious. Recognition isn't a question. It's a *guarantee.*"

At that, Kalithea finally tilted her head. "Of course you'll be recognized."

Kipp sat straighter in the saddle. "And you don't see a problem with that?"

Her lips curved, faint and maddening. "A problem?" she mused. "Or an opportunity?"

Jaymes grimaced. "Kal."

But she only hummed under her breath, the sound low and satisfied, as though she were already ten moves ahead of them, and they were just now catching up.

Kipp leaned forward over his pommel, exasperation warring with reluctant amusement. "Alright then, oh great queen of chaos. Enlighten your humble servants."

Her smile deepened, sweet as honey and completely unpredictable.

"It's simple," she said lightly. "When we arrive, I'll tell the court you're my new handmaidens. You'll be fitted for lace and silk before the hour is out."

Both men recoiled at once, their voices crashing in horrified unison.

"Absolutely not."

Kipp looked personally wounded, jabbing a finger at his own chest. "Do I strike you as someone who wears lace?"

Jaymes' glare could have cut glass. "Over my dead body."

Kalithea laughed.

The sound startled them more than her threat. It broke from her without guard, bright and unrestrained, and for an instant the weight she carried seemed to vanish. It was the kind of laugh that left them both rigid in their saddles.

Then she winked, the picture of calm devastation.

"A queen," she said airily, "does not concern herself with such trivial matters."

With a flick of the reins she urged Nyra forward, the mare's black mane tossing in the wind as she pulled ahead.

Kipp stared after her, still half-struck. Jaymes was slower to follow, watching her with a frown that held more than irritation.

"I hate her," Kipp muttered finally.

Jaymes dragged a hand through his hair and sighed. "I knew it was a joke. And yet–g*ods help me*–I saw the lace."

Kipp shuddered theatrically. "Powdered wigs. Ribbons. I'm telling you, she'd do it."

Jaymes gave a reluctant chuckle. "Do you think she actually has a plan?"

Kipp shook his head, grim. "She probably has ten. That's the part that should terrify you."

Jaymes grunted, spurring his horse to follow. "It does."

Kipp and Jaymes had spent so much time stewing over Jarreth and Raoul, sharpening plans, bracing themselves for politics and the inevitable clash of past versus present. In all their worrying, they had overlooked the most immediate threat waiting for them at the palace gates.

Liam.

Kipp's jaw tightened. He edged his horse closer to Kalithea. "Hold on. We've been talking nobles, shadows, your noble admirers–"

Jaymes groaned, already weary. "Not this again."

Kipp ignored him, fixing Kal with a pointed stare. "But we haven't discussed your brother."

At the word, Jaymes stiffened in his saddle. Right. Liam. The very definition of a walking death threat.

Both men turned to her, waiting for something, *anything*, that might reassure them.

"Your *very* overprotective, *very* lethal, *extremely* possessive brother," Kipp added, rubbing the back of his neck, "who is unlikely to welcome two rather handsome, wildly talented, questionably lawful individuals riding at his sister's side."

Before Kal could respond, Arjun let out a short, cutting laugh.

Both Jaymes and Kipp snapped their attention to him instantly.

"What's so funny?" Jaymes asked, suspicion sharpening his tone.

Arjun grinned without sympathy. "Just picturing Liam's face when he sees you."

Kipp winced. "That bad?"

"Oh, worse," Arjun said cheerfully, far too pleased for their liking. "Liam has spent his life guarding Kal's every breath. Protecting her from anyone who so much as looked at her wrong. Bleeding for her. Killing for her."

Jaymes rolled his eyes. "Yes, yes, Liam the Noble Martyr. We get it."

Arjun's grin only widened. "He's... particular," he said, almost pitying. "Very particular about the company she keeps."

Kipp narrowed his eyes. "Particular how?"

"Let's just say," Arjun mused, "I'd start practicing your most harmless, innocent smiles now. Not that it will help."

Jaymes exhaled through his teeth. "So he's going to hate us."

Arjun nodded once, unapologetic. "Oh, with his whole blackened little heart."

Both men turned back to Kal, waiting desperately for a denial.

Kalithea only shrugged. Then nodded, calm as the sea at dawn.

Jaymes dragged a hand down his face. "Fantastic. Just what we needed. Another shadow with a sword."

Kipp sighed heavily. "Does he at least have a sense of humor?"

Arjun considered. "He laughs," he said at last. "When he's gutting people."

Kipp groaned. "Wonderful. We're doomed."

Kal smirked, utterly unbothered.

Jaymes blew out a sharp breath. "So let me get this straight. We're about to walk into a court that would hang us if they could, stuffed with nobles who'll bleed us dry, facing two men who already despise us by default–"

"And," Kipp cut in, hand flashing upward, "on top of that, a viciously loyal brother who will carve us to pieces on principle."

Arjun grinned, merciless. "That about sums it up."

Kipp shook his head, muttering, "I knew I should've stayed on the ship."

Jaymes sighed, "I should've let you."

Kalithea finally spoke, her tone dry as dust. "Are you two finished?"

They turned matching glares on her.

"You could have warned us," Jaymes said pointedly.

Her brow arched, elegant and imperious. "And would that have changed your decision?"

Jaymes opened his mouth. Kipp mirrored him. Neither found an answer.

After a beat, they both sighed in grim, defeated unison.

Kal's smirk sharpened. "Exactly."

The palace loomed ahead, its towers rising over the city like spears of stone. Kalithea rode at an unbroken pace, every line of her body carved into the shape of a woman who belonged to no one. Her mind should have been turning through plans, the next steps, how to weave herself back onto the path now that Arjun was once more at her side. But her thoughts were not on strategy. They lingered instead on the two men riding behind her.

Jaymes Blackwell, born of storm and sea, who bowed to nothing save the tide.

Kipp Harlow, the King of Thieves, who slipped through the world like smoke through a keyhole.

They had not merely entered her life; they had carved out places she had not meant to leave vacant. And now, whether they understood it or not, they were hers. She had given them her word she would not leave them behind. And Kalithea did not break her word.

They hadn't asked for her protection, would probably bristle at the very thought of it, but that mattered little. The moment she had stepped aboard that ship and they had refused to let her face the dark alone, she had claimed them. They were under her care now, these reckless, impossible men who would follow her into the jaws of court politics armed with nothing but sharp tongues and sharper smiles. She would protect them, even if it cost her life.

The city blurred past in flashes of color and sound, but Kalithea's focus never wavered. Walls could not contain the men who rode at her back. Nor crowns. Nor thrones.

Jaymes would always hear the call of the ocean, feel it tugging at him like a second heartbeat. And Kipp, with his restless spirit, would never be content inside marble halls or gilded cages. No matter what promises they made, no matter how fiercely they swore to stay, the world would always pull at them.

And that was why she admired them. Trusted them. More than anyone she had ever known, save Liam and Arjun.

Because they were wild. Untamed. And she would never ask them to be anything less.

But the palace would. It would try to grind down their edges, polish them into something palatable, fit them into neat, acceptable roles. And in doing so, it would destroy the very things that made them extraordinary. She would fight to guard that, just as she would fight the ghosts waiting behind those gates.

Her thoughts turned to Jarreth and Raoul.

Men who had stood at her side, who had fought to be seen by her, and who would now be forced to reckon with the woman she had become.

Kalithea did not delude herself. They would not welcome Jaymes and Kipp. Jarreth and Raoul were men of principle, polished and proud, who would balk at sharing their place beside her with rogues, no matter how hard-won their titles. And the rogues in turn would not yield their claim.

If no blood was drawn within the first week, it would be nothing short of a miracle. She allowed herself the ghost of a smile, sharp and fleeting. It would almost be worth the trouble, just to watch it.

Drawing a slow breath, Kalithea crossed the first of the gates into the city. She tasted freedom one last time, and pushed all softer thoughts aside. The woman who had laughed on the deck of a ship, who had gambled knives against pirates and thieves, that woman belonged to the sea.

The woman who passed beneath these walls wore a crown of flame and ash.

There was no room for hesitation. No room for longing.

Kalithea lifted her chin, her mask sliding into place like a second skin.

Let the court come for her. Let Jarreth and Raoul test their claim. Let Jaymes and Kipp fight the world itself to remain at her side.

She welcomed all of it. She had never been afraid of battles.

ABOUT THE AUTHOR

J.D. Marcella has been writing since she was a teenager, scribbling half-formed worlds into notebooks instead of doing anything remotely practical. After the loss of her father, she realized it was time to stop hiding her stories in drawers and start bringing them to life—both for him, and for herself. She lives with her infinitely patient husband and stepson, a miniature version of herself in her daughter, and a brain that runs on a unique blend of caffeine, hyperfocus, and ADHD-fueled chaos.

When she's not writing emotionally complex characters or orchestrating tangled plotlines, she's likely annoying a very small but devoted circle of friends who've endured countless rants about lore mechanics, emotional beats, and the color of a character's shirt in chapter seventeen—with alarming grace. The Queen of Light and Shadows is her debut epic fantasy series.